BROOME STAGES

BY

CLEMENCE DANE

Novels

BROOME STAGES

REGIMENT OF WOMEN

FIRST THE BLADE

LEGEND

WANDERING STARS

THE BABYONS

(With Helen Simpson)
ENTER SIR JOHN

Plays

A BILL OF DIVORCEMENT

WILL SHAKESPEARE

THE WAY THINGS HAPPEN

NABOTH'S VINEYARD

GRANITE

MARINERS

ADAM'S OPERA

Criticism

TRADITION AND HUGH WALPOLE

THE WOMEN'S SIDE

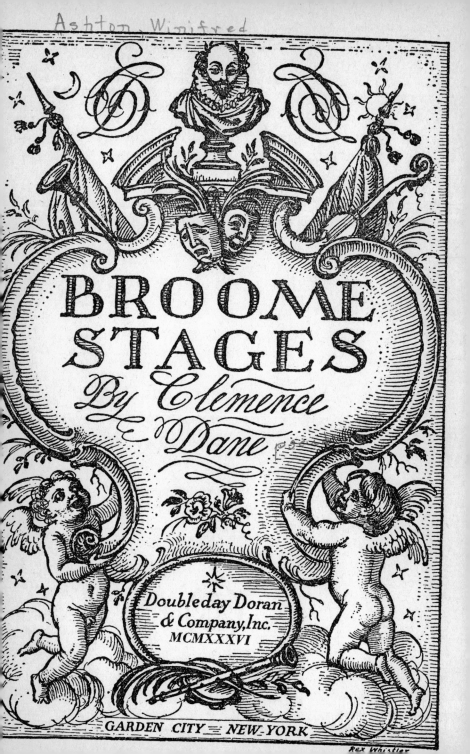

BROOME STAGES

By Clemence Dane

Doubleday Doran
& Company, Inc.
MCMXXXVI

GARDEN CITY · NEW·YORK

Rex Whistler

PRINTED AT THE *Country Life Press*, GARDEN CITY, N. Y., U. S. A.

Dear Dick,

But for your conviction, expressed cautiously but with irritating frequency, that a play about the Plantagenets was really a novel about the Broomes, this book would not have been written.

So now you must take the consequences, dedicated to you cautiously, but with much affection, by

The Author.

Tavistock Street,
Covent Garden.

CONTENTS

CHAPTER		PAGE
I	ALL THE BROOMES	I
2	THE FIRST RICHARD BROOME IS TAUGHT A CHARM	3
3	RICHARD BROOME HAS A STAGE FALL	8
4	TRIALS OF A GRANDFATHER	13
5	ROBERT BROOME AND HIS SON WILLIAM	24
6	THE WYBIRDS TALK IT OVER	44
7	THE LADY'S BATTLE	54
8	A BROOME HUSBAND AND A BROOME WIFE	69
9	WILLIAM BROOME AND HIS SON RUSSEL	90
10	LETTICE'S SONS AND LIONEL'S DAUGHTER	103
11	HARRY BROOME IN MANAGEMENT	123
12	'MY SON'S MY SON TILL . . .'	136
13	DEAR MAUD	142
14	DEAREST MAUD	152
15	ROBIN BROOME, PLAYWRIGHT	155
16	MYRTLE AND ORANGE BLOSSOM	165
17	THE CRYSTAL PALACE	171
18	EDUCATION OF A MARRIED COUPLE	182
19	THE BROOMES ARE TOGETHER AGAIN	202
20	NEMO ME IMPUNE LACESSIT	230
21	CAN A BROOME BE TOO CLEVER?	241
22	SUMMER IS OVER	246
23	HARRY BROOME AND HIS DAUGHTER DOMINA	253
24	MOONLIGHT ON A BROTHER AND SISTER	277
25	OBERON	293
26	DONNA HAS CHARM AFTER ALL	307
27	THE EARTHLY PARADISE	318
28	'WHO MOURNS FOR ADONAIS?'	324
29	HARRY BROOME WRITES TO HIS DAUGHTER	333
30	LETTICE LOOKS ON	342

CONTENTS

CHAPTER		PAGE
31	SNOW IN PARADISE	348
32	HARRY BROOME IS GENEROUS	352
33	SNOW EVERYWHERE	369
34	THREE BROOME WOMEN	374
35	STEPHEN HAS IT OUT WITH DONNA	378
36	FEVER	398
37	BROOMES' BENEFIT	407
38	'THE ELDEST HATH BORNE MOST'	416
39	INTERLUDE IN A NEW WORLD	430
40	EDMUND—A BROOME	440
41	THE PRICE OF WAR	446
42	THE PRICE OF PEACE	470
43	A NEW BROOME SWEEPS CLEAN	482
44	ELINOR	500
45	ENGAGED TO LEWIS WYBIRD	512
46	RECKON, BECKON . . .	522
47	A WEDDING DRESS	534
48	DOMINA BROOME'S LAST MANAGEMENT	545
49	KINGDOM COME	553
50	EDMUND BROOME AND HIS FAMILY	563
51	A REHEARSAL	582
52	ELINOR WALKS HOME	592
53	RICHARD, HENRY, GEOFFREY AND JOHN	598
54	ELINOR AND HER SONS	618
55	JOHN'S WAR	627
56	ALYS BROOME	642
57	EDMUND AND HIS SON RICHARD	652
58	RICHARD'S STAR	662
59	EDMUND BROOME WATCHES TWO SHOWS	676
60	TAKEN IN EXECUTION	690
61	RICHARD AND JOHN	695

BROOME STAGES

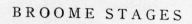

CHAPTER 1

ALL THE BROOMES

ALL the Broomes have charm: it is their epithet. The Broomes, indeed, may be said to have established charm as a social asset, just as they have established the stage as socially virtuous. This last achievement has taken them some two hundred years to accomplish, and in that time their charm has become part of them, like their air of living serenely and royally in public. The Broomes do not thereby lose their sense of personal privacy, nor allow the spectator to persuade himself that by gazing he has become intimate. He may know them all, their ancestry, the interlacing facts of their lives, the ebullitions of their genius, the zig-zags of their eccentricities, their amazing and diverse charm, as well as he knows the history of the Macbeths. But though the spectator has watched Macbeth's wife in her nightgown, washing her hands, in no world can he ever claim intimacy with her because he has seen what he should not. The footlights divide eternally his world from hers.

Even so do the footlights lie between the Broomes and the rest of the world which they entertain. Even in their own stage world they are difficult to know, perhaps because they have ceased with the years to be true stage folk. They are, by persistent playing of the classics and constant intermarriage with stage-struck superiors, long since grown into gentlefolk who use the stage as a profession. Since the War, say the critics, the Broomes have grown, indeed, too gentle for their job; for in the theatre they refuse to raise their voices, but instead charm the public into applauding their art of being natural. Yet, met socially, they still strike you as flamboyant: you can spy the invisible footlights throwing fantastic looks upon their actors' masks.

Domina Broome, for instance, in spite of her long years in retirement, still stalks into the popular drawing-room of her daughter-in-law Elinor Broome like the Tragic Muse paying a visit of condolence to Comedy, and young John Broome flickers to and fro among his mother's guests, quiet and dangerous as a flame. As for the second Richard Broome, that popular hero with the callous tongue and the heavy heart, we know all about him, or think we do. Flattered, fêted, the calm centre of all behind-the-scenes embroilments of his day, and long since shorn of reputation, he is the darling of the gods in all our eyes. If in his own eyes he is not much better than a parricide, nobody knows it, though young John guesses.

But even young John, whose bright eyes watch everyone, whose quick ears hear everyone's secrets, only guesses at his brother's: for Richard, of all the Broomes, is the least accessible. A mere straight line of footlights divides us from Edmund and Elinor and their other sons, and we can skirt that barrier and get to them, at a pinch, by the pass door. But Richard Broome for us is but a beckoning shadow on a white sheet, exciting, intangible, the female world's Synthetic Sweetheart, but the lover of no flesh-and-blood woman. And so, there being no-one to listen to his secrets and betray them to us, what can be said of Richard Broome save that the cinemas of England and America are his to fill, that he lives very simply in spite of his huge fortune, and that young John adores him. To understand him is possible, of course, but only if we first see something of all the Broomes and their wars.

To do this we must work backwards through time. We shall pass and re-pass the figures of Elinor and her husband the great Edmund Broome, and his arrogant mother, Domina, ever at war with the fathers of her son. We shall pass, too, the hardworking, early-Victorian Broomes in their playhouses, re-writing Shakespeare to suit themselves; but contributing also their own comedies and tragedies. We shall pass the Regency Broomes and the Wybird contingent and begin our history with the figure of the first Richard Broome, earning his name as well as his keep on a Devon hillside.

CHAPTER 2

THE FIRST RICHARD BROOME IS TAUGHT A CHARM

THE first Richard Broome was born in 1715 and spent his childhood making brooms. He sold them to the lazy gypsies and brought the halfpence to his mother. From her he had his letters and his knowledge of the Bible, and so his pure speech. But whence did he get his fairy-tales? For he would as soon have doubted the existence of the Virgin Mary as the existence of the fairy mistress who might any day speak to him from the middle of the burning broom.

His chief source of enlightenment was, according to his own account, the notorious Lucy Godfrey. Her curious commerce with the fairies had taken place some sixty years earlier: she had been barely twenty at the time of her disgrace and imprisonment as an impostor. But as an old woman she had been the small boy's crony. Richard Broome, in his own old age, liked to tell stories of little Dick Broom-maker and Lucy Godfrey, and their community of dreams. He had actually heard her talk of her invisible ring of playfellows and had drunk from the silver cup the fairies gave her. She had even given him a morsel of her fairy bread and nothing so delicious had ever passed his lips.

"For how should I know the taste of cake?" demanded old Richard who had once been little Dick Broom-maker. But as a child Dick had believed Lucy when she swore that she had the secret of her bread-making from the fairies in the orchard, and that the fairies abandoned her because she had talked of them too openly. She was sorry enough afterwards, said pitiful, toothless Lucy who had once danced with the fairies. Nevertheless, though she had been warned so sharply of the perils of blabbing, she had taught the little boy a spell or two. One he remembered and taught to his grand-daughter Hilaret—for the charm must go from sex to sex if it is to work. The Broomes have lost belief in it by now; but little Dick Broom-maker believed, as he sat on Lucy Godfrey's three-legged stool, saying after her with much more fervour than he said the confession in church:—

> Dickon! Dickon! Cats and mice!
> Crook your finger and beckon thrice!

3

By the Father and the Son,
        Reckon up and beckon on!
    Reckon, beckon——

Then came the two secret lines that set the Broome charm working.

On the day that Dick learned the charm he accompanied Lucy Godfrey on one of her rare scuttles down the hostile village street and so was present at her death. The village louts had always thrown stones at her for a witch; but she was not too much afraid of them. The recent Atterbury Plot, however, had stirred the populace into general murmurings against papists, Jacobites and heretics of all sorts. Poor, tolerated Lucy, hobbling down the street with outcast Dick tugging at her skirts, suddenly became the symbol of these abominations. A mob of women, men and dogs threw themselves upon her, and her death was a beastly one. For they dragged her to the sea-shore at the end of the lane, stripped her, swam her till she choked, and then trampled her to death beneath her own house door wrenched from its posts to serve as a coffin-lid.

Little Dick belaboured all the bodies he could reach and was kicked and cuffed out of the way till at last, exhausted and sobbing with rage, he climbed the cliff-side and watched out the tragedy from a thicket of broom. After which he was sick all by himself in the broom. When the last of the mob had wound out of sight down the shore lane and all was quiet, he crawled out, green-faced and shaky, and looked about him. He felt too weak to walk, but he was afraid to stay alone any longer in the dusk within sight of the trampled quiet pale beach, and the quiet pale evening sea, and the unstirring hillock of pinkish wreckage that lay, quieter than beach or sea, between them, and, as it were, rejected by both. He took, indeed, a few uncertain steps towards the wreckage and watched the glassy lilac ripples change colour as they broke smoothly against the obstruction. He watched them drain away again, drawing red weed after them. At last a gull flew down and settled on Lucy Godfrey. Then the sky began to fill with shapes and to scream and Dick turned and ran, unsteadily, like a day-old calf, and scarcely slackened till he was at home and weeping out the whole story in his mother's lap. But though she was motherly to him she was on the mob's side, and so he heard the truth about Lucy Godfrey and fairyland.

He had found his mother in her grand dress that she would not wear in the village, and found with her the elegant parson who did the fortnightly duty. When the parson came he lodged with Dick's mother, to the anger of the parish. Why should God's minister lodge in a beggarly widow's cot when ten farms would have been glad to offer him free lodging?

There did not seem to be any answer: at least the parson offered none: nor did Dick's mother. Dick, who had had the village gossip flung at him like stones by the better fed children of the hamlets, kept a watch, and saw odd glances pass sometimes that did not match the sober, lodger-and-landlady talk. But he never heard the pair speak of anything but clean linen and the fear of the Lord until he came home crying with his tale of Lucy Godfrey. Then he heard the truth about fairyland.

Fairyland, then said his mother, while the parson nodded approval and watched her and the boy alternately with his secret, gleaming smile—fairyland was a real country, situate on the high-road to hell. Fairyland was the devil's paradise, all a glamour and a sham. Its money was dead leaves: its wine ditch-water: its food toadstools, horse dung and pig-swill: its towers and royal halls were the standing stones of the moor. Dance with the fairies by night and at dawn you found yourself on a swampy hillside with ague in your bones. How did they trick you? By glamour! Oh, fairyland was a right enough place, and no doubt Lucy Godfrey had been there; but make the sign of the cross and the glamour peeled off the fairy folk like onion peel off an onion, till naught was left but a company of haggard humans, swept brides and unwilling prisoners.

And then the parson chimed in with a dreadful tale of Mr. Kirk, himself a parson, and of all that the fairies did to him. And the boy listened and believed, for a parson was a parson: besides, he liked him. The parson, in fact, was much more to Dick's taste than Dick's mother, who was a fierce, handsome woman, commanding obedience but demanding no affection.

Nevertheless, if the small Dick could have shaped his thoughts into words, he would have answered thus—Lucy Godfrey's wicked fairyland may be mere muck-heap by honest sunlight. All the same, by touchwood-light the muck-heap must be beyond desire beautiful. Lucy Godfrey had told Dick that if she could go back to her enchanted orchard she would do so, though she paid for it in hell. For, she told him, once back she would look no more than thirty and feel seventeen.

But Dick could not say what he meant: he could only dissent and rebel. The more fiercely his mother inveighed against Faery, the more fiercely the boy made up his romantic mind that one day he would go where Lucy had gone and see what she had seen. He would hunt till he found the four-leaved key—and then, in he would march, and never come out again, parson or no parson, mother or no mother. And Dick, the first of the Broomes who would have what they wanted, in the end had his wish and his way.

He did not find his lucky clover at once. First came long years of broom-making to turn the pretty five-year-old into a handsome, idling boy, bored by his trade, ignorant and curious, ready for adventures. He spent lazy hours lying on the hillside, staring up through the yellow banners of broom into the blue sky. The song of birds, the thunder of the wind, the yellow banners tossed into the melting sky—he hugged these things into his mind, ate them, drank them, swallowed them down. Yet there they remained, sky, wind, broom bushes, though he had eaten and drunk them, and he would stretch out his arms and draw them down again to wrap them round him like the mantle of a king. Thus clothed he would go strutting down the hillside, throwing out his arms in magnificent gestures of indignation and defiance, or slash at the yellow besoms in a frenzy, and in another frenzy pick up from the earth the drooped bruised plumes of beauty and shake out the tousled petals. Then, with a wild whoop, he would race up the hillside till he was breathless and fling himself down again under new broom bushes to begin his crazy play once more.

He did not know what was the matter with him. He lived in a passion of pretence, yet could not be contented with his pretence. He wanted flesh and blood to pretend with him. Pretend what? Dick Broom-maker did not know: did not know until, going into the village one evening to sell his day's work, he stopped at the tithe barn outside the town. In that moment his life was changed for him.

He had no premonitions that on this, his lucky day, the spells were beginning to work, though he should have guessed; for not only was it the thirteenth of May and his birthday, but it was his thirteenth birthday also. Lucy Godfrey had told him that thirteen was the Good People's lucky number, and would be his lucky number too because he had eaten fairy food. Let him never be afraid of ladders, black pins, crossed knives, spilled salt or the number thirteen! Other men's ill luck would always be luck to him.

But young Dick, with his arm full of bright, unstripped broom besoms, stopped at the tithe barn, not because of any premonition of luck to come, but because there was a crowd about it, and he could never see a crowd without his mind flashing back, sickly, to the harrying of Lucy Godfrey. The hideous picture formed in his mind anew and he hung on one foot, while the brooms slid unnoticed to the grass, as he fought the black heroic impulse to charge down into the mob of children and do damage, pound away the memory. He dramatised the possibility while his mind clothed him in the armour of the man in the church window: and yet another part of his mind gathered up blue sky and yellow broom afresh, and wove them into a banner to be carried in his left hand. His right held the reins and between his knees he felt the warm sides of his charger. But when he saw the charger, not in his dream but through his dream, fifty yards ahead of him, sheer urchin curiosity dispersed the vision. For the charger was the rector's grey cob and the grey cob was a friend of his, and it hung its uneasy head over the broken-down wall that divided the highroad from the nettle-grown paddock.

Now the grey cob, Dick knew, was too old and wise to browse for choice among nettles. Someone had turned him out of the barn in which he stabled and had bundled him through the gap in the wall, and put up a hurdle to prevent his getting out. Now who could have dispossessed the grey cob? Who was hidden in the barn? What had drawn the village children from their usual playground? Why had they gathered at the bolted door? Who had bolted the door?

Dick had to find out.

CHAPTER 3

RICHARD BROOME HAS A STAGE FALL

THE huge barn door was bar-locked, and the children of the village, among whom he was already an outcast and a man, crowded round the crack talking their nonsense. They said the actors had come. What were actors? He had never heard the word. He wrenched a slobbering farmer's youngest from the door-post, peered through the crack himself, and saw a fairy queen.

She was sitting in the middle of the barn on a golden chair: she wore a crown and strings of pearl about her neck: had a book in her hand and spoke spells in a voice like the fiddle in church, while with her free hand she chafed her naked foot. Beside her stood a lady, draped like one of the white marble ladies in the Squire's gardens. She was busily darning the fairy's stocking. Other creatures moved behind the pair and he thought he saw a donkey with a man's body and a winged child.

Here the crowd pushed him from Paradise by sheer weight of numbers, and he found himself lying in the nettles with the grey cob's soft muzzle touching his cheek. He lay still, wondering at the stir in him, not knowing that 'the Broome rage' was being born. He only knew that he was hurt and must hurt back. So he got to his feet and headed back into the mob like a young goat, ramming his way to the desired spy-hole. The crack was his crack and he would have it!

Once again he was toppled into the nettles: once again Dobbin nuzzled his stung cheeks.

Then to the Broome rage succeeded the Broome calm. He lay on his back, ignoring his bruises and smarting hands and face, and stared up at his blue and white sky, its surface torn by the wind. Then he noticed the sharp outline of the barn roof thrusting into soft pale flurries of cloud, and he remembered how often he had lain within the old barn itself upon last year's hay, staring at the same sky through the broken rafters. Remembering he shot one of his gleaming looks at Dobbin, and sprang again to his feet. Let the brats huddle before their crack! In five minutes he would be inside and laughing at them.

Twisting a hand in his friend's mane, he dragged the kind beast along with him, unobserved by the mob of children, till the east end of

8

the barn was reached. Here Dobbin gave him a back to the first branch of the elm which shadowed the rotten, lichen-stained roof. The rest was easy, though he was afraid of the treacherous upper branches, fancied a dozen times that the limb he straddled would give suddenly under his weight. But the elm was in a good mood. It swayed and dumped itself against the roof, displacing a tile or two, but it did not crack, and let him slide gently and easily from its arms to the ridge-pole. Straddling this he paused, breathless.

He was so high up that he could see the coast. The sea lay like a looking-glass reflecting the darkening sky but distorting it a little, too, as a looking-glass does. The fields were spread out over the hills like his mother's best quilt humped over the pillows of her bed. He could see rabbits like ant-grubs in the open fields directly below him, and cockle gatherers with gulls shrieking over them on the strand where Lucy Godfrey died, and a horse in the act of lying down, and little figures of labourers threading the needle-eye lanes, and the loafers playing morris on the hard ground before the inn. He gave them all a hasty fearless glance, to be sure that they did not see him, and spent no further time upon the view. For under his feet he could hear the fairies : and he wriggled and slung himself along the roof ridge in painful excitement that he might see as well as hear.

The marvellous noises of fairyland grew louder. He could distinguish songs, laughter, deep growls, and the voice of the fairy queen, which made him once again think of the fiddle in church. He could not hear the words she spoke, but he was sure that she said words. That was why he liked the sound of her voice better than music ; for music would not shape into words.

"I know a bank whereon the wild thyme blows—" said another voice not so beautiful as hers—"Where oxlips and the nodding violet grows !"

Dick knew it too : and they were right about the musk-roses and the eglantine ; but they had said nothing about the bee-orchis which grew there. So he hitched himself forward, for he wanted to tell them about the orchis, till his chin was level with the gap that yawned in the roof. His mother had just such an ugly gap in her mouth. Then the thought ran idly through his head that since his mother had lost her two front teeth they seldom saw the smiling parson, and that his mother had grown almost as vague as Lucy Godfrey. Nevertheless he was glad she could not see him perched up so high nor watch what he was doing, for, vague as she was, she still had her harsh rages and her arm was like a flail. One day he would flail back at her! What would she do then?

His eyes brightened wickedly and he giggled, for he loved to devise strange situations, to imagine himself hunting where he had been hunted. And all the while he worked at the slates with his free fingers, heaving one after another recklessly downwards till far-off Dobbin snorted and flung up his heels.

Thus Dick cleared himself a convenient space, for he was to create the tradition observed by all his descendants that other people's comfort and other people's property meant nothing at all to a Broome. "Get out, Dobbin! Get out, slates." Out of the way they went, till at last he looked down upon the fairyland of his desires from a height, giddily, much as in years to come the gallery gods were to look down at him and his children, and his children's children.

The great disused barn was roomy as the parson's church. Its east end was still piled high with trusses of hay, and on the hay in turn were spread some dingy gaudy coverlets. On one of these a baby sprawled: on the other a woman, small and naked to the waist, kneeled upright, combing out long fair hair. She shone like silver against the rafters where darkness wove the straws and cobwebs into a hanging for her beauty. The long gold shaft of light from the pigeon-hole shot past her without so much as grazing her shoulder. But it flung a mote-peopled mist upon the hay, and her body rode in the mist like a swan breasting a pool from which night fogs are rising. When she leaned suddenly forward over the rampart of hay to speak to one of the dancers below, so that Dick saw no more of her than her white back and her cataract of hair, she reminded him once more of a swan plunging its neck suddenly into the water. Presently she righted herself, flung up a white arm and felt blindly for a shawl that hung from a rafter, tore it down, crossed it about her, tied it behind and in a whirl of clicketing hoops slid down to join the rest of the company. These broke their circle as she came and rested panting: while two tall young men and another woman came up and the four began to quarrel in rhyme. But Dick saw that though they ran about and were angry enough to draw swords, they moved always within some fifteen feet of space and, like the other dancers, observed the line of an invisible barrier which they would not or could not pass.

Dick's enchanted eye, however, was free: it wandered from the half-naked woman and the dancers in blue and green satin and the lady with flowers in her hair and the sulky winged boy, to the other side of the barrier. There men, men fairies as he still thought them, were busy clearing away enchantments. The donkey's head had tumbled off the man and was tied into a bundle with spears and a drum and a banner. The stone house with pillars and pink flowers was moved as easily as if it were one of Dick's brooms, and tilted with its door in the air against the hay. He spied pots and pans like those in use in his mother's cottage as far as shape went, but made of gold and silver and flashing with jewels. The boy noticed, however, that when one of the green fairy men drank, he drank from a common pipkin and poured his drink from a bottle just like the bottle the parson had once left behind him. The fairy queen had taken off her crown and was pulling on her stockings : old women (one of them so like Lucy Godfrey!) hung over a fire built in the centre of the floor-space. His country wits said : "Fire so near hay? Wicked!" only to recollect that touchwood fires do not burn. Nevertheless there floated up from this ethereal fire pale blue curls of smoke and good poacher's cooking smells : and he wondered that oak-apples and horse dung could so counterfeit roast rabbit. Then he turned from the wonder to watch the fairy queen again.

She had borne down the barn on light feet, had circled the invisible barrier and re-appeared among the dancers, waving her arms and beckoning, while the tall boy with wings ran after her, till at last the crowd melted away and left her alone. Then he saw her stamp her little foot, and her voice, her beautiful fiddling voice, rose shrill and fretful on the air—

"I tell you she is as clumsy as Jacko!" said the fairy queen. "You may send her back to her charity school, and so I tell you! I'll not play Titania even in the provinces until you get me a proper Oberon. Jack would play better. Here! Jacko!"

At her call there was a noise like the clink of a chain, and through the window of the tilted house leapt, plain for the boy to see, Brownie himself.

Brownie was a little old man in a red flannel coat with a red cap on his head and a chain round his waist. The loose end of the chain was gathered up over his skinny hairy arm like a garland. As he came skipping to the queen everyone began to laugh except the pink boy with wings, who, snivelling, struck out at the creature. It raced to the queen for protection and so intercepted the return blows which she was aiming at the winged boy. Then Brownie snarled, gnashed his teeth, ran up the fairy queen's dress to her bare shoulder, caught at her powder-clogged curls, then in a cloud of white dust leaped for the cross beam.

"Come up! Come up here!" shrilled Dick crazed with excitement. The monkey heard and made a second leap to a higher beam, ran along it and paused, grinning, four feet below Dick's outstretched hand.

"Oh, come up!" besought the boy, oblivious of the cries below, "Here, take my hand!" and stretched a second hand downwards, craning and yearning towards the chattering fairy beast, till a crack and a fall of slates warned him of danger. But it warned him too late. In vain he scrabbled for a foothold with his bare toes: in vain he strove to brace and straighten his body. He had leaned too far and the yielding slates slid him gently forwards and down, as the elm twigs had done. He felt himself going: clutched wildly at space and caught in passing the coat of the terrified ape. Then the two of them, escaping the cross-beams as by a miracle, dived neatly downwards into the hay. What happened to Jacko he did not know, but he himself bounced wildly and rolled over the edge of the hay trusses to fall again, and finally, on to the improvised stage of 'A Company of Comedians from the Theatres of London.'

CHAPTER 4

TRIALS OF A GRANDFATHER

AT this point old Richard, with his professional instinct for a good curtain, liked to break off the story. But the end of it could be coaxed out of him by questions and tentative mis-statements. It ran thus.

He had fallen luckily. Young as he was he had already the handsome looks he lived by, and quick eyes, a quick tongue and quick wits. So he did not waste time in lamenting over his tumble or feeling for broken bones, but, a wiser and more wakeful Eutychus, set himself to the task of conciliating the creatures of glamour among whom he had thus dropped like a wind-fall apple.

It was easy. He had white teeth in his large but well-shaped and softly curved mouth: he had the Broome smile and the Broome glance, and was quick to use his young charms as all the Broomes use them, on men and women alike. Lucy Godfrey's spell was in his eyes, his carriage, his walk. He had but to reckon and beckon: especially when he discovered, as he pretty soon did, of course, that the glamour of these magnificent creatures was an artificial enchantment, to be bought at fairs. For the fairy queen was one of your petting, stroking, kiss-mama ladies when a hurt and handsome boy was in question. Within five minutes his cheek had received its first smear of paint and his mind its first social lesson. He was always a quick learner and a slow forgetter, and he learnt then and never forgot how to manage pretty women older than himself and plain women cleverer than himself. And never forgot, either, to prolong his welcome by wise confederate glances at the men folk of the plain and pretty women.

But he did not like his hosts the less for finding them flesh and blood, and showed it. Indeed, he must have been a touching young Pan, wild and friendly, smelling of the hills and dewy with life as a cluster of blackberries. So the players adored him as English men and women always adore young wild creatures, and petted and comforted him, the women with kisses, the men with a taste of brandy. The unknown spirit fired him anew. He soon had them exclaiming at his bright looks, and, when he answered questions, at his clean Bible speech.

The fairy queen cried—"Saved, an Oberon!" and while the swanwoman hugged him in turn, fell upon the sulky pink-satin child and

stripped it to the skin. Young Dick stared in astonishment at a
wretched young girl left shivering; but he made no bones about
wearing grand pink satin, and took his place in the play with a strutting
delight that made the women laugh and the men nudge each other.
One older man who had from a distance watched the scene with
complete dispassion, here knocked his pipe against a flat, slouched over
to the group and addressed the fairy queen, calling—

"Will he suit you, my dear? Then you shall have him! He can
convoy the drum." And to the flushed Dick—"Will you come with
us? Who's your father? You don't know? Why then, your mother'll
sell you cheap, I take it. You stable up the hill? Then I'll go and clinch
the bargain—we'll call it an apprenticeship to save Goody's feelings.
And it's that, eh, Cynthy? Well, teach him his tricks! He's not too
young to begin."

"And he swung out," said old Broome, "as great as a king. And
that," he'd finish, "was how I first fell in with a management."

The boy's luck held. Before he had been a week with the strolling
players he realised that he had indeed his wish and his way, and
was safe in the only fairyland left in a Protestant world. For the
know-alls, said old Richard, though they could banish the belief
in magic, could not banish the desire for it. And, denied fairyland,
where could poets and dancers herd but in the Middle-land of the
theatre? For, demanded Richard, waxing eloquent, is not the theatre
the land of sham and glamour, of cardboard battles, learnt-by-heart
nobilities, clockwork monsters and pinchbeck virtues and jewels? Is
not the sloping floor behind the footlights so drenched with dreams,
so perfumed with glamour, that a man who treads those boards can
continue to look and feel twenty till three times seven years pass in
the outer world?

Then, indeed, the spell may fail him, and through the eyes of a
newcomer into his world of enchantment he will see that he himself and
his fellow players have grown old just like the common men and
women who know nothing of spells. Then, indeed, lest the hell of
oblivion claim him, he will fight to keep his place within the charmed
circle of the illusion as fiercely as ever do his unbeglamoured neighbours
of the daytime streets. More fiercely; for the stage gives as well as takes.
It gives an ampler gesture, a quicker hope, an easier despair, a larger
vanity, a sordider poverty, a more prodigal fortune, than is to be found
in the humdrum outer world. Moreover it bestows upon its families and
hangers-on an aptitude for spells. Richard Broome hugged the thought

of his own, and the knowledge that time had not yet weakened it.

"Beckon, Dickon! . . ." he would quote, and protest that the art of acting was but the art of beckoning.

And, indeed, when a house rose at him as it sometimes did, bodily, with a frightening forward surge, it was as if the whole concourse of tired men and women desired to bathe in the transfiguring theatre light. "Let them!" ended Richard on a large gesture. If the light faded and the glamour passed away like dew in the next dawn, what matter? Fairies and players sleep away the sunlight.

Old Richard Broome (Broom-maker was no sort of a name for a playbill) had long since forgotten, perhaps never knew, how the bargain was struck with his mother. He had always wondered why she let him go so easily, and thought that the parson may have had some say in the matter. He was sure that the parson was his father. Richard had met him again years later wearing a bishop's apron, and hand in glove with the great. The cleric was not civil enough to the Roscius of the hour; so it pleased Richard to recall himself. He said that his lordship took it well, thawed, drank more port, and in the end confessed paternity; but could tell him little of his mother save that she was dead, and that she had once sold oranges in the theatres. She had always been a dark, melancholy she-devil with a beckoning eye and a long nose in her long face, and she called herself Charlotta. Richard could make what he liked of that! Good King Charles's blood ran in too many hackney veins for it to mean much: still, there it was, the magic Stuart drop, and Richard might as well make the most of it. The bishop was inclined to be apologetic because, having at last encountered his offspring, he had neither place nor purse to offer. But Richard said that he didn't care: he would rather found than inherit. They talked a good hour and were friendly, but never met again. "And a good thing too!" said Dick's granddaughter the Duchess of Bedenham.

Yes, Dick Broome, the strolling player, may or may not have been the grandson of a king, but he certainly ended as the grandfather of a duchess. And this is how it came about.

Richard Broome married twice, and the first time as foolishly as Will Shakespeare himself and for much the same reasons. He enjoyed his years with the strolling players, and at fifteen prided himself on being a young man of the theatre, toughened and reliable. But he was not so tough as he fancied. He had once seen a loved creature die horribly and the experience left him with a skinned heart and a sensitive imagination. And ever since his tumble into the midst of the barn-stormers there was etched on his memory a companion picture to the picture of Lucy Godfrey on the sea-shore. It was the picture of a weeping, shivering girl, older than himself too, plucked of her pink-satin clothes as a live goose is plucked of its feathers. He saw her kicked aside, creeping half naked into the hay, bowed into herself, her thin arms crossed over her breast. He hated the picture, he hated being the cause of it, and he eased his acute discomfort by taking the white, snivelling creature under his special protection. He was everybody's favourite: it was right that he should have his own favourite also.

So he was good to the drudge and naturally she adored him, though he treated her as a weaker and inferior boy and fagged her to death and seldom gave her a thank-you; but he was a fairy-tale companion to the frightened girl. On their interminable ramblings from country town to country town he always drew her off from the main gang. He would take her by by-ways and short cuts over a hillside or across a river and carried her on his back when she shrieked at the cold water, or, if the mood took him, splash on without her and leave her to follow or not as she chose. And sometimes, when the day was hot and the next town not too far away, he would go in bathing and she, with her poor little feminine instincts shooting up like sick plants under the warm rays of this sun-god come to earth, this incredible Dick Broome, would wash his dirty shirt in the stream for him and keep him by her, lying half naked in the grass while the sun dried it. Then he would tell her stories about his mother and Lucy Godfrey and the fairy food, and she would tell him fairy tales about filthy London.

But when he was fifteen and she a year older the harshness of the age wrecked their curious alliance. For the crazy girl, who month by month must do more, ever more, for her idol, was mad enough one day to steal a roll of linen, a pitiful three yards of it, from a good-natured farmer's wife, and had not even sense to get away with her booty. She was caught and locked up in a barn till the constable could be fetched, and if Dick Broom-maker had not come in just then with a hatful of plovers' eggs and his own smile and a sprig of broom stuck behind his shapely ear, there would have been an end of Phoebe. Stealing linen was a hanging matter.

Dick knew it and was sick with fright; for he heard again in his ears the screams of Lucy Godfrey. But he was a man now, a fifteen-year-old man, and Phoebe was his property. He would half kill her for it afterwards; but he was not going to have her touched. So he tackled the farmer's wife.

Reckon, beckon——!

For the first time Richard consciously set the charm to work. And what with his piteous beautiful looks, his childish reliance on the mercies of the farmer's wife, his grown-up reliance on the effect of his own charm on the farmer's wife, and his brilliant inspiration of confiding to the farmer's wife a long, improbable, but most fascinating story of his own antecedents and the wretched Phoebe's antecedents, he succeeded. For he convinced the good soul and himself that here was being lived out before her in the flesh the story of Romeo and Juliet—only she had never heard of Romeo and Juliet—and the Babes in the Wood.

So he got the key out of her and, what's more, a hamper of good food and a decent gown for Phoebe, and was even allowed to keep the linen. For these things he paid, as he could pay, with exquisite decency, giving nothing but a look and a laugh, and perhaps a kiss and the promise that he would allow himself to be spoiled and cosseted and helped out of his next great trouble by the farmer's wife—if ever he were in trouble again. And so amid blessings and laughter they escaped from that Valley of the Shadow. For Death had been brutally near. Dick knew it, and the knowledge turned him into a man, and he looked at his poor dependent with new eyes and looked twice, for in the new gown her pale silvery prettiness showed for the first time.

She needed a beating for her folly and he told her so. But she only clung to him and wept, and when he kissed her for the first time she kissed him back. And after that it was not long before poor Phoebe, who knew so little and poor Dick who did not know so much as he thought he did, found themselves in a fresh difficulty. They loved and they were happy. But to save a girl from hanging, and take charge of her and make her happy was not the end of a man's responsibilities, it seemed. There came a day when Dick discovered, through the coarse talk of the women and the laughter of the men, that it was also necessary to make an honest woman of her as well as a happy one if she were not to endure, even in that crude company, Lucy Godfrey's stonethrowing. Well, it was a new adventure. What it is to be a man and earn shillings and have a woman of your own! Dick with a grin marched his Phoebe off to the parson and brought her back a proud girl, wearing on her finger a brass ring that one of the more good-natured theatre queens had flung them.

And so Phoebe was happy, ludicrously, pathetically, crazily happy.

She had never very strong wits. And then she had a baby. And then she died: which, as everybody said, was the best thing that could have happened. But Dick cried, for he had childishly loved her. And now here he was, a bare sixteen, with a live, squalling baby and no Phoebe.

He went straight off to the farmer's wife. And the good woman, who had a son or two but no husband and no daughter, was good to him, and took charge of the child. The relieved Dick went back gaily to his company, a single man once more, and soon after found his way to London and began his own prosperous career. That he took much further interest in his state of parenthood is doubtful, but he did send money and once in five years or so came down, glorious, to beglamour his country friend with his London ways, to display his real gratitude and affection, and to eye his small daughter with growing distaste. For she was like Phoebe, but without Phoebe's grace of helplessness and poverty. But his good friend told him she could marry the girl easily if there were a little money behind her. Dick vowed there should be money, and by the time the girl was twenty and Dick nearing the forties, money there was—enough at least to marry her well to the local schoolmaster. Dick came down for the wedding and was polite to the schoolmaster, who was inclined to make a virtue of marrying an actor's daughter. But Dick overwhelmed him by his close acquaintanceship with Shakespeare and Mr. Addison. All the village heard that the king had attended Dick's last performance in person and that the great Duke of Bedenham himself was his patron, not to say his friend.

"Well, my girl, bless you and be happy."

Off went Dick, and by this time the faint scar in his mind did not so much as itch. If he thought at all of his daughter when he was an hour from the village it was to congratulate himself on the fact that at last he was quit of a responsibility. With that his mind went off to excited canvassing of his own affairs, private and particular. He had fallen a little in love with a plainish heiress and a great deal in love with her very considerable fortune. And he had hopes.

It was mere malignancy of fate, which always insisted on treating Richard Broome as a comic figure, that his daughter beat him to the altar by a year. When Richard did at last capture his heiress, he received with mixed emotions the news that freakish chance had chosen to make him a grandfather on his second wedding day. He thought it a good joke that his new wife should be a grandmother before she was a mother; but the new wife who, early in 1751, made him the father of a fine boy, was not at all pleased. As for fetching up granddaughter Hilaret from the country as a companion for son Robert, the notion struck the second Mrs. Broome as almost improper. "What! Acknowledge a grandchild older than one's own child? Horrid!" So Richard promised a dowry for his granddaughter and then thought no more of daughter or granddaughter. The son of his old age was naturally more to him than the daughter of his youth. As for granddaughters, let 'em marry lest they burn! And he heard, some sixteen years later, of granddaughter Hilaret's betrothal with placid satisfaction.

But granddaughter Hilaret, with her father's small library to fire her and her grandfather's roving blood in her veins, wrecked all schemes made by her elders. She loathed her selected bridegroom and said so. The day came when, denied money, she robbed her father's pockets, travelled to town in dubious company and boy's clothes: then headed straight for old Broome and his theatre. Behold Hilaret, pretty Hilaret, in Richard's managerial den, demanding as her right her place in the disreputable world behind the scenes!

Old Richard Broome, to do him justice, was all for packing her back to her home, though the manager in him itched to exploit her—her bloom, her pale yellow hair, her lovely narrow eyes so like his own, her grace, her extravagant egoism, her simplicity. Nevertheless he was prepared to play the decorous grandfather: a new rôle always enthralled him. But Hilaret was not prepared to play granddaughter. There was a tussle. She won.

She did not ask for acknowledgment, for favours: she would neither return to her home and her disconsolate Benedict nor appear upon the stage as Dick Broome's heiress apparent. She wanted to be a beggar-maid, to take the town by the mystery of wild-flower charms: and pointed out to her grandfather how he, of all people, ought to be aware that to spring from the soil is the surest way to disarm criticism and attract the Cophetuas. Therefore she would not be the respectable granddaughter of the great Dick Broome. If she must have parents they should be street hawkers, highwaymen, brothel keepers. With serious eyes she weighed origin against origin and plumped for the romance of the brothel.

Richard Broome was charmed by the wise little pretty fool—besides, his business sense was tickled. So, though he was proud of his brief twinge of responsibility and often referred to it later as a creditable sensation, he nevertheless flung himself with enthusiasm into his granddaughter's schemes. She made him laugh. How could he resist

her? Besides, Robert, his only son, took to her from the first: and the
elder Broome had a great respect for the younger Broome's judgment.
If Robert wanted to play with this niece who was a year older than her
uncle—well, Hilaret should stay and play with him. It was no question
of the nursery now. Robert was sixteen and Hilaret seventeen, and the
theatre was their nursery, that was clear.

So Hilaret hung about the theatre, protected, though not acknowledged, by her grandfather Richard and her youthful uncle Robert: and
had her romances, adventures and quarrels with the underlings, and
thus learnt a great deal about life, men and women. From the first she
played brilliantly the part of the guttersnipe, and shocked her grandfather so much, yet continued to make him laugh so much, that it was
not long before he gave her small parts. She played them well. Dick
Broome thereupon decided to gratify his granddaughter and at the same
time turn the tables on her impudence by playing a trick upon her. It
was not to be thought that the great Richard Broome was going to allow
himself to be directed by his own flesh and blood! So he hired a playwright to write a play with a part much better suited to Hilaret's charms
than to those of the leading lady. On its delivery he publicly called up
his granddaughter and, condescending to no argument, thrust a copy of
the script upon the astonished young woman and bade her go home
and learn all the women's parts, and within a week too, if ever she
desired to prove that she could earn her living.

Hilaret, with a giggle which shocked the company, took the script
and vanished to one of her lurking holes; for she liked the carpenter's
workshop, the prompt corner, even the flies, better than the fairly
decorous second green-room. In her corners, with an ear cocked for
her call, she devoured the manuscript, and being well acquainted with
her grandfather's little ways, was soon aware of what he planned.

Rehearsals for the new play began inauspiciously. It became evident
soon enough how little the new part was suited to the leading lady's
dignity. Richard Broome, who had neither scruples nor chivalry, contrived so to criticise the injured woman's quite gallant performance,
that she herself threw up the part and her right to compensation in a
Mrs. Bracegirdle rage, two days before the first performance. Who
then so despairing as old Dick?

"What's to be done? Who's to be got in time? I gave the understudy
to—— Here! You! Mistress! Little Miss what's-her-name! I gave
you a script, but I'll swear you've not looked at it! Come now,
Mistress—confess!"

Hilaret, so timid, with such faun's eyes, but with laughter trickling from the corner of her lips like flowers from Flora's mouth, assured the great manager in a gossamer whisper that she had looked at it. Indeed she had tried to learn all the women's parts, though she found the long words hard, and there were some, she ended in a splutter of laughter, that she did not understand.

"Don't giggle at me, chit!" Old Broome could scarcely keep his own handsome countenance. "It's folly to put a baby into such a part, as we all know. Still—needs must, so we'll try you! Speak up!"

Hilaret spoke up.

Within a week she was the toast of the town. Her gaucheries provided the drawing-rooms with new jests: her simplicities charmed the clubs. She came to harm once or twice, but neither she nor Dick Broome cared. Nor did the absurd prodigious pair care when Hilaret's forsaken bridegroom came to town and showed his Bottom's countenance behind the scenes. It certainly dimmed for a moment the fairy lights, as reality always does; but he was challenged by an unsuccessful worshipper within a week, and so two nuisances were got out of the way.

It needed but the rumour of the duel for Hilaret to be mobbed flatteringly in the streets and parks, and as she and old Broome were generally seen together her success did even the great Dick no harm. The pit adored her because she was one of them, and showed their approval by following her about: the ladies in the boxes liked her because she did not pretend to be one of them, and showed their approval by following the fashions she set. Then the Duke of Bedenham, the proud duke whose first wife had been his equal in rank and who had died of his ceremonious indifference, came one evening stalking as of right, for he was Richard Broome's patron, into Richard Broome's dressing-room.

There he found old Broome absorbed in making up his handsome face while Hilaret sat on his knee and lightened his labour with ridiculous tales of her unfortunate lovers. The duke, assuming, like the rest of the world, that she was Broome's mistress, treated her as was suitable.

Then Hilaret looked at her grandfather and he at her. They always understood each other without words. Broome knew that it was the moment to reveal the secret of the relationship, and did so: and the duke was immensely tickled by this revelation of the town befooled and by the fact that he himself was in the know. The fact of the relationship, however, set a certain barrier of good manners between him and Hilaret. The little supper parties that he forthwith arranged, and which Broome and his granddaughter were happy to attend, ended so decorously that within a week the duke had fallen into a fit of love. With a full consciousness of the enormous honour he was doing the beggar-maid, he offered his protection.

At this point, however, the play ceased to run as the actors had planned it. For the ridiculous beggar-maid, without any affectation whatever, was wounded to the quick by the offer for which she so ardently schemed and which did indeed represent the height of her ambition. She broke into a passion of wild-flower weeping, to the ruin of her make-up, the confusion of old Dick Broome and the absorbed interest of the duke.

He made his peace with her at last, but on a new footing. They were still seen much together but there was no scandal: the duke was too well known for a woman hater, and Hilaret was in no hurry. Having secured her Cophetua she employed her exquisite skill in putting off the beggar-maid so gently, so quietly, so imperceptibly, that nobody stared when, a year later, she was playing Ophelia instead of Miss Prue.

In 1770 she married the duke: and nobody but old Dick Broome guessed that she married him and that he made her his duchess for the simplest of all reasons—a passion for each other, a passion which lasted till his death. She had twelve children, of whom eight lived—George, Edward the ambassador, Hubert who did nothing, Bartrum the great banker, Charles the dilettante, virtuous dull Rosina— Wybirds all—and Lionel and Lettice who had far too much of their mother in them. But their mother nevertheless brought up the pack as decorously as if her great-grandfather the bishop had had a hand in it.

But she took them sometimes to see Mr. Broome play, and later in her life let the secret of the relationship leak out. Indeed, as an old woman she would make merry over the carefully created legend of her beginnings, and point out to the young daughters of the aristocracy that to make your market you must at all costs avoid the trite. "Be an imp, be a changeling, or be dropped in Houndsditch," said the duchess—"and it's all according to your talents whether you end with a coronet or die in a ditch. But be born in Clerkenwell and you'll finish in Clerkenwell, talents or no talents." And then the duchess would tell the story of how her grandfather had fallen through the roof of a tithe barn into a midsummer night's dream.

So much for Hilaret, who set a fashion in her day for lupin yellows and periwinkle blues, and persuaded the blondes to forego powder: and in her old age went journeying to the East with her youngest child, the elegant Lionel, and was heard of in Persia, and then, with him, dropped out of knowledge. Some said that he and she together had penetrated Marco Polo's country of invisible men and that she saw him crowned there, king of a white elusive tribe. But these legends come echoing back after any lost traveller.

The disappearance of Hilaret stirred London for a morning; but she would have been speedily forgotten for a newer sensation had not her uncle Robert Broome seized upon the chance that these romantic rumours gave him to behave outrageously.

CHAPTER 5

ROBERT BROOME AND HIS SON WILLIAM

ROBERT BROOME was born, like his elderly niece Hilaret, with an immense capacity for intrigue. It amused his father to foster this trait much as it amused him to foster the calculations of Hilaret. Robert, colder, cleverer, less handsome than the dark-eyed, fair-cheeked boy who had once enchanted the strolling players, was nevertheless much more attractive than his father to sophisticated people, just because his good looks and his skill were less obvious. He always declared that it had done him much harm in his youth to be known as the son of the great Richard Broome instead of being allowed to earn his own fame. Nevertheless, he did in the long run make more money than his father, played better parts earlier, and contrived to be on intimate terms with highly-placed patrons whom Richard had been wont to control only by sheer flamboyant display of handsome looks and insolent humours. Richard, in fact, ruled by turning his back on a prince of the blood when it suited him. Robert, on the other hand, took care to be attractive to those invisible rulers of England whom even princes fear. Thus it came that he could meet Royalty on terms which rendered it unnecessary for him to indulge in the sort of self-assertion which made his father a figure. The polite world always said that nobody could have the heart to snub Dick Broome: he was too attractive. But it never occurred to the polite world that it must excuse itself for not snubbing Robert. Robert, though he might elect to be an actor, was of course one of themselves. If you wanted to be sure of meeting him you called on the Duchess of Bedenham.

And indeed Robert's smile, his beckoning air, and his curious capacity for attracting confidence and directing the emotions of anyone with whom he came into contact, had long since given him his sure footing in the duke's household. The family could not do without him. He treated his niece Hilaret as an elder sister, was on cousinly terms with his grand-nephews and nieces, and, in an age ceremonious in the use of titles, would not burden his clever tongue with Graces, Lordships and Ladyings. It was a natural consequence of his popularity with his niece's family that he should unthinkingly be accepted by a society that was opening its doors to the picked wits of literature and the stage.

24

All this Dick Broome, strolling player to the last and much more at home in the dressing-room of his leading lady than in the boudoir of his granddaughter, watched, understood and approved. For the first of the Broomes was born with a capacity for frantic, ruinous paternal affection. All the males of the family show this feeling for their sons, though in some of them the impulse can pervert itself and become a jealous hate. But Richard, a sweet-natured creature, had no jealousy in him. He was not in the least embittered by the successes of Robert. He was not even humanly pleased that the successes were less flamboyant and the glories less popular than his own. He loved his boy and sunned himself in the young man's noon, unfretted by the glare.

And Robert returned the old man's affection, though of course he used his influence to possess himself in good time of available theatre rights. He was also firm in pointing out what happened to a paying concern when the old will not take their ease and leave the burdens of government to be borne by younger shoulders. When he first spoke thus old Richard stared angrily, but he soon began to chuckle and, pressed to explain his amusement, wheezed out that "sermons ran in the family!" But he saw his son's point of view and soon abdicated with a good enough grace. Why not? He would be a man of leisure at last like his father the bishop. He would be able to forget his figure, drink port, and enjoy himself.

So he went to Brighton for the rest of the season, caught cold one day because he insisted on paddling as he used to do when a boy, and died of it, handsomely blessing his good son. Robert found that it did not take much wire-pulling to get him buried in the Abbey. And he put up a fine monument to his father, with a bust, and ordered a duplicate of the bust for the entrance-hall of the Gloriana.

The Gloriana was Robert's monument. He had built the play-house under the very nose of the jealous patent theatres, defying them and the eight-mile clause by tinkling a piano at intervals during the show: and during the duchess's powerful reign in London he had been safe enough. For his aunt Hilaret was his refuge and strength. They were on a brother and sister footing—Robert was actually older than his half-niece—and they understood each other well and humorously. She adored him because he was witty and could keep his mouth shut, besides being the best company in the world. Dearest Robert! He relied on her judgment and liked her giggle, and found her much better company than his wife. Dear Hilaret!

When she left England he was furious. He was always jealous of her affection for her own children. When Lionel took his mother off with him as a matter of course and lost her and himself in the rose-gardens of unreality, Robert was bitter in every coffee-house in London about the selfishness of the younger generation. He refused to admit that dear Hilaret had as carefully intrigued to be taken as he would have intrigued to keep her at home, had he got wind of her plans.

"Dragging a feeble old woman to her grave!" raged Robert, who was longing for the feeble old woman's invaluable support in his perfectly outrageous scheme: which was nothing less than the performance of a play written by himself about his niece Hilaret, her duke and her world. It was a piece as scandalous as it was effective, for he had most of his facts from Hilaret's own lips, and, knowing her, he had no doubt of her cynical approval. But he wanted to read the play to her and hear her laugh at its best lines.

However, his irritating young great-nephew had withdrawn dear Hilaret: so he had to be content with the laughter of boxes filled with her relations, and the bewilderment of the pit. For three nights the laughter increased and the bewilderment lessened, as Demos slowly recognised the fact that its rulers were being stuck full of gay-headed pins. On the fourth night the government absorbed the fact also, and closed the theatre, and Robert found that his licence was in danger. He had forgotten his weak point. Neither the Lane nor the Haymarket loved him, and here was their chance to rid themselves of their rival.

The sequel in the law courts stirred London up. Officially, of course, the new duke, Robert's grand-nephew, was against him. But his niece's children were a clannish lot and had not forgotten that, though their father was a duke, their mother was a Broome. Besides, they had inherited the wicked Broome giggle, and were of course aware that whoever reproached their irresponsible relative for his indecorum, the injured duchess would not do so. So, on the whole, influential London was in Robert's favour, and the mob are always for the rebel. Relatives and mob came to hear him plead his own case in the witness box. Robert had never played a part better, they said, than he played that day the part of injured innocence unconscious of offence.

He lost his cause, of course; but by much wire-pulling his licence was preserved to him, for the Duke of Bedenham was welcome at Carlton House, and Mrs. Fitzherbert had ever a soft heart. The business cost him, indeed, a pot of money; but what he lost in the afternoon he got back next morning; for his adventures had made him better worth seeing than the Skeleton Man or the Authentic Elephant. With the money he made he discreetly bought himself into one of the patent houses and so legitimated his other enterprises. Thereafter he flourished as his father had flourished before him, till his tremendous son, William, ousted Robert Broome from his own boards.

Robert thought it right and natural that his ageing father should abdicate; but when Robert in turn began to age and his own son to press for a similar abdication, Robert was outraged. His point of view is understandable. Townsmen preserve the illusion of youth later than countrymen. They refuse to lend an ear to Old Age when they meet her on the street. As for taking her home—never! Father Richard at sixty worked because he had to work and was glad enough when his reign ended; but son Robert at sixty still enjoyed the sweets of management and the applause of a crowd. He enjoyed too, like every other ageing actor, the sheer enjoyment of using nightly his perfected art. He thought he had a right to keep a son waiting. But younger William, like his grandfather in mien, much more like his aunt and his father in character, well read, well bred, with immense ambition, could not bother to wait.

For years he harried his father. Robert fought a losing battle from the start. Dismayed, he confronted himself in the person of his son and saw his own special qualities alive again in a countenance that might have been his own seen in a looking-glass. It shocked Robert to see his own face staring at him so observantly, with such hostile, comprehending eyes. He began to intrigue against his son.

But if he could intrigue, so could William. Once, when Robert called in Hilaret to admonish his son, it was conveyed to him in a look, a laugh, with the flirt of a fan, that a jealous father was an amusing spectacle on the stage, but as a social spectacle was neither amusing nor seemly. William, divining the processes of his father's thought, had been before him with Hilaret, who always took sides and never could resist a handsome young man. It was inevitable that as the years went by Robert should find himself forced to concede, here a right, there a privilege, till, by the time William was twenty-five, all the threads of management were gathered into his acquisitive hands. Robert found the situation less trying than he expected; for William was capable and strong, and his assumption of authority certainly left Robert more time for amusements and his art. But two powers Robert would not resign. He still controlled the purse strings and his parts.

But it was precisely those purse strings and those parts which William desired to have. For father and son intrigued and marketed for the same reason that a poet does hack-work. Only so could they purchase the right to practise the art they both adored. Old Richard's acting had been an affair of looks and personality; but Robert was a conscious artist, and William undoubtedly a genius. Richard could have been happy in a dozen professions; but Robert and William had to act. It was their reason for being alive.

There should have been room for them both. There had been room for Richard and Robert, but then Richard had a golden comic vein: he could afford to share tragic parts with his son. But Robert and William were best in tragedy, and in the same sort of tragedy, and this fact lay gnawing at the root of their differences. For it followed that old Robert's big parts were the parts which young William necessarily hankered to play. Robert, of course, was violently sure that the boy was too young for them, and to-day might have been justified. But a boy of twenty-five in the early years of the nineteenth century was a decade older than a boy of twenty-five today. The youngsters of the Regency knew that their fathers had been well governed by a boy of twenty-four, that he had stood between the country and the mismanagements of a dodderer. Pitt, Chatterton, Keats, Shelley and Sheridan all cried to youth—"Twenty-five is the Golden Age!"

Small blame to William if he listened to that cry in an age that was odd in its attitude towards its actors. For it put inordinate value upon bloom, and rejected women when their charms began to fade and men when their vigour failed them, with the senseless fury of a modern audience hooting the loser at a prize fight. But it had no objection to seeing youth representing eld. To see an old actor play Romeo was unendurable; but to see a boy attempt the passion of a Lear was merely to witness an exciting test of his actor's art. The age, in fact, liked minds and bodies better than it liked souls and spirits, and could always be enchanted by a *tour de force*.

William understood his age and was dying to take his chance in parts too old for him. But Robert clung to his stage sovereignty as to an imperial crown. Robert was enough the proud father to enjoy seeing his young hopeful play Romeo and Orlando, but he was less able to endure William's triumphs as Antonio and Leonato. As for surrendering Hamlet and Othello to the younger man—that was to lose half his kingdom! In the end, overborne by public opinion and his son's superior force of will, he did surrender those very parts; but further along the path of resignation neither his public nor his William could coax him. He would not give up Shylock and he would not give up Lear.

Now the part of Lear William was ready enough to leave his father as one leaves the old dog a bone; but he wanted to play Shylock, and he wanted to play it on lines of his own. He had a fixed idea that his father's notion of a villainous old man in a red wig was not the only reading of the part conceivable, and he wanted to spring a novelty upon London. Besides there was his promise to Lettice. His cousin Lettice, the youngest of Hilaret's brood, had engaged to bring half the town with her to his own benefit (Lettice could pull wires as well as her mother!) if he would promise her that Shylock should be played, not nastily, greasily, but as a gentleman. "Married we'll be in any case," said his cousin Lettice—"but the family will take it less hard if you have been behaving nobly in the evenings."

For Lettice was a romantic young widow of twenty-three, and had made up her mind to elope with William at the proper time. Everyone knew, of course, that she had been in love with him since her early teens, and everybody had pointed out to her that, cousin or no cousin, the youngest daughter of a Duke of Bedenham would never be allowed to marry an actor, though a Duke of Bedenham might with propriety take an actress to wife. A man may do as he pleases, but a Mrs. Thrale becomes a Mrs. Piozzi at her peril. Lady Lettice had accepted the fact as coolly as her mother Hilaret might have done, and accepted at the same time the elderly suitor with the large fortune proposed by her family as the alternative to cousin William and romance. She knew he would not last long, and she was sure of William. It would suit William to wait, just as it would suit him to marry above him and to marry money.

Everything turned out very well for Lettice. Three years found her rich, childless, free to please herself and still in love with William. His successes, too, had made it easier for them to marry. She was aware nevertheless that she was taking a social risk and that it was a question of eloping tactfully rather than of marrying defiantly in Hanover Square. So, as she did not intend to lose her position, she continued to point out to William that romance was much more likely to placate society than realistic art.

But though there were all these good reasons for wanting to play Shylock romantically, William's inmost reason was the desire to beat his father at his own game. He wanted to put an end once and for all to the old man's tiresome assumption of superior artistry, and yet more tiresome habit of quoting the good old days when grandfather Richard learnt his job by strolling the country and sleeping in a barn. How tedious are the old men! William hated his father for being slow in speech, for telling long stories and laughing at his own jokes; but hated him most of all for sometimes, at a crisis, ceasing to be old. Young William could be tender enough when his father made a fool of himself; but there were times when William was aware that he himself had been the fool. Robert could be wonderfully generous at such moments and his advice would be so obviously worth taking that William, who was never a fool for more than a moment, usually took it. Then William would feel intensely humbled and intensely grateful, and would show it by turning sullen: and would like as not fling out of the theatre with his mind or his pocket full of benefits received, and stamp down the Strand jostling passers-by and muttering till people turned to stare at him. And his mutterings ran thus—

"He is a prince! He is a wise old tartar! But oh, why can't I be allowed to make my own mistakes?"

But as time went by William made fewer mistakes, and Robert made more mistakes, till it came to pass that William was always in the right and Robert, fuming, was always in the wrong. Then it was William who kept his head and Robert who muttered and flung out: till many such scenes had occurred and been witnessed, too often, by far too many underlings. At last William decided—Lettice helped him to decide—that something must be done to put an end to an old man's follies.

Throughout the season of 1815, with the Waterloo rejoicings obliterating all other interests, William lay low and matured his plans. But in 1816 he judged the public ready for a new theatrical sensation, early in the season announced the last appearance of his father as Shylock in *The Merchant of Venice* and his own first appearance in the same part two months later. Within a day half London knew that dear old Bob Broome was retiring on a cool two hundred thousand, while the other half was equally certain that it was all a dodge to stave off bankruptcy and the Fleet.

As the cousins said to each other—it was all astonishingly easy once William found courage to take the audacious step. It taught one a lesson, said William: taught one that no situation need be endured if one only had the courage to cope with it wisely and with foresight. And after all his father was being outwitted for his own good. Everybody knew that Robert's great days were over. Could it have been so easy to trick him unless his great days were long since over?

William was right. Ten years ago Robert Broome would have

scrutinised every announcement, would have smelt out mutiny and quelled it before the malcontents had so much as considered the tactics of revolt. But now it was the simplest matter in the world for an enterprising young actor-manager to control the future of the theatre and old Broome.

William kept his father occupied with the production of the play, was the meekest of Antonios, and did not stint the old man of cash or credit. As Robert had for years complained that William impudently criticised his acting and would not let him spend enough upon the setting of his acting, Robert naturally beamed upon the reformed penitent. William was seeing sense at last, bless the boy! Well, William should see that his father knew what he was talking about.

So Robert threw himself with fresh vigour into the part of Shylock: raved, cringed and slavered till the over-rehearsed company fainted with boredom; but was quite content that William should see, unhampered, to 'the business side.'

William did see to it.

'Business' included the printing of the play-bills. They were handsome bills, better printed than was usual: and they were plastered over the town. But William took special care that, though the town saw them, his father should not. It merely meant printing two sets of bills, one for the theatre, one for the town. For Robert, in a heavenly turmoil of professional activity, was eating on the stage, sleeping in the dressing-room, and in three weeks did not stir ten yards from the stage door. It was as if, sub-consciously, he felt a crisis upon him. The theatre felt it too. Most of all William felt it; but he continued pleasant to the old man.

The first night of the season opened fairly. In the opening scenes Robert as Shylock acted well, though William Broome as Antonio acted better. But Robert did not know it and so was not ruffled. It was not until the interval before the Trial Scene that a toady of William's, out of temper with his master over some mis-use, contrived to pin a town play-bill to the green-room notice-board. The bill announced in all the startling vulgarity of lamp-black capitals the last appearance of Robert Broome. It was inevitable that Robert entering, and as long-sighted as most old men, should instantly catch sight of it.

Yet the design was almost frustrated, for Robert had gone to his dressing-room directly after his exit in order to renew his make-up. Had he been resting in exhaustion after one of the earlier scenes he would certainly have stayed there till his call came. But he had not greatly agitated himself in the brief street scene. By the time Jessica and Lorenzo were in the thick of their fooling with Gobbo (he could hear their voices ringing down the passage) he had adjusted his wig, mopped his face, renewed the exaggerations of his own crow's feet which excitement and sweat had blurred, and, bored with waiting, strolled across the passage to the first green-room in search of company. The green-room, however, was empty; for every player not actually on the stage was hovering on the stairs within ear-shot but out of sight, in order to avoid the old man. Though William was too powerful for them to show it, many felt sympathy with the old dog who was to be hanged, and, anyway, nobody wanted to brave Robert's anger. And so there is no actual account of what Robert said and did when he noticed the new play-bill. But that he did notice it, did read it, and did completely appreciate the magnitude of the evil trick that had been played upon him, is clear enough by the records of what followed.

There are many accounts left by eye-witnesses of the extraordinary occasion, and in all one can read between the lines. The most intimate is that of the actress Miss Beverley, whose memoirs still amuse the curious. She had once, for a month or two, been one of William's mistresses, and was that season's Portia: and her account, allowing for some partisanship and some feminine flights of sentiment, is credible.

The performance, she says pathetically, was the most difficult that she had ever been called upon to give—

"We actors were at our wit's end, for news of the great Broome's retirement having spread through the town, the crush was very great and but a third of the audience could be accommodated. Our manager, Mr. William Broome, could not endure to see the half-tendered money returning to the pockets of disappointed patrons, so he hit upon the extraordinary notion of admitting the audience to the stage itself at a charge of three shillings each. It is said that he took more than forty pounds at the stage-door and that some two hundred and fifty persons were accommodated behind the scenes. Of that I cannot speak with certainty, but I may tell you that the public thronged every passage and even swarmed into the flies, and clustered so thick round the walls of the stage itself that it was impossible to change the scenes. Indeed we were completely encircled by spectators and forced to act out the play after the fashion of pugilists or fighting cocks. But it was useless to protest, and the good-humoured excitement which prevailed among our admirers encouraged us to do better than our best."

Miss Beverley goes on to describe the first entrance of Robert Broome as Shylock.

"The house had roared a welcome. Broome, totally ignorant of the rumours spread by the play-bills, took it as his cue, but without particular emotion. Indeed the crowded stage displeased and incommoded him to such an extent that it damaged his performance; for, as always, he showed displeasure by a languor better suited to his son's part of Antonio than to the paternal and pecuniary furies of the Jew."

Antonio seems, indeed, during the first part of the play to have been the more interesting figure of the two. "But"—proceeds the actress-authoress, warming to her theme—"after the fatal interval 'a change came,' as Lord Byron would say, 'o'er the spirit of our dream.' Not that the younger Broome flagged. His entrance in the Court Scene was dignified. His 'Ready, so please your Grace' touched by the simplicity of its delivery. No, the change was in the elder Broome. Never shall I forget his entrance. Because of the press of people the Court Scene could not be built, so the only exit was the stairway of some four brick steps on the back wall of the stage. These ended in a door. Pull this door open and you stood facing the green-room in the long passage with its dressing-rooms and distant stairway. Two inferior actors, dressed as attendants, stood on either side of the uppermost step and so controlled the doorway; but on this occasion old Broome gave the appointed sentinels no opportunity to do their duty. Long before his cue was spoken he pulled back the door so that it clanged against the passage wall and swung to again with a second clang while he remained on the uppermost step between the sentinels, staring upon us all."

It must have been a singular spectacle so strongly to impress the not too sensitive Miss Beverley. There is no doubt that it did; for she says (strange simile for her to use) that as he faced the blaze of light he reminded her of—"a panther that once I saw forced out of its cage at a village fair. It had been taught to leap through a blazing hoop, and it did so, but not without many imprecations and threats from its keeper." Then she goes on to speak of Robert Broome's furious carriage which in her opinion—"did not consort with the part of the mock-humble Jew." Yet she goes on to confess—"customary or not, I shall never forget him leaping the three steps in his rage and then stumbling upon the tails of his gaberdine so that he fell down at full length on the carpet. None went to help him, for we did not know that he had not intended the fall; seeing that he would constantly intro-

duce new tricks and gestures without warning his company. But the
surrounding spectators thought it a common mishap, as indeed it was,
and though the main audience sat quiet, those actually surrounding
us, being drawn from the lower orders, had not modesty or manners
enough to refrain from laughter. Then raising himself up upon his
hands (for he was still kneeling) Broome spat against them, snarling,
as if he were indeed the Jew and they were all the Antonios of his hate.
It was so vicious and yet so absolute a putting on of the part that
the whole house was stirred and began to applaud. As for the ring
of onlookers upon the stage, these drew back in as much haste as
if a wild beast had snapped at them, and we poor players breathed
easier for it.

"Meanwhile Broome had got upon his feet again and stepped
forward to stand before the Duke like a sleep-walker; for all the
while his eyes were fixed upon William his son, who, as Antonio,
was opposing him at the Duke's other hand. He carried himself
bent, but though he cringed he was more dangerous in looks than
any Shylock I ever saw, and I have seen Kean and his son Charles,
and Kemble, and Macready, not to speak of William Broome himself
in his great days. All indeed could rival him in the earlier scenes
and Kean and his own son far surpassed him. But none surpassed
him in the Trial Scene on that one night. When he spoke his lines—

> 'So can I give no reason nor I will not
> More than a lodged hate and certain loathing
> I bear Antonio, that I enter thus
> A losing suit against him——'

his speaking of the line—'I give no reason'—was so proud, and 'a
losing suit' so pitiful, that he touched us all with discomfort and every
eye turned (against the sense of the play) upon William. For a moment,
indeed, I feared that the house would catch the infection of our pities.
But William was even then a handsome man, though he was handsomer in his later years: he grew grim, but grimness suited him. In his
youth, however, he had a sweetness of countenance that was soft and
taking. He smiled gently upon the loathsome Jew, as if he said—
'Pray have patience with him!' Then he won back more than half the
sympathy which Robert Broome had gained.

"As for me, what with the oddity of the situation, my care for
William's reputation with the house, and my fear of old Broome's

anger, I could hardly speak my lines. I was the more troubled because
Broome did not play as we had rehearsed. He had never before
touched me; for he said that Shylock would be careful not to touch any
Christian. But when he spoke the Jew's line—'On what compulsion
must I? Tell me that!' he came up to me, caught me by the wrist, and
held it so hard that I was bruised a week. All the while he was thrusting
his greasy matted wig under my nose, and turning up his face from his
bent shoulders to fix me with his cunning angry eyes as if (forgive me,
reader, the comparison), as if I were a roosting pullet and he would
have foxed an answer out of me. And when I made shift to reply with—
'The quality of mercy is not strained'—still he would not let me go,
but continued forcing me to speak to him alone, while he listened to
me alone, till I came to the line—'Teach us all to render deeds of
mercy!' Whereupon with a snarl he flung away my hand so roughly
that had not Antonio, my William, been t'other side of me I must have
fallen. As Broome treated me so he treated the other actors, even the
Duke. He raged through the scene like a madman and put us all in fear,
save William, who still smiled at him and said the little that was in his
part gently and was the more moving because of it. When William
said, with his slow and very sweet smile, but sighing a little—
'I am armed and well prepared'—then the whole house sighed:
and when he sent Portia the last message—

> 'Say how I loved you, speak me fair in death;
> And, when the tale is told, bid her be judge——'

then it was hard for me as Portia to keep my manly look. Indeed there
are some that say I did not keep it, that my cry, quickly suppressed, and
my starting tear as hastily wiped away, touched the house to sobbing.
But I must not make too much of these partial comments. If for a
moment I outshone those two great players, it was a moment 'brief as
the lightning in the collied night.' On the next word of my William's,
poor I was clean forgotten.

"But Broome's great moment came at the end, though even then
William robbed him of half his triumph. You will remember how
Shylock cries—

> 'You take my life
> When you do take the means whereby I live——'

At that his voice softened, as it were in a lull of tempest and he put out his hand gropingly to William. The change from rage to grief was more than common touching: I could have cried at it. But William turned his back on him to answer the Duke. He had always a low voice, but full. Audiences could hear him though his back was turned. Broome knew that it was in William's part to do this; but yet he stared and drew back as though William had intended an insult. Then I said to Shylock—'Art thou contented, Jew?'

"And here," says Miss Beverley in a professional ecstasy, "came the great trick of the night. For Broome had still the knife in his hand, and instead of answering me he took a step forward upon his son, his clenched fist with the knife in it raised high, and I thought, and I heard it said that many in the audience thought, with the Jew's feigned rage so possessing the old man, we should see a new ending to the play. So, out of my part, I ran forward and pulled old Broome by the cloak, and I think it was my action that halted him. William for his part still smiled on his father but did not stir. There the three of us stood a minute like figures in the new French waxwork exhibition: it seemed at least to be a full minute. Then down comes Shylock's raised arm as slowly as he had lifted it, and the knife clatters to the boards and old Broome says to me in his own voice—'I am content.' After which, ignoring the true run of the text, and before I could say my next line, he went on with—

> 'I pray you, give me leave to go from hence:
> I am not well:'

"Then, clean against the exit as we had all rehearsed it, he dropped his head in his hands, sobbing, and so wandered off the stage. We could hear the loud sobbing continued as he walked down the passage to his dressing-room, long after the door had swung into place.

"Then the sound was drowned, as indeed all after-words were drowned, in the applause of the house. They clapped till it might have been a hail-storm, and we played out the rest of the scene in dumb show. As for me I was much praised afterwards for my presence of mind, and showed my bruises to my friends as a trophy. I wore a blue velvet band knotted over my wrist until it faded, and at once the 'Beverley bracelet' became so much the fashion that the very serving-maids wore a twist of tape."

But we need not follow Miss Beverley further at the moment, though she crops up again later in the history of the Broome wars, a figure of some importance. But on the evening of Robert Broome's farewell benefit she appears to have made, in spite of her own account, no great impression on the house. The two Broomes dwarfed her. When she spoke the specially composed epilogue on behalf of Robert, the excited house barely let her finish it. They wanted Shylock, not Portia, and continued to call and call again for Robert till there was something like a riot; for a Waterloo audience was accustomed to be gratified in its least demand, and it demanded a sight of Robert Broome.

But Robert Broome did not come: and at last the younger Broome, much agitated, appeared before the curtain instead, to convey his father's humblest thanks and farewells. The audience's magnificent reception had been too much for his father. The good old man was utterly broken down: as he himself had told them, he was not well. William bore a message, however. His father prayed them to excuse their old, their most faithful servant his first act of disobedience, and to accept his humble greetings, his thanks and—his loves. On which word—and though it came more easily to the lips of a Regency actor than it could to a modern, it was an odd word to use in such a situation —the younger Broome in turn faltered and could say no more, and has been in consequence reproached for his hypocrisy.

This is unfair to William: he was sincere enough. But he was an artist who might have made a mark in the world of letters, as his diary shows: an artist whose instinct for the right word was exact and passionate. He could always intoxicate himself with words. Besides, William had fought and won a great battle, and he was feeling the strain. But above all he was an actor playing the most strained and ticklish part of his career, and he knew it. One word, one gesture of repudiation from old Broome, and William was ruined. He had gambled on his knowledge of his father's character: he thought he knew how his father would behave; but how could he be sure? He could not be sure until, in his father's shoes, he faced the audience. He did not let them fetch Robert. He did not dare to send a messenger. Could he be sure? It was no wonder that the emotion of a crowded theatre roaring itself hoarse loosened William's own self-control.

The useful Miss Beverley records that when the speeches were ended half the audience turned away, not caring to wait for the after piece—

"Whereupon the spectators who had been drafted on to the stage streamed back into the body of the house, and were given seats there for the farce. Behind the curtain the scene-shifters scuttled about like spiders, while my fellow-players also hurried to change their costumes. But I had no part in the farce. Lingering a moment at my ease, I observed that William was still standing in the centre of the stage, to the great annoyance of the scene-shifters, who found it almost impossible to avoid him. I went up to him and saw with concern that he was extremely white; for there was by then but a vestige of paint left on his face to disguise his condition. I took him gently by the arm, saying that he must make room or he would delay us all, on which he suffered himself to be led aside. I asked him if he felt ill and promised him, if he would come to the green-room, to fetch him a restorative. Thereupon he fixed his eyes on me and replied as one in a trance—

'I? I'm well enough, but I have to go to my father.'

Then he said, taking my arm—

'Come along! We don't make it better by delay!' and walked me off the stage and up the steps. As he opened the door for me, he looked down the long passage that stretched before us and, pointing to the narrow doors to right and left, he addressed me again—

'Did you never think that a theatre is very like a prison?' and pointing to his father's door, added—'There he sits in his cell, and is not glad to be released.' Then he dropped my arm and said angrily—

'But why do you keep me? I have to take him home.'

I offered to come with him, but he made me no answer, so, being uncertain of his wishes, I followed him down the passage. But outside Broome's door he stopped and said—

'Don't come!' But he still kept his left hand on my arm as he put his other hand to the door-handle and turned it softly to and fro, and let it go again unopened. At last he said—

'I would give a thousand pounds if I had not done it. Well—it is done!'

Then he dropped my arm and turned the handle again, opened the door and went in, and I heard him say—

'Father, I'm sorry you are ill.'

Old Broome was laid on a sofa, half dressed, and had his man bending over him. I could not hear what he answered, but he looked very ill."

And indeed Robert was literally and physically ill with rage, prostrate with rage. He lay green and shaking on the day-bed, much as his father Richard had, long ago, lain shaking in the broom. But Robert was not a broken man: there was far more fury than grief in his sensations; for he still thought of himself as a strong man tricked by another strong man, rather than as an old man overwhelmed by the superior energies of a young one. This invincible vanity of his, as well as his family pride, the clan loyalty which makes the Broomes impregnable, bade him conceal his son's treachery when, by revealing it, he could have so easily had the public on his side. But his son had beaten him in a contest of wills and wits, and, for all his bitter anger, Robert took a sort of delight in William's boldness, heartlessness and secrecy. Anyway, the war was between two Broomes: it was no affair for outsiders.

So Robert admitted defeat: received his son's solicitudes with courteous fury, and replied to the farewells of his players with such an air of cold amusement that they went home whispering—"What is the old fox up to now?" But he made no further protest and, on the next day, actually allowed himself, his manservant and his personal belongings to be shifted by his wary son into respectable retirement. William could hardly believe it.

Father and son drove down together to the villa at Dulwich, sitting side by side in an open chaise, not speaking, but each glancing now and then at the other out of narrow eyes. William thought—'What a handsome old devil my father is still!' Robert thought—'He's a handsome young devil, my son!'

The Dulwich villa was charming: and Robert's man Morgan was there before him to make all snug and familiar for the old man. Robert's pictures, Robert's books, his relics of former triumphs, were all disposed about the well proportioned rooms, and the garden showed like an Eden. A meal was laid. William stayed for it and heard his father praise his care and taste, and confess himself perfectly content. The two parted decorously at the garden gate, shaking hands, and each smiled at the other as a Broome does when the other Broome is an enemy. It is a smile that shows the invariably excellent teeth and does not disturb the rest of the facial mask.

William went back to the Gloriana and his swelling success: and Robert endured Dulwich till the end of the season, living very quietly, though once or twice he drove into London. But he avoided his former haunts, saw no friends, and indeed he seems to have gone to London, Morgan in attendance, merely to make a purchase or two. The shopman wondered what the flaming old gentleman wanted, at his age, with duelling pistols.

But on the day of his son's much advertised appearance as Shylock, Robert dressed himself elegantly and drove off in the dusk to the theatre, the famous 'Royal Gloriana,'—the Glory Hole, they called it—in which two-thirds of his life had been spent. It has been noted as pathetic that he had bespoken his box secretly through Morgan, as if he feared to be refused admittance. But here these critics do both father and son injustice. William would have received the old man with all the honours of war: and Robert knew it. But it did not suit Robert to be expected. He had other plans.

It was well after six (for he would not arrive till the last minute) when his carriage rolled out of the Strand and into the by-way at the tail of the stream of chariots, coaches, cabriolets and meaner vehicles which contested with the foot passengers the right of way. The foot passengers, link-boys, servants, coach touts, play-bill sellers, hawkers, Italian image men, costers going home and ordinary wayfarers caught up unawares in the turmoil, were thick enough temporarily to block the oncoming carriages as sand-heaps block the tide. As Robert's carriage drew near the theatre the pest of the play-bill sellers increased. They hung upon the steps, thrust their ill-printed, gaudy leaflets into the vehicles, bawling their wares. When a crack of the coachman's whip dislodged them, the relief was but momentary, for each dropped back into the stream only to change places with a mate at the next carriage. Robert would have paid his penny ten times over to be quit of the nuisance; but the play-bill seller knew him, and not only refused to take his fee but excitedly proclaimed to his neighbours his discovery:—

"Bob's back again, boys! Buy a broom! Buy a broom! Bob's back again!"

Instantly the nearest bystanders took up the jest which three generations had hallowed into a salute—

"Buy a broom! Buy a broom!" Within two minutes the whole street re-echoed the cry. The delighted mob fought its way to Robert's carriage, surrounded it, wrenched off the harness, and by sheer weight of numbers headed the coachman and the terrified horses down a side street. For the rest of the short distance Robert Broome was drawn forward by patrons, while the street yelled—

"Buy a broom! Buy a broom!"

He was not disturbed. He did not, in any case, suppose that he should ever use his horses again. He had planned otherwise. So he smiled and waved his handkerchief at his admirers coolly enough. If a wave of homesickness flooded him as he saw again the beloved frontage, if his eyes filled and his throat choked him, till he twisted in his seat half sick with frustrate passion, the worshippers never guessed it.

Arrived, he forced his way with difficulty through his own coach door, was borne forward by the thrusting hands of his admirers and received into the foyer by scared attendants who could not imagine what the riot was about. One glance at the new arrival, however, explained the situation, and then the mob's cry was taken up by the crowded forecourt and filled the passages—

"Buy a broom! Buy a broom!"

And when Robert reached his box and showed himself through the brand-new curtains, the gala house itself did not disdain to join the cry.

William behind the scenes heard the yells of welcome, and thought that the Regent must be in front. But the Regent had honoured the theatre only four nights earlier, arriving magnificently-corseted and cravated at the head of a formal company. William himself, taper in hand, had backed before him to the Royal Box. Besides, warning would have been given, for fat George's Haroun-al-Raschid nights were long since over. Then who could it be? In his decent black suit and wig of honourable grey hairs, so different from Robert's greasy dishevelment in the same part, William hurried to the prompter's corner. Prying open the crack in the curtain with practised fingers, he peered into the house. The noise had redoubled. Who was it? Who could it be? Then, six feet away from him, directly opposite Lettice and her party in the family box, he saw his father standing upright and bowing to the house.

Involuntarily William's hand tightened on the curtain, and in that instant he caught his father's eye. For Robert had marked the tremor. He knew of the pry-hole—had he not slit it himself many years ago?—and knew, too, who would be behind it at such a moment. So he turned him about and grinned at his invisible son. Then, as the fiddles struck up, he pulled forward a chair, still grinning, and settled back to watch the performance. The pistol box lay on the broad red velvet parapet. Ladies in the box above peered down upon the parapet and tittered wonderingly at the open box. But they had no notion that there was anything to do but titter, and the rest of the house could not see its contents. Besides, what could anyone do with a brace of pistols in a theatre?

But Robert knew what he could do. In the mad letter he left behind him he very clearly avowed his intention, which was to put a bullet through his son should William fail as Shylock and so disgrace the Broome tradition. But should William indeed prove a finer actor than

his father, and the greater man, then Robert knew even better what he
intended to do.

It turned out, however, to be William's night. William had done a
great deal to the Gloriana during his short reign. He not only painted,
decorated and new furnished, but he abolished some of the cumbersome
stage boxes, installed more comfortable seats in the pit and took pains
to bar out undesirables from the gallery. The new regulations had
caused an initial squall, but as they really made for the general comfort
they were, in the grudging English fashion, presently endured and in
the end approved. They were approved the sooner because the new
management, lavish and inventive, was in every other way popular.
Loose-haired, glowing Miranda Beverley was the idol of the pit that
quinquennium, and William's light touch and natural flow of emotion
suited the after-war temper and taste. Given a free hand he could build
up his own popularity, and did so. He was aware that his new reading
of Shylock would be a test of it, but he need not have been afraid. The
audience came curious but prepared to be pleased, and he was not half
way through the Court Scene before he felt with glorious certainty
that he was having the success of his life.

A news-sheet of the day records the triumph, not without a sly hit
or two at William's innovations—

> New brooms sweep clean! The lively bills invite
> Critics and pit to "Buy a Broome!" tonight.
> Son Bob to that grim closet must return
> Where father Richard long since lies in urn:
> While grandson Will reforms the pit and boxes
> And keeps a rod in pickle for the doxies.
> Will dedicates the swept and garnished boards
> To Lady L..tt..e and related Lords:
> "A Broome to sell!" cries Will. My Lady buys,
> While worn-out Robert hugs his injuries.

It is to be assumed that the critic, like his brothers of our later day,
had left the theatre before the performance was over in order to be in
time with his notice. Had he stayed to the end he would have known
that Robert did not hug his injuries long. As the curtain rose for the
tenth time Robert Broome, too, rose up, put out his hand towards the
pistol case, closed it with a snap, tucked it under his arm and retired
to the drawing-room at the back of the box. There he must have
re-opened the case, for later it was found upon the floor. One of its

pistols still nested, but the other was in old Robert's own hand and held as tight as he had once held the reins of management. He had turned it upon himself, and so ended with dignity, and unobserved; for the applause his son was still earning drowned the report of the shot.

CHAPTER 6

THE WYBIRDS TALK IT OVER

THE scandal of Robert's death and William's consequent unpopularity looked like dividing the lovers for ever. But Lettice since her childhood had regarded her cousin William as her special property, and Lettice never gave up her hold of a property. She was a gay, brittle woman with some heart, but more humour. She was remarkably like her mother Hilaret, but she inherited also her father's callousness and the strong will of them both. She was possessive to a degree. She had always intended to marry William : she owned him : earthquakes would not loosen her grasp. Besides, he had always been physically attractive to her, and, though she had sufficient hard common-sense to delay her love affairs in order to secure a fortune, she had no intention of being cheated of any desire or right. Some instinct, too, told her that William could not always be as much under her control as he was at the time of his father's death, and it is possible that her inherited delight in a combat made her look forward to the time when William would struggle to free himself from dominance.

And so the new turn in William's affairs but intensified her liking for the match. She had three main problems to solve, her family's disapproval, society's shrugged shoulders, and the extraordinary change which had taken place in the character of William since his father's death. The first problem did not much trouble her. She was rich, independent, and her brothers and sisters had made over to her much of the delighted homage that they had been used to pay to her mother. Her brothers had their father's heavy figure, slow tongue and his exaggerated sense of physical dignity, but mentally they were half Hilaret's children, in love with laughter, wit and shamelessness, and with a passion for physical beauty. They could not resist their mother, because, even as an old woman, she so pleased their eyes as well as their ears. And Lettice was even prettier than her mother. The fashion was coming in for neatness and grace, and Lettice was a sugar-plum creature with fine bones, bed-post waist, graceful neck and a snow-drop air. Her eyes were shaped like her mother's, were the narrow eyes of all the Broomes ; but they were large and in colour lilac-blue, and her mouth, though shrewish, gave character to her face. Her lips were very red.

It was easy for Lettice, looking so pretty, tears in her eyes and her quick tongue lashing out unexpected answers to expected criticisms, to make a good case for Cousin William. She did not defend William's judgment to the grave circle of brothers sitting in the duke's library; but she did defend his integrity. Hadn't he been distracted by the prospect of financial ruin daily brought closer by an old man's stubbornness and folly? She recalled to them how Uncle Robert Broome had kicked over the traces ten years earlier, involving their mother, pillorying them all. "That reprehensible play, Bedenham—humorous, of course—Mother would have died of laughing at it—and the family had certainly condoned the affair—but had the family enjoyed it? And could it conceivably have happened if William had been in charge?"

Then, said Lettice, let them remember William's superior sense, let them consider with what William had had to contend! Forcing the old man off the stage, they must see, had been absolutely necessary. "Remember that Uncle Robert was irresponsible. Let us face the fact, the Broomes are irresponsible! They have a changeling humour. Our mother prances off to Persia, Robert turns the family honour into a play, because she—he—all the Broomes—are puckish, all except William, of course, and ourselves. Oh, I've long realised that I'm more Wybird than Broome. That is why I've been able to urge upon William that Uncle Robert must go. I saw much more clearly than William could see that such ranting as his had no place in the modern theatre. Didn't his last appearance prove that his day was done, his departure overdue? Ah, yes, Bedenham, he certainly wrought up the house into a frenzy, but it was a farewell frenzy, now wasn't it?"

The duke, rolling a distracted eye on his doubtful brothers and finding no support among the Wybirds, hastily agreed that it was undoubtedly a farewell frenzy.

"But, Lettice, all the same, we did not like it that William should be so nippy with the old man! We feel——"

Lettice would not let them feel. Feel! There was too much feeling about the business altogether. It was relying on mere feeling that had ruined Robert. His Shylock was all feeling, yet who remembered the performance now? William's had eclipsed it. William's Shylock had been greeted three months later with a very different sort of applause. Then a cool, critical house had been carried away by genius. "Yes, brother, genius!" Oh, after seeing his Shylock how could the world doubt William's powers? Certainly his father had not doubted them. Just because he was so sure of William's superiority Robert had jealously refused to resign his parts. When William, by trickery if you like, but by justified trickery at any rate, had won his chance to show how he could act, then Robert had known himself beaten. Then, hating his son for beating him he had aimed his cruel blow at William's career—"A fantastic idea? A fantastic revenge? Not for a Broome! Don't we know that my mother might have done just such a thing? Look at her own history! Yes, look at Mama, gadding off with Lionel, at her age! Is not that just as much a form of suicide as my uncle's pistol shot? William the injured one? I hear my uncle's ghost laughing at you. I know, I am sure, that my uncle shot off his pistol with a giggle. If our mother were here she would tell you so, too. No doubt they are laughing over the business together now. I beg your pardon, Bedenham, Edward, Bartrum, Hubert—I mean no disrespect to our dead, Rosina—you know I don't, Charles—I loved Mama as well as all of you, and I shall never forgive Lionel for abducting her, or letting her abduct him, which would be nearer the truth of the matter. Nevertheless Mama cannot be alive now—why, she would be eighty! Of course she is buried long ago in a rose-garden and having the laugh of our father because of it. Don't you remember how she hated the family vault and vowed she'd sooner be burned and have her ashes scattered to grow flowers? Dear, great, absurd Mama! I wish she were here to take her own cousin's part. She, at least, was never afraid to stand by her own flesh and blood in face of opinion!"

The duke said, flushing, that they none of them wanted to consult outside opinion, or, for that matter, were afraid to face it. But he, for his part, had not yet made up his own mind.

"Oh, slow, slow, slow!" cried Lettice, and laboured to prove to them that while they hesitated the damage was being done. The town had chosen to raise an idle cry against a Broome. By their hesitation they, the family, his own cousins who knew the facts, were flinging William to the mob. "Has that ever been our way? Remember our great grandfather and Lucy Godfrey! He stuck by his friend, the poor little boy! But we have grown too grand to be loyal!"

Here Lettice tore her handkerchief in two and stood up, to make it more clear to them that if they washed their hands of William they must renounce her too. For, she told them, she had once, for all their sakes, foregone a romantic, youthful dream of eloping with William. But now, soberly awake and of age, she meant to marry him if he would still have her. It was a matter of loyalty as well as of affection now. Well, what were they going to do about it? She had married once to please them. This time, when her happiness, her whole future depended on their approval (here Lettice dissolved in a crystal flow), were they going to support her, or were they going to run with the rest of the sheep?

She did not win them then and there; for all Wybirds need time and room to turn, and all Broomes love to bone their least spratling of an idea or a situation. Of Lettice's brothers, some were more Broome than Wybird, and some were more Wybird than Broome, but they all discussed the problems of Lettice's marriage with passion. They divided into sub-committees. There was a duel in the morning-room between the banker brother and the china-collecting brother while the duke walked in the garden with his brother the ambassador and his sister Rosina. The duel having ended in a reconciliation and complete agreement, Rosina was called in from the garden to ratify terms and convey them to Lettice. Meanwhile the duke, left alone with the ambassador, recalled all his pronouncements to Rosina, wiped them out, stamped them under and, meeting her as she quitted the banker and the collector, said so very slowly and firmly. Rosina, primed by her brothers, took "the liberty of disagreeing with you, Bedenham! The others say that it is no affair of ours. Lettice is of age."

"Where are the others?" demanded the duke.

The banker and Rosina went off to fetch them and were waylaid by the china collector. He, since the duel in the morning-room, had encountered Lettice, and, by way of a chat on Flaxman's medallions, had become a convert to an entirely new view of a blameless William, and now felt very strongly that poor William had better give up the stage altogether and settle down quietly with Lettice. The stage, after all, is the house of the showman, not of the artist: which, as the banker brother remarked sharply to Rosina (whom he walked off to look at the peacocks and talk the business over quietly), was a direct reflection on their mother. It was acknowledged, said the banker brother, that whatever the position of the stage forty years ago, their mother had adorned it.

Rosina hurried to tell the duke of the reflection on their mother, and found him once more in the library in the company of Lettice and the ambassador, and the brother who farmed his wife's estate and who had come up specially for the conference. They were discussing with a good deal of acrimony the fact that their uncle Robert had never nominated a Wybird to the theatrical council which patron'd the Gloriana. After all, Lord Byron had taken similar duties very seriously.

Considering what the family had done for Robert, Robert might at least have called in one of them as adviser. "So what about this affair of Lettice and William, Rosina? I think we'd better countenance it, eh? The others seem to think we should."

And the banker and the collector entering, arm in arm, at this point, to explain that on the whole they would rather see Lettice in her grave than married to an actor, found Lettice kissing the duke, and were told that he had promised her all the furniture from their mother's boudoir and half her jointure on the occasion of her marriage to William. Whereupon they put away in their minds for future use the fact that they had never approved of the marriage of second-cousins, and they politely and affectionately wished their sister joy.

"It is understood, of course," remarked the duke to the reassembled and reunited family, "that in no circumstances does Lettice act with him!" And he took his handleless cup of tea from Rosina with patient resignation, for, disliking tea, he only took it when Rosina visited him, because Rosina was incapable of understanding that anybody didn't drink tea.

Lettice was willing enough to promise. She had a passion for the art of acting, but she could always satisfy her passion in private life.

So next day in the gayest spirits, leaving her brothers to discuss measures for solving her second problem, the coolness of society, she put on her prettiest mourning, ordered her carriage and drove out to Dulwich. William had not been near her since the discovery of Robert's body and she knew by sure report that he had not appeared in any of his parts since then, nor even been seen at the back of the theatre. But she did not hesitate: she had an instinct that she would find him at Dulwich. She took with her her dear sister Rosina, who would far rather have stayed to continue the discussion at the duke's, and also her sister-in-law Mary Moone; for, though Lettice and William were cousins and betrothed, decorum had to be observed. William was particular in these matters. Indeed, as Lettice remarked in explanation to Rosina and Mary, stage people as a rule were extraordinarily pernickety in their ideas of how people who did not belong to the stage should behave. "The truth is," said Lettice, "the stage nowadays makes the gulf between itself and us as wide as it can, and with good reason. If once it allowed that you and Mary could give as good performances in your own drawing-rooms as Mrs. Jordan and Miss Beverley can give upon the boards, the glamour is gone. No, no, the stage lives by contrast with the rest of us!" declared Lettice, "and if it can only persuade society to be prudish it need not then bother itself to be vicious. And think what a relief that is to the English!" finished Lettice agreeably. "We find it such an effort to be vicious, don't you think?"

"But surely nobody is vicious except as a matter of pleasure?" began Rosina indignantly, and continued—"I mean, one's always vicious from choice, surely? Then how can it be a relief not to be, I mean?"

Lettice giggled; but her attention was wandering.

"Vicious is a nasty word, I always think," said Mary Moone politely.

"Look at the lilac," said Lettice eagerly. "I wish I could have it made into dresses. Smell it! Shall we stop the carriage and pick lilac, Rosina? It's in somebody's garden. I like picking my lilac from other people's gardens."

"I wish you would talk sense," said Rosina despairingly. "It's bad enough to be driving on Sunday. I never knew anything like the dust on one's black. How much longer does this road go on?"

"Exquisite road! Unparalleled road!" chanted Lettice.

"It's just like any other road," said Mary Moone staring.

"I suppose it *does* lead to Dulwich?" said Rosina crossly.

"It's lined with lilac and it leads to Paradise," said Lettice. "Where else should one drive on Sunday? Dear William!"

"William's father—" said Rosina heavily—"died by his own hand less than a week ago. How can you mock at William?"

"Mock? I?" said Lettice, turning her blue eyes full on her sister: and Rosina saw with amazement that they were swimming with tears. "Do you think I'm not in agony for William? Why else am I driving down to Dulwich instead of letting him come to me? Why else? And the dust, as you rightly say, ruining one's mourning!" finished Lettice, her voice lilting suddenly upwards, as it always did when she desired to change the key of a conversation. She wiped her eyes with her lace handkerchief and let it flutter from her fingers to dry. When they drove by the Effra Arms she waved it at the publican's little boy open-mouthed in the doorway, and was later with difficulty restrained, as they drove past the Dulwich Gallery buried in pyramids of mulberry bloom, from stopping the carriage in order to visit the picture of Mrs. Siddons.

"And suppose William is in town? Robert was buried from the theatre, didn't you tell me? Suppose William has not returned to Dulwich at all?" demanded Rosina, continuing the conversation implacably. "What shall we do then?"

"Why, then—" returned Lettice—"there's always the gallery and Mrs. Siddons!" And rising suddenly from her seat she reached at, clutched and secured a puff of double-cherry bloom that swung from a low-drooping bough. "But he will be at Dulwich," said Lettice. Then, as she pinned the white froth of petals against the laces at her throat—"Look! I don't tan much, do I? Yes, he'll be there—I know William. He'll have gone into mourning in his own way. He'll be wanting to kill himself too. And he'll be wanting company, my company, nobody's company but mine!" said Lettice, smiling to herself as the coachman pulled up his horses with a jingle at the neat iron gates of Robert's house.

The three ladies descended with flutterings and shakings like sparrows after a dust bath, and made their way up the long flagged path to the point-device house itself with its delicate fan-light, its narrow-pillared Corinthian portico, its windows with curved panes that looked as if they were polished. To the left and sweeping round to the back of the house lay the garden, a garden of flowering shrubs, cedars, and dark lawns lengthening down to a stretch of water, too big for a pond, too small for a lake. A brook flowed in and out again, sluggishly, and on the further bank overgrown elder bushes, white with panicles of bloom and pink with encroaching dog-roses, showed that here the gentleman's pleasure-grounds ended and the farmer's fields began.

"Sweet spot," said Mary Moone sentimentally.

"Damp, though," said Rosina.

Lettice, who had run up the steps ahead of them without waiting for the footman, rapped out a tattoo.

"Your master is in!" asserted Lettice fiercely to the man-servant who, almost on her knock, opened the door.

She was right. The man, Robert's dresser Morgan, beamed a welcome, was punctilious in escorting them into the formal reception-room, and zealous in finding the right chair for each of the ladies, in spite of Lettice's emphatic—"I can go straight to your master. Where is he?"

Lady Rosina took the best chair graciously. Miss Moone took what was given her meekly. But Lettice, as usual, got the better of Morgan. She knew the man so well, knew that it was his vanity to carry himself and dress himself so as to be mistaken for an actor. It amused her to play upon this family vanity and family loyalty, just as it would have amused Hilaret to play.

"No, Morgan, I don't want your chair. I've been sitting these two hours. I want to talk to you, Morgan! Well, these have been sad times for us all, my friend. And how are you yourself? Are you thinking that it is time for you to rest and dig your grave, Morgan, near your poor master? Ah, I daresay you do. Very hard for you, Morgan, after all these years! Yes, we know that, but you mustn't die just yet. Gracious me, you are only—what are you? Forty-five? And besides, there's Mr. William to be considered. What would he do without someone who knows all our ways? You must think of your duty in another way, Morgan! How is Mr. William? Were you with him at the funeral? Where has he been since?"

Thus she plied him, to the horror of her sister, who would not talk to an underling if she could help it, and to the vague discomfort of Mary Moone, who did not mind talking to an underling but did not know how to do so. But Lettice cared nothing for their stares. She had it out of Morgan in no time that Mr. William had come straight home from the funeral and had gone to his room, and there he had lain upon his bed ever since. It was two days now, and he had neither eaten nor drunk nor taken off his clothes. The servant observed with some pride that it was just the sort of fit that his old master would take on occasion, and that nothing ever cured Mr. Robert but to be left alone till the fit was over. Nevertheless he would go upstairs and tell Mr. William that their ladyships were there, if her ladyship wished it. He didn't know, he couldn't say what would be the result, but Master William was after all but half a Broome, and so might be easier to rouse than Mr. Robert.

Thus spoke the servant, letting off obliquely his far-away, unforgotten dislike of Robert's city wife. The poor lady had done her duty by bringing William into the world, but had not otherwise distinguished herself in the brief five years of her reign, before she again did her duty by relieving her husband of her quiet company. The body-servant had hated her because she was merely another servant, with superior rights, a simpleton, good enough to keep a house and sew her husband's ruffles. He could not understand that his master had loved her because she was a simpleton and his sweet and willing servant. But then Morgan had once allowed that Mrs. Siddons might have been half good enough for his master, and, in his Victorian old age, he often pointed out that if the Duke of Clarence had stuck to his true wife, Mrs. Jordan, the country would have been ruled by a king that was a king instead of by a chit. But with these two exceptions there were no women on the stage good enough for Morgan's Mr. Robert, and he had never quite forgiven William for not being the son of the great Sarah or the demi-royal Dorothy.

So he sniffed and muttered while Lettice regarded him with a cool look of amusement. Jealousy in other folk always amused her. She often declared that she had too much self-respect to be jealous of any man or woman. But when Morgan mumbled an offer to go up to his master, she stopped him, declaring that he had better get her ladyship and Miss Moone a glass of wine. For they had driven for two hours and were choked with spring dust. As for her, she would wake his master herself!

And so she rustled out of the room, leaving a trail of perfume behind her, faint and delicious as the lilac-laden air of the gardens itself, while the ladies and the serving-man blanched at her audacity. She would go to a man's bedroom? Morgan, naturally, was the more shocked. He cast an agonised look upon Lady Rosina, and dropped his eyes. Lady Rosina and Mary Moone had already dropped theirs. "She would go to a man's bedroom!" shrieked the silence that followed Lettice's departure. Then Morgan hurried away for wine and biscuits. But the silence continued to shriek that Lettice had gone to William in his bedroom, until Lady Rosina could bear it no longer.

"I wish my husband were here," said Lady Rosina.

"But what could he do, Rosina?"

"He could wake William," said Rosina tartly. "What do you suppose would happen if it were known that Lettice——"

"I always said that it was an unfortunate connection," returned Lettice's sister-in-law. "It's the stage, you know. The lights—the complexions: an actor deludes the judgment. I have felt it myself. And yet so coarse in the hand—I mean in the street. You know what I mean. They say Mrs. Siddons drinks stout. Horrid. I confess that to see a woman on the stage——"

"Our mother performed upon the stage, for that matter," said Rosina, again tartly.

"Do you think that Lettice," said Mary, "if she marries William——"

"Lettice must marry him now," said Rosina with resignation. "She is in his room at this moment." And they paused, contemplating the moment and the ceiling wistfully.

"—she is likely to join him in his performances?" resumed Mary Moone.

"Of course not! She promised us!" returned Lady Rosina uneasily, her eyes still on the ceiling. It shook under a footfall, and the chandelier swayed. "Somebody's moving about the room," said Rosina.

Again the two women regarded each other.

"I think somebody ought to go up," said Mary Moone timidly.

"They're bound to be down soon now," said Rosina hopefully. The chandelier tinkled.

"If they aren't down in five minutes," said Mary Moone with unexpected firmness, "I shall go up myself."

"I'm the one to go up if it comes to that," said Rosina. "I'm a relation and married. You're a connection and not."

A bell pealing through the house checked the retort rising to Miss Moone's lips, and as of one impulse both ladies crossed to the window.

"It's a strange woman," said Mary, getting there first, "and in mourning."

Rosina peered in turn.

"And what does a strange woman in mourning want with William?" demanded Rosina, "and on Sunday? Is Morgan letting her in?"

There was a stir in the hall. The ladies became aware that they were to be invaded, and re-seated themselves in haste as the door opened.

"At any rate," said Miss Moone triumphantly, "somebody will have to go upstairs now, and quickly too!"

Here Morgan ushered a beautiful, strange lady into the room and found her a chair. The ladies in possession curtsied; but, all three being English, nobody smiled and nobody spoke.

CHAPTER 7

THE LADY'S BATTLE

MEANWHILE Lettice, who had advised William in furnishing the house for his father, found her way up the stone staircase, with its elegantly turned rail, and paused by the landing-window, whose red rep curtains darkened the whole floor. There was a breakfast tray on the marble-topped table which stood outside the best room of the house. It had not been touched, but there was a litter of torn paper on it. It had been set down in a hurry by Morgan, that was clear. Was it possible that William had already taken over his father's room? What else brought the tray there? She came to the door: stood a moment listening. The room within was quiet, but it was a full, inhabited quiet. She rapped. Then, getting no answer, she called softly— "William! Are you there? It's Lettice."

But there was still no answer: so, putting her hesitation behind her, she opened the door of Robert's room and walked in.

She found herself in semi-darkness. Indeed, although the funeral was over, the blinds were still down all over the house save in the saloon, whose curtains had been hastily pulled on the entry of the three ladies. But she could see well enough the dead fire on the hearth, the tallboy that used to stand in Robert's dressing-room, and the elaborate table for make-up that had been made for him by the actor-son of a cabinet-maker who worked for Chippendale. She could make out too the portrait of Robert's wife over the mantel, the caricature of Richard Broome as Jafir, two prints of the Gloriana, a lovely likeness of Hilaret by Romney and the Reynolds sketch of William himself as a boy. But here Lettice started and looked in horror again, for the glass of William's picture was broken and the sketch itself scrawled over, and utterly defaced by daubs of grease-paint. The actual stick of paint that had done the damage lay beneath, soiling the pale brocade of the sofa.

Very angry, she whipped round to the bed. On it lay her cousin; but the curtains were pulled forward so that, what with their shadow and the darkness of the room, she could hardly see his face. It angered her the more.

"William!" she cried indignantly.

54

"Who is it?" said his voice.

"Who is it? It's I myself! It's Lettice!"

"Have you come? You had better go again," said William, not moving. "You can do no good here."

"William!" She stood over him, quivering with annoyance, concern, and a certain alarm. "William! What have you done to your own picture? How could you do it? How dared you do it? Are you mad that you lie here like this? I'm ashamed of you. This is to be weaker than your father. Get up at once and answer me!"

He repeated dully—"You can do no good here."

"Good!" cried his cousin indignantly, "I can do this much good!" And she swept across to the window, pulled aside the blinds and flung back the half-closed shutters. The pleasant light flooded the room and lighted her beauty, and, as she struggled with the window-sash, she grew lovelier still; for agitation and exertion made her rosy. She left the window at last and came back to the bed. "And now, my dear William," said Lettice, puzzled, angry, but sweet enough, "you will tell me the meaning of all this nonsense. Morgan says you have sulked here for two days."

Still he did not answer.

She was not a pitiful woman: but as she observed him she felt pity. His eyes were deep in their sockets and dull, as if his soul as well as his body had been fasting: his face was disfigured by fatigue, emotion, and a three days' beard, which gave him the air of a Sebastian made up for a ruffianly part. But above all, his effect of an obstinate boy who had found obstinacy useless, of an angry boy who had found in anger no stay, of an adult who had only just ceased to be a young and commanded creature, touched her guarded heart. She forgot her indignation and her impatience, and gathered him into her arms, crying—

"My poor William! You blame yourself too much. Don't be a fool, my darling! Don't be such a fool!"

She felt him shake in her arms and clutch at her hand. She did not know what to do with him, but her common sense told her that, in any case, two days without proper nourishment on the top of such emotion was as much the cause of his collapse as remorse. So she pulled upon the embroidered bell-rope, and when Morgan appeared, stately and startled in the doorway, sent him flying for fresh food and drink: and when it came, stood over her cousin till he had eaten and drunk, which he did meekly enough. Then she said to him—

"Well, now, William, out with it! Let us be rid of it! I know why you are breaking your heart."

"Do you?" said he dully.

She continued petulantly—

"You have too soft a heart."

"A soft heart! I?" said William, knitting his brows: and she was glad to see the familiar look of mockery come and go for an instant in his eyes—"Is that your word for it?"

She smoothed her tumbled ruffles lightly as she answered—

"It is my word for it. You get this softness from your mother. City folk, soft folk! I'm ashamed of you! You did what you did for the best and it broke your father's heart, or his temper, or his wits: and it is very sad, and I'm sorry, and you, of course, are much more sorry. But can you alter things by being sorry, by lying in a dark room, listening to those melancholy church bells which I hate, while you brood over the Confession—'done those things' and so forth—till I daresay you've thought of using the other pistol on yourself. Haven't you now? Of course you have! Oh, how weak men are! And all the while, William, there's so much to be done. You know that you have the whole town against you, don't you? Well, the town has got to be fought. I've done some fighting already. The family's not pleased; but it will keep its displeasure to itself. It will do what it can, though I think it will be a year or two before you can play in London again."

"I shall never play in London again," said William sharply. "I've sworn that. You may goad me, Lettice, but I'll never play in London again." And he got up and stood facing her, and already his air of collapse had left him.

"Well, let that wait," said she, pleased with the effect of her careful work, but disliking his dishevelment; for she was super-sensitive in such matters, and it was a test of her affection for him that she had so far endured his disarray and the stuffiness of the room. She, too, rose. But her work was not done.

"Well, you didn't come to me, so I've come to you," she said, "and there's much to be planned. But we've talked enough here. Put on fresh linen and wash your face and hands, and come downstairs to me. There is our marriage to be talked about. Have you forgotten?"

He sneered at himself and her.

"I am so soft-hearted, ain't I? Am I soft-hearted if I've forgotten it since my father shot himself? Or am I soft-hearted if I've remembered? Oh——" he fretted up and down the room, touching and picking

restlessly at the appointments of the dressing-chest, the mantel ornaments, the trail of clothes flung across the bed, taking up and putting
down this or that trifle as he talked. "Oh, what do you say 'forgotten'
for? Why do you engineer this conversation between us? What do
you want me to say? Forgotten? What else have I thought about? But
why talk of our marriage—now? I'm cut off from London. My income
is gone. Is it in any way conceivable that we can marry each other?
Father has put an end to that! If you were prudent you perhaps would
be thankful."

Lettice's easy temper flamed at his tone.

"Are you suggesting that you perhaps are thankful?"

He flung up his head in a fury of irritation.

"You need not coquette with me. We've understood each other too
long for that. But is it seemly—now?"

"Seemly? Grant me patience! What has seemliness to do with it?
To announce our marriage now, with my family's approval, is good
tactics, William, seemly or not! It gives the world something new to
talk about. If we are to marry, it is now or never. One shock nullifies
the other. Besides—" then she flushed in turn—"I will not wait for
ever, William!"

He said sulkily—

"So far I've done the waiting."

She said in a low voice—

"If I didn't know, if you hadn't assured me so often that you did
wait for me, that you did desire me to marry you, I would go downstairs
and drink my glass of sherry and then walk out to my carriage and
drive back to town and never see you again! That I'd do, William
Broome, if I didn't know that only your father's death makes you seem
thus indifferent to me. I please myself, as my mother did, over what
you call seemliness; but if I discovered that you misread me—if you
thought that I could not sell in any market——"

"Lettice!" he cried angrily and, still angrily, caught her by the
shoulders, and kissed her with a roughness and an air of possession
that satisfied her. She had not been in any doubt of him, but she had been
doubtful whether she had let him be too sure of her. It was monstrous
that his grief should not be at least lightened by her coming. But having
angered him into an expression of feeling and thus restored their relative
positions to her liking, she could relax, and did so, in his arms. Indeed
the scene might have ended not at all according to her plan if at that
moment a knock on the door had not separated them.

Morgan stood bowing on the threshold.

"Miss Beverley, sir," said Morgan, "is below."

At which there was a pause, and a double hesitation such as you see when two polite people give each other precedence in a doorway. William opened his mouth to speak, and thought better of it. Lettice began her—"Who, pray?" and stopped because it was not her house. Then Lettice looked at William and saw that he was vexed, but not at all surprised, yet endeavouring to assume an air of complete surprise: and she giggled, though, feeling Morgan's reproachful eyes upon her, she turned the giggle hastily into speech.

"Were you expecting her, William? Who is Miss Beverley? Perhaps she had better not come upstairs." And she giggled again, for she knew perfectly well who Miss Beverley was. Being completely a woman of the world she was pretty well aware that William would necessarily have persuaded an accommodating charmer or two to help him while away the long years of waiting for herself. Indeed she would have thought him a milksop if he hadn't; but she was not therefore going to make a ticklish situation easier for him. She loved to see a man flounder. She thought, too, with some vexation, that if William had not given way to this amateurish fit of remorse when all his affairs were unsettled, when energy and a bold front were supremely necessary, it would not have been possible for his stage ladies to hunt him out. She was quite sure that Miss Beverley was there to show sympathy and proffer consolation. Then Lettice bit her lip and darted an angry glance at William, for was she not there herself to show sympathy and proffer consolation?

"You must not keep her on the door-step, William!" said Lettice softly. "And I think Rosina will be tired of waiting and I think we had better be going." And she picked up her gauze cloak, clouded it round her and stepped towards the door, a little prancingly, as if she were picking her way down a muddy lane, as if she were very glad to be out of the littered, untidy man's room and all those littered, untidy man's affairs.

But William took no notice of her airs and graces except to say curtly —Lettice was pleased to observe that with the mention of the actress William's capable business-manager air had returned to him—

"You had better go down to Rosina. I'll join you in five minutes. Of course you must not go yet. I have a great deal to say to you still."

"And if Miss Beverley also should have a great deal to say?" Lettice demanded.

"That's my affair. Don't be troublesome, Lettice! You choose to be in the thick of my affairs and you know they are tangled. Miss Beverley, no doubt, brings me news of some fresh difficulty at the theatre."

"A kindly woman!" murmured Lettice.

He gleamed at her between annoyance and amusement.

"Damn it! Draw in your claws, Lettice! Is this a time—I think you would dance on a grave. Save up your mockeries till we are out of this house at least. And now go down to Rosina while I get rid of the Beverley. Where is she?" He turned upon Morgan.

Morgan stepped aside to let Lettice pass.

"I ushered her into the parlour, sir! The dining-room is not fit——"

"Are you mad, Morgan?" William was genuinely shocked. "Miss Beverley and—oh, my God, Morgan! Stop laughing, Lettice! Miranda and your sisters! What's to be done? You're to stop laughing, Lettice, do you hear?"

But Lettice was incapable of stopping. The bland Morgan, the outraged William, whose social sense was very much more sensitive than her own, and the picture which she made for herself with infinite glee of the trio in the parlour below, was a dose of the absurd that went to her head.

The interview with William, brief as it was, had excited her, for, in spite of her common sense, she was intensely susceptible to the emotion of drama and the drama of emotion. This unexpected absurdity following on tragic airs had on her much the same effect as a glass of champagne on an empty stomach. The livelier William grew, the more she laughed. Not until she saw with a certain discomfort that there was no answering amusement whatever in his face, did she realise that there was a time for all things, and that this was not the time to laugh at William.

Still much flushed she did her best to repair the error, and, smiling at him sweetly enough but with a suspicious trembling in her voice, she suggested that she had better join the party downstairs.

"After all, William, I, at any rate, shall have to know your stage loves one day," said Lettice, "though I don't suppose Rosina will care to pursue the acquaintance. It's Mama we need now, William! If Mama were here how well she would carry it off. She would know how to talk to your Mirandas. Go and put your coat on, William, and brush your hair, and don't stand there looking like Kemble. This is not the Gloriana." And then, in a new voice—"William, you're not annoyed, are you? Is anything more the matter?"

"If you will go downstairs, Lettice," said William furiously and with complete courtesy, "I will follow you almost at once."

He held open the door for her. She walked out. He shut it after her.

Lettice did not know whether she had had the best of it or not as she went downstairs. But one thing she was sure of, that Miss Beverley should not have the best of it. Then she opened the parlour door and stood a moment surveying the scene, and found it so humorous that again she wished for her mother, or indeed for dead Robert himself. Those two would have enjoyed the jest with her.

She sighed in her heart and blew a farewell kiss to the last generation that had frolicked through life as she and William would never be allowed to do. Looking at her sister and her sister-in-law, seated to right and left of the beautiful Miss Beverley, she had a prophetic vision of the coming half-century and the boredom it was to bring her. Every year, reflected Lettice, life grew more respectable. The rift between her father's blood and her mother's blood was widening into a gulf. Her father had married her mother, and what a lot of amusement they had got out of the match and how well Society had taken the business! But look, only look how her sister-in-law and dear Rosina were regarding the beautiful Miss Beverley whom their mother in her youngest days would have been very glad to know. It was true that Miss Beverley carried herself with an air of assurance that was irritating, though she had not sat down, perhaps because Morgan had offered her a seat too near the door. Curtseys, no doubt, had been interchanged between the three, Lettice was sure of that; but she did not think that Rosina had asked the stranger to draw near. Miss Beverley, however, with the unerring instinct of her profession in selecting a noticeable position, had taken the centre of the hearthrug. There she stood, looking remarkably handsome, one shapely arm resting upon the mantel-shelf, and her foot just a little stretched out to the fire. The pose was perfect, though it was clear that Rosina, regarding the intruder with gooseberry eyes, thought it familiar.

But Lettice appreciated it. It was exactly like a print which she had seen recently of Religion mourning for George II, though Miss Beverley made it very clear that she was in mourning for someone much more recently deceased. Indeed, as far as mourning went she outdid them all. Lady Rosina's bonnets and shawls were always black, always dowdy. She was far too much at home in her black for it to look grievous. Mary Moone had contented herself with a black pelisse and veil worn over a purple and comparatively cheerful sprigged muslin:

and Lettice herself, though her mourning was mourning, and her mourning was new, had also the air of a cheat. She was a black figure, certainly, in her clinging muslin with the double flounces of chantilly, her floating veil and gauze cloak; but how gay, how gossamer were the materials employed in mourning for Robert! Her charming movements displayed alike the flow of her figure and the airiness of the new summer fashions: and her little white face, whipped into almond-pink over the cheek-bones by the late encounter with William, was more alive than was seemly in a house of grief. With that all-observing, all-enjoying countenance framed in the bonnet of cobweb-straw and massed sable plumes, Lettice had such an air of gleaming starrily out of her gloom like the first fairy lamp of the evening to be lighted at Vauxhall, that Miss Beverley undoubtedly bore away the palm for sorrow. Besides, Lettice looked very well indeed, looked as if she had eaten and drunk: nor, it was clear, were either of her companions much bowed. But Miss Beverley, the artist, had enhanced the suitability of her attire by a careful blanching of her handsome features and a becoming blue shading of her large white eyelids. Nothing, her bearing declared, should induce her to fail in rendering the last tribute to a head of the profession, and, on Lettice's entrance, she lifted the delicately tinted lids and rolled on the three women distracted eyes pearling with tears. At which Lettice, all the while admitting that tears suited Miss Beverley, lost her sense of humour and her temper, and did not stop to search for either.

She was amazed that she had not instantly recognised the outrage of the visit. How dare the woman stand there dripping unrequested sympathy? How dared she be able to cry unquenchably without her eyelids and her nose showing pink? How dared she be there at all? How dared she exist for that matter? To appear on the stage as an underling of Uncle Robert's was one thing; but to appear privately at Dulwich as a friend of William's was another: as she should learn. She was welcome to claim acquaintance with the Broome in William, for that matter, but how dare she be intimate with a Wybird?

"I think you are Miss Beverley?" said Lettice in her charming high voice. "Won't you sit down?"

Miss Beverley curtsied and took a step forward.

"Is he here?" she demanded deeply, and the large pear-drop tears made faint runnels in the rice-powder smoothness of her cheeks as she let them fall at last from her long lashes.

Lettice looked at her with an expression of puzzled helpfulness in her own eyes, which might be dry but were equally bright.

"He?"

"Broome!"

"Oh," said the enlightened Lettice briskly, "you mean my Uncle Robert! You're a day late. He's in heaven, I think."

"Don't, Lettice!" murmured Rosina.

"Mrs. Beverley wants to know, Rosina. Don't you, Mrs. Beverley—or Miss? Miss, of course! It's so kind of you to enquire. You knew my uncle well, didn't you? Weren't you one of his Portias? Portia is such a difficult part, I always think, especially in the Court Scene, because, of course, everyone guesses at once just exactly what she is, don't they? And then they have to pretend ignorance. Very difficult for everyone. But I thought you did it so well."

"Lettice! Lettice!" Rosina, that nice woman, half rose.

"What, Rosina? Oh, of course. I forgot. May I introduce Miss Miranda Beverley to you, Rosina? Miss Beverley of the Gloriana Theatre and—where else do you come from, Miss Beverley? York, Dublin, Edinburgh—they all know you, I expect, so well! You must not mind if we stare at you. It's a new experience for my sister and my sister-in-law to meet anyone so celebrated. Will you have a glass of sherry before you go, Miss Beverley, or would you rather see William? He'll be down some time or other, I daresay."

And Lettice, drawing breath, smiled at the dumb, affronted creature, who swayed under the attack like a loose-petalled, over-blown peony when a bright angry bee kicks and claws a ruthless way into its secrets.

But the stiff, kind Rosina was genuinely shocked. Turning to the actress, whose tears now needed no forcing, she smiled at her as politely as her shyness would allow and began pointing out the beauties of William's lilacs and young laburnums while Lettice, scarlet cheeked and quite hoarse with rage, turned abruptly from them to the table and with shaking hands poured out glass after glass of sherry for Mary Moone.

As the fifth brimmed over William came in, grasped the situation and, briefly greeting his relations, withdrew the Tragic Muse with professional adroitness. He pulled-to the door upon his exit; but the three women could hear his voice faintly in the passage, beginning angrily—

"My good Miranda, you can't come here! This is my home!"

They pretended not to listen for the reply. It came clotted with sobs, high and extinguished—

"I couldn't stay away, Broome dear. You looked so ill at the funeral. How should I know that your relations would be here, your terrible relations! That cruel woman! She took a whip to me, Broome!"

"Lady Lettice is to be my wife," said William's voice in the passage, irritated, apologetic, triumphant. "You know that, Miranda. Can't you be quiet? Well then, come away into the air."

The click of the latch let in garden sounds, the song of the birds and the boisterous sweet spring wind. Footsteps sounded on the steps and died away with Miss Beverley's sobs in the distance.

"Strumpet!" said Lettice fiercely.

"Oh, Lettice!" said Mary Moone.

"I'm ashamed of you, Lettice," said Rosina.

"Will you tell me why?" returned Lettice, lifting her chin and staring down at her sister.

But Rosina remarked that the tears were now pouring down her sister's cheeks as freely as if Lettice had been a mere soft, foolish Miranda Beverley: and Rosina, who understood nothing of the subtler emotions, knew at least what tears meant. She had shed her own natural portion in her time. So she turned to the table and the glasses of sherry and tut-tutted over the spilling of good wine; but said no more to Lettice, stationed at the window dabbing her eyes with her lace handkerchief.

It was some twenty minutes before Miss Beverley's departure occurred. Lettice watched it from the curved panes of the parlour bay. William helped the lady into her carriage, but their farewells appeared to be formal. Nevertheless, when the coach had driven away and William had closed the little gate and come up the narrow path, he did not ascend the steps to the house but strolled off into the garden.

When Lettice against her judgment, because she was tired of waiting and angry afresh at being made to wait, went out to him, he was strolling to and fro under the mulberries, absorbed in thought.

She came to him over the grass.

"Well?" she addressed him as she rounded a flower-bed and held aside with her white, pink-tipped fingers a pink and white spray of Japanese cherry that barred her path, "Well, so you've got rid of her!"

He looked at her in abstraction.

"Who? The Beverley? That was easy enough."

Relief descended upon her like dew. She fell into step beside him. They walked up and down in silence, she lifting her skirts and controlling her fluttering laces, he with his hands clasped behind his back.

"What did she come for?" said Lettice lightly. Her fever of angry curiosity was gone, but she hated a silence. When he did not answer she added with a half laugh—"I mean, what was her formal excuse for coming?"

But he refused to understand the implication.

"She's an old friend and she'd heard some absurd rumours," said he coldly. "She feared that I was ill. She feared even that I——"

"That you'd followed your father's example? I daresay that is what your Miss Beverley would call a good curtain to an act. Was she greatly disappointed?"

Said William impassively—

"Lettice, it's time you went home."

"I daresay," she returned with equal phlegm. "But I thought you had things to discuss with me?"

"So I had," said he gloomily; but volunteered no more: and they continued to walk up and down the paths together while she said to herself, "These artists! Six moods in six minutes! What have I done now?"

For she was beginning to be aware that he was really angry with her and had a glimmer of a notion why. She was quite sure that it was not concern for Miranda Beverley's feelings, though she was equally sure that he would pretend to himself that it was precisely that. No, the injury had been done him earlier, thought Lettice, cheering up. You should never laugh at a Broome. Dear William! She glanced up at him. Rigid—quite rigid! Dearest William! But the immobility of his profile should not prevent her from making a fresh advance. In her own eyes, which were the world's eyes, she was his superior in birth and fortune, and, though his talents brought them once more upon a level, her initial advantage gave her, she felt, liberty to humour him more than otherwise she could have done. She could not cheapen herself to William: she had too much to give. Therefore she enjoyed being generous in taking the first steps towards reconciliation.

She glanced at him again and this time found him glancing also. Detected, he sustained her gaze hardily and tightened his lips. "Yes," she thought, "he is certainly angry." It did not displease her. On they strolled again, he lowering, she smiling to herself. At last she stopped dead on the path and put her hand upon the lapel of his coat.

"Are you sulking with me?" Lettice demanded. "Why are you sulking with me, William?"

He glowered at her.

"I don't like your notions of humour," said the future Hamlet of his generation.

"Because I laugh at Miss Beverley?" she demanded, a little ashamed of herself, but not prepared ever to admit it. "But we're even. She weeps much better than I do."

"She was weeping for my father," said William harshly, "and for me. But you—you laugh at us all."

Lettice flung up her pretty hands with a Heaven-send-me-patience gesture that her mother had used as Lady Teazle; but none the less she was alarmed. She had known William since her babyhood and their friendship had been based upon the fact that they always saw each other's jokes. Even in their romantic first meetings as lovers and most tragical partings, still they had laughed at the same jokes.

But now she saw, suddenly, that it was part of her fatuity as a human being and a woman (Lettice was always in the superlative) not to know when a joke ceased to be a joke and became a piece of bad taste. Continuing to think in the new dawn, she now saw further and with blazing, blinding clearness, that she was a much shallower creature than William. She had always known that she was a much cleverer creature. She had not known though that the polished, sparkling surface of his mind, on which her own had sped along so gaily, like a skater on a sparkling strip of ice, had deeps. But now she had come upon a rough surface, tripped over some silly sunken branches, the ice had cracked all round her and she was of a sudden up to her neck in water. It was all very cold and alarming. But though she knew herself capable of floundering ashore in the end, she would not think of doing so, not yet. She had done wrong and she intended to be penitent and nobody should stop her. A stranger, indeed, might say that William was showing ridiculous vanity, an absurd lack of balance, instability and a dozen other inconvenient traits. Not so Lettice! Pish! These surface irritabilities meant nothing. They were straws on a dark current, a deep current. The vanquishing of Robert was having a result that even she, the foresighted, had not fore-dreamed. So this, gasped Lettice, was the real William! Robert's death was having results! It was already profoundly modifying the character of his victorious son. She thought to herself, "This is very serious indeed! This business may kill him. He's a stripped creature. A little thing like a giggle is a public flogging to him. I must never laugh at him again. What a fool I was to laugh at him! If he were playing Hamlet tonight he would break our hearts. He could never touch Hamlet before. But now he has lost faith in himself, yes, now he could play it!"

Thus Lettice, a trifle exaggerated in her conversion, as she had to be in all she did, but with a clearer view of her cousin and betrothed than had yet been vouchsafed her: thus Lettice, getting a foothold but by no means ashore.

So she began vaguely, even with a certain timidity, merely to be walking with him mentally, merely to be in step with his thoughts—

"William, I'm sure that Miss Beverley is really nice and kind."

But William stopped short, and the look on his face startled her. For the moment it showed pure dislike, as he said—

"Please, Lettice, please! I don't want to discuss her. I would rather not."

"But—" she began.

"Please!" said William with considerable emphasis.

The snub hurt astonishingly. Also it sent her into a panic. She had been so sure of him. She could not bear to be reproved and it surely was not right that he should detect in her anything reprovable. Yet, of course, angry and hurt as she was she had to see that her failure to control the situation was a fault deserving punishment. And all the time, while her cheeks burned and she lost her breath, another part of her mind said, "I'm falling in love with him all over again. I've never been in love with him—properly. I knew him too well. But this William is a stranger. I'm not sure that I even like him. But I'm certainly falling in love with him. How I hate the Beverley! But I needn't have troubled. He's not thinking of her, he's thinking of his father. But now I must make him think of me."

All these things flashed through her mind while she stood in front of him, looking up into his face. Then her affection taught her what to say.

"William, do forgive me! I didn't mean to laugh. I didn't mean to be hateful. I was worried about you and I wanted to rouse you. I hadn't any more intention of offending you than of marrying the man in the moon. I love you too much. Do believe it!"

Never before had she owned herself wrong. But even now he was too absorbed in himself to understand the implications of the surrender.

"I don't need apologies," said he remotely.

"No, but I give them to you, so you must take them. Love hurts without intending it. You hurt your father without intending it. No, don't wince, it's better to talk it out. We may as well know what we are facing. We did worse than we dreamed, without intending. Good God, my dear, we didn't want him dead!"

He cried out at that—

"No, no! I didn't want him dead, Lettice! You know I didn't. I only wanted my own way."

She smiled up at him, the most intimate of all his possessions.

"Oh, how I understand you!" she said. "I want my own way more than anything in the world. But look, William, we shall get our own way still. You will have them hauling you back with golden chains if you play your cards well. Turn this disaster to your service. What's done cannot be undone."

He stared at her, then broke into a great laugh.

"Will you play the part for me?"

"What part?" said she, not following his thought.

"'Come, come, come, come, give me your hand: what's done cannot be undone. To bed, to bed, to bed.'"

"William, don't be so horrid. Let go, William!" and she struggled fiercely in his arms.

"Yes, you would play it if I let you," he said, still staring at her. "It's in you to play it, you pretty iron-willed creature, and you wouldn't walk in your sleep afterwards either. Well, you're right, I suppose, just as she was. Women are so damnably right always. No, it's no good looking back. What do you want me to do?"

"Do?" Lettice's eyes sparkled. "Snap your fingers! Take your chance! You have money, reputation, control of a company. The very notoriety will help. Don't shiver at me! Wouldn't your father say the same thing? He wasn't squeamish. Look how he exploited Mama! He'd say to you as I do—all you need is variety of experience. You need to try yourself against a hundred audiences. Well, now's the moment! Tour!"

He was waking up.

"I was on the northern circuit years ago. He—my father—insisted on it. He said what you are saying—I needed the rough and tumble. Besides, there's America—Australia—"

"Yes," she said, "London's local after all. London will have forgotten what it thinks of this business in a year. Then it will be 'Buy a Broome!' again. Meanwhile—I've always wanted to travel."

He stopped short.

"You, Lettice?" He was moved. "Would you? Could you? Lettice—" the cry was dragged out of him—"Lettice, I can't endure to be alone!"

Upon which, to the scandal of Rosina watching from the window and to the edification of Morgan at his observation post in the basement window behind the ferns, Lettice, tip-toe on the garden path, put her arms round William's neck and kissed him fair and full.

"But of course I'm coming with you," said Lettice sharply. "I wish we could go to Persia and find my mother. It will be odd to be one of a company. I shall drop my title, of course, but I think—" said Lettice, who always reverted to any subject on which she had suffered defeat and did on a second trial generally level matters up—"I think that your Miss Beverley had better stay at the Glory Hole."

William shot a look at her of comprehensive amusement, yet in it there was enough appreciation to satisfy her that he was once more satisfied with her conduct of herself and his affairs. Lettice, well ashore, congratulated herself on her safety. But she resolved to keep a better look-out for the notice-boards when she went skating again.

CHAPTER 8

A BROOME HUSBAND AND A BROOME WIFE

LETTICE had her way, and the English theatre may be grateful to her; for William did much for it before he died and the three sons Lettice bore him did more. She was right in all her prophecies. Sentimental London was for the time being finished with William Broome; but the provinces adored him. He earned his success; for having leased his interests in the Gloriana for a period of years, he settled down to harder work than he had ever done in his life.

But though Lettice had her way and was justified of it the pair were not in the first years of their marriage at all happy together. It was no fault of his: no fault of his wife's: or perhaps it was the joint fault of their past. Robert's death was not to go unavenged, and Lettice's very sanity drew down their punishment upon them. For in an emergency Lettice was unsurpassed; but she could not long breathe easily on a height. Her nature craved gaiety and throve on common sense. So she allowed William six months to be melancholy in and then she demanded a return to the normal. William, however, never returned to the normal, and Lettice never accustomed herself to the change.

Yet the change was part of his hold upon her. It stung her, yet intrigued her to discover that she was no longer able to manage him by her wit, her spirit, her social grace. These charms of hers had no effect on him: he loved her, if he loved her, for reasons that he would not give her. His temper, always uneasy, became with the years a devil beyond the control of either of them, a sullen third at their table and bed. She knew that he had never fully recovered from Robert's death: and yet her own temper revolted against the need to make allowance, allowance, and again allowance. Each time that she revolted there would be periods of black estrangement when the very civilities fluttered away like scared sparrows. But though the skirmishes might go on for a day or for a month they ended always in a full dress battle and the complete defeat, now of William, now of Lettice. William won on his power mentally to cut himself off from the humanities, to be a mad bull in the field of his own emotions, charging down upon the intruder, his wife. Lettice won on the fact that she was quick-witted, evasive, that she slipped away from his rushes of rage and re-appeared unshaken, merciless in attack and, more often than not, in the right.

But they were, of course, neither of them ever wholly in the right. Their battles were without cause, without object, mere attempts at mastery. They were wrestlers of the emotions who enjoyed a trial of strength; though each, afterwards, blamed the other for the personal exhaustion of energy. Yet in each the taste for drama was inextinguishable and each provided the other with the stimulant that made life worth living. Each was the other's champagne; but after a drinking-bout, each, in a frenzy of nervous exhaustion, reviled the champagne.

But though they thus constantly wore out their mutual patience, their mutual passion suffered no diminution. No fury of battle, no after-wounds, no humiliation of the vanquished could kill it. They were in fact completely happy had they but known it; but they did not know it.

In the first five years of their married life Lettice bore William two sons, Russel and Robert. The birth of Robert (they called him Robin) left her delicate. She had long since outlived her amusement at the odd conditions of life in a travelling company, and she was left disliking the hardships. William's gloomy pride would not allow her to use any of her own plentiful moneys to ease their way, and in one of their earliest quarrels he told her plainly that she could lodge by herself in the best room in the best hotel in every town they visited if she elected to do so; but while she lived with him he paid the bills. His unexpected firmness pleased her, for, like most strong-minded women, she enjoyed the unusual sensation of being ordered about. Nevertheless she intended to have her own way.

But William would not let her have it. His order was no gesture. He had made up his mind. He would live as his company lived. Submitting out of affection for him, she yet found theatre lodgings and dirty dressing-rooms tedious, and the social humiliations which a duke's daughter masquerading as an actor's wife could find amusing when they first occurred, became in time as much a nuisance as rusty bacon and bugs in beds.

When her first confinement drew near she decided to go home. By 'home' she really meant the house of her brother the duke, for between him and her the family ties were strong and she had almost a daughter's reliance on him; but to please William she went instead to the little house at Dulwich.

It was a well-planned house: she brought down good servants and was comfortable. The birth of her first child endeared it to her and she ended by liking it so well that, though she returned to William and a touring life six months later, she went back to the pretty village and the pretty house for the birth of her second child. This time she did not return to William: instead he came to her. There was no quarrel at all: on the contrary, the arrangement suited them both and proved their marital salvation. Their professional separations merely enhanced their need of each other. Not only did William spend the intervals between his tours with her, but he snatched every opportunity which the chances of travel afforded to get a glimpse of her, while to her these strenuous visits were the supreme events of her smoothly ordered existence. She looked forward to them as a child looks forward to Christmas. She developed also for this dramatic William disinherited from her London world the special tenderness that a woman of the dark ages might have entertained for an outlawed lover, forced to visit her by stealth.

Thus they met with the delight of parted lovers, and parted eager for new meetings: and meanwhile did not disdain the reliefs of a complete change. He gleefully indulged the Broome in him, the eccentric, the egotist, the beckoning Will-o'-the-wisp. She was pleased to be a Wybird again, to slip into the formalities of London life: had Mary Moone to stay with her as sheep-dog, and was welcomed by her adoring family, who always spoke most affectionately of William.

Indeed Lettice, in her second venture into married life, could look upon her work and find it good. Two fine children, her husband still her lover and her social position unimpaired—these were her personal gains. For her William the gains were even greater. He was at the head of his profession as far as the provinces were concerned: news of his triumphs had intrigued London: the old scandal was half forgotten, and he had a fabulous offer for an American tour. Had she not reason to be proud?

When William decided to accept the fabulous offer Lettice thoroughly approved. "And when he comes back," said Lettice to her intimates, "we'll think of London. For, of course, sooner or later William must come back to London."

But when she said the same thing to him on his latest flying visit he was furious with her. He could not even yet bear a reference to London, as she ought to have known. He made her feel that she ought to have known. And indeed she did know it and could have whipped herself for her error of judgment. So she, too, was sore: and before they had time to protect themselves, before they knew, the difference between them had blown up into the worst of all their quarrels.

When William left her he was still raging. Lettice, who knew herself in the wrong and was ready to be conciliatory, took his sullen departure without too much anxiety. She thought she knew her William. He would have cooled in a week or two and be writing to her affectionately as usual, or be asking for comments and advice on his new venture. However fiercely they quarrelled he never left her long without a valentine.

Then he wrote. "Just as I knew he would," said Lettice, smiling over the envelope and the abrupt handwriting. The letter was affectionate enough; but he wrote that, hurried by circumstances, he had been forced to engage his company for the American tour without her advice and that his leading lady was Miranda Beverley.

The news outraged Lettice. Not once since their marriage had he given her cause for jealousy. She had not the faintest doubt that she was as necessary to him as he to her, even when he told her that she was the Maria to his Malvolio and that he wished he had her on the stage. She might be the light comedy in his life, but she reflected that comedy and common sense are not far apart and that her poor William was singularly lacking in common sense. From the house in Dulwich she had controlled the common-sense side of William's ventures. She was perfectly aware, for instance, of the terms of the Bath bargain, the sum gleaned in the York benefit, the salaries paid to the members of his company, and the need for fresh blood every year or so. It was she who, not content with the enormous reputation which William had made in five years, had urged on him that the time had come to seek a fortune further afield. When the offer came from the American impresario she had insisted that William should accept. She had quite resigned herself to missing his company for a year at least.

But it hadn't occurred to her that William would dream of providing himself with a substitute for wifely devotion. Here, however, from the list in William's slanting decided hand (never before had she realised how firm was William's hand) stared up the name of Miranda Beverley. Why Miranda Beverley out of dozens of promising leading ladies? Oh, it was clear enough! There could be but one reason. Why were such women allowed to prey upon decent societies? If she had power she would have such women whipped.

Thus jealousy and possessiveness for the first time in Lettice's life fought a winning battle with Lettice's common sense. She was exceedingly unjust to William, who had engaged the actress for two very good reasons. Being a little past her prime Miranda was cheap, and he considered that her Junoesque physique and her slightly démodé methods were more suited to barbarian audiences than the other leading ladies within reach of his purse. Though, questionless, he had a kindliness for her, it was much more vivid in Lettice's memory than in his that Miranda had once been his mistress.

But Lettice was moved, though neither of them realised it, by a passion for him stronger than she admitted even to herself. Torn between the wish to accompany him and the knowledge that her children and her settled order of life held her fast, she eased herself of her hesitations and contradictory wishes by concentrating all the resources of her nature on getting rid of the woman she disliked. Lettice could not go herself, surely that was clear. Then Miranda Beverley should not go either.

Surprise, businesslike disapproval, retail of gossip and vicious innuendo having no effect upon William by letter, she tackled the matter on his last visit home. After conscientiously wrecking for him the holiday in which he had hoped to rest and enjoy himself, after rousing his temper and exasperating her own, she ended by losing her head, making it a matter of threats. He must choose between her and the Beverley, she told him. She did not tell him so prettily. In all their wars she had been the one to keep her temper, but now she surrendered herself to the intoxication of jealousy, and the effect upon William, whose conscience was perfectly clear, was inevitable. He was amazed at his wife's fury and despised her for it. Hardening his heart, he shook off with extraordinary sensation of relief his respect for her judgment and began to wonder if after all he would not have done well in his young days to have married—not Miranda Beverley, of course, but— well, a Miranda Beverley.

He left his home after a final pitched battle which had raged from parlour to saloon, from garden to pond, and back again to Lettice's dressing-room, and ended in the nurseries with Lettice thanking God that at least she had her children left her, and William furiously assuring her that though he left them with her for the present because he had no way of accommodating them elsewhere, she might be sure that he would take possession of them according to his legal rights as soon as he returned to England. Two days later he sailed, without sending her any reconciling message.

She could hardly believe it. But she had the satisfaction of most jealous wives. She was shrewd enough to realise that she had probably put it into his head to do the very thing that she would have given her heart and soul to prevent his doing. She was right. For news trickled through from America, not merely of his triumphs, but of the fact that he was much more closely associated with Miss Beverley than their professional partnership made necessary: and when he came back to England having made something like forty thousand pounds, the association was openly admitted and continued for a couple of years longer. Yet, had Lettice but had the calm to realise it, it was an association that did her very little injury.

William did not take his art lightly. He had long since perfected his technique, but his creation of a part never became a thing of habit. Nightly he went through a curious process of self-hypnotism. He would call up the character out of his own inner consciousness and lend it the clothing of his body. For the three hours that ensued he was not William Broome but the creature he represented, and it was as dangerous to speak to him during the progress of the play or jerk him suddenly back into a discussion of outside theatrical affairs as it is to speak to a medium in a trance. The company who played with him acquired the habit of leaving him completely alone. If it was necessary to address him the players would use a studiedly monotonous voice or even continue in the characters of the parts which they happened to be playing. No visitor was allowed behind the scenes during the performance under any pretext whatever, for, on the one or two occasions when the rule was contravened the effects had been alarming. Broome, hauled back to the surfaces of consciousness, behaved like a man woken out of a faery absence. He would stare about him without knowledge of his whereabouts or recognition of his friends: would stammer, stumble, rub his eyes, talk at random, and be entirely ineffective as an actor for the rest of the evening, even when he did not actually give way to a fit of hysterics. Then the unfortunate understudy would be pushed into the part while William was helped to the dressing-room. There he would stay all through the night and all through the next day, huddled on a sofa in the darkness, impervious to remonstrances, refusing food, screaming out in a nervous frenzy at the lighting of a candle and slinging the curtains across the window when the raw morning sun streamed in on his self-chosen prison.

But left to play as he pleased and guarded from disturbance, Broome would come out of his part at the end of a performance as naturally as a man awaking from a sleep, and pay no greater penalty than profound exhaustion. What he needed then was not wit, gaiety, charm, diversion nor even love. What he needed then was a nurse. Miss Beverley was a good one. She was indeed a far better nurse than an actress, and he owed the preservation of a career for whose beginnings his wife was responsible to the interloper's care for his comforts. That he had an affection for her is not to be denied; but though he thought of her with relief, he thought with the same relief of the supper, the good fire and night's rest that awaited him. She had no share in the life of his mind and, indeed, had no desire to possess that part of him. She was fond of him and it suited her very well to be in charge of a genius. She thought Lettice was a fool to let him travel alone.

So the breach between the husband and wife remained for four years unhealed. During these years they never met, though William wrote at formal intervals about money matters and Lettice reported regularly on the children's welfare. William, in spite of his threats, did not interfere with her possession of them, till one day Lettice wrote to remind him that Russel would soon be nine and that it was time to think of school. Then the father insisted on an interview with the boy and the mother made no objection.

So William came to Dulwich to spend an hour with Russel and Robin. But even then the two parents did not meet each other, though it is possible that each expected the other to contrive or insist upon a meeting.

Lettice, of course, did not appear. She shut herself instead into her sitting-room that had once been Robert's bedroom and watched from behind the curtains the arrival of William, welcomed by the children at the garden gate. But she thought to herself that he knew the ways of the house. If he wanted to see her, her refusal to see him could easily enough be brushed aside.

William on his side was determined to show his invisible wife that he was not the man to take advantage of an awkward situation; but he, too, hoped for a sign.

The children took him first to the parlour; but presently Lettice heard familiar footfalls, for William, though he was in his prime, took his stairs slowly. Then she heard the excited voice of Russel showing Papa the way to the nursery. At that she knew how immeasurably she had missed him. She put her hand to her throat, suffocated. So he was coming after all! He was coming! She knew that she would forgive him everything if he opened the door and came in. But the footsteps went slowly past and the door of the nursery opened and shut. Then she could have burst out crying with the sickness of her disappointment. Nevertheless she beat down the hysteric lump in her throat with the conviction—On his way back he'll come to me! He can't leave the house without coming to me! He'll find me out!

Not he! He spent an hour, and then she heard him pass her door once more and go down the stairs, the children at his heels.

Incredulous of such cruelty she went again to the windows and watched the farewells. Dark, jolly Russel was all for clambering after Papa into the dog-cart, but, stout child that he was, the step was too high for him. She saw William bend down and lift up his son, hug the child to him and drop him again to the safety of the pavement, as the younger Robin, who had been madly tearing at the tough stems of the iris blooms which glorified the edgings, came pelting into view with a bundle of the purple flowers in his arms. He threw them with all his little strength into his father's lap as the equipage drove away, and so Lettice's last sight of William was the familiar professional one. She was always to see him fêted and acclaimed as the public idol, the great William Broome.

As she stood at the window, staring at the billow of white dust which William's carriage had left behind it, Lettice, who loved beauty in a man and held that it rubbed out an alphabet of faults and wrongs, said to herself—"He's handsomer than ever. Older, but more handsome for that. He looks more than thirty-seven though! He stoops a little. It's effective. He was always a little too tall." Here she moved from the window and moved about the room aimlessly, saying—"William, William!" under her breath and sighing. Her heart was as empty as the empty road. "William, William!" Then she went down to the excited boys.

They could talk of nothing but their father. "Did Papa—? Could Papa—? Will Papa—? When does Papa—?"

She answered them vaguely. "And now run and play, children! Be careful of your brother, Russel, if you're going near the pond."

But how empty the garden was when the children had disappeared behind the elder bushes! "William, William!" If anybody had told her that she, at her age, with her advantages, with her poise, would find nothing better to do than sit in the garden, with her hands in her lap and say "William!" to herself, she would have thought them merely silly. Such an unromantic name, too—"William." She shook the name out of her mind and ordered her carriage and drove into London and shopped a little and stayed the night with the duke, and was put to sleep in the vast state bed-chamber. The ceiling was busy with dropsical cherubs, Leda and swans. The Leda exactly resembled Miranda Beverley. Lettice woke up in the middle of the night crying "William, William!" to the emptiness about her.

As for William Broome, he no sooner got back to his company than he found it necessary to write an extremely long letter to his wife all about Russel's future. He discussed in detail the problem of the stage as a profession for one's son and heir, and told her with great particularity where he proposed to be for the next three months at least. Later, he said, he had good hopes of settling down: at any rate, he meant to buy an estate in Kent. He must have some home to return to. He had his eye on that pretty place beyond Plaxtol. Lettice would probably remember it. They had looked it over when they had last stayed at Bedenstead.

And Lettice remembered. The last time they had stayed at Bedenstead had been upon their honeymoon.

So the strange half-meeting did in the end help to a reconciliation between those cautious individualists, William Broome and his wife, though at the time it seemed the very flourish to their signatures of estrangement. Russel went to school, and his school reports and the new need of a tutor for the solitary Robin led to a more frequent letter-writing. There came a day when William informed his wife that his fortune now exceeded seventy thousand pounds and that his doctor had warned him that his heart was over-strained. William hastily added that he was not thinking of leaving the stage, but that it was clear that a prolonged holiday was necessary. He also added that at the end of the summer he would be disbanding his present company—"which has, as you doubtless know, long since lost its principals."

Lettice set enquiries afoot on receipt of that letter and learnt that Miss Beverley had more than a year ago been married to a well-to-do manufacturer whose acquaintance had been made in the last northern tour.

William's letter, in fact, was one that she could have answered without too much hurt to her pride, but it was not an absolute appeal for reconciliation. That appeal he, in turn, had too much pride to make, and she admired him for his inflexibility. But how could she be expected to put her pride in her pocket without being asked to do so in so many words? She beat herself that she had not taken her chance when she had it. But she had been taken by surprise, amazed and overwhelmed by her own capitulation at the mere sound of his voice. Her own weakness had frightened her. She had thought herself so superbly indifferent. She had been so sure that he had no longer the power to attract her. But at the mere sound of his voice her old delight in him had returned. She had ached to open the door and catch at his arm and say—"Let's forget this nonsense, William! Kiss me and forget it all!"

But to do so would have been to forego her advantage, her very status. He had deserted her, not she him. Tell him she was sorry that he had left her for that woman? No! Yet she wished she had been prepared for her own emotion when he had come to Dulwich. Then maybe she might have handled the situation so wisely that William would have owned himself wrong. Then this letter would not have arrived to disturb her and make her like him so much that it took all her strength not to answer it as he doubtless hoped she would do.

But, thank God, Lettice always knew what was due to herself and her position, and she did not answer it. It was tucked away in her writing-desk and fell out every time she opened it, a passport to happiness that she would not use. And the year came round again and the flags bloomed unplucked and spring lengthened into summer, and William's letters grew once more formal. Indeed, it is doubtful that a reconciliation would ever have come about between two such obstinate creatures had not the stick of very chance stirred their pudding for them.

Chance intervened at Bath. Lettice had gone thither in pure friendship for her sister Rosina, who had settled there for the season with her dull, elderly, religious husband, and had not even her London charities to amuse her.

Poor Rosina! Lettice despised Rosina affectionately, and Rosina disapproved of Lettice admiringly; but the two relied on each other. Besides, Lettice had the gift of gratitude. Rosina had stood by her at the time of her marriage and had never since reminded her of the fact. So Lettice reminded herself of it instead and, though she disliked Rosina's maid, Rosina's pug and Rosina's husband, when Rosina wanted her Lettice would put aside her own affairs and come.

True, she made it very clear to Rosina that it was a sacrifice to be out of London in June. Still, she came and brightened life for her sister, as she knew how to do, with her gossip and her quick tongue, her pretty clothes and her insistence that even poor health and a husband with religious mania should not prevent one from amusing oneself. And Rosina, in whom the Broome spark had also once burnt dimly, though it had long since been husbanded out of existence, enjoyed trying to satisfy the bountiful, condescending creature by drives, picnics, stately expeditions to Beckford's Tower and Beechen Cliff, and an occasional box at the theatre. Nor did Rosina purchase the tickets purely out of good nature. She shared the family passion for a play : though she got a little tired of hearing Lettice point out how very much better the leading business was wont to be when it was in the hands of William Broome, and more than tired of the agitations of Lettice when the leading man skipped half a dozen lines, mangled a metaphor, or substituted for some traditional gesture a county-town reading that had pleased the groundlings but offended her taste.

And so it came that Rosina, to entertain Lettice and polish off some acquaintance, purchased one day a box for a performance of *Othello*. But the principal leading man at the last moment fell ill and the Bath manager was aware that he himself was too familiar to his fashionable audiences to provide the requisite novelty. So he sent an imploring post to William Broome who, he knew, was playing at Bristol: and William, to oblige an old friend, posted over on the morning of the performance.

It is a fact that he got himself into considerable trouble with his Bristol public for doing so ; but, after playing a week to a passionately enthusiastic house, he had been re-engaged for a second week, and then for a third. But, much as Bristol loved him, towards the end of the third week the receipts began to drop. He knew well enough that he had not outstayed his welcome but only the capacity of the Bristol purse. Still, it would do no harm to teach Bristol the difference between William Broome and an understudy. He would have the better houses on Friday and Saturday for giving them a change in the middle of the week. They would not like it. There would be a scene in the theatre, like as not, when he came back; but what did William Broome care for scenes? He had never yet met an audience that he could not tame; for he had learned in those first months following his father's death that an actor must know how to face and tame a hostile house, not on one night only, but nightly, weekly, sometimes for months. But while he was still strong and handsome he did not fear any audience. Old age was another matter : he dreaded the coming of old age. He had been brought up on the tales of what an English audience could do, when the mood took it, to a toothless lion. Well, it had never tried it yet on a Broome! Not on Richard! Not on Robert! And he, William, was not yet toothless.

He flashed a critical look at himself in the glass as he scribbled his answer to the Bath manager, and the face in the glass showed teeth still white in an answering smile. "Beckon! Reckon! No, you are not toothless!" He reckoned that he could beckon back an audience for another twenty years. He wished he could be as sure of beckoning back his revolted wife. Why had he been fool enough to go to Dulwich? He had got over missing her; but once back in their house, their home, he had instantly wanted her again and as much as ever. He had known where she was. He had heard her dress rustling on the other side of the half-open door as he passed, and there had been an elusive suggestion of perfume in the air, too faint to be noticed by anyone a stranger to her. But he knew that she had been using what she called her 'best' scent, the ridiculous creature! He wondered what she was doing at this moment. "Oh, my Lettice, why must you be what you are!" And with a gusty sigh he signed his note and sent the messenger flying.

Even sophisticated Bath was agog at the news of William Broome's advent; for it will be remembered that London could no longer see a Broome whenever it pleased. But Lettice and Rosina held themselves aloof from the town gossips, and, as the whole subject of the theatre and theatre-going was avoided in the earl's company, it came about that neither sister knew of the change of cast till their party of guests had joined them and they were all seated in their box and perusing the unwieldy, splotched play-bill with its lamp-black print that soiled Lettice's gloves. Then Rosina clutched her sister's arm.

"Lettice, do you see this?"

Lettice had seen it a moment earlier and was quite composed.

"Let's hope he knows his part," she said. At which a guest exclaimed horrified—

"Dear Lady Lettice! When he is the greatest Othello of his day? How can you talk so?"

"Well," said Lettice with resignation, "he never used to know his words as Othello, I can tell you that."

Rosina looked at her inquisitively.

"You talk of him almost as if he were dead," she said in a low voice.

"He is dead to me," said Lettice with dignity; but she, too, lowered her voice, for though the family knew all about the quarrel and as usual took sides over it whenever two members met, the public fiction of perfect friendship between husband and wife had to be maintained.

Rosina nodded approval of the attitude and perhaps wished ruefully that her own husband would give her occasion to assume so comfort-able a pose. She envied her sister the drama of her marriage, envied her at the moment the fact that Lettice was sitting in the stage box and would soon be within three feet of her own husband whom she had not met for over four years, and be taking it as a matter of course that people should tell her that he was the greatest Othello of his day. She had never seen him play Othello herself and apart from her vicarious excitements was as eager as the rest of the house.

And indeed the house was eager; for in those days each town had its own notion, taste and fashion in matters theatrical, and its own gallery leaders who told the performers pretty freely what the house thought of them. Such leaders particularly enjoyed telling the favourite of another circuit what their gallery thought of him, or her. Besides, William Broome's reputation as an innovator had preceded him. Bath, indeed, was inclined to grumble because Broome was giving himself to them in one part only; for length of bill was still the rule. Midnight often found the players but half-way through the prologue to a last piece and the audience placidly prepared to sit through the three acts yet to come.

William, whose repertory was, of course, as vast as in those days was necessary, thought it a holiday to play Othello only, and leave the minor pieces to the locals; but Bristol had worked him hard and he was certainly tired when the Bath curtain went up, especially as he had been forced, after his arrival, to spend a good part of the day running through his own scenes and adapting the business of the Bath company to his own notions. So he opened the night scene with a little less than his usual fire-through-smoke of enthusiastic gloom.

But the spectators roused him. They 'went for him,' as he phrased it, on his first entrance in such an ecstasy of pure expectation and good-will that he went for them in turn, deeming it necessary (but when did he not deem it necessary?) to give them something just a trifle better than his best. This led sometimes to accusations of over-acting, but it was for such over-actings that his own public loved him.

So, in the second scene, William unloosed his genius upon the panting, critical, expectant house, swooping disdainfully and im-partially upon the attackers and defenders of his person, like an unfallen Lucifer dominating the lesser angels.

"Keep up your bright swords, for the dew will rust them."

Instantly the house unloosed its enthusiasm upon him in return, and so it went on, ding-dong, till mob and actor between them had created a general hysteria of emotion almost beyond the power of the actor to control.

He did control it, however, according to his habit when he was physically exhausted, by drawing the more recklessly upon the very forces which it so exhausted him to employ. Always he met the inevitable spiritual depletion which this entailed by yet further demands upon his own demoniac power to loose power upon the spectators. He was not for nothing one of the beckoning Broomes.

Beckon? He reached out, he clutched, he caught the mob to his breast like a hundred-armed god of death and torment: tore out each heart in turn and flung the carcase from him. And yet the dazed house was aware that in that dreadful clutch upon its pities he did but faintly teach them how his own heart was torn by his own frantic hands. He was his own god of death and devoted himself to his own torture. Iago could be flung half strangled to the rubbish heap where rats end, but still that unrelievable, striding figure could not, could never more be eased of the rat that gnawed at its heart. So much for noble rant! The house cowered gloating over the spectacle as over the wounding of Leviathan.

"Is there anyone like him, anyone in the world?" demanded Lettice relaxing her strained position of attention as she leant back in her chair. Then she began to laugh hysterically as she observed that upon Othello's exit half the audience had walked out also, leaving the unfortunate Cassio and Iago to continue their scene unheeded.

"What is happening?" Rosina, slower in feeling the pulse of the house, gaped apprehensively at the sudden emptying of the benches.

"They are going out to talk him over," said Lettice. "Only listen to the noise in the passages. They won't bother themselves about the local lights. But they'll be back in their seats for his next incoming, and then we shall truly know what they think of him."

She was right. The house came back with an appetite and was ready for Broome's next entrance long before he was. What is more, there were added so many late-comers whom rumour of the new Othello had raked in, that not only was all standing-room at the back of the house invested, but the very gangways were choked. Seated ticket-holders whose view of the stage was thus blocked by these irregulars, protested by rising. Better stand than lose their clear view. So of course it soon came about that the whole floor of the house was standing. Then began that creeping movement which

Lettice instantly recognised with a cold and private pang of fear. Only once before in her life had she seen it: it was the preliminary movement of a house half mad with excitement about to besiege the stage itself. More than one of the great actors of the day could boast of having caused it: it was none the less an uncanny spectacle, this manifestation of the popular mind played upon by noble rant.

Staid Rosina shivered as she watched: while Lettice drew a breath of furious, unpleasurable excitement for she remembered well enough when she had last seen Birnam Wood moving towards Dunsinane. And indeed, the urgent, unceasing yet scarcely perceptible encroachment of the whole house upon the sphere of the performers was almost as gradual a business as that famous greenwood shift.

Looking down upon the orchestra Lettice observed that it was no longer filled by its legitimate occupants. The gangways had already overflowed it, crowding the musicians under the stage. But still the forward pressure continued, till, by easy stages, for the carved gilded front of the apron and the fat cherubs that upheld the boxes afforded easy foothold, the sides of the stage itself were reached. Then the pioneers, edged forward by the pressure of those behind, encroached yet further, sidling down and along the flats themselves. These were ringed with onlookers and the scenery swayed and rocked under the backward pressure of so many human shoulders. Silent, curious clusters of spectators lined the inner stage, already filled by the great bed. And on the great bed lay Desdemona's pillows and Desdemona's twisting body, and William Broome's arm and agony were flung across it.

"Great God!" Lettice felt the blood drain from her lips till she could hardly move or shape them to words. "It's the Gloriana business over again, Rosina! It's Uncle Robert's last performance at the Glory Hole. That's how they crowded in on Robert. And William doesn't even see them. He's rapt. Look at him! He doesn't see anything, anyone. Did you ever see him so wrought up? If they crowd in upon him now and wake him anything may happen. Oh, why doesn't somebody stop the fools?" And here Lettice, reckless of her dignity and her draperies, stood up in her seat and leant forward over the parapet of the box and stretched out her hands in vague, helpless flutterings of warning and proffered support to her husband.

For Broome playing Othello did not for one instant rouse in Lettice a response to his supreme art. His complete surrender to the part disguised him from her as little as the pale mulatto tinge of his skin or

his barbaric garments. Othello he might be to the world and to himself
in that ecstatic moment of creation; but to her he was solely William,
needing her though he did not yet know it, depending on her, though
he did not yet dream it, to avert a catastrophe which she alone foresaw.
For, to the eternal credit of her five wits, she had instantly recognised
that the tragic scene in which he and his fathers had once played such
ominous parts was now in process of duplication. This recognition was
for Lettice her supreme effort of imagination and sympathetic understanding : she would never make such an act of imagination again : she
was not born for the heights, nor at home there. Nevertheless she made
it, and that was much.

But at such a moment, also to identify herself with the other
William, the actor who was Othello, Shakespeare, mankind, was beyond her. Othello's agony touched her not at all. But it did move her
to see her husband, not two feet away and unconscious of her,
triumphing in his art : and it would have moved her just as little, just as
much, if he had spoken in a language she did not understand and
played a part with which she was unacquainted. It was his power to
achieve and yet be William, her own husband, that thrilled her. And
now her memory of the past and her fear for him in the event of a shock
turned her thrillings to tremblings.

> "When we shall meet at compt,
> This look of thine will hurl my soul from heaven,
> And fiends will snatch at it. Cold, cold, my girl——"

cried the Othello, William Broome, and his desolate eyes fixed and held
hers, but without recognition. And while, in spite of herself, she
muttered in return she knew not what of consolation and applause, yet
it shot a jealous pang into her to realise that he did not know her. It
was intolerable that the theatric passion could obscure his eyes, that
the mere literature of a wrong could forbid his recognition of her, his
own wronged Lettice. Then she forgot her own strange pain as he,
in a fresh access of agony, reeled down the steps of the daïs on which
stood the murder-laden bed and staggered across the stage.

> "Whip me, ye devils,
> From the possession of this heavenly sight!
> Blow me about in winds! roast me in sulphur!
> Wash me in steep-down gulfs of liquid fire!
> O Desdemona! Desdemona dead!
> Oh! Oh! Oh!"

cried William and collapsed in a sort of fit against the pillar of the stage box in which his wife was sitting. And on that last aching 'Oh!' there came softly, horridly, an echoed sigh, a general exhalation from the spell-bound house. "Oh—oh—oh!" quavered the house, released from the actor's grip upon its emotions. "Oh!" sighed the house, breathing again and began to stir and rustle.

Now in his frenzy William Broome the actor had been oblivious of the encroachment on his stage. It had, indeed, so automatic a quality that it did not need to be noticed. The invaders had flowed forward as in a dream, whispered, stumbled, jostled, ranged themselves as in a dream, their eyes never wavering from the circle of the drama even while their bodies jostled for a better view. But as the teasing touch of a grass leaf on a sleeper's cheek can in a certain mood be more startling than a heavy blow, so the sigh which, tremulous, flowed out from row after row of the relaxing audience, woke the player to a state of consciousness when the general movement earlier in the scene had not been able to do so. And as, from the side of the scene, Lodovico and his party entered pompously, the bound Iago in their midst, Broome, with a dreadful start, lifted his head, looked about him, realised the unusual nature of his surroundings, swung up blind hands to his forehead and then stood dazed.

The gesture implied the bewilderment of a man aroused from nightmare to a worse reality. It was so in keeping with the nature of the scene that the house stiffened to attention anew. "See now, our idol has not finished entertaining us: there is yet a new refinement of hideous grief to be displayed!" Thus the audience, who by this time had drunk horror till they were as crazy as a Roman audience glutted with the blood of beasts and the spectacle of beautiful men fighting and torn. They loved their Broome for what he had given them. Now they were to have more. Now, out of final horror, beauty was to come. "Cold, cold, my girl!" Was not that the pinnacle of horror and beauty? But with this piteous and awaking air he promised them yet more of the pity and terror of pure beauty slain.

But Lettice knew better: she saw what they did not see. She saw Othello die out of the actor's face and her husband's own spirit return to it, bewildered, but bringing his own capacity to recognise and to remember. In her great fear for him, for she knew what such a sudden emergence meant, she gave a soft cry, half warning, half mere hysteric sound, then beat her fists against her mouth to stifle the folly of that sound. She was too late. He saw her, and now he recognised her. His eye-balls, unnaturally white and prominent in his darkened face, shuttled from her to the tense circle of onlookers. He stretched out a trembling finger and, as one pointing to landmarks, with that wavering digit identified her own face, the position of her box, the crowded walls, the positions of his fellow-actors, and the commanding figure of Lodovico in his robes of a Venetian senator, till his outstretched finger rested at last on the opposed figure of Iago, red-haired and villainous as Iago had to be for a country audience, his mask snarling and foxy. At that the great Broome staggered back and whimpered as one in fear, less of death than of his enemy's hand upon him.

Lettice caught at her sister's arm.

"He's going to faint. Get me out of this! Let me get round to him!" and then stayed frozenly, on the half turn of her rise, to stare again at the stage. For Broome had dropped his hand and was now looking down upon himself, puzzled, frowning, as if his clothes were strange to him or he were ill-arrayed. Then he began to fumble with the button of his shirt, loosened it and tore open the folds with a martyr's gesture, till half his breast was bare, which done he lifted his face again, blank and innocent.

The house was enchanted. You could hear its acquainted thoughts willing him on—"Go on, Broome! Give us more! Yes, yes, dazed, ignorant, thus would Othello look! Watch him waking up though! Soon now he'll know what he's done!"

But it was not in the strong dark accents of the Moor that Broome replied to the Venetian's—

"Where is this rash and most unfortunate man?"

He answered instead in the tones of his comedy days, in the tame, self-conscious, martyred bleat of Antonio, Merchant of Venice, answering his Duke. Nor was it merely the tone that startled Lettice. When his eyes seeking Iago were the fascinated eyes of the Venetian, seeking, dreading the gaze of Shylock, as he said—

"Ready, so please your Grace—"

"No, William, no!" the horrified Lettice winged her words to him very softly and intensely, but he continued stumblingly—

"I am armed and well prepared—"

and paused, feeling for words.

Then Lettice, concentrating her whole will and her memory on the part of Othello, prompted him—

"Come back, William!

> If that thou be'st a devil—"

But he went on unheeding—

> "Say how I loved you, speak me fair in death;
> And, when the tale is told, bid her be judge—"

"No William, no!" As she spoke Lettice caught the eye of one of the actors and hissed out her orders viciously—"Get on with the lines, you fool! Give him any line!"

At that Lodovico, who had long since recognised her, flung into the scene at random with—

> "Did you and he consent in Cassio's death?"

But the Cassio boggled, and she herself had to give him the next cue again—

> "Dear general, I never gave you cause."

At this Broome started and went off into a wild fit of laughter that did not ill suit the scene and the part. Then, sobering—

> "I do believe it, and I ask your pardon,"

said he, still in the voice of Antonio, but returning at last to the actual lines of his part. Then he stalked up to the box's side and eyeing his wife swung out his arm against Iago—

> "Will you, I pray, demand that demi-devil
> Why he hath thus ensnared my soul and body?"

"Go on! Go on!" commanded Lettice in her fierce whisper—"Go on, all of you!"

And Iago went on with his "Demand me nothing!" and the rest followed: and William Broome himself, marking his part in the scene with the mere exclamations which his wife hissed into his ear, was steady enough when the time came to ask his question concerning the handkerchief and to subdue the house to tears again with his—

> "O fool! fool! fool!"

After which he died well enough almost at Lettice's feet, and took his triumph with decorous decision afterwards, though it was noted as singular that he bowed, not from the centre of the stage but from the pillar that flanked the stage box. This was an odd thing to do and people talked of it so much that only a few remembered to remark on the fact that he had for a moment needed the prompter's help. The prompter who, as everyone knew had his own little box just behind the pillar on the left of the stage, had skipped a line or two. It was no great matter in those days for a gallery enthusiast to prompt a favourite actor whose memory was a fume on pay night. There were at least fifty people in the house that night who could have prompted William Broome had they known he needed it : yet even of those enthusiasts not one had identified the alien lines with which William Broome had bolstered his lapse of memory. As for the mass of the house they thought the collapse intentional. They had seen, not William Broome breaking down in his speech, but Othello witless and astray.

And so the major part of the house, as drunk with drama as once an English audience could be, streamed out into the cool air, clattered home over the cobbles under the dark blue night sky of June, perfectly satisfied on the whole with their evening's entertainment. They would have been puzzled if someone had told them that their great William Broome had not yet quitted the stage, that he still leaned against the pillar just as they had seen him before the curtain fell for the last time on their enthusiasm. But it was so.

William was still so close to his wife that she was able to put aside the curtain that had fallen between them and speak to him.

"Go to your dressing-room, William! I'm coming round at once." She turned to her sister, ignoring the cousins. "Rosina, have my maid pack some night-clothes and send them over to William's lodgings as soon as you get home. Why? Because I'm staying with William. But of course I'm staying with him. Don't you see that he's in a state of collapse? His lodgings? Ask anyone in the theatre! Don't fuss, Rosina! Don't gabble at me! Yes, I'll see you tomorrow. Let me pass, please, everyone!"

She sailed out of the box and made her way by the pass-door into the confusion of the emptied stage. The hurrying stage-hands stared at the great lady in her pale elaborate gown and her white cashmere shawl, and the late Lodovico, now a mere flustered factotum of William's who travelled with him, hurried forward, knowing very well who she was.

"Your ladyship? Here in this dirty place! You want Mr. Broome, of course. He's there against the pillar. I've sent for his dresser: I don't like to disturb him myself. You know what he is when he is in one of these fits of his. But your ladyship, he must go to his room. You know he must. There is still the afterpiece, and the sets for it to change."

She flung her casual enchantment over him.

"Yes, yes, of course! But now I'm here. You will help me with him, won't you, Mr.—Mr.—" and she remembered the name—"You were with my husband in America." Then she went up to her husband, smiling and easy—

"William, aren't you coming down to your room? It's me. It's Lettice. Come with me!"

She slipped her arm through his and turned once more to the anxious underling—"I'll see to him. I think you'd better get his dresser to help me. Yes, get Morgan! It will be all right." And then—

"Come along, William, you must change. It's time to go home."

The late Lodovico, hurrying ahead of her, crowed out his admiration.

"Morgan! Her ladyship's here! Now we shall run smoothly again. Look lively now! Make yourself useful! Get the governor's street clothes together! Have you his brandy and water ready? No fear, she'll pour it down him. It's her ladyship back, I tell you! She's tackling the governor for us. So now we're all right again, Morgan! Curtain's up! We're off!"

CHAPTER 9

WILLIAM BROOME AND HIS SON RUSSEL

AND that was the end of Lettice's objection to the hugger-mugger of life behind the scenes. She joined William, bag and baggage, in spite of forlorn Rosina's protests, and they got on delightfully till the end of the tour, when William came home to Dulwich and for three months amused himself by pottering about the neighbourhood and damming the Effra to make fresh ponds in his garden: while twice a week or so he drove into London *incognito* to observe how completely the lessees were mismanaging his property.

In 1828 their last son was born. And with the coming of the youngster, whom they called Harry, the last uncertainties between the pair vanished. It was as if Robert's death had cast a spell for a term of years upon them, and that at last William had worked out of the enchantment. Even his style lightened again as he came once more under the influence of his wife. Gradually comedy reclaimed him, and in his older years he was as well known for his Surface, his Overreach and his Malvolio, as he had once been esteemed for his Shylock and his Lear. It was as if the deep waters had been skimmed over at last by smooth ice on which the sun sparkled very pleasantly.

One obstinacy remained. Nothing would induce him to play in London. He had a superstition about it. He once told his wife quite seriously that it would be fatal to him. She understood him to mean that it would be fatal to his reputation, and, having learnt wisdom in the wars, forewent this particular ambition, contenting herself with his unvarying successes in the rest of the kingdom.

Yet fate proved too strong for William's superstition and for Lettice's late-won wifely tact. William did once again enter the Gloriana, and it did prove fatal to him, though it was no fault of his wife's. The years had shifted her point of view. By the time Russel left school it was she who fought against William's itch for new enterprise. For as his health weakened his urge to be at work increased.

"A bad sign," said his doctor. "He drives himself unreasonably, insanely. Why? What's behind it?"

"It's William," said his wife between pride and despair. "Have you ever tried to stamp out a heath fire, Doctor?"

"Have you, Lady Lettice?" said the medico, his eyes slipping from her tiny low-heeled satin slippers to her bare shoulders, and the tucker of lace above the striped gauze day-dress, thence to her alert countenance and back again to her shoes. "You have stamped on hearts, dear madam, in your time, that is easy to see; but I shouldn't like to see those little slippers of yours contend with burning hill-tops."

Lettice laughed; for the doctor who had brought her into the world was privileged. But she continued—

"All the same, I have seen such smoulderings. You can't do a thing to check 'em, Doctor, any more than I can check William. If he will act he will."

"It's true. He must be humoured," her old friend agreed. "Rages aren't good for him. But I doubt whether you'll find it easy to be meek, Lady Lettice!"

But Lettice, the triumphant matron, laughed again.

"I've reared three sons," said Lettice. "What! Can't I manage a husband and his health?"

And it is a fact that she never again allowed herself and William to quarrel grandiosely and with enjoyment. William could not quite understand why Lettice had grown so gentle, and missed the older version of her as much as he was soothed by the new one, and shame-lessly took advantage of her meekness to get his own way unfairly fifty times a day. But she was sharp with her sons in those later days, was Lettice.

"Why does Papa still go on circuit, Mama, when the Glory Hole's his own? When I go on the stage I shall stick to London." Thus Russel.

"Ah! When!" Lettice took a deep breath and loosed her suppressed anxieties in wrath. "Don't trouble yourself, my dear! You'll never cut a figure upon the stage. You haven't the talent, you haven't the looks—let alone the intelligence. You haven't even the sense to understand that your father does not like to be cross-questioned. If he doesn't choose to play in London, whose affair is it but his, I should like to know? He has been implored to play, often enough."

"I only meant—" muttered Russel. And then—"Whether you like it or not, Mama, I mean to be an actor."

"Do you want to drag away your life playing utility in some fit-up? Do you want to be stranded in some remote American town, left behind because you are sick and not worth nursing? That's what happens, my dear Russel, to youngsters like you who think they have talent. They see their elders reaping a harvest and think they can glean after them. You would get an engagement, I daresay, because you are called Broome; but there it would end, believe me! My dear boy, for the stage you need genius or you need training, and you do not call yourself a genius, I hope? And for the rest? Have you knocked about in barns and fairs as your great-grandfather did? Have you hung about London theatres as a boy, as your grandfather did, and known all the ups-and-downs and ins-and-outs of a great management? Have you spent your time, as your father did, in study? There was not a part of your grandfather's that your father could not recite by the time he was twelve. But you—you don't occupy yourself much with the arts, I fancy!"

"Hang it, Mama, I'm at school."

"Yes, I'm sure you're very good at games; but throwing balls and catching them again and running along the road scattering paper won't get you a London engagement or any other engagement, even if your father entertained for one instant the notion of allowing you to go upon the stage at all. No, no, my dear boy, be thankful that he has other ideas for you and is prepared to spend money on furthering your career and that your mother has some influence. Why, my dearest boy," cried Lettice, warming to her new theme and entirely forgetting her former one, which was the complete, the idiot incapacity and general worthlessness of her first-born—"with your talents and the Wybirds behind you, of course you would be wasted on the stage."

"Is my father wasted?" said Russel sharply.

"He is a genius."

"Yet, when he was young, people said he would never be as good as grandfather," muttered Russel. "Morgan told me so."

Lettice was indignant.

"Not as good? My dear Russel, your grandfather could not hold a candle to your father."

"Well," said the boy hardily, "maybe Papa won't be able to hold a candle to me in twenty years. I don't know why you're so vexed about it, Mama. Grandmamma and Grandfather were on the stage, let alone Papa. Why are you heading me off?"

Why was she? She had begun the attack as a mere sally to prevent the boy from cross-questioning her about his father's horror of the Gloriana. She supposed that he would one day hear the story of Robert's suicide; but she didn't want to be the one to tell him. But now she had silenced her son's questioning only to start another question in her own heart. She had discovered that she did indeed dislike the idea of the stage for Russel.

She thought that she knew why. Lettice was aware that, though the barrier between the stage and society could still be overleaped, it was certainly higher than it had been in her mother's time. The young Victoria's rule was already having some slight effect upon social values. Lettice herself, of course, could be at will inside or outside the pale, and William had genius: genius goes anywhere. But— had Russel genius? He was an athlete, handsome, no fool. Yes, he could take his place on the stage and keep it too, for a time, on these things. But could he keep his social place on these things if he lost his figure and could not prove himself to have something of his father's quality? Russel acted well enough, certainly. The boys were always acting. Scenes, charades, improvisations were the habit of the house. He had pleasant movements and a certain stage sense, and always that amazingly proportioned figure which made men and women watch him as they would watch a race-horse or a yacht. But genius? No, not a sign of it! Lettice knew the divine flicker when she saw it. She had burnt her fingers often enough in sheltering William's flame against the draughts of time and chance. But Russel's lamp was not alight. When his looks were gone he would be a Wybird, woefully on the wrong side of the barrier. It must not be. Russel would be well enough in politics; but he should not, if she or William could prevent it, go upon the cruel, sacred stage.

She said so to her husband, whose face fell. He wanted his son to follow him.

"But there's Robin and Harry to come along," protested Lettice. "Though Robin is too delicate. Robin will write, I believe," said Robin's mother. And then, with her look of a Dresden china pythoness—"I see Robin in the Civil Service, and writing in his spare time, like Lamb. That's how we'll have it, William! Russel in politics, for he's a fighter. Robin safe, for he's not——"

"And Harry?" said William, cocking his eye at her in sudden suspicion.

"Harry's an astonishing child for his age," returned Lettice reverently. "I hope I know my children's faults, and I don't want to use the word genius lightly," said Lettice, who used the word genius on every possible occasion when her family was in question, "but——"

"But he's the youngest," said William smiling at her.

"Ah, you may laugh! But do you remember giving him a handful of old grease paints? Well, my dear, he's learnt the trick of make-up since then. The things he can do with his little face! Coaxed Morgan to teach him. Morgan, of course, is quite foolish about him. But really, his imitation of you as Mark Antony is very funny, William. He has hit you off to the life. He does it after his bath, with a towel. And I daresay we should catch him at it now if you came up to the nursery."

Thus Russel's ambitions were tucked out of sight by his elders, and the boy himself said no more either of them or of his father's refusal to play in London. But though Russel might lack all that Lettice said he lacked, and Lettice was generally right in her estimate of those she loved, he had at least his mother's strong will, and he did not for an instant falter in his plans for himself. Because he took what school and university had to offer, his parents thought that he acquiesced in their plans for him. It was not so. At the end of his third year he made up his mind to delay no longer in seeking an engagement, with or without the family's consent. Better without. They would only fuss him.

A month's holiday at home confirmed him in his decision.

The Broomes had long since moved from Dulwich to a pretty country house, rented from Lettice's eldest brother, among whose properties could be reckoned a smiling Kentish valley, the two lines of hills that ruled it, a toy village, a mansion, some handsome lesser houses, and several miles of a river, placid as the duke himself. The duke's official seat, Bedenham Castle, was famous for its lily ponds, its zoo, and its view over the Bristol Channel; but it was built in the English-Grecian style. Its vast chimneys scorched your knees while the rest of you shivered. It had formal gardens: its trees were but quarter grown: the wife of his youth had died there, and the duke hated it. But the Kentish mansion was comfortable and near town: and though it had two ghosts he had been accustomed to them all his life. "Leave a ghost alone, and it'll leave you alone!" said the duke cheerily. "They've never bothered me yet; though Welkin hates 'em," and he would pull the spaniel's ears in affectionate contempt. "Welkin ought to know by now," said the duke, "that all the Wybirds walk a bit when they're dead. I shall walk myself one day and then Welkin will want to come along."

Thus the duke, when his sisters-in-law and his maid-servants gave notice. So the house continued pleasantly free of unnecessary women, as he explained to Lettice, who promised him that he should not be asked to entertain on her account. But, of course, the fact that she was settled so near him did lead to entertainments. Lettice, set down among relations and connections and family friends, enjoyed herself as heartily in the country as in London, and saw to it that the duke enjoyed himself too. And to William, home for brief periods, Kent was Eden.

But country life had always bored Russel: and when, one chilly Easter vacation, he had dutifully stayed at home a month, had invited sets of friends and seen them leave again till he got tired of playing half-host, he ended by going to town on particular affairs. There he stayed a fortnight, returned home at the end of it, and was enchanting to his mother during the evening of his return, but was not able to get said to her what he wanted to say. He slept badly, and, between naps, rehearsed the dialogue that would not get itself spoken between himself and his mother. The next morning he ordered his trap, saw his boxes were packed, and then marched into Lettice's bedroom, very nervous, but with his mind made up.

"Mama, I've got news for you!" But he got no further.

His mother was sitting bolt upright in bed, her pillows piled up behind her. The rose-lined curtains of her bed threw pink lights and shadows on her charming face, a little wrinkled now, but wrinkled like a rose-leaf. The colour deepened her eyes from middle-aged grey to their former youthful lilac, and her blue peignoir enhanced that lilac. Over the lace-edged pillows her showers of straw-coloured hair spread out like a waterfall. Twenty years had altered Lettice but little: indeed she still had a bloom of second youth when she was excited, and she was, as Russel could see, at that moment headily excited and much occupied. The feather-bed was littered with opened letters and in a hollow of it nested a porcelain ink-stand with a porcelain butterfly poised on the lid. Her ridiculous lady's blotter with its mother-of-pearl inlay was propped against the neglected breakfast tray and Lettice herself was writing a letter. The scrawled sheets already inscribed she had piled upon the coffee cup.

But at his entrance and words she looked up, her eyes dancing.

"News, my darling? But I've got news! Russel, Russel, Lionel is home! Lionel himself, my brother, your uncle! Home at last, Russel, and I thought he was dead long ago. You must not interrupt me, Russel, I'm writing to your father. What will your father say? But let me read you Lionel's letter. I never thought I should see Lionel again. My dearest Lionel! My favourite brother! Look, this is what he says! But you may read for yourself. I wouldn't show it to everyone, but you may read it, Russel."

And then, as he took the letter from her, she pulled him down on the bed beside her and read it again over his shoulder.

When you have decided upon taking the step of your life and your foot is already lifted, it would irritate you to be obliged to hold it poised for an indefinite period while you are told about an elderly, unmet and entirely unimportant uncle. It irritated Russel. But when Russel mastered his impatience and the difficult handwriting, he found that the letter, after all, was not likely to interfere with his professional plans. Lord Lionel was commendably independent. There was no hint that a nephew would be required to dance attendance. Nephew? This uncle did not appear to be aware that he had one. The letter was all about himself and a remote sister Lettice, whom he was fondling by post, and an unknown 'Mama' who 'died, of course, years ago, as you will have realised—in 1830 to be precise. It was her eightieth birthday. A peaceful end, dear Lettice, though it was not peaceful for us. Dear Mother! Her deathbed was purest theatre, and how she enjoyed the performance!'

"What a brute, Mother!" said Russel.

"No," said Lettice softly. "You don't understand. He adored her. Read on."

'You could not have counted the instructions she gave me before-hand. She had thought out all the details—grave-clothes, bier, coverlet, the very flowers and trees she wanted planted round herself. Yes, and artificial nests to lure the nightingales. Dear Mama! Dear absurdity! But I don't think I forgot a single command of hers. Have you grown old, Lettice? Will you say sentimental to my scrupulosity? I don't care if you do, for you know well enough that I am not a sentimentalist. Nevertheless, I grieved for our mother unspeakably. I miss her still. She was the perfect companion.

Once, Lettice, I saw her ghost. I did, I assure you. So like Mother, my dear sister, to come back. She wouldn't be cheated of her fifth act. This is how it was. I was sitting in the courtyard of my house one evening thinking to myself that, without her to share it, there was no fun in foreigners. I resolved on going home to you, though I had never thought to turn westward again. Then I heard her laugh, an unmistakable sound: quite clear above the gurgle of the fountain and rather like it, but higher. I leant forward and between dusk and night I saw her, Lettice, sitting beside the fountain watching me. It was her favourite seat. I could not speak. Then she laughed again as if at my resolution to be gone. She always said I should return to the British fold in the end. I stared. She wavered like a mist rising.

Behind her the moon rose also over the roofs, and with its first beams Mama was gone. You don't believe it? Nevertheless it is true.

That was two years ago. Yes, my dear, I have been two years coming home. That is because the cities of the world still fascinate me. I find in each of them human beings to detain me.

Why do I write of these things when I shall see you so soon? I have taken rooms in the Albany. Where are you, Lettice? I want to come and see you. You have married William, of course. He and I used to get on well enough. I hope the alliance continues, because you will not get rid of me: you are the next best thing to Mama in the way of home. I shall expect you to do a great deal for me.

I send no messages to our family till I know that we are all on speaking terms, or to yours till I hear that you have one. Am I an uncle? I am long since a father; but of that later also.

Write at once to me, Lettice!

Your affectionate brother
Lionel.'

"Cool!" said Russel hotly.

"What?" Lettice stared at her son as if for a moment he were a stranger: then she laughed delightedly.

"Cool? It's Lionel. You don't understand. It's only Lionel's way. Lift the tray off my bed, Russel! I'm getting up. I'm driving straight up to London to see your uncle. The dear, dearest creature! But no—leave it! I forgot. First I must tell your father that Lionel has come home."

"Will you also tell him," said Russel, resentful of his uncle and his mother's inattention and the general unawareness of the fact that he had an important announcement to make—"will you add, only as a postscript Mama, only if you have room, that I'm appearing at the Glory Hole next Monday?"

"Absurd boy!" murmured Lettice affectionately: and then still writing, over her shoulder—"Hairs in the pen again! Call Mitcham, Russel! That woman refuses to wash out the ink-pot when she refills it, obstinate, brainless slug. Ring the bell!"

"It's a good little part," continued Russel—"and the understudy of the lead. They are both old parts of Father's."

"What are you talking about, dear boy?" Lettice was still irritably squawking her pen over a spare sheet. "You had better pass me a pen-knife. Is it some Oxford theatricals? Yes, I must cut it."

Russel unlinked his own pen-knife from his watch-chain.

"Give it to me," said Russel, holding out his hand for the quill;

for he had the pleasant family trait of helpfulness to a woman in minor difficulties. But Lettice would never be helped.

"Not at all! Bless me, child, I trimmed pens before you were born. I always trim your father's. Well, my dear, what are you going to see on Monday? Your uncle and I may join you. Dear Lionel, he always adored a play. He was a very good amateur actor too. How strange he will find it to go to the Glory Hole and see no Broome acting there."

"He'll see me, Mother."

Lettice lifted her head from her papers and for the first time gave him her full attention.

"You? What are you talking about, child?"

Russel sighed heavily.

"You never listen, Mama."

"Listen? Of course not—that is unless there is something worth hearing. There seldom is when your father's away. You children have none of you the art of conversation. Mere egotistical starlings, all of you! Listen? Your poor mother's entire day is spent in listening to nonsense."

Lettice's retort was as automatic as the flash of a cat's paw when the puppy gambols too near her dignity. The box on the ear did not ruffle Russel, nor the exertion his mother. It was all part of a game which both enjoyed.

"Still," continued Russel, "I should like you to come and hear me. Old Manton is stage-manager at the Glory Hole now——"

"Manton? How time flies! He was one of the juveniles under your grandfather," cried Lettice, a reminiscent note in her voice. Russel heard it with alarm and hurried on.

"Yes, he said so: and he said 'chip of the old block' when he saw me."

Russel did not suppress the fact that the exchange of courtesies had ended in grog for old Manton at Russel's expense: he quite genuinely forgot it; for Russel believed that everyone liked him, and was perhaps right. He was a generous child, generous with his personality, his handsome looks, his smile, his confidences, his modesties: generous with his likes and dislikes. He was generously in love with life and all the exciting people in it. No, it cannot have been merely the grog.

"And, sincerely, I don't think I'm too bad, Mama," finished Russel, proud, apprehensive, yet, though he did not know it, with a wistful note in his voice—"so could you come?"

That wistful note pierced through Lettice's personal preoccupations, and the mother in her responded instantly, automatically.

"Dearest boy, of course I'll come. Is it a party? Have they lent you the theatre? What do you want me to do? Entertain for you? Dress up? I have a new oyster-coloured moiré, by good luck, just home from Désirée's. You shall see it. Ah, Mitcham, there you are. Yes, I want ink, not mud—ink! But first go into my dressing-room and take out the Paris dress! Packed for London? No matter! Unpack it!" And then, as the maid scurried off and she took up her pen again—"Well, Russel, what else?"

"Mama, you don't understand."

"Your mother is a stupid woman, I know; but it's not her eldest son's place to tell her so."

"But Mama, do listen! I've got an engagement at the Glory Hole and I've been rehearsing for a fortnight. We open on Monday and the dress rehearsal is tonight. And so I must go up to town, Mama, at once, or I shall miss everything—I should have started half an hour ago, and I'm sorry you and Papa don't like my going on the stage, but I'm twenty-one, and for me to be a diplomat would be absurd, Mama! I'm not one by nature. Only snobs despise the stage and anyway I'm my own master. And, Mama, I will, I intend to do what I want to do. That's what I want to say. Why shouldn't I? That's what I want to know. Well, I must go now. I've to go to the fitter's again and a hundred and one trifles to see to. You know what it is, Mama, before a first night, and this is the first time, and—oh, Mama, be pleased about it, and tell Papa! You know how to tell Papa so that he will be pleased too. Do! Please do, Mama! Won't you? I can't help it, you know. I can't help being a Broome."

Lettice drew herself together for an outburst, but Russel was too quick for her. He gave her that special look which, as he knew, she found irresistible. It was the look which admitted his sins and invited her and nobody in the world but her to know all about him and them, and to enjoy the fun that sinning could be.

"No, stop it, Mama! Now stop it! And don't scold! Give a fellow a kiss and say 'good luck'!" And with that he clambered from the bed-steps on to the high bed itself just as the small Russel used to do who once was Lettice's whole world: hugged her till she was breathless: leaped down again, sending the tray flying as he did so, and so ran out of the room with a last call to her over his shoulder—"Make Papa approve! You know you can."

Quite stunned by the fireworks of youth the mother sat perfectly still after her son's departure in the equally stunning quiet; for when youth leaves a room, it leaves a husk in which older people hear their own souls rattle as they move. Her middle-aged beauty shone for nobody's eyes just then, not even for her own, though the pier-glass showed her herself and her litter of papers and her overturned tray. But for once the disorder of the room did not disturb her housewifely soul. The disturbance was in her mind.

'It won't do,' thought Lettice, in the strangest mingling of amusement and real pain. 'But it's monstrous! The wretched, selfish child! And how handsome he looked! But it's flat disobedience. How am I to tell William? It isn't right that William should be bamboozled like this. It makes a fool of him. But what's to be done? It's too late to stop him now, of course, but I shall never forgive Russel. He must be taught a lesson, a very severe lesson. Well, his father will do that. William will be so angry. Yes, and of course Russel comes to me, the wretched boy! Well, as long as he comes to me! Poor boy! But I can manage his father: he knows that. I'll tell William myself about it. With that heart of his he must not hear it from strangers. Now if I dressed and started almost at once, when should I reach York?' And then, aloud—

"Mitcham, come here! I want you! Oh, there you are! What on earth are you doing with that ball-dress? Oh, did I? Well, I don't want it now. I want to dress, and while I'm dressing order the horses and pack me some clothes. Pack for yourself too! Don't argue with me, woman! Pack!"

And so Lettice decided on her course of action. Necessarily she left her letter to William unfinished; though she found time before closing her letter to Lionel to scrawl the shocking news in a postscript, and to beg him to attend the disastrous Monday performance. "For we must rally round the boy, of course, all of us; but my own duty at the moment is William." She sealed and dispatched it to London by one of her servants, sending at the same time a parcel to Russel with forgotten linen, a furious, scribbled scolding, and some of her own pin-money— "for necessary tips and so on; for you are no doubt short of money, worthless child that you are! I send you no good wishes, and I daren't think what your father will say."

Then she gave some necessary orders to her household, annoyed the coachman by accurate calculation of distances to be covered and the times needed in which to cover them, and incredibly soon was driving towards her William.

But when she had accomplished the long, exhausting journey she

found William's Company and an agitated understudy rehearsing parts;
but no William himself. William, too, was a traveller.

For just about the time when Russel broke his news to his mother,
a well-meaning underling had shoved under William's nose a cutting
from a London paper. The cutting announced that Mr. Russel Broome,
eldest son of the famous actor, William Broome, was to appear for the
first time upon any stage on the following Monday night. The cutting
pointed out further that the Gloriana was the family theatre: recounted
the triumphs of Richard, the tragedy of Robert, and opined that the
evening might prove a turning-point in theatrical history.

Now, if Russel had himself broken the news to his father William
would have been angry enough; but to have it thus thrust upon him
by strangers was more than a blow: it was a wound. In either case he
would have suffered and been angered as a father; but, as a professional
actor, anger itself paled before his horror at the technical imprudence
of the step. Didn't the mad boy realise that he could not possibly have
been engaged upon his own talents? The lick-spittle management
had taken him on simply and solely because he was a Broome! If he
must go upon the stage, let him at least be properly trained: and to
whom should a Broome go for training if not to a Broome, and his own
father? Oh, it was a monstrous business! It would do the boy good, of
course, to fall, and fall heavily: and yet—could nothing be done to save
Russel the fall? Nothing, of course. It was too late. Well, at least he,
William, must be there to see what sort of a fool the boy was making
of himself. A father must back up his son. Besides, how could he sit
still and wait for bad news?

So William, after his own performance ended, travelled south,
unaccompanied, and in haste. He had no time to notify his wife when
he reached town; but unshaven, exhausted with lack of sleep, hurried
straight to the theatre and dropped into his seat, the heavy, excitable,
anxious man, not three minutes before the curtain rose.

He suffered in the half hour that elapsed before his son's appearance.
The anxiety of a father mingled with a thousand recollections of his
own youth which stirred and tormented him. He leant forward (he had
pushed his way into the pit) and grasped the pillar which flanked his
seat so that the whole attached bench creaked under his clutch. When
the boy did at last come on, William was so strained with anxiety that
he could hardly hear the nervous young voice.

But Russel did not utterly disgrace himself. He had watched his
father often enough, and he gave an innocent young copy of the older

man's work, with one or two interpretations of his own, that were not
too bad either, thought William, relaxing with relief. Though there was
nothing great, nothing heroic about his performance, Russel hadn't
made an utter fool of himself. His voice carried well. His appearance
was good. He could stand still. He would pass, he would pass!
William heaved an exquisite sigh of relief and leaned back in his seat.

For once he had been unaware that everybody surrounding him had
recognised him, and perfectly understanding his special interest in the
performance, found him at least as interesting as the stage. But now
he began to turn in his seat and look about him, to puzzle over the
new decorations, frown at the unfamiliar painting on the curtain and,
his professional instinct waking, to reckon up the money in the house.
"Sixty to eighty in the stalls," he thought to himself.

Then he lifted his eyes to the boxes and, in the management's box,
the old Broome box, as it was still called, saw his own father, Robert
Broome, sitting, very drawn and pale, his eyes fixed upon him. Moreover, as William stirred, tried to rise and cried out chokingly, his own
dead father smiled at him and beckoned with his hand.

CHAPTER 10

LETTICE'S SONS AND LIONEL'S DAUGHTER

WILLIAM's death from heart-failure in his own theatre, at his own son's début, hurt many people. His companies mourned him unfeignedly, for, if he was self-absorbed, he was also fantastically generous to those who would stand up to him and show him, not only their wrongs, but their rights. They rightly surmised, too, that his wife would be no more seen in their world: and this was a second loss to be mourned. For, jealous of the Broome dignity, easily resentful of gaucheries, seeing no point of view but her own, she had yet a sense of duty to God and her neighbour, that is to say to her husband and his innumerable dependents. She was often just and generally championed distress, put her hand in her pocket without a grumble, scolded with a twinkle and saved souls and bodies at considerable personal exertion. She was respected, feared and adored: occasionally she was hated. But, loved or hated, at least she was always greeted with excitement when she interrupted a rehearsal, appeared on the threshold of a dressing-room, or penetrated into theatrical bed-sitting-rooms. Would it be a blessing or a box on the ear? You never knew till you got it, but you generally deserved what you got.

But William's death ended that wholesome, lively reign; for Lettice in her wild grief turned her face from the stage, the murderous stage which had lured their boy on to it, and lured her husband to overtax his strength in order to see their boy and so had killed him. Yes, killed him. What a journey for a man of his age after such a day's work and the shock of Russel's disobedience! Hadn't the doctors warned them all? Didn't Russel know it? Yet he had persisted in his wilful courses, and so he and the stage between them had killed his father. She would not speak of it to Russel unless he drove her to speech, but she would always remember in her heart that Russel and his acting had killed his father.

Thus Lettice in her restless, caged grief, flinging herself to and fro against the bars of the facts that imprisoned her. 'William is dead. I loved William. William is gone. I shall never see him smile at me again. I shall never hear his voice. I have lost him. He is gone. I loved my William. William is dead. He is gone.'

And so round and round it went in her poor vigorous, rebellious mind, till the agony relieved itself in curious twistings of thought and emotion against, always against the memory of the too much beloved dead. Indeed, none of the Broomes care to remember their dead over-long, though they have prodigious memories for every detail of their own lives and their living neighbours, and keep strict accounts; for it torments a Broome to be in debt to a neighbour. If it is no more than a laugh behind the hedge when a Broome slips on an orange peel, that laugh will be recorded in the debit column and the account will not be closed till the little debt of mockery has been paid. It may take thirty minutes, it may take thirty years before the account is closed, and meanwhile the debtor and creditor can be the best of friends, the dearest of friends. Nevertheless a Broome always pays his debts in the end with a bow and a charming smile.

Thence, perhaps, has arisen the belief that the Broomes are not to be trusted in their relationships: that they turn on their friends too easily. This, of course, is quite untrue. The Broomes never forget their friends, would defend them against a world in arms. 'Our friend, right or wrong!' is the Broome motto. But if our friend inadvertently treads on our toes, then we retaliate upon his toe, and a trifle more heavily. How else are we to keep our account with him balanced? And when our friend is dead we forget him as quickly as we can. How else can we punish him for hurting us by dying? Friend or no friend, we must punish people who hurt us. Otherwise keeping accounts becomes a mere farce.

So Lettice squared accounts with the adored husband who had so cruelly hurt her in dying, by putting him fiercely out of her mind and memory, him and his fame, him and his English stage. It was a sign of her wild, inverted misery that she could not be persuaded to wear mourning for him, though black and lavender were particularly becoming to her fading beauty. She flamed with anger when Rosina reproached her, and quoted the returned beloved brother. Lionel himself had said that he didn't see why she should wear mourning if she didn't want to: for his part he despised such conventions. Lettice, who had become a little conventional like the rest of the early Victorians, was pulled up short when he said that, though she quoted him so securely to Rosina. Did Lionel hate conventions? Oh, she would show him that she could keep pace with his hates and loves.

For already the atmosphere, which had rocked a little with the removal of its centre, was steadying again and centring round the returned Lionel, her comfort, her only oracle now. Thank God for Lionel, still blessedly young in mind though he had certainly aged in looks. To look at, he was an old sixty rather than the young fifty that he ought to be. But, at least, he had aged like a Broome not like a Wybird. The Wybirds grew so heavy: their lines were never sharp in any case: they were clay busts, not marble ones, and time smudged their features to the indistinguishable menacing benevolence of an English bloodhound. But Lionel had aged like a Broome: he had dried and sharpened. Indeed, since his return, Lettice had been more than once struck by his likeness to poor Uncle Robert. Time had left him with just the same precise porcelain look, his mouth had thinned as Robert's had thinned and as with Robert, all the life of his face was now concentrated in the all-observant eyes. Lionel was much more like Uncle Robert than Robert's own son William. Poor William! Poor dear Uncle Robert! Dearest Lionel! It was just like dearest Lionel to return at the right moment. He was always so effective. Not so solid, but much more at home in life than William. William had been a size too large for Lettice's drawing-room; but Lionel suited it like an Empire chair, one of those delicious thin-legged chairs that the duke had given her only the week before she married William. Lettice was thankful to remember that she had secured the chairs, though she had never used them. But they would come in now. Lionel used to admire them. She could turn the nursery into a parlour for Lionel.

For if she made everything delightfully easy for Lionel it was just possible that he would make her house his headquarters. She was afraid that he had too much fortune to be content with living in some-one else's house, but she might suggest it. With the nursery and William's own room made over to him, and at a pinch the library, she could make Lionel very comfortable, and she would not mind seeing him in her William's rooms. Her poor William! Of course she would mind; but better Lionel than Russel who had brought about his father's death. (Yes, he had!) So Lionel should have the rooms: it was always better to make a clean sweep. She thanked God that she was not sentimental. She hated to see the once prized relics of the dead littering the rooms which they no longer used. She could not bear to have William's tastes ruling the place now that William was gone. He must go, utterly! She could not endure missing him so. Good-bye, my poor darling—go quickly!

Yet she wondered what Lionel would have thought of William. She wished that he and William had met once again: it would have enormously amused her to hear from each his opinion of the other. Of course they had met again in a sense, but it was not certain that William had recognised Lionel. "Or did he know you, Lionel? Tell me again how it happened!"

But Lionel could not tell her much. He had, as Lettice knew, gone to the theatre because of her note. Naturally he took an interest in the young scamp his nephew. Naturally he would back up a Broome. He had taken the stage box because it was nearest to the stage and he wanted to see all he could of Russel's make-up. It was just after young Russel's final exit that he had seen William himself sitting in the pit and had said, not recognising him in the least—"There's a striking creature!" ("Ah, so he was!" said Lettice.) Then an attendant had overheard him and had whispered the news. The stranger at whom he and, for that matter, the rest of the house was staring, was William Broome himself. The attendant opined that he had come to see his son's first appearance, and added that it was a great day for the house; for William Broome had not been inside it, his own theatre, close on twenty years—"Not since his father died, sir, in the very chair you are sitting upon!"—which, said Lionel, "was a tactless observation of the fellow."

So Lionel had shifted to another chair backing the stage, from which he could observe William more easily, and had given his card to the man and bidden him take it down to William in the pit. Meanwhile he continued to watch him and presently, catching his eye, had smiled at him, waved and beckoned: at which William clearly recognised him. Lionel was sure of it. William had risen to his feet with a vague shout that turned all heads and then, as far as Lionel could make out, had fallen forward over the bench in some sort of a fit. "And as you are aware, Lettice, when I got round to the ante-room where they had carried him, the poor fellow was dead. Well—he had his day! He did more with his life than I've managed to do. I wish I'd seen him in his prime. But did you know of this trouble with his heart? Did he know? Such a great handsome heavy strapping fellow! It was very strange to me to see him puff out like a dandelion. So that's what heart does to you, does it? Don't cry! They say it's the end of so many actors. Kean went that way, didn't he? In harness. Best way, Lettice! But didn't he know? Shouldn't he have taken more care of himself?"

Lettice nodded absently.

"He'd been warned against strain, excitement; but what was he to do, Lionel? An actor must excite himself. They wanted him to leave the stage, but you know he would have died of ennui. The Broomes must excite themselves. You're enough of a Broome to know that. Look at my mother! Oh, it's quite clear to me what killed William, Lionel, and I shall never forgive Russel."

Lionel cocked his bright eye at her.

"My nephew Russel? Dear Lettice! Is he your new scapegoat?"

She flushed angrily.

"Scapegoat? I don't know what you mean. But I do know what killed William. First the shock of the news: it shocked him enough that Russel should be on the stage at all: then the anger he felt, just as I felt it, Lionel! Keen anger at the defiance, the disobedience, the wicked insolent disobedience of the step: and then, naturally, anxiety as a father. I felt it myself enough as a mother, though I would not countenance Russel by watching him play. But here comes William pelting down from York: no sleep, no rest, and I daresay no food. And what's the result? With his heart any one of these agitations might have killed him, and on the top of it he has the excitement of watching Russel play, and play very badly, I hear. Believe me, I shall never forgive Russel. I shall always say he is responsible for widowing me. But one day God will punish him, or if God won't I will. I am not to be robbed of my husband. Russel forgets his duty to his mother and his father at his peril. He doesn't know it yet, but he has ceased to be my son. Don't be ridiculous, Lionel! Of course I've not told him this. What, within a week of his father's funeral! Do you think I have no heart? But one day I shall make him know it. I'm a very patient woman, Lionel, but it is possible to try my patience too highly, as Russel shall find: as my darling William found for that matter. Once, when my William was insufferable, I taught him a lesson too. He thought I could not do without him. I showed him. I did without him very well indeed for five years. But then, of course, he was sorry and I thought he had learned his lesson, so I forgave him. He was the best of husbands to me and my life is over. Thank God I have Harry left, and Robin and you! I'm glad William saw you before he died. But why are you so sure that he recognised you when you didn't recognise him?"

Lionel could give no good reason, but he was quite sure that William had recognised him. As he answered his sister he could see in his mind's eye William's face with the look of recognition stamped upon it like the mark of a heel in wet sand. He shuddered as he recalled that livid face. But why had it been so livid? Why had it borne a look of such horrified recognition? Lionel could think of no reason, and as the problem was a disagreeable one he very shortly put the matter out of his mind.

For he had much to occupy him.

Lionel, back in England, found himself a busier man than he had ever been in his life, though he had not been idle in the East. As a younger son his inheritance was small; but Hilaret had given him a generous allowance. She would have enjoyed seeing him fritter it and come to her for fresh supplies; but Lionel was prudent over money. He trained his taste, and used his allowance to buy lovely nonsense— Tanagra figurines, Limoges enamels, rugs, embroideries, intaglios, manuscripts. And he made his profits and yet kept the best of the loot for his one-day house in England, till, in twenty years of leisurely trading and travelling, he had accumulated a considerable fortune. Now he had to turn it into respectable English cash. He had bought new clothes in Paris, but he found himself monstrously out of date in the matter of snuff-boxes, walking-sticks and cravats. It was not a matter of purchase: he had to learn a new, a Victorian, idea of dress. And there were rubies to be re-set for Lettice, and so many relations to visit. There was the duke and the rest of his brothers and Rosina, all requiring attention, leisurely attention, and a detailed account of the career and death of the duchess their mother. And they had all aged, and the account had to be very strictly supervised and pruned. And when he had satisfied his relations he still had his friends to consider, all the young bloods who had grown into fathers of families and flourished whiskers and a morality. And he had to go to court: he had to find a house: he had by the way to run over to Paris sometime that spring to see his daughter.

"Didn't I tell you in my letter, Lettice, that I was bringing you home a niece? Sixteen years old, but looks twenty-five. You know how it is in the East. Blue eyes, but otherwise the duchess over again. Oh, yes, she's sufficiently white. Her mother was a Circassian, a slave. Yes, it's different out there. Mama bought her for a whim—the mother, I mean. And she was a very remarkable creature: devoted to Mama: devoted to me. There was a boy too, but he died and she with him. Mama adored Georgina. Yes, she would have the child called Georgina. She said it would have so greatly annoyed our father to have such a granddaughter, born in such circumstances, that she could not refrain from perpetuating the situation by christening her after him. Well, Georgina is now in Paris. I put her into the first convent I could find— the problem of clothes, you know, and table manners. For after Mama's death I could not be perpetually arranging for her to travel with me, and so I left her to be brought up with very worthy people, cousins of the Shah, and of course they did not train her in European manners. Perhaps I should have left her with them altogether. It would have been easy to arrange a local marriage. But somehow I could not fancy that Mama would approve. So I brought Georgina home with me and there she is now in this convent which was recommended to me by some of the Legation people, and no doubt the poor little soul is suffering the tortures of the damned. You must tell me what to do with her, Lettice! To be sure, I don't think you will like her, but you had better do something. Besides, it would do you good to go to Paris. The life is amusing and such hosts of our friends live there. Even Charles has settled down: I saw him on my way home. He collects minor poets at the moment—live ones. Yes, he said he had not seen you for two years. We grow old, Lettice, as I told Bedenham. Oh dear me, yes, Bedenham was hospitality itself. But what's happened to him, my dear? He reminds me of our father. Eh, isn't he like the old man? He has ruined the town house, or so I think. I can't relish his red rep and his mahogany. And all my mother's furniture has gone from the blue room! Where, oh where are those delightful French chairs that I helped her to buy? Do you remember?"

"Calm yourself! I have them," interpolated Lettice. "You shall see them again."

"Bless you!" He lifted her hand and kissed it. "I might have known. Our tastes always ran together. But Lettice, our brother's taste is an offence! There were five dogs in the library when I arrived. I came in saying, 'Don't you remember me, Bedenham?' and he arose from his chair and a bloodhound and a spaniel rose with him, and upon my word he stood like a cross between the two and bayed at me—'To whom am I indebted for this honour?' and I was responding with— 'Sold you, my boy. It's Lionel,' when his infernal hound began baying and my lines were lost. And I had amused myself on that confounded crossing at Messina, with Georgina sea-sick and the pirate scare, by planning to myself how I'd work up my entrance upon Bedenham. But I admit he was surprised enough. He pulled me out a chair (Heaven and earth, how pompous he has grown, Lettice! He makes a ceremony of pulling out a chair!)—and induced me with the utmost fraternal affection. I believe the old boy was really pleased to see me. And for that matter, so was I to see him. And down we sat. Then says Bedenham—'First of all, Lionel—Mama? Have you brought

her home with you?' I gaped at him—'Why, Bedenham, she's been
dead this ten years and more,' I said : and he answered me very stiff and
straight—'I was referring to the body.' And then, you know, Lettice,
it would have been all over, for—no disrespect to Mama—I nearly burst
out laughing at the idea. For Mama had her own notions of where she
should be buried, and I carried them out like a good son. But after all
these years, you know—to demand the body! But at that moment, to
save me, one of his great hounds lurched up against the bust of Byron
and over it went, pedestal and all, and Bedenham was so much touched,
he nearly wept. Not at the breakage—he didn't care for that. It was
the way the beast apologised. He said it was human. He was as pleased
as Punch. It's odd to me how you can all fondle dogs. I've
been too long in the East to relish touching a dog. But the long
and the short of the story is, Lettice, that I'd thought of quartering
myself on Bedenham; but I see it won't do. Bedenham and I are poles
apart. So where am I to live, Lettice? You'll have to take pity on me.
What's fashionable now? Harley Street? Bloomsbury? Or are you all
still shifting west? I'll tell you what, Lettice, you'll have to find me a
house : at least, unless you find me a wife. I've no great wish to marry ;
but you know, Lettice, I must have someone to look after me."

He looked at her sideways. For Lionel also had his ideas for the
future. Not only to Lettice had the idea occurred that old age spent
with Lionel might prove entertaining. But it was much better that the
suggestion should come from her, thought Lionel ; it would give him
the whip hand. For, though he was prepared to share a house with her,
he didn't intend to be controlled in his comings in and goings out by
Lettice. His mother had never attempted to control him, which was
the reason that they agreed so perfectly together ; but he had a suspicion
that Lettice, for all her strong resemblance to Hilaret, was much more
possessive. He was quite sure that she would try to control him,
which might lead to a quarrel, which might lead to a separation, which
would wreck his delightful plan of spending the rest of his life in being
amused by everyone when he walked abroad, and being amused by
Lettice when he felt like staying at home.

"So I'm afraid I shall have to get married, Lettice," said Lionel,
"unless you can find me a house." And he lay back happily in his chair
and let Lettice, with infinite skill, tact and precaution, outline to him
that scheme for their mutual future which he intended her to adopt.

It was adopted. The brother and sister were rich enough to do as
they pleased : and it pleased them to buy a vast house at the corner of

Park Lane. In it they amused themselves very well. Lionel leisurely and gracefully began to take an interest in politics, and Lettice had a salon; at least when she was in the mood, for she would have scandalised a Mlle de Lespinasse by her casual ways. Such gatherings of prize plants in their seasons need more gardener's toil than Lettice cared to give.

But it is a fact that she could always indicate to London that she would be at home: and London, though she had neglected it for months, was always delighted to call again.

For she had a genius for annexing human beings. She would go into a drawing-room, attend a garden-party, make a morning call, and be the centre of the entertainment or a mere shadow in the shadow of her hostess, according to her mood. But, sun or shadow, before she left she generally lifted her finger once, to draw after her the man or woman, boy or girl, who on the occasion had best amused her or most sharply tugged at her hair-trigger curiosity. She was faithful to her own tastes, and generally picked out a man for his fair looks, his grooming or his wit, a woman for her dark looks, good temper or originality. She would devote a week or so to riveting her hold and was then affection-ately and contemptuously sure of her prize for life. She often neglected, but never abandoned these captives of hers. A little starvation is good for everyone; but she never starved them to death, and was kind and pampered them when need arose. They were her human toys, her half-loves, the diversions of her life, though the centre of her life was still her family. She would have tied all her friends and toys together, neck and heels, and laid them down like paving-stones to make a causeway for the triumphal car of her family. Let 'em bruise! Let 'em crush! Way for the Broomes!

Reproached with this, she would cry—"No such thing!" indignantly, but with a giggle, and continue to be enchantingly intimate and tender when she felt like it, and to be as cool and slippery as an eel when she didn't. When her weekly salon became a daily one or invitations too insistent, or her friends squabbled with her and made scenes, she knew what to do. She retired to the country and the bachelor duke, and was delightful to him, giving a fine performance of a maiden aunt, playing cribbage: or she went up to see Robin at Oxford and was the perfect mother, radiant, asking no questions, submissive, perfectly but dis-creetly clothed, low-voiced, fit to be taken about: or she ran away to Paris with Lionel. The truth was that she liked to possess but could not bear to be possessed. A claim, even on her own acknowledged affection, drove her frantic with nervous irritation. She must always be giving and taking, but she must never be asked to give or take.

It was this shying, arrogant resentment of claims which widened the breach between her and her eldest son. She had directly after William's death severed herself with finality from her immediate stage interests. William had left all his property to her with directions that the three theatres should go to their three children on her death, but that she should dispose of his other stage interests, his houses and his cash as she pleased. Lettice was no fool in money matters. She was perfectly aware that she could not control her theatre interests without devoting to them the personal attention which she was no longer prepared to give. So she leased them to other managers for varying terms of years, regardless of the protests of her eldest son, who, on the strength of a six-months engagement was perfectly prepared to go into management. But she told him coldly that he must learn the trade first, as his father and his grandfather and his great-grandfather had done. Though one of the three theatres must be his in the end, she would not raise a finger to help him to earlier management. Let him go on circuit! Let him sweat as his father had done! Russel stuck out his chin at her but said no more.

Lionel, watching, said to his sister later—

"That youngster of yours has mischief in his eye. Don't try him too high, Lettice! After all, it's natural enough that he should stick to the stage."

"William had other plans for him," said Lettice coldly, "and so have I."

"Plans for him? That's the Wybird in you speaking. But he's a Broome, and the Broomes have plans for themselves. If you thwart him he will intrigue against you. I see it in his eye."

"And what could he do?" said Lettice disdainfully, but interested. Lionel laughed.

"That stirs you, does it? You love a fight."

"As if I would fight my own son," said Lettice again coldly.

"What else are you doing—" said Lionel—"now?"

"I don't want him on the stage," said Lettice fiercely. "There's a different attitude towards the stage nowadays."

"Snob!" said Lionel. "Of course, you were at Windsor last week. I'd forgotten."

"The stage," said Lettice, "is an illegitimate profession. You know that, Lionel! I want Russel to realise it in time. If he went into politics or the church he could have all the amusements of the actor and yet be taken seriously."

Lionel was interested.

"Ah, you've always looked upon acting as an amusement. You, my dear, don't need the stage for that, any more than Mama did. To quote our income—'All the world's your stage!' But of course it is, silly darling, silly woman! Don't deny, Lettice! Don't pose! But with Robert and William and, I suspect, with our forefather Richard, the stage was not an amusement at all. It was a passion, my dear. They were love-sick about it. They were pixie-led. And I think my nephew has inherited their passion. I've watched your Russel, sister, and it's for your own sake as much as for his that I say—Don't try to stop him! Make it easy for him instead. If you fight him he'll beat you. Don't forget he's twice a Broome."

"What could little Russel do against me?" asked Lettice in genuine wonder. "I'm his mother. I hold all the cards." Then she stiffened. "He can come to me and say he's sorry for his disobedience and cruelty to his father. He can do that first, and then, perhaps—I'm not sure— but then, perhaps, I'd give him an allowance and some arrangement might be made about one of the theatres. But if he shows fight—well, I hold all the cards."

Lionel shrugged his shoulders. He was perfectly convinced that Russel had a card up his sleeve of which his sister was entirely unaware.

And Lionel, as usual, was right. Russel's card was young Robin.

Robin Broome hero-worshipped his elder brother. Russel was a good deal solider than Robin, quicker tongued, a better athlete, a warmer personality altogether. Robin had his mother's brittleness and his father's melancholy, an impossible combination in a child but an attractive combination in a young man at Oxford. Russel and Robin, in spite of the year between them, had gone up to Oxford together, for Russel had been tempted to delay leaving Weston because of the important positions he held there, while Robin had been tempted to leave Weston early because he held there no position at all. But though Russel was the king of his world throughout his school-days and Robin a stranger in that gate, nothing shook the affection between the brothers. Russel protected Robin. Robin adored Russel.

At the university the situation altered. The frailer Robin began to find out that he had gifts of his own, that he could buy old prints judiciously, decorate his rooms attractively: that he enjoyed playing host and was in demand as a guest. He found that a flow of words does as well as a flow of wine if you want to make a party go, and that if you can dispense both you are sure of friends. To play two or three instruments extremely well was, he further discovered, an asset instead of a drawback: to have a gift for turning verse was another asset. It was amusing, too, to find that if, smiling, you lifted up your finger and beckoned—once, twice, thrice—friends fluttered up like winter birds at a scatter of crumbs.

Timid Robin was pleased to discover these things, but scarcely more pleased than Russel to watch Robin's discoveries. Russel, secure in his position as an athlete, was delighted to observe that his young brother's more peculiar talents were at last properly appreciated. He very genuinely appreciated them himself: and Robin's brains relieved him, too, of certain responsibilities. It was soon clear to Russel that it was quite impossible to work and enjoy himself at the same time. However, Robin could do the work and glorify the Broome name. What it was to have brains!

Thus Russel, beaming benevolently upon the family Ariel; for there was no jealousy in him. When, characteristically, he began to find himself bored by his own unvarying athletic successes: when the fascinating, unreal drama of university life suddenly appeared to him a childish business: when he was given the chance of plunging into the real drama of stage life and decided to take his chance—his only regret was the separation from Robin which his plans involved. But the regret did not alter his determination to put away childish things. For though Russel was in character by far the most childlike of the three brothers—small Harry, still in the nursery, would never be as guileless as Russel—yet, like all the Broomes, Russel was old for his age.

So he took his step: and in the brief month of rehearsals so attuned himself to his new world that the Russel and Robin of Oxford seemed to him as remote as the Babes in the Wood. His father's death had aged him yet further, had hardened him, accentuated his wilfulness. He was a man; but still people treated him as a boy: and yet they blamed him for his father's death. That was cruel. That was complicatedly unfair. Had anyone, even his mother, suffered by it more than he? His father's death made him secretly indignant, because, as Russel felt and saw it, it had happened with such wilful spectacularity on the fair night of his first venture. He felt himself cheated, ill-treated, bedevilled by ill-luck. None of these fools understood how he felt about his father. Indeed it is doubtful if the boy himself understood his own passion, understood that his worship of the stage and his hero-worship of William were one and the same thing. He could never disassociate the man from all that the actor represented—power, glamour, the Shakespearean conception of the tragic man. But he thought that he loved his father—that was one reason why a management ought to trust him with Hamlet, only one couldn't say so. But Hamlet ought to be played by somebody young enough to understand Hamlet's attitude to a magnificent king of a parent. 'I think I see my father . . . Hyperion—' Yes, Shakespeare knew how one felt to such a father as William Broome, remote, incomprehensible, strong, melancholy, beautiful William Broome—"my father and the greatest actor in the world!"

And now his very love of his father was put wrong, belittled, set a-squint by the circumstances of William's end. He ought to be thinking only of the loss of his father; but how could he help thinking of the spoiling of his own happy, joyous start in life? He was furious with fate—and the dead: he could not forgive his father for dying and so spoiling everything and putting him, Russel, in the wrong.

And when he found that his mother, unreasonable and eccentric in her grief, was allowing it to curdle into antagonism to him and to the stage, he resented her attitude fiercely and at once began to consider what measures he could devise to frustrate her. He understood her well enough to bear her no personal grudge. To herself she was much more Broome than Wybird, but to the boy she was Wybird entire. He identified her with all antagonism to his chosen profession, with the tightening of social etiquette, with the growing belief that immorality was an ingredient of art.

"People chatter! What do they know of the stage?" fumed Russel, three months old in that world, and his uncle Lionel listened sympathetically. Lionel was of opinion that his nephew had not more brains than were necessary, that he had, indeed, the natural stupidity of the good actor as regards ideas. Still, he was sure that the youngster was in his right place, and had the capacity to be, if not as great an actor as his father, at any rate as good an actor as any. He thought his sister was treating the boy unfairly, and said so to them both. Lettice responded with indignation: Russel with confidences.

"Uncle Lionel, I'm desperate. I shall do something she doesn't like soon. I shall, Uncle. I'm as obstinate as she is if I'm roused. I'll show her."

Lionel shook his head.

"You'll never get anything out of your mother by violence, my boy. Tactics—tactics!"

"Damn tactics! I'm talking of my rights! It's so obvious what Father intended. It's my own property, and she ought to let me learn to handle it. I'm not a fool! I don't want to run before I can walk; but I want to put my work into my own property, not another man's. 'Apprenticeship leading to management,' that's my war-cry! Isn't that reasonable, Uncle?"

"I think so," said Lionel. "I've told her what I think."

"I know you have. You've been a trump, Uncle. But, Uncle, you must go on telling her. Mother's as difficult to turn as a runaway horse, but she can be turned. You've got to be in her graces, though: and I never was. I'm not her favourite."

"No—too much like her," said time-calmed, elderly Lionel, smiling at his impetuous nephew.

"Me? Not me! I want peace, Uncle. I hate Waterloos. That's why I bore Mama. She loves them. No, you've more influence than I have, sir, with a woman like Mama. So has Robin, for that matter. That's it! I'll get hold of Robin. He can do anything with Mama and I can do anything with him. So, if she won't listen to the three of us I'll——" He broke off, his eyes alight with mischief.

"What, nephew?" Lionel's eyes sparkled in sympathy.

"Robin's my rod in pickle," said Russel simply and solemnly. And off he went. Lionel could hear his loud young voice down the passages, shouting for his man and explaining to anyone who cared to hear that he was going up to Oxford for the night.

"My poor sister!" murmured the father of a daughter, and began with some complacence to dwell upon an ideal picture of Georgina embowered in nuns. Some day soon, thought Lionel, he must run over to Paris and take Lettice with him. Lettice was a trifle invincible in this matter of sons. Well, she should see that there was something to be said for daughters. Yes, it was time to consider the future of Georgina, who must be, when he came to think of it, nearly eighteen. Marriageable! Hm! The nuns would have done the rough polishing. It was time that Lettice took the girl in hand. Not that she would be difficult. She had given him no trouble whatever in the brief weeks of their journey home. Indeed, he had scarcely seen her. She was always in her cabin with the duenna. They took meals together, and she went over gangways and entered inns on his arm, certainly. Nevertheless he knew her more as livestock to be carted, watered, wisped and fed than as a daughter. He saw her as a dumb, shy, docile heifer, who ate life with her large blue eyes, and was as handsome as her mother, but with a whiter skin. She was, in fact, too white. It was the Circassian sherbet, not the Nordic snow. But they would not know the difference in London. Dressed and dowered, the girl was fit to marry a younger son, at any rate, in spite of her irregular birth. Besides—irregular? How regular was the affair of John Smith and Pocahontas? Pooh! It would amuse him to turn matchmaker and circumvent the matrons with dowerless, legitimate daughters to sell. Besides, he faintly missed the girl. She represented, she was all that was left of the best twenty years of his life: and the good Lettice did so flourish her sons at the universe.

"Dear Lettice, I, too, am a parent! You need a holiday. Shall we go over to Paris and take a look at Georgina? They will have made a good little Catholic of her by now. At least, I gave instructions to that effect. Don't you hate Protestant women? They have such scrubbed, un-powdered souls. Women and religion should always paint a little. But every woman ought to know how to pray. Mama didn't. Nor do you, Lettice. So come and take a lesson from my Georgina."

But at Paris the gay, parental Lionel received the finest shock of his life: which hurt him, for he liked giving shocks, and was not accustomed to getting them. His Georgina had not approved of her convent. So she had left it.

When?

Two days ago.

How?

By a window, it was surmised.

With whom?

Nobody knew.

Well!

"But can you blame her, my poor brother?" breathed the enchanted, sympathetic Lettice. "It's just what Mama would have done. Indeed, you both did it, didn't you, when you were Georgina's age?"

Fortunately, she spoke in English. If she had said it in French, in earshot of those magpie women, it is possible that Lionel would have killed her. Instead, he was charming to the magpies. They had been resentfully on the offensive, for Mlle Wybird had been intractable, had a passion for smuggled sweetmeats, and wouldn't say her prayers. But Lionel's helpless, heart-wrung parenthood would have won him any woman except Lettice, and in five minutes the nuns were on the defensive and distressedly his allies. But Lettice could not be bothered to watch an exhibition of Lionel's little ways at such a moment. She hurried him off to the Embassy, where she put all his little ways, feminised, into action. Soon all the notabilities were running. Paris was stirred up as with a stick, and there were fished up from the depths of that pond handfuls of muddy, wriggling creatures who were exhibited, questioned, and flung back again. Lettice, sincerely and decently anxious about her niece, for she had a sense of duty and a lively imagination, nevertheless enjoyed the fuss. But Lionel, doing his utmost to play the part of distracted father as it should be played, found himself, at the end of the month, much more relieved than angered by a formal letter from far-away Buda-Pesth.

In it a son-in-law with an unpronounceable name assured him that Georgina was safe and most securely married. Then did Lionel remember the handsome young Jew on the Mediterranean boat, who sat next to him at table and had a better cabin than Lionel's. The young Jew had treated the Englishman as a fellow dealer. Lionel, who had the art of hobnobbing remotely with everyone and never used his own name in his trading, had seen quite a lot of the Jew: liked him: found him a bit of an innocent when it came to a deal. An exquisite Chinese carpet had changed hands, and had been brought home to grace Lettice's boudoir—one of Lionel's bargains.

And now it appeared that, after all, it had not been quite such a bargain, nor had the young Jew been quite such an innocent. That stung. The young Jew and Georgina had laughed at him, and Lionel was furious, and kept a hand on his sense of humour much as you keep your fingers round the muzzle of an intelligent terrier who will not be quiet.

"So after all my care and trouble the minx goes behind me! With a Jew, a huckstering Jew! And I thought she was sea-sick. Why, I never troubled myself with her for a moment. So that's what was behind her blue eyes and her nonsense with her veils. And it means, I suppose, that I must drag myself off to Buda-Pesth to thrash my son-in-law." And Lionel's face grew longer still. Like all great travellers, he hated being shifted by other people's whims. He glanced down at the letter and sought comfort in it.

"I tell you what, Lettice, he writes with a certain distinction. The French is perfect. Well, there it is. I have to be glad, I suppose, that he has married her, for I'm sure he didn't know who I was, and the girl's ideas of our family are misty. She called Mama 'Princess.' That's as near as I got her to 'Duchess.' No doubt she has transferred the rank to herself, and told a great tale to her husband. Husband! That Jewish rug-seller my daughter's husband! What a come-down! And nothing to be done, I suppose?"

He hesitated: he shot a glance, tentative, entreating, at his sister. Then, petulantly—

"Oh, don't tell me that I ought never to have transplanted her! I'm fully aware of that. But now that she's pigeoned East on her own, ought I to interfere, Lettice? Would it not be better, perhaps, to let things be?"

Thus the airy Lionel, and was amazed to find himself instantly called to order by a really angry woman.

"Let things be? Have you no heart at all, Lionel? Do you want to be known as a monster? You let your motherless daughter—more than motherless, and far worse than fatherless, and my own niece too—be brought up by natives! You drag the poor child to Europe un-chaperoned! You leave her to be sea-sick and fall in love as she pleases. You shut her up in a convent, poor Eastern creature, like a peacock with its tail strapped to a board, week after week, month after month. And then, when the poor child sickens of being a jail-bird in a foreign country, and makes a bolt for it, you say 'Let things be!' In another minute you'll be saying to me, 'She has made her bed, let her lie on it!' You sound like a low-church dowager. I'm ashamed of you, Lionel. Of course you will start for Buda-Pesth tonight, and if the man is really fond of her you will give them your blessing, and if the man is a rogue (for we don't yet know which it may be and never shall, if you take your responsibilities as a father so lightly), then you beat the man and bring the poor child home to me. I should come with you and see you do it if I hadn't Robin coming home for the vacation and Russel in this 'mood. You'd better see about passports at once."

Thus spoke Hilaret's daughter, and Lionel recognised the tone and obeyed.

He was rewarded by finding his truant in a comfortable Jewish home. Not only was the husband innocent of designs on an English fortune, but Lionel found himself received with patronage, as the father of a beggar-maid, and warned almost as soon as he was welcomed that, though the girl would be accepted by the family, he need expect nothing for himself. To reverse the situation was irresistible. He did the business well, and, as he told his sister on his return, they took it well.

"Nice people. But I always liked the Jews. These are half oriental still, but heading west. Georgina has fallen on her feet. She would never have gone down in England, I see it now. But these people keep their women in subjection, and yet pamper them. They've got Georgina into step already. This elopement of hers will be her one independent action. The rest of me will come out in her children. But, as my son-in-law has ambitions—he is a second son and has his eye on South America—well—I may still do the world a good turn yet, Lettice, by proxy. Yes, I'm well satisfied. I may say that I have left my new relations purring."

"How much did you settle on her?" said his sister.

" 'With half my worldly goods . . .' "

"My dear Lionel!"

"Well, I didn't endow her mother. I have a conscience, Lettice, though you wouldn't think it."

"But—half!"

"Well, I like giving presents, and they were so sure I had come for a pension. Why shouldn't I amuse myself? Besides—don't let's mince matters. Georgina might have come to a bad end. I've been a bad father. So let me at least enable my son-in-law to be a good husband. He will be. Georgina's money will be doubled in five years. He promised me that, his eyes downright religious. I like Jews. Trustable. They like me too. I suppose because I'm not."

With a large gesture he shook off parenthood, and turned a fresher smile on his sister.

"And now your news, my dear? I hope you have kept me in countenance by being equally extravagant with Russel? You'll enjoy yourself, Lettice. It's most amusing making people happy. They present a singularly pleasing expression. I don't know what it is, but make them happy and the very skin acquires a bloom. It's a patina of the spirit. You cannot fake it. So little trouble to create it—just the stroke of the pen. That's what money can do. Is there anything it can't do? You aren't listening. Why, what's the matter, Lettice? My dear sister, what in the world is wrong?"

He had been so happy in his return, full of his affairs, so triumphant in the telling, that he had not looked at his sister with any attention. Now he saw that her eyelids were swollen with sleeplessness again as they had been in the first weeks of her widowhood, and that her eyes were dumb.

"Russel? I have no son of that name. I have only one son left to me, Lionel. That's my Harry."

"My dear Lettice—" He rose from the easy-chair. She rose too. She flung her news at him as if it were a javelin.

"Your daughter has given you anxiety; but my sons have broken my heart."

"Sit down, Lettice Don't speak so theatrically! What has happened?"

"Happened? They have defied me. Russel has corrupted Robin. Robin has gone on the stage now. That's the latest folly. He threatened me that if I wouldn't concede—oh, I spare you the details—but unless I helped Russel to do all the things that his father most disapproved, Robin would throw up the university. He will not 'take advantage of Russel'! That is the cry. If Russel is to go without, so will he. Go without, when they know that I'm prepared to allow Russel any sum in reason if he follows his father's wishes. But no! He is to do as he likes and I am to pay for it. Well, I will not. Lionel, I will not. And Robin sits in judgment! Robin dares! Robin—let him beware of judgment on himself! 'Honour thy father and thy mother'—what sort of honour do they give me—after all I've done for them? I tell you, Lionel—they have a devilish spirit. I hope God will break it."

"Lettice, Lettice!"

"What's the good of saying 'Lettice, Lettice,' like a parrot? Don't talk at me, Lionel! Don't I know what's best for my children? If Robin chooses to throw up an assured career because Russel lifts his little finger—if Russel thinks he can break his mother's heart as he broke his father's—— Ah, he would be glad to see me dead too, I daresay. But I am not so easily broken. They have made their beds and there they can lie!" And Lettice broke into a storm of weeping.

Lionel did what he could. He sought out the two young men, interviewed them, represented the mother's point of view to the boys and the boys' point of view to the mother, till both sides hated him. But the young men stood firm. They wanted no help. They wanted no advice. They were both hot against their mother. They would make their fortunes in six months at latest. Uncle Lionel was always welcome as an ally, but they did not want his advice though they were gratifyingly confidential about their plans.

"It will all go back to Mama, you know," said Russel to Robin: and Robin had answered with a gleam in his eye—"Let's give him something to take back!" And languidly, reluctantly, suffered a story to be dragged out of him of prospects so roseate, of finances so complicatedly secure, of promises so magnificent, of theatrical allies so exalted, that Lionel, reducing the dimensions of the tale by two-thirds, was yet immensely relieved. He told Lettice that the boys seemed to have plenty of friends at any rate: they were to travel with old Kendal himself: there was a world tour in prospect. He supposed it was the Broome name, impudence and good looks—"But surely, Lettice, you had better give them your blessing. They are ducks in the pond at last, it seems to me. You can't keep them from swimming."

But Lettice, who would have melted at a tale of panic and lean meats, hardened her lips. She would not see either of them, and would not answer their letters, though she could not resist reading them. After a time, even that pricking comfort was denied her. The letters ceased. Stray news of the boys continued to come in, however. Russel was in America. Russel was doing very well. Russel was going to be, was married. (That shred of gossip drove Lettice into a frenzy.) Then no more news of Russel. Robin sent home to his uncle a story in the Monk Lewis manner printed in a country magazine, several poems cut from newspapers, and one long letter describing the climate of California, reflecting adversely upon God, and asking for news of home and Mama and Russel. So Robin and Russel were no longer together! "I thought that wouldn't last," said Lettice, triumphantly, bitterly. Uncle Lionel wrote, and with a wry mouth and a pitiful eye enclosed money orders. But there was no more news of Robin.

Thus it was that Lettice lost, in the days of their youth, her two elder sons.

CHAPTER II

HARRY BROOME IN MANAGEMENT

SHE suffered: the more because, as her history shows, she was not a woman to cry over spilt milk. If her sons did not want their mother, if they did not appreciate their mother, why then, let them go! "It's finished, you understand, it's finished!" cried Lettice furiously to her pillow, beating it with her soft white fists as she wept and yearned for her sons in the long hours before dawn. "What? Write to them when they treat me like that—me, their own mother? Do they think because I'm their mother that they can treat me like that? Let them learn!" cried Lettice, agonising and implacable. And when she had wept herself quiet she would slip out of bed and wander across to the dressing-table and dab her eyes with expensive toilet water and brush out her hair and re-plait it smooth and cool. Then she would wrap her trailing, floating, rainbow-coloured dressing-gown round her and slip across to the room where her youngest son lay asleep, or, like as not, awake.

For Harry was a sickly child and accustomed to enduring hours of wakefulness in which he lay planning his own future. Harry at twelve knew exactly what he was going to do with his whole life. And it is a fact that, though Fate the disciplinarian did its dark best to prove to him that he lived by God's wits and not his own, Fate had no sort of success with Harry Broome. Fate withered flowers in his hand: nevertheless he picked his flowers. Fate turned fruit to ashes in his mouth: nevertheless he ripened, plucked and ate the fruit. Fate was as cruel as a cat to Harry Broome; but it was not able to alter by one hair's breadth the plans which the little boy made for himself as he lay awake in the light summer nights, listening to his mother's movements in the next room, and preparing, with a faint smile, to cope with her, calm her, and send her back to bed soothed when she came across to him, as in those first weeks after the defection of his brothers, she always came.

He was a great comfort to Lettice, was Harry. Firstly because he loved her and the child in him clung to her; but secondly because he profoundly understood her. In his heart he thought his brothers two fools to quarrel with Mama, when it was so easy not to quarrel with her, so easy to make her do exactly what you wanted. Harry thought to himself—"When I'm grown up, when I've been abroad—because I don't intend to go to Oxford—then I shall come home and go on the stage: and what's more Mama will back me! She'll be there on my first night. She'll want to travel with me when I tour, and sometimes I shall let her and sometimes I won't. But either way I'll keep her perfectly contented and happy. Anyone who listened to my thoughts would think me a beast," continued Harry, "but I know I'm not. If I'm going to be an actor I have got to learn to act: and if I'm going to be a manager I've got to learn to manage people," concluded the child, arranging himself on his pillows with a pathetic air, and kicking his bed-clothes into a disorder that would agonise any woman as he heard a step in the passage and saw the gleam of a candle shooting through the key-hole.

Lettice, entering noiselessly, would meet his dark, patient look, and it would shoot into her heart and rankle there till she was a-quiver with tenderness and delight in him, and yet filled too with vague home-sickness for she knew not what—for the baby, perhaps, that he had once been.

"Why aren't you asleep, Harry?"

Harry would toss on his pillow with a shrug and a twist of the mouth, and counter her with—"Why aren't you?" And then—"Mother, give me some water."

She would fetch it for him, pleased to be active, and he would watch her with a child's pleasure in the pretty colours of her wrap. When she came back to him he would catch at her long pig-tail and pull her down upon the bed.

"You've got to go to sleep, Harry," Lettice would protest. But it was generally an hour before she left him, and in that hour she would have talked to him of his babyhood, and her own youth, and William—your father, darling—and people she disliked and people who had wronged her. Thus she led up invariably to a re-discussion of the character of Russel and a lament for slight Robin led away by Russel, and, if she were in a soft mood, with an anxious recapitulation of the hardships they were both enduring as wayfaring men. But it ended always with the harsh formula—"Well, they've made their beds! Let them lie!"

"When I'm a manager—" said Harry one evening.

"Nonsense!" said Lettice sharply.

"When I'm on the stage," resumed Harry calmly, "I shall take you with me. Can't one have a lady dresser? After all, you did it for Papa. Morgan said so."

"You don't want to go on the stage," said Lettice fondly.

"Russel and Robin are. And I can act better than Russel already," said Harry. And then and there he sat upright in his bed and launched out into one of the speeches for which William had been famous. It was his favourite game, and Lettice would prompt him in spite of herself, and they would work each other up into a fine frenzy, which would end with Harry tumbling back into the pillows in a state of exhaustion so like William's that Lettice would be in a maternal fuss, and there would be soothing drinks brewed: and the next day Harry would stay in bed and play with his toy theatre, and be adored by the servants and visited by his uncle Lionel. And Lettice would tell Lionel how impossible it was to prevent Harry from using his brains, and how she wished that Lionel would do his best to knock the absurd idea of becoming an actor out of Harry's head. He hadn't the physique, and, besides, what sort of a career could the stage provide? But there was no doubt that Harry was a genius. He was Robert over again, but with William's fire added. But of course nothing would ever induce her to send him upon the stage.

Thus it was that Harry Broome began the training of his mother. He continued it with such success that he was able to evade the rough and tumble of a Victorian school and, instead, sucked dry the not inconsiderable brains of a private tutor selected for him by his uncle. He went on to Paris to acquire French and there showed his future showmanship by running mad over the early tentative Fechter, and taking enormous pains to become acquainted with him. It was his young passion for Fechter's art that in 1846 took him to Berlin, where the Frenchman was experimenting. Once in Germany he roamed for some months from state to state, from theatre to theatre, acquiring the language and that astonishing knowledge of stage technique which he found so valuable in later life. When he returned to England he assumed, as a matter of course, that now his stage career would begin.

His absence had completed Lettice's education as well as his own. She was magnificently willing to let him do anything that made him happy and kept him at home. So Harry was given his own suite in the Park Lane mansion, and an allowance that would have turned the head of a less prudent young man: and every wire, social and theatrical, that could be pulled was pulled. Soon London talked pleasantly of the promising youngster who was carrying on the great Broome tradition, and Harry found himself worshipped by his mother for his success in the profession which she had disinherited her two other sons for following.

"You'll spoil the boy, Lettice," said Lionel. But then, Lionel was not so fond of Harry as he had been of the elder boys. He regarded his youngest nephew with a certain jealous disfavour because of his ridiculous influence with his mother, and considered him a young man who would always look after himself first. Lionel was growing old. Lettice thought that he grew more like Robert, forgotten Robert, every day. He was actually jealous of her and Harry, just as Robert had been jealous of Hilaret and Lionel himself. Time was as whimsical a trifler as Lionel; but Time's jests were bitterer. But she did not say this to Lionel, grumbling that Harry was being spoiled.

He was wrong. Harry was not spoiled, in Lionel's sense of the word. Harry, that cool, astute, long-headed young man, had certain qualities of which neither his uncle nor even his mother was aware. Lionel was convinced of Harry's cautious attachment to Harry and Harry's interests: Lettice was convinced of Harry's passionate attachment to her and no-one else. Neither of them conceived that Harry's attachments to other human beings would be equally tenacious, cautious, and passionate.

But so it was. And the fact had kept the boy fresh-hearted. Harry, as a ten-year-old, had a sort of hero-worship for his brothers, Russel and Robin. What a sun and moon! He circled the fringe of their mysteries, respectful, all-observant, thrilled. When they were together they talked a language that Harry could not understand, though he understood well enough the language that Lettice and Lionel used to each other. But his brothers referred to experiences such as you read about in books: they smoked: they had marvellous waistcoats: they sat up all night and talked of their uncles by their Christian names, and they threw money about with mad ease. Lettice constantly took Harry to this or that entertainment, and Lionel was good to him. But when once Russel took him out, did the gorgeous adventure compare with any commonplace treat devised by his mother or uncle? No!

"When Russel took me to see the prize-fighter—"

"When Robin and I went to Madame Tussaud's—" These events stood out in Harry's mind, white-lighted, like glimpses of futurity. Thus his brothers walked beglamoured: and it was one of the boy's secret plans, fulfilled in every detail later, to seek them out, and if possible re-instate them in his mother's graces. He had a dim feeling that it was disgraceful to have a family breach, and perhaps he saw himself, this born child of the theatre, as the central figure in a grandiose reconciliation scene.

At any rate, Harry, after his establishment as a hope of the English stage, did take real trouble over Russel and Robin. It astonished Lionel to observe the trouble selfish young Harry took! Here he was plaguing his uncle for seven-year-old news of his brothers, spending time and money on locating the strayaways. Lionel liked Harry better than he had liked him for years, and for once did not pass on the news of his nephew's activities to Lettice.

To locate Russel was an easy matter. Harry got into touch with him almost at once. Russel was still in America, and doing remarkably well. His letter in reply was most affectionate, but not in the least plaintive. Russel had found himself. Russel was a star. Some day or other he meant to come to England and bring his company. No, he was not married—"You're mixing me up with Robin!" He wrote as he used to do when he was a schoolboy and Harry a baby, in an easy hand, using short words. Simple Russel did not in the least realise, it seemed, that his brother had grown up.

Harry wrote again to enlighten him. Russel wrote back charmed at belated interest arriving out of England, and this time he was full of enquiries as to young Harry's doings. Was Harry getting on? What sort of a future was there for a young actor in England? If Harry wanted work at any time or fresh experience he had only to come over : he was always to remember that he had a brother in New York, fond of him, with some little influence. What was Harry's line? Shakespeare? Modern stuff? Comedy? For himself he stuck to Shakespeare like all the Broomes. And what news of Robin? Robin and he had been separated these three years : not by any wish of Russel's. But Robin had wanted to strike out for himself. "And the truth of it is, Harry, Robin is not cut out for the stage. He has not the health nor the drive. And that business of his wife has cut him up pretty badly. Poor old Robin!" Russel had done his best to prevent Robin from leaving him, but Robin always did as he chose. Was he reconciled with Mama? Did they see much of him? Russel's letters to Robin had not been answered for ages. Was that Mama's doing? You couldn't be hurt with Robin because Robin was different from other people, and yet he was a little hurt, was Russel, that Robin never wrote. "Tell Robin to write to me, Harry! Send me news of you all, there's a good fellow! I wouldn't be sorry to have news of Mama. If it wouldn't madden her, tell her I'm doing well. I'd like her to know I'm doing well. If she's in a good temper tell her I'd like a letter. But most of all I want news of Robin."

Thus lightly did Russel skim over old agonies. But it was long before Harry could send out to his successful brother in America any news of Robin, though he did in the end trace Robin back across America and as near home as Ireland. But in Dublin the company had been reformed and Robin, it appeared, had not been kept on. Then all information ceased: and though Harry, who was a great collector of gossip, was liberal with time and money in all likely quarters, for months he heard nothing new of Robin.

But in the end chance stepped in to help the hunt with a direction. A cousin of the Kembles visiting Mrs. Siddons' grave in Paddington churchyard thought he saw Harry, thought he was cut, was hurt at the cut and wrote to expostulate. But Harry had not been near Paddington. Yet the Broome countenance was not easy to mistake. Could it possibly be Robin?

There was a cluster of theatrical lodgings not far from the Green and old Morgan, Lettice's pensioner and Harry's slave, had gone post-haste thither to make discreet enquiries. He had come back with great news. It was undoubtedly Mr. Robin, though Morgan had not seen him. Mr. Robin's door was barred against strangers, but Morgan had talked to the landlady. She was paid but curious. She could swear that no food had gone into the house these three days save milk. Old Morgan, who insisted on valeting his young master as he had valeted his father and his father's father, was at Harry's bedside at seven o'clock with the news: he had known it over-night, but Mr. Harry, who slept so badly, must not break his sleep even for Mr. Robin. But at seven Harry heard, and, half awake, whipped out of bed and began to dress, though he scarcely took in the meaning of the babble. But he packed off Morgan to traverse the distance at his own slow pace, and by the time he had finished dressing and swallowed some coffee, excitement began to wake in him and he set out at last, an eager brother, affectionate and not a little stirred.

But he was not stirred purely by fraternal emotion: the irony of the situation gave him an æsthetic thrill. Here was the mother at the corner of Park Lane spending her five thousand a year: there was the son, half a mile away, starving in a slum. Between them lay no more than a quarrel and Tyburn, the ill-omened acre. Harry had always wondered to himself if any good luck could come of living so near Tyburn. He never came out of his mother's door, with its stone urns overflowing with geraniums, never closed the gate on its small garden, precisely gay with seasonable flowers, and crossed the wide space between it and the Edgware Road without a feeling of oppression.

And on that fine summer morning, agitated by the news of his brother's return, his imagination, at work already on the dramatic possibilities of that dubious return, deepened the oppression into panic. The open Tyburn space was never empty. He felt it thick with death, noisy with voices crying for help and choking on the cry. The gallows was gone, but the air was thick still with human agony. 'Horrible to hang' thought Harry to himself—'any way of death but the choking way. Hang or drown—either's horrible. But it's worse still to drown. God save me from ever drowning,' cried Harry. And indeed, the fear of that particular form of death had been such a nightmare of his childhood that crossing Tyburn as a grown man, thinking of the hanged and thinking of the drowned, he felt sick and had to catch at a railing to steady himself.

The green uncut grass of Hyde Park spread before him was billowing in the summer wind; but he saw it in his agitation as the green sea and his lively imagination turned a dropped branch into a floating spar and a flurry of daisies into a drowning face. He shivered. For he felt descending upon himself one of those strange isolations of the spirit which in his childhood he had feared as some children fear ghosts, though he had known nothing of that horror, for his clear mind rejected the supernatural as completely as oil-skin rejects water. It was not that his imagination was small or starved; but it was an imagination incapable of dealing with abstractions. Facts were his bricks: give him bricks and he could build you a Troy. But he must have real bricks to build with. Reality, he adored reality: his imagination was entirely occupied with the re-arrangement of reality. As unknowable, he put the unknown out of his mind.

Yet Harry's mind remained, for all the owner's careful ordering of its activities, an immensely sensitive mind, a mind of such devouring energy that it fed itself as fiercely as a raging fire on all fuel that came its way. Certain fuel it rejected; but the fuel of personal contact, of ideas, of relationships, of the mere spectacle of other people's reactions to life and to him was fuel upon which his mind fed and throve.

But sometimes his appetite glutted itself. He had not learned the art of transporting his appetites into a world of pure thought, and so, being no mere sensation-monger but a fastidious spirit, was very capable of satiety: and then there came upon him in dreadful retribution for his immunity from the terrors of the spirit, a terror of another sort. Even as a child the capacity to desire would cease suddenly, sometimes for hours, sometimes for weeks. In the midst of his enjoyment he would feel descending upon him all-enveloping isolation, till he stood like a ghost, able to observe, yet cut off from all contact with the chattering, hurrying, quarrelling world that he so passionately loved and despised.

To fall asleep in a rose-garden and to wake up in a frost-bound landscape with the unbreakable silence of snow about you would be a dreadful experience even to an adult; but it was nevertheless the experience of the small boy Harry Broome. As a child he had a toy, a globe of glass with a little figure standing inside it. When the globe was shaken up snow whirled over the little figure and settled again to stillness. He saw the little figure as himself: he knew what it felt like to be in prison, silenced, frozen. All the warm kind hands in the world shaking his prison could not break it: the shaking merely stirred up the implacable snow and set it falling again as silence falls.

The mood came and went of its own will, not of his, and became a more frequent experience as he grew into a man. He dreaded its oncoming: he was a sick man after its going; but while the mood lasted it was his chief terror that he was incapable of being terrified, his chief suffering that he was incapable of feeling. He would plunge into any sort of wild gaiety, or exercise all his wit and his charm and his ingenuity on gaining the affection of someone, anyone (the silliest chit, the heaviest lout was good enough for him then), till his very soul sweated with the exertion. Thus he lulled his fear; but no sooner was the entertainment over, no sooner did the need for his own exertion cease, than his curse fell on him again and through the walls of his glass prison he saw men and women, yes, those he loved and hated best, as shadows too thin to be hated or loved. And, as his gifts were the gifts of the business man, the organiser, the planner and the teacher rather than the creative artist, he found no escape in his art as his father had been able to do. For it is unquestioned that he inherited the bedevilments from William. But William's melancholy was warm and generous, a rich despair like flowing blood, and the blood fed his art. But Harry was too wise to be very warm-hearted: he believed in prudence, and so his hell was a cold one.

Shivering in the May sunshine he felt the cold air of his hell blow over him as he crossed the road where Oxford Street met Edgware Road. He had been eager to see his brother a moment earlier. It was like his special destiny to send down snow upon him and chill the human kindness in his veins. His face had a still, despairing look as he walked down the deserted Edgware Road, and he pitied himself as he might have pitied a hanged woman in her agony if he had crossed by the gallows fifty years ago; but all his pity did not help him. When he caught up with Morgan at the Green he had to imitate most carefully his own accustomed half jocular, half filial greeting to the old man. He did it successfully, but he mocked himself for doing it. They walked on together, Harry charmingly suiting himself to the old man's slow pace, while inside his mind he was thinking—'Why do I trouble myself? What's Hecuba to me?' The petals of the full may-trees drifted past in a warm wind, and he thought—'How nature plays up to me! The snow-scene, you observe!' Then he hoped—'Perhaps seeing Robin again will shake me out of this. Surely I shall feel something when I see him? When Russel or Robin came into the nursery I used to be blissfully happy. I used to live for the holidays. It's impossible that he should give me the old feeling, but oh! if he could! His face was the most beautiful I've ever seen in my life, man or woman.'

And Harry began calling up pictures of his brother, of his brother's face framed in a doorway or bending over a paint-box, or lit by the candle as he sat at the end of the bed in the night-nursery and told Harry stories. Harry could always get a pang of affectionate sensuous pleasure out of the mere recollection of that beautiful face, so like Lettice's, so like Lionel's, yet with the mark of its own soul already upon it. Harry had the humility of the irregular-featured in the presence of formal good looks, and Robin's looks were amusing as well as regular. He was the first man of the Broomes with blue eyes, and his nose and his chin were tilted, which gave him a defiant air as if he said— Pooh to you and the universe! Harry, whose own features had the Wybird heaviness, thought that it was a weakness in his brother to give his thoughts away so easily in look and poise, and yet he admired and envied him that weakness. He never realised that his own countenance, for all its heaviness, was as mobile as his brother's, and that his dark grey-green stare and his resolutely shut mouth betrayed him as completely as Robin's forget-me-not glances and lips that twitched so easily in laughter and pain.

Thus, visualising his brother as a man visualises the messenger who causes his prison door to be opened and stands upon the stony threshold holding the order of release, Harry zig-zagged through the village slum of Paddington, thinking his thoughts and keeping Morgan happy with the sort of talk the old man enjoyed. But all the time another part of his mind was saying—'This land will be valuable one day. Who owns those rabbit hutches, I wonder? Buy 'em and pull them down— that's the thing to do! Put one's capital into building good terraces and decent squares, and save a site for a theatre! If I could borrow capital— if Mother would advance me—yes, I must look into this.' And so he went off into complicated speculations which entailed the remapping of London and the settling of theatres at strategic points, and the organisa- tion of a series of companies who exchanged guests and planned seasons with strict reference to each other: till he arrived at the dismal lodging- house where, according to Morgan, Robin had hidden himself.

'Why?' Harry asked himself again: and then—'and why on earth has he not written to me?' and felt his own mental pulse on the question, hopefully. 'Was not that a generous pang? Am I not concerned for Robin? Am I not feeling and thinking and plotting like other folk for the good of those I love?'

The snow settled down again. 'I don't know,' said Harry wearily, 'why I am concerning myself about Robin? Why do I dress? Why do I eat? Why do I breathe? Instinct, no more!'

He glanced at Morgan in distaste. 'How could my father have endured Morgan all those years with that snuffle of his? Use your handkerchief, Morgan!' Then aloud—

"So this is the place, is it? But of course, of course you are to come up with me. You think my brother won't want to see you? Don't be so modest, Morgan!"

The old man snuffled with pleasure as he knocked.

There was no answer to the knock; but after a few moments they became aware of slight sounds within the passage. The door-knob turned to and fro weakly, but still the door was not opened. Then Morgan, observing that it was made cupboard-fashion, in two pieces, swung open the upper half with a push of his hand. They looked into the tunnel-like passage. Ill smells poured out on them, but they saw nothing. The door-knob continued to shift uncertainly.

Then it occurred to Harry to look over the lower half of the door. Within, pressed against it, he then distinguished an extremely small male child whose hands could reach the clumsy handle but could not turn it. But the child was so absorbed in the attempt that it was only when Harry put a hand over the door-top and himself released the catch that the little thing upturned a face to receive the strangers. But he received them with an air of recognition, and, though he seemed to be not more than four years old, he spoke with extreme ease and polish.

"I saw you from the window," said the infant. "My father said, 'That will be your uncle Harry! You can tell him to come up.'"

Harry stared down at the child and then glanced swiftly and coldly at Morgan.

"My brother's child? You said nothing of this." And then, still more suspiciously—"He knows you?"

For the child had turned from Harry and slipped his fingers into Morgan's hand with an air of confidence.

"Knows me? He's seen me once, sir. I thought he was the landlady's child. She never said."

Harry flared suddenly.

"'You thought?' God! are you blind? Look at his eyes!" And indeed the child had Lettice's eyes, set unmistakably in pink cheeks above a tip-tilted nose. And the mouth, though Harry did not see this so clearly, was the soft full mouth of his own childhood. "You need spectacles, Morgan!" decided Harry cruelly, for Morgan was very proud of his un-ageing virtue. He turned to his new nephew. "What's your name?" Harry asked, stooping to him.

"Stephen," said the little boy, and his face lit up with delightful mischief, as if in presenting the stranger with his name he was presenting him, against orders, with a secret of unimaginable value. But a flood of shyness overwhelmed him and he scampered down the long passage and darted up the stairs. As the men followed, stumbling against each other in the half light, he peered at them between the upper banisters with one childish finger thrust out and beckoning. But when they reached the place where he stood he was already up the next flight, peering and beckoning again, and so led them from floor to floor till they reached the attics. There the struggle with the door-handle renewed itself. The child was not clumsy, but the handle was set too high.

For a moment Harry watched him, unhelpful, stirred by a strange emotion, while he repeated to himself with incredulous delight that it was actually an emotion. Imperceptibly, causelessly as it had come, his fit was passing from him. The invisible walls of his cage were melting. Noise was noise again and colour was colour, and the frozen world that had stood still began to revolve once more around the central figure of Harry Broome. He drew a deep breath of exquisite release. Poor old

Morgan! Nice small boy! Dreadful rabbit-hutch of a house! And God! how he wanted to see Robin!

The baby, scarlet now with temper, was still fighting the door-handle. Harry stooped, put his large hand over the little one and the two hands together turned the handle easily. At once the child's comical rage ceased. He gave a chuckle of delight, pushed open the door, ran forward to the big, old-fashioned bed that dwarfed the attic, flung himself against the curtains and began clambering up them like a little cat. A long thin arm shot out from the tangle of bed-clothes and hauled the child up on to a level with the pillows. A head turned weakly.

"Is that you, Harry?" said Robin, delight in his voice.

But it was almost with horror that Harry answered him from the doorway.

"Is that you, Robin?"

"I daresay I look pathetic," said Robin. "I hope I'm upsetting you, Harry!"

"You are," said his brother in a choked voice, and he came to the bedside and stooping down kissed him, and then said quickly and awkwardly—"Here, the child's too much for you." And he would have moved away the grave infant sitting cross-legged at his father's shoulder, but Robin's thin arm tightened round the mite, so absurdly huddled in a grown man's coat.

"He's my son," said Robin with some pride. And then—"Harry, I think I'm dying."

"You? Rubbish!" said Harry coldly; for the words stabbed at his heart and he hated pain. "But you've staged it very well, Robin. How much of it's real?"

"Most of it," said Robin weakly, "is lack of food, and the rest is what my landlady calls an ague."

"Do you mean you're hungry?" said Harry awkwardly.

"Yes," said Robin flushing. "At least—I was. Too tired now."

Morgan snuffled. Harry turned on him ferociously.

"Stop that, Morgan! My brother's very ill. Can't you see it? Get out of this and get me a coach! We must fetch her ladyship. He's got to be got home."

"I've been out of work for six months," said Robin huskily, "and there was the child."

"Where's its mother?" said Harry, furious against all women.

"Gone off with a wage-earner," said Robin. "I could only write plays."

"If you'd written a letter or two instead—" said Harry furiously and nearly in tears. "Are you all right for twenty minutes? I'm going to fetch Mama."

"If you can arrange for Stephen," muttered Robin, "it would be a weight off my mind. And I wouldn't mind a doctor, though he can't do much. It's the lungs."

"More theatre!" sneered Harry, almost in tears. "You only want nursing, you know that. Mama will deal with you."

"She's alive then?" said Robin feebly, but his eyes began to dance. "She sent me a dying curse five years ago, bless her! I'd be glad of some help from you, Harry, but there's no good asking Mother. She's done with me. She made that clear enough." And then, restlessly— "We never did get on."

"You never understood her," said Harry impatiently. "You were a fool over Mama. However, that's neither here nor there. I'll go and get her down to you."

"You won't budge Mother," said Robin, shutting his eyes, and did not open them for the sound of hoofs in the street and the jingle of harness.

"Morgan's got a coach," said Harry, regarding the indifferent mask on the pillow. "I'll be back in twenty minutes. Hold on, Robin, it's all over now!" And he ran out of the room crying. For though he had never seen death he thought he knew death when he saw it.

The child scrambled down from the high bed and trotted across to the window, scrambled in to the seat and watched Harry enter the vehicle and drive away.

"Uncle Harry's crying," said the boy.

His father smiled beatifically. He felt very ill. His eyelids were too heavy to lift. But oh, how good it was to be the centre of attention again! His mother would not come, of course. But there was Harry. Oh, in an alien, hateful, mazy world, how good it was to hear a Broome voice again!

CHAPTER 12

'MY SON'S MY SON TILL . . .'

HARRY, in the brief drive from Paddington to his mother's house, worked himself into a rage against his mother for stubbornly refusing to come, prepared his arguments and ascended the platform of scorn.

'How can you, Mama, be so heartless? Your own son dying! If you could have seen him, like a smiling ghost. His face is a mere skull, and yet it is still Robin, still beautiful. I could hardly bear to look at him, the change hurt me so, and yet it is still Robin. He looked ten years old, as if he'd been cruelly beaten, as if he were a child in a grave. Mama, you've got to come!'

Thus he rehearsed his arguments, because it eased his extreme trouble at the sight of his brother. He knew well enough that it was unlikely that he would ever use them. Nor did he use them.

He left the servants to deal with the ramshackle coach, ordered their own, and ran up the stairs to his mother's sitting-room. There sat Lettice, the centre of a lavender circle nigh three yards deep, for crinolines were in and they suited her. Lavender suited her too, and her fine lace cap set off the unconquerable carriage of head and neck, and hid the fact that her hair was thinning. There was a net-work of lines round her eyes and the eyes themselves were a little less blue; but she used them as whimsically as ever as she looked up from her breakfast.

"Well, my own? Late as usual! How did you sleep?" Then— "Harry, what's the matter?" and she half rose.

"I've found Robin," said Harry with an ugly look at her, sticking out his chin. His tone was a threat. It said, 'Don't you dare play tricks with me now, Mama! I can't bear it.' But he might have known that the tone would have no effect on her.

She resumed her seat and sliced her toast with precision.

"That's no reason for bursting in on me. I take no interest in Robin."

"He can't get work," said Harry.

"I'm not surprised," said Lettice, helping herself to butter.

"He's in an attic at Paddington, half starved," said Harry.

"I warned him," said Lettice, adding marmalade. But she did not eat.

"There's a child," said Harry.

"And a woman, no doubt," said Lettice.

"He says she's deserted him," said Harry.

"Then he knows what it feels like to be deserted," said Lettice.

Harry's lip quivered suddenly.

"He's very ill indeed, Mother. He wants you to come."

"What!" said Lettice, rising to her feet. "Ill? And why couldn't you say so at once?"

"I think he's dying," muttered Harry.

"Don't dare to say it!" cried Lettice, white to her lips. "Don't dare! Can he be moved? You had better go for a doctor. No, send Mitcham! What's the address? Where's Mitcham?" And then, as that meek woman hurried into the room—"You take a hackney-coach, Mitcham, and you go straight to the doctor. You don't come on without him. Yes, in his carriage if you like, what does it matter? What? What shall you do with the coach? Pay it, woman! pay it! I don't care how you come as long as you bring the doctor. Bring him to—the direction, Harry! Write it down here on my note!" She had been scribbling at her own desk as she talked.

Harry wrote hastily. His mother snatched it from him unblotted, and thrust it on the bewildered maid.

"You give him this note and you bring him on with you—to this address, you understand me? Have you got that clear in your stupid mind? Don't argue with me, Mitcham!" said Lettice. "Go! Wait! First send me Hetty!" Then, as a couple of maids came flying she continued—"Some wraps and cushions! And tell Derek to get up a bottle of champagne! I'll see him and the housekeeper later, tell them! Have you ordered the carriage, Harry? Ah, you have had that much sense. Bonnet? I want no bonnet."

She took a light shawl from the sofa and twisted it round her hair while the household hummed about her, like a hive disturbed.

"Hurry with those blankets! What—the linen cupboard's locked? Then take them from my bed, girl! Will you be all night?" Then, to the solemn butler—"Oh, Derek—yes—is that the champagne? Put it in the carriage with the hamper. Oh, and Derek—tell cook to have invalid food ready—arrowroot, beef-tea, fruit of all sorts. I'll see her later too. Oh, is that you, Mrs. Drew? The maids are to put clean sheets on my own bed. Yes, and fill a warming-pan. You can make up a bed for me in my dressing-room. Mr. Robin is ill. Mr. Robin is coming home. Where's Lord Lionel? Out, is he? Send a footman down to his club. Tell him where we've gone. Tell him Mr. Robin is home.

Now Harry, why do you keep me waiting?" And she sped down the stairs like a rushing mighty wind.

Harry followed her, a small boy in disgrace; but once in the closed carriage, once rolling swiftly down the Edgware Road, she turned to him, quiet again, and put her hand in his.

"You're my comfort, Harry! You found him for me. He isn't going to die, Harry, is he? We shall make him well between us?"

Harry, looking at her, thought—'There is that in her still which could raise a man from the dead.' And then, so curiously was he made, he could not refrain from patting himself on the back for his own shrewdness. 'I knew. I understand Mother. What fools Robin and Russel are! Of course she would come.' He looked at her, smiling affectionately. She caught his hand again.

"Not starving, Harry?" she said, horror in her voice.

"I'm afraid so," said Harry.

"But he's my son," said Lettice: and spoke no more till they reached their destination.

The arrival of the fine carriage caused a commotion. The comings and goings of Harry had already prepared the door-step housewives for events, and Lettice's lavender billows sent the windows flying up, till the whole street chattered like starlings in a tree-top near sunset. Harry's professional eye ran over the crowd expertly; but his mother saw nothing, heard nothing. With her hands pressed to her sides to hold down her crinoline, she hurried into the narrow passage and undulated, as only a Victorian woman could, up the twisting stairs ahead of her son. But on the top landing outside Robin's door she paused, a hand on her heart, and caught at his arm unsteadily.

"You're out of breath, Mama! You shouldn't hurry yourself so. Look at you!" said Harry, always concerned for her. But she ignored utterly his tedious concern.

"Why didn't he write to me?" said Lettice, a wail in her voice.

'What a schoolgirl she is still,' thought Harry, pressing her hand reassuringly.

As if she heard his thought she wrenched her hand out of his, stood a minute visibly growing older, visibly assuming the competent woman, the worldling, the wife, and, last of all, the mother. Then, composed, looking her years, Robin's mother went in to her son, stooped to him, kissed him reassuringly, twitched his bed-clothes straight, sank into a chair beside him and turned upon Harry.

"Go down to the street! There's a basket of jellies and wine. Can't you see that your brother's faint for want of nourishment? Don't stand there staring, Harry!"

She turned to her elder son again.

"My lamb, this is nothing. You aren't at all ill, you know. You only want home-nursing. In a trice we'll have you home. Darling child— what have you done to yourself? But you aren't so ill as you think, Robin! Wait till Mama gets you home. Ah, is that you, Harry? That's right! Put the basket there! Gently, don't shake the bed, Harry! And now go down and watch for the doctor. Not that you need a doctor, Robin, but for precaution's sake we are sending for Dr. Burton. Now, Robin! Now then, my child!"

Her cool hands were busy with plates and jars and bottles as she murmured: and presently, slipping her arm about his shoulders, masking her horror at the sharpness of his bones, she had him lying against her breast, and so fed him—a peeled grape, a spoonful of jelly, a sip of wine. Robin swallowed and tasted as she told him. Then, suddenly, he relaxed, turned round luxuriously in her arms while the plate and the jellies went crashing, and his head fell against her neck and his long tired hand clutched her shoulder.

"Mother, you smell so sweet," said Robin, and with a sigh of utter contentment lay quiet and half-asleep, while she held him tightly, reliving the pangs that he had cost her more than a quarter of a century ago and thinking that these new pangs were sharper.

Then her eye fell upon the small figure huddled in the window-seat, watching her. She had forgotten the grandchild. She had forgotten Robin's son. "He's Robin over again," said Lettice to herself. She opened her lips to call the baby to her, and shut them again with no words said, for fear she should disturb the exhausted creature lying on her breast, half stifling her with his clutch. But she talked to his son with her eyes, and presently the little thing rose and slowly, shyly, yet with an air of confidence, crossed the room to her and leaning against her knee began fingering the shining changeful flounces of her dress. She sat as still as if a bird had alighted on her knee. What next?

The silk rustled under the small fingers and instantly the child lifted delighted eyes to her face and imitated with an enchanting smile the lisping crackle of the material. She smiled back and at once they were intimates.

But the sound, tiny as it was, roused Robin from his momentary drowse, and at his first movement even the child was forgotten.

But he stood watching as she laid his father back upon the bed and fed him again.

"Had you no money, Robin? None at all?" said Lettice softly.

"Well, Mama, a little," he temporised, seeing the look in her eyes. "But one can't eat when one's ill, and I've been pretty ill. But the child's been fed," said Robin flushing. "And I'd have sent him to you if it had gone on much longer. But every day I thought to be better."

"How long have you been like this?" said Lettice.

"I don't know," said Robin feebly, as Harry and the family doctor appeared together.

The doctor was non-committal. He spoke of neglected chills, underfeeding, weakness; but he was grave enough to agitate Lettice anew. She drew him into the passage and besieged him with hurried questions—What was it? Lungs? Heart? Tell her the worst! And then swept her own questions aside to cry—"But, Doctor, first let me get him home! Why do you keep me here chattering when we ought to be getting him home? It won't hurt him, will it, to get him home? He can't breathe in this hole. How can I nurse him here?"

And the doctor agreed with her that while it might be a risk to move him it would be scarcely worse than the risk of letting him remain.

So Robin was bundled in the wraps that Lettice had had the inspiration to bring, and the tall footman who stood behind the carriage was summoned to carry him downstairs, and found it patently too easy a task. Lettice put out her hand to the little boy who took it trustfully, and the two fled down the stairs ahead of the sick man, while Harry and the medico followed. And Robin, half fainting, yet with a blissful smile of content on his face, was laid in the carriage with Harry propping his knees and his mother once more pillowing his head on her shoulder. Then, at a snail's pace for fear of jolting him, the carriage rolled him out of the back streets into the sunshine and the mild air.

When they reached Park Lane there were Derek and Mitcham and a scatter of anxious maids in the hall, and Morgan and the doctor, who had preceded them in a swifter vehicle, in equally anxious attendance on the doorstep. And presently Robin was in his mother's bed as he had always been after a little boy's illness, and the fire danced on the ceiling as it used to do, and there were cool drinks on the bed-table and warmth at his feet, and the portrait of his father staring at him from the opposite wall. Stephen had been spirited away. He fetched a deep sigh as the burden of Stephen fell from his shoulders. Stephen would be safe enough with his mother. What a fool he had been to escape so perkily from his mother! This was better. Was there anything better than lying still and doing as you were told?

He opened his eyes at a shadow of sound in the room and beamed weakly.

"Is that you, Uncle Lionel?"

It was Lionel, and Harry beside him.

"That's right," said Robin. Then, as one counting his possessions— "Lionel—Harry—Where's Mama?"

"Seeing to Stephen," said Harry.

"Will she be back soon?" said Robin querulously.

His uncle chuckled.

"Don't you know your mother?" said Lionel. "I wonder she allows either of us in here."

"You mustn't—" said Robin with the slurred dignity of extreme fatigue, which is not unlike the dignity of drunkenness—"say a word against my mother. I won't allow it. You don't understand her. Nobody understands her but me."

Harry's eyes, for all his anxiety, began to dance with pleasant malice.

"You can take that look off your face," said Robin with drowsy indignation. "I don't like it. Mama's an angel, I tell you. She's been an angel to me."

"She can afford to be," said Harry, with deep appreciation of a marvellous woman. "She's won."

Robin did not hear the murmur, but Lionel glanced at his nephew critically.

"Has she?" said he. "Don't be too sure."

Robin opened his eyes again, glazed with sleep.

"Where's Russel?" he demanded, and closed them again.

"Has she won, eh?" said Lionel to his nephew.

There was a lizard-quick look from Harry in return.

"Eh?" insisted Lionel.

Then the two Broomes eyed each other, each reading the other's thoughts, each foreseeing, dreading and delighting in the possibilities of drama yet to come.

CHAPTER 13

DEAR MAUD

ROBIN never recovered, though he lingered. Over-work, travelling in difficult conditions, lack of proper food, and, for that matter, luxury, had ruined a constitution naturally delicate. The lungs were in a deplorable state. The doctor, moreover, spoke of the effects of shock and prolonged emotion on a nervous temperament, and everybody knew what he meant. Everybody, of course, was dying to know the exact details of Robin's marriage, and his later separation from his wife; but nobody had the nerve to enquire upon a subject which a Broome did not choose to discuss.

For weeks Lettice could hardly speak to her son without the question trembling on her lips—"What was she like? Did she leave you, or did you leave her?" But she never asked it: and Harry bided his time. Harry thought: 'Robin will never tell Mother the details, of course. She's too merciless. But he'll tell me one day.' Meanwhile neither he nor Lettice showed any consciousness of the fact that Stephen, to have existed at all, must have had a mother.

Nevertheless, Stephen, for all the dubiety of his history, was pretty soon the darling of the house. When Lettice bore away her elder boy to the south of France, Stephen as well as Lionel went with her; for there was in the sentimental fifties no notion of guarding from contagion the family of a man or woman in a decline.

Harry did not travel with them. He was prospering in his work, and it was beginning to be wondered whether, though he was a safe actor, his true talent did not lie in stage-craft, as much as in performance. In the fifties a 'producer' in the modern sense had yet to be born. The actor-manager coached his flock when he thought this or that member of it needed coaching, and the more competent were left to their own devices, unless, indeed, they interfered with his own conception of his own part. But the stage-manager was a person of importance, and Harry was now stage-manager in one of the family theatres, learning, as heir-apparent, to govern what would, one day, be his own kingdom.

He enjoyed the work the more for the contrast between theatre life and life in his own home; for the Broomes kept in touch with the

Wybird cousins, and Harry Broome had none of that sense of being on sufferance of which Mrs. Siddons once so bitterly complained. His social world was the world of the Wybirds : his place of business was the theatre : and so he led an innocent double life. No, Harry would not go to the south of France with Lettice. He had far too much to do at home, for at last, at last, the Gloriana was being rigged out properly with gas lights. Save the Haymarket, it was the only theatre which still held out against the new invention : and Lettice, though she took interest in the stage again now that Harry was on it and doing so well, thought it a pity to lose the cachet of 'as it was in the beginning.' But the antiquated oil lamps vexed Harry's soul and he could easily persuade his mother. The lessee was not so easily persuaded, and the man's miserliness had at last driven Harry to the examination of the terms of the lease and thence to the perusal of his father's will.

Its contents set his mind working furiously. So the theatre was his own at his mother's death! He couldn't bear to see the valuable property leased away and thus entirely unexploited. He resolved to tackle his mother when she came home. Meanwhile he was able, with her lawyer's help, to force through the point about the gas installation. The lease was badly drawn ; but not, he was gratified to know, drawn against the Broome interests.

The tussle did more than improve the property. It taught him how keen was his interest in the facts and the figures that control an enterprise. It roused in him new ambitions. To cut a figure in the world as an artist—yes, this was good. But to control such artist figures—was this not better ? Harry meant to do both. It was about the same time that he bought, out of a legacy left him by his grandfather the duke, a tumbled-down property in Paddington where he had found his brother. It was the beginning of his habit of taking up odd parcels of land all over London.

In theory, he was happy enough to stay at home, ready enough to let Robin be the centre of attention abroad. But in practice Harry felt rather chilled, rather lost. It was strange that his mother should be able to take him at his word and roll off to the Riviera with her son and her grandson, and her brother, and her staff. Harry was not accustomed to have his family get on without him, and he was utterly unaccustomed to live without the affection of a woman. He missed Lettice absurdly and, being an extremely practical young man, he began saying to himself that his mother would not live for ever and that one day he supposed he should be alone unless he married. He had never thought of marriage, perhaps because he found it so easy to manage women. 'Reckon—beckon!' Lettice had taught him the rhyme in his babyhood. Neither maids nor matrons at the theatre gave him the faintest trouble. But he was bored by the theatre women and Lettice had not been particularly eager to surround him with young ladies eligible as well as attractive. Now that she had left him to himself, however, he began to say to himself that he needed a wife.

So soon as he began to consider the matter he found, to his surprise, that he knew exactly what he wanted. His wife must be extremely beautiful and preferably fair. Not red-headed on any account. He detested red-haired women. Brown eyes—blue-eyed women were too shrewd. 'I adore Mama, but fancy being married to her! Whew!' No, she must have peaceful, peaceable brown eyes. She must waltz well, for he liked dancing. She must move gracefully and wear clothes as well as his mother wore them. He must be able to rely upon her to play the hostess for him perfectly. He must be able to be proud of her at the head of his dinner-table, in his carriage, on his arm. She must have a sweet and soft voice. She must understand him. He did not want a stupid woman, but he did not think it would be suitable for her to have any active talents of her own. For Harry was fair-minded and saw that a wife would have no time over if she did her duties properly, and he would not like to see her unhappy because she had to forego her natural bent. She must be ready to have children if ever he wanted children, but she must not degenerate into a mere nurse. She mustn't be too religious. She must make him able to fall deeply in love with her and keep him deeply in love with her. She must be extremely beautiful. Ah, there he was back again at the beginning of the catalogue!

Surely there must be some woman in the world—in England—in London? She was probably in London at this moment: it was merely a question of hunting her down. Harry, in the absence of the unsuspicious Lettice, ordered new clothes from his tailor and began paying long-neglected calls.

He found her, of course; for Harry always got what he wanted: and except for the fact that she had auburn hair, blue eyes instead of brown, and had been brought up in a convent, she was exactly what he wanted. Even Lettice, who naturally did not like the girl at first, had to admit that socially and pictorially Maud Blythe was impeccable.

She was the granddaughter of an Irish baronet, an orphan with a little money of her own. She had been brought up in a convent and was now being given a season by Rosina. Lettice could not imagine why Rosina had let herself be bothered with the girl. But then Lettice, for all her sharpness, did not know everything about the elderly Rosina.

Lettice was still in the nursery when Rosina's youth had bloomed a shy bud or two. Rosina had been firmly married to her elderly earl at the end of her first season, by her redoubtable mother: nevertheless, in the brief spring allowed her, Rosina had contrived to fall stiffly and despairingly in love. It did not affect the duchess's plans for her. Rosina was never even aware that Hilaret's mocking regard was sharpened by any knowledge of her green-salad secret. "She'll get over it," said the duchess comfortably: and was right. Rosina was soon resigned, did her duty by her husband and the estate, bore a sufficiency of children, and became in time as high-church as her husband, though they never went over to Rome.

Nevertheless there remained in her heart a tender spot, literally a tender spot: she could not bear to have it touched or pressed. She would flush at the sound of an Irish accent: she read, the strait-laced elderly lady, such novelists as Samuel Lover and Charles Lever. When, thirty years later, 'he' wrote to her, touching on their early meetings, recounting his own ill-fortunes—an impoverished estate, a daughter's death, a young granddaughter on his hands who, he understood, must have her season in town if ever she was to be married—and besought Rosina's help in placing his little miss, then Rosina the dowager broke through the austere habits of a lifetime. She was a widow, moneyed, free to do as she pleased: she, too, was a Broome. So off she went, the staid Rosina, to Ireland. Moreover she thoroughly enjoyed her visit, for she was really welcome and her advice was listened to with considerable respect, whether she spoke of piggeries, of tenants' cottages, of grandchildren or the marriage of granddaughters. And when she returned she brought with her convent-bred Maud Blythe, having given her promise that the girl should be turned into a fashionable young lady, and should not be returned upon her grandfather's hands until she was a fashionable young matron.

But, oh dear me! how was Rosina to set about being fashionable? And how was a lovely young lady from the country to be made happy by a dull old one in town? After her astonishing sojourn in the ramshackle lavish establishment over which 'he' reigned goutily but with a swagger, she found her London house singularly calm, almost stuffy. 'His' place had been overrun by dogs that ruined the fine needlework of the chairs, muddied the good torn carpets, and diffused about the all-but-state apartments the odours of the kennel. Rosina had been very firm during the whole length of her visit on the mistake of letting sporting dogs into the house, and reforms had been promised. But coming home to Portland Place she found her pug unpleasantly obese and his yap displeased her. The rooms smelled respectably of camphor, for naturally the furniture had been shrouded in linen dust-sheets during her absence, and she found that she disliked the small of camphor even more than she disliked the smell of dogs. Her house was full of magnificent furniture, beautifully kept, but it seemed to her that she had allowed knick-knacks to accumulate till the rooms looked as if no man had used them for twenty years, which, of course, was true. But one missed the feel of a man in the house, and there was no view from her window! Now in 'his' house you could see twenty miles from the window of the state bedroom.

She began nervously to distress herself over the letters that Maud would write complaining of her and her house, and her failure to keep her promises. For she had promised to dress Maud and give her pleasures, and marry her well, and how was it to be done? She thought of her sister. Lettice would know how to deal with young people, would tell her where to take Maud for clothes and gew-gaws. But Lettice was in the south of France with Robin. Besides, Lettice would ask questions. Rosina at fifty-five was still painfully shy, and she thought that if her sister mocked her, though only with her eyes, she might take up the pretty little gold scissors from her tortoiseshell *étui* and drive them into her sister's breast.

Yet to whom should she go? She was singularly bare of female friends. Her husband's connections were all discreet, religious folk, full of good works, and there were no young people. Her adored eldest brother was dead and she did not get on with the new duke and duchess. And her own daughter was in India. It was easy enough to take her protégée to court, of course, and fairly easy to get her asked to the right parties; for though she might not like the new duchess, nevertheless she had but to lift a finger in that quarter. But clothes! Clothes were the problem. If only Lettice were at home! Rosina talked it all out with Mary Moone who, of course, was worse than useless, and visited some shops herself and was appalled by the prices and the styles; but found no solution to her problem till in casual despair she turned to the person most concerned.

"I really don't know what we are to do about your dresses, my dear!" said Rosina to her young guest, and discovered to her charmed amazement that her young guest knew exactly what to do.

Maud Blythe had been educated at a convent, certainly; but the convent was in Paris, and all her holidays had been spent with impeccable friends. Maud, with her Irish colouring, her soft voice, her adaptability, had been popular in her convent, not only among her mates but also with their mothers; for there had been an inter-marriage or two in the days of the Young Pretender between her family and French sympathisers, and she knew her way about one or two Bourbon strongholds. So when her special cronies had gone away to be married they had not forgotten her, and she had stayed with one and another every holiday, and had learned from them how to dress, how to choose her setting, how to pick her steps in a society stiff with etiquette.

Her training showed in the tact with which she relieved Rosina's distresses. If Maud was dressed delightfully and not too expensively, Rosina never realised that anyone was responsible save herself. If Rosina abandoned her mourning for handsome dresses that made her look ten years younger, Rosina never guessed that the initiative did not come from her. If Maud Blythe's first season was a modest triumph for all concerned, Rosina, writing fully and freely to Ireland, never dreamed that she was not justified in taking all the credit. Indeed, she enjoyed telling Maud that she must learn to think for herself, "As my sister Lettice says, 'You need to know a great deal about everything before you can look as if you knew nothing about anything with success.' Which of course I want you to do, dear. I wish my sister were at home to help you. She is a much cleverer woman than I am."

But Rosina was lying, for she was afraid of Lettice's sharp tongue and her power of shredding up into fragments Rosina's pleasures. Rosina was thankful that Lettice was on the Riviera. She would never have been allowed to go to Ireland and adopt Maud Blythe if Lettice had been at home.

Yet as the season passed and Maud's success became unmistakable, Rosina could not help wishing that Lettice were witnessing the triumph. Rosina's own daughter had been well enough married, but there had been no triumph, and Rosina knew that Lettice had thought her a bungler. But Maud Blythe shed lustre on her chaperon. Miraculously, she contrived to be popular with her own sex and, in spite of a proposal a week, to keep the goodwill of the dowagers: and she brought her proposals dutifully to Rosina and listened meekly to Rosina when Rosina urged her to accept them, and yet contrived to make Rosina feel relieved when she refused them all.

Then, just after Maud had been presented, Rosina capped her own conception of herself by giving a ball for her darling. And as she dealt with all the people who ought to come, intended to come, and pulled wires to come, Rosina realised that she was giving the ball of the season —she, the dull dowager! Oh, delightful days! When one has never been a success as a young woman, it is doubly sweet to shine in one's dull old age! And how pleased 'he' would be.

"Have you written to your grandfather this week, my dear? Don't let him think I am plunging you into dissipation. Perhaps it would amuse him to see a list of our guests? Why don't you write this morning? The drive with me? Oh, my dear, I can wait for you. I am in no hurry. What does half an hour matter? Give your grandfather my kindest regards."

To Rosina's ball there came, of course, Harry Broome, because he was not a young man to miss the ball of the season, and because, though he had adroitly contrived to evade tea-table invitations from his Aunt Rosina, to have refused to come to her party would have been an open slight, and he had an affection for her, dry old stick as she was. And he knew perfectly well that she was already a little hurt with him for so successfully evading Maud Blythe.

For, of course, he had heard all about Maud Blythe. At least a dozen acquaintances of his were in love with her, and Lettice in her letters was full of enquiries. Even Lionel had written demanding lightly an unbiassed description of Rosina's incredible cygnet. Social success always interested Lionel, and, aware that it interested his nephew almost as much, he was a little hurt that no gossip had reached him.

But Harry, alone in London, had fallen into one of his moods again, and though he paid his calls religiously and danced a great deal and had even once or twice been at the same balls, he had not lifted a finger to effect a meeting with Maud Blythe. His mind in its frozen mood yawned at the rhapsodies of his friends, and yet was bitter against them for falling in love where he could not. For it was a grievance of Harry's that he had never been in love: was eternally having to retreat very hastily from the results of his own too hasty beckonings. He found his interest in the paragon whetted by all he heard, and he despised his own interest and marvelled at it, and continued to dance with a string of partners, and dislike them all. For he observed with disgusted detachment that a beauty in pink did not know that the colour turned her yellow: that a fine figure of a girl in blue had hot hands and flushed unbecomingly: that the pretty little butterfly with such pots of money wore her hair over velvet pads so that, when she bounded in the schottische, her hair lifted and the pads showed unpleasingly: that the girls who could dance well did not know how to talk: that the girls who talked well leant against his arm during the dance as if it were a rail of a chair: that the mothers of penniless beauties made it clear enough that they would overlook the Broome in him for the sake of the Wybird: that the mothers of heiresses made it clear enough that the Wybird was all but obliterated by the Broome, while handsome married women asked him why he was not acting any more, and then made clear enough their consciousness of the fact that ceasing to act had set his evenings free. So, although the impression he made on the society in which he moved was utterly different from that which he imagined, and although he had half-a-dozen pretty girls in love with him and the Wybird influence solidly in his favour, still he felt the season and himself a failure, did Harry. But he did not even care, because he was in his glass prison once more, and heard, saw, and felt nothing at all but the beat of his own heart and the sound of his own fists beating against the glass barrier, and the sight of his own face reflecting his solitary boredom from his prison walls.

He was still in his cold limbo as he dressed for Rosina's ball. He arrived late, and the hall was crowded with guests ascending and descending the curiously balustered double stair-case which led from the handsome mausoleum of a hall to the ball-rooms above.

Harry knew so many people that it took him a long time to reach the top, where even his quiet was a little staggered by the splendour of his aunt. Who on earth had dressed his aunt, and re-arranged her hair, and divined that green suited her, and was the only colour which suited also her old-fashioned emeralds? He was amused by this rejuvenation, and Rosina was pleased with him for making no bones about telling her that he had observed the alterations. She liked the way he did it.

"If Mama were here," remarked Harry, gazing at his aunt, "she would pick a quarrel with you, Aunt Rosina. Oh, she would be out-raged. I shall write to her to-night."

His aunt blinked at him benevolently.

"Maud chose it," she said, smoothing her dress. "Step back a little, Harry! There are the Brutons coming. But don't go yet!"

She did her duties, and turned again to her nephew.

"You've not met Maud. You've never come near me this season, you wicked boy. I'll introduce you later, but I doubt if she'll have a

dance for you! She's a very much sought after young woman, Harry.
Did you see that paragraph in the *Post?* Unsuitable, of course, for a
young lady to be mentioned in any news-sheet; but it was written from
the point of view of an artist. They say that her head is Greek, pure
Greek. Maclise is painting her. Maud! Ah, you see, she did not hear
me, and I expect, Harry, her programme is full."

Now this speech of Rosina's was very good for Harry. He was not
accustomed to young women whose programmes were full. His eyes
snapped with annoyance. But Rosina did not leave well alone. She
continued naïvely and quite untruly—

"Besides, I daresay she won't dance with you, in any case. She's
vexed with you, I think."

"With me?" Harry, relaxing, permitted his eyebrows to lift
benevolently. "We've never met."

"No, you've never called," said Rosina sharply and triumphantly,
considering that she had administered a reproof, but not considering
that to tell a young man who is popular and thinks well of himself that
he has been expected and missed is hardly a reproof.

Harry shrugged. So Maud Blythe was like all the rest of them! He
had thought as much. Certainly she danced well. He caught sight of
her in the distance. She was very light on her feet, and though she was
listening to her partner she did not look up at him with any rapt air.
The dance drew to an end, and Rosina put her hand on his arm.

"I'll introduce you now," she said.

Harry followed her, prepared for any entertainment that would make
him for a moment forget the weariness of his state.

Maud Blythe, returning to her chaperon, was enough to make him
forget it. He watched her gracious descent of the shallow flight of
stairs that led from the ball-room to the ante-chamber with wondering
appreciation. He had never before been near enough to distinguish
her features but—when had he dreamt her or foreseen her?

She was poised: she was graceful: her figure was perfect, yet on the
slight side, and she was not too tall. She wore white gauze thickly
worked with sprigs of daisies, and this film of whiteness was spread out
over a flounced under-dress of pale green. Her white shoulders were
scarfed in white lace and her little green bodice fitted her as smoothly as
her white gloves fitted her arms. He particularly noticed her gloves.
He had a mania for freshness in a woman, and those gloves of
hers, though the evening was more than half over, did not show
a trace of use. Her hair lay loosely on her forehead, but was

not disarranged by dancing. She looked as cool as a snowdrop.

His swift look as he bowed over her hand took in the background of other young women, and he thought that in every way she was their superior, and yet that she entirely conformed to the pattern. Her one departure from the exactitude of the mode was in her arrangement of her hair. There was no pomatum in it, and instead of the conventional wreath she wore a circlet of silver and jade leaves. Harry was looking at her, into her face, into her eyes, and found that these were dark blue, set rather deeply under strong brows between lids so straight that her eyes had the look of an Egyptian wall painting. For a moment he suspected her of producing the effect artificially; but he knew too much of the art of make-up to suspect it for more than an instant.

He thought her the most lovely woman he had ever seen. He was still haunted by the likeness to something known in dreams as he asked her for a dance. But he forgot about dreams when he found himself refused. He was sure she had no intention of snubbing him; for she showed him her programme; yet he felt unreasonably angry. They talked a little: then a partner claimed her.

He stood staring after her, slowly realising where he had seen her before, had been seeing her for months. He had built her up in his own heart, long ago. Auburn hair or no auburn hair, blue eyes or brown—she was the woman he wanted to marry.

CHAPTER 14

DEAREST MAUD

HARRY always got what he wanted and Maud did not give him too much trouble in getting her. He had at once acted with his usual decision. Rosina had been hustled into introducing at least four extra dances into the evening's programme: he had danced one with Maud, sat out with her for the three others, and disarmed for ever her prejudice against him.

For she had had a prejudice and owned it. What was her prejudice? He hardly dared put it into words. Could it be possible that she was piqued that he had not made himself one of her pursuers? Was it possible, feeling so mean a pique behind her heavenly-pure mask, that she should have the timidity or the stupidity to own to it?

He was prepared to be instantly disappointed in her, and was defeated, as throughout his life he was to be defeated, by the complete simplicity of her avowal. She had heard so much of him from his aunt Rosina, and—she flushed faintly—from other people. But he had never come near them—"and Aunt Rosina—she lets me call her 'Aunt'— Aunt Rosina felt it, I think: though she would not own that you were unkind. But I thought you were unkind," said Maud firmly, sweetly.

Unkind! It was a new word to him. Unkind, eh? Kindness and unkindness were virtues and vices that did not exist for the Broomes. Love and hate—yes! But to refrain from wounding if you were in the mood to wound: to soothe a fool's foible out of affection for the fool, this was not a Broome habit, this was not in the Broome tradition. But 'kind' was Maud's word. Where Harry would say—"He has wit or looks or charm," Maud said—"He looks kind."

The trait in her pleased him, amused him a little, fitted in with his conception of her. He spent his evening in falling in love with her and in compelling her to fall in love with him. He did it very easily: he talked to her about himself, and Harry on himself could be inspired. Next morning he broke the habits of a life-time to get up early and ride with her in the Row, and, much as he liked her in her ball finery, he liked her still better in her tight-waisted riding habit with the full skirts, Byron cuffs and collar, dove-coloured gloves, and the veiled man's beaver tied under her white chin with long black velvet strings. He specially approved of her neat boots, and the fact that, though they galloped, her knot of hair did not come untidied.

Thereafter he saw her daily and sometimes thrice a day, for when he wanted a thing he wanted it. But, though she was charming to him, it was a fortnight before he got her to love him.

But one night at the opera, withdrawn at the back of the box, they attained intimacy, and, singularly, it was the gentle, pliable Maud who swiftly took the opportunity afforded them by Rosina's mental absence. For Rosina had in charge her niece by marriage, the new Duchess of Bedenham, and the duchess was inclined to be pert to Rosina, and Rosina, for all her Wybird thumbiness, had the Broome temper if she had not the Broome tongue. She was never vanquished by the duchess; but their encounters were always battles. However, the duchess could be exceedingly useful to Maud Blythe, so Rosina fought her with the buttons on and gave her the better place in the box, and allowed her to display her proud little parrot-profile crowned with diamonds to the house without asking for the crimson box-curtains to be drawn against imaginary draughts. Instead the curtains hung limp behind the duchess, enhanced her white shoulders, and sheltered Maud and Harry.

"I envy you!" said Maud, looking past him to the buzzing house.

He looked at her in flattered surprise.

"Isn't this your own theatre?" she went on.

"It will be one day," he said, puzzled by the turn of the conversation. And then she said, flushing—

"What you'll be able to do! Oh, how I envy you!"

"I didn't know you cared particularly for acting," said he.

"You don't, do you?" she turned the tables quickly. "Your aunt says you've left the stage."

"The stage is not the theatre," he corrected her. "Never the theatre. I, we, all the Broomes are theatre people, though my aunt would never admit it." He glanced at Rosina's erect back. "Our history goes back a hundred and fifty years. My great-grandfather first fell on to a stage in George II's reign, and here we are in 1850 still on the stage. No, Miss Blythe, I'm not a good actor, but my work will always be the theatre."

She picked out a phrase,

"You aren't a good actor, do you say? But I think you are."

"When have you seen me?" demanded Harry, not too pleased; for he had no illusions as to the quality of his performances.

"At the ball," she said. "The ball your aunt gave for me. But whenever I have caught sight of you I think you have always been acting."

"I'm not acting now," said Harry, staring down at her, amused, incredulous, yet behind these sensations with a blissful feeling of a man climbing the last steps of a tower, and coming out upon a view of heaven.

"No," she returned, calmly. "You stopped acting—oh, I can remember it exactly—at our second dance. I couldn't help noticing the change," she said, flushing. "Till then it had seemed to me that you spoke to me from a distance—to everyone, not only to me—as if there were a glass wall between us."

"What?" He felt himself whiten. He stared. "What do you mean?"

"My grandfather has a glass top to one of the hives, and inside you can see the bees running about. It's exceedingly interesting to watch them," returned Maud sedately. "But they don't know that we are watching, and however closely I watch I can't distinguish one bee from another, and I scarcely want to! Well, you were looking at everyone that evening as I look at the bees."

He said, with an air of distress assumed to provoke her further revelations—

"All this sounds as if I had been a most intolerable bore."

"No," she said, falling into the trap. "But I thought you looked very unhappy, and that you concealed it very well. That was why I said you were a good actor. When you changed to me half way through the evening, I knew how well you had been acting."

He could hardly believe his ears. She had put her soft finger on his private horror and behold, it was no longer horrible to him! Now he could share his horror. He had never thought to find in a wife the sort of understanding that her criticism implied. This was shrewder than wisdom. This was better than beauty. This was more gracious than grace.

He began to tell her what he thought of her.

Rosina, some echo from her own youth making her aware of what was happening, took the button off her foil, and engaged the duchess more vigorously than before.

CHAPTER 15

ROBIN BROOME, PLAYWRIGHT

LETTICE returned to England with all her train pretty soon after the receipt of Harry's letter announcing his engagement to Maud Blythe. She was conscious that she had erred in letting her revived affection for her frail elder son blind her to the dangers of leaving defenceless Harry alone in London. As she put it to herself, she must not be guilty of favouritism. Harry had his rights just as much as Robin. Robin was getting better and he must learn to adapt himself to the English climate. He could, of course, stay out with Lionel if he pleased, but he'd be better at home with his mother—"don't you think, Lionel?"

Lionel thought so indeed. Lionel, who had no intention whatever of being left with an invalid on his hands, protested that, much as he would have enjoyed staying on a little longer with Robin and Stephen and Robin's two nurses and Stephen's *bonne,* it was absolutely necessary that he should pay a visit to his daughter in Buda-Pesth—for the Argentine scheme was maturing much against her wishes and she had written for advice and, if possible, his personal support. This was true enough, though Lionel forgot to mention that the letter was four months old.

So he posted off with charmingly expressed and, for that matter, sincerely felt regrets that Lettice's responsibilities prevented her from accompanying him on a visit to her niece. Nothing would have suited Lionel better than a jaunt to Vienna with Lettice—after all Buda-Pesth is a mere excursion from Vienna—Vienna is the place to make your headquarters! For his sister's company had not palled on him with the years, and he resented the resurgence of her maternal instincts. But he knew better than to suggest to Lettice that she should do anything she truly didn't want to do at the moment. Instead he bought her the seed-pearl earrings, brooch and knotted necklace for which she had been hankering a week: bought Stephen a French poodle puppy that nearly died of train-sickness on the way home: tipped the *bonne:* bestowed immense boxes of bonbons on the nurses: and, on the very eve of his departure, presented Robin himself with a large writing-case made of light-weighing wood, not too heavy to lie on a sick man's knees.

Accompanying the desk was a second box filled with quire upon quire of easy, smooth-surfaced, lined writing paper.

"You're ready for this medicine again, I should say," observed Lionel to his nephew, "and I don't think you need mind going home to England. You've been bored here, haven't you? Too much sunshine: too many women. Try my medicine and talk it over with Harry when you get home. That'll cure you."

But to himself he said that Lettice might travel the boy home to England, but she would scarcely be able to shift him again. His bones stuck through his cheeks in spite of Lettice's jellies and creams and expensive French doctors. He's burning himself out, thought Lionel— consuming himself. Well, let him put it on to paper! Maybe fuel is what he needs. He turned to meet Robin's bright stare.

"How did you know?" Robin was asking suspiciously, excitedly, as he caressed the paper's tempting surface. "Have you and Harry been rummaging in my papers?"

"Harry brought home a basket full of scripts," returned his uncle hardily, "but he was too upset to look at them. But I wasn't. You know what I am. Never can keep my fingers off other people's papers. Besides——"

"Yes, I used to show you things," Robin conceded. Then, expressionlessly—"But these—did you read any of them? What—what did you think of them?"

"Well, as a matter of fact," returned his uncle with his air of malicious enjoyment, "your handwriting is beyond me. But I took the liberty, thinking you'd probably be dead before the job was finished, of sending them to a transcriber and they've all been copied out in a fair hand. They're waiting for you at home." And thought, with a chuckle at his own cleverness and a pang of affectionate regret for the need of such a tonic—'That'll get the boy back to England if nothing else will.'

"But you didn't read them?" persisted Robin, the flush on his cheeks deepening and his blue eyes burning.

"Only enough to know that they were worth trouble," returned his uncle. "But take my advice. Give them to Harry when you get home, and whether he likes them or whether he doesn't, go on writing!" He stooped to his nephew, kissed him, and went off cheerfully.

But now Robin was all in a fever to be in England, and, because he wished to, stood the journey well, for change was a form of health to him. Settled once more in Park Lane he could see that Lettice was right in saying—Home is what you want! It was true—until he tired of it.

Oh, for the stimulus of change! Robin thought sometimes that death might be just the change he needed. Meanwhile—oh, lovely England! Lovely home! Pleasant servants! Comfortable English lavendered sheets! Where's Harry? How I like my brother! I want Harry! Yes, and Uncle Lionel has left some parcels for me. Where are they?

He had not been in the house an hour before he had opened his parcels. He lay hugging them, happy, when Harry came to sit with him. For Lionel had been better than his word. The dozen manuscripts were not only transcribed, but bound and tooled.

Harry came in, a halo round his head and a frown on his forehead; for, though he was a happy man, Maud's grandfather did not write too cordially from Ireland. Maud's grandfather was inclined to confuse a Broome with the less reputable type of Dublin player, such players as had attacked Mrs. Jordan in the old man's youth. He had seen the affair and been horrified. Now he had no notion of allowing his granddaughter to marry an actor, and wrote with such indignation that Rosina was in tears and Lettice, equally indignant, refused to discuss the business with Harry at all in the first week of their reunion. As usual the sight of Lettice in the flesh sadly disturbed Harry's ideal picture of a melting mother, and the plan that had seemed so simple in her absence, the plan of persuading her to turn over to him immediately the control of the theatre property which he must inherit at her death, had another aspect in her presence. In fact, Harry, though in no doubt whatever of his eventual victories over all opposing forces, was very much in need of brotherly counsel and support. But Robin was absorbed in the flights of his own butterflies.

"Hullo, old fellow! Don't you think I look better?" began Robin.

"Better! It's time you dropped this invalid pose altogether. When are you coming to act for me, you luxurious devil?" improvised Harry glibly; for he did not think his brother looked better. He was shocked that three months' rest and nursing and affection could be so completely without effect on his brother. He said to himself—'I was right! He is going to die!' And for the moment the thought of his own joys and worries left him as Robin, with the optimism of his disease, went on to tell Harry how much stronger he felt in himself, fitter for work than he had ever felt in his life. Of course he was a little tired by the journey, but that was natural. He had been up and about quite often in the south, out in a bath-chair and sitting in the sunshine while Steenie played with litters of French children: the little fellow picked up French in a way that was amazing. Steenie always made friends anyway.

"It's Steenie that's on my mind, Harry. That's the problem—how to provide for Steenie?"

Harry smiled at his brother.

"I shouldn't worry about Stephen, Robin. He's put all our noses out of joint with Mama as it is."

Robin scowled suddenly.

"How long will it last? Russel was Mama's favourite once," said Robin.

"You've never been just to Mama," said Harry coldly. "But if you don't trust her, I expect you'll trust me. If Mama leaves him out of her will, I'll see that he's in mine."

"You're going to be married yourself, I hear," returned Robin equally coldly.

"Certainly! Do you object?" said Harry.

It was as if a sudden sharp wind had sprung up and was driving like a knife between the two brothers.

"Huh! Married and marred," said Robin bitterly. "A will's not valid once you're married, don't you know that? And when you make another your wife looks over your shoulder. No, Harry, until I see some provision for my own child I can't——" He broke off suddenly with the air of a man who has lost the thread of his speech.

'Can't die in peace, you mean!' thought Harry, his anger dropping as suddenly as it had arisen, and wondering for the hundredth time on what rock his brother had wrecked himself: and thinking for the hundredth time that if he ever met the woman who had driven him upon the rock he would do his best to punish her for the hurt she had done his brother. But he said mildly enough—

"When you meet Maud you won't be afraid for Stephen. Besides, there's your share of the property at Mama's death."

Robin paid no attention.

"Oxford, and whatever he chooses afterwards," dreamed Robin, "though it's bound to be the stage, of course, with me and his mother in his blood."

"Was she an actress?" asked Harry casually; but he could not resist asking.

"What else?" said Robin. "You don't think I married a publican's daughter, do you? Stephen has her hands. She used to do a dance of the hands. But look here, Harry, I've got to have money for Stephen. How am I to get it? Mama?"

"I've got to have money to get married. How am I to get it? Mama?" retorted his brother.

"How much money have you got of your own?" demanded Robin. "Have you saved, or do you always spend your allowance? You used to be a miserly infant. But now——" He hesitated, looking at his brother up and down in amused appreciation. "You go to a good tailor; but there's a certain expense of thought as well, eh? Dove-grey discretion."

Harry laughed, but he was pleased. He had not altogether lost the old passionate hunger for Robin's approval.

"Well, go on!" said Robin, the gleam fading.

"I've saved enough to pick up a little property that's going to be valuable one day," said Harry. "I could mortgage on it. It wouldn't do to sell. Why?"

"Well, I might have an investment for you—at least Uncle Lionel seemed to think so."

"Uncle Lionel's no fool," said Harry.

"Then I wish you'd take a look at these," said Robin fretfully, and the heavy handsome volumes slid from the bed to the floor with a crash as he twisted his tired body. Harry picked one up and began to handle it.

"Rivière bound this," he remarked with sudden interest. "He does all Uncle Lionel's work. What is it?"

"A play," said Robin, watching him. "Read it! Read it now!"

"I was going to tea with Maud," began Harry. Then a glance at his brother's hectic cheek decided him. He thought, with a throb of exquisite pleasure—'She'll know without being told that I didn't come because I couldn't come, the blessed darling!' Then on a second unloverlike but exceedingly characteristic thought, he said to himself—'Ought a woman to be so placid? Well, if she is, I shall have to stir her up.'

He pulled forward a high-backed chair, sank into it, and settled down to the manuscript. He was at first uncomfortably aware that Robin was watching him with unnatural intensity, but he speedily forgot Robin in the play itself. He read quickly. Twice Robin stopped him with an anguished—

"You're skipping. Read every word! How can you judge if you don't read every word?" But presently Harry was reading every word.

At the end of an hour he slapped down the book and answered the unspoken question of his brother, whose head indeed had sunk back on the pillows but whose gaze had never wavered.

"Have you got any more like this?" said Harry coldly, in the voice he had never used to Robin, the voice of the business manager striking a bargain and concealing eagerness and appreciation for fear a bargain should be spoiled.

But Robin recognised the tone, and the relief in his face tore Harry's heart-strings.

"You can use it?" was all he said, however.

"I can use it," returned his brother. And then—"Let me read the rest, though. Then we'll talk. I'll take them away with me and——"

"Read them now!" commanded Robin.

"But——"

"Now!" said Robin. "I don't believe in tomorrow." And then, in a strangled voice—"How can I? Look at me!" The tears began to roll down his cheeks.

"Robin, Robin——"

"I buoy myself up, but do you think that I don't know I've got to die?" cried Robin. "Why, it's one of the symptoms to pretend you're getting well, isn't it? Isn't it? Didn't you say so to yourself ten minutes ago when I babbled? I heard you. As if we couldn't hear each other's minds! But if the plays were any good, they'd make a nest-egg for Stephen. If I'm not there to look after Stephen and his mother gets hold of him——"

"She shan't. You lie quiet. Which shall I read next? You choose, Robin!"

Weak, panting, so quickly pacified, so quickly exhausted, Robin chose: and Harry, knowing how he would be observed, forced his mind to steady, critical reading. It was the only way to quiet Robin, he knew. And indeed, after watching his brother for a few minutes, Robin, like a moth in a killing jar, quivered, relaxed, fell sideways on his pillow, and before the second play was half devoured, had fallen lightly asleep.

But Harry read on, finished the second manuscript: then, putting it down, leant back and stared at his brother. So these papers were the true Robin—not that petal of a boy, colourless and wilting. So it was these pages which Robin's spirit intended to haunt. So Robin was more a man of the theatre than any of them! Harry was awestruck. He had been right then, as a child, to think of Robin as the remote mystery who knew everything, who did everything superlatively well, and, with a laugh, took a small brother by the hand. Robin a stick? A phrase from one of Russel's letters came into his mind—'The truth is Robin, the dear old fellow, can't act!'

Maybe not, my good Russel! But he knows more about the stage than either of us. Why, he knows as much as our father did. More, Russel! And while you strutted, old fellow, Robin watched you from the prompt box and took you down. What parts he has written you, Russel! How your mouth will water! Why, they make mine water and God knows I know my limitations as an actor. Finding women will be the job. He's got a lot about Mother in, of course, and old Rosina. Oh, I can match them. But I don't understand his minxes—*or* his mistresses. Kitty Develin could play the older one—or could she? No —too refined. It's an odd type. I wonder what's in the rest of the stuff. Where has he met the original, I wonder. She's half bar-maid, half snake. She's fascinating. She's beastly. It's his wife, I suppose. But if it is how can he bear to write down that last act? Oh, of course it's a triumph, that last act—and he does know his public. *Clever Kate!* Good title—keeps the thing light. That's the genius of it—keeping it comedic. He isn't bitter either: he's such a sweet-tempered devil. He ought to be bitter. He can't have invented that auction scene. What happened to Robin? I could kill that woman. I'd like to shame her publicly. Well, please God old Robin shall earn a guinea or two out of his torments. That's only fair. That's what he's written it for, I suppose, to earn a guinea for Stephen. 'Child of shame!' That's a woman's phrase. But Stephen is the child of Robin's shame, it seems to me. And now he's peddling his shame to give Stephen a future. I wonder what she *did* do to him?

As if in answer Robin opened his eyes.

"What is it, Harry? What do you want to know?"

Harry caught his breath.

"What did she do to you, Robin?"

"My wife?"

"Yes."

"Well," said Robin harshly, "you've read *Clever Kate*."

Harry blanched.

"What? Is your wife the original?"

"More or less."

"Was she ten years older?"

"She was."

"Robin, you fool! But the rest, Robin?"

"Well?"

"It didn't happen, Robin? It can't be a fact?"

"That she auctioned me? Certainly. I wasn't present, Harry, but I understand that the bidding was keen. I fetched quite a good price, I heard." Then as the complete silence lengthened, Robin smiled gently at his brother as you smile at a child who needs some reassurance. "I heard in time, Harry."

Harry fumbled.

"You haven't got to tell me that."

Robin was still gentle with him.

"Haven't I? You don't know much about this sort of thing, do you? I didn't either at twenty-three—that's when I—when she married me!"

"What did you do?"

"Took Stephen off—and myself. She never wanted Stephen. Technically, though, I deserted my wife because I heard some filthy gossip, and wasn't man enough to ask her if it were true."

"But why didn't you, Robin?"

"No necessity: it rang too familiar. But in my play, you see, the hero doesn't hear in time."

Harry clutched at any spar in those cold waters.

"No, old fellow, and that's what we shall have to alter. The public won't stand that last act. But if you can soften it down a little—prettify it, you know——"

"I know," said Robin.

"Well, then," said Harry after another long pause, "well, then there's money in both of them. I'll read the rest to-night."

"These are the best," said Robin.

"But I think I see my way. As you know, the Genista lease expires next month——"

"How should I know?" asked Robin wearily.

"Well, it does. Suppose now I could persuade Mama to make it over to us or lease it to us if she won't let us have it outright; but I think she may——"

"You mean," said Robin languidly, "that, as there is no possible chance of my inheriting later on, she might think it fair——"

"It's no use talking of what is fair to Mama," said Harry firmly. "That would merely irritate her. But she'd give it you fast enough if you wanted it to play with."

"Why, haven't you asked her to give it to you?"

Harry flushed.

"You think I'm scheming, Robin, but here's fact. I wouldn't ask her until I got into touch with you and Russel, for fear you'd say precisely that, for fear you'd say 'Jacob!' But now you're home, and we've got these comedies to barter with, don't you see what a game it can be? We'll put on the *Clever Kate* first and see if they like it. And if they do— I know my little Genista public pretty well, and I think they will—then we risk *The Lemnians* and then we're really launched. We beat Tom Robertson at his own game then. And what's more, old fellow, this is a Broome venture. My management—your plays—and if I could get Russel over, why then, we should be complete. Eh, wouldn't that be a notion?"

"I thought you'd forgotten Russel," said Robin with a certain bitterness.

"No," said Harry. "Oh, no!"

Robin raised himself on his elbow and stared at his brother.

"You're a queer customer. I used to think of 'little Harry' as the cuckoo in the nest——"

Harry shook his head, amused.

"No you didn't. The idea has only this moment occurred to you. But it would have been an effective idea if it *had* occurred to you, of course, very effective. The Rival Brothers! do you think only in terms of scenes, Robin?"

"What do you think in?" returned Robin.

Harry chuckled.

"Terms of intervals! Terms of salary lists! I wonder what Russel thinks in?"

"Terms of parts," said Robin slowly.

"Then he's a real actor, eh? The reports don't flatter?"

"Oh, no! Russel's a fine actor. He's more, he's a stupid genius: just as I'm a brilliant fool."

"What am I?" said Harry.

"As yet, nothing! But wait till you've been married a year," said Robin, suddenly bitter. "Then I can tell you exactly what you'll be for the rest of your life."

"Why did you marry that woman?" asked Harry bluntly.

"I was in love with her," said Robin. "Odd, isn't it?"

"Where did you meet her?"

"She was the leading lady in a touring company. She drank. She was a devil."

"But why? Then why?"

"I can't explain to you, Harry. You've never been in love."

Harry was indignant.

"Never been in love? What do you mean?"

"Oh, I don't know. I don't want to argue," said Robin. And then—"Don't bother about me, Harry. I'm sure you and Maud will be entirely happy."

"We shall. Oh—" cried Harry, blandly anticipating the exquisite conversations which would presently be held, between him and his brother, between him and his love—"I do so want to know what you and Maud will think of each other. You've got to like each other. She likes you already."

"And if I don't like her?"

Harry looked at him compassionately, and Robin was restless under the look.

"If I don't like her, Harry, what am I to do? Fake? You'll see through it, of course, but she needn't. Or would you take it as an insult? Because—" he shivered—"except for Mama—and even Mama sometimes gets on my nerves—I don't much like women." He ceased. He looked old.

"You'll like Maud," Harry assured him, looking young.

CHAPTER 16

HARRY's schemes prospered. When did they not? Lettice, whose business instincts, long dormant, were not in the least dead, astonished her sons by re-appearing as the Lettice whom William had once relied upon. Neither of them knew this new Lettice who understood figures and did not need to have facts told her twice or the plan of a theatre elaborately explained. Harry read her the pick of Robin's manuscripts. He read extremely well, and needed to; for Robin when he wrote abandoned the graces, the whimsies, even his own charm. His lines glittered with opportunities for the actor, but had little literary value. Nor, be it said, has all Robin's work survived; but in its day it satisfied thousands.

Harry from the first was eager over the possibilities of the new Broome line.

"You see, Mama, the Broomes are William, and William is the Broomes. I don't mean Papa, dearest, I mean Shakespeare. William and the Gloriana—that's our safe investment, don't you see? That will last for ever. When the Broomes stop thinking in terms of Shakespeare it's the end of everything. Oh, by the way, did you hear, Mama, that Russel's Othello is the talk of New York?"

"Russel's?" Lettice's eyes flashed. "You should have seen your father's." Then, belatedly—"I don't want to hear about Russel."

"No, Mama, of course not! I know. But I have just had a bundle of press notices. They are on my desk. Well, as I was saying—nobody can disassociate us from Shakespeare. But Mama, they should! I want a second line—a little theatre to turn somersaults in, eh? Wouldn't it be fun? And if Robin's plays take, it would build up an inheritance for Stephen."

"I can look after my own grandson's future, I hope," began Lettice; but he checked her—

"Of course, Mama! But don't you see, it's not the money. It's a theatre for Stephen to use later in Robin's plays. Robin's stuff is too slight for the big theatres. Besides, Mama, think what it would mean for us, the Broomes, to create a new tradition, and house it—a modern house, up-to-date, every detail perfect! That's my dream, Mama, to build a new Broome theatre. If I could stand outside one day and say 'I built this,' I wouldn't care if it bankrupted me."

"I should. Let us confine ourselves to the theatres we possess," said his mother dryly. Then, relenting—

"But if it is understood that you don't plague me over the Glory Hole—well, I don't mind so much what you do with Robin's inheritance. Yes, I've always looked on the Genista as your special inheritance, Robin! And if you and Harry choose to risk it, if you believe in yourselves sufficiently——"

Thus the mad scheme took shape and in time, for Harry in action was as cautious as he was rash in planning, was a success. He began rebuilding the Genista at once; but he had been married a couple of years before Robin's first play was put on.

Yes, in spite of the indignant grandfather, Harry married his first and only love, though Lettice, for once, would not help him to his desire. She held herself cool in the matter and would give no advice. Indeed, she protested that it would not be decorous for her so much as to make the young lady's acquaintance until the engagement was hallowed. Lettice secretly was hopeful that the dreaded death-by-marriage of Harry might be postponed, perhaps avoided altogether.

Not so her sister. Rosina adored her match: Rosina agonised at 'his' attitude. When Harry posted over to Ireland for his interview he took—serenely contriving to make it a perfectly natural thing—his aunt with him.

They were received coolly: it roused the Broome in them both, and Harry prepared himself to play Ferdinand; for he intended, though the Irish heavens fell and Lettice disliked the idea, to marry Maud Blythe. He was, however, amazed to find that his important affair was become a secondary matter, that the true war was between an unknown, incredible Aunt Rosina and an elderly gentleman who plainly regarded her as a tempestuous petticoat to be controlled by the solider sex: and regarded him, Harry, as a mere figure of the nursery. "Should little Miss Maud be allowed to go to tea with Master Broome?" "Frankly, my lady——" But at that my lady conveyed, with raised eyebrows, her surprise that the matter should be discussed before one of the children in question, whom, however—"I brought with me that you might see for yourself, Almeric—though I may say, stage or no stage, I had hoped that Harry, as my nephew, would be welcome. Besides, what have you after all against the stage? This is no question of the lesser fry. The Broomes are stage history!

If you had even hinted to my mother—oh, Almeric, do you remember her and the Regent at the Peyton ball?"

At that the old gentleman laughed.

"Oh, if you have the courage to talk of the Peyton ball, Rosina——"

"Harry, you ought to explore the gardens this fine afternoon."

And the little boy, Harry, was sent out for a walk while his elders talked over his affairs and their own. Their own appeared to them considerably more important.

"The Peyton ball? Good heavens, Rosina, do you remember the Peyton ball too? Why, it was at the Peyton ball——"

Once more the two old fogies began to get on very well indeed.

"Do I remember your mother at it? I should think I do! The duchess was a hard woman, Rosina. Say what you like, if I hesitate over that young fellow of yours, is it not altogether natural? I am thinking of your mother. The stage hardens a woman. The duchess was very hard. I shouldn't like it if Maud——"

"But my dear Almeric, you don't suppose that Harry would allow his wife to associate——? I was never behind the scenes in my life! Mama may have been hard, but if so, it was in re-action from all you term 'theatre.' My dear Sir Almeric, the theatrical thing after the Peyton ball and your interview——"

"Whew!" interjected Sir Almeric. Even after thirty years he remembered that dusty, dead interview.

"—would have been 'Bless you, my children!'" Rosina went on, eyeing him wistfully. "But did Mama behave so? No! Why, she never so much as told me of that interview. Until you yourself spoke of it six months ago I hadn't a notion. If I had dreamed—if I had known—' Rosina sighed.

"What then, Rosina?"

"I don't know. I never had Lettice's courage. That's my sister—that's Harry's mother. Yes, you're right, Almeric! Mama was a hard woman. It was half her charm. But are you going to punish Mama's sins on Harry and Maud? It would make me wretched, Almeric, if you did. I've had—not too gay a life. Until you charged me with dear Maud, all this—" she made a vague gesture which included the sunshine pouring in through the high clear windows, the blue distances, the green lawns brilliant with bedding, the tumbling puppies on the terrace—"all these pleasures, these adventures—such things as these dear children's love affair—they've never come my way. I am born again, Almeric, old woman that I am. Life, your soft Irish weather, so much more laughter than I ever knew existed in the world, all this your little Maud has brought me! I must confess it would make me very wretched, Almeric, if I saw our own—what shall I call it?—mishap repeated. Yes, mishap! It was too slight a business, wasn't it, for tragedy?" said Rosina drearily.

"It was tragic enough," volunteered the old gentleman suddenly. "Believe it or not, Rosina, I nearly blew my brains out one evening in the gun-room. I can show you the gun-room."

"Yes, yes! It was all very needless and cruel. That is why I beg of you, Almeric, allow this match! Harry and Maud—Maud and Harry—they are good for each other. I should like you to let them be happy."

"They are so young——"

"Yes, Almeric, that's why——"

So it came about that at the week's end Harry was allowed to return to London an engaged man. But Rosina was persuaded to stay on a few days longer.

"What on earth can Rosina find in the bogs to amuse her?" wondered Lettice fretfully, as she wrote an extremely sweet and cordial invitation to her future daughter-in-law to come and stay with her till Aunt Rosina returned. "Well, she will have to come home for the wedding!" For the grandfather, capitulating, had made no petty conditions, and Maud and Harry were to be married at the end of the season from Rosina's house.

Harry, once Maud was in his mother's possession, drew a deep breath of relief. Now the two women might fight it out: he backed both to win. He believed in giving his mother her head soon and swiftly, and he could trust his placid Maud. Meanwhile, what on earth was dear old Aunt Rosina doing in Ireland now that he and Maud were safely plighted?

Rosina told them defiantly, when she came back a fortnight later and resumed possession of Miss Blythe, what she had done in Ireland.

"Well, Lettice——?" she began, and her eyes strayed questioningly to the figures of Maud and Harry on their distant sofa.

"Well enough!" said Lettice grudgingly. And then—"The child wants to be married very quietly in a travelling dress! Did you ever hear such nonsense? I put a stop to it at once. I said to her—My dear child, your wedding-dress is my affair!"

"Mine," said Rosina sharply.

Lettice stared. The meek Rosina!

"It's very kind of you, Rosina——" she began. Lettice was not often at a loss, but Rosina puzzled her. This air of determination, this gleam in the eye—what was it?

"I am in charge of Maud's trousseau," continued Rosina firmly, "and her wedding-dress I am giving her myself."

"Oh! Oh, just as you like," said Lettice, frightening Rosina anew by giving in so easily.

"We shall be glad if you will superintend the making of it, of course, my dear," conceded Rosina hastily. "Maud will be glad of your taste. So shall I, for that matter. I admit a trousseau is beyond me."

"I have worked out lists already for the child," said Lettice. "But she is too scrupulous. She looks at every penny."

"They are so poor, you know," said Rosina.

"Of course I know. I have never said that I considered it a good match for Harry, though the girl is well-bred, and I think appreciates her luck. There is no doubt that she is attached to Harry. She has all the proper ideas. But she must learn to spend, or at any rate to let people spend for her. I told her so. I said—my dear you must learn the gracious art of *taking*," said Lettice, who had never in her life practised it. "If your future mother-in-law can't amuse herself by choosing you a couple of frocks and a dozen pocket-handkerchiefs——"

"She will want much more than that," said the literal Rosina.

Lettice clicked her tongue.

"Yes, Rosina, of course she will. But we mustn't overwhelm the child. We must let her down lightly. She is not very clever, but she is pleasant and presentable, though I admit I have never admired the lymphatic type. However, that is Harry's affair: and carefully dressed she will do well enough. But I do beg you to leave the trousseau to me."

"As long as I pay for it," said Rosina.

"Well, we can discuss it later."

"As a matter of fact, Lettice—" Rosina hesitated and began again— "I shall be wanting a few things for myself."

"Oh, a dress for the wedding," said Lettice, not greatly interested.

"I know I'm over sixty——" continued Rosina, fidgeting and unhappy.

"Maroon, I fancy!" Lavender Lettice, all filmy laces, eyed her solid sister critically. "Or green? Yes, dark bottle green would be best for you."

"I should like green," said Rosina sentimentally. Then—"What should you say, Lettice, if I said to you, 'I mean to marry again'?"

"I should say you were a fool," said Lettice, busy with her lists.

"I am going to marry again," said her sister loudly, and waited with discomforted cheeks for Lettice's surprise, for Lettice's gay, savage mockeries.

But Lettice, after one sharp look, continued making her lists. It was a full minute before she said in belated answer—

"Are you really thinking of marrying again, Rosina?"

"I am," said Rosina, unnerved by the pause, but defiant.

"The Irishman?"

"Yes."

"Well!" said Lettice, amiable, non-committal.

"Well?" relaxed her sister, questioning piteously.

"Are you sure you like Ireland—bogs and rain and all that? Are you sure you like being cut off from London and us all? But after all you ought to know: you've stayed there twice."

"I suppose people will laugh," said Rosina wretchedly.

"Laugh?" Lettice frowned.

"Laugh at me," said Rosina.

"Laugh at you?" repeated Lettice indignantly. "Why should they, I should like to know? If you like it, my dear, I think it's a very good thing. When does he come over? Laugh indeed! What an idea! But you are quite right, Rosina—I must see about your clothes at once."

Ah, one liked Lettice! There was no doubt about it, faults or no faults, bullying or no bullying, one liked Lettice. She had a tongue, said poor soothed Rosina to herself; but oh, she was—she was dependable!

CHAPTER 17

THE CRYSTAL PALACE

THE marriage of Harry and Maud was an immense success from the wedding day on. Indeed the two suited each other so well that Lettice, who would not have allowed any daughter or daughter-in-law of hers to criticise, much less to withstand any son of hers, was apt to point out that dear Maud was absurdly meek and that it was very bad for Harry to be thus humoured. And indeed, growing very fond of Maud with time, though always reserving to herself the right to hate her if she should ever cease to do her duty by Harry, Lettice spent a good deal of energy in rebuking her daughter-in-law for her too exact obedience.

"You should never," said Lettice, "spoil a man." And she would prove to Maud by humorous anecdote how she, Lettice, had always set her face against spoiling William. Maud—continued Lettice—did not yet fully understand the character of Harry. Harry was an angel of unselfish consideration. "Never—" said Lettice, and spoke truly—"has my dear boy wilfully distressed me. Had I disapproved of you, my dear," said Lettice on a sudden and entirely unwarranted inspiration, "had I said to Harry that I could not receive you as a daughter-in-law, I don't believe he would have gone on with the affair. I am sure, sure he would not," said Lettice, watching to see how her daughter-in-law would receive the statement.

Maud took it for gospel, but remained unruffled.

"So you see, my dear," continued Lettice, highly satisfied with Maud, "I can hardly be said to be prejudiced *against* Harry. And yet I say to you—take care!"

"Oh, I do," said Maud.

Lettice shook her head and explained that one could be too gentle, too sweet, too yielding. It was not good for any man, as she, Lettice, knew by bitter experience. Harry might easily grow selfish if Maud spoiled him, gave in to him, waited on him and worshipped him as she so obviously was doing. "I have always understood Harry's faults," said Harry's mother, "and always pointed them out to him. I don't pretend he liked it, but what do I care whether he liked it or not? My duty is to tell him the truth about himself, and I don't think it has made him love his mother the less," finished Lettice. "But you, you'll be boring him, my dear," said Lettice, "if you humour him so absurdly. He should be humouring you. Bless me—you haven't been married a year! Why do you give in to him so?"

Maud smiled her slow smile.

"I don't always," she said. "He wanted me to stay at home this morning. Some sort of a theatre magnate from the States might be arriving. But I told him that I was engaged with you."

"Now that, I don't mind saying," said Lettice swiftly, "was inconsiderate of you, my dear. If Harry asked you to entertain a friend of his it seems to me that it is ungracious of you to put a mere morning engagement before his wishes. A woman can be a great help to a man in these matters. I wonder what William would have done," cried Lettice in mounting indignation, "if I'd been out and about every day of my life, never there when he wanted my co-operation. What time is this engagement of Harry's?"

"The man arrives about twelve," said Maud, glancing at the clock.

"And you are letting them lunch alone? I shouldn't do that, my dear. Harry needs a hostess. I'll ring for the carriage and you shall get off at once."

"I suppose you couldn't come with me," said Maud hesitating.

"You can manage very well without me," said Lettice, rising briskly. "You must do your own entertaining. You can't always be running round my skirts, asking my advice. However, I don't at all mind coming if you really want me," conceded Lettice, her finger on the bell. "What is this man's name? Where does he come from? New York? I hear that Russel has had a certain success in New York. I don't wonder. There is no doubt that he is the handsomest of my sons." Then, when she had ordered her carriage and summoned her maid— "Yes, you may come up to my room with me while I change my dress. No, my dear, I am not going to lunch with you and my son in a frumpy morning gown that I should not be wearing at all if I hadn't the flowers to do. I have some self-respect, I hope."

"Wear the lavender silk," said Maud. "Harry loves the lavender silk."

"Yes, my dear," retorted Lettice sharply, "and I may tell you this— he has no great fondness for blue. You should take Harry's advice when you are choosing your dresses if you won't take mine. Blue is common-place," said Lettice, surveying her daughter-in-law's azure muslin. "Now I have a length of silk that I have not yet had made up. It is a little too young for me. We will take it round with us and see what Harry says to it. The foxglove coloured silk that I put aside for

Mrs. Harry, Mitcham! Nonsense, my dear, it won't clash with your hair at all. Two wrong reds together make a right. Trust me! You're a mere milkmaid in blue or green, but this combination has distinction. Ask Harry! Yes, my dear, if Harry likes it I'll have it made up for your birthday."

Maud, pleased as usual, smiled her slow smile again. She loved Harry so much that she had a great deal of affection left over for her mother-in-law. And she knew, too, that Harry particularly wanted his mother to join them that day at lunch.

And Harry was indeed delighted with his wife for bringing the decorative Lettice, enlivener of stiff gatherings and enhancer of intimate ones; for his American visitor was a man of extreme importance to him. He was an American of the fifties, naïvely pleased to be in the old world, to be in London, to be talking to a duke's daughter. He was a man considerably older than Harry, and in his own business world was a professional where Harry was still an amateur. But socially he was no match for Lettice, whether she graciously liked him or glitteringly disliked him.

Fortunately she liked him, and the vague toothache of desire for news of her son, her first-born, her own handsome Russel, his father's murderer, made her much more interested than an English great lady of her time was likely to be in the stranger and his huts. What was New York like? How big was it? What sort of people lived in it? Had it shops now? Theatres? What sort of theatres? Tell me all about New York and its theatres, its actors and its actresses!

The American spent a happy half hour telling her all about New York and its theatres, its touring system and adventures of the road.

"You don't know what we mean by 'the road,' Lady Lettice? But then I daresay you know as little of the touring system on this side of the ocean."

"Herring-pond," corrected Lettice graciously, and continued to ask wise-foolish, provocative questions till Harry turned to Maud in delight.

"Mama is marvellous! Look at her now! She's doing all the work for me. What made you sure that I wanted her? I thought we were to lunch without you."

And his eyes danced with delight; for the arrangement had been made with formal care between the two of them. It had been one of his little traps for her, and now he knew that she had known it to be one of his little traps. He had not been quite sure, though, that she had known when he said—"I've a guest for lunch, Maud. A New Yorker who brings me news of Russel. I'm very sorry you won't be there to give him lunch, but you're going to Mama's, aren't you?"

"That was the arrangement," Maud had responded.

"Give her my love! Now if she had been lunching with us—but she never likes altering her plans unless she thinks of it herself."

Maud had smiled gently.

"Shall I tell her that there is news of Russel?" she ventured meekly: and he had answered with his stare—

"Yes—no—yes! Well, at your discretion, Maud!" Then the stare had broken up on the acknowledgment—"I've set my heart on getting Russel over to play in Robin's stuff."

"I know," Maud had responded to that, and departed, and Harry had watched her go, wondering just how well his wife had understood him: and almost, but not quite sure that she and his mother would be there to help him out long before the lunch bell rang. And now he knew how well Maud understood him: and so he was charming to her as they stood together by the aviary that Lettice had insisted on installing in the little conservatory room which led out of the saloon.

"Angelic woman!" said he, smiling at her. "How did you get Mama to come?"

"I think she wanted to," said Maud, smiling back at him.

"Did you mention Russel?" said Harry, ready to reprove the angel's indiscretion if she had, and regret the woman's omission if she had not. For he wanted his wife perfect, did Harry.

"No, but she did," said Maud. "You see she has put on the lavender silk, the new one."

"She doesn't look a day over forty," said Harry admiringly. "Well then, we can bring up the subject of Russel at lunch without discomfort. Between ourselves, Maud, he may be in England next autumn."

"Shall I like Russel?" asked Maud, thrusting a bit of groundsel through the bars to a tamed, darting wisp of blue and red feathers. It perched on a convenient bar, and pecked, and cocked its eye at her and at Harry alternately, till Harry, greedy for her attention, took away the groundsel impatiently.

"Listen to me, Maud! You can feed the bird at any time. We shall be going in to lunch in a moment. Look, this is the situation—Russel is coming to England in any case. This is his agent, his manager, his impresario, his advance guard. Russel has made a fortune in New York, though I daresay we shall find him a little provincial. They rant, you know, on that side of the water: they're all superlatives. Russel will have been infected: he was always impressionable. However, he's coming to England for a season and, no doubt, will do here very well. I'm told he's grown as like our father as one ship of the line to another. But, you see, he must come to us. He must not act anywhere but at the Glory Hole. It would be monstrous if a Broome should come back to London and not to the Glory Hole. And there are parts for him in three of Robin's plays. But it's a question of terms. Russel wants to come, but he's in his agent's—this man's—hands. And the terms are a tooth-pull! It will pay me almost certainly, but it is a gamble: and, as you know, I am not yet in full control. My mother has acquiesced, confirming the general venture, but what will happen if now I spring Russel on her against her will?"

Maud laughed, confidently.

"My dear, she wants to see your brother. Of course she will manœuvre to see him. You have no cause to worry."

But Harry's mind shot back to his childhood and the midnight sessions with his mother, and Lettice's bitterness and despair. "Never again, Harry! I'll never see his face again. His disobedience killed your father. He can come home with every excuse that his clever brain cares to make: I won't listen. He can never wipe out what he did. I have no son Russel. I say this to you, Harry. Naturally I shouldn't discuss my son before strangers, whatever he has done to his mother. And if he ever returned to London, if he ever dared to come to this house, I shouldn't deny myself because that would disgrace him publicly: no, I should see him and I then should tell him all that has been in my heart since his father died. He wouldn't want to see me a second time, believe me! But of course he will never come near me. He knows well enough what I think of him."

So the grown-up Harry said to his wife—

"Yes, indeed she wants to see him, but only to discharge her feelings on him. I tell you she'll shoot off her feelings at him like a shot-gun at two yards range. You can kill a man with small shot if you fire close enough—blind him anyway. She's capable of breaking his nerve deliberately: and what's more, Maud, she might forbid him the theatre. You don't know my mother."

Maud shook her wise head.

"She won't forbid him the theatre. You Broomes stand by each other. Your God is a jealous God, but He visits your sins on you in private. I've learnt that much about you already—all of you. But I think you don't understand your mother. I think she's longing to see Russel."

Harry nodded.

"So do I. A part of me agrees with you; but another part of me knows another side of her. Mother's a grasshopper: you never know how she'll jump." Then as the gong sounded through the house— "Look, Maud, shall I put my cards on the table?"

"Won't he?" Maud nodded at the American offering his arm, and looking as if he would very much like to add to it his heart, his fortune and any other trifle that Lady Lettice cared to touch with her finger-tips.

"I've not told him to hold his tongue. Russel has written to me privately that he merely gave him an introduction to me as to a useful management. He knows we are brothers; but nothing, of course, of any estrangement. And, of course, he has no idea how very much, professionally, I want Russel, and how ready Russel will be to come. Well, we must feel our way. You will be alert, won't you? Humour Mama!" He smiled at his mother as he hurried to help her to her chair, and pushed the elaborate epergne with its golden broom-pods and silver leafage out of her way: Lettice always managed to disarrange a table. Then, settling down beside her, he smiled at her, satisfied.

"Mama, I wish you came to lunch every day. And I wish you would speak to Maud about going across to you so often. Whenever I want her she is with you. I think we had better come and live with you. Can I have my old rooms, Mama? Maud and I would do very well there." Then in his discreet voice, as Maud engaged the visitor—"Dear Mama, your amethysts are a little too grand for the occasion, but if you hadn't worn them I should have been irritated. And why don't you make Maud wear lavender?"

"That's what I tell her—only country ingénues wear blue."

"Of course! But she does look well in anything, doesn't she? And what do you think of my importation?"

"He knows Russel," said Lettice. "Did you know that he knew Russel when you asked him, Harry?"

"Yes, Mama," said he, meeting her keen look. "Russel sent him to me with a letter of introduction."

"To you and not to me?" said Lettice, winging a glance at her daughter-in-law which could be interpreted, 'Hold to your guest, girl, and dither him well! I'll relieve you later.'

"Well, Mama darling, Russel would think, I daresay, that you would consider it an impertinence."

"Russel ought to know," said Lettice indignantly, but keeping her voice as low as was compatible with good manners, "that however abominably he behaves to me in private, to send his friends to you and not to me is to suggest a public breach. We are not a family to advertise our quarrels, as Russel ought to know if he is a Broome at all, which I sometimes doubt."

"Mama, dearest! What private cupboard are you opening now, to your appalled son?"

"Don't be silly, Harry! You know perfectly what I mean. I merely say that I should never dream of letting the world know how wickedly Russel has behaved, as he ought to have realised. There is decency in these things. The man should have been sent direct to me," said Lettice.

So Maud was right! Harry felicitated himself anew on his wife and on the progress of his affair and Robin's, as he watched his mother skilfully taking possession of the visitor, and that quite clearly to the visitor's gratification. For the American had found that his gracious young hostess made him work very hard. She was a sweet young lady, but she said things which required all his attention to digest, but digested, did not seem to leave him in a much more agreeable mood than he was before. Her conversation did not tease him, tickle him, leave him in a pleasant glow: it merely left him a little better informed than he was before about the Irish church, the new Harley Street college, the writings of Doctor Tilt, the salaries of the young ladies of the London pantomimes, and the reform of the Royal Coburg Theatre in which Mrs. Broome seemed to take a great interest. He did not think it at all nice for a young matron to know about gin palaces and sanitation, or be aware of the fact that young dancers find it difficult to live upon their stage earnings: and yet she was a very gracious young matron. He liked to look at her, though she was much more simply dressed than the young married women of his own aristocracy, whom he never met, but saw, with patriotic pride, driving in their carriages, and sitting in the boxes of the theatres in which he had lounge rights. These ladies would not have admitted him to their table, let alone have talked to him about sanitation and slums. He knew perfectly well that these English ladies would not have talked to him either but for the luck of his letter of introduction. They were not of his world. But how he enjoyed his privilege! Young Mrs. Broome moved him, respectfully, as the sight of Westminster Abbey moved him. She was that well-known institution, the young British matron,

icily beautiful, splendidly something or other, and he was proud to
have met her, proud and—low be it spoken—bored.

But if young Mrs. Broome was Westminster Abbey, her mother-in-
law was England herself. He understood that this elderly lady was the
daughter of a duke, and he realised that she could be terrifying if she
chose, as England was terrifying. But she did not frighten him at all, and
she most certainly did not bore him. She was not icy, she was familiar :
she excited him as the whole country of England excited him, and she
took him for granted just as England took him for granted.

Yes, and therein lay England's power to terrify. England terrified by
her mere difference, by her phlegm, by her air of having existed and
continued exactly as she was for a thousand years : and in that time
tourists and flies had settled on England's forehead and been brushed
away so often, so unconsciously. If you were a stranger you travelled
up and down England half mad with excitement, and England smiled at
you and displayed herself familiarly, so familiarly that you had dreadful
moments of wondering whether she were aware of you at all. Was
Lady Lettice aware of him at all, the American wondered? And yet how
delightfully she was entertaining him by her mere personality, by her
dress, by her movements, by the sound of her sweet, high-pitched
voice and by her conversation with its hither-and-thither of interests,
its casual references to people and things that to her were life and to
him were mere books.

It seemed that there was no-one she had not met and talked with—
half a dozen queens, a king or two, let alone that young man who
would be emperor of the French very soon now—"I give him a year
myself—" and Nelson's Lady Hamilton, and the king and queen of the
Sandwich Islands who died so miserably of measles in the Adelphi when
Lettice was a gay young widow on the edge of re-marriage to the great
William Broome. Yes, he noticed that she spoke casually of both
Napoleons and reserved the epithet 'great' for William Broome. Astonishing woman—glittering, incalculable, magnificent, absurd! Yes, she
was England—England diamond-crowned by the Great Exhibition.

The American snapped his fingers with delight because he had got
her docketed for his diary at last. Yes, now he could describe Lady
Lettice. She was all England heading for London : all roads running to
Hyde Park. She was Hyde Park with its trampled grass and its secluded
glades, its formal flower beds, its carpet of spring daisies, its sheep,
its elegant idlers strolling towards the great glass palace to which
all the world hurried, marvel of the age, centre of the universe,

a Victorian greenhouse enshrining two noble elms and the Kohinoor.

The romantic American enlarged his idea as he drank champagne and listened to Lettice. He saw for a moment the curve of the world that was England, blood-stained and buttercup-stained : its earth invaded by dungeons, wine cellars, mines and the eternal plough : its surface a recurring loveliness, white for winter, yellow for spring, green for summer, orange-tawny for autumn—a spread Royal Standard of the English year with cities like smuts upon its pure and ardent weave. Yes, cities like smuts ! Then he put his glass to his mind's eye, did this romantic American, and saw each smut enlarged : saw England again, but now translated into terms of towns, serene country towns, sleepy religious towns, stinking factory towns, towns ancient as evil, raucous as youth : towns quaint or horrible or serene. Then he twiddled the lens in his glass and lo, all these soot-flecked cities ran together into one blur, one blot that was London, the London of his brief three days' acquaintance—a mad city, fast asleep, but restless with dreams. And all the dreams streamed down the roads behind the dumpy little queen-dream in her carriage, as she hurried to open the Great Exhibition.

For this absurd, transparent piece of trumpery was the newest ideal of incalculable England, so gleefully exchanging art for commerce, nature for artiness, love for philanthropy, stability for speed, humour for zeal, and so solemnly boasting of the bargain. There it stood, the Crystal Palace, the Great Exhibition, and the whole glittering piece of nonsense would be carted away in a few months to make room for—what ? What memorial would they erect to immortalise this particular whim of the strange woman England, who was so full of whims ? One of them had been the Tower, another the Eleanor Crosses : and the latest was the carefully curved roof of the Great Exhibition, curved to protect the lives of the elms which happened to grow where England wanted her whim built. So England saved her elms and had her whim as well, and beckoned in the universe to see the result.

Oh, transparent England, determined since the beginning of time to eat her cake and have it ! Was not England transparent, transparent as the great lady sitting beside him ? She did not care two pins about him, probably had never grasped his name. She had been so enchanting to him that he was half in love with her, all because, it was beginning to dawn upon him, she had a son in America and wanted to hear her son's name mentioned, but would not mention his name first. And he would have never guessed that she had any interests in the matter if he had not been studying her face with such fascinated attention for the last half hour. Thus he had begun to learn its laws, and could be made aware by her sudden stillness of pose, by the sudden slowing of her feminine output, that something in him was interesting her at last. The champagning cascade of bright looks, amusing speech, soft enquiries and quick detaining glances, had been no more than the glitter of the sun on the glass walls of the Crystal Palace. The Palace scintillated indifferently for all beholders and dazzled their eyes; but now, he thought, pleased with the conceit, he, a beholder, had walked up to the Palace wall itself and was looking through one of the glass panes into the marvellous interior.

'A letter to you that your brother Russel gave me,' was the phrase that transformed her. He had addressed her son, and her son hesitating, had turned to her: and she had no longer been able to restrain herself from active betrayal of interest.

The son had said then—

"You know, don't you, Mama, that our friend here was sent to me by Russel?"

"You know my son, sir?"

"I have that privilege, ma'am!"

"Ah! And what does America think of my son?"

"Well, ma'am, I'd say he has made a hit with us. His father was very well known in the States, ma'am, and we don't forget our friends. Russel—well, Russel does pretty well what he likes with a New York audience. And he's popular on the road, too. Yes, he does what he likes."

"And plays what he likes," put in Harry, "from what he writes me."

"But Shakespeare mainly, though he likes change, Russel does. We are close acquaintance, ma'am. I advise him when he will listen, which isn't often. I say, 'Stick to your line!' But Russel, he likes change. He's all for this scheme of a season here in London—"

"Ah!"

"That's why I'm over, making preliminary enquiries. I'm his business brain, as you may say. Yes, ma'am, at this moment, speaking officially, I am your son Russel Broome. And I'll say I've been gratified at my reception. There's been great curiosity expressed in various quarters, and I'm hoping to take back several advantageous offers."

"Harry, do you hear this?" Lettice was moved. "What step have you taken?"

"None at all, Mama, without consulting you. But of course Russel has written to me privately of his wish to play in one of our theatres."

"Naturally! Where else could he play without looking foolish— making us all look foolish?"

"Ah, Mama, but these wild schemes mean capital." Harry nodded blandly to the American. "Isn't that so, sir? But it would be pleasant to have my brother with us, of course."

"It is no affair of mine, of course—" Lettice had recovered her light serenity—"I do not pretend to understand business. I never have. But I cannot imagine—" she spoke slowly, her eyes speaking to her son—"I cannot see that it would be difficult to procure capital for any sound venture. But you are quite right, Maud, my dear, it is time that we leave them to their cigars. I will say goodbye now, sir! Harry is not likely to let you go early and I have an appointment. Yes, Maud, I am taking Charles and his wife to the Exhibition and I am to call for them at Brown's Hotel at four and we have sat so long talking—— But Harry must bring you to dinner with me, sir. Harry, arrange it! Was that four striking, Maud? I am lost. Sir—my son—!" For all her smiling haste Lettice's gesture of farewell was elaborate. Then she was gone, sweeping out her daughter-in-law in a superb swirl of silk and lace.

The two men sat down again, intimately, nearer to each other, the American agonised by the desire to comment, and Harry amused to watch the struggle between good manners and vivacity.

"Well, sir!" said his guest at last—"Curtain's down! Let's go into the office!"

Harry, who looked extremely tired, offered a cigar.

CHAPTER 18

EDUCATION OF A MARRIED COUPLE

BUT though he was tired Harry was a satisfied man and brother when he returned to his Maud: and he had news for her. The American had succumbed: they had agreed over terms: there was no doubt that in a year's time Russel would be over in England playing the lead. Yes, that was the delightful idea—Russel was to play lead in Robin's *Clever Kate*.

"It completely fulfills my ambition, Maud! Think of it—a Broome theatre, under my management, Robin's play, and Russel plays the lead! Do you see what it will do for Robin?—how it will revitalise him? Robin less than any man I know lives by bread. If we keep him with us, Maud, it will be by tempting him with every word that proceedeth—"

"Don't, Harry!" said Maud uncomfortably.

"Don't you, then, be starched! You know well enough what I mean. We must pin down his soul as you pin down a butterfly's wings, with the finest needles. Coarse reality, you see, is no more than a great four-sided kitchen skewer stuck through his body, smashing, obliterating. Life has mangled Robin. He's nearly gone as it is. If we are to keep him a little longer we can only do it by pinning down his spirit. How to do that now? Why, by putting on his plays. For, don't you understand, Maud, to see your own conceived world created upon the stage, real as the kitchen skewer, that's the playwright's seventh day. That's to be God. That's what we all want—the power and the glory. But why should Robin flit to heaven when he can be a god here on earth? A little god, I daresay, but still saying to his world—'You're good!' Well, you see, I can do this for Robin. D'you see what it means for me to do this for Robin? I've always envied him so. What I would give to have his beauty, to have a face like his, to have eyes like his! But it has not been a hateful envy; and to renew that beauty, to make that face light up, to make those eyes sparkle again, would make me—peaceful-minded. He was a wonderful creature, Maud, once. You see, Robin has a creative quality that I have not, and I delight in it. It's a refreshment to me. Why, Robin—sometimes I think he is the half of my spirit as you are the half of my soul. Yes, I love my brother. And I tell you,

Maud, Stephen shall be like our own son, shan't he, if—when—anything happens to Robin. And you see, Maud, to get Russel home, that's a triumph too. Robin feels to Russel, I think, much as I do to Robin. You'll like my brother Russel. He's solid and strong. He's good and kind. He has not so much humour as Robin, but he's dependable. Oh, how I like Russel! But with Robin it is more than liking. Robin worships him. At least he used to, till that woman spoilt everything for Robin. You see, Robin thinks nothing of himself. He hates his own frailty: he doesn't see his own charm. He would like to be like Russel. And now Russel's coming home to play in Robin's play and I've managed it all for both of them. Oh, Maud, I am so happy!"

She smiled at him. Nevertheless she said her say—

"What about your mother?"

And she said it with a look of amusement which the over-tired Harry disliked and resented. In fact, the more he thought of it, the more he took in the varied implications of that look, the more he resented its mockery. From Maud, of all people in the world, and of the Broomes! Monstrous!

And Maud, of course, knew quite well that it was monstrous, that though she meant no harm, Harry was hyper-sensitive about his mother. But she also was tired, for late nights never suited her. She endured them graciously; for, as Lettice had said to her—"You have married the theatre, my dear. If you cannot be ready to have supper with Harry when he comes home tired after his day's work just because his day ends at midnight, why then, as I see it, you're no wife at all. Better have stayed in Ireland where nobody, I hear, does any work. Sleepy? Perform your slumbers in the day-time. You've got most of the day to yourself. Gracious me, child, adapt yourself!"

Maud, who had no intention of doing anything else, who adored adapting herself to Harry, said that she would try.

But though she tried she was always an unusual Maud at night. It was the result of fatigue when she had been at the theatre with him, and the absorbed enchanted expectation of his speedy return when she had stayed at home. And in that first summer of unaccustomed marriage the flickering late-burning candles were for ever reminding her of June nights in her scarce regretted home, when the Aurora lights flickered round the horizon like candle-flames leaping from their hidden wicks. Sleepy Maud was much more Irish at night than by day. She woke up at English midnight as a cat wakes, into a new creature. When she greeted her Harry returning so late from that Lilith the theatre, her

Eve's eyes shone round and inscrutable and gay. She would be in a
mood to chase her own shadow. There would be electricity in her hair
as she brushed it out at night: it would rise and lie clinging along
Harry's fingers as he played with it. Yes, Maud could get Harry
through his supper, as Lettice phrased it, even better than his mother
could. Lettice, occasionally present, owned that. And who was better
acquainted than Lettice with the routine of getting a man through his
supper? Who could better appreciate the technique—"A man too
tired to eat when he comes home will drink too much, and where's his
genius and his digestion then? But if you can soothe him into enjoying
his food and sparkle him into forgetting his wine, why then you know
your business as a wife, my dear!"

But when Maud was just a fraction too tired: when there was just a
spark too much of electricity in her hair or thunder in the sky, then
Maud failed in her business as a wife, and could say, as she said then,
meaning no harm and yet with a dangerous intonation—"What about
your mother?" You see what it did to Harry. It underlined the
complete understanding of the luncheon party. It rammed home the
fact that Maud knew how to manage Lettice just as well as Harry did.
Now though Harry would be the first to own that his mother needed
managing, and although it was a perpetual delight to him to display his
virtuosity in managing her—it was his daily exercise that kept him fit
and in training for managing the rest of the world—still it was monstrous that slow, beautiful, sleepy Maud should take it for granted.
Tactless—Maud must not be tactless! He could not allow her to be
unaware that she, even she, could occasionally be tactless. She ought to
know that you can say a thing to a man one day that you can't say on
another. Tactless, dear Maud—but she must be taught!

So he said—"What about my mother?" unsmiling.

Maud beamed.

"Why, Harry, if Russel comes home in such triumph, he won't need
to be forgiven."

Said Harry, icily—

"I don't follow you."

She bubbled along happily—

"You ought to know your mother by now!"

He flared.

"I do know my mother by now, quite well. I know her so well that I
should never dream of discussing her flippantly."

She flushed. There was a long pause. Then she said in a low voice and the sparkle had gone out of her—

"This is unfair."

He lifted his eyebrows, politely, but, making no other answer, went on with his supper.

She said again, in some distress—

"You've discussed her with me by implication, by manner, over and over again. And now, all of a sudden—I think you're unfair."

He thought so too, now that the flash of irritation was over; but still she should not have taken the lead. If she had trodden on his toes, though he had put them out to be trodden on, still she should be prepared for the indignity of a stumble. Besides, he enjoyed hitting out at something when he was tired. So he said, smiling at her—

"Dear Maud, are you trying to get up a scene with me? Honestly, I'm too tired for one. Besides, there's no need, so long as we leave my mother's failings alone."

He looked up at her, his odd, insolent smile suddenly softening into boyishness, impishness. It had been fun, the little battle, and he felt better. How pleasant it was to hit out at somebody who loved you! How it refreshed you! Darling Maud!

"Darling Maud!" said Harry aloud, smiling up at her.

She stood a moment looking down on him: then she shook her head slowly, thoughtfully.

"Good-night, Harry!" said Maud, and walked out of the room.

Well, that was that. She was not quite pleased with him evidently. He was not entirely pleased with himself. However, he knew how to manage her. He would put it right when he went upstairs. He lit a cigar and leant back in his chair, thinking to himself that he did enjoy being married. There were a thousand reasons why he liked being married, but most of all he liked having someone, an equal, to play with. For Maud was practically an equal, though of course he was the stronger and quicker and adroiter of the two. It was so delightful to have to play with every ounce of yourself in order to win, and yet to know that, of course, you always would just win. If only by a point you would still win. And Maud was generally an admirable loser. He had played rather roughly just now, and he knew it. To go and tell her that he was sorry would relieve his conscience, would put an end to this strange feeling of strain between them, and would be a new and most adroit way of winning the game.

Dear Maud! He would go upstairs soon: no, he would go upstairs at once.

He went upstairs at once, turned the handle of the bedroom door rather softly, entered quietly, and stood, questioning, half smiling, attractive, in the doorway.

"Maud?"

There was no answer. There was no Maud. The room, lit by one candle (and that needed snuffing) showed Maud's beautiful order. Her decorative arrangement of her personal belongings enhanced the noble crimsons of the bed-hangings, ivoried the perfectly smooth sheets and unpressed pillows of the broad Victorian bed. But there was no Maud to be seen.

"Maud!" said Harry sharply: and thought, 'It is an hour since she went upstairs. She ought to have finished her undressings by now.' He turned to the dressing-room, tapped, got no answer, turned the handle. The door did not open. The door was locked. He rapped loudly and said softly—"Maud?"

No answer. But he heard the couch in the dressing-room creak. Then followed faint movements. The line of light under the door blinked out and there was a faint tinkle as if a hand had touched a glass candle-shield, and then again a stir as if a sleeper were settling afresh, very comfortably, upon pillows. But there was no answer.

"Maud!" cried Harry, wrathfully, and hurt his knuckles against the door.

No answer. The candle-wick on the dressing-table was streaming up an intolerable thread of ill-smelling smoke. Angrily he turned upon it. Was this housewifely, to leave a candle burning so that the bedroom became impossible, besides the danger of fire? He disliked a guttering candle. He caught up the elegant snuffer and snuffed savagely, so savagely that he put the candle out. Now where were the lucifers? He could not find the lucifers anywhere and he had to fetch them at last from the deserted dining-room. He was irritated, morally and physically out of breath, by the time he got into bed, but he was careful to undress quietly. Maud should never say that coming to bed late he had been so inconsiderate as to move about the room noisily and disturb her. So he lay quiet, rehearsing what he should say in the morning, but with a lump in his throat. He thought he should never quite forgive Maud, or forget either. Oh—he was very angry indeed!

He did not sleep well, but he did doze off as the birds began to sing. When he opened his eyes again, dear Maud, as fresh as an apple-blossom in her white muslin wrapper, was brushing out her long hair before the looking-glass.

"Maud!" said Harry, sitting up in bed.

She turned, threw him a charmed and charming look. They were extremely pleased to see each other. Each thought that there was no advantage in discussing what had happened last night and neither did discuss it; but Harry, at any rate, had made up his mind that such a thing should not happen again. So had Maud.

It was a pity that, though their resolution was mutual, they were not resolved about precisely the same article of conduct. Harry had resolved that never again should his wife lock him out of his own dressing-room. Maud had resolved that never again should her husband be rude to her at her own supper table. Therefore, they continued to enjoy each other's society, to find an added zest in each other's society just because the little matter had never been thrashed out between them. But neither of them was in complete possession of the other's feelings, therefore the real problem remained unsolved. Who should win the game? Harry was shocked that Maud, though a woman, should rate the winning of a game higher than the pleasure of playing it. Maud, much simpler, did not see why Harry should be able to make her so completely miserable whenever he felt like it, and resolved that he should learn that it was not pleasant to be made unhappy by anyone you loved. So there remained a soreness in the heart of each, yet each thought the other was much more attractive now than in the incredibly remote days of their engagement, and admired how marriage could improve a human being.

'She's twice the woman she was,' thought Harry. 'Dear Maud! And that's my doing.'

'When I've finished with Harry there will not be a man in England to hold a candle to him,' thought Maud.

Meanwhile the theatre found its manager a little difficult, a little fretted; but brisk. He got twice the work out of his company that he had ever done before, and gave them less thanks. "Not at all sure that Harry Broome is improved by marriage," was the verdict of the dressing-rooms: and so Maud, who came to the theatre on occasions with her husband, was coolly received by the principalities and powers. They were elaborately courteous to her. But it was known that Harry did not wish his wife to embark on intimacies, and the star dressing-rooms made it quite clear that Harry need have no fear on that score.

But the lesser folk liked her. Harry, bringing Maud down to watch a rehearsal and glancing up occasionally to the dust-sheeted box in which he had installed her, would sometimes see with a frown and a laugh that Maud was too busily occupied in chatting with a cleaner or a stage hand to have any eye or ear for the star of the moment, momentarily improving under Harry's instructions. And when she drove home with him afterwards he would learn the name of that cleaner and the number of her children. For he always listened to her gossip, and when Maud wanted money he put his hand in his pocket, and when she explained to him indignantly that the little top attic where the supers dressed had a choked ventilator or a window stopped with brown paper or a floor that had not been scrubbed for months, he was ready to promise to reform.

For he liked her philanthropies: and though he had so sternly resolved that his wife should be protected from knowledge of the sordider side of his profession, he could not resist indulging her in her good deeds, and being rather proud of them. Maud, thought Harry, was a good housekeeper—even his mother admitted that. If Maud wanted to housekeep in the theatre as well as at home it did no-one any harm, and he liked knowing that she was within call. He liked eating a meal with her after a tiring rehearsal and driving home with her after a matinée, even if it meant an almost immediate return for the evening show: and if Maud's crinolines were being ruined by the dirt and disorder, it was easy enough to prevent that by engaging new cleaners and paying the old ones better. If she wanted passages repainted, if she was right about the sanitation, well, it would only improve the property to put things right.

So he put things right and naturally reaped the credit, though he was willing enough for her to have it.

He liked her to be popular with his stage hands and the hangers-on. It was a relief to him to turn over to her the problem of the wardrobe and the wardrobe workers. If she chose to organise regular meals for the staff, why shouldn't she, so long as her activities did not upset the larger discipline? Her popularity increased, and he was proud of her. But it only made him more firmly resolved that in his own house he would be master. Almost he hoped that Maud would soon give him occasion to emphasise this resolve to her. Almost it seemed to him, sometimes, that Maud was soft and yielding, and meekly stupid and intelligently repentant, on purpose. This, he felt, was mean. How could you prove that you were master in your own house if you were given no rebellion to quell? There were times when he eyed his Maud with real suspicion. There came one Sunday afternoon at his mother's when he told himself, as he watched Maud being meek with Lettice, that, really, gentleness could be cloying. How admirably his mother rattled! How startlingly she attacked! How imminent was danger! You walked with her down so smooth a path and tripped on the smallest stone and at once you sat down on a nettle-bed, and she did not help you up. But only once had Maud ever pushed him into a nettle-bed, and then she had been almost too ready to help him up. Now his mother . . . ! Sitting over their dinner that Sunday evening after such a pleasant afternoon at the Park Lane house, he found himself once more irrevocably, fascinatingly, but dangerously involved with his wife in a discussion of his mother.

"You don't know how glad I am, Maud," Harry had begun very affectionately and graciously, "that you and my mother get on so well. I always hoped you would; but frankly, knowing Mama, I wasn't altogether sanguine. But you have a way with her. It is amusing to see how she likes your way with her. By the way, what were you talking about all the afternoon? I thought you'd never come in." And, as he asked, Harry was reminded that he had a faint grievance. Continuing, he voiced it—"Yes, Robin said so too. There we both sat, waiting for our tea. We never knew it was tea-time. We weren't called down and when we came—neither of you there! It's unheard of for Mama to be late for tea. What did you do to her?"

Maud smiled at him, but had not anything particular to say, it appeared, in answer.

"No, but as a mere matter of curiosity," persisted Harry, "what were you talking about? I watched you as you came in from the arbour. You know, Maud, I've never seen Mama give any woman the affection she gives you. And she dislikes being kissed."

"She kissed me," said Maud flushing.

"I know, I saw it. Amazing! But, Maud, be a little careful. Mama is capricious."

"You are all capricious," said Maud.

"Yes, but you like it in us, don't you?" said he.

"Yes," said Maud.

"Yes, you like us! That is it. We are all of us quite helpless against the honesty of your liking. Lionel, Robin, Mama—they all accept you for your wisdom in liking them so much. As for me—but then I adore you!"

"You mean that you adore adoring me," said Maud placidly.

He looked at her.

"You've picked that up from me, that sort of cleverish speech," said he.

"I'm a good learner," said his wife.

"It's not true, you know," said he.

"Half true," said she.

"No."

"Yes. But I don't mind. I like you as you are, all of you. I wouldn't alter you."

"Don't lie, my darling! You know you try to improve upon me. You're much wiser with Mama."

Said Maud slowly, but with a gleaming eye; for it was true—she had picked up a good many of her husband's little ways—

"You didn't think I appreciated your mother three months ago, did you?"

Harry produced a blank look, and gave his head that vague characteristic shake that disclaimed all knowledge of the subject under discussion, knowledge even that anything was about to be discussed.

Maud chuckled.

"Don't look so bland," said she. "I did stumble somehow in discussing your mother, and you did snub me, and it hurt me very much."

"Dear Maud! It's all over and forgotten."

"Yes, of course, dearest Harry! That's why we can speak of it. But now that it's quite over and forgotten and a thing to laugh at, I would like to know how it was, why it was, that I vexed you. I never intended to. You must have realised that."

"Of course," said he affectionately.

"Well then, what did I say, and why were you so remote with me?"

"I was not."

"Oh, but you were. You—removed yourself, in spirit: you punished me—for what? What did I say?"

"Nothing. I was in a mood."

"Nevertheless, you may as well tell me what I said."

"Oh, leave it, Maud!"

"No. I want to get rid of it. It's a thorn that still rankles. What did I say? Why did you make me feel that I'd taken a liberty?"

"You had," said he suddenly, the former sensation once more obscuring his common sense.

Maud flushed in turn.

"I? But I'm your wife. Can we take liberties with each other? Is it possible? It ought not to be possible. But if you say that I can and did, then of course I have formally to express regret."

Now what had come over the placid Maud? Maud with flushed cheeks and eyes sparkling, Maud on the edge of temper and tears, was a new incarnation. Harry leant forward, picked up her white, well-shaped hand, and turned it over.

"What's the matter?" said she.

"I was looking for claws," said he. "You mustn't have claws out with me."

She pulled her hand away across the polished table; for the table was between them, and they faced each other as grimly as opponents at a business meeting.

"You won't discuss this thing because you know that you were in the wrong," she attacked him. "You would always rather smooth over things and pretend that they're not there, and pretend to forget them. You would smooth over an injury for years, or what you fancied was an injury, a non-existent injury: and then, when one is lulled into security, then, I know, you would choose your time to spring and tear me. You talk of cat's claws. It's you who have cat habits. But I am not a plaything that you have caught and carried home. I won't be gentled and then struck down."

So now Harry had his scene, all he could wish to cope with, and he didn't like it at all. She was entirely unreasonable, of course, and that should have made it easier for him to retain his own calm. To a certain extent he succeeded. The more angry poor Maud grew, the calmer was he, the sweeter his voice, the colder his look, the more elaborate his restraint. But within himself he, too, was losing his temper, fully and finally.

"Oh, well, we needn't discuss it any more," said Maud, veering suddenly from anger to weakness. "I was a fool to begin. I tried—I wanted something of you—but it has all gone wrong. I'm not saying what I mean and you say that I have taken liberties."

She put out that withdrawn hand again in her favourite gesture, palm upwards, half appeal, half a disowning of responsibility. But he would not look at her hand. He saw that the time had come to teach Maud her lesson.

"I don't think any of this is at all necessary," said he coldly. "But if you insist on discussion, why then, my point of view is this. Close as we are to each other, I can say things to you about my own people, about Mama that is, with perfect propriety. But when you say the same sort of things to me—no! That jars. It may be foolish of me—it may be hyper-sensitive—and I am perfectly ready to admit that I am unreasonable; but when you say things to me about Mama, I resent it, even though I have said precisely the same sort of things to you. I know what Mama is, I know her weaknesses. I know that you know them. But when you, even you, criticise Mama to me I feel it's a liberty."

"I will not take any more liberties," said Maud.

"And another thing," went on Harry, a little heightened by success. "If it comes to liberties (your phrase, Maud, not mine!) I may as well tell you that I resent being made to look a fool."

"I don't know what you mean," said Maud.

"Of course you know what I mean," said Harry hardly.

"Well, what do you mean?" said Maud.

"I mean—" said Harry, and now he, too, was coming to the core of his grievance—"that to lock yourself into a room, to lock me out of my own dressing-room—"

Suddenly Maud began to laugh. There may have been a touch of hysteria in her laughter, but Harry did not notice that, though his ear caught the completeness of her amusement very correctly.

"Oh, but it was funny, that night, Harry!" said Maud. "I could hear your expression, through the wall. It was extremely funny to listen to." And she laughed again, because it eased the tension for her and she was extremely frightened and unhappy at the vastness of the scene in which, all without intending it, she was playing so startling a part. She laughed to reassure herself and to make it clear to herself that it was only a little scene and that it was not going to shatter her entire relations with Harry for ever after.

But of course she should not have laughed: as Harry, beaming upon her politely, made clear.

"I'm so glad it amused you, Maud, because I'm afraid you won't have that sort of amusement often. That sort of joke happens once."

"If I want to be by myself, Harry, I shall be by myself," said his wife sharply.

"Oh no!" said Harry. And then, as the servant came in with the coffee, he rose from his seat. "Excuse me, won't you?" said Harry to Maud.

She nodded graciously. She was not alone two minutes; but two minutes was long enough to make her wonder why the wretched business had happened, to make her wonder at her own nerves, her unaccustomed sensibilities, her almost uncontrollable desire to quarrel with Harry, for whom, at that moment, she was nevertheless feeling an affection so intense, so overmastering, that to break into irritabilities seemed to be the only way in which she could preserve her own dignity. She longed for him, when he came back into the room, to come up to her and kiss her and tell her that she was important to him. She thought with horror that, on the contrary, it might be she herself who would, in spite of her own will, be the one to make love, and that he would probably snub her. She thought that if he did that, life, all the rest of her life, would be a daily and nightly remembering of the snub, that for ever after she would feel like one of those women in Uncle Lionel's picture, stifled in a sack, muffled and shamed. She put her hand to her head, saying—

"I must control myself better. I am behaving very foolishly. What is the matter with me?"

Then she began to pour out the coffee with a hand that shook.

But Harry, re-entering with a certain unexplained buoyancy, saw her sitting cool and gracious as Demeter, and thought with an instant fall back into the former pit of anger—

'How impervious she is! She doesn't even know that there's been a scene. She's crude, that's what it is—she's crude. Well, I will break this stupid obstinacy of hers if it takes me a year.'

And he went back to the table, and she gave him coffee, and, as though mutually ignoring the fact that there had been any difficulty between them, they began to discuss agreeably the happenings of the day. Thus the wise room which had witnessed so many domesticities, witnessed now the singular spectacle of host entertaining hostess, of hostess responding to host. At the end of the hour they were, as far as manners went, on perfectly good terms again: and when Maud went to bed she presented her cheek graciously, and gracefully Harry kissed it.

"I'm very tired. I think I'll go up early," said Maud, not looking at Harry.

"I shan't be very long," said Harry, looking at Maud as he held open the door for her. Then she did look up and nodded. He displayed in return an effect of lips and teeth. She went on. He watched her swim across the black and white chessboard of the entrance-hall and disappear into the darkness of the upper staircase. Then he went back to the table, poured himself a glass of wine and drank it. Then, fetching himself a book, he settled down into the chair before the fire. It should have been a relaxed and comfortable pause; but it is a fact that Harry did not relax. He read; but he read with a certain tenseness. The clock ticked away half an hour.

He put down his book. Ten o'clock! Absurdly early, but he thought he would go upstairs, nevertheless. He rose and poured himself another drink. As he did so there came a rush of skirts in the hall and the door was flung open and closed again with a certain violence as his wife came in and up to him. She was quite composed, but her eyes blazed with anger and she held out her hand to him with a movement that, though it turned palm upwards in its furious appeal, was definitely one of command.

"Harry!"

"Yes, Maud?"

"Please give me the key of my dressing-room!"

They looked at each other for a long moment. He was taller than she and she had to look up to him.

"No," said Harry softly, at last: and smiled at her happily.

"You will please give me the key of my dressing-room!" she repeated, as if he had not spoken.

"No," said Harry, still smiling, and thrusting out his chin. "Oh, no!"

"At once!" said Maud, on a high note.

"No!" said Harry brightly. His eyes were bold, dark, opaque as pebbles. He looked ugly, and he looked old. She was in an agony of pain at his air of hard and satisfied alienation; but she was also in an agony of anger. If he said it again—

"Oh, no!" said Harry again.

At that, so exactly repeating her former gesture that he wondered for an instant if he were not dreaming their former quarrel, she turned from him and went quietly out of the room.

And now, of course, having achieved and completed his victory over his wife, Harry began to feel tenderly towards her. He was wildly excited and half ashamed of himself, perfectly ready for the next stage of the quarrel and the latest development of their relationship, but anxious, too, to be magnanimous now that Maud knew at last what it felt like to be made to look a fool. It was necessary that she should learn that lesson, but now that she had learned it he would make things easy for her.

So, though he would have liked to follow her upstairs, he deliberately idled away a couple of hours in order to give her time to become placable: or rather, for he was incapable of wasting time, he spent it in virtuous concentration, in preparing a prompt copy of Robin's latest play. He enjoyed scissors and paste, and red ink and black ink, and ruled margins and the smell of foolscap. He was as relaxed and happy as a small boy over a stamp album till midnight struck. Then he went, rather slowly, just a little uncertain of the next step, upstairs to his room. She was not in the bedroom and the dressing-room door was shut.

For an instant he hesitated outside it, then, with a gleam, turned away. Maud, of course, expected him to come in. She would be mistaken. He had won on principle: now she should learn how unnecessary it had been to fight. He would say to her in the morning— "My dear Maud, perhaps now you realise—" And, lying in bed by himself and staring at the moon through the unblinded window, his mind flowed off into a series of admirable remarks. He made up scene after scene, rehearsed, acted, scrapped each in turn.

Dear, silly Maud—ridiculously banishing herself: he didn't suppose she was feeling very happy.

He would have liked to go in to her quietly, without lighting a candle, and slip his arm under her shoulder and say—"Darling, what fools we've been!" He half thought he would: he didn't believe he should sleep well until he had.

The moon slid behind a tree and slipped smoothly downwards from gap to gap in the branches, leaving a snail's track of silver on his eyeballs. Somewhere near the moon a clock struck three. He got up and slipped on his dressing-gown, and strolled to the window. A bird was stirring in the eaves above him. The morning poured in and blew about him. Suddenly he realised how cold and quiet was the night and the room.

"Maud?" said Harry sharply, loudly.

If she had been awake she would have heard him. Then, how cruel, how resentful, not to answer! If she was asleep, then how cruel, how insensitive to be so little moved by all that had passed between them!

He must go at once to see if she were awake or asleep, and so know for good and all what sort of woman he had married.

He turned to the dressing-table and lit a candle, and taking it in his hand, opened the door of debate and, slipping in, held the candle high above his head, to let the light fall on the narrow couch that fitted into the alcove behind it.

"My darling—I think we've been rather foolish—" he began, and stopped abruptly.

Maud was not there.

Here was a situation for a husband and a lover! Maud was not there. The bed had not been slept in: there was no sign of folded clothes on the chair. Maud was not there. He went solemnly through the farce of flinging open the cupboards: and then he perceived that Maud's new sealskin coat was not there either. He could not fail to observe its absence for he had just given it to her and it had its place of honour.

So now what do we do? Harry didn't know. He was extremely upset: he was very angry: he was just a little frightened: he was entirely taken aback. But his principal sensations were helpless irritation at having been diddled, and real dismay, dismay so strong, so panicky, that it wiped out at last the frantic protests of his injured vanity. This was serious: this went beyond a joke: this was the sort of thing that shouldn't be allowed to happen. And it had happened, and what on earth was he to do next? And where, in the name of folly, had Maud gone?

He was a calm and sensible person, nevertheless there were a few panicking moments when Harry saw Maud, flowery as Ophelia, in the Regent's Park canal. And yet—would she have put on her sealskin coat if—? He had better go out, though. She was probably in the garden, through which, let us not remember, ran the canal. And, though he never admitted it even to her, the morning stars knew that a hatless and frantic Harry did make his way down the garden to the canal side, and did run like a hunted man up and down the neat banks and across the little bridge and down the other side and back again. But that was a folly of the night and of a conscience which, though it still could not see what else Harry could have done, was annoyed with Harry. Harry, returning at last exhausted but relieved to the house, to the staircase, to the abandoned sleeping-quarters, had a cold bath and re-dressed and felt better; but was not very happy. For the night panic did but give way to the more common-place panics of plain, sane morning. This was a serious business, and Maud had got to be found. Well—where was she? If she had indeed taken the whole business so intensely seriously it was just possible that she might have bolted to Ireland and Rosina.

But that was impossible: Maud would have too much pride and sense. What—when she had led dear, chirping Aunt Rosina by the nose, managed her, dressed her, and shipped her to Ireland to cherish a deserted grandfather, would she to such a one admit defeat? Maud was too clever for that.

For Harry was now in a mood to admire Maud and to attribute to her a Broomeish ingenuity of which she was quite incapable; for thus did a Broome right himself in his own estimation. If an opponent got the better of him, and especially a woman opponent, how full of wit, cunning, charm and technique must that opponent be! Love your enemies, after all, is one of the commandments. A Broome always has a fighting weakness for his triumphant enemy. And Maud, the enemy, was certainly triumphant.

Whither had she vanished? A public lodging was unthinkable. Could she have gone to the theatre? Ridiculous idea! A horrible idea, too, to think of a woman driving alone in the London streets at night. Or had she walked?

For he was now possessed by the sober anxiety of a Victorian husband and protector. Maud alone in the streets, walking! This was awful! And couldn't she realise the awful impropriety of the position in which she had put him? What would the servants say? To desert her house, to desert her husband and her home, on a whim, on an irritation —oh, it was monstrous! Desertion—that was what it was—a monstrous desertion! And women had been divorced for just such desertion of their husbands and their homes.

And for an instant Harry toyed magnificently with the idea of divorcing Maud. But he saw her in the witness-box, meeting his eye, and felt that this new Maud might have something to say. She was capable of—Lord, of what was Maud not capable if she was capable of running away from home? And it was past seven and he was exhausted, and to ring for an early breakfast, would it not expedite the inevitable gossip? Where was breakfast? Where was Maud? That was the worst of being married, you had nobody to consult. For loyalty forbade you to discuss your wife with your mother. To begin with, it wasn't dignified, and secondly Maud would never forgive him, and thirdly if once his mother got her knife into Maud she would twist it horribly. *Coup de cornet*—first to the left, then to the right. If their intimacy survived the wound, still his mother could be relied upon to fix her eyes upon the scar whenever the mood took her. No, he couldn't give away Maud to his mother; but there was no reason why he should not go and see his mother. He would be able to think more soberly when he had had some breakfast; because, of course, Maud must be somewhere. Where *was* Maud?

He would not rouse his coachman, but went out to the stables where his mare was already saddled for his morning ride and got away into the main road. Once out of sight he galloped. It did him some good to ride the beast tired. The milk cans were still enlivening the crisp morning as he jumped down at the gates of the Park Lane house, and, handing the reins to the loafer who patrolled as if by right the twenty yards of pavement that divided the house from the Park, went hurriedly up the steps. It annoyed him to have to ring and he was curt with the maid.

"Go up to her Ladyship's room and ask if I may see her! What? In the breakfast-room already?" Harry was not in the mood for fresh shocks. Maud had run away from him: his mother was down to breakfast at half past seven! What next?

He went hastily into the cool, cavernous room. Its black and white tiled floor, its walls painted with Jacobean trees and flowers, its green furniture, its three windows, each a framed picture of the bright, formal garden beyond, greeted his eye pleasantly. So did the smells of a British breakfast-table. So did his mother, who sat behind her silver and porcelain in the pale pink of a fine-weather mood. Her face showed dark against the bright window behind her. She looked agreeable, yet severe. She was busily de-calyxing the best of a fine pile of early strawberries, but not for her own eating; for the meek butler held a breakfast tray already laden, though not over-laden. A transparent slice of ham on a plate, two pieces of toast in a silver toast-rack, a dab of butter crowned with parsley in its platter, a dish of dark marmalade, a Georgian tea-pot and a Dresden china cup, were set out on a strip of sprigged embroidery. A pink rose in a glass, decorated with a picture of the Great Exhibition, completed a breakfast that the ravenous Harry would have enjoyed.

"Ah, Harry?" said his mother, as she settled the plate of fruit in the place reserved, and dabbled her stained fingers in the finger-bowl beside her. And then—"Maud takes strawberries, doesn't she?"

She gave him a bland look and had the pleasure, as his eye met hers, of seeing her son, for once in his life, taken aback. He did not show it, save by a certain expressionlessness. There was not a pause, but there might have been a pause if Harry had not his face under such excellent control. Only the fractional stiffening, the fractional arrestation of mobility, betrayed him, and they would not have betrayed him to anyone but his mother, as he answered, ready, amiably—

"They're her favourite fruit."

"Take Mrs. Broome's tray up to her," said Lettice to the butler: and then, rising to minister to her son—"What will you have, Harry? Bacon and eggs? Or shall I cut you some ham?"

"Some ham, please," said Harry.

"You had better have bacon and eggs first," said his mother, and placed in front of him that which it was good for him to eat. "Tea or coffee?"

"Coffee, please," said Harry. "No milk."

"Of course you will drink milk in your coffee," said his mother. "If you have been drinking coffee without milk it fully accounts for that yellow look. Poison! Toast?"

Meekly he took toast.

She sat down again and poured herself out a cup of coffee (she herself never took milk) and put it down beside her plate. But she did not drink it. He looked up from his plate and caught her eye. She smiled at him. Slowly, unwillingly, he permitted a smile to appear in return upon his own face.

"Yellow," said his mother agreeably. "And your eyes popping out of your head. If I looked at myself in the glass and saw a countenance like that looking back at me—"

"Hang it, Mother, I'm only rather tired," said Harry irritably.

"Yes, and so is Maud rather tired," said his mother. "And has been crying her eyes out. However, she has slept, for I have seen her this morning already: which is more than you have, I should say. And serves you right! Really Harry, a child of ten would have more tact and patience than you seem to have displayed."

"What has Maud been saying?" began Harry angrily.

"Maud hasn't said anything at all. Don't throw away your napkin. I am peeling you some strawberries. Maud arrived here last night with perhaps the most elaborately unconvincing reason for calling on her husband's mother that I have heard on the lips of any woman. You, it appears, were in the library so absorbed in hard work on Robin's manuscript that she could not even ask you for a restorative when she felt faint. So she walks, mark you, a twenty minutes' walk, at half past nine at night, alone, unaccompanied, to my house: and nearly faints when she gets here. And was proposing to walk back if I hadn't put my foot down. I put her to bed, of course. And I told her that I should let you know where she was and why."

"And why didn't you?" said Harry, angry and humiliated, hating his wife and his mother.

"I didn't because I thought that a little uncertainty would do you good. And I must say, Harry, I am surprised that you did not knock up the house five hours ago. Suppose she had not been here!"

"Good God, Mama," said Harry, "don't tongue-lash me! I only missed her this morning."

"Missed her! Is Maud a glove or a stud?"

"If you must know, Mama, though I don't think it's anybody's affair but ours, I thought she was in another room and I didn't choose to disturb her."

"Separate rooms? This is very modern. And do you usually go to bed without saying good-night to your wife, Harry?"

Harry, wildly angry, turned to the door.

"Mother, I shall go and see Maud now. She will probably be ready to go home."

"She should never have left her home—at this time of all times!" Lettice, too, had risen. She sailed up to her son in a majesty of silk and trailing cap-lappets. There were danger flags in her cheeks and her eyes were bright: and yet Harry could not help realising that she was not half so angry as he. It checked his own exit, this air of weakening in the hand that held the thunder-bolt. Something there was yet behind the scene of which he was not aware. So, though furious, he controlled himself and continued to submit bareheaded to the storm.

"At this time of all times? What do you mean, Mama?"

"What do you mean, Harry, by letting her get into such a hysterical state? Why must you quarrel? For of course you quarrelled. And of course she thinks that she has avoided telling me that you quarrelled. And you, it seems, think that I have no sense either. But I tell you, my son, that you should know better than to pick a quarrel with your wife when she has just found out that she is going to have a baby."

"What!" said Harry: and his weight, as he leant suddenly back against it, clicked the door shut—"What are you saying, Mother?"

"A second grandchild!" said Lettice triumphantly. "Isn't it lovely? I'm so pleased that I don't know what to do."

So that was the radiance behind the storm! And now the storm had ceased as suddenly as it had begun: and Lettice, refreshed and dis-burdened, stood before him, most maternal. "He must be called William, of course," said Lettice.

"Mother, don't talk so quickly," said Harry irritably.

"If you talked a little less yourself and thought a little more of women's feelings," retorted his mother, "Maud would probably have told you last night.   But you pick a quarrel with the poor child—"

"But how was I to know?" said Harry indignantly.   Then his face softened.   "Forgive me, Mama! Where have you put Maud?"

"In your old room," said his mother : and smiling at the closing door, hoped that Maud was properly ashamed of herself. Dear Harry!

Harry, racing up the stairs, came upon Maud fully dressed, rather white, very glad indeed to see him—charmed to see him.   There was no cloud between them.   They had not met for months, and now they had met again.   They were both very happy and extraordinarily anxious to get home.   It struck Harry, with an odd little shock at the change in himself, that he no longer thought of Park Lane as home.   He hurried his wife out of the bedroom as if they had a train to catch : and they did not delay long in farewells to Lettice, who, most thoughtfully, had ordered the carriage.

"But the mare, Mama?"

"John took it home half an hour ago," said Lettice.   "Good-bye, my children!   I shall be round some time this afternoon, Maud.   I am not at all pleased with either of you.   And as for the poor infant, if you are as selfish and inconsiderate parents as you are husband and wife, I am sorry for him.   There is not a chance for him.   Go home at once!"

"Harry—" said Maud in the carriage—"I do appreciate you, don't I? You know I do.   Your mother said I didn't.   She said I was incapable of appreciating you and that I had a vile temper and no tact and didn't deserve to have the bearing of your child.   I mean, Harry—it's all new to me—"

"Darling—if you don't know Mama by now—"

"Yes, I do know.   And you know I like your mother. Indeed, I love her.   And I am not saying a word against her, Harry, but you don't know how brutal she can be."

"She is getting old.   We must make allowances," said Harry.

CHAPTER 19

THE BROOMES ARE TOGETHER AGAIN

THE old year rolled blandly into the new, like an Atlantic breaker heading for a golden shore of success. Harry crested that wave of success and Maud rode, triumphant as a sea-goddess, beside him.

For in that one outburst Maud seemed to accumulate and disperse all the troubles of her pregnancy. She had no more hysterical humours and few physical disabilities. She was one of the women, indeed, whose beauty pregnancy enhanced. Her carriage was magnificent: she bloomed her way into maternity like an orange-tree, white and golden, bearing flowers and fruit at once.

Lettice, who was impatient of weakness and thought the mention of bodily ailments indelicate, beamed approval, could not see enough of Maud and yet contrived to lay all the credit for Maud's successful maternity at Harry's door. Her son knew how to manage his wife. He was not too proud to take his mother's advice.

"Dear Harry! So like his father, and yet in one way, my dear, with far more brains. Look at the way he is managing the theatre. Look at the new interests he has brought into my poor Robin's life! But, Maud, you haven't been to see Robin these three days, and that, I think, is unkind of you. Harry, busy as he is, cannot be expected to run in and out at odd moments; but you, I think, should come when you can. But I have always noticed that healthy people, grossly healthy people, never have much sympathy with the sick. God gave you your health, my dear! It is not your own doing; though I must say I do think that you owe Harry a lot. It is not every husband who would be so gentle, so thoughtful. Even my own William had not Harry's beautiful delicacy. By no means. Harry is wonderful with you, my dear! I don't say it because he is my son; but I have been married twice and I know what I am talking about. And with all your blessings, Maud, I think you might spare a little thought for the less blessed. Robin has asked after you twice."

Maud, smiling happily at her mother-in-law, accepted the invitation to tea and a good gossip in Lettice's room, perfectly understanding the form in which it was cast: and when Lettice had done with her, went upstairs to see Robin. She found Lionel with him.

Lionel was bronzed from a sea-voyage to Brazil; for his daughter Georgina had been at last exported with the rest of her husband's goods to the New World: and all his life Lionel had travelled in the East. How then could he resist a legitimate opportunity to explore the West? He had, indeed, hankered to accompany the emigrants: and would have done so, as he explained to Lettice, but for his affection for Harry, his curiosity to see Maud, and his knowledge that his sister needed a man in the house to help her through the wedding fuss. On the other hand, as Lettice instantly pointed out, it was much more comfortable to visit them later when they were established. Perhaps he had thought of that as well as his sister: at any rate Georgina and her Adamovitz had departed accompanied only by bundles of poor relations and goods: and Lionel, following them two months later, contrived to go to so many out of the way places before he reached Brazil that Georgina was installed, delivered of her first child, and the Adamovitz son-in-law had become a popular figure in Rio society before he overtook them. He stayed long enough to realise that his daughter had become entirely one of her husband's people, to bestow one of his mother's possessions, a valuable and curious ring, upon his granddaughter, to contract a form of malaria peculiar to the district, and to find out, decidedly, that he was getting an old man who could not throw things off as he used to do.

Like his sister, Lionel fiercely hated illness and despised the sick in his heart: and he assured her several times on the first days of his return that she need not be afraid that she would have another invalid on her hands. Nevertheless it was pretty generally understood that 'poor old Lionel Wybird' had brought home a travelling companion who would not be shaken off again. He was not much older than Lettice, but the malaria had aged him prodigiously.

"So that's Uncle Lionel!" said Robin to Harry. "Did you ever see such a change? Shall we come to such changes, Harry? I don't think he'll last long, poor old boy! It's odd to me that people never realise— Oh, Harry, did I tell you? I've got a new idea for the play after the next two are done. New York setting—do you think the public'll stand for a New York setting? What are you looking at me like that for? Are you saying to yourself—'Lazy brute to stay in bed!'? But you know, Harry, I work so much better in bed. And you know, Harry, I'm in a fever of work. I've got ten years of work planned out."

"Well now!" said Harry, not looking at his brother; but Lionel, entering, caught the remark and shook his head unseen by Robin, and his eyes signalled to Harry—'Poor devil! I suppose he doesn't in the least realise——'

Then Robin looked up and saw Uncle Lionel and gave him his looked-for welcome. For Robin, sorry for poor old Uncle Lionel with his notice to quit in his pocket, always made a point of giving him a grand welcome. He had even persuaded Lettice to establish a special arm-chair and a special table for him. And Uncle Lionel, sorry for that poor, cheated, dying devil Robin, spent so much of his time in Robin's company that they began to be restless apart. Stephen was in his nursery, Lettice much occupied with them all; but Lionel and Robin sat together day after day, each with his travelling companion at his elbow.

Maud found them both lively and voluble over the latest letters from America, and she had not been with them an hour when Harry walked in to confirm the news that Russel had sent over his signature, and that, God willing, he would open in *Clever Kate* next autumn.

"Autumn?" said Maud sharply, and made a calculation: and then, with a sigh of relief—"Autumn will be lovely. I shall be able to come to all the rehearsals."

"Where will Russel stay?" asked Lionel suddenly in his Tithonus voice. He was but little altered in appearance: a little dryer, a little more bent; but the fever had affected his throat.

"Mama had a letter from Russel this morning," said Harry, twinkling at his uncle.

"You don't say so?"

"I do. And I understand the partition in the night-nursery is to be taken down and the whole room is being re-decorated."

"Where are they moving Stephen?" said Robin jealously.

"Your mother says," said Maud, "that Stephen is quite old enough to sleep by himself, and that it is not at all desirable that he should be tied to his nurse's apron-strings. He is to have the dressing-room next to her so that she can have him under her eye. Where she's putting the nurse I'm sure I don't know. All I know is that we've been choosing wallpaper for the night-nursery-that-was this last hour."

"Did she say she'd heard from Russel?" whispered Lionel.

"Not she," said Maud, smiling at him. They shared the joke.

Meanwhile Harry was explaining to Robin that he had completed the provisional cast for *Clever Kate,* with the sole exception of *Kate* herself.

"And there, frankly, I'm at my wit's end, Robin. I've tried out a dozen women, early as it is. I can't get the quality. I would send a batch of them up for you to see, but I think it would tire you too much."

"It would tire me too much," murmured Robin, cutting off upon the instant his fountain showers of smiles, glances and verbalities, and sinking back into exhaustion and his pillows. "Yes," he repeated, in a voice thready as his uncle's—"it would tire me too much. Surely you can find her for me, Harry? A thin devil, every line of her face ugly, eyes like innocence itself, full mouth. Do you know those paintings of the Indian goddesses—curves, the tiny waist, curves again, hands and feet like flowers? That's what she should be." He pulled down his brother to a whispering level—"I'm awfully tired, Harry. I ache with tiredness. Harry, without hurting their feelings, d'you think you could make them go away? Not Uncle Lionel—I don't mind Uncle Lionel—but the rest of them."

"Of course," said Harry, smiling at him. "We'll go at once, Maud and I."

"I don't mind you and Maud," said Harry. "But I'm damned if I can do with all these women. Take them away, there's a good fellow." And before his brother could answer him he had drowsed off into one of his sudden, gossamer fits of sleep. Harry signalled to his wife and together they tip-toed from the room.

"I don't like it," said Harry to his mother, as he paused to greet her on his way out. "He blows about like a flame in a high wind. He excites himself, he writes a most brilliant scene—did you hear what he was reading me, Maud?—then, flat he goes, almost rambling—'All these women!' Did you hear that? He talks out of a dream sometimes. I told him I'd send him a pack to interview and already in his mind he's going through all the interviews. No, I shan't let them come near him. It's not worth it. He excites himself too much. What does the doctor say, Mother?"

"Russel's coming home," said Lettice, deliberately evasive. "Russel will do him good."

"He's written to you? I'm so glad, Mama." Harry's face lit up.

"But of course he has written," said Lettice superbly. "And, as I hear, he is sending you all the necessary confirmations of your plans. He is to arrive in the first week of September and I am having the night-nursery done up for him."

"September will be lovely," said Maud for the second time.

No wonder Maud was pleased. For Maud's children, a boy and a girl, had arrived with the New Year's snow: and after seven or eight months of subsequent close attendance, even Lettice could not object if Maud spent a certain amount of time at the theatre once more. For she had good nurses, and she was not one of those women who put her babies first. Harry came first.

But all panned out nicely. The children were weaned, her nurses reliable, and Lettice liked to supervise. Maud, who loved her children reasonably rather than passionately, was not in the least jealous. Certainly the boy should be called after William. Lettice kissed her for that; but soon found it very painful to hear the name 'William' on everyone's lips.

"You mustn't think me unkind, Maud, but if he is called William it will chill me to the child."

Maud understood absolutely. They would name him after her own grandfather then. But then Lettice was hurt.

"But of course he must be called after Harry's father—the first son! What are you thinking of, my dear?"

Maud was thinking of a compromise; for her own French grandfather was a Guillaume.

"Could we name him William, Lady Lettice, and call him Gilly?"

"I've told you before to call me 'Mama', my dear!" said Lettice, who had carefully refrained from any such order. Harry, overhearing, knew, and Maud knew, that she was now and forever a Broome indeed.

As for the little girl's name, that was easily settled. None of the Broomes minded what a girl was called, and Maud's grandfather wanted the family name of Domina revived. Gilly and Domina—Donna for short—yes, it would do.

"And you, my dear, can trust me to keep an eye on your nurses, if Harry really needs you at this time of strain. He is not very strong, my dear, for all his energy, and if you ask me, a good mother has first to learn to be a good wife."

So Lettice guarded the nurseries while Maud went to and fro between the theatre and her home: and both women were happy. And indeed if Maud had not been able to go to rehearsals she would have scarcely seen her husband in the six weeks before his brother's arrival.

For Harry lived and not infrequently slept at the theatre in those heady last weeks. He was putting the whole of his capital in invention and originality, and quite half his private capital in money, into the venture. He thought the public was ready for a new type of play. He thought that in his brother's tragic farce he had found something that would shock, outrage but, probably, in the end, delight. We know now that he was right, though it is difficult, three quarters of a century later, to realise just why the sixties found it all so shockingly outspoken, so revoltingly new. The mild little masterpiece has to be dressed in the period and delicately burlesqued to please the London wit of today, though the provinces revive it much as Robin planned it, much as Harry arranged it for performance. And the auction scene, no longer blue-pencilled into Victorian propriety, still holds its own as the test of a rising star.

Harry's trouble, of course, as he told Robin, lay in the fact that he could find no rising star to put over the ticklish woman's part. He was faced with the reverse of the Juliet problem. He had to find a woman at the dubious age of thirty who would not only look her age but add an extra ten years to it. He wanted lovely, vicious Female Experience that could flash back for brief moments to the Age of Innocence. A true fair-and-forty was too old for his purpose. Robin's great line, the famous—'I have not yet experienced youth!' must be delivered by a creature in whom the sap was still rising.

But he could not find such a creature; for the mid-Victorian actress aged fatly and soon. So he gave the part, provisionally, to his latest pretty young discovery, the sprightly Lily Altamont, whom the world knew later as the sensational Mrs. Deemer. She did well enough; but he still held the word 'provisional' over her, even though he worked her like a hackney. The play on the whole had certainly shaped well, considering that Lily was mis-cast, and that a lively young provincial star was under-studying the part which Russel was to play on his arrival: and would, no doubt, play very differently. But Harry did not worry. The actors, at any rate, adored their own parts and enjoyed the play—"That, of course," said Harry to Maud, "is usually the worst of signs!" He himself was sufficiently effective in a minor part, though— "I hate to see you play a hunchback, Harry!" said Lettice. Also the Altamont was improving. She was still intolerably coy, but she was building up to her big scenes successfully, if you only allowed her her coyness. Russel was the unknown quantity; but Russel, at his worst, could not much upset the balance of the well-knit whole. And Russel at his best, if it were anything like hearsay, would probably have a triumph.

"But that won't help us," said Harry to Maud, as he munched sandwiches and bolted steaming coffee in the Broome box instead of sitting down to a proper meal. But he was in the mood to run races with time, and there was real danger that he, as well as the company, would be worn out a week before the night. He had no mercy when he was in a working fit, and expected his lively young *jeune premier* to play Hamlet

at night with undiminished vigour though he rehearsed from ten to
six. Moreover he would sometimes call the company after the evening
performance, and flog them through scene after scene till the morning
twilight filtered down from the flies and the players not actually
dancing through parts in frantic evasion of Harry's cracking whip,
fell frankly asleep in little huddles in the wings. The only hope of the
exhausted company lay in the fact that Mrs. Broome always refused to
go home without her husband. Mrs. Broome, giddy with lack of sleep,
had her own way of dealing with the all-night rehearsals. Somewhere
about dawn she would cook up, in a paint spattered corner of the
property room, a hearty English breakfast of steaming coffee and fried
eggs and bacon, with loaves hot from the early baker. Mrs. Broome,
sweeping on to the stage, a vast frying-pan in her hand, followed by her
own special consistory, the jolly wardrobe-mistress, the two lean
dressers, the fat dresser, the dresser who drank, the cleaning woman,
and her own ally the all-important stage carpenter, was the herald of
release, welcome as a day-star, popular as Queen Victoria. Even Harry
knew that his night-reign was over when Maud Broome, still a lovely
lady in spite of her frying-pans, skirted the dead footlights to put a hand
on the back of his hard chair and whispered—a blessed, powerful
whisper that reached every corner of the wings—

"Breakfast, Harry, and then home we go!"

"I've just got to finish the scene," Harry would begin, and the voices
of husband and wife would drop a minute: and then Mrs. Broome's
voice would rise again—

"I don't often ask you anything, Harry! But just this once, as a
favour to me——"

And Harry would get up wearily and call out—

"Breakfast in the green-room, ladies and gentlemen! It's later than
I thought."

Then would come breakfast in the green-room, at the two battered,
magnificent Hepplewhite tables with the brass-edged inlaid tops and
curving brass-tipped legs. The Prince Regent had given them to Perdita
Robinson, and Perdita had sold them to Sheridan, and William Broome
had picked them up at the Sheridan sale in 1816. The tables had been
in more than one fire, and one had a buckled surface and the other
a crazy leg; but they had survived with other glories—the Garrick
candlesticks and the curtains that Hilaret Broome had worked for
her grandfather's own managerial parlour. The curtains hung now
on either side of the portrait of the duchess herself who, like her

nephew Robert, had patronised Sir Joshua. Grandson William, who had sat to Lawrence, fared larger but more gloomily : while old Richard Broome winked at them all from his own corner as if he said— "Hogarth for me !"

And indeed Hogarth had given him as lively and rakish an immortality as ever his mortality had been. On any summer morning old Richard was far more vivid than the close sitting company on which he looked down.

For so tired were the players that the younger members used to sit like exhausted school-children, heads on arms, waiting to be fed : while the older men and women preserved their dignity little better. Only old Mrs. Reilly was upright, dapper, roguish, at four o'clock in the morning. Harry, dead weary, but equally indomitable, always sat down beside her and summoned up for her benefit the naïve midnight charm that as a little boy he had used upon his mother : and old Mrs. Reilly in turn summoned her own ghost of girlhood to play the part for her. So he preserved, in that gathering of the de-vitalised, his semblance of conquering energy, and she re-lived her indispensable days. Thus, while Maud fed and comforted their weary subjects, the two royalties— the young king of but a quarter century and the old queen in her fifth decade—gave the cheer.

And the old queen made an excellent breakfast herself when her job was done and the party freshening again to gossip and good humour. But young Harry never took more than a cup of coffee. Then he would depart, his arm through his wife's, a last word flung over his shoulder, brilliantly, charmingly. And driving home in the carriage he would be wide awake, hectic with fatigue and over-stimulation, pouring out the problems of their rehearsal just past to his white-cheeked Maud.

"We're in for a failure, Maud ! We can't possibly get away with it. I must talk to Robin. He'll have to re-write the last act. The Altamont can't get near it. The girl drives me mad. Why will she be a lady ? Did you notice how she quirked her finger just now as she drank her cup of coffee ? She does that to the part. I need a vulgarian, Maud, or else a great lady. Either could play it. Mama could have played it. D'you see what I'm driving at ? Can you imagine Mama a trollop ? Then, my dear, then, what an actress we should have had ! What an auction scene we should have had ! As it is we haven't a hope, and I daren't tell Robin. Otherwise the play doesn't go too badly."

"Badly ? My dearest Harry ! It has never gone so smoothly. I watched you with amazement, my dear ! You were hovering over it, hands outstretched, as if you were engaged on that new Eastern trick of healing tired bodies—what's the name for it now—massage? Yes, you massaged the play. I loved to watch you."

"Ah, you say that to comfort me."

"I do not. Your stroke at the window after Kate's exit straightened out the whole tangle, Harry. It was the worst scene before, now it is the best."

"You are being very clever, Maud! It is just what I like to hear. But I don't believe you for an instant."

"Why should I say so unless I thought so? I don't pretend to understand the theatre, as you know; but at that moment I could have screamed with pure excitement, tired as I was."

"Could you really, Maud? I did think that bit at the window was fresh. Did it really strike you as fresh?"

"I was so relieved that I said to myself—Now I needn't watch any more! Now we are safe!"

"Did you? What did you think of the Altamont's new reading there?"

"You managed the Altamont most amusingly, Harry. It was very neat."

"Yes, it was neat, wasn't it? I've fought her for a week over that bit of business. But now, you see——"

"Oh yes, I see, my dear love!"

"You do think she will do, Maud?"

"I have always thought she would do: and since you have been training her——"

"Oh, I don't pretend that the part isn't safe with her," said Harry, restlessly interrupting, "but I would have liked to create a new star. Maud, I think I shall drop you at home and I shall go on to breakfast at Browntree's. He has been scouring the country for me. He heard of a young woman playing at Ipswich last week who might do. He went down specially to see her. I think I'll go and breakfast with him and so straight back to the theatre. The call is ten-thirty. It is not worth while undressing and going to bed."

But Maud put her hand firmly on his arm.

"You will do no such thing. You will come straight home and rest. It is only five o'clock. You can get four and a half hours."

"Can I? I shall never sleep. O my God, Maud, I am so tired!" And down his head would go on her shoulder in sudden complete abandonment and he would hardly rouse as the carriage stopped at their own door, but would reel drunkenly into the house, Maud's hand on his arm behind the elbow steadying him to his room. And she would put him to bed as if he were a child and then go across to the nursery and stand in her cool voluminous wrapper, looking down at the sleeping babies, at the dark, sturdy Domina and the waxen boy, the pink and golden Gilly. She would heave a sigh of pure satisfaction, touch them, kiss them, leave them: noiselessly return to her room, undress, bathe, brush out her long hair without haste, slip on a nightdress made, Victorian fashion, long-sleeved, high-necked, elaborate: and then, with a stretching gesture of comfortable but not too great fatigue, lie down beside her husband and in a moment be as dreamlessly asleep as her own babies. She had magnificent health, and she did not regard herself as at all an over-worked or injured person. She adored her life, she adored her husband: she was an exceedingly happy woman. If she did indulge in any dream, it was the dream of herself reviewing (unperceived) the applicants who daily thronged the stage-door and the box-office door and pushed in at any other momentarily unguarded door of the three theatres, of herself selecting unerringly, out of a mob of full skirts, demure jackets and mask-like, pink and white faces under the pork-pie hats, the one actress—'Indian goddess' of Robin's fantasy, 'ugly creature' of Lettice's sharp comment, 'statuette in mud and gold' of Harry's phrase—who should satisfy Harry and incidentally reduce the importance of that objectionable young woman, Miss Lily Altamont. For Maud, who was tolerant of all the weaknesses and most of the sins, found it difficult to forgive gentility.

But that dream was not fulfilled. It was Harry's agent who discovered the paragon and brought her along to see Harry ten days before Russel's arrival. "Can't think why I never thought of her before, Mr. Broome! But I'd lost touch with her, that's the truth. She says she's been in the States. As I said to her—'Why not let me know your whereabouts?' But there, I always found her secretive. She came to me first when she was twenty—not my business to inquire—but they do say her grandmother knows why she was called Caroline. Not that I believe it! I was always on the Queen's side, poor lady. Why shouldn't she be crowned? But this Madame Caroline, she carries herself with an air! Always did! When I first knew her she was a friend of old Lord——"

"You are speaking," said Harry icily, "of a second-cousin of my own."

"I'm sorry, sir! Rumour's rumour, and it's always a dirty night when she flies. What does it matter? Well, as I say, Madame Caroline—La Rayne was what she called herself in those days—had her living to earn for all her fine airs, and got her first piece of work through me. She toured in Australia, did well enough, and, they say, went about like royalty, till there was a fuss with the Governor, and the lady was hopped out of the colony like a flea, biting wherever she landed. Now she says she's a star in America. Of that I know nothing, but she looks shabby. And she hasn't a cutting to show. You could write your brother, I daresay, sir, or I could write. But it'll take a month to find out, and with him here in a fortnight and knowing the theatre lists, we'll do better to save postage and wait. Meantime, sir, would you like to see her? Coached by you, sir, and knowing what I do of the part she'll do you better than the Altamont filly, and she's not asking a fortune neither. Then I've a young thing, pink and white. I found her in Ipswich. She's worth using for a year. By then, no doubt, she'll be fly-blown—you know the sort, sir! But for the next year, at least, she's worth the retaining fee."

"Send her along," said Harry coldly. He disliked coarse tools, but was far too shrewd not to use them.

The affair in pink and white he engaged at once, turning her over with a chuckle to his Maud who, he knew, would think her well worth saving. Well, let Maud try! Lost or saved, her bloom would be over in a year. If, then, Maud preferred to chivvy the pretty tired thing on to a flinty path instead of a primrose one, well, that was Maud's affair. For himself he hated a weak mouth, and her eyes were the wrong blue.

But Madame Caroline La Rayne—preposterous name—was another matter. Hard as nails, theatrical, hysterical—and yet—joyfully something in him rose to meet a worthy antagonist—and yet, here was something uncatalogued, undefeated, perhaps undefeatable. Coarse Browntree was right. She was Robin's list of qualities and points rendered in flesh. Here were the curves and the slenderness of the experienced body. Here was the ugly, unforgettable head. And, yes, behind the raddled cheeks and the emphasised air of languor, the sap was still rising.

"How old?" said he harshly, not at all in his usual manner, for it was said of Harry that he could refuse a favour more ensnaringly than any man alive.

"Twenty-five," said she, her chin up but with lilting eyes.

"Thirty," wrote down Harry. She laughed at him, sprawling her elbow well over the table that divided them, cupping her chin in her beautiful hand with the bitten nails, and shamelessly reading what he wrote before she said—

"Better put thirty-five."

"Thirty serves," said Harry inscrutably. Then, running his eyes over the full mouth, the gaunt cheek-bones, the amazing width between the eyes, he added—"You are sure of your make-up?"

"Oh, yes," said she. "I'm not sure of the English taste, but I'm sure of anything under twenty-five—with my make-up."

He said—

"Will you say a line for me?"

"What is the line?" she drawled.

" 'I have never experienced youth!' " Harry made his voice entirely expressionless. The woman's eyes glowed: they reminded him of his young son, sucking his mother's milk with glazed eyes.

"I have never——" she began. Then—"Who wrote this? What does it belong to?"

"A part," said Harry courteously—"that I think you might be able to play if I could persuade you to drop your mannerisms. I don't want languor."

"I've never played in London," said she greedily.

"That—" said Harry—"is precisely the note I want. Will you try the line again?"

She looked at him angrily. Her eyes dropped.

"I have never experienced youth," she muttered sullenly.

"Again."

She lifted her large light eyes in extraordinary appeal. "I have never experienced youth," she said sighing, and her eyes were brimming.

"I'm afraid that's not at all what I want," said Harry gently. "If you are to play the part, and I think it is possible that you might play it, you must be able to say that line greedily."

"I don't know the play," said she roughly. "I can't work on a few lines. Never could."

"The play—" said Harry, rather bored, for he found her stupider than he had expected—"is a very light affair. A very guileless and innocent youngster is bewitched by an older woman. She comes near to ruining him."

"She is hungry for youth," said the woman. "I see! Go on!"

"Naturally she soon tires of his youth: is perhaps afraid that she will be herself de-vitalised. Anyway she barters her interest in him for a considerable sum of money to another woman. That is the big scene of the play."

"I could play that," said she. "Who is the woman?"

"His mother."

"Oh, his mother," said Madame La Rayne, bored. "That's not the way to handle it. I could tell you how to handle it."

"I'm sure you could," said Harry charmingly. "I'm sure you could play the part—that is, if you can cope with the line at all. For her justification, her confession, her vice, her whole history past and future, lies in her last word to the boy's mother—'I didn't know what I was doing. I have never experienced youth.'"

"I have never experienced youth," said the woman hungrily, and her eyes flickered. He thought to himself, regarding her with professional interest—'When the locust passes, what's left? I read that somewhere. The creature's filthy. She probably can't act. But she's exactly what I want.'

Then to her he said coldly—

"You had better come down and read the part tomorrow. Here it is. Do what you can with it."

"Am I paid for rehearsals?" said the woman. "Will you advance it?"

"We don't pay rehearsals," said Harry coldly.

"I'm hard up," said she with a brilliant smile. He hesitated, then scribbled on a paper.

"You can take this down to my manager," said Harry. "It is half what you will get on Friday, if I entrust the part to you."

"And if you don't?" said she, hardly.

"Call it a gift," said Harry, smiling at her for the first time.

She flung out her arms in a gesture of relief, excitement, pleasure. She looked twenty-five.

"I have never experienced youth," said she, perfectly: and thus rewarding him, went out like a mote dancing in a sunbeam, so lightly, on her small, shabbily shod feet. Harry looked after her.

"She's got it," said Harry with satisfaction. "Charm, charm, charm! She's the only person I've ever met, not a Broome, who had it so strongly. Even Maud—Maud couldn't hold a candle to the filthy creature! I don't like professional women. I wonder if she'll let me train her. If she doesn't, charm or no charm, she goes," said Harry. And then—"I don't think I'll tell Robin. It's an experiment. She may not be able to do it. I'll see what Russel says first, anyway. And what am I to say to the Altamont? Well, I told her it was provisional. I must put her into Perdita at the Glory Hole, that's all. That will level things up. I'm probably making a fool of myself," said Harry. "I shall probably sack her tomorrow; but if she can get it over the footlights we're made. So's she, for that matter. The charm will wax for another ten years. After that she'll go flaccid. She'll be nothing—a nut-cracker old woman. Aren't people interesting? And aren't people fools? Look at that woman's eyes. I wouldn't waste my substance if I were a woman. I'd be ashamed to run about the world crying 'I'm hungry.' She's like an ogre's child with her gold hair and her white teeth and her red cheeks. She's a child-eater. Yes, she'll do," said Harry: and thought about the ugly, red-lipped, hungry woman all the way home. But he told Maud very little about her.

But Maud, at the first rehearsal, nodded to him her admiration. "The half was not told me," said her nod. And indeed, it was clear to him in five minutes that his instinct for casting had not failed him, though the company grumbled at the amateur in the manger. They made it clear enough that they thought that she had mistaken her profession, and resented the fact that she dressed like a woman who calls herself an actress, but on the stage itself had no such air.

This, thought Harry to himself, probably accounted for the fact that, for all her experience, and he could see that she must have had a variety of theatrical experiences, she could return to her own country no better known than when she had left it. But within her type she could do no wrong: and by some marvellous intuition on the part of his agent, and, he modestly congratulated himself, as the result of a certain flair and courage of his own, here she was, the right woman in the right place. It interested him, too, to see that her boldness, her vulgarity, was mere off-the-stage acting. She had evidently been given a hint of what he would probably require and had set herself to create the effect in advance. Now, having got a hearing out of him, she reverted to the stately amateur, to the actress cast upon the stage by circumstances, and bringing with her in every rustle of her draperies, in every movement of her shoulders, the flick of her hand as she unbuttoned a glove or adjusted a bonnet string, an air of drawing-room, luxurious travel, of all the punctilios and all the conventions. The story of her illegitimacy occurred to him. It might even be true. She was exactly his idea of authentic but really vulgar royalty. And it was odd to note that she was unpopular with the actresses of the company, not for her vulgarities but rather for her authenticities. They could forgive her certain lack of money, her probable lack of virtue; but not her grace and her well-bred wrists and ankles.

But her effect on the actors was electric. The young provincial star was doubled in value before she had been a week in the theatre: the other men over-played till Harry shouted himself hoarse, and Harry himself began to enjoy his own rôle though it was the most weak and conventional of all the parts. Therefore he had kept it in his own hands; for, like his father and his grandfather, he liked to do his own gilding and polishing, and could never be hampered by too nice an adherence to the author's intentions. But even he, playing the part more because it kept him on the stage at the moment when his young provincial needed a little help than for any other reason, found himself looking forward to his one scene with the newcomer: and, he soon realised, she too looked forward to the scene with him. He knew flattery when he heard it, and knew that she would like to flatter, but also knew that they played with mutual appreciation.

"Must you play it as forty-five?" said she abruptly to him one day. "A hunchback is any age, isn't he? Why don't you play it twenty? A hunchback of twenty in love with me—don't you see what it would do to the play?"

Of course he saw. Instantly he saw. From a hanger-on the part would be the foil of the main character, the other boy of twenty, the beautiful boy. And she, how she would gain!

"You would have two youths to play with," said he. "Is that it?" She shook her head.

"That's crude. Don't you see that you are my shadow, not the boy's? With an ugly face and a hunched back you echo me. You, too, have never experienced youth. I wish you would play it that way."

"I'll think about it," he told her.

She flashed at him a look of satisfaction.

The look stayed with him. The creature had been licking her lips. The female side of his nature shot up into his brain and endowed him with instant comprehension of the reasons for her satisfaction. So that was her method, was it? Sympathy, comprehension, subtlety, domination, and a conveyed appreciation of the beauty of his ugly face (for Harry had no illusion about his Wybird countenance)! So that was the lay!

He countered at the next rehearsal by playing the part older than ever, and waited for her next move: though why she was so anxious to play at double or quits with him he did not know. He was aware, of course, that she must have a certain purpose as far as he was concerned, and dimly guessed that by mistressing his interest she hoped for stage pre-eminence and metropolitan success. He supposed that she knew him to be married; but he found himself rather glad that an ailment of Gilly's had kept Maud at home for the last few days. He missed Maud badly: indeed was peevish at her continued absence; for he had long forgotten his bridegroom's promise to keep his wife free of the theatre. It had been inevitable that she should be involved: and he always admired her maternal attitude to the people of the place. It was an achievement to know the theatre world so intimately and yet to remain so entirely unconnected with it in looks, manner or ways of thought. But now, suddenly, he was relieved at her absence: he found that he did not want her to encounter his new find. Now why was this— Harry asked himself. Had he not always angrily despised the Puritans who looked on the theatre as the devil's meeting-house? He had heard once of a fellow-actor's child being refused admittance to a public school, and had impersonally raged. Such an absurdity could never happen to a Broome: but that it should happen to any actor was outrageous.

But watching his new find he experienced a revulsion of feeling, a sudden understanding of the Puritan point of view. She represented the theatre as they thought of it—a synthetic muse, a mere concubine of the true gods, a creature who destroyed but who could never experience innocence.

Well, there was no need for Maud to meet her. Thank God, Maud was an understanding creature. He would tell her quite frankly that the La Rayne was not the type of woman who could be met socially. Maud could be as kind as she liked to her poor little harlots and reformed trollops, but this elegant Duessa was another matter. It would be easy to keep them apart. Once rehearsals were over and the run started they would be doing much less work in the theatre for a season, and with Russel to entertain there would be many claims on Maud's time: and at present there was this most fortunate feverish cold of Gilly's. Yes, it would all work out very nicely: and he was not likely to engage the woman again. If she made her hit other managements would be angling for her, and my word! they could have her. They would put her into Kate Hardcastle and lose a lot of money. It would teach them not to fish in his waters.

"Meanwhile——" Harry pulled himself up short—"I am behaving like the milkmaid, spending my money before I sell my milk. I shall spill my pails if I'm not careful. Now, let me face facts. I am taking a great risk with Russel. I think I am mad to take the risk. He pleases the trans-Atlantic taste, but he never had any brains. Suppose they do not like his New York developments over here? Over goes my pail! Still, he's a Broome, and he can't have lost all his charm in the States."

Harry was right. Russel had not lost all his charm. Russel, arriving a day before they expected him—for he had been too impatient to stay the night in Liverpool—Russel, arriving at his mother's house gracefully and conveniently round about tea-time, Russel in Robin's room, surrounded by his family, a little embarrassed, a stranger yet the same Russel, had lost none of his charm. But he had added to his looks. He was as handsome as a young lion and carried himself like one. There was a kind of stupid nobility about him. He had the actor's head and the actor's toss of the head: he was incessantly flinging back his very thick brown hair. His eyes made Robin's bright eyes look cold and pale: his teeth were as white as his mother's. Indeed, he was in face not so much changed as either of his brothers; but his throat, his shoulders, his whole presence, was solid and broad: and the tan of the voyage enhanced his massiveness.

Thank God he has kept his figure, thought Harry. He would be a mountain if he hadn't. What a Brutus he must make! My God, he shall play Brutus under me at the Glory Hole or I'll know the reason why.

"Mother—" he said aloud—"couldn't he play Brutus?"

Lettice did not answer. Lettice was crying, quite openly and sincerely crying. Russel had kissed her and said—

"Well, Mama——" And then, hesitating—"Is it all right, Mama?" And she had choked and nodded and kissed him back; but she had not yet spoken to her prodigal. Her eyes instead had sought Harry's, and Harry had at once come across to her. The comprehension between those two never failed, and it was to Harry that she said, fierce tears rolling down her cheeks—

"He's William over again! That is how your father looked. He's even handsomer, Harry." And then, with the inevitable smack of her hand against an irritation—"And stupider, too, for that matter. There's no rancour in him."

"Rancour?" said Harry, puzzled.

"Power to be rancorous," said his mother. "Yes, he could play Brutus." Then, and he felt her hand grow tense in his—"Harry, look at Robin!"

He looked, saw what she saw, looked back at her and shivered. Body and soul—the lamp and the flame—the crocus in the snow—the beacon on the hill-top—all these figures rose confusedly in his mind as he watched his brothers—the Hercules, Russel, on the sofa by the Hylas, Robin. Robin was half mad with excitement. His mind glowed behind his face: his thoughts flowed up and down it as light flickers in an alabaster lamp. Nothing in him was still—hands, eyes or lips: he was a spiritual flicker: he fought his own substance like the jet of gas flaring above his head in its primrose demi-lune.

"He's—what is he, Harry?" said Lettice watching. There was an alarm of tears in her voice that took her son back to early days, to a Lettice new bereft of a young Russel and a younger Robin. "What is happening to Robin? Harry, he is dreadfully young. I mean 'dread'. It's a dread thing to watch. Russel has aged into the thirties as he should. He has grown up and has changed, as is right and natural. But Robin is still eighteen. Look at him! He belongs to yesterday. He is not in our time at all. Then what have we kept with us? Am I nursing a ghost?"

"Now, Mother—" Harry soothed her—"you and Robin feel too much. That is what is the matter with you both. You are exhausting yourself with feeling and so is he."

Old Lionel's whisper threaded its way to them—

"The worst was this: my love was my decay." It was unheeded, as all their surroundings were unheeded, by the absorbed brothers. But Lettice heard and turned on her brother—

"What? What's that? What are you saying, Lionel? Decay! What a phrase! You needn't talk, Lionel! You, at any rate, have lost the art of taking care of yourself." Then, lowering her voice piteously—"Do you think Robin looks so ill? Surely he looks better than he's looked for months? I don't know what you mean by decay. I say Robin looks well. I knew that once Russel was home he would begin to improve. Their separation was a disaster." Then, raising her voice—"Russel, talk to us a little! My dear boy, are you glad to be home? Are you glad to see your brother again? He has been so ill, Russel, but he is strengthening daily, aren't you, Robin? Robin, don't you think you're a little tired? Don't you think you've had enough? I think you should have your tea quietly up here and we will go downstairs for ours. You mustn't be selfish, Robin. The rest of us have hardly seen Russel."

What, stay in this stuffy room and let them tell all the news without him? Robin wouldn't hear of it.

"Well then, we will all have tea with you."

"No!" And Robin wouldn't hear of that either. He was not bed-ridden. Russel would be thinking him an invalid. He was coming downstairs with the rest of them. "Russel, give me your arm. I've been a little shaky, but it's over now. I've only to get up my strength. Isn't that so, Harry? Isn't that so, Uncle Lionel? It's such a mistake to cosset oneself. Why, the first night is in a fortnight's time! D'you think I'm going to miss Russel's début, let alone my own play? We have so much to tell you, Russel. Of course you will be starting rehearsals immediately; but I did want, Russel, to talk over the part first. Tonight, perhaps? After dinner?"

Lettice caught at Harry's hand. She was looking old and tired. It was as if the confrontation with the solid, vigorous piece of her own flesh and blood, the mature and independent Russel, had shaken her grip on authority. Here was something which had outgrown her control. Her own self had escaped herself. And here was her Robin, drunk and inspired with rebellion, openly worshipping this counter-authority, this second masculine self. Instantly she fought her own usurping flesh and blood, not with all the usual rattling, bustling weapons, but in a whisper.

"Harry, can you do nothing? Consider your brother's state of health. He has not been downstairs these three weeks. He is possessed. If he insists on dining with us and then has a late session, he will be prostrate to-morrow. You know what you boys are when you get together late. Do something about it, Harry!"

Harry nodded.

"I say, Robin, give me a minute. If you are so much better, if you are really planning to come to the first night, I shall be wanting more than that of you! Would it be possible for you to come to a rehearsal?"

"I don't see why not. I could drive down with Russel. Russel, do you know that I've never seen the Genista either? We left it together and we come back together. Yes, Harry, if I rest in between whiles, I don't see why I shouldn't. Do you, Mama?"

Lettice, not following Harry's thoughts, but assured that he had his scheme, nodded non-committally. "It might be managed———" And left him to continue—

"Well, old fellow, I put it to you. You must make yourself ready to be used this fortnight. Lie up in between! We can't afford to have you fagged out. Tonight now, I shall want Russel to read over the part with you, and I shall want you damned critical, I shall want you fresh. So I say—let Stephen have tea with you up here and cut out his time with you later. Eh? Get your rest then! Dinner with us if you feel like it, of course. But I think it would be wiser to have a tray up here. Keep you out of the noise! Keep you fresh! And Russel and I will come up to you afterwards and we can go through the business. It sounds selfish, I know, to ask you to forego all the fun; but I do need the help, Robin. I shouldn't ask you if I didn't. Do you see—this is the stuff I want you to look at. (Russel, go down with Mama! I'll be along in a minute.) Now, can you do anything with Act II, Robin? Because, now I've seen Russel, I'm sure that something must be done with the part. Russel can't play it as young as you've written it. Don't you think so yourself? Yes, get back on the sofa, old fellow! That's it. Here's the scene that's worrying me. Ah, there's Morgan with your tea. Now then, Robin, listen while you drink it."

And Harry sat himself down in the low chair by Robin's couch, and he talked technicalities in his slow, measured voice till Robin's incandescence dimmed to an easier glow, and the hectic, feverish energy slowed down, flowed back and retired upon itself, making way for that patience, that pathetic resignation to the stronger will which was the other half of Robin's charm for his brother. Stephen, coming in, completed the work. Stephen intended to be played with. Stephen refused to be ignored. Robin, crying after Harry—"Send Russel up again soon!" turned to his duty as a father quite happily.

But Harry was not so happy. Coming into the saloon where his family sat he saw, however, that he would not find it necessary to say to Russel those things concerning Robin which he had intended to say. For Lettice had been crying again, Lionel had withdrawn into himself, and poor Russel had lost his air of delight at being home. He was anxious and distressed.

"You ought to have told me, Harry," said Russel. "You ought to have warned me. I'd have been over six months ago. He's a ghost: he's a phantom. It's the most cruel thing I've ever seen. You all seem to take his state very lightly. Is anything being done? Davos?"

"Of course that's where he ought to be. But he won't go. And we daren't force him, daren't risk the agitation. Besides, you can't force a grown man. Anyway it would only prolong, not cure—if it did. I don't think it would. He'd die of—lack of will to live. No, you're the last throw," said Harry.

"I?"

"You know how he feels about you. And it seems to me," continued Harry, "that the disaster of his marriage has thrown him back emotionally into his boyhood. He only lives by feeling: and he daren't live in today. He's wrenched himself back ten years to make you the centre of things again as you used to be. He can go on living that way for a little while. All this business, his play being put on, it's what he dreamed for himself ten years ago. That's why, whatever I say to him, I don't want him to go down to the theatre. It would become a real play then, not a dream, and I don't think he could stand it. We've got to keep him in the past to keep him alive at all."

"Do you follow all this?" said Russel, turning to Lettice.

Lettice's face was cold; but she answered—

"Harry is quite right. He's got to forget about that woman."

"Oh, I see." Russel looked relieved. "Now I see what you're driving at. Yes, I suppose it was the woman who finished Robin."

"Couldn't you have stopped it?" Lettice turned fiercely on her eldest son. "I can't forgive you that you didn't stop it."

"Why, Mama——" The old defensive manner was creeping over Russel—"It wasn't my fault. It all happened after he left me."

"Why did you let him leave you?"

"Why, Mama, we were men. We couldn't sit in each other's pockets. Robin wanted to go. He wanted a three months' trip on his own. And for that matter, Mama, it's I who have the grievance. Robin didn't treat me well. He knew I'd hate the whole business of his marriage and so he told me nothing, nothing at all! First thing I knew they were married. And I don't know to this day what made him do it, the mad ass. Did he ever tell you, Mama?"

"You don't suppose," said Lettice, "that he'd ever talk to me about such a woman?"

"Why then, Mama, how do you know what sort of a woman she was?"

"She left him, didn't she?" said Lettice icily.

"Well, Mama, you know, you left Father."

Lettice's face flamed.

"Russel, you've been at home only two hours and already you've contrived to insult me."

Harry rushed in with—

"Mama! Dearest—no!"

"He has, Harry! He compares me with that woman who deserted my son."

"I only said, Mama—" Russel ploughed on unhappily—"that we don't know the rights and wrongs of it, that's all. Harry, tell Mama that's all I meant. That damned woman—" said Russel unhappily—

"whenever her name's mentioned she gets us all upset. Look, Mama, I didn't mean anything at all. Do listen, Mama!"

"Shut up, Russel!" muttered Harry between his teeth, and flashed a look of muffled reproach, condolence and 'For God's sake leave it to me!' at his brother. "Come on, Mama, don't be down on Russel! He can never say what he means." He had her arm in his and was coaxing her to the tea-table. "We all want our tea, Mama!" Then, in an under-tone—"Don't you see how Robin's upset him? Dearest, pull us all together!"

Thus he caught at her, coaxed her, appealed, gentled, jockeyed her back on to her throne, and the tea went well enough, with a slightly subdued Russel headed back on to the path by the united efforts of his brother and old Uncle Lionel, who might be frail and thread-voiced, but had not in the least lost his appreciation of tight-rope walking in a nephew, and would always help, if only with appreciation and applause. Russel did not at all know what they were doing, but he was quite happy by the end of the meal and gained confidence as he told them about America or about as much of America as had assisted in the career of a Broome. He became extremely entertaining, and Lettice's pride awoke. Her eldest son would always irritate her; but still, she could be proud of him. But it was her youngest son to whom she looked every now and then. When he brought her his tea-cup to be refilled she told him what she thought of him in her own way.

"I wish Maud were here," said Lettice delightfully to Harry. And then to Russel, the bachelor—"Harry's wife is the comfort of our lives, you know—and such a complexion!"

"And you're a proud father?" Russel was delighted to be pleasant to useful, sensitive Harry. "I can't see you somehow. But of course I haven't got accustomed to you yet, Harry. I can't think of you as much older than Stephen. By the way, I haven't seen Stephen."

"He's with his father now," began Harry; just as the quick-eared Lettice held up her hand.

"Hush, that is Stephen calling. Isn't it Stephen, Harry? Is anything wrong?" She was at the door before they could anticipate her quick movements and pulled it open in time to receive the full fling of Stephen's inrush: while Harry thought—'Do the people of other families have this perpetual half awareness of each other? We all thought of Stephen just now. Why? Because something was wrong with Stephen. We are queer!' And he turned to look at his nephew and to listen to Lettice scolding him.

"Steenie, love, I've told you before not to run across the hall like that. You'll slip on the rugs and kill yourself. What is it?"

Stephen was breathless, but he did not lose his composed and careful speech.

"Papa is coughing again," said Stephen. "And he sent me for Morgan; but I can't find Morgan, Grandmama." And he stood quietly panting like a little thirsty puppy.

"Quiet him, Harry!" said Lettice. She was out of the room in a flash.

"He's quiet enough," said Russel, eyeing his small nephew. "Oughtn't we to help Mama, Harry?"

"She knows what to do," said Harry. "Quiet? A bit too quiet, Russel!" and he took the child on his knee. Stephen leant against him instantly, easily, naturally. His small hands were clenched, his mouth firmly set. He leant against his uncle unrelaxed, with the rigidity of a wooden doll, his large grey eyes shifted from speaker to speaker. Russel was amazed to find himself engaged in the lightest of chit-chat with his brother, found himself, he did not know how, engaged in humorous anecdote and reminiscent anecdote. Why on earth did Harry want to discuss his remote nursery-days at such a moment? But he did own that he remembered the pond at Dulwich, and how he had been pushed in by Robin and had chased Robin all over the garden but had not caught him, and how Robin had pulled three hairs out of the pony's tail but had not been kicked, and how Robin's cat had jumped from the second-floor window and had landed as cool as you please, not hurt at all. He found himself admitting to Harry that Robin had always been the lucky one and he the clumsy. He had had measles much worse than Robin, though when they had whooping-cough, Robin's cough had gone on twice as long. It was the joke of the house, Robin's cough, and he had still got a scar on his forehead where Robin had stumbled against him sliding, one Christmas, and brought him down heavily on a flint.

"Can I see it?" inquired Stephen, and slipped down from Harry's knee and went across to the fascinating uncle, and was soon exploring the scar with a shy finger.

"I'm going up to Mama for a little," said Harry. "Will you be all right with Stephen?"

Russel nodded. Only the child's presence prevented him from saying how extraordinary he thought it that Harry had not gone five minutes ago.

Later, indeed, he spoke of it to Harry. Lettice was completely occupied with Robin, whose attack, too familiar to be alarming, did nevertheless wipe out the little festivities that his mother, that eternal little girl, had so eagerly planned. But Maud dined at Park Lane and met her new brother and liked him, mildly and in spite of herself, for she had a long-standing resentment to combat. She had heard so much from Harry of Russel's virtues, looks and charm. She had always been irritated to find Harry, so sure of himself as far as the rest of the world was concerned, accepting Russel as the one Broome whose physical power of attracting fellow humans he could never rival: just as he invariably counted Robin his born superior in charming by wit. All this fuss and to-do about a mere Farnese Hercules, thought Maud: a prize ox at the Agricultural Hall! A strong, docile creature, very likeable indeed, was Russel; but it was absurd to compare him with either of his brothers. However, she would not be prejudiced, and indeed, watching Russel's pleasure at being at home again, amused, touched by his half timid, half paternal friendliness to 'young Harry,' and his wary politeness to his mother, she did feel her prejudices dying away. Harry was right. Russel certainly had a sort of coarse charm.

She began to talk to him with more ease, and then with still more ease; foɪ he so plainly found her easy to talk to. Lettice dashed away to Robin's bedside after the meal ended and left Maud to deal with the coffee-cups, and Russel settled himself happily beside her. Harry, hovering between the drawing-room and the sick-room, bestowed upon them glances of triumph and amusement. He had been perfectly aware of Maud's prejudice, but Russel was indomitable. 'And it isn't even a trick,' thought Harry. 'He just does it to the women and down they go! Even Maud! I did think Maud would hold out; but not a bit of it. It's because he's so simple.' Yet sometimes he found Russel's simplicity irritating, and he guessed that Russel irritated Lettice in precisely the same way.

"You don't take this business of Robin's very seriously then?" said Russel to him later in the library.

Harry stiffened.

"Seriously? I take it so seriously that I've got to joke about ıt. He's hanging on by a thread, Russel. Surely you must see that? This is not the first hæmorrhage."

"Yet—" said Russel, who was observant in his own way, "you ᵴat quite a long time telling Stephen stories. I couldn't make it out. I wanted to go up to his room only I thought I'd hamper Mother. But I couldn't make you out, you were so cool."

"Stephen would have had hysterics if I hadn't been cool," said Harry.

"That quiet little chap?"

"Too quiet for comfort, Russel! He has a life of his own, you know. He's secretive. He doesn't give much away."

Russel beamed at him.

"Well, you ought to understand. You were an unnatural baby yourself. Oh, you were a funny little chap, Harry—an ugly little chap. And now you're at the head of two theatres, and I'm not because I'm a star who doesn't care to be bothered with properties. Ain't that a joke, Harry, my boy? And Robin writes plays for us to put money in and get money out of. And here we sit, you and I, and Robin's dying upstairs by inches: and Mama's ageing, and Uncle Lionel's a straw. Ain't it queer, Harry? And now you tell me Robin's child has got the family failing, has he?"

"Failing?" Harry was puzzled.

"Well, Harry, where I have been for the last ten years, people have been much solider somehow: brighter, coarser, like the colours in *Struwelpeter*. But over here you are all faint, pretty-pretty like Uncle's aquatints." He looked round the room. "There—that one now, on the wall. Look at that hill! I could walk into that blue hill. It would melt for me. It's so transparent."

Harry flashed him an odd look.

"What? You know that feeling?"

Russel nodded.

"I ain't so ignorant, old fellow, as I sound to you. I read a lot. I couldn't keep English if I didn't. His voice suddenly lost the faint American twang and rhythm that lay like a tarnish on his daily speech. It became an instrument of music, played by a professional—

"And I awoke and found me here
On the cold hillside——"

murmured Russel: and the room hummed as if a finger had been run round a glass finger-bowl. Then, relaxing into drawling, comfortable speech—"That's how I feel about England. I hadn't been back twenty-four hours before I remembered the old chilly feeling. English people live in a mist, especially us Broomes, Harry. They say old Dick Broome used to see fairies. And Grandpa Robert shot himself, and that isn't sane, is it, to shoot yourself? And talking to our father—you don't remember him, of course—was like talking to a room lined with mirrors. I never knew which was father and which was just a reflection. And Mama, too, for all she's so brittle and harsh, is a she-will-o'-the-wisp. I don't know where I am with her. And Robin—well, we know all about Robin. And you, too, Harry—you used to walk away from us all like a sick cat. One couldn't find you, though you were always as good as gold, just like little Stephen. And now you tell me Stephen's got a private life like the rest of us. He goes into the hillsides too, does he, like Great-grandfather Dick? 'Reckon—beckon——' Well, well, we're a mad lot. That's why I like America—all solid and bright and newly varnished like a Noah's Ark. I do like it. I think I'm a hark-back to Grandmama Robert. I don't like being a Broome. I'm going to marry an American. If I stayed over here I'd make a queer marriage like the rest of you. I admire your wife—milk and roses. I think you're in luck, my boy. But she's Irish, isn't she, and you've got twins. How are you sure one of them isn't a changeling?"

"Well, Russel," said Harry with emphasis, "if I hadn't heard you with my own ears——" He left the sentence eloquently unfinished.

Russel laughed.

"I know, I know! I'm drunk on English air. I've never talked like this in my life. I didn't know I could. It's a rush of family to the head. It won't happen again. America suits me. I can stand it. I'm not like Robin. We ought never to have let Robin go to America, Harry."

"We?" Harry lifted his eyebrows.

"Oh——" Russel actually blushed—"It was my fault. I took him—to spite Mama. I know that. But how was I to know it wouldn't suit him? It suits me—America. I'm not so stupid in America. I know just how dull I am, old fellow, believe me! You and Mama, and Father too, let alone Uncle Lionel, you all make me feel like a plough-boy. But in New York I pass for a wit. Yes, I do. I make epigrams. I think about you all at home and remember something you've said: and then I repeat it as if it were my own: and then I have a success. Besides it's quite true what everybody says, there's something in the air of the States. You live twice as fast. It's good for a slow cove like me. But it wrecked Robin."

Harry nodded, bright-eyed, intelligent, very grave.

"Yes. To accelerate Robin, that's farcical, that's mad."

Russel grew more confidential still.

"Good Lord, yes! I see now I shouldn't have taken Robin. But how could I foresee that the life would spoil him when it suited me? And how could I foresee that damned woman?"

"Couldn't you have fought her?" said Harry fiercely.

"Me? I only met her twice. How was I to guess? You know what we were to each other. If his little finger ached he told me of it. We couldn't breathe without each other. And then in a week she'd changed him, changed him under my nose, and I never knew, never guessed what was going on. Of course I knew she was an adventure for him. He talked of her quite freely. I thought it would do him good to have adventures. Why not? Of course when Robin got his job in her company—Oh, yes, she ran a company in those days—I did give him a word of warning. I thought I knew what she was after. I know that type. I keep clear of 'em—too bitter, too hungry. Magnificent eyes, of course—temper—large movements, you know, fine and free—this one had breeding, too, from somewhere. Too much for American provincial audiences: they like 'em Siddons and blue ribbons. Still she had her company and filled it up with youngsters who paid her for the experience. Oh, yes, and they got their experience. You see, there were half a dozen women like her at that time in New York—managers' wives, rich professional amateurs—you don't have them over here, I think. They all knew each other. They pounce on the youngsters. We, the professional stage, we don't touch 'em. But I didn't know all that then. Robin and I, we were both such youngsters, Harry. You were never young, were you? But we were two young fools. Still, I knew more than Robin, and I did warn him to look after himself, not to let himself get caught. And he laughed at me, Harry! Yes, he did— laughed at me—lied to me by laughing. Would you believe it of Robin? Up to the very night he left we talked just as we had always done. He left me thinking there wasn't a thing about him I didn't know. Yes, Robin had the heart. He acted it so well to me, his own brother—you know how we felt about each other, Harry—that even when I was on the platform and saw the pair of them in the carriage together, still I thought it natural enough that he should be fussing about her rugs and her travelling bag, and letting her talk, playing background, if you know what I mean. Still I thought it was all right. I thought it an affair that would pass. And then, my boy, just as the train was shaking itself, she says to him—not he to her, mark you, not he to her—'Shall we show him, Robin?' And he says—'All right!' And she puts out her long hand with a wedding ring on it.

I can see that round streak of gold now. It had a diamond guard. The sun caught it. I couldn't say anything, Harry. I just looked at Robin: and he stared back at me with not a rap of feeling in his whole face, and says—'We've been married a week, Russel!' And she laughed, and then the train drew out. And I haven't seen Robin since till I saw him this afternoon. That's my side of it, Harry. I don't know what he's told you."

"It's incredible," said his brother.

"I don't know about incredible. It happened."

"Was she—did anything in her account for it? What quality had she? How did she net him?"

"I never saw anything in her," said Russel. "Good figure, tall, that's all. Years older and red hair. But I can never be fair to a woman with red hair. Don't like red hair."

Harry rose to his feet.

"Well, I suppose he got his plays out of it at least. But Russel, he's got to have those lost years given him back. I've set my heart on it. It's our responsibility, making this play of his go. I hope you realise that."

"Don't worry. I'm safe on the stage," said Russel. And for the first time Harry realised that there was authority in his brother. Simple, unwitty, he yet had a capacity to labour along at the tail of a thought till he arrived at the same place which Harry reached in grasshopper leaps and Robin by thistledown flight. Russel was still the eldest of the three. He had weight. He had capacity.

"I'm not so anxious as I was," confided Harry to Maud as they drove home. "It's a great relief to have Russel over at last. He shares the responsibility. His experience will be invaluable. And say what you like, Maud, he's ten times more attractive than any man of his age on the London stage today."

"Oh, yes, I like him," said Maud.

CHAPTER 20

NEMO ME IMPUNE LACESSIT

"I TELL you what, old man," said Harry next morning as he drove down with Russel to the Genista, "you'd better watch a run through from the box with the understudy in your part. You'll see how we've shaped it. Then you can give me your criticisms and we can agree over minor alterations. We needn't trouble the company until we're agreed. We'll run it straight through for you. We haven't got props yet."

Russel nodded, and sat quietly enough in his box during the run-through of the first act. But before they could run into the second he appeared at the swing doors. Harry, from the stalls, heard the click, rose and edged out.

"Carry on, ladies and gentlemen! Don't let me interrupt you, Madame La Rayne." He reached his brother. "What is it, Russel? Would you rather sit down here?"

"Come out!" Russel gripped his brother's arm and pulled him out into the corridor. "What's all this, Harry? Are you playing a trick on me or don't you know?"

"Know what?"

"Who that woman is."

"What woman?"

"Your lead. The Kate."

"What, the La Rayne? That's Caroline La Rayne. My find."

"I don't know what she calls herself or how you found her, but her name's Broome. She's Robin's wife."

"You're dreaming."

"I'm not dreaming. Her voice alone— I confess I didn't see it at once. That black hair's a wig, I suppose, or else she's dyed it. But as soon as she spoke it was unmistakable. What the devil are we to do?"

"Do?" There was a note in Harry's voice that made Russel stare, and staring, take his brother by the arm again and pull him forward to the better light of the foyer.

"Harry, what's the matter with you? You're shaking."

"I've been had." Harry laughed aloud.

"I know. But what are we going to do?"

230

"Do? There's only one thing to do."

"Carry on?"

"D'you think we ought to carry on, Russel?" said Harry, eyeing his brother narrowly—and Russel flushed.

"Well, it's a week to the night and frankly, Harry, I've my reputation over here to think about. I can't afford a scramble. It might be better to carry on—get rid of her later. After all, it is a masquerade on her side: you can trust her to carry it out."

"And then, after the night and the success, announce herself publicly as Robin's wife?"

"And a Broome!"

"And a Broome!"

"I suppose that's the game, Harry?"

"I suppose it is, Russel! It gives her standing, you see, for ever after."

"Hm! It's a damned clever trick. We should have to acknowledge her."

"Exactly."

"Well, I think she's got us in a cleft stick. I can't endanger my first appearance here, though I tell you frankly I don't relish appearing with her. If there were any alternative——"

"You shan't appear with her," said Harry.

Russel hesitated. Then he said again, uneasily—

"I can't afford to fail, Harry!"

"I know," said his brother.

Russel hesitated again.

"You know, old boy, it's the chance of stage life. Get the first night over and we can cope with her somehow."

"I don't ring up for that woman, Russel," said Harry, "not if I have to sell the Genista."

Russel wavered. Then—

"Well, I'm in your hands. Have you an alternative?"

"Oh, yes, I have an alternative," said Harry firmly. "Come along! Come down into the pit with me."

"What are you going to do?" said the older man uncomfortably.

"You'll see," snapped Harry: and, pushing open the door for his brother with a pomp and ceremony that wrecked the rehearsal, ushered in his star.

The dialogue on the stage wavered and dried up.

"What's this?" Harry's voice shot through the empty theatre like an

arrow. "Whose dry-up? Madame La Rayne? Carfax, give Madame
La Rayne her lines. Carry on, Madame! And a little louder, please, I
can't hear you."

He turned and whispered to his brother, and not only to his brother.
He was in complete darkness as far as the vision of the players was
concerned; but he was the centre of a lively darkness. He conversed in
a powerful whisper with emissaries from the box-office, the manager's
room, the bar: he found occasion to call up the stage-carpenter, and he
sent the stage-manager steadily to and fro from his seat to the stage,
clattering up and down the wooden ladder with disturbing energy. He
did not interrupt the run of the scene, but occasionally he interjected
courteously the unvarying cornerer—"A little louder, Madame La
Rayne! I can't quite hear you." And then, as the scene flushed and
broadened to its climax, he rose in his seat.

The tired but beautiful voice of the actress was swelling towards the
goal-line of the scene—'I am hungry for experience, and I have never
experienced youth—' but Harry did not let her finish it.

"I am hungry for experience——"

"Just a moment, Madame La Rayne! Do you mind going back a
little?" Then, addressing the stage-manager, hovering on the edge of
the scene—"Carfax, you've set that table too far up stage. It's swallow-
ing the sound. I can't hear Madame La Rayne."

The stage-manager, shading his eyes against the hot, blinding
footlight glare, shouted back—

"It's on the chalk marks, Mr. Broome."

"I daresay. But I want to make it easier for Madame La Rayne.
Can't you hear how she's cracking her voice? Move down the furniture
and the props."

Aggrieved, patient, fully aware that a scene was brewing, the
manager and his assistants shifted the stage furniture forward.

"How's that, sir?"

"It doesn't look so well. No—it won't do at all. We can't have that
crowded fore-stage. We shall have to shift the mantelpiece, Carfax, I
expect. I'll talk to you about it later."

"It'll mean remaking the flat, sir."

"Well, we must remake it. This scene has got to be heard. You
ought to know by now, Carfax, that I won't have sound swallowed.
Those curtains had better come down too. But not now, Carfax!
Come back to me now! Come and listen!" And Harry waited, and all
the theatre waited in dead silence till the factotum was once more at his

elbow. Then—"Now, my dear—" he addressed his leading lady amiably out of the darkness—"is that comfortable for you? Is that how you like it? Now then, will you begin the scene again?"

"From the beginning, Mr. Broome?"

"Yes, please."

The scene began again. The butler came and went. Maud's one crony among all the women, Linda Reilly, once blue-eyed and adorable, now an old lady in the grand manner, was ushered in, and the La Rayne glided down the long staircase to greet her. The placing of the staircase displayed the star's figure and concentrated the eye upon her movements.

"It's an amazing shape," muttered Russel appreciatively. "She'd make a hit, Harry."

"I know," said his brother grimly. Then, raising his voice—"I want that line again, Madame La Rayne. I didn't catch it. Just come in again, will you, Mrs. Reilly?"

Mrs. Reilly, who had seen many managers come and go and had worked for years with Harry's father, shot a keen look into the darkness. Then she glanced at her companion on the scene. Madame La Rayne held herself erect: her lips were compressed: she had whitened about the mouth and eyes as violent natured people do when temper takes them. Mrs. Reilly coughed, the faint cough of warning that had sometimes had its useful effect on Harry's father. Then she retired and came on again, and was relieved to find herself greeted by the La Rayne in the proper accent, with the proper composure, and very loudly indeed—'Is this an intrusion or an honour?'

"Once again, please," said Harry patiently.

The La Rayne whirled.

"I'm speaking as loudly as I can, Mr. Broome."

Harry rose apologetically.

"I beg your pardon, Madame La Rayne, I don't catch what you said. Will you come down to the footlights? Russel, come down with me."

He made his way forward, Russel following. Harry reached the railing in front of the orchestra pit, and his face was lifted in concern.

"I'm afraid you're finding it difficult, Madame La Rayne. It's a big theatre, I know. Would you like to rest for five minutes? No doubt you've strained your voice a little: or possibly a chill—let us call a halt: let us have a breather, eh, Russel? Oh, by the way, is Mrs. Reilly there? Mrs. Reilly, here is an old friend of yours. Come, Russel!"

The brothers clattered up the wooden stair and Mrs. Reilly ran up to them and caught Russel's hands.

"My dear Mr. Broome! After how many years? I welcome you home—" she weighted the welcome with a preliminary pause—"in the name of the English Stage. I am one of its oldest members, you know, or you ought to know. I played Ophelia to your grandfather's Hamlet, and now I am to play mother to you. And in your brother's play, too! And thus the whirligig of time, as the bard says. . . . You make me want to cry, indeed you do. So like poor William Broome. Has not your mother told you that you were like our William Broome? There was no-one to touch him—no-one. Well, that's a long time ago. Golden lads and girls all must—like chimney sweepers, you know. Dear me, how glad I am to see you! But I must not keep you from the rest of the company. They are all in the wings. It's one of your brother's new little rules, you know—he will not have anyone in front."

"Who is that then?" Russel, a little embarrassed by the old lady's warmth, though he liked it, was glad to find another subject of conversation. He was rather tired of being told that he was like his father, and he did want to know who the pretty glimmer of a woman in the stalls might be. He had not noticed her come in.

"That?" The old lady peered. "Where are my lorgnettes? Yes, my dear, you may well look at them. They were given to me by Queen Adelaide, a pair of her own. I'm very proud of my lorgnettes. Inlaid, you see. Ah, now I can see. It's too far for me but it looks remarkably like Miss Altamont. She plays our pretty young ladies as a rule. She is at the Gloriana just now as Perdita." Then, lowering her voice— "Between ourselves, your brother tried her for Kate. She did rehearse the part, and very good she was in it if you ask my opinion. But your brother didn't think her enough of a woman of the world. And there's no doubt Madame La Rayne has a strangeness—Your brother can judge much better, I'm sure, than we, who are actually in the scene itself. Still, little Altamont wasn't at all bad, my dear, not at all. I don't know what she is doing here. Well, I daresay she will come and talk to us if I beckon her. Shall I?"

But here Harry's voice interrupted them.

"Russel," said Harry, "you have not yet met Madame La Rayne."

Russel turned. Oh, no, he was not mistaken. Seen at close quarters, how could he be mistaken? She had dyed her hair jet-black and her brows were plucked, which singularly altered her expression, and she, too, was consciously altering her expression. But of course he knew her, and of course she knew him. Staring in her face as he would stare at a predatory bird on a perch, presented for his inspection, and meeting her unwinking stare, watching, as she turned for an instant to his brother, the upward thrust of her profile as it cut the intervening air like a scimitar, seeing her thus, expectant of his recognition, disdaining it, daring it, braving it, holding herself ready to outface it, he felt a pang of admiration. He saw her as a bird of prey with a body under its claws, defiant, scared, but not ready to relinquish its prey, no, not though thereby it risked capture and maiming.

Then he remembered that it was Robin's body which she had gripped and paralysed, and hated her, so that when she addressed him softly with—"So we are to play together!"—he could not for the life of him say—"I hope so," or—"So it appears," or some such phrase. Instead he dropped his eyes to her left hand. There were many rings on every finger, but he noted the wedding ring.

"I'm sorry your voice is troublesome," said he, talking quickly, with no conscious intention of aiding Harry, but blindly taking the first subject that came to hand.

But it annoyed her. She shrugged her shoulders and answered coldly, though she smiled—

"It is the first time I have heard of any trouble with my voice. I am perfectly well."

Then Harry at her elbow slid in—

"It is possibly the pitch of the hall."

"I don't know at all what it can be," said she coldly. "You have not spoken of it before."

Harry nodded.

"Ah, but I've been on the stage so far. This is the first time I've taken a rehearsal from the back of the house. We must try again. But you will have to exert yourself a good deal more, I fear, if you are to be heard."

"I shall be heard," said she: and then, glancing with some dislike at Mrs. Reilly, she added—"Some players pull one's voice down, I always find. But with Mr. Broome's voice to pitch to—" she turned to Russel slyly, radiantly—"Mr. Broome will rescue me from inaudibility. Our scene comes next, you know, our first big scene. Are you equal to it today, sir, or are you but just arrived? I think we shall find the scene amusing. It is surprisingly written, don't you think?"

"Surprisingly?" said Harry quickly, interrupting.

Her eyes flickered.

"I understand that the author—another brother, is he not?—is still so young that I can hardly believe he wrote it. The play is so witty, so true to life."

"He is a good deal older than I am," said Harry.

She laughed, and was deprecating to Russel concerning Harry, with a graceful gesture.

"But one's manager, one does not think of him as old or young. He is the ageless law. One listens, fears, obeys: one does not criticise. I will speak much louder, Mr. Broome, I promise you."

"I will hold you to your promise, Madame," said Harry, on a full smile, all teeth.

For an instant she stared at him, puzzled, then she laughed again, valiantly, and continued to chatter and demand attention, while Russel turned from the duellists uncomfortably and sought out the safe Mrs. Reilly, and wandered over with her into the wings to be introduced to the rest of the principals. No sooner was he out of earshot than, with a glance at his back, Madame La Rayne dropped her voice to a confidential note. Her interest in Harry's brothers was, she conveyed, merely an approach to interest in Harry.

"Are you really so young?" she whispered. "That interests me. I have never—" She broke off.

Harry finished her line.

"You have never experienced youth?"

"Is that how you want me to say it?" she exclaimed, flushing: and her bright eyes bored into his.

"How did I say it?"

"Mocking, icy, terrifying—oh, quite terrifying." And then—"Have I done anything to displease you, Mr. Broome? Is anything the matter?"

"I think you must make a great effort, Madame La Rayne, to suit your voice to the theatre. You seemed to me this morning harsh, yet indistinct."

"I've played in every theatre in England and the States," said she more angrily, so much more naturally, "and nobody has yet complained that I could not be heard."

"No? Well, I'm only concerned with my own theatre; but my rule here is audibility. Every word must be heard. No beauty, no grace, no power of interpretation can outweigh distinctness. Well, shall we begin again? Where is my brother? Russel, will you come with me or will you go into the box? No, come with me. I want you to meet Miss Altamont."

And he made his way to the bench where the lady sat, a little breath-less from her hurry, pretty, talkative in whispers, all flutters and lace veil, unable to imagine why she had been sent for, post-haste, from the Gloriana. Her loud whisper, unchecked by Harry, penetrated the theatre powerfully, and everybody on the stage knew that Miss Altamont had been summoned from the Glory Hole within the last half hour. Caroline La Rayne, re-opening her scene with old Linda Reilly, had patches of scarlet on her cheek and carried herself more magnifi-cently than ever, but when she spoke she, too, was breathless, and her voice shook a little.

"A little louder, please, Madame!" came Harry's voice from the stalls: and then, as she continued, ignoring the interruption—"Begin again, please!"

Again the two women went through the scene, again the star found her confidence and swept on to her climax. But when she came to her critical line it was inevitable that she should flinch from it. And all her watchers knew that she would flinch: the groups huddled in the wings knew it: so did the cleaner in one of the scarlet boxes, arrested in interest, her mouth open, a pail swinging and a brush dripping with dirty water: so did the worried manager, who hated just such trouble as was now blowing up because it would fall to him to soothe down the combatants: so did the assistant stage-manager who dreaded the recoil upon himself of his superior's irritation: so did the players in the wings, fearfully rejoicing in the excitement and maliciously relieved that trouble was coming to the unpopular alien woman, to the steal-job who had ousted a favourite member of the company. All these watchers awaited the inevitable moment. It came. Her voice flagged where it should have swelled, she took too short a breath, forced it a moment too late and achieved a scream.

Harry put up his hand.

"I'm so sorry to stop you, but do you mind giving me that last line again? I couldn't hear it."

Her voice came clear then. It sped over the footlights like a bird flying low, angry, beautiful, perfectly clear.

"I can't play the part, Mr. Broome, if I'm not allowed to feel myself in it. You must let me rehearse in my own way."

"Oh, certainly," said Harry soothingly. "So long as I can hear you."

"I can scream, of course," said she sullenly.

"Oh, no," said he. "That would be too loud. Try again."

She put her hand to her throat, choking. Nothing happened. Everyone waited.

"Where shall I go from?" she said at last.

"Give her the line, Carfax!" said Harry wearily.

She ignored the manager's hasty prompt.

"I must have a cue given me," she said angrily to everyone. "I can't pick it up without help."

"We are all helping you as much as we can, Madame La Rayne," said Harry gently. "Linda, dear," he addressed the old actress, "do you mind going back a line or two?"

The old lady, her eyes bright with amusement, sailed securely into her previous speech, her voice soft, dove-like in the part of a conventional English stage mother, who has white side-curls and is always sixty years older than her adolescent. She, at least, thought every listener, was safe. All London loved Mrs. Reilly as a mother, and ignored the fact that she was a grandmother a dozen times over.

" 'I understand that you are fond of money,' " began Mrs. Reilly, that soft, strong, safe actress. " 'Yes, fond of money. So I wondered if you would care to sell me back my son?' "

The La Rayne flamed out her answer.

" 'There is already another bidder. What will you pay?' "

She said it so magnificently that she obliterated even experienced Mrs. Reilly. She stood, as greedy as a French peasant, as implacable as hunger.

Harry mourned over the need to discard so perfect a thing as her interpretation, but it did also strike him that if he had not discovered who she was, if he had allowed her to continue, though she might have a personal triumph, she was hardly likely to emphasise the play's comedic possibilities. She was far too true to sour life. But if the play's success depended on her and her alone, still she was unpunished, still she must go. For since he had heard of the hurt to his brother he had made up his mind that the human being who had hurt his brother should not go unpunished if ever that human being came his way. Now she had come his way.

So he broke in upon that remarkably fine piece of acting with a shout to his brother at the other side of the theatre.

"Could you hear that, Russel?" His strong voice echoed and re-echoed in the empty place.

Russel's voice rolled back like a distant thunder.

"Not very clearly, I'm afraid."

Harry turned to the stage.

"Ladies and gentlemen, I'm very sorry to hold you up like this. I must ask you to be patient. Now then, Madame, take the speech again—'There is already another bidder.' And speak up, please!"

She took the speech again.

" 'There is already another bidder.' "

"I can't hear you," said Harry wearily; and at that she began to scream her lines outright. She tossed back her fine head and the hair swung loose and tumbled. She flung out her arms with a fish-wife gesture, made a trumpet of her hands and bawled the answer through it. "There is already another bidder. What will you pay, pay, pay?" She flung down her hands again, she stalked to the footlights, she gesticulated, she raved. "Is that loud enough for you? D'you want it louder still? Shall I climb the Monument and shriek to you from the top? Is that what you want? Would you like me to break my voice in two for you? Would you like me to ruin it? I've had enough of this farce. I think you want to get rid of me. What will you pay, pay, pay, to get rid of me? Oh, but you shall soon find out. I'm not unprotected. I will send my lawyers to you. You complain of not hearing me. I assure you, there will be plenty to hear by the time I've done with you all. Am I speaking clearly enough now, or can't you hear me yet? Speak up, Mr. Broome! Do you hear me? Speak up!"

Harry crooked a finger at his manager.

"We'll have hysterics in a minute. Stand by!"

"I'm no doctor."

"No, you'd better get hold of the dresser."

But already Madame La Rayne, fulfilling his prophecy, had ripped her last rags of control into pieces. She raced to the proscenium exit, clattered down the little wooden stair into the stalls, and clawed her way to her enemies in the pit benches, crying—

"Conspiracy! That's what it is! Speak up, can't you, all of you? If you have anything to say about me, say it so that I can hear!"

"Now then!" The manager caught the frantic woman by the arm. She wrenched it away.

"Don't touch me! How dare you touch your betters? Haven't I a right in the theatre? I have as much right as any of you. Author's wife! Author's wife!"

"Demented," said Harry.

There was such venom in his tone, such boredom, such dislike, such complete contempt, that the word was like a pail of cold water flung in the face of her hysteria. She checked, went limp, and stood trembling like an exhausted horse. Sanity, caution and fear flowed back into her face. She hesitated, peering up at her enemy. The candle-end floating in its saucer on the bench by the pile of prompt books gave so faint a light that she pressed in upon him in order to read his expression.

He stood still, not recoiling. She might read before she ran, thought Harry. But his face was completely expressionless. She saw it as a series of planes—the double planes of the cleft chin, the block of the mouth, expanded nostrils, cheek-bones, brows. On these her eyes dwelt in turn as if they had been the separate stones and boulders that went to make up an arid hillside. She was suddenly terrified, and showed it.

"I am sorry——" she began.

"Get out of my theatre!" said Harry. And not watching to see whether or no she obeyed him, he turned to his lighted stage and addressed blandly, benevolently, the clusters of thrilled faces that were to be seen behind the unglazed windows of the painted flats, in the cracks of doors and about the prompter's box.

"Now, ladies and gentlemen, shall we begin again? I am sorry we have delayed you. Russel—" Here he turned to the boxes—"Russel, are you coming down? Bring Miss Altamont with you. Oh, there you are, Miss Altamont! Will you read Kate for us? You know the lines, don't you? Will you help us through? Now, ladies and gentlemen! Act I, Scene I. Oh, Carfax! Shut that door!"

A flash of light flickered over the theatre like a summer lightning as the great swing door at the back of the pit, whose inner side was a mirror, swung open and swung to behind Caroline La Rayne.

"That's finished," muttered Harry to his brother as he shepherded him on to the stage.

"Won't she fight?"

"Who cares? She can't get at Robin. That's all I care. Come along, Russel! Give us a taste of your quality!"

But Russel looked long at his brother.

"After a taste of yours I'm nervous."

"That? I've dreamed of doing that these three years. God, how well I feel! I feel as if I'd had a hot bath. I can't fail now, Russel, nor can you. Ready, ladies and gentlemen? Very well, then. Ready, Miss Altamont? Now then, Mrs. Reilly, it's your entrance!"

And indeed the company settled down to work as gaily as if a heavy day had ended in a thunderstorm and left the air uncannily fresh and sweet.

CHAPTER 21

CAN A BROOME BE TOO CLEVER?

"Maud, have you been giving Harry a tonic?" said Lettice to her daughter-in-law at the dress rehearsal a week later. "Iron, I suppose. It's very wise of you. It's done him good. I've never seen Harry look so well. He ought to be exhausted after the strain of the last few months, but look at him! He's carrying them all on his hands—he and Russel, that is. I'll confess to you, my dear, that Russel has surprised me and pleased me too. A most finished performance! Great charm! When Harry read me Robin's play, you know, I was not at all pleased. I thought it morbid. I don't like grossness except in Shakespeare. And even there I think it would be better away, though William would not see it. I could have told Harry from the start that Robin's comedy would not do as it stood. But Harry is old enough to judge for himself. Of course he must stage it in his own way. If I am asked, then I say what I think; but I don't interfere. But I told Russel what I thought and, you see, Russel has listened. As for Russel's own part, he has gilded it! And your Miss Altamont, though her accent is doubtful like all these young women's accents nowadays, she certainly makes the part acceptable. That scene with the mother made me cry, and I don't often cry. Dear Robin, he understands women! The mother is exquisite. I think we shall see a success."

Lettice as usual was observant and was right. The play had materially altered since it left poor Robin's clutch: what had once been an ugly farce was now a very pretty comedy indeed, and Russel was responsible for the change. Harry was the first to admit it. Daily Russel became a more admirable figure in his brother's eyes. He might not be a genius, but he was a very good popular actor, had no conceit, and did understand, as he was fond of telling his brother, when to stop making a reputation and think about making money.

"I am glad the La Rayne has gone," confided Russel at the end of a couple of rehearsals. "You can't have two stars in this sort of comedy. Her going frees me. I can improve upon the part now."

And, indeed, Russel had been as good as his word. Stronger grew the character, more ample the repentance, more and more satisfying the escape from vice: and Miss Altamont seconded him nobly. The ugly hungers of the older woman became the prettiest languors and languish-ings in the world. "Cherry ripe, cherry ripe—ripe, ripe cherries!" warbled Miss Altamont: and looked much more ready to be eaten than to eat.

Only Harry kept his previous reading of the hunchback. Why, he didn't know, except that something in his own nature, something bitter and astringent in his taste, wanted to preserve the ugliness that Robin had endured and had tried to record. And he had a reward that he did not expect and hardly desired. He made a success, not so much as a manager but as an actor.

He could be pleased with himself as a manager also, of course. Robin's first play was a success: it became a fashion: it made Russel as popular in his own country as he could desire. The favour of London was upon the Genista and the figures in Harry's separate account, the account earmarked for Stephen, increased and multiplied at a great rate. Robin would not take any money for his play nor let a banking account be opened in Stephen's name, and told his brother why.

"I shan't live long: and God knows what will break out in Stephen by the time he's twenty. But I can trust you, Harry. You've done well by me so far." And he looked across at his brother over the litter of news-papers and letters and 'floral compliments' as old Morgan called them, very happily, yet with a gleam of amusement. "And I trust you the more because you do look after yourself too. Russel's very pleased: so's Mama. But you know well enough who's made the real hit, Harry!"

Harry knew. His Hogarthian thumbnail sketch had not gone unnoticed by the judicious. There had been complimentary references and more than one broad hint that the family talent had not entirely accompanied the family good looks. One paper had gone so far as to point out that the business management of theatrical enterprises was a fine occupation for a man of talent, but that a manager was not at his best unless he took the lion's share in the actual acting of a piece as well as its presentation.

"And all because," said Robin, his eyes dancing, "you chose to be the black patch on the pink and white cheek. If you had seen to it that the play was played as written, Harry, your own little outburst wouldn't have startled them so. You played your own part as I wanted it. God knows what you've let the rest of them do. Russel's doing, I suppose. He understands the sweet tooth. But I didn't think you'd emasculate me, Harry. Oh, you needn't deny it: you have! It's icing sugar—" he tapped the papers restlessly—"and I wanted powdered arsenic."

Harry laughed. He knew well enough what Robin meant. But he knew that he had done well by his brother in extracting the poison and leaving only the sweet. He knew what he had given his brother—the taste of fame, money for his son, self-respect restored. Robin knew it too. But there was one thing Robin didn't know. He didn't know, he never would know how completely Harry had paid Robin's debt to life and Robin's wife. For every humiliation that Robin had suffered, for every robbery that had been done him, for every blow that had bruised him, for every disappointment that had sapped him, for every cruelty that had flayed him, payment had been rendered. Humiliation for humiliation, theft for theft, blow for blow: hope lost for hope raised, torture for torture, scorn for scorn—all things had been rendered and interest paid. 'Get out of my theatre!' It was Harry's sweetest memory.

He smiled radiantly at his brother.

"I did my best," said Harry, seeing the woman's stricken face in front of him. "I did my very best."

"I know," said Robin, returning his look. "I sound ungrateful. I'm not. But from the notices I know perfectly well what hampered you. Your Altamont, of course, could never play my Kate."

"She wasn't perfectly right," Harry conceded.

"No," said Robin wistfully. "There was only one woman who could have played that part."

"Who?" said Harry, knowing the answer.

"My wife," said Robin, "could have played it. She was not a good actress, but she could have played that part. I knew how to write parts for her—once. If she'd played it—" his eyes began to burn—"then we should have had a triumph, Harry."

Harry was regarding his brother with an amazement verging on horror.

"But you wouldn't have let her——"

"Let her?" Robin whispered, and laughed.

"Tell me," said Harry, picking up a paper and turning the pages idly as he spoke—"if, putting the inconceivable for a moment, if she had been in England and had applied to you for the part, would you have let her play it?"

Robin went on talking as if he had not heard.

"She had a raging hunger for success," said Robin. "And if she had been patient with me I could have made her a success. I knew how to write her parts. She was useless outside her own line, but I understood her line. Well, I suppose she's still touring in America: smaller parts, less salary: decay, decay, decay. If I'm dying of consumption—" said Robin.

"Robin, Robin—" protested his brother.

"Aren't I? You know I am. But so is she, Harry, so is she! And if she'd been patient I could have made her a star." And he smiled, weakly, blissfully, as people smile out of a dream.

Harry could not bear his look.

"You'd have given her the part if she'd asked for it?" said Harry blankly. "After everything, you'd have given her the part?"

"How often I'd planned it," said Robin. "While I was writing it, afterwards, even this last month when I heard you discussing all the possible women, I used to picture her asking you for the part: you sending her to me, not knowing. Childish," said Robin—"childish! But think of the exquisite pleasure——"

"Of refusing," said Harry quickly.

"Refusing? Use your imagination, Harry! Ah, you are so upright, you are so generous, you don't understand the cruel, petty impulses one has, lying here all day. I can't forgive injuries lightly. I've wanted my revenge, Harry."

"But I mean just that," broke in his brother.

Robin continued, impervious.

"She thought me such a weakling." He twisted his hands on the counterpane. "And now, now she has to come to me. I have the power to make or break her future. She broke mine. But I—I laugh, Harry, and I give her what she wants! That, Harry, would be a divine moment of vengeance. She was not a fool. The coals of fire would have burned her thin skin. Refuse? No, Harry, I wouldn't have refused her." He looked at his brother, his mouth quivering. "Oh, Harry, I wish it had happened," said Robin childishly. "I wish it had happened. It would have made up for everything. It would have been such an exquisite revenge." Then he ruffled his papers impatiently. "I talk a lot of nonsense. It's because I'm ill. Take no notice of me. I'm desperately grateful to you, Harry. All this—" he touched the witnesses of success—"is more than I ever thought would come to me. It's my justification. I'm not so utter a failure. I have provided for Stephen. I am not what she made me. I've provided for Stephen. I've provided for Stephen! And you made it possible. Can you imagine, then, how I feel to you, Harry? With what a passion of gratitude?" His eyes filled with the easy tears of weakness.

"Yes, yes, old fellow! Lie quiet a little. Give me your papers."

"Don't go away," said Robin fretfully.

"I'm not going away. I want to have a look at them too."

And Harry, though he was particularly needed at the theatre to deal with all the matters of business that must arise during the first weeks of a successful venture, and though he had not been leisurely with Maud for days and had not seen his children at all for a fortnight, stayed quietly in the sick-room another hour, reading notices to Robin, and telling him all over again the story of the first night's success. And all the while another part of his mind ran over the steps by which, because he was Harry Broome, so clever, so quick-witted, so adroit, so merciless, so super-subtle, he had been able to rob his brother, his darling, his adored, of the one thing his brother wanted before he died—his exquisite revenge.

CHAPTER 22

SUMMER IS OVER

HE could not forget it, his miserable, arrogant slip. In the hour of success the memory of it stood at his elbow like the skull at a king's feast, warning him. The memory opened its lipless jaws and spoke, saying—"Thus it will always be with you in the hour of your triumph." And he would turn upon it in horror, crying—"I know it. I've always known it. Let me have my hour." Then the memory answered—"Yes, but remember me."

And so his longed-for, his achieved success was embittered for him by dread. He had never been able to believe altogether in his little successes. His very arrogance, the arrogance that was his charm, was a protest, a disguise, a protection. He carried himself to the world as a Broome unconquerable, because he did not believe that complete success would ever be his. When he first saw his future wife he said—"She is too good to be true. There is a flaw somewhere." And when he found her as flawless as a human being need be, then he said to himself—"She could never love me." And when she made it clear enough that she thought him loveable, then he thought—"Something will prevent our marriage." And when they were married it was long until he was lulled into a blessed reliance on her love and duty. But being at last lulled, his ground of fear shifted and he said to her—"Everybody thinks I shall succeed; everybody expects me to succeed: everybody knows that I am to do great things. Only I know that I cannot do them. What is the good of you all believing in my success when I know myself and know that I have not the gift of succeeding?"

And then, after that successful first night, he had flung his fears from him. Success had swept up to his door like the overflowing Thames and had drowned out the cellars of his doubts and fears. He had launched himself on that happy tide and splashed in it rejoicing. He had been proud of himself as a swimmer until he had talked to Robin. Then he had felt the cramp: then he perceived that though he was floating on a sea of success, he was within his glass prison again. The glass walls of his prison were buoyant indeed. They lifted him above his own success: success meant nothing at all to him any more.

Well, he had Maud nowadays. She knew at a look what was wrong with him. To her he could even talk of his enemy horror.

"Maud, it's come on me again. Have patience with me."

"You are so overwrought, Harry. You are so overtired, so overstrained. Think how you have worked. Think of the burden you have carried. This feeling of yours is the way the strain shows itself. Believe me, my darling, it has nothing to do with you. It's only your poor tired mind refusing to carry its burden any more. It will pass again, my darling. It always passes. You must have patience."

"Yes, if you, too, will have patience."

"I will. Kiss me, dearest!"

No, he would not. He put his hand to her cheek, touched it clumsily then turned away. She watched him a little while. Then—

"Dear, I was going up to the children. Will you come?"

"No. I'm going out. I'm going for a long walk."

"Shall I come with you? I should enjoy a walk."

"You are not very subtle, Maud."

"No, I love you too much. Let me come, Harry!"

"I don't want you," said Harry with quivering lips, and waited, chin lifted, defiant. She smiled at him with unwounded eyes.

"Yes, you go off by yourself. I shall be here when you come back, I expect."

"I thought you were going to the bazaar?"

"No," said Maud, smiling at him.

"You were to open it."

"I have excused myself."

"You needn't on my account, you know."

"I know," said Maud.

Thus it was with Harry in the first weeks of his success. The mood wore off in time, for Maud had rightly divined that it was a mood induced by fatigue, a mere reminder that he had not outgrown his visitations rather than the visitation itself. Hard work helped to cure him. For he soon won the complete confidence of Russel and became not only his impresario as far as his English engagements were concerned, but his partner. Russel was content. Like all the family he trusted Harry completely: and their business alliance continued indeed till Russel, overtaken by stoutness in later life, and too lazy to cure it, left the stage for good.

But though Harry's mood left him, its warning remained. The future spread golden before him, but yet he distrusted fate and feared the future. When Robin died, in the summer of 1853, he felt in the midst of his deep grief a certain actual relief. He had known that some heavy trouble would come and mar his pleasure in living. Well, now the trouble had come. He had lost his favourite brother. There could scarcely be a heavier blow in store for him than that. And, after all, it was a normal, unfated grief. No-one had expected Robin to live long. His death was a clean wound inflicted on his friends. There was no poison, no fester in it.

Nevertheless the loss of Robin was a milestone in Harry's life. He was now past his quarter century, and Robin's death told him that his youth was over; for he had lost the living reminder of his own young power to love. Loving Robin had been such a lovely experience. Love had grown in Harry like a thick, curled, sturdy, yet delicate bracken frond, thrusting up towards maturity in a young world of blue and green mists. And then the impulse had changed: the strong, downy growth had uncurled, had opened itself like a hand opening, had spread out into the exquisite open leaf, into the full spread of true love, the summer love of man for woman, of his love for Maud.

And now Robin was dead, stupidly dead, because a vicious female fool had once chosen to pull off his wings. Robin, like any other lovely fly, could not live without wings. And with Robin had died all Harry's youth and charm. For he had learnt to charm from Robin: he had stolen the smile, the bright look, all the tricks, gestures, approaches from Robin—who else? He had been a fair learner, too. Now that the charm was gone, he could dogmatise quite coolly over that beckoning gift which he had once possessed. Reckon—beckon. . . . Lettice had taught him the rhyme: and as a silly boy, self-conscious, craving for liking, delighting in mastery, it had given him a sort of confidence to say over the last two lines of the rhyme, which nobody knew but Lettice and himself.

Reckon, beckon. . . . His admired brother had no need of any charm but that of his own fresh spirit; but Harry's mind had fingered the actual spell, just as he had fingered the lucky sixpence with a hole in it that Robin had once given him. And now the spell was wound up. Robin was dead. He, Harry, was a successful man of the world: his theatres were full: he was married: he had two children: his youth was over.

He said all this to Maud and Maud laughed at him openly, which comforted him a little; but still he was afraid. What would be the next stroke? Charm gone, Robin gone, what would life take away from him next? Not his theatre: that could hardly be. In the theatre he was

Midas. Farce, comedy, melodrama, turned to gold at his touch: not for him did Shakespeare spell ruin and Byron bankruptcy: nor did the Crimean War affect his prosperity. By the time it ended he was controlling five theatres, had an interest in a couple of seaside enterprises, and had bought the Syracuse, that scandal of the slums, for Maud to play with. A million was a large sum in Harry's day, in Harry's world; but there were times when he dreamed a dream of being the first theatre millionaire.

And then he would shrug his shoulders at himself to think how his dreams changed. Once he had dreamed of bringing home his brothers. Once he had dreamed of avenging Robin. Now his dream was to write a cheque for a million. Was cash then the end of all dreaming?

But the money was not for himself. It was for Gilly and Stephen and the girl. And then, one day, he knew his new fear. If anything went wrong with little Stephen? He was responsible to the bright ghost of Robin—for he still saw Robin sometimes, at noon, as a strand of sunshine on his floor, as an aggregation of motes dancing in the beam— responsible for Stephen: and he took the charge with passionate earnestness. There was almost an estrangement between him and his mother because Lettice insisted on keeping the boy with her. When Maud agreed, he was angry with her also.

"But, dear," said Maud, "there are six years between Stephen and the twins, and he is accustomed to your mother's house and she would be miserable without him. He has always been an only child. Sudden, perpetual company would not be good for him. Let him come and go as he pleases and he will come the more readily, and your mother will not feel sore against us. Don't you see that she wants him in the house at nights? And it is good for the boy to have to consider her."

"Uncle Lionel is bed-ridden, and my mother is getting old. It's not a natural life for a child," Harry would protest.

"But Stephen is here nearly every day. He is fond of the children. Don't force his affection for them."

"Gilly adores him," said the father.

"So does Donna," said Maud quickly.

"Does she?" said Harry indifferently. "Maud, are you taking the children down to Kent next month?"

"I had thought of Ireland," said Maud.

But Harry frowned, as a new fear lifted its ugly head.

"What, risk a crossing for Gilly? I'd much rather you didn't. A delicate little chap like that——"

"My dear Harry, you are fantastic about Gilly. He sleeps well, he eats well, he never catches cold. Donna gives me far more anxiety. I thought our soft Atlantic air would suit them. Aunt Rosina is very ready to have us."

"You could send Donna and the nurse if you like, if you think it would do the child good to run wild. I leave it to you, my dear, as regards Donna. You should understand your daughter. But I won't have you take risks with Gilly. He looks so like Robin sometimes that he frightens me. He's much more like Robin than Stephen himself."

"But your mother says——"

"I don't care what Mama says. I won't have risks run with Gilly. But Donna can go back to Ireland with Rosina, by all means."

"Rosina's maid is excellent with children, certainly," said Maud.

"There you are, then."

"Very well, and we will go down to Kent. I had a long letter yesterday from the duchess. Uncle Barbrim has sent down little Lewis to her. He is terribly backward. As bright as a needle, but they are afraid to let him learn."

"How old is he? Eleven? He will do for Gilly to play with. Anyone would say that Gilly was eleven. I think you had better go. Have they asked Stephen?"

"Of course. I fancy Mama is going down too. It is one of the grander summer parties, but you know what Lucy is. She plans her house-party round the nursery. Well, another idea, Harry! I would take the boys down, and if Nurse gets on as well as last year with Lucy's nurse, I could safely leave them there for a few weeks. There is no need for me to stay with them."

Harry chuckled.

"You are hankering for the Syracuse."

"Well, there is to be a Committee Meeting on the tenth. I should like to be there."

"I don't know what you want with a committee," said Harry. "They do as you tell them in any case. You give them infinite trouble in driving down to Syracuse Street."

"A slum makes them ashamed of themselves," said Maud placidly. "But they feel important, too. The two feelings together produce cheques and discourage interest. Oh, wait, Harry, wait two years! How easy I shall sleep in my bed in another two years!"

"Well, as long as you don't leave the children too long," said he.

She laughed, and he laughed with her. She was not a woman who left her children too long. Nevertheless she was not passionately maternal in Lettice's way. She was kind and just, and loved her children, and would have put her head in the water and held it there till she drowned, if thereby she could have insured to her little son and daughter the sort of future that she wanted for them. But her passion was her husband, and her main interest her charities.

She had great intelligence, organising power, common sense and, her detractors said, the meddling instinct: her friends called it a passion for tidying. She had tidied up her husband's theatres, and if she meddled, at any rate the health of her husband's employés was the better for her meddling. Nor did the staff resent her interferences; for she had the gossip's art of making friends. Harry could be fairy prince, but he was squeamish; he hated dirt and snivelling children and unnecessary squalor. But Maud would take a charity child on her lap and blow its nose on her own handkerchief, and think nothing at all about the matter save to note in her practical mind that the children must be provided with handkerchiefs in the future and taught to use them.

And one day, hunting down one of the theatre cleaners who had failed to appear for a fortnight, she had discovered, on the wrong side of the Thames, a down-at-heel music-hall called the Syracuse. The dresser's husband was bar-man there and Maud, in half a dozen visits, had heard enough about the conditions in which he worked to come to Harry crying out that something must be done. The place was a festering dust-bin: all the miseries of the neighbourhood prowled about it at night-fall, like the lean cats of London seeking their meat and their prey. It bred vice, filth and disease: it was a blow-fly centre of poverty and shame.

But Maud did not put it so poetically. She said that it was a horrid dirty place and needed clearing up: and said further that she was prepared to do the clearing if Harry would help her, and that she saw no reason why there should not be a Broome theatre on the south side of London.

This was getting the ear of all the Broomes: they had a passion for theatre property. Harry and Lettice were charmed to gratify Maud: and together bought the place outright and cheaply, and gave it to Maud for—"your tin wedding, my dear, for it's a gimcrack place," said Lettice.

"Married ten years, Maud! I can hardly believe it," said Harry.

Maud liked her present, especially as it was one that she could not enjoy without her husband to help her. Together they rebuilt, cleansed and purged. It was their joke to call their disreputable investment the New Broom. The joke became known and the name stuck. Today South London still goes to the New Broom, uses the comfortable temperance restaurant (Maud was strict on temperance) and listens to much the same plays that Harry put on in those first hostile years when the audience brought eggs and dead cats along with it as a protest against the closing of the bar and the shutting up of the promenade. For Maud and Harry built strongly and built well. The dressing-rooms that they thought so modern have long since been scrapped as 'rabbit-hutches' and the apron-stage is gone, and gone the great curtain made of looking-glasses; but the famous roof survives, and rehearsals are still held there in fine weather. And the stone pillars at the entrance still stand, and the marble entrance-hall is scarcely changed: and the picture of Maud herself, young and sweet and prim in her graceful, middle-aged clothes, still hangs facing the ticket-buyers. It is like her, though Lettice always said that there was something wrong with the eyes.

But then Maud did not sit for her portrait, and never knew that they had hung her up in the entrance-hall of the New Broom. For two years after its re-opening she died of a fever caught on one of her charitable expeditions, and Harry Broome's happiness ended like a candle blown out.

CHAPTER 23

HARRY BROOME AND HIS DAUGHTER DOMINA

His acquaintances said—"At least he has the girl and boy." His intimates said—"At least he has the theatre and the boy." Harry said—"I've still got the boy." For in him the fatherly passion, strong in all the Broomes, was brought by the deprivation of his wife's death to a pitch that made those who loved him best fear for him and the boy alike.

For Harry Broome was not an easy father, any more than he was an easy husband. The circumstances of his childhood had matured him early. Indeed, part of his charm in early manhood had been the mixture in him of extreme sophistication with the sparkle of youth. His gaiety had masked a quite relentless will: his audacious egotism did not disguise the fact that in a crisis he would be reliable: and the many men and women who fell under his spell and did exactly what he wanted them to do, comforted themselves after their surrender to his freshness, his unspoilt manner and his physical charm, by telling themselves that they were humouring the boy for the sake of the man that he was about to become. When, at twenty-five, they saw the boy the successful controller of a great business, they said that it was no more than they expected: that Harry Broome was a Pitt turned business man. The women perhaps lamented that the sparkle died away so soon, but admitted that the charm remained, and blamed his wife's sedateness for the early passing of her husband's attractive youth.

And it is a fact that Maud at sixteen had been a young woman, not a girl: and at eighteen was a sweet matron, as Harry at twenty-five was a man of affairs. But Maud was hardly to blame. He was as hard to influence as any other genius: for there is no doubt that he had a certain genius, the genius of the actor-manager. He was in fact the organiser visited by creative ideas: and his early habit of self-reliance, his early training in the necessity for managing the human beings who surrounded him, made it easy for him to impose an inspiration upon the unwilling, the unbelieving, the hide-bound and the lazy. The behind-the-scenes of the theatre was his natural territory. Though he seldom acted he.enjoyed acting, and had a family understanding of the varying actor-types and actor-temperaments. His sound business capacity, inherited from Robert's obscure city wife, found expression in controlling the finances of half a dozen theatrical enterprises. So prudent was he that they called him a cheese-parer, and so shrewd that he not only had a unique record of success in his own concerns, but was supposed to bring luck to any man or woman who served under him.

And though he practised economy he could be generous, impulsively generous: and Maud had taught him to be inquisitively generous also. Besides, it was in the Broome tradition to regard the private fortunes of the actors employed in Broome theatres as, to some extent, a Broome concern. Harry could help with money and he could fire with comfortable words. He paid good wages and he could be generous to folly as well as to distress.

Yet though he was said to be the best loved man on the stage he was also the best hated. Women complained of his fickleness and men of his periods of non-fellowship. For legend said that Harry Broome, who would lend you fifty pounds on Monday, thrash a pat into you on Tuesday, and take a risk by starring you on Wednesday, would as like as not cut you in the street on Thursday morning, and, if you came into the office huffed on Friday and talked of resignation, would pay you your week's wage and let you go out like a candle on Saturday without a smile or a regret.

Yet the worst offended admitted that if you gave Broome time, if you could be patient and refuse to recognise cause for offence, sooner or later Broome would be himself again. Indeed it says something, I think, for this strange Harry Broome that he had but to lift his finger to the worst offended and they very joyfully returned to their allegiance. Perhaps the reason was, though no-one but Maud had ever known it, that his fickleness was not mere egoism, but the working upon him of the familiar curse which not even his affection for her and her understanding of him had been able to disperse. Loving her as he did, there were still periods when his snow mood came upon him and wrecked life for himself and her: and after her death the mood came oftener and oftener upon him.

Even while he watched her die he had felt the familiar inhibition of all emotion. He had stood at the dressing-table fingering the long plaits cut off in a last attempt to relieve her fever. He had coiled the shining bracelets of hair over his hands, in and out of his fingers, twisting them, turning them: observing each variation of colour, sunburn, gold, brown: dropping them into the open drawer and then lifting them out again to finger then. And, as his fingers played with the severed soft beauty of his wife and he remembered how often before he had let his fingers tangle it when it was part of her, he thought to himself coldly—'It is a sign. I'm cut off from her for good, just as these plaits are cut off. She is going to die.' And then he thought—'And I shall survive it. It won't be so bad. I'm feeling nothing.'

It was awful to him to be insensible, but he had a dreadful, conscious 'told-you-so' pride in it too. He took his own flesh at the wrist between finger and thumb and twisted it till he stopped because of the sharp pain, and said to himself—'There, you see, that's pain! I can feel that well enough. But I feel nothing because she is dying.'

He dropped the plaits of hair and turned to the bed and studied Maud's face with the closed eyes and the air of false peace, and listened, still with the same unfeeling curiosity, to the faint, hurried breathing. He thought—'She breathes as if her soul were running a race. Maud, I am losing you and I feel nothing. Maud, make me feel—make me feel——'

Then his wife stirred and made a vague movement of her weak hands, and he pushed aside the nurse whom he hated, and stooped over her. She put her arms round him as he lifted her in her bed, and clung convulsively; but it gave him no comfort. He thought—'This is a mere clutch of her bodily arms. She doesn't know me. We are cut off from each other: cut off like her hair. How long is this to go on?'

And he put her back on the pillows and sat down again in the chair by her bed to watch her and listen to the ticking of the clock and her curious, agitated breathing. And sometimes he heard one and sometimes he heard the other, till at last he heard only the tick of the clock.

Then his mother came to him. He had not known that she was in the room.

"My darling, she's gone," said Lettice. "We've lost her." And she began to weep on his shoulder.

"I know," said Harry indifferently: and went laboriously and successfully through the business of comforting his mother. He preserved that indifference throughout the nightmare week that followed, and made all the funeral arrangements himself with great care: and a fortnight later put on a new play at the Gloriana. It was the success he had intended and when it had run a week he sat by himself in the box to watch how it went. He always watched his plays at regular intervals. If he was playing then he handed over to his understudy for that night.

And as he listened to the applause of the house he thought— 'Since Maud left me I've not heard a sound, except muffled. How dim all that clapping sounds. I can hear it well enough, but it doesn't reach me. Odd! When Midas swallowed food did it turn to gold in his throat and slip down in tasteless lumps? How he must have retched and choked at every meal! Shall I ever feel again? My soul can't be completely dead or I should not care for the fact that I cannot care. I should not care that I'm an outcast from all feeling. It's all there is left me—to care that much.'

And thinking thus he rose and went through the withdrawing-room where Robert had died, and out through the foyer and on, all the way from Covent Garden, to flowery, bowery Regent's Park. And still the only thought in his head was—'How solitary I am!' And indeed, once clear of the hot little Soho patch that had teemed with midnight life like a patch of old cow dung, he encountered no gaze that rested on his, no passer-by who so much as jostled him. He walked, a substance among shadows, or, he thought, a shadow among substances. If he wanted peace, surcease from the pain of living, then, at that hour, he had it. Yet he moved with gingerly content, like a man whose mortal wound is frozen. For with the return of feeling, will not his wound flow afresh? Will he not bleed to death?

But when he got home he remembered that tonight his boy and girl were returning from their prolonged visit to their grandmother, and that he had to pick up the life of the house again. Going upstairs to the nurseries, coldly, because he coldly knew that this move would be expected of him, he found his son in bed, but not asleep. The boy had wakened at his movements in the darkness and begun to cry and stammer out vague terrors of vague dreams and as he stooped to soothe him, he remembered suddenly his own childhood and his own wakeful midnights, and the sound of his mother stirring in the next room. A warm rush of pity for that small boy who had been himself flooded him like a wave, and thawed to thinness and to nothingness the cruel world of ghosts and snow. He heard no longer the dreadful breathing of his dying wife and the ticking of a clock; but he heard mortal sounds again—the purr of the lamp, the heavy breath of the sleeping nurse in the next room, the leap of the fire, the drowsy chirp of the canary, and his own child's voice. He was warmed by the feel of his own child's body nestled in his arms, and so came to himself at last, and kissed the boy and went away to his own room and his loneliness. Then, indeed, his dreadful wound began to bleed anew, and

Harry, flinging himself down upon his bed, cried out for his dead wife.

And for many nights, when he could bear the misery of it no longer, he would steal back, as his mother had done before him, to the nursery, and would sit half the night watching his darling: but would smile to himself bitterly sometimes to think that the little boy Harry had always lain awake for Lettice, but that Gilly never lay awake for him.

Thus year by year Harry Broome worked out his trouble, feeling alternately the recurrence of his strange immunity from feeling and the return of his capacity for grief: and with each return his passion for his son increased. For his son could make him forget his loss: in his son he could see himself again miraculously unburdened. Ah, his son was to have life so prepared for him by his father that he should escape his father's miseries and double-taste his father's joys. Harry said to himself that he knew well enough how easy it was for a father to be foolish about his children; but it was not possible that he, Harry, was anything but sane in his feeling for Gilly. Was it he alone who loved Gilly? Hadn't old Lionel made a superstition of the boy, and left him half his money when he died? Weren't the Wybird lot for ever inviting him? Besides it was not merely a question of biassed friends and kindred. Was there anyone whom the boy met in his daily life, his nurses, companions, tutors, Harry's own acquaintances, the theatre people, country folk at Bedenstead, who did not love him? The very crossing-sweepers and street beggars could not resist the boy's charm. And Harry would glance at the photograph on his desk with such pride.

For the new fashion of little neat, three-inch, brown photographs had superseded daguerreotype. Lettice herself in her spread of crinoline had been accurately reproduced: and she then had the two children taken with Stephen on the twins' fourteenth birthday as a surprise for their father and uncle. And indeed the three inches of pale glazed paper revealed even to strangers two personable boys: and to the father's eyes they were a reminder of a beauty which custom never staled for him. He had for his nephew an inherited affection. Stephen was so like Robin. He was sturdier than Robin, more delicate than Russel, cool in glance, with a temper redder than his red-golden hair. His delicacy, his air of possessing the Broome charm feminised, but all the more sparkling and intense for that, was a phase of adolescence. It would glide off in a year or two as morning bloom glides off the daytime earth, and leave him solid and real and mature, and a help to Harry in the theatre.

But Gilly—would Gilly ever grow into a solid human fact? Surely his precisely similar delicacy was a quality rather than a phase? Harry, looking at his boy, would murmur to himself the word he mocked at his mother for using. Genius? No, no, cried his common sense. But if not genius, then at least a flame burning in an alabaster lamp. It was not possible that Gilly's looks should be no indication of his personality. He was not Stephen subtilised for nothing.

"He's a younger Stephen, but with less character, I find," said Lettice bluntly: and Harry hated his mother for her stupidity.

Less character! If you wanted to be modern, as his mother liked to be thought, and if you thought you could be modern by patronising these new pre-Raphaelite amateurs, then it was understandable that your eye should prefer Stephen's corn-red shock to Gilly's smooth cap of silver gilt. "But character is not a matter of colour, Mama—I grant you Stephen has more colour—but of line, expression, of—how shall I put it?—transparence. Give me a face through which thoughts shine dimly like shadows seen through a blind. Gilly's thoughts flit about behind his face. Character!"

For the word rankled in the father's mind, and he would number over all the signs of superlative excellence in Gilly that should in good time transfigure the dull Broome mould. "The dull Broome mould," repeated Harry wearily and with complete sincerity: and continued to catalogue his son's qualities as some men finger their collection of rare coins or stand in front of a picture bought at great cost.

Item—the Broome eyes, as far as narrow shape, full swell of eye-ball and decisive brows went. But in colour Gilly's eyes were his own, a greenish hazel flecked with brown: and the droop of the lids, sleepy yet without insolence, was his own. The fullness of his mouth he got, of course, from the Wybirds; but how laughing and sensitive were its large curves. Harry thought of the perpetual smile that hovered on that young mouth, and sighed. Already Gilly had his delightful secrets: only fourteen, yet he had his secrets. Did he tell no-one his secrets? Did he tell Stephen? He, Harry, had always told Robin his secrets. Now his son and Robin's son were repeating the story.

But not exactly. Stephen was less emotional than his father—curiously like Russel in that matter as well as in looks. But still he had the proper attitude to Gilly, protective, though a trifle impatient of Gilly's delicacy and inclined to hustle him. Harry wished, not for the first time, that Lettice had not insisted on keeping Stephen with her after Robin's death. There was Maud and the nursery, and a welcome waiting; but Lettice would not hear of losing Stephen, especially when Lionel's death had compelled her loneliness, and now, of course, that Stephen and Gilly were schoolboys there were only the holidays to consider. And it was perfectly true that wherever Stephen slept, the boys were still together all day, for all the six years difference. But Gilly, of course, had always been as old for his age as Stephen was young, reflected Harry: and his slenderness and the long lines of his face make him look older still. Stephen is rounder faced and it takes off his height; but otherwise how alike they are! Much more alike than Gilly and Donna. Donna is not like any of us—nor tries to be.

And Harry turned with impatience from the picture of his daughter —dark, silent, scowling, then as always with a book in her hand, but without a smile on her face or a caress in her nature, thought Harry contemptuously. She was more like a heavy-eyed boy who plays games well but sullenly, without pleasure, and goes back to his books and his secrets so soon as the mob lets him. Yes—a dull, masculine, new-womanish type, thought Harry uneasily. No charm. He pronounced sentence on his relationship with his daughter in those two words; but he could not help himself, for Harry, like every other Broome, held charm to be the prime virtue. The other virtues, and kindness, and beauty, even genius, they could withstand; but not charm. Beckon, beckon—they who had beckoned so many, could themselves never resist a beckoner. But Donna had no charm for her father.

And so, though he was not an unkind father to her, though her wants were supplied and she was well groomed, well dressed and well taught, he had no affection for her, and pretended none. How could he?

"Look at the two children together, Mama! Gilly is constantly doing little things for Donna; but does she respond? Never! At least I never see her respond. And yet she has but to lift her finger and Gilly runs to do her bidding. He obeys her before he obeys me. The boy is so affectionate. I hate to see him checked and chilled."

"It won't hurt him," said Lettice comfortably.

"Well, I won't have it. I won't have his nature soured."

"Oh. Harry, children must be left to cure each other."

"It used to distress Maud," said Harry sullenly. "And I won't have it. When Donna gave me this—" he pointed to the little photograph, the cause of the whole discussion—"do you think she had a natural smile and look? No, she looked exactly as she does in the photograph—sulky. I ask you, Mama, look at her beside Gilly!"

And indeed beside him Domina showed like a blackamoor. Photography is unkind to a dark skin and heavy features, and Donna, though she grew later into beauty, was an ugly child: or rather her face was too old for her age. Her straight brows met over the strong nose: her lips were full and heavy: her chin deeply cloven: she had, indeed, the head of a woman of twenty-five on the still awkward body of a girl. The Broomes, accustomed to take the delicacies of Lettice and Hilaret as a standard of family attraction, foresaw no possibility of beauty in Harry's child.

"She's all Wybird," said Lettice: and then repeated, softening Harry's own damnation—"She means well, poor child. But you are right, Harry, she has no charm."

It became the family excuse for the ugly duckling. The boys heard it and used it as a teazle. Donna soon knew the phrase by heart and told herself that she didn't care what her grandmother thought, what her brother thought, what her father thought: that she hated them all.

She had not hated her mother, though it was inevitable that Maud's first tenderness should have been for her son. Like the rest of the world, had been a slave to his light touch, his affection and his laughter. Maud had puzzled grievously over her daughter. The heavy temper, the sullen ways, the inaccessibility, the uncontrollable explosions of passion, these things had alarmed her and estranged her. She had seen the same things in her husband without recognising them, so gilded were they by his charm; but ungilded they disturbed her. Her nature was, at root, deeply superstitious, though education had translated superstition into religion, and so sweetened it. But nevertheless the superstitious vein in her took a fear against her child. What was this changeling?

The modern side of her mind had fought her fear. She had been educated by her very charities, through the friendships to which they had led with the women pioneers of the Victorian sixties—nurses, would-be doctors, missionaries at home and abroad. Instructed a little by them her mind groped confusedly among the mysteries of conception and racial inheritance. She thought of her husband's isolation of spirit. It was on the crest and the breaking up of such a mood that her child had been conceived. Was it possible that that dark mood had been transmitted along with the heavy features and the narrow eyes? A text had come into Maud's pious mind—'The twilight I desire is turned into trembling.' Was her daughter walking in such a twilight?

Her own simpler spirit drew away in horror from the possibility, even while her maternal instinct drove her spirit back again to rescue the lost creature.

Donna felt alike the aversion and the return, and so her passion for her mother (for she was in all things passionate) was a grudging and a suspicious one. Yet it saved her childhood. For Maud had contrived to love her daughter the more, because she believed in a jealous God, and was troubled, not only at her daughter's lot, but at her son's immunity. Gilly walked in the sun. At Donna's expense? Maud half believed it. And because of her relief at the unfair decrees of God-heredity, was the tenderer to the scape-goat.

And so, though Harry's daughter was a natural solitary, she was not truly aware of it until Maud died. Then, indeed, her isolation was complete: and between her tenth and sixteenth years Harry knew his daughter only from the complaints of the nurses and the governess. For she was an intractable child, and the natural quarrels of the nursery were intensified by her jealousy of her brother's general popularity. When Gilly went to school he brought home plenty of friends of his own and Stephen's; for Gilly's instinct was always to make friends with boys older than himself. Gilly was so docile.

But Stephen found Donna less docile, and he very naturally teased her till she raged: and when she raged she was as uncontrollable as a wild animal. Stephen would go off home laughing after a teasing bout, but Gilly, still laughing, stayed behind to carry on the war. But Donna was a stronger build than he, and in their wars he got the worst of it. As a result she hardly encountered her father save as a creature to be punished.

Harry came home one holiday afternoon to find his son with a cut eye, and a lump on his forehead as big as an egg, lying half unconscious at the foot of the stairs, while his daughter, still white with fury, stood over him, crying—"That'll teach you!"

How the struggle began Harry did not enquire. It was obvious that Donna had pitched her brother down a full flight of stairs. He was in terror for his son, and indeed it proved to be a mild case of concussion. When the doctor had gone he faced his daughter in the study as furious as she.

"You're fourteen years old, Donna, and I've never beaten you yet; but now I think you must be taught. You might have killed your brother."

"I wouldn't have cared," said Donna.

"Then I shall teach you to care," said Harry, and taking her chin in his hand, cuffed her repeatedly on the cheek and ear. She twisted in his grip and caught at his hand, digging into it with her nails, tearing and ripping, in an ecstasy of fear and pain. With an exclamation of excitement and anger he released her chin, caught and mastered her two hands in his large grip, and with his free hand struck her again and again till she and he were alike dazed by his violence. Then, contemptuous, he turned her out of the room. She went upstairs raging with anger and pain. She never forgave him for his lack of justice; for the squabble had not been of her provoking and he had asked no questions. And he never forgave her for his son's closed eyes and catching breath. That they were alike did not occur to either the father or the daughter: and not even to shrewd, anxious Lettice, deploring the lack of sympathy between her son and her granddaughter, did it occur that they were suffering from the same disease, that each was slowly dying for lack of happiness.

But the encounter had a very remarkable effect upon Harry. He awoke belatedly to the fact that his daughter had as definite a personality as his son. He disliked her personality, disliked it the more because her revolting obstinacy and her maddening dumbness did at times and in spite of himself remind him of the lovely dumbness and the attractive obstinacy of his adored wife. This, of course, he would not, could not admit. But he said to Lettice (for though he talked to her less, he still talked to her) that it was quite clear that something must be done about the child.

"And I tell you what, Mother, I've a mind, young as she is, to break her in to the stage."

Lettice was shocked; but not so shocked as she would have been if she had liked her granddaughter.

"My dear, I would rather see a girl dead than on the stage," said Lettice perfunctorily. "It's not what it used to be. In your grandmother's time, yes, then there were compensations. But now there's no glamour left. It's either respectable and dull, or impossible from every point of view. You know that, Harry, better than I do. It has become a business."

"There's got to be a Broome on the stage," said Harry obstinately.

"There's Stephen and there's Gilly," said Lettice smiling at him.

Harry twisted uneasily.

"Stephen? Yes, there's no doubt that Stephen is a born actor. I'm very pleased with Stephen. Robin would be pleased. But, Mother,

Stephen is not my own flesh and blood. I'm building up a great heritage. I won't have it frittered away. Stephen—I think I know Stephen: it would depend upon Stephen's wife whether his talent continues or fizzles out; but he has no business head. Now Gilly——"

"You want Gilly on the stage?" said Lettice softly.

"I'd rather have him behind the scenes," said Harry.

"What, with his looks?" said Lettice. "Do you imagine that you'll ever keep him behind the scenes, Harry? He's born for the stage, and you know it. That voice, those movements—oh, I confess, he's a little slight——"

"I'm not considering the stage for him for the present," said Harry. "He's doing very well at school—extremely popular by all accounts."

"Whose accounts?" said Lettice casually.

"At any rate," her son rode her down, "I shan't hurry him. These child actors lose as much as they gain. With a girl, of course, it's different. His sister at fourteen years is as tall as I am, and she showed me a side of herself the other day that shocked me. I'd had to correct her. But, Mother, she flattened her head at me like a cat: she crouched like a panther. I might have been a trainer instead of her father. It came over me that she needed training of another sort than her mother's. The convent would be no good to the girl: as well put a cat in a pigeon loft. No, Mother, she's got the Broome temperament, plain as she is: and I mean to use it. I'd just as soon see Gilly in parliament as on the stage. He'd do well in parliament: he's damned persuasive," said Harry, half in pride, half ruefully. "He won't though: he'll come to the Glory Hole, of course, when he's ripe, like the rest of us. Meanwhile the girl can keep the name alive. There's an actress in her somewhere. I caught a look as she fought me. If I can break her in she may be useful. I want a young star, and why should I pay a stranger when I can make one of my own daughter?"

Lettice fidgeted, hesitated.

"I'm not at all sure that you don't outrage me by your attitude," she said. "You ought to be thinking of getting the girl married. Who'll marry a girl from the stage?"

"I don't think she'll marry," said Harry coldly. "It must be pretty obvious to you, Mother, that she has no—no——"

"Charm," supplied Lettice, irradiating it. "I see what you're driving at, Harry. Off the stage—no—none whatever. But these big young women come up well behind the footlights."

"Exactly!" said Harry. "It is not the charming faces that make up best, and she has good features."

"You mean," said Lettice, "that she may have another sort of charm?"

"I don't know what I mean," said Harry heavily, "except that she wants breaking in. And what's more, Mother, she wants using. There's something in the creature—" said Harry coldly—"going to waste. And I hate waste."

"The truth is—" said Lettice—"your business instinct is roused, isn't it?"

Harry shrugged.

"Something's roused," he said.

"You remind me—" said Lettice thoughtfully—"of Robert Broome sometimes, in his relations with your father."

Harry's heavy face broke out in a smile that youthened it by ten years.

"Gilly's the apple of my eye," he said. "I thought my father and my grandfather didn't get on?"

"Do you and Donna get on?" asked Lettice. "Yet I daresay she'll learn as much from you as William learnt from Robert, and give you much the same sort of thanks. Can I come to the lessons?"

"I wish you'd come and live with us altogether," said Harry. "It's a gloomy house nowadays, Mama!"

But though he said it and meant it, he never took the further steps that would have induced Lettice to break up her own household for the sake of being with him. He had, to tell the truth, got accustomed to his solitude. Lettice was a refreshment, and he loved her dearly; but he no longer missed her, and would have found her perpetual presence in the house as irritating as the presence of a cat with a bell round its neck. But he made every opportunity to persuade her to come and go, and the education of Donna, which he proceeded to put into practice, was lightened for them both by Lettice's constant presence.

For Harry was deeply in earnest in his plans for the girl: and, though the closer companionship between father and daughter which was entailed did not lessen their mutual enmity, it did lead to a certain professional understanding between them and to a certain respect.

He called her into his study a week after the accident to Gilly.

"Well, Donna?"

"Well, Father?" She never called him 'papa' and Gilly, as usual, followed her lead.

"Where's your brother?"

"I don't know."

"You should know," said Harry sharply. "It's the last week of the holidays. Have you no affection for your brother?"

"No," said Donna hardily. "But if you want me to find him for you, Father, I think he's in the garden with Stephen and some of their friends."

"Do you never play with them?" said Harry.

"No," said Donna. And then—"They don't want me and I don't want them. I'd rather read."

"What do you read?" said Harry.

"Books," said Donna.

"What sort of books?"

"Whatever I can get," said his daughter.

"Do you ever read plays?"

"Yes," said Donna.

"Shakespeare?" he hazarded.

"Yes," said Donna.

"Do you ever learn Shakespeare by heart?"

It was becoming more and more an interview between a manager and an applicant for a part, and he found it, with every new question, the easier to conduct. He smiled at her, his professional, engaging smile.

"Do you learn by heart at all?"

"I know my catechism," said Donna wearily. "But I'm not going to be confirmed."

He lifted his brows: his smile dwindled.

"Why not?" Then—"You'll do as you're told, my child!"

"Not if I scream," said Donna. "You cannot drag people to church screaming and get them confirmed," said Donna, "any more than you can drag them to church and say they are to be married."

"You won't be much use to me professionally if you take up that tone," said Harry coldly. "But you'll be confirmed, of course," he added, with a sudden appeal in his voice that startled and curiously enchanted her, "because it would have pleased your mother."

"Would it?" she demanded, with Maud's own serious brows bent over the problem.

Her father winced and sighed.

"You must know," said Harry in a low voice, "that your mother was a deeply religious woman." He could not bear discussing Maud.

"If you think she would have liked it, I'll do it," said Donna, finishing the discussion; for she, too, hated talking of her mother.

The two looked at each other. It dawned on them both that they were enduring similar feelings of discomfort.

"Don't do it for me, you know," said the father awkwardly.

"Oh, no!" said his daughter. And then—"It's just a bit of acting, Father."

"I daresay," he conceded, hiding his relief by a yet more professional manner. "We need not discuss it further. I have other things to discuss with you. I propose training you for the stage."

"Why?" said his daughter. "You aren't hurrying Gilly to go on the stage, are you?" And then, astounding him—"I think you are right not to. It would not be good for Gilly, though, of course, he would be exquisite in women's parts."

"Women's parts?" Harry stared.

"He's very girlish," said his sister. "And boys always played girls' parts, didn't they, in Shakespeare's days?"

Harry gloomed at his daughter, startled into interest. She was perfectly right about Gilly. The fashion of the age made it, of course, impossible to put him into women's parts, but she was right, he could have played them. As it was, in such parts as Oberon, Ariel, he would make a hit. A pity not to use him before his voice broke! Then he put aside the consideration and returned to a more interested contemplation of his daughter.

"Boys don't play girls' parts nowadays," said Harry less coldly. "But what about yourself? Would it interest you to play girls' parts? Would you like to learn?"

"Why, Father—" she stood up and stretched out her arms a little with such boredom that again he stared at her—"if you've made up your mind that I'm to go upon the stage, I suppose I shall go, shan't I? It doesn't much matter what I think."

"I'm not going to waste time on you if you don't work," said he.

"Oh, for that matter—" said Donna—"I don't dislike work. I like something to do."

And as she stood facing him he recognised anew his own wisdom in recognising the immense energy that was locked and restless in her strongly built body.

"Get down Shakespeare," said Harry. "Turn up *Macbeth*."

"Which scene?" said she, not moving. "I know them all. 'The raven himself is hoarse——' Is that the scene you want? 'Come, you spirits——' "

"Go on!" said he sharply.

She went on and interested him. Young, crude, ignorant, she had yet a force, vitality, and a sexless fury of intelligence. She would never be a great actress, he thought: or rather, though she might have the elements of greatness in her, though she might in her maturity be able to play a Volumnia or a Lady Macbeth or even a Hermione outraged, she would never have that quality which his audiences were year by year more eagerly demanding. The grand manner was going with the grand figure and the grand face, with blank verse, candle-light, the apron-stage and noble rant. She, deriving as she did so directly from their ancestor the strolling player, would be out-dated before she was truly come to maturity.

Nevertheless she would have her public: there would be a woman of the Broomes upon the stage again at last. Gilly and Stephen could undertake modern comedy and modern romance; but Domina Broome, as he envisaged her in later life, majestic, black-browed, unmoved by passion, would be a foil for their intelligence and charm, and a perpetual reminder that the house of Broome would now and always be, as it was in the beginning, the reigning house.

So he began training her, to the dismay of her governess, who was not accustomed to the hectic pace that Harry set. The Child's Guide to Knowledge, Mrs. Markham, and the use of the globes, the needlework and the blackboard were banished from the schoolroom. Instead the girl, with an air of neither liking nor disliking the innovation, went to French lessons, German lessons, singing lessons, to her dancing and fencing masters—and to the theatre!

It was dreadful to treat the usual accomplishments seriously. And then the governess had to endure hearing the girl her 'words', words which often enough had no place in the vocabulary of a lady. The governess had never before realised how unintelligibly coarse William Shakespeare could be. Who would be a governess in a theatrical family? It was the last straw when she was asked to accompany her charge to the Gloriana: to sit bored, resentful, with her skirts pulled together against the dirt and her ears pulled together against the noise, while ten yards away scenes were rehearsed out of all context, and ill-bred, passionate men and women clasped each other publicly, burst into tears, swore, ate sandwiches, drank stout from bottles in dark nooks of the wings, and then repeated the business again, again, and again until her head reeled.

Her charge's father moved through the din at least a gentleman, said the governess : and there were one or two women upon the stage who had the air of great ladies. But when her charge was introduced to these masquerading great ladies, when her charge was not only allowed to leave her side but incessantly called away from her, when she saw her re-appear upon the dusty stage itself, a victim driven to the altar of some insane cathedral, what could she do but resign?

She went in despair to dear Lady Lettice who had originally engaged her. And Lettice, who was always brusquely kind to her underlings, was once more brusquely kind, and presented her with a dress of puce silk with at least thirty yards of stuff in it, and a fringed velvet dolman : and packed her off as a companion to a cousin's cousin of her own, an impoverished Wybird who lived in Cheltenham, and whose eighteen-year-old daughter Adelaide sometimes came to stay with her little cousin Donna. And the governess earned her keep and a certain standing in the new society by her vigorous descriptions of the horrors that attended a young woman criminally encouraged into entering upon a career which could have but one ending.

Donna no more noticed the departure of her governess than a stone knows when the lichen on it peels and dries and is scattered by the breeze. Ill-trained, ill-guided, she despised underlings. Kindness to servants was no virtue of the sixties, and kindness was not a quality ingrained in Donna. Her father influenced her more than she realised. She imitated his harsh, imperious intention of having his own way at whatever cost in justice or in mercy. She was too young to realise that it was a way assumed as a protection against the uncouth and undisciplined world he ruled, and in which he had created, by sheer force of character, and disregard of sentiment, so rigid a sense of order and discipline. He was a great producer, to use a word coined long after his day, and a ruthless one. His strokes of justice and injustice, of pitiless decision, of shameless coercion, were celebrated. His daughter watched him ceaselessly and envied him his power of dominating and hurting. She made up her mind that when her day came she would bethink herself of his methods and use them, if need be, against himself. "Two can play at your game, Father !" said Donna in her heart, savagely.

For though she admired and imitated him, though he, in a sombre, possessive way, had in return a certain impatient admiration for her, they remained mutually antagonistic. Indeed, Harry found that there was a certain pleasure in training a creature who would, he was perfectly aware, at the faintest show of weakness, turn upon him uglily.

One effect of the training he had not foreseen. It was inevitable that he should supplement her training in the theatre itself by a certain amount of private coaching; but he did not expect such coachings to awaken in himself his long forgotten delight in acting. For many years the business side of his theatrical enterprises had absorbed him. He had no particular footlight ambition: he had been content with minor parts that kept him upon the stage, able to watch and control his company without overtaxing his always delicate physique. Like his mother he had found sufficient satisfaction for his actor's passions in daily life. But now he was solitary, bored, cut off from normal passions; for he had found no woman to stir him as his wife had stirred him, and his passion for his son was strictly limited by the terms of the boy's education. He was too austere, too fastidious, to fall into Russel's weakness, and he had so much money already. Yet, like all his race, he craved incessantly for stimulant

In Donna he found his singular stimulant. It amused, interested, exercised him to train the reluctant girl. He set her to study the huge rôles that he was contemptuously sure she would never be able to play. He wrestled with her obstinacies. He beat down her cold reserves and lighted her vast stupidities. He would wrestle with her till they were both exhausted, and he himself, utterly discouraged, would be on the point of rejecting her altogether. Then, in the very midst of his disdain, he would be pricked suddenly to attention by some sword-sharp utterance of hers, by some uncouth young outcry of raw passion, by some untrained, laughable, and yet majestic young effect of dignity, of tenderness, of rage. Then he would find himself so stirred, so challenged by her crude artistry that inevitably it quickened his dormant interest in his own capacities. He could not teach pedagogically: he had to act. He began running over rôles with her that he had never attempted, or attempted only in a youth comparable with hers. Then the rôles began to fascinate him: month by month he took more interest in his public engagements, and from time to time put himself into a more important part than he was accustomed to play. Forgotten ambitions stirred anew, and he began to say to himself—

'Why leave these parts to other folk? I teach them how to play. Why should they take the credit for my thoughts and my gestures and my business? I know my business and I am still young. The theatres are mine. Why shouldn't I play leads in my own theatre?'

By the end of the year he had stolen upon the public, not as the manager of the Gloriana who was a sound actor, but as a personal draw who happened to be manager of the Gloriana. It began to be urged upon him that he ought to be playing bigger parts still. Then his leading man fell ill, and he played the vacant part at a moment's notice: and with such success that in the next Shakespearean production he cast himself, not for Casca, but for Cassius. He did it timidly, dreading ridicule. But nobody laughed. And when, suddenly flaming into enterprise, he began playing Cassius and Brutus on alternate nights, the town streamed to see him. Not for nothing had he coached his companions for fifteen years: not for nothing had he excelled in all the little parts that nobody cared to play: not for nothing had he dammed up his own genius and, half unconscious, watched others' failures while he waited for this hour.

Now his hour had idly dawned, and found him ready. That autumn he put on, at unprecedented expense, the pageant of *Henry VIII*. He made a fortune: and, as Wolsey, a name that is not yet altogether forgotten. How good for a man's soul is a late supreme success with its silly press cuttings, and commands to act at Windsor, cables from Russel growing easy-going in America, and the spectacular joy of Lettice, daughter, wife and mother of stage kings! Oh, and it pleased Harry well enough; but it pleased him most that he had at last discovered how to light a fire in his own cold world at which he could warm himself a little. And this warmth, this refuge, he owed, and was aware that he owed, to his unloved daughter: and the knowledge gave him, not a tenderness for her—that he never had—but a certain sense of her value to him and in his life. He was as harsh with her as ever. He took, indeed, increased delight in thwarting her, in forcing her to do what she found difficult; but he had pride in her none the less. She was his daughter and got her wits from him.

Yet his new feeling towards her was no simple one. If she roused his pride, she also roused his pleasure in tormenting. He liked to put her in positions where she must sharpen her sluggish wits if she would not be made ridiculous, knowing how she hated to be shamed. He watched for his chance to humiliate her as an artist: and she knew that he watched: and in order that he should not take the chance, she made prodigious efforts. The results showed soon enough in her work, which improved startlingly. This pleased him anew, and he rewarded her in his own fashion by ceasing to force upon her parts that, as far as her years went, she should have played. He still insisted that she should understudy Rosalind, Ophelia, Miranda, as well as dozens of contemporary ingénue rôles: just as Lettice, who was in charge of her granddaughter's wardrobe, insisted on fitting out the girl with pinks and blues and whites, in muslin, tarletan and illusion; for these the taste of the day considered proper wear for an ingénue. But Harry was wiser than his mother in that he never asked his daughter to play the parts in public save in emergency, while Lettice insisted that the dresses should be worn. Harry knew well enough that the sweetnesses, the gentlenesses and the gaieties were not for his girl, and indeed, the big dark young woman with her penetrating voice, her decided movements and her perpetual frown, was a ridiculous and clumsy giantess in white muslins.

Yet in her white muslin she had to come down to the library when her father sent for her, knowing herself ridiculous: and in her white muslin she had to do what she could with Rosalind or Viola. She would fail, fail, and fail again, and Harry, grinning, would show her precisely how she failed, and old Lettice would watch the pair of them with curious enjoyment, and sometimes break out in defence of her granddaughter.

"Harry, you don't give the child a chance! It's cruel to expect it of her at her age."

Harry would narrow his eyes at his mother.

"But you expect her to be girlish. Yes, you do. Look how you dress her. If I'm to let her off Ophelia, then do you put her into middle-aged maroons and velvets."

"That's a different matter. Maroon velvet would make her ridiculous at sixteen. A girl must be dressed suitably. When Donna is married then she can wear crimsons and brocades."

Her son would flash back at her:

"Yes, and when Donna's an experienced actress then she shall play Cressida and Lady Macbeth; but she must learn to play schoolgirls first, and learn not to be ridiculous as a schoolgirl."

Then Lettice would turn to look at her granddaughter through her lorgnettes, and say placidly—

"What can she do with her big bones? But it's good training for you, Donna! Don't mind him, my dear!"

And Donna, waiting dispassionately till the discussion about her looks and personality should be over, would return her grandmother's amused smile with a look of complete uninterest, and answer—

"Mind? Why should I mind? Go on, Father!"

And Harry would go on, for he was a fine teacher, and with every sharp word, every darting criticism, every unendurable imitation of her deficiencies, he would be rounding, smoothing, remodelling the strange personality that professionally so greatly interested him. He had never had such a pupil: she could actually stand a beating. He could beat away at her faults like a cook beating a steak, and she improved, constantly improved in quality; but nothing else happened. If he had so harried one of his company there would have been an explosion: not the meekest would have endured the incessant harrying.

But his daughter took it all very calmly and continued to improve. Indeed, the only fault that he had to find with her as a pupil (though the faults he found with her performances were innumerable) was her lack of interest in her own wrongs. It infuriated him sometimes that he could not flush her vanity into her cheek by any mockery: that she was so little concerned with her own failures in the parts that she ought to be playing easily—the sweet parts, the gay parts, the gentle parts, the silly innocencies. She could do nothing with them, and yet she could not play Juliet either. She lacked passion: he could not get a natural love line out of her. Yet she was not tame. There was vigour. There was fierce determination in her dumb refusal to open herself to the words, to the mood of Juliet: and though she was no born ingénue, yet in her large-featured, smooth young face, innocence bloomed fiercely like some leafless japonica of January flowering upon the house-wall— a clear, red flower clustering stemless on its dark branch without a softening leaf, a red flower from which icicles drip, a flower that rejoices in its stone pillow and unvisited, unplucked and quiet, dreads the melting rain and defies sun and spring. Harry thought to himself that the only part she was fit for was Isabella in *Measure for Measure:* and would have put it on for her if either Lucio or Angelo had tempted him.

What was he to do with her? Go on training her, he supposed, and mark time till she was ripe for Goneril. Meanwhile, when a small part came along that suited her, let her try her hand. There were always parts going at the Syracuse, Maud's theatre, where he tried out his young stuff. So he gave her Phœbe in *As You Like It,* and she did not do so badly. But when he tried her on Jessica she drove him to despair.

" 'I'm never merry when I hear sweet music!' "

Harry flung up his hands in his mother's fashion: and his mother, who watched, lifted her eye-brows and sighed, smiling.

"My good girl, speak low!" cried her son. "Don't be so conversational. In such a line there must be tears in your voice and a tremble. Listen—'I'm never merry——' " and his own voice shook.

"I'm never merry when I hear sweet music," said Donna sulkily, and her voice had no expression whatever. But a gust of emotion, the mere tune of the words, caught up her father and spun him round, and she watched unsmiling as he expressed his own passion for his own art.

"Stop! Such a voice to use! Listen to me, Donna! She, Jessica, is listening to music. She—you—you as Jessica are realising how much there is in the world that you greedily desire and will never experience. What do you hear in music? Tell me!"

But Donna shook her head.

"Oh!" His silence destroyed him: he had to speak. "I tell you that you hear the pleasure of pain, the pain of pleasure. What else is music but an ache and a tug at your heart, a reminder that you are alive and will soon be dead, and that alive or dead you will never, never, never hold anything in your hands for more than a moment. Life is golden water by day and silver water by night, that you scoop up in your hands and watch run through your fingers again. When you hear music you know this, and when the music ceases you forget again, and yet there is something in you that would rather hear than forget, and so you listen. But yet how can you be merry listening, knowing what you lose? And yet how exquisite it is to be told that you will lose, are losing, even as you listen. 'I'm never merry——' Smile, girl! But have tears ready in your eyes! Look! Like this! Let them run down and then brush them aside with your hands! Look, lift both your hands so—brush them away and all tomorrows and yesterdays with them, and look up and smile again at your ridiculous Lorenzo! 'I'm never merry——' Oh, but you—" cried Harry raging—"you talk of music as if it were the dinner-bell."

"So it was, for Jessica," said Donna, watching her father's admirable impersonation with detached interest. "You don't understand Jessica at all, Papa: any more than Lorenzo did. How could you, either of you, and do all the talking too?"

Lettice giggled; but father and daughter, for once sharing a sentiment, looked at her stonily, while Donna continued—

"Jessica doesn't understand a word of what you are talking about, silly little thing!"

"You'll play this part as I tell you," retorted Harry; but with still an eye on his mother, who was sewing again. Lettice was always sewing beautiful, useless things. "How many Jessicas have I played to?"

His daughter eyed him coldly.

"You always play to Mama in your mind," she said contemptuously: and Lettice dropped her work as her son whitened in a silence that drew itself out ominously.

Lettice broke in—

"Donna, Donna, my dear! You don't understand what you say."

"But he does. Why, he teaches me to play all her tricks. He does it at the theatre too: he makes all the women play like Mama, smile like Mama, move as she did: he teaches them to do it. But I tell you, Jessica would never be like Mama. Jessica was just a greedy little Jewess, and this is how she would speak it—'I'm never merry when I hear sweet music——'" And she lisped and gave a high laugh that curiously echoed Lettice's own silvery trill of a moment earlier.

"Did you do that on purpose?" demanded Lettice sharply, and her eyes began to snap. Then her son's face checked her. He had not moved, and his hand held the back of the chair so fast that she thought she saw the rung bend under his grasp. She struck in again hastily, for she knew in three generations the signs of storm—"You've both done enough for today, I think. Donna, will you fetch me my cloak? It's time I went home."

She rustled to the door.

"Donna stays here for a little," said Harry, colourlessly.

Lettice, at her brightest and pinkest, smiled upon her son.

"Oh, but I want her, Harry."

"Later, dear Mama."

"Come, Donna!"

"Donna stays here," said Harry.

"Which of you am I to obey?" enquired Donna dispassionately.

Lettice looked from her contemptuous granddaughter to her son, who regarded her with a set face, not troubling to repeat his order. And then, very quietly, with the pink flush turned true carnation, she left the room.

For the moment Harry had won; though, if Harry thought that he had won for good, Harry was mistaken. So much her elaborately quiet exit said to anyone listening. But neither the father nor the daughter was listening. They remained staring at each other. Twice Harry opened his lips: twice closed them again. His face was perfectly white and his voice, when he did at last control it, was hoarse.

"Donna, if you ever mention your mother to me again in that tone—if you ever speak of your mother to me again at all——"

His voice was so strange that he frightened her; but she stood her ground.

"Then why do you do what you do, Father? You know that all I say is true. I hate it so when you do it."

"Be quiet!"

"And when it isn't Mama it's Gilly."

"Be quiet!"

Then she struck at the air in front of her with her hands as if, had he been near her, she would have struck him.

"I won't be quiet. Need you show so plainly that you think of no-one else? Mama—Gilly—Gilly—Mama! Are they always before your eyes? Then what am I? I might not be your daughter?" She waited an instant for an answer, then saying sullenly, half under her breath—"Well, after all, it doesn't matter!" she turned from her father and with a movement so like Lettice's movement that it was laughable, went quietly (for all her size she could move very quietly) out of the room.

But Harry stood on where she left him, rolling a pen to and fro between his fingers. Presently his mouth began to shake. He said—"Maud!" to the quiet room: and again—"Maud!" And on the second word his voice broke and his eyes began to fill with tears, and presently, after a restless turn or two about the room, he put his arms down against his standing desk and burying his head in them, eased himself of a passion half hysterical yet none the less agonising.

Then, as the storm lessened and he began to pull himself together, again he lifted his head, and saw his own face in the mirror behind the desk, and instantly, instinctively, began to examine with professional interest his own distorted features, and let his mouth quiver again deliberately, and thought how he would use that movement of the mouth when he played Leontes next month. But then, he thought, he must be careful as to the sort of beard he put on. He must wear a beard, he supposed? Yes, of course he must—'For 'tis a bastard, so sure as this beard's grey——' Still, it need not be a heavy one. Then he began to repeat to himself the lines he had been getting by heart before Donna's lesson began—

'We enjoin thee,
As thou art liege-man to us, that thou carry
This female bastard hence, and that thou bear it
To some remote and desert place, quite out
Of our dominions; and that there thou leave it,
Without more mercy, to its own protection
And favour of the climate. As by strange fortune
It came to us, I do in justice charge thee,
On thy soul's peril and thy body's torture,
That thou commend it strangely to some place
Where chance may nurse or end it. Take it up.'

He thought he would speak the passage, not as Phelps did, on a last rush of hate, but coldly, with an air of indifference more dreadful than malice. But it was a troublesome passage. In it, he had always felt, Shakespeare had outraged the possibilities. But Shakespeare, he reflected, had deserted his children and so could conceive such heartlessness more easily than most. But it was not easy for a normal human being like himself to get into touch with the unnatural mood. But still—the greater triumph if he feigned with success a state so outside the ranges of his nature. Let's see now!

Once again he turned to the looking-glass, and, getting interested, ended by doing an admirable evening's work.

CHAPTER 24

MOONLIGHT ON A BROTHER AND SISTER

It was the morn of midnight when, in a gorgeous exhaustion, Harry put back into his celebrated cabinet of Shakespeareana the cut copy of *The Winter's Tale,* well and truly rewritten by four generations of Broomes. Then, yawning, he stepped to the French window and flung it open. A garden could still be a garden in London in the fifties, and Harry still lived in the Regent's Park house which he and Maud had chosen. Time had done marvels with the shrubberies and young trees: and the house and long green lawns were so embowered in bloom that here town could fancy itself country.

The midnight was brilliant with moonshine, strong bleaching moonshine that put a glamour over the world. The apple-blossoms had lost their pink tinge through this same moonlight: the paved flags of the walk and the strip of water beyond the garden shone white in it. But this white was not no-coloured: it was a white in which all seven colours passionately sought and found sleep, and so robbed the rest of the world of its sleep. For moonlight does not lull. It is, to most people, an exciting light, begetting an intolerable restlessness. It strikes upon the mind of the human creature as a horse's hoof strikes sparks out of pebbles.

Harry, least of all men, could find peace in the moonlight. With that fierce, muted radiance pouring down from space upon him, it was absurd to think of sleep. Exhausted as he was he had to be moving. So he stepped out on to the verandah and down the iron steps to the gravel path. Then, annoyed at the clatter of his own footsteps, crossed to the lawn. Slowly he strolled down the stretch of moon-greyed velvet, his hands behind his back, not in the least aware that even in that isolation he was using his stage gait, as noticeable as a sailor's. Up and down he paced, thinking of his past and of his present, and of the effect he intended to produce in the trial scene: thinking of Donna and how the outline of her cheek-bone always reminded him of Maud's quick turn of the head: thinking that the receipts had gone down in the last week at the Syracuse and that he would have to get rid of that damned fool at the box-office who was insolent in his receipt of customers: thinking that it was on just such a moonlight

night that he had first seen Maud and talked to her: thinking that the
dew was soaking through his thin evening shoes: thinking that cherry
blossom was the purest white in the world, white as Maud's dead face:
thinking that he had yet another forty springs to see, but that then he
would be out of it all, thank God: thinking that it did not much matter
after all either way: thinking that he had forgotten to file his nails that
morning: thinking that he heard a noise beyond him in the mulberry
trees.

Harry was as inquisitive in observation as a wild animal, and as
cautious. It was pure instinct in him that drew him instantly into the
shadow of the lilacs on his left. Their night-chilled scent drifted across
his face, vague as a rumour. As vague, as soft, there drifted across his
hearing the sound of voices: and then he saw two figures, bleached like
the rest of that world of shadow and ivory, pass along the cross-walk
behind the mulberries. Dim as they were, and swift in their passing,
they were to be seen as young figures, a boy and a girl like saplings
walking.

He stood still, startled. Donna in the garden at this hour? And who
was that with her?

But he had not time to get into the proper state of paternal, moral
indignation at the sight of his daughter in talk with a man, before the
two figures were near enough to him for him to recognise the slighter
figure. It was Gilly, his own Gilly, Gilly, who should have been in
bed and asleep in his dormitory at school.

Then the two came so close to him in their to-and-fro pacings that
he could begin to distinguish snatches of the conversation.

It would have been natural to another man to step out and confront
them, but it would not have been natural to Harry. Instead, insensibly
delighted by anything dramatic and mysterious, inevitably charmed to
be in a position to discover that which he was not meant to know—
what could he do but stand still? Thus he would be able to gather and
hold odd threads of knowledge blowing idly as a spider's loosed fila-
ments against his hands. Later he would pick out one of the caught
threads to wind about a puppet, later still he would pull the thread and
make that puppet dance. How then was it possible that Harry should
step out into the open and confront his son and daughter whom he
adored and hated, whom he could never master, whom he delighted to
master? What could Harry do but stand still and listen to the alien
conversation in the alien tones of his own flesh and blood?

Besides, the cold currents of curiosity and excitement were warmed by good human fatherly anger at these children's impudence. What were they doing, and how dared they be doing it? Hush! Listen! Gilly speaks in the golden coaxing voice with the latent chuckle tinkling through the vowels.

"I swear to you, Donna, it's as safe as houses. I've got a friend keeping cavé. Goodness, girl, I've done it a dozen times before. Half a dozen times, then. Well, once. All right, only once. Anyhow I shall be back at the school gates by six and then I come up from the baths with the rest of them. It's great sport, but of course I won't do it again if you say not. But look here, Donna, you can surely let me have five pounds. I'll pay you back the first day of the holidays—swear to God!"

Donna's slow, contemptuous voice, harsher than the boy's, came very clearly, floating across the lawn.

"If I buy something from you for five pounds, Gilly, I don't have the five pounds back as well."

Then Gilly's answer, too, came floating.

"Oh, Donna, you darling, will you give it to me? Have you it here?"

And hers—

"I have it here, but I don't know whether I shall give it to you, Gilly."

And his again—

"Well, Donna, you said I was always to come to you——"

Then they passed out of hearing but not out of sight; for Donna paused under the cherry tree, leaning against the shining trunk whose varnished, rich red browns were ennobled but not obliterated by the moonlight.

Cautiously Harry stepped nearer. The father in him, spying out his young pair as they stood thus together, felt in spite of his anger and his curiosity a pang of pure pride in their beauty. His boy swayed as he talked eagerly like the bough above him laden with flowers of the double cherry, the barren, colourless double cherry that has so opulent a bloom. His young, smooth, perfect profile was without strength, but fierce as a knife-blade now that the moonlight had drained it of its girlish colour. The soft full mouth was dulled to the grey of a half-open rose in the bed beyond. The light eyes shone as the dew shone at his feet. The father thought—'How lovely my son is: and he's asking for five pounds: and he's asking his sister. He doesn't come to me.'

And that sister stood beside the brother, strong and straight as the sapling tree itself. The boughs that carried the weight of barren bloom were shaken by a faint night-wind; but the trunk remained unshaken: and so did she. He could just hear her voice.

"Gilly, I think you're such a fool. I do despise you so. Yes, I'll give you the money. You don't suppose I believe what you tell me. Of course you don't owe it to anyone at school. You've made that up."

"Ask Stephen if you don't believe me," said the boy sulkily. And Harry thought—'Isn't it strange that his face can't assume an ugly line? The shape of his mouth makes the words he says beautiful. But what does she think about him? Has she any affection for him? Why is she here at midnight, helping him, conniving, giving him money?' And, angry as he was with Gilly, Harry's real anger concentrated on Donna because of the contempt with which she regarded her brother as she put her hand into her breast, drew out a small clinking silken purse and weighed it up and down in her hand.

"I don't know why I give it to you," said Donna with an air of faint interest, as if she really did not know and would be amused to hear.

"You're an angel," said Gilly, watching her hands playing with the purse. It was a knitted one, ringed in the middle, its full ends hanging down on either side of her long fingers.

"What do you do with it?" said Donna, coldly curious. "Your allowance is twice mine. You can't possibly spend all that money at school. You don't think I believe one word, do you, about lending it to Stephen? And what sort of debts can you have in the town that you can't tell Father? Look here, Gilly, tell me how you spent the last lot I gave you, and you can have it. There are ten pounds here, not five. But you must tell me truthfully. You needn't make up stories. I always know when you are lying."

"I'm not lying," said Gilly sulkily.

"Then you can go to Father. If it's just silly little schoolboy debts, do you suppose he'll care? He adores giving you money."

"Yes, but he'll make enquiries. You know what he is. He'll come down himself. He'll be angelic. He'll say—'Give me the bills and I'll deal with it—' and he'll come down himself, Donna, himself! And he'll go to every shop in the town. I can't let him do it. Besides——"

"Exactly! That only accounts for half," said Donna. "Fifteen pounds is a lot of money, Gilly. Tell me how you've spent it."

Gilly's beautiful eyes searched the daisy stars on the grey lawn for an inspiration.

"Well, as a matter of fact——" he began, suddenly radiant.

"I don't want your facts," she interrupted relentlessly. "I want to know how you've spent it. Who came up with you?"

"Donna, what does it matter? Anyway, Donna, I can't tell you now. I must go, Donna! They're waiting for me. If we don't start back within an hour we're nabbed. Of course I ought not to ask you, but if you'll help me this time—— Look here, I'll pay you interest!"

His sister laughed suddenly. The father thought—'I've never heard that girl laugh before.' And indeed, it was as cool a sound as any in the garden.

"You are a fool, Gilly! Of course you've spent it on someone or something. Why do you like coming up to town? What do you do? What sort of adventures? Pay me interest! I don't want your interest: I want to know how you've spent it," said Donna. Then, straightening suddenly her vigorous young body and stretching out her arms in a gesture half yawn, half protest—"Gilly—you do things, and I don't do them. Can't you see I want to be amused?"

"Oh—" said the brother sullenly, with sudden and extravagant bitterness—"my affairs are certainly amusing!"

She caught his arm and spoke with savagery—

"Gilly, Gilly, tell me things! You won't shock me. Gilly, I'm so bored. From the moment I get up to the moment I go to bed I wear pink and white muslin and I'm under somebody's eye. Even when I'm acting with Father I'm ruled and regulated. I shall break out of it one day. But I shall do it openly. I shan't be furtive like you."

"Don't talk rubbish, Donna!"

"No, you'd hate it, wouldn't you, if I made myself conspicuous? You can do the—the queerest things, but if I——"

He shrugged his shoulders impatiently.

"You don't in the least know what you're talking about, Donna."

"That's it! I want to know."

There was an anguish of eagerness in her voice that made Harry suddenly see her mother in her: and so, with a sort of terror, recognise how nearly he had misjudged Maud's child. He did realise then, listening, that a human being's own words and phrases do not necessarily give the truth about the speaker. How prurient in expression was her curiosity and how pathetically innocent in intention! She was a fierce Eve deciding—'I will have knowledge!' but with no knowledge whatever of the meaning of knowledge, as she cried—

"I shall find out the exciting things somehow. I shall. I shall. And when I do it'll make a scandal, and you won't like that, Gilly: so you had better tell me what you've been up to, and if it's exciting enough it may satisfy me: and anyway, you know I've never given you away."

"One can't tell a girl," said Gilly, obstinate but charming.

"All right," said Donna: and began to move slowly, majestically along the path. Instantly the boy was after her, as swiftly as a ripple of water slips over and round an obstruction. His voice came urgently—

"Donna, Donna, don't be so headstrong. Of course I mean to tell you all about it. I meant to all along. Dearest darling Donna, do listen! You see, Donna, it was like this. There's a friend of mine called Arkwright, an older fellow—as a matter of fact, Arkwright's left—and his cousin, another friend of mine——"

The voice died away in the distance as the two beautiful young figures melted into the lilacs.

Harry did not follow them. He had his own emotions to master before he could pursue and master the inherited emotions of his children. For his own spirit was as young as theirs: and all three spirits were tricky and determined as young convolvulus spirals insinuating their way upward to the surface of life. For a convolvulus spiral will squeeze through brickwork, wind itself about stones and shards, inter-penetrate fleshier roots than its own, transfix the white underground stemmage, smother the frailer sort of seedling stuff, enwreathe what it cannot strangle, evade and surround what it cannot overcome—so bent is it on control and triumph, on displaying to the rest of the world of plants and to the adored, changeable sky, its particular grace, its particular subtlety of colour, its own evanescent and restrained charm.

This convolute spirit of Harry, so young, so chaste in intention, so Jesuitical in action, so ruthless in effect, this eternally boyish spirit of Harry masquerading in the body of a man and assuming, with the conscious importance of a dog carrying a bundle of papers, the heavy responsibilities of fatherhood, this naïve spirit of Harry was outraged, and astonished by his children's exhibition of duplicity. Donna and Gilly had actually been living a life of which he knew nothing. They had not displayed to him every detail of their minds. They had thoughts, ideas, points of view, systems of conduct which they had acquired without consulting him. Moreover they criticised him, their father, the—a Victorian phrase rose instinctively to his lips—the author of their being. And they lied to him as easily and as instinctively as he lied to an agent, a suburban manager, or a pretty lady of whose attention he was tired. O monstrous, O horrible, O incredible revelation of the baseness of human nature in one's own flesh and blood! He revolted from the business with the real distaste of a nature innately pure, which has set up a double standard of morality in order to cope with the business of living. Harry was the best liar in England; but he never lied unnecessarily: and the one thing which quite genuinely revolted him was discovering that he had been lied to. And now his own children had acted a lie.

Disgust was tempered also by considerable curiosity. Harry very much wanted to know what Gilly was doing in the garden at midnight when he should have been asleep thirty miles away: and he intended to find out—from Donna, not from Gilly. He called it—giving the girl a chance to tell the truth. But in his heart he hoped that Donna would so represent the truth that it would not be necessary to lose his temper with Gilly.

As for bursting out upon the two conspirators and having an explanation with them there and then, that simple piece of effectiveness never occurred to him. That was not Harry's way. It was his way to go into the house as the moon dropped behind the cherry trees, tiptoe to his room, and spend the rest of the night in brooding over the situation. Miserably wakeful he lay, planning, devising, obscuring the issue, clearing it up again, cocooning his grievance with fresh threads of remembered injury and wrong foreseen, till the morning and the morning tea came. Then up he got and came down to breakfast extremely white, his eyes drugged with sleeplessness till they glowed like agates, and was extraordinarily agreeable to his daughter over the bacon and eggs.

The central window of the small octagonal breakfast-room was wide open, and the beautiful, early air, cold with morning dew, swept gustily into the room and made Harry shiver. But it helped him to make his effect.

"Your shoes must be remarkably wet, my dear, from the dew. I hope you changed them?"

Donna glanced down at her slippers indifferently, but she made no answer.

Harry went on.

"One must not be deceived by the morning sunshine. There is always a nip in the air when the dew has been heavy in the night."

Donna rose quietly and shut the windows. Her billowy white dress, dappled yellow-white by the sunshine, imitated the grace of the cherry trees far down the garden, and brought the scene of last night yet more vividly into Harry's angry mind.

"Come and eat your breakfast, Donna!" said the father, still more agreeably. "How did you sleep?" And waited, eyes narrowed, for the answer.

"Badly," said Donna.

Harry was disappointed.

"What do you do when you can't sleep?" he enquired.

She gave him a direct look.

"Sometimes I get up and go out into the garden," said Donna. "I did last night."

"I was in the garden, too, late last night," said Harry amiably: and at that a scared look stirred in her eyes; but she did not flinch. "The moonlight was wonderful," he continued. "Moonlight is like snow, I think. One hears with such distinctness, and so much further than usual. Will you have some more bacon?" and left it at that for the rest of the day.

But that night, driving home from the theatre in their comfortable closed carriage, he put his hand on her wrist and asked her—

"Who was with you in the garden last night, Donna?" Then, with a pressure that expressed the intensity of his harboured irritation— "I've waited for you to come to me all day. Now answer me!"

But she said nothing.

"Who is Arkwright, Donna?"

She closed her stubborn lips.

"Answer me!" said Harry. And then—"I shall punish you if you don't answer me."

"How?" asked the girl hardily.

He thought for a moment.

"I shall put you into Viola and I shall bring Gilly up from school to play Sebastian," said Harry.

"You mean you would make a laughing-stock of me," said Donna.

"Yes," said her father. "I haven't noticed that anything except ridicule affects you. It's no punishment to you to know," said Harry with intense bitterness, "that you grieve me and disappoint me. You have a hard nature. Withdrawal of affection means nothing to you."

"Affection? Are you so fond of me, Father?" said Donna out of her bitterness, and looking exactly like him as she smiled.

"I'm your father, amn't I?" said Harry coldly.

She shook her head.

"Oh, Papa, why pretend? Gilly's eaten my portion. But that's not the point. Of course you can make me ridiculous, and I daresay you're rich enough to afford the amusement. But I don't think it would be good for Gilly."

"What?"

"Father, you're hurting my hand. I suppose you saw us in the garden. And of course you're furious. I told Gilly you'd find out. One can never keep things hidden from you. But it is amusing that you should be angry with me just now, because I have just now been making up my mind to warn you about Gilly. Not that I really care about him," said Donna disdainfully, "but you do, don't you? So you needn't threaten me. I'm ready to tell you what I guess."

"Why?" demanded Harry suspiciously.

"I hardly know." This was true, and she checked and puzzled over the problem a moment, before she shrugged her shoulders and went on with a certain impatience—"Of course I met Gilly in the garden. Of course I gave him money."

"Why?" said Harry again.

"Why? Oh, he wanted it, and I had plenty."

"Why doesn't he come to me?"

"But, Father, of course he's terrified of you!" said Donna.

She hurt him so. He could hardly bear the hurt that she inflicted. He said for the third time, but so humbly—

"Why?"

She shrugged again.

"It's something about you. How can one talk to you?"

"But you are talking to me now, Donna," said Harry in a choked voice—"talking to me quite easily."

"Yes," she said. "We can talk to you once we're started. But Gilly and I, and Stephen——"

"Stephen, too?" said Harry, still in that low voice.

"Oh, yes."

"Well?"

"Why, we are afraid to begin. How can we know what your mood will be? And Gilly least of all will risk—risk—" she hesitated—"risk a loss of favour. He *must* walk in the sun, Father. He must."

"You see that? So you love him too?" said Harry suddenly.

Her face hardened.

"I don't love anyone. You said so yourself. And Gilly doesn't care tuppence for me. But he comes to me. There's no-one else to come to.

He trusts me. And, Father, if you tell Gilly that I have told you these things, then I think I could kill you. But I want to say this. He's in the wrong set at school. I think you ought to take him away. If you don't he'll be sent away. I can see it coming."

Harry was gentle enough now, his irritations, angers, jealousies blown away by the mere breath of this danger. He leant to his daughter in complete confidence. He knew when to trust, and he knew her at that moment for his ally, his equal. There they were, two Broomes discussing another Broome.

"He exaggerates his adventures, no doubt," he said, but with a question in his voice. "A little showing off to a mere sister?"

"His friends are horrid," said Donna flatly. The phrase was the phrase of a schoolgirl; but he felt with dread the suggestion of hidden knowledge in the tone. She said no more. He waited a moment: then—

"Well, go on!" said Harry impatiently.

She turned on him frowning.

"Oh, I'm not going to tell you tales, Father. I only tell you what I think. I think that Gilly is one of those people who's got a grown-up mind although he's only just sixteen."

"We're all like that," said Harry. "When I was sixteen——"

"Yes, Father, but you didn't go to school, and you weren't weak."

"Gilly's not weak," said the father passionately.

"Weak," said the sister dispassionately. "He does what I tell him when he's with me, and when he's back at that place he does what they tell him. Ask Stephen if you don't believe me. But Stephen isn't there now to look after him. He's there by himself now—always about with older boys who like him and flatter him. And of course he likes it. He does love to enjoy himself. It's a mania with him. Poor Gilly!" She ended abruptly.

"Go on!" said the father.

"Oh, Father, I don't know how to go on. There's no more to say. But——"

"But what?"

"I think," said Donna, "that Gilly ought to be treated as if he were old. Grown up. Not petted so. I think that if Gilly left at the end of the term, and trained under you for the stage, were trained hard as you've been training me, and given enough money so that he didn't have to cadge, and were allowed to do silly things when he felt like it instead of having to break bounds as if it were an adventure, and if he were given parts in which he had not always to be handsome—well, I think Gilly would be nicer."

"He's at the best school in England," said Harry defensively, as to an equal.

"Yes, but Gilly's a Broome," said Donna.

"I'll think about it," said Harry. Then he gave her hand, still lying under his, a gentler pressure. "Thank you, my dear," said Harry, lightly, affectionately, but abstractedly, for his mind had already flown to his beloved. He was making new plans for the welfare of that beloved, rehearsing explanations, arguments, methods of attack. He was foreseeing a reconciliation and a new golden era of mutual under-standing, ending in a vision of Gilly playing juvenile leads at the Gloriana—a glass of fashion, a mould of form, observed of all observers.

Donna, watching him, withdrew her hand and shivered.

"Cold?" said Harry kindly.

"I'm always cold," said Donna.

"The boy's mad about acting, isn't he?" said the father.

"They both are," said Donna. "Did you know that Stephen is coming down from Oxford to play in *A Midsummer Night's Dream* this term? He's running it."

The father turned.

"And Gilly? Have they left Gilly out of it?"

Donna was flushed to a faint indignation that Harry should know so little.

"Left him out of it? Why he and Stephen are behind the whole thing. There's a master, one of the French masters, who runs it; but our boys are behind it all, Father. Of course they are."

"And what's Gilly playing?" said Harry eagerly: and because he got no immediate answer, turned sharply to question his daughter's face. The young moonlight could not enlighten the darkness of the carriage, but the street lamps, walking by at rare intervals, would shoot their yellow gleams in at the open window long enough to light the girl's face but never long enough for Harry to make sure of what was written in that face. But something was written there: and, for the first time since she was born, he looked at her with a pang of startled interest. What was she, that Gilly should come to her instead of to his father? Her night countenance with the eyes mere skull-shadows of blackness, was not to be read, and her doubtful unwilling smile was a flickering thing not to be understood. Her personality was incessantly new—

created and destroyed again by the passing lamps. There she was, and there she was not: she appeared and disappeared like a crinolined Cassandra, prophesying nonsense about Gilly: and her thoughts and her knowledge appeared and disappeared with her.

What more does she know? wondered the father. What more does she think she knows about her brother, about me, about herself? If her mother were alive—down, wantons, down!

Well, he would talk to Lettice about her. This he resolved; for there were faint stirrings of fatherly conscience in Harry Broome's breast, though they were quickly enough smothered by his jealousy.

So Gilly talks to his sister, does he? And she smiles at me—damn her insolence!—as though I ought to know by instinct what part they've given the boy to play. Well, but I ought to know. How should I myself cast him in *A Midsummer Night's Dream?* Lysander? Too robust. Demetrius? Too robust. Theseus? Too robust, too old. Then how should I cast him?

In the father's mind rose a picture of Gilly swaying under the swaying double cherries. Gilly's golden voice hummed in his mind—or was it Robin's, or sweet selfish Lionel's? Dead both, and dreams now of the night. If it is Gilly speaking, what are the words which he says, as he flits beneath the double cherries by moonlight, all the dreams, the graces and the goblins in his train?

'I do but beg a little changeling boy . . .' 'Quite over-canopied with lush woodbine . . .' 'And with the juice of this I'll streak her eyes and make her full of hateful fantasies . . .'

"Then he is to play Oberon, is he?" growled Harry, frowning to conceal his delight at the picture of Gilly playing Oberon. And Donna smiled at him in return, yet with her faint air of disdain at his slowness in arriving at the only possible conclusion. Then, as the horses drew up at the house door, she said, rather shyly—

"Father, would you like to see a drawing of Gilly in the clothes they want? Stephen did it. I promised I'd find the right sort of thing."

"And where, may I ask?"

Again she smiled.

"There's the theatre wardrobe. I took what I wanted."

"Didn't think fit to ask me first?"

Then she laughed outright.

"Oh, Father, you're never petty. I knew I could have what I wanted. Besides, it was only a fawn's skin and a bit of gold ribbon."

She was speaking to him over her shoulder, as she led the **way**

upstairs, treading softly in the sleeping house. His producer's eyes
took in the effectiveness of her setting; for the crimson rep curtains
of the landing had turned an unnatural raw violet, the garden seen
through its window was white and luminous: and the near staircase
and the upper landing became in consequence a charcoal drawing on
brown wrapping paper. On the marble console table between the doors
of their bedrooms, a nightlight floated in a frail coffin-glass. Its unreal
and useless flicker dulled the darkness of the recess to a mere boredom;
but it could not banish it, and Harry waited in the doorway till Donna
had struck a match, turned on and lit the gas jet over the mantel-piece.
The two beautiful peacock-eyed flames lit up the room royally:
nevertheless she turned to the dressing-table, and presently the lesser,
finer flame of candles sprang from the wax, like crocuses bursting up
through snow. Then she went to her writing-table carrying a candle,
and opened and searched the small walnut desk that stood upon it:
while Harry leaned against the end of the bed, waiting.

Presently he said—

"Where's your maid?"

"I never let her wait nowadays," said Donna, but her attention was
on her search.

"I thought your grandmother gave orders that she was to be there
with a hot drink for you when you came home late?"

"She bothers me," said Donna absently.

He understood that and said no more, but began surveying his
daughter's room. He had never been in it before. It was singularly
unfeminine: there were no pictures, no flowers, no ornaments, no
fallals. He went to the bed-table and turned over the pile of books.
There was *Jane Eyre* and Lemprière's *Classical Dictionary,* a Charlotte
Yonge, Murdoch on *Elocution, Die Jungfrau von Orleans* and *King
Lear*. The *Lear* lay face open. Harry picked it up and began turning
the marked pages, glancing from them to his daughter as a thought
struck him. But at the moment she found the object of her search and
brought it across to him.

"There's the picture, Father!"

He scarcely looked at it. He put his hands on her shoulders, his eyes
scanning her face. She smiled faintly into his anxious eyes, but she
said nothing. A moment they stood thus. Then—

"What's the matter with him, Donna?" said the father humbly.

She shook her head. Suddenly she felt herself childish again, with
no more to give.

"I don't know. I don't know any more, Father. It's only that I don't think school is the right place for Gilly. Look how old his face is getting." And her finger traced certain lines about the mouth and nose which the rough drawing had accentuated. "I think that if he were at the theatre under you he'd think more of himself and other people wouldn't think so much of him. But that's muddled. I don't know how to put it. I don't know what I mean. Good-night, Father!"

But he continued to hold her by the shoulders and stare at her, while she moved uneasily under his hands. At last he said—

"What do you think of me, Donna, as a player?"

The question startled her, excited her. But she said again warily—

"I don't know, Father."

"Don't know?" Harry's grip tightened impatiently. "Nonsense! Tell me!"

She pulled her mind together.

"Yes, I suppose I do know, really. I know that it excites me to watch you act. I see all your weaknesses and then I think——" She paused, flushing.

"Well?" said Harry, his eyes glittering.

"Why, I think—" said Donna—"that if I were those women on the stage playing with you, I would take advantage of the things that I know about you, as Goneril did. I would make such a fool of you," said Donna, eyeing her father. "I would make it so difficult for you to act."

"Would you like to play Goneril—" said he—"if ever I played Lear?"

She shrugged her shoulders.

"Miss Altamont would never let me."

"Miss Altamont?" said Harry sharply. "What is it to do with her?"

"She's the lead—and Goneril's the lead. She'd resign," said Donna.

"Pooh!" said Harry.

"No, Father. We can't afford to lose her, not this season," said Donna seriously.

"We?" commented Harry, seriously delighted.

She moved her head impatiently.

"The Broome management. You know what I mean. She'd be difficult to replace, at this stage."

"But she couldn't play Goneril," said Harry confidentially, as to an equal. "And I don't propose to let her try. We can't have a pretty Goneril"

"I see." Donna frowned again. "But she'd be jealous and make trouble. And anyway, Father, everyone would say I was too young."

"I suppose you are too young. And I doubt if you could play Cordelia."

"I could play the beginning of Cordelia," said Donna, "but not the end."

Harry actually laughed.

"No, I can't hear you saying to me—'No cause, no cause,' " said he.

"And I can't hear you saying—'Pray you now, forget and forgive,' " she retorted. And then—"No, Father, if you had come to me mad, making a fool of yourself, as Lear did to Cordelia——"

"What would you have done?" said he greedily.

Her eyes gleamed.

"What should I have done?" said Donna, and she too spoke greedily. "I should have said—'Who is this? I don't know him. Send him to Bedlam!' Yes, that's what I should have said. No, I'd have done better than that. I'd have said—'Put the old man in a litter and send him back to Goneril.' " Then her voice dulled, as if she were suddenly bored—"No, I shouldn't, Father. I shouldn't have troubled. I suppose I should have just had you looked after."

He did not answer her; but continued to observe her with bright-eyed interest. She met his gaze: she understood it perfectly.

"I amuse you, don't I?" said Donna, "in school-time. How long is it to the summer holidays? A month now. Then Gilly will be home and then I shall not even amuse you." She flushed. "But I know Gilly better than you do, Father. When I see you and Gilly together in a year or two I shall be amused then, I promise you. He's going to make such trouble for you."

"That's enough now," said Harry sharply. "Listen to me! You are to understudy Goneril, do you hear? You never know what may happen, and it would be a fine chance for you. I think you could play it."

"Oh, I could play it," said Donna: and she looked at herself in the long glass with the gold eagle at the top. Harry coming up behind her laid his hand on her shoulder again: and though she hitched her shoulder impatiently and would have wriggled it off, he kept it there as he contemplated the picture the two of them made with sardonic satisfaction. Then he spoke his new satisfaction, awkwardly, into the looking-glass.

"Donna—you have been a help to me tonight."

" 'An interlude!' " said she in turn to the looking-glass: and her voice was high and insolent.

Then he stared indeed. He could not believe his ears. He was so unaccustomed to rebuffs.

"But Donna—my dear—my dear little girl—" began Harry.

"Good-night, Father," said his daughter politely, and offered her forehead for his formal kiss.

CHAPTER 25

OBERON

He was bitter against her for her strangeness; but he found himself acting on her advice. He went down to see Gilly and found that Stephen was also paying his house a flying visit, for he took his producer's duties seriously: and the two made his short stay so pleasant that his bitterness dried like dew. But his anxiety remained. Stephen and Gilly were so much alike that they acted as standards of comparison to each other. Stephen's handsome countenance had the delicate flush natural to his years and his fair skin, but it was a flush of pure health. His eyes were untroubled and he carried himself as if he had been swimming in champagne. But Gilly was Stephen reflected in a mirror and, like all reflections, was a little dulled, a little shadowy. Harry was troubled, but he was too wise to ask questions. He had tea in Gilly's study and saw a rehearsal, and once again said to himself that Donna was no fool. For Gilly, dulled a little in daily life, was not dull in his part: on the contrary, as an actor, he was already over-ripe. Even in a form-room, barricaded with desks, with two square yards of dais for a bank whereon the wild thyme blows and a happy lout of fourteen for his Titania, he could create a glamour about them both. He moved like a spirit, and he bargained like a petulant god—'Give me the boy and I will go with thee!'

Was not the voice, the movement, the smile, irresistible? Would not all London find this Broome irresistible?

Harry gloated over the picture of his irresistible son and tried to put out of his mind the memories of his boy moving like a spirit against the snow-white cherry trees, crying, as he bargained with his sister—'Give me five pounds, Donna, and I'll tell you all about it.' Yes, young as he was, it was time that the boy was under his own eye. Besides, how opportune it would be. For mingled with the father's pride and anxiety was the manager's delight in a new discovery. Harry remembered a play in his desk at the office that had been tossed aside as useless because there was nobody in London fresh enough, yet sufficiently sophisticated to play the leading part. It was not a part that required experience but it did require stage sense, good looks, delicacy and freshness. Harry made up his mind before the rehearsal was half over: and ten minutes later was buttonholing the college authorities. Whatever they said against it, he meant to remove Gilly at the end of the term.

He was half relieved, yet disconcerted, that the protests against his decision were but formal. The authorities had an air almost of relief. There was regret, certainly, but a relieved regret.

Harry asked no questions, although he was bothered; but he had always found it better to let sleeping dogs lie. He could find out the trick of a latch noiselessly in his own time, so why trouble the kennel? Then his nephew gave him a shock.

"Are you taking Gilly away, Uncle? I'm jolly glad. He'll do tip-top in London. He's been hankering after London. But you don't want me yet, sir, do you?"

"Do you want to come?" Harry prided himself on being scrupulously fair in his treatment of his brother's child whom he loved almost as well as his own son, and spoiled as much for Robin's sake.

"Lord, no, sir! Not unless I must. I want to get abroad first."

"You shall," said Harry indulgently. And then—"But don't you think Gilly ought to go up?"

"I expect you know what's best for Gilly, sir," said Stephen lightly.

"I think I do." But Harry frowned. He distrusted such limpid simplicity. But all he said was—"By the way, Stephen, you'll say nothing of this to Gilly. I don't want him to know just yet."

Stephen nodded. He knew his uncle's delight in mysteries. And knowing his Gilly, he approved. He knew that he would get no work out of Gilly if Gilly knew he was leaving. Why trouble to shine in a school play if you were leaving the school? But Stephen was honestly absorbed in the venture, for school ties had not yet been weakened for him: he desperately wanted the show to be a success. To that end, Gilly must shine.

"Very well, sir! I won't say a word. It would only take Gilly off his work. Not that that matters, for he don't work, you know—but off his part. You'll come down for the show, Uncle, won't you?"

Yes, Harry would come. Of course he would come down to see Gilly act.

And he came, prepared to be gracious, amused, bored: not at all realising that he was assisting at the birth of a new era, and also witnessing his nephew's first victory in the first of many battles that Stephen was to fight against tradition. But it was so.

For the school, once famous for its yearly performance of a classic, had for a century ceased to encourage the acting tradition. The taste as well as the religion of the period was against such enterprise. But it so happened that one of the French masters had been, like Harry, a friend of Fechter, and brought his enthusiasm for Fechter's art to England with him. His pupils laughed at him; but they liked him, and found French drama much more amusing than French grammar. Presently a young English house-master caught the infection of his colleague's enthusiasm. French plays began to be acted in his house, and English plays—farces, principally, and ingenious concoctions by the boys themselves, followed in two or three of the others. The innovations shocked the older masters: nevertheless, such informal evenings became customary.

The two Broome cousins, however, as they grew more important in the school, had grown tired of *Ici on parle français* and *Box and Cox*. Stephen had a taste for literature, knew something of music and could sing. He had been a leading light in the reading society, had written most of the school paper, and still found that he had time on his hands. For games had amused him sufficiently, but had not at all absorbed him: he had a horror of boxing, but he had taken up fencing with furious energy, and could dance. The truth was that the family passion for the arts showed itself early, and naturally showed itself in the family form. Stephen, equipped and energetic, had begun to clamour for more prolonged excitement than singsongs could provide. Why not a Shakespeare Society? His house-master, a sound Shakespearean, had rejoiced, and backed him. There were, of course, combats and delays, but Shakespeare is always Shakespeare, and the house-master undertook to see that the bowdlerisations were drastic.

So the Society formed itself, was successful, and worked mysteriously for a couple of terms. Stephen, indeed, had left before the venture was fairly started; but he contrived to run down from Oxford occasionally to continue the good work. And at the end of the autumn term it was announced on all the notice boards that two performances of *A Midsummer Night's Dream* would be given by the Society. The second night was for the school: the first for parents and visitors. It was not for many years that the mere towns-folk were allowed a glimpse of the mysteries.

Then the parents, of course, came down like Assyrians: and the head-master had his life made a misery to him by serious-minded mothers and evangelical fathers who saw in play-acting the devil at his tricks. But the Society itself, on that cold December afternoon, was not concerned with the views of parents. It was much more concerned with the fact that it had undertaken to open at eight o'clock of the evening, and that the hour and a half allowed it for dressing was proving less than adequate. Everybody had been magnificently garbed at dress rehearsal, but it had not occurred to the nominal producer or to the sanguine Stephen that the make-up would need rehearsal. Stephen had provided grease sticks and powder enough for twice the company: and those children of the stage, the Broome cousins, were both of them perfectly capable of making up themselves or anybody else. But they had not reckoned on the time it would take to conceive and create a dozen elderly faces upon the smooth young masks gigglingly presented, to turn hobbledehoys into girls and elves. Stephen was incessantly called off to arrange a chiton, reassure a stage hand, tie a fillet, or send a crowd of servitors in search of forgotten stage property, and of all these difficulties he discoursed agitatedly to his uncle. For Harry, as the privileged parent, the great actor Harry Broome, arrived by invitation an hour before the curtain rose in the drawing-school which was turned into green-room and dressing-room combined.

Harry listened sympathetically as his nephew piloted him to the foot-high dais at the end of the room. On it stood the make-up table. Groups and queues of boys stood beside it, awaiting their turn to be painted: and whiled away the tedium by fingering the paints and experimenting privately with powders and rouge. They were agile and irresponsible as monkeys, and drove Gilly brilliantly and plaintively demented. This amused Harry; but he was careful to take little public notice of his son. Instead he devoted himself to observing every detail of his son's background.

The room was high, oblong, echoing. It was shaken, and the spaces filled, by the perpetual overhead din of clattering footsteps; for its ceiling was the floor of the main upstair corridor of the building. Its walls were painted the liverish terra-cotta still to be seen upon the walls of the British Museum. The colour lessened the beauty of the busts, casts, friezes and torsos that stood upon dusty shelves or hung from nails, as cruelly as the Museum decorations lessen the loveliness of the originals. Between the drab of the upper walls and the terra-cotta of the dado ran an emphatic black line; but the dado was, of course, defaced as completely as any street wall or railway station waiting-room, by the scribblings of the generations. Apollo Belvedere, Venus of Milo, the little David with the hat, and a broken-winged Victory, had been pushed together into a far corner and served usefully as clothes props. On the blackboards were remains of the morning's work: and fifty desks that should have run in rows up and down the room were now ranged nose to tail along the edges of the walls, but were broken at intervals by a faun, a battered Hebe, or a table with a carefully arranged group upon it consisting of a peacock's feather, a loaf of bread and half an orange.

But all these details Harry saw brokenly, with no certainty, because desks, statuary, blackboards and tables were incessantly revealed only to be submerged again in a surging sea of boys in every stage of undress. The gas jets, flaring nakedly, threw their strong wild light upon the absurd, magnificent groups.

Then Harry became aware that he was in Stephen's way.

"Shall I go, my boy? Do I hinder you?"

"Oh—oh no, Uncle, not at all. It's only—— Gilly, put Lewis's wig on again: he's got it back to front. Micklethwaite, find me the blue—the light blue pencil. It's there somewhere. I tell you I was using it a minute ago. Don't tread on it. Ah, thanks! Careful there, Hippolyta! Pick up your train, boy! Don't draggle it! Gilly, show him how! No, Uncle, not at all! Gilly, Hermia hasn't changed his boots. Bedroom slippers will do. Let him fetch them then. There's a box of coloured tape—tie it crosswise. Broome will show you, Jackson—the same colour as the fillet. Uncle, can you tell me the time? Now then, you, who are you? Snout? I told you I wasn't ready for the beards till I'd finished the women and the elves. Be quiet a minute there! Are there any more fairies not yet made up? I say, stop rotting! Listen! Shut up over there! Are there any more women?—well, come along then! Seven-thirty, Uncle? And we ring up at eight! Gilly? Gilly, can you do Peaseblossom while I get on to the men's beards? There are eleven to do still. Quiet, please! First act make-ups first! And who are you? Mustard-seed? Yes, but you're not first act: besides, Puck's much more important. Go across to Broome. Where's Puck? Do for God's sake stop fooling, all of you, and leave the grease-paints alone! We've only got half an hour left. How are you getting on, Gilly? I say, don't make him too red. He won't need eye-lashes either, it's half light. Hurry up, Gilly! I want you to do a couple of groundworks for me."

"I've got myself to do, you know," said Gilly good-temperedly, but with a certain passive resistance in his voice.

"You've got the whole of Act I."

"I know, but———"

Harry turned to Stephen with a certain shyness, for it was not his world.

"This is my line, you know, young man———"

But before Stephen could answer, Gilly flashed into the conversation, and Gilly's relief was delightful to watch.

"Father, do you mean you'll help? Could you? Then look, here's all my lot, waiting." And he whirled off the willing Harry to the neighbouring make-up table and was assiduous in pointing out the position of towels, grease-sticks, eyelash-black, wet-white and powder. His little queue of actors, their faces dripping from too liberal applications of clarified lard, were commanded to 'wipe off that muck' while their parts and requirements were explained. Harry, not needing explanation, nodded good-naturedly and set to work with the swiftness of life-long experience on a Peaseblossom.

Gilly hovered a moment, watching with intense approval: then, as Stephen called to him, spoke hurriedly—

"I say, Father, will you do me when the curtain's up? You needn't see the first scene."

"Isn't Stephen in it?"

"I suppose he is. He's Theseus."

"I wanted to see Stephen."

"I know. But do make me up, Father! I shall only wreck it. Do, Father!"

"Won't Stephen be hurt?"

"Look, Papa, you'd have time to slip in at the back before the end. He'd never know."

"You ought to be able to make up yourself, Gilly."

"Yes, I can, of course. Only—oh, do do me, Father! I shall look twice as well. Father, could you do something to my eyes?"

Harry tried to be off-hand as he examined his son's excited face.

"What's wrong with your eyes, Gilly?"

"Nothing, only there's a special look I want painted on. I can't tell you now, but do do me! I'll come as soon as you've done these chaps, Father." Then, delightfully, over his shoulder—"Yes, it's all settled, Stephen. Father's doing them. No, I can't come. I wish I could. But I've promised to help some other people—awfully sorry!" And he flashed away like a dragon-fly.

The glorious noise grew steadily for the next twenty minutes, then dwindled again as Stephen and Harry dismissed boy after boy, and the laughter, the skirls of excitement, the shrill of cracked and cracking voices and the rumble of raw new basses faded in the distance. But Harry noticed neither the noise nor the lull. Harry, so accustomed to shine that he never thought about it, now was filled with anxiety to shine in his son's eyes, and he had turned with caution and respect to his selected string of fourteen-year-olds. His own effect made his mouth twitch with amusement, for at his glance and question the yelling conglomerate of demon puppies stilled, dissolved and was instantly transformed and re-presented to him as a meekly charming group of shy-voiced incorruptibles, tongue-tied until he had bestowed the power of speech, then flatteringly garrulous, incredibly fidgety, but also incredibly obedient. He, unaccustomed to youth, marvelled at the dazzling white necks, lustrous eyes and extravagant eye-lashes of picked male childhood, and found it easy enough to turn the artless little grubs into creatures of sexless but startling beauty. As he worked on face after face with care, swiftness and certainty, he was following out a colour scheme of which Gilly was to be the brilliant centre. Oberon confronting the frightened sprites and their childish queen, must be much more alive than they, must reduce them to mere effects of moonlight. 'Where's Peaseblossom? Cobweb? Mustard-seed? Where, indeed? But there stands Oberon!'

"Aren't they a bit pale, Uncle, for our lighting?" asked Stephen coming across, his handsome face shining with heat, for his make-up and his wig were alike heavy. "They look transparent."

Harry smiled.

" 'Following darkness like a dream!' Why not? But these belong to Titania's train. I've done Oberon's. There they are. Like 'em?" And he jerked his head at a second group whose members were fighting each other for best places round the heavy iron stove whose funnel climbed the wall and disappeared into the ceiling. The glow from the stove reddened yet further the Eastern faces, gold, bronze and Indian red, liquid-eyed, slant-eyed, scarlet-lipped.

"Oho!" Stephen chuckled in turn. " 'Spirits of another sort!' You are allowed to stretch the text, Uncle. I shouldn't dare."

"I don't stretch the text, confound you!" cried Harry delighted. " 'Farthest steppe of India. . . . I with the morning's love . . .' Think, Stephen, think!"

"I see, sir! Titania the moon and Gilly the sun. Of course I like it, but I shall have to be careful of my lighting. Well, thanks awfully, Uncle, you're a brick. Will you come with me now and I'll show you your seats?"

Harry hesitated.

"As a matter of fact, I half promised to make up Gilly."

Stephen's face fell.

"Oh, but you'll miss my first scene, Uncle."

"Only a bit of it, my boy. You don't care, Stephen, do you?"

"He might have done himself. He's had nothing to do but tag around." Stephen's eyes sparkled angrily and he began to shout across the noise-filled space—"Here, Gilly, come out of that! Arkwright, I made you up first of all. You ought to be dressed and on the stage. Come on now, all of you. And I do think, Gilly, you might have done something about your own face. Come along, now, at once. Where are your clothes? In the other room? Well then, get 'em! What are you here for? Don't you see Uncle's waiting?" Then, his brief spurt of temper over—"It can't be helped, Uncle. Only see as much as you can, won't you? I'm rather proud of my grouping."

Then, after a hasty last powdering of his handsome, determined face, he began shouting at the top of his voice and clapping his hands.

"Be quiet, everyone! Listen! Curtain's up in five minutes. Does anyone still want help before I go? Is anyone not made up yet? Only you, Gilly? All right! Come on, the rest of you. And listen to me! If anyone looks through the curtains or talks behind the scenes, I'll——" He surged out, a visible high wind, brisk and balmy, shepherding all the clouds of that sky.

Peace descended on the gaunt, dishevelled room. The clatter of steps overhead had all but ceased, though an occasional single footfall thrilled the full silence as a ghost's might have done. For the room was now so quiet that you could hear the roar of the stove, distant as the roar of the sea in a shell. The gas flared cruelly upon the general confusion. The raised, flouted dust was settling everywhere again on shelves, furniture, ledges, busts, and on the desks already piled with shirts, waistcoats, trousers, coats and theatrical finery heaped huggermugger. Braces and ties festooned the backs of desks: collars crooked over them and one encircled the neck of Clytie whose plaster petals were freshly chipped. Fragments of plaster lay beneath her pedestal on the floor which was already patterned with ground-in and soaked-in substances—blackboard chalk, bread and butter, smears of greasepaint, spilt macassar oil, red ink, black ink, mud. On it lay also small possessions, dirty handkerchiefs, packets of sandwiches, orange peel, school books, letters in torn envelopes, pencils, combs and a good deal of crêpe hair dropped by Stephen at his beard-making and wafted like thistledown by the icy blasts from the incessantly opening doors hither and thither about the room.

But now the draughts had ceased and at once Harry began to realise the thickness of the atmosphere. What with fatigue, gas-heat, stove-heat, shut windows and the smells of dust, grease-paint, beeswax, black frost, coke and schoolboy, he began to feel so dizzy that he sat down to wait for Gilly, who had darted off crying—"Back in a moment, Father!"

He found it very pleasant to sit there and rest and wait for Gilly, in spite of the closeness. It was absurd that he should be reminded of a summer's morning that he had once passed lazing on a windless hill-top, that he should translate the glare and hiss of the gas into the glare of sunshine and the buzz of bees, that the sudden lull should seem to him a noontide lull, and that the sweet artificial reek of the spilled hair-oil should remind him of a natural scent, the exquisite scent of golden broom in flower on that same hill-top; but the illusion was a very pleasant one and extremely vivid. He shook it off, however, and called, refreshed and smiling, to his returning son—"Come along, Gilly! Hurry now! Let's look at you!" And then, chiding as a parent should—"Why did you dress before I made you up? The powder will spoil your clothes."

"That's only a cloak I bagged," returned his son, letting the gaudy length of embroidered stuff slip from his shoulders. And as he did so, his father started. For when the drapery fell away, there flashed across the surface of the mirror Oberon, sudden in his coming as the sun. And indeed he appeared to stream upwards, slender as a shaft of light. His eyes shone beneath his golden cap of hair, bound to his brows by a golden fillet. His cheeks were sun-flushed, his body bare. The long line of beauty from ankle to knee, from knee to thigh, that line of beauty incomparable and evanescent as a boy's singing voice, was broken only by a skin swung about him. He stood a moment displaying himself to his father, then stretched out his arms like a young morning and laughed.

"Well, do you like it, Father? I think it's good." And he looked at himself again critically but with pleasure as he continued—"A skin's much simpler than a tunic and Oberon wouldn't wear much. We got the idea from that Roman faun."

Harry glanced in startled recognition from his son to the plaster cast. Gilly was right. Plaster and breathing flesh resembled each other. There, duplicated, were the small hips, thin waist, broadening shoulders and the miraculous run and play and shift of the lovely line as the spectator moved about the statue, or as the boy took up a fresh pose in front of the looking-glass.

"Oberon should have wings," said the father with a catch of the breath.

"So I have." Gilly showed his Mercury sandals. "Well?"

"You're very tanned."

"Oh well, that's make-up, of course. It took ages to rub in. But I was far too white. I want to look golden, all sun and air—'Come unto these yellow sands—' I don't see how she can resist him—I mean, that's the effect I want. But you'll have to do my face for me, Father! I can't manage it. But it will be good, won't it, the whole effect?"

"It isn't the stock costume for Oberon," said Harry severely.

"I should think it isn't," returned Gilly, delighting in the withheld praise.

"Who designed it?"

Gilly laughed.

"Well, I know what I ought to wear."

"I daresay you think you do. Don't screw up your eyes."

And Harry began to dip his fingers in the lard. But Gilly stopped him.

"Don't use that on me. I've got some cold cream of my own."

Harry shook his head over his son's niceness, completely understanding it and pretending not to, as he accepted the substitute.

"You'll come to cocoa-butter like the rest of us before you've finished, Gilly."

But Gilly wrinkled his nose.

"Lard smells so. Doesn't this room smell foul too? I hate dirt. Father, what are you going to do? Are you using No. 3 to start with? Let me see what you've done, Father."

"You may as well learn," Harry indulged him.

Gilly surveyed himself closely with intense interest.

"I don't want to be pink and white. I want to have a strange look. I want long slanting eyes. Can't you paint a sort of beckoning?"

"Beckoning? What makes you say that?" Harry was working away indefatigably as he chatted. He was hardly listening to his own words, so intensely were his fingers delighting in Gilly's face. He had the fine bones under his hand to feel at leisure, could trace with pressing thumbs the vault of the temples, the inner arches of the brows, feel the true character of the chin, sharp, delicate, wilful, reveal itself beneath its smooth disguise. He felt as if his whole soul were housed at that moment in his fingers: the fingers of his memory were learning Gilly's face by heart. 'Thus and thus was Gilly shaped in 1867. I shall grow old. I may become blind or paralysed: and Gilly will one day be emptied of youth and beauty and dependence upon me, his father. But still, in that day I shall remember, my ten fingers will remember for me, this year 1867 and this December of the year, and this present face of Gilly's. I have seen him and touched him as he is. I am learning him by heart. I know him for ever, my dear, dear son.'

Meanwhile he continued to fantasticalise the fair face, turning it from the face of the boy Gilly into the countenance of Oberon, king of dreams and enchantment. It was easy enough. He had but to lengthen the eyes, tilt the line of the brow and deepen the soft, contemptuous curve of the upper lip.

"I say, Father—"

"Don't screw up your eyes. What did you say, my boy?"

"Papa, do something for me, will you? Promise!"

"I never make a blind promise, Gilly."

"No, but promise me. It's quite easy for you, Father! Do, please, Father, promise me."

"Promise you what? Don't blink. Am I making your eyes water?" For large clear tears were welling up in the large clear eyes and overflowed the lids.

"Sorry, I can't help it." Gilly laughed unembarrassed. "You're not hurting me a bit, but my eyes will weep. They always do. But listen! You know I said 'beckoning'. Well, what I mean is—I do want to play Oberon well. Now if you were playing Oberon wouldn't you just crook your finger at 'em?"

"I could never have played Oberon, Gilly. I haven't the physique."

"Well, but if you were coaching me, Father, wouldn't you play it on those beckoning lines? 'Come here!' 'Go there!' 'Come here again!' That's the effect I want."

"I daresay you'll manage it," said Harry grimly, thinking to himself —'He must not learn from me how easily he can get what he wants.'

"But I can't, Father. I have to persuade, lay plans, arrange the stage, when I want to influence anyone. But Stephen, he just beckons to them—'Come here!' says Stephen, and they come. It makes me mad. I have to take trouble; but he doesn't have to take trouble. I want to beckon, not reckon. So I thought—I'll ask Father to teach me the Broome spell. Will you, Father? I wish you would."

"Spell? What nonsense are you talking, Gilly?"

"Spell—charm—the Broome charm. I know the first four lines, of course; but do teach me the rest of it, Papa! Grandmama says you know it."

"I can't, Gilly." For a moment Harry was serious. "It has to go from a man to a woman." Then he bethought himself. "Besides, it's pure nonsense."

"I could beat 'em all tonight if I knew it," said Gilly obstinately.

"You'll play very well, I'm sure. Look at yourself."

Gilly twisted round and stared intensely into the mirror, large and swinging, that he had wheedled from the spare bedroom of his housemaster's wife: and Harry, wiping his stained hands on a towel, peered over his son's shoulder. Gilly was enchanted.

"It's a miracle. I look so much older."

"Oberon is ageless but not young," said Harry.

"That's it. Rippingly old. I might be you if only—" He broke off.

"I am a plain father; but you—" said Harry, delighted to be ugly if it enhanced the boy's pleasure—"you—"

"No!" Gilly flushed so violently that it showed through his make-up. "I don't mean that, Father. I mean just the opposite. Paint won't give me what you've got. You still know the charm. Oh, you might tell me."

"Dickon, Dickon, cats and mice—" began Harry dreamily. And then—"You're making a fool of me, Gilly."

"Go on, Papa!"

> "Crook your finger and beckon thrice!
> By the Father and the Son,
> Reckon up and beckon on!
> Reckon, beckon—"

"Go on, Father!"

"I can't, dear boy. It's a silly superstition, but why should I break the chain? Your great-great-grandfather got it from an old woman, and he told it to your great-grandmother the duchess, and she taught it to your great-uncle Lionel. You still remember him, don't you? And he taught your grandmother and she taught me. But it's all nonsense, of course."

"Then tell me, Father, if it's just nonsense."

"I'll tell your wife, Gilly, one day."

"I'm not going to marry," cried the boy flushing.

"Of course you'll marry."

"I won't, Father. I swear to you I never shall. I'd hate it."

"Well, if you never marry, Gilly, I shall have to teach Donna."

"Donna?" Gilly was furious. "Father, you couldn't! You wouldn't! Can't you imagine her jeering? Besides, she isn't a Broome as I am. She'll change her name when she marries. I shan't. It's got to be me, Father! Do tell me, dear, darling Father!"

"And bring the Broomes bad luck, Gilly?"

"But it won't. It can't. There's no such thing as luck. You know you don't believe that, Father. You know you don't believe in anything."

"Gilly, Gilly, you mustn't say that," and Harry was troubled. The boy was fantastically excited.

"Well, I don't believe in anything anyway. A friend of mine's a Free-thinker. I am, too, really. As a matter of fact I'm an atheist."

"Gilly, I won't allow this. Control yourself!"

"Well, Father, what about you? When do you go to church? Aren't you an atheist too? Don't pretend to me, Papa! You are, aren't you? It's a sort of secret between us. There's no harm. It's just that we both despise silly superstitions. And this about the Broome charm is just a silly superstition; so tell it to me, Father, oh do! Do!"

Unseemly talk for the 'sixties—wild, whirling, blasphemous talk, and a father's duty was to obliterate a child who talked thus to the author of his being. But oh, the flattery of such talk! 'He's terrified of you, Father!' He could hear Donna's voice and remember the pang that her words struck into him. Now he could retort—'Well, Donna, does this look like terror? For Gilly had been watching him, it seemed, with sympathy and understanding, had childishly comprehended his mature disillusionments. His own little son had penetrated his secret hells and was not a bit afraid. Since he had stood here this last half-hour, painting Gilly's face, listening to Gilly's chatter, how real and warm and touchable the walls of the world had become! Here was an end of isolation. Atheist? Absurd boy!

"Don't we both despise superstition, Father? Don't we? I do and I know you do. So tell me the rhyme, Father! Don't tell Donna! Tell me!"

A clang of doors, a nearing murmur of many voices announced the end of the act.

"Go on, Father, they'll be here in a second. Reckon—beckon—go on!"

"Gilly, I—"

Then a pack of boys flung into the room shouting. At the sight of them Harry could resist no longer, or was it the sight of Gilly's disappointed face? At any rate he stooped and whispered the queer final couplet in his son's ear.

"Aha!" Gilly's eyes blazed. "So that's it, is it? Thanks awfully, Father! It'll bring me luck, Father, you see!" He darted off, plunged into the whirl of returning actors, sought out a quarry, dragged him off and disappeared in the turmoil. Harry was left for Stephen.

"Well, my boy, how has it gone?"

"Didn't you see any of it, Uncle?"

Harry was confused.

"I'm afraid I missed it. But I'll be there for the next act. Better get to my seat now, hadn't I? Have you time to show me?"

After all, what right had Stephen to be disappointed? Stephen was Harry's dear nephew, but not his son.

CHAPTER 26

DONNA HAS CHARM AFTER ALL

THE show went very well, though Stephen was more and Gilly less effective on the stage than in the dressing-rooms. However Harry was pleased, for he expected nothing from an amateur performance, and schoolboys' performance at that. Yet he had brought away two valuable facts with him—Stephen could act, and direct actors: and Gilly could look beautiful and speak verse, not intelligently perhaps, but in a voice that made again the sense that his inexperience destroyed. But he badly wanted training and Harry was quite sure that he was right in beginning the training at once. As for school not being the place for him, he intended to forget that nonsense. He had seen for himself that Gilly was obviously popular and happy; but he needed instant training. Harry was glad that he had arranged for him to leave. And Gilly was too docile to raise objections, especially if Stephen broke the news to him.

"Stephen, I leave you to tell Gilly. He is too excited to be told tonight. See that he is pleased with the idea!"

"I'll talk to him, Uncle."

Thus the Broomes always arranged the fortunes of other Broomes. Sometimes a William or a Russel rebelled; but Gilly, as his father said, was docile. He acquiesced joyously in the new scheme, and left the school where he had intensely enjoyed himself and made more friends than there were days in a term, with scarcely a regret.

But Lettice was shocked when she heard the news. William had always said, and Lionel had always said, and everybody had always said that three years at the University were indispensable. What was Harry thinking about to deny the boy his chances, and especially to do so without consulting her first?

But Harry's reasons were not reasons that he could disclose. He had been disquieted by a girl, but he could not pass on his disquiet to a woman. And Lettice, for once at fault, did not perceive that his hesitation, his troubled, withholding air was genuine. She thought that he was getting his own way for the sake of the theatre, and because of some private whim or ambition of his own. She compared unfavourably this strange eagerness of his to have the boy upon the stage with

307

her own William's refusal to help Russel to a stage career. Instantly she revived, for Gilly's benefit, the forgotten attitude; for she had the true grandmotherly passion for her son's son. She was not quite sure that his father, her strange, stupid Harry, fully appreciated the virtues and the charms of Gilly. Harry had made his decision and he was the boy's father, and it was not for her to interfere, and no doubt he knew what was right, and she would not dream of saying a word: nevertheless Lettice was not pleased. Besides, only recently Harry had quite definitely overruled her in the matter of Donna. He had made her look a fool. She had proposed at the time to teach him that he could not do this to his own mother, but had softened to him in the morning, remembering that Maud was dead. Now, however, she recalled that vague slight and, unable to convey her disapprobation of his treatment of Gilly and quite resolved not to be hurt with him for this, was fortunate enough to remember the former slight and to be hurt with him for that.

Harry had gone over to see her on his return from the school knowing that it would please her; but she had no sooner kissed him than he knew that she was not pleased, and that her response to his account of his new plans for Gilly lacked vitality.

So then he knew where he was; for it was Lettice's little trick to behave when she was annoyed as if she were a watch with a broken main-spring. The only way to mend her was to provoke her into a statement of her grievance: and this also Harry very well knew.

Dutifully he began the healing process.

"What's the matter, Mama dear?"

"Matter? I am sure I don't know."

"You've been doing too much?" he hazarded affectionately.

"Too much? I am not given an opportunity of doing too much. My son is swallowed up by the theatre: my granddaughter whom, I must say, I did once look forward to introducing into society, is taught to neglect me: Stephen, dear child, is at the University and writing me that much against his will he will be forced to travel these holidays. Have you heard of this? Do you approve of his gadding off? Not that I want to stop Stephen. I like his friends. He has been seeing something of Lewis Wybird and Mary Lawburn's boys. Dear Mary Lawburn and I were at school together, and though I never knew old Lord Deeming, Rosina knows them well. It's the best thing in the world for Stephen. So is Oxford. How else can he make the right friends? It's good for him to be among his cousins. If he is a Wybird he may at least have the advantage of it. I hope Gilly won't feel later on—but you are quite right to do what you think best for the boy, Harry: though whether your idea of what is best is wise—however, it is no concern of mine. But Donna is another matter. Not that I blame the girl. But another time, Harry, if you want to teach her to slight my authority, to show her how little you value my opinion, I shall be glad if you would do it in my absence."

"But, dearest Mother——"

"We won't discuss it, dear boy. It's all over and forgotten. If I was hurt I have got over it."

"Dear Mama, if you would like Donna——"

"To come and see me? It's very strange, isn't it, that I should wish to enjoy my granddaughter's company? Soon after Christmas, for instance, I am entertaining Rosina's relations who are over for a month or two. She wrote to me to do what I could, and I shall. No, I didn't trouble you with it. I know better than to disturb a busy man. Your father taught me that. Besides, you haven't given me an opportunity, have you, for a long time now? But it would have been natural to have my granddaughter by me: I am sure that Rosina would have liked it. After all, if it had not been for Rosina you would never have met poor Maud. Dear Maud! Ah, there was no-one like Maud! And I think, Harry, that if Maud had been alive she would have seen to it that Donna had her chances. But as you know I never force my opinion. If you ask me I say what I think; but I am not going to step between father and daughter. Do me justice, Harry, I never interfered between you and Maud. When she asked me for advice I gave it. When she came to me that night and told me the whole story I did not mince matters. I said—'My dear, he is your husband and he is five years older than you and he loves you dearly. That is enough to expect of any man. For the rest, if he is arbitrary, it is for you to submit.' That is what I said, Harry. I did not tell her that my sympathies were all with her, as they were, believe me! I thought you very high-handed with Maud."

"Mama, for pity's sake—" said Harry: and he got up and walked about the room.

It was the sign of defeat. It was all she wanted. She changed in an instant to another woman. That curious inheritance of hers, that streak in her of the male desire to torment, not out of cruelty but out of curiosity, ceased to show itself. She was wholly the mother, the Mother of the Churches, hanging horror-stricken over wounds—'My dearest child, are you unhappy? Do you still miss her so after so many years?' She did not say this aloud, but with her gesture, the expression of her face. Aloud she said—

"Dearest boy, are you worried? About Gilly? There is something, isn't there? No, don't tell me. There is no need. I am not curious, only distressed for you. You would tell me if I ought to know. It's enough for me that you are troubled."

"I'm so tired, Mother," said he, sitting down again nearer to her.

"Yes, yes, yes," she crooned. "It's the price you pay, my poor lamb, just as your father paid it. Are you playing this week? I have not been down yet to see you. Are you good?"

"Better than ever," said Harry, mocking and truthful. And then— "Mother, what is this about Donna? Should anything be done that I don't do?"

She soothed him.

"You do all a father can."

"But not what a mother could do? D'you want me to marry again?"

The wary cat-look, jealous, fierce, warning off all women, changed Lettice's eyes more quickly than words rose to her lips. But when the words rose they were gentle, kind, dispassionate.

"Dear Harry, if you found the right woman how I should love her!"

He smiled at her, understanding her profoundly.

"Would you, Mother?"

"Yes, Harry."

They stared at each other, he whimsically, she defensively. Then, because they were Broomes and had known each other intimately for some forty odd years, they both began to laugh.

And the upshot of it all was that though Harry could not give himself leave of absence, Donna was released from her duties as understudy early in the new year, and packed off to her grandmother's house in Park Lane. And on the evening of her arrival Lettice's maid dressed her in a creation of white gauze which Lettice had ordered from Paris a month earlier, for she had always intended that Donna should attend this particular dinner-party.

It was a very grand dinner-party and it was a very grand dress with flounced panniers and a swathed pointed waist. And the maid who took hair-dressing lessons every season, parted the young lady's hair smoothly across her brow, then loosely plaited the long mass that hung down her back into an immense coil upon the arch of her head, drooped the end of the great plait on the nape of her neck and caught it up again. On this Athene's helmet of shining hair she would have further placed a wreath of white rosebuds mounted on gauze. But her young lady who like Gilly knew what she could wear, though unlike Gilly she did not always take the trouble to wear it, pushed it aside frowning. She stood up, surveyed herself, shrugged her bare shoulders, nodded—"It'll do!" and walked out: leaving the maid with a necklace and bracelets still on her hands and a fine fear upon her of a midnight interview with her ladyship. But her ladyship ought to know that one could not persuade Miss Donna against her will: and, after all, Miss Donna's bare neck and arms needed no hiding. Yes, she would say that to her ladyship, secure in the knowledge that for once she was not flattering nor fibbing.

But Donna went down the staircase, cold as one of her Uncle Lionel's statues on the half-way landing, quite indifferent to her looks. She hated dinner-parties and had nothing whatever to say to a man, besides being convinced that her own awkwardness would infallibly prevent any man from wanting to speak to her. She managed the gauze billows of her skirt with the ease of her profession, but this she did not know for a virtue, or know that passers-by in the hall were staring at her. Down she came, casting looks of dislike at the portraits on the wall. How tired she was of the eternal stories of the sombre duke and the sparkling Hilaret, of warm-cheeked Richard Broome and his son and his grandchildren!

She entered the drawing-room still with that schoolgirl scowl upon her noble young countenance, and Lettice, gracious on the hearth-rug, wanted to beat her. She said so to the tall, middle-aged Irishman who had passed Donna in the hall and was now standing beside her.

"My granddaughter!" said Lettice, and then—"Oh, my dear Sir Joscelyn, don't look at her as if you admired her, just to please me! Of course she is beautiful; but look at her sulks! Where do these young things acquire this ferocious shyness? For that's what it is, you know," continued gallant Lettice, loyal to Harry and his brat, "a ferocity of shyness. It is real suffering, I daresay. But I can't tell. I was never shy."

"I remember her mother," said the Irishman, his eyes still occupied. "But Maud Blythe was a gentler goddess."

"Gentler, that's the word. The young are so harsh. Oh, I could beat her with my fan," cried Lettice, pluming the air so that the soft wind of the ostrich-feathers touched the attentive cheek of her listener in a caress. "Why can't she be like all these other pretty little dolls?" said Lettice with a contemptuous gesture for the pink-and-whites whom

Donna was ungraciously greeting. "But you can't beat a great girl of sixteen."

He looked from her to her fan and laughed pleasantly.

"I don't think Miss Broome has much to fear, Lady Lettice."

She admitted with a chuckle that she was less terrible than her words.

"And now may I meet her?" said he.

"If you have the courage," returned Lettice: and having now put her principal guest into the one mood in which it would be possible for him to take an interest in her granddaughter, she blew them together as lightly as a child telling time by a dandelion clock.

"Donna, my dear, may I present to you Sir Joscelyn Pallas, a connection of your Aunt Rosina. He is to take you in. I think you will find things to talk about."

But the couple did not at first find much to talk about.

"Yes—yes—no—no—" said Donna stonily in answer to his polite questions—Did she ride? Did she dance? Did she mind the cold weather? Would she have an olive? But, as he dived for her table-napkin and returned it to her, something in his pleasant questioning smiling look thawed her.

"What did she mean," said Donna suddenly, awkwardly, "that we should have things to talk about? We are just talking weather, aren't we?"

He laughed outright: then answered her with a gravity that suited her.

"She meant, I think," said he, "that I used to know your mother when she was about your age."

Her eyes strayed to his greying temples. She was at the age to approve of grey hair.

"Where did you know her?" demanded Donna fiercely.

"In Ireland."

"Ireland?" She abandoned her knife and fork, swinging round upon him, and lost her napkin again: then cried—"Leave it! Leave it! I don't want it," as he stooped.

But he picked it up again before he answered—

"I live there, you know."

"Where?"

"In the far west, four miles from the sea, under the hills."

"Oh!" She flushed brightly. "Is it possible that you know my home—I mean my mother's home?"

"My home is further north," he said. "But I have been to your grandfather's place. I danced with your mother there too when she was your age and I—not so old as I am now."

"You are not so old," she said, considering him. It was a statement of opinion without intent to please, and so it pleased him: though without further comment he went on—

"And what's more I've taken her in to dinner and she used to lose her table-napkin." He dived a third time.

He did not see Lettice at the end of the table lift her eyebrows at her granddaughter; but he came up to find his partner once more in gloom.

"I wonder how Mother could stand them," said Donna, her eyes sweeping across the table. "Oh, thank you! D'you know how she managed to stand them?" There was ferocity in her accents.

But again he laughed.

"Dear Miss Broome! What is the meaning of your 'them'? Who? Which? What?"

She eyed him warily. Was he laughing at her? It appeared that he was. Then she saw with amazement that though he was laughing, he really wanted to know what she meant by 'them'.

"All these people," said Donna half sulkily. "All these London drawing-rooms, London streets, all these ladies like my grandmother. What did my mother want to come to England for? What does anyone come to England for? Why have you come?" There was no impertinence in her tone. She was as guileless and assured as Sarah saying scornfully to the angels—'What are you doing here among men? You can't change my lot for me.' Yes, she looked at him enviously, he realised, because he had come from Paradise. He leant forward to her.

"What, do you know Ireland yourself?"

"I was there once." She shone out at once like a sun bursting from a cloud, and went on eagerly—"I'm half Irish."

"And you feel yourself more Irish than English? Is that it?"

"I don't know," said Donna, shy again, and hiding her sunshine in sullenness. But her sullenness no more dispelled her beauty than sun-obscuring clouds can deny the grand curve of the sky itself. He could not take his eyes off this beauty. But a pretty girl was twittering on his right and he turned unwillingly to agree that the weather was fine and that Queen Victoria was dumpy and without taste in dress, not to be compared with the wonderful French empress. Then he was free again.

"Would you like to go to Ireland?" said he.

She shot him first a dark look that moved him, for it told him that his question was cruel—'Would you like to have the run of the fields?' One does not ask that question of the wild things at the Zoo. But before he could soften his question—

"Would I like to go to Ireland?" repeated Donna, considered him a moment, laughed joyously and began to tell him why she would like to go to Ireland.

He listened enchanted, knowing that because of his race, or his look at her, or for some other reason, simple and inexplicable as the reasons for sympathy between two people always are, he was being made free of a sanctuary. 'There are dreams in my house,' said Donna's look. 'Come and play with my dreams.' He came willingly: and continued to be enchanted by her. For, once begun, her Irish blood gave her ease and eloquence. She chose to tell him about his own home and contrived to make him homesick. Where had she got her notions? Could all this dreamery spring from one visit in early childhood? Her geography was a dream, yet undoubtedly she knew his familiar valleys, though it seemed to him that she had seen them in a dream, peopled with gods not men, and laughter-starred instead of lily-starred. She remembered the look of his hills, though she pronounced them wrongly: and she had the most extraordinary tangle of legends and tales at her finger-ends, and the familiar names sounded as strange and comical and pretty in her alien English voice as his own speech with its Irish flavour sounded comical and pleasing to her when he talked to her of her familiar London. But half her talk was questioning. She was trying to fill in the gaps in her memory: she wanted new knowledge: she was hungry: why shouldn't he feed her?

So he began to tell her about his home with its plantation of laburnums, its rookery, its beechwood, its primrose-carpeted groves, its fairy fort in the walled garden, and the high hill behind crowned by the cairn of an Irish queen.

"Maeve's tomb? Mother told me. Mother saw it. And on the mountain across the valley there's a doorstep and a doorway into the hill itself, and the river by it runs uphill in windy weather. Mother must have been to your house once to see it all," cried Donna, and her eyes were shining.

So that was where she had got her passionate half-knowledge! But why these guesses? What was wrong? A girl should be contented in her own home. But this young woman called her mother's once visited province 'home', and hated London. Strange! But a lovable strangeness in this stranger to be in love with his home!

"Was your mother homesick for Ireland," said he, "after she left it for good?"

"No," said Donna, "I don't think so. She never said so. She was a satisfied person. I used to worry her."

"You ought to come to Ireland," said he.

"I should like to come," she said, quite deliberately, her cheeks slowly deepening in colour but her gaze perfectly steady.

"I'd like you to see my home," he said slowly.

"I should like to see it," said Donna. Her eyes considered his friendly face with its middle-aged look of amusement that all young people encounter and its other look of humility that all young people fail to understand. She liked his mouth and the wrinkles at the corners of his eyes, and the way he showed her that he thought her beautiful, and the way he was peeling her a peach, and the way he picked up her napkin as a matter of course without implying, 'How careless you are!'

"I should like to see your home," said Donna again. "I think your sisters sound kind." She hesitated. "I should like them, though I don't expect they would like me, would they?" And again her tone convinced him that she was saying exactly what she meant and feared.

"I think they would," he returned: and she accepted his plain statement in turn with confidence and went on eagerly to her next question.

"What do they do all day?"

"Well, I don't know," said he. "Just now they will be picking snowdrops and tying them into bunches and sending them off to the market. They get money for their charities in all sorts of ways. They're great gardeners."

She looked down at her long white hands.

"I should like to dig and delve," said Donna.

"You would find it very dull."

"I shouldn't."

"There are no young people for miles."

"I'm not young," Donna answered him passionately. He laughed. "I could show you," said Donna eagerly. "Will you come and see me play?"

"The harp?" said he—"the piano?"

"No, no—a part. I am playing Olivia in a month," said she, "at the Glory Hole. It's my first big part and I shan't be good in it. But will

you come and see me all the same? Then I could show you at least
that—"

"Donna! Donna, dear!" said Lettice's voice. All the rest of the
ladies had risen and were rustling to the door. The Irish guest sprang
to his feet not at all embarrassed, but the girl was crimson.

"How long are you going to be in England?" whispered Lettice to
her guest as she passed him : and her eyes were dancing with amusement.

"It depends," returned her guest evenly.

"I see," said Lettice.

She said nothing more, said nothing to her granddaughter in the
ladies'-hour that followed ; but when the Irishman came across to her on
the entrance of the men and picked up the conversation exactly where
he had left it, he did not fence.

"Lady Lettice, what do you see?" he asked her defiantly.

Her wicked grey eyes swept the room.

"I see," said Lettice deliberately, "that my granddaughter is sitting
on a cloud and has nobody to talk to."

It was undeniable ; so he went and talked to her—talked to her all the
evening.

The next day he took her for a drive and they were together daily for
the rest of the week. But though her stay with her grandmother was to
end on Sunday evening, Donna did not resume rehearsals on the
following Monday : and Joscelyn Pallas never did see her play Olivia or
any other stage part. For on Sunday morning he had a long talk with
Lettice. He began it gloomily, after breakfast, fidgeting with Lettice's
spools and scissors as he talked : and he did not give her time to be
tactful beyond a smile and a preliminary—"Well?" but leaped back to
the week-old understanding, expecting her to follow. Being Lettice
that gave her no difficulty.

"Well?"

"I'm too old for her," said he.

"Not at all," said Lettice coolly.

He continued uneasily.

"And we are an impoverished lot."

"She will have a fortune, of course," said Lettice practically, "if she
pleases her father."

"Would such a marriage please her father?"

"My dear man, he won't care tuppence," said Lettice. "He's
wrapped up in the boy."

"And you?" said he.

"Oh, well," said Lettice impatiently—"I like to see people happy and the girl is miserable. I was fond of her mother. She reminds me of her mother. It's the Irish obstinacy over again; but Maud had set her heart on being happy in London and so she was happy; but this child—" said Lettice—"she was born homesick and a failure. She fights to be free of us all. She always has. I don't know what to do with her. I thought the stage might be the way out. Not a bit! So the only thing," said Lettice practically, "is to get her married."

He laughed.

"To an Irishman?"

Lettice looked at him laughing also.

"Of course! I'm not shocking you, I know. As soon as I saw you I said to myself—'Now I understand Maud.' Maud always puzzled me, or rather, it was the Irish in her that puzzled me. You Irish, you're the theatrical profession among the nations. You are businesslike about the passions. As the daughter of actors I think I understand you. So go and talk to my granddaughter."

"I never meant to get married," said he, staring down at her.

"Nobody does," said Lettice, "unless they're unattractive."

He strolled out of the room, amused, not in the least displeased, for he had the Irish attitude to marriage as a bargain needing careful thought, much discussion and the interested intervention of all the family.

Donna lifted her head as he came to her in the morning-room, welcome incarnate. They went to church together primly and afterwards strolled in the Park. But it was not till the evening that he told her what was in his mind. Then, in the little conservatory behind the Park Lane morning-room, he proposed to her while the bells rang for evening service. And in the deep six o'clock silence that succeeded them she accepted him with an enthusiasm which would have much astonished her grandmother.

CHAPTER 27

THE EARTHLY PARADISE

DONNA met her elderly Irishman in the January of 1868. In April she was married to him and disappeared for nearly three years from the world of the Broomes, which is the world of the theatre : and forgot about that world as utterly and callously as only a happy woman can. For the marriage was a success : and Donna, for that brief three years, knew happiness.

What is happiness? The Cleopatras and the Juliets might have laughed at Donna ; for hers was no great passion. She was not wildly in love with her courteous, placid, elderly husband : she was achieving no ambition : she could look forward to nothing more, as her husband was careful to explain, than the mistress-ship of a ramshackle Georgian house set in a remote countryside, and the companionship of a couple of elderly women and a middle-aged man. And she was sixteen. It was not to be wondered at that London, Lettice's London, thought the match mad, supposed that it was for the title. No doubt Lettice Broome had realised at last how disastrous it was socially to let a young woman become a player. They said that Lettice Broome had tackled the situation admirably and supposed the fortune given with the girl was immense. Pallas was certainly a good name, and the Pallas's were connected with everyone in the world—a very good match. But Lettice was always clever.

Lettice allowed them to say what they liked. She herself saw the situation clearly, astonishing the doubtful Harry by her unworldliness. "They suit each other, my dear," she said to him, and was right : though it was not in her to understand, and Harry absorbed in Gilly did not choose to understand why the marriage of young Domina Broome and her middle-aged lover was so successful.

It was successful because, throughout her brief married life, Donna was in a state of mild intoxication. Was it not intoxicating to find herself a perpetual success? Her husband idolised her and made it plain that he did : made it plain that he thought her beautiful, thought her witty. And he never criticised her : he sought means to please her, and at the same time took as much care of her as if she were a queen, or her own marvellous grandmother who at sixty-five still held a court by

318

merely coming into a room and flashing her look, her laugh, at the
people in it.   To be treated as the world treated Lettice, how enormously, how simply Donna enjoyed it!   She was liked, she was thought
a marvel.   Very well, then, she would be a marvel.

And with that she bent her strong young brows and will and desire to
pleasing and delighting the middle-aged man who, though nobody else
did, thought her delightful.   He had liked her in the dresses she hated.
Very well, he should be enchanted with her in the dresses she liked.   He
had found her worth talking to at those horrible dinner-parties where
she had been sullen and vapourish, always aware of her grandmother's
eye upon her.   Very well, then!   Now that she was alone with this
friend, now that she had all the hours of this long journey through
Ireland and all the days of the long journey through life in which to find
herself and retrieve her mistakes as she made them, uncriticised,
unblamed by anyone but herself—oh, how at last she would let herself
go!   How she would please, how she would strain every nerve to
please this amiable, delightful person who thought her in turn amiable
and delightful!

And it was indeed not conceit but rather gratitude at relief from the
charge of inadequacy, of coldness, of charmlessness, that produced in
the young wife a mood of revelling happiness, a mood of which her
husband was to enjoy the charming fruits.   If the sun shines, and the
flowers come out, whom do the flowers thank?   The sun, not the
gardener.   And Donna had no thanks for Lettice who had with such
care planted her where she could blossom, or for her father who had in
his own fashion done his best by her brains, though he could do
nothing for her heart.   But she turned in a fervour of feeling to her
husband: and he, an ageing Perseus, and a little afraid that ardours
might be expected of him, was entirely satisfied by her dutiful affection
and redoubled his pleasant care of her: and thought to himself with
pride and tenderness that he had waited a long time for his happiness
but that now he envied none of the young ones: he was only overwhelmed by his own good luck.

He had gone to London with no more intention of marrying—and
look what he had done!   He had fallen in love and married a wife—
from the stage, too, of all places in the world! And now there was only
one problem left to disturb his pleasure.   Would his fierce, affectionate
young beauty ever be content in the wilds with him and his sisters, and
would his sisters get on with her?

But he need not have troubled himself.   From the first she was content. Her misery had lain as much in the withholding of her racial inheritance as in her pettier, childish, personal troubles. For she, too, was a Broome with the instinct to beckon and respond to beckoning, to act as if the Broome whim were the universal law, and complete personal freedom the Broome inheritance: and she had raged against the conventional education meted out to her alone, as it seemed to her, of all her race. Gilly did as he pleased, Stephen did as he pleased, her father had always done as he pleased: and as for Grandmama Lettice and the incessantly quoted Great-grandmother Hilaret—how those flibberty-gibbet women had done as they pleased and had been admired for it and loved for it too! But she, Donna, had been denied her birth-right. It had been her elders' whim to turn her out a pattern young woman. She had conformed because she had inherited her mother's placidity and there was nothing else to do; but, inheriting also her mother's stubbornness, she had never submitted.

Conceive now this young creature in her spotless fashionable clothes, with her enforced maiden gentility, the more severely enforced because of her stage training, suddenly dumped—but how tenderly and admiringly dumped!—into that poverty-stricken, ancient, remote Irish household with its handsome peasant housemaids, its butler, toothless, deaf, pottering over the silver, its ill-dusted magnificent rooms, and its robins flying in through the windows of the dining-room at meal-time to peck at the butter. But the disorder had its grace, and the decay was stately. Ill-kept lawns stretched softly like spoiled velvet to the very stonework of the house, and these lawns were not outraged like the tidy lawns at home by heart-shaped, diamond and oblong beds filled with the calceolarias, lobelias and geraniums of old England. Rather were they infested by lively hares, and in sultry weather, in thunder-purple weather, by impudent thunder-purple cuckoos. These flew low and close and alighted first on the teak garden seat. Rested they would fly on to the very window ledges and there sometimes one would hang upon a latch poking forward a woodenish Noah's ark head and cocking an eye as round, bright and unwinking as the eye of a narcissus flower at the people in the room.

Behind the house towered the rookery. Its low branches beat on the roof in wet or windy weather, and it was always wet or windy: and its trees were alive with black shapes and hoarse murmurs. The rookery led to the hanged-man's wood, birdless, dank, full of nettles and bright green bramble saplings that never fruited; but in front the beech woods were airy and golden as a Sicilian temple. The ill-kept gravel path that ran round under the windows of the square, creeperless house was gravelled, not with the yellow gravel of Regent's Park but with gravel full of shells because it came from the sea three miles away. The path led to the stables where it turned to cobbles, and so on to the walled garden.

So far the place, though beautiful, was masculine and austere; but once inside the garden Donna was in a female world. So spacious was the garden, so richly clothed, so richly lighted, that it was to her as if she were once more in her own domain of the theatre. So vast were the poppies that summer, so pink the roses, so luxuriant the apple-blossom and apple fruits, so rich a rose colour the walls, so tangled and tapestried and battlemented with every flower that grows—wallflower, snap-dragon, arabis, alyssum, fronds of fern, seeded eglantine, honeysuckle—that the place was like a jumble of pantomime sets into which life had been willed. The very disorder was exaggerated, luxuriant, theatrical. The box hedges that edged the flower-beds were broken by overflowing weeds and flowers—variegated parsley at one season, at another red anemones. Lilies of the valley were a weed against which there was no struggling: lemon-scented verbena, that chill and chancy delicate, fought for room and beat the nettles hollow. Peaches were everywhere, in autumn the apples rotted on the ground so plentiful were they, and even the bare-foot children let in to gather and feast seemed scarcely to diminish them.

Yet in spite of the riot a certain control obtained. Weeds there were everywhere, but the weeds were not allowed to choke and utterly lay waste the garden: decay was everywhere, yet it was a decay that enriched the rich ground. Over that happy acre aired by the Atlantic winds, yet protected from those winds by its walls of brick and its ramparts of hill and wood, the generous sunshine was spread as thick as butter, as golden as butter. Early morning there was an inspiration to live: the noontide was a dream of plenty: and the evening a blessing.

And to this asylum Donna came direct from Regent's Park. Yet un-prepared as she was for such natural licence by her daylight life, she was to a certain extent prepared for it by her nightly life, by stage natural-ism and the licence of the imagination. It was perhaps a necessary preparation. Certainly the differences in the two ways of living would have been too mad for a house-kept young Englishwoman of the late sixties to endure with patience. But Donna had been a spectator dream-ing dreams and an actress acting dreams: now it was easy for her to live dreams, be their governess and mistress. Here was her kingdom as the theatre was her father's kingdom, as the social world was her grandmother's. Here she came into the possession of something which her youth desired, for which her womanhood longed, for which her nature starved.

And that which she desired, she obtained. The lovely garden and demesne and the old house awaiting its mistress, the old people awaiting their darling, their pet, their young plant—all these made her welcome and showed her that she had come home. It was little wonder that she loved her home, and loved too the simple kind old ladies—old to her though one was but fifty-five and the other fifty-odd—who made her so instantly welcome.

"Do you think your sisters will like me?" she said to her husband as they drove the last twenty miles of their journey. And he had answered very seriously—

"I don't see how they can help it."

"They could easily help it," said Donna sadly.

And he laughed and told her that though she was so handsome, handsomer than her mother, he had really fallen in love with her for her voice, so dark and soft. And yet he wasn't sure—it might have been the way she moved as she came across the room in that first evening in her white evening dress.

"That dress!" said Donna, but already half reconciled to the dress. "But don't you like this better?" And she touched her new, half suitable straw-coloured travelling dress trimmed with magenta pipings. She was proud of it, though she had never before been proud of her clothes.

And he said that he did like it better, of course, but still he had liked the white; but that, when he thought the evening over, he remembered that he had not fallen in love with the dress nor even the way she moved in it. He had really fallen in love with her frowning face at the moment when she decided not to frown at him any longer.

"Well, but you made me laugh," said Donna. "I don't remember what it was, but you did make me laugh. Nobody else does. But you— I suppose it's your accent—I bubble when I'm with you. And you never think it undignified. You never say—'Donna, not so loud!' It's the being liked," said Donna with a warm sigh of relaxation and pleasure. "Gilly says you must be a fool. So does Stephen. Stephen says that I am a Mrs. Siddons without the genius and that's not the sort of woman men want to marry in our century," finished Donna. She looked up at her husband. "I can't help it, Joscelyn. One's born as one's born: and I wasn't born with the power to attract. You're the first person in the world who hasn't said to me—of me, I mean—'That's a fine young woman! What a pity she hasn't any charm.' Oh, I love you for not noticing that. Oh, and now if your sisters are disappointed with me what shall I do? You've lived with them all your life. You must be much fonder of them than you ever will be of me. It must be rooted in you—fondness for them—family fondness; for I have that for Gilly, though I do despise Gilly. Well, if they should say to you——"

"Wait till you see them," said Joscelyn.

"What are they like?" she asked for the twentieth time. And again, delighted to talk to her of his own folk and his own life, he told her what they were like.

Laura was the eldest, had grey hair and was religious, but could be very funny sometimes on purpose. And Lucy, five years younger, was not so strong-minded, had been pretty once, was a little fussy and did the accounts.

When Donna saw them she found them, as described strangers always are, like his accounts of them yet quite different to the pictures she had built up from his accounts. She was stiff with them for an evening, and heard her stiffness explained, infallibly, as pure fatigue, and heard Joscelyn scolded for over-tiring her. That was strange, soothing hearing. Hearing, she ceased to be so stiff though she was still shy: but next she heard her shyness applauded.

"So young! So different! So sweet! So unlike the girl of the period!" How could she be afraid of these angels who turned her faults into virtues for her? And then they petted her, fussed over her. How could she help enjoying the novel experience? She melted still more, melted altogether: and at the end of the week had taken the elderly women into her life and her heart. She had always wanted aunts like other girls—these sisters-in-law were as good as good aunts. They spoilt her. She loved them for it. Joscelyn, Laura and Lucy—these three were one home.

CHAPTER 28

'WHO MOURNS FOR ADONAIS?'

She was embedded in the new life: week by week her roots struck deeper. She was all root: she lived in her roots, stretching sensitively downwards into the dark secrets of the soil. Her surface life was a delightful swaying in the wind, a delightful reception of sun and rain and a giving out again of idle, thoughtless perfume. But her vital forces were centred in her roots, striking down, down, deep, knotting round hidden roots, interlacing with other roots, struggling downwards into safe sub-soils where were food, protection and secrecy.

"She blooms," said the sisters.

"I think she's happy," said her husband.

And they would smile at her as she came in from the garden, her hands earthy but her dress, as always, composed and spotless, or passed out of the French window with the family parrot on her shoulder, or sailed down to take her place at the head of the dinner table and entertain the dull families of the neighbourhood whom she, so singularly, did not find dull at all. And she would smile back in complete understanding of their loving patronage, in complete understanding of what it was in herself that called it forth. She knew why they loved her though she did not put it into words. Why should she? The garden plants have no speech, and she was at last an established plant, blooming freely, rich-leaved, with weeded space about her, in a soil that suited her. It was with actual agony that she thought sometimes of the possibility of disturbance. If they shifted her now she would scream like a mandrake, she thought. But there was no chance of that. They had forgotten her in England.

She had written to her father, a first formal letter announcing her arrival, and she acknowledged every three months the receipt of her allowance with a thankless coolness which implied—'You be thankful too! You are rid of me cheaply.' But she never wrote for the pleasure of writing. Indeed, as time separated her further from her father, she found that, so far from softening her feeling for him, it hardened anew the resentful dislike which the last months of their mutual life had softened.

Alone with him, united by common interest in the theatre or in Gilly, she had at times been affected by his charm. His very ruthlessness, his insensitiveness to her feelings had at times excited her. She, so masterful, had even felt a certain angry enjoyment in being mastered. It was a mere momentary thrill of her theatrical blood : it did not affect her permanently. Now, married and gentle, and remote from the world of the theatre, she looked back on those childish tussles, those vehement, precocious scenes with embarrassment and fresh resentment, hating the troll-girl she had been, and began to think of Harry again as a mere tyrant to be paid out one day for what he had made of her. For freedom had gone to her head, happiness had made her touchingly arrogant, and the gentler she showed herself to these strangers whom she loved, the more truly unselfish she was in her dealings with them, the more concentrated grew her retrospective hatred of her father.

Like all the Broomes she had a passion for paying debts, and like all the Broomes she never forgot a debt. It was as if the house of her mind were now so aired and sweetened that all the shadows, glooms, dank airs, dust, damp and creeping parasites of the woodwork had been driven inwards towards the centre of the house, to some airless, understairs closet. There too she kept her account books. Donna would turn the key for months on that closet door and go about her sunshiny rooms very proud and happy. But whenever she had occasion to fetch a rag or a broom-handle of memory from that closet under the stairs, then it seemed to her each time a darker and ranker place. That the place should exist at all enraged her, and that, too, was a fresh debt that she must pay her father.

So when Gilly wrote to her for money (that was a habitual matter between them) she sent him ridiculously large slices of her scarcely touched allowance. It was inevitable that he should beg of her and she had no personal alarm for his welfare, just as she had no illusions whatever concerning his probable courses; but she did think to herself with pleasure that sooner or later her father would find out that she was giving Gilly money and that the discovery would anger and humiliate him as much as a blow.

Then she would write more affectionately to Gilly because of the thought and urge him to remember that, if ever he were in any sort of difficulty, he had a sister in Ireland ready enough to listen, help him and not grudge. And she would seal her letter and sit staring at it and feel her father's long strong hand holding her chin in a vice, and see his cold, implacable face in front of her, and feel again blow after blow on her cheek and hate him for it in a sick black rage. Then she would shake off the obsession and cross to the window and stare out on the loved familiar scene. There was the bright lawn and the cedar, the spread tea-table under it: there in their shabby chairs in the black velvet shade sat her darlings, with laburnums blazing behind them like joys incarnate. Grey-haired Laura would be knitting: gentle, fussy sweet Lucy nipping the covers off the tea-cakes and waving away flies. Joscelyn would be playing with his bitch and her puppies. All three would be peaceful, yet vaguely expectant, waiting for someone, waiting for her to complete them.

"Darlings! Darlings! My own darlings!" she would cry silently, passionately to them from the window. "My own people, my own darlings, I do love you so!" And she would shut her account book and turn the key on the closet again and whirl down the stairs and out to them.

"It's extraordinary to me that she can be so contented with old people like us," said Laura to Lucy, and said something of the kind quite often to Donna herself. Donna beamed at them in return, but she did not break into protestations. She was not a woman who enjoyed expressing herself, though she could express herself convincingly when the need arose. But her instinct, until that need arose, was her father's instinct for silence. She could be radiantly silent and darkly silent. In either case one might be sure that she was feeling intensely.

And when the day and its need came her husband and her sisters-in-law gave her credit for feeling intensely. For Joscelyn looked up one morning from the *Irish Times* with a grave face.

"My love, where is your brother just now?"

"Gilly? He was to have gone on tour this summer. He wrote me of it. I daresay he will have started. I can't tell you where he is. Why?"

"Then he is out of England," said her husband, his face still hidden by the open sheets.

"Out of England? Oh no, Joscelyn! It will be the Southern Circuit. My father has a great notion of the provinces as a training ground. I was to have gone with Gilly if it had not been for you. But that does not mean abroad. A world tour is no mean undertaking, you know, though it can bring in a lot of money. My uncle Russel made a fortune by his last venture and he's to start again this summer, Grandmama wrote me."

"Was your brother to go with him?" asked her husband gravely. And at that she came up to him and put her hand on his shoulder.

"Why? What is it? Why are you asking these questions? Is there anything about Gilly in the paper?" She leant forward, following his finger and his look. "Joscelyn, what's this? The *Sylvania* foundered? Is this a list of passengers? Yes, it's Gilly's name, but it must be a misprint."

Her husband looked worried.

"You're quite sure that Gilly was not joining your uncle Russel, for instance?"

"Oh, quite sure! Gilly would have told me. I heard from him only three weeks ago."

"Any particular reason?" said her husband.

"He wanted some money," said Donna ruefully, half laughing. She had no secrets from her husband. "For once I did not send it—my allowance is late."

"You are quite sure, Donna—" he began again—"he was not going abroad?"

"Quite sure. After all, Joscelyn, William Broome is not an uncommon name."

"But it says—" he repeated—" 'understood to be the son——' "

"Does it? Let me see!" Her face began to lose its colour, but she continued a little breathlessly—"But Joscelyn, this is a weekly paper. Then the disaster is at least a fortnight old. I should certainly have heard. It's preposterous to be alarmed, isn't it?"

"Is your allowance often late?"

"Oh, Joscelyn, you don't think—? Oh, my poor Gilly! But it's fantastic. There is no conceivable reason why Gilly should be aboard the *Sylvania*. Joscelyn, may we telegraph to my grandmother? May I have the horses? I know it's thirty miles, but——"

"My dear Donna, I'll send a man at once to the town. I'll see to it for you. In any case it would be better not to worry your father. But we will telegraph to Lady Lettice."

"Will you? You are so good to me, Joscelyn. I'm not worried in the least—but you are so good to me. Don't speak of it to your sisters, will you?"

He laughed.

"I never tell them anything troublesome until I am sure——"

"No," she said. "And we are not sure. I'll come with you to the stables. And we know it's a mare's nest, don't we, Joscelyn? We're all but certain it's a mare's nest."

"You know you must be patient," he said. "It's a long business. We go half across Ireland before we link up with the telegraph.'

"When shall you be back?" said Donna restlessly.

"I? I will take the opportunity to do some business in the town, but I will be with you again by dinner-time. I'll arrange the return service. We should hear by tomorrow night or possibly the morning after."

"It is good of you to trouble," she said again. "Especially as I am so sure it is a mare's nest."

He stooped and gave her his hand. She caught it and kissed it.

"You are good to me," said Donna for the third time.

Her eyes were full of tears as she slipped away from him to open the gate, and she came back slowly towards the house, her mind packed with fears and selfish pain. If anything happened to Gilly who was so young—why then, anything could happen to people who were not so young. O God, take care of Joscelyn! Take care, take care of Joscelyn! She had not time to cry even once—O God, take care of Gilly!

She worked through the day in a fever, waiting for dinner-time and Joscelyn. But he was home by the afternoon, for sending the telegram had proved a sleeveless errand. Joscelyn, making enquiries at the Post Office in the town, had had his own post handed over the counter to him for quicker delivery: and one shuffle of it, one glimpse of a black-bordered letter was enough for him. He rode home at once, much shocked, grieving deeply for Donna's grief. He could not at first find words to tell her of the black-bordered letter.

But she took the news quietly. It was the two sisters, not Donna, who were most concerned and pitying when Lettice's letter was opened and its main contents told them. It was they who talked in shocked whispers of the poor bereaved father, and that poor young life cut off. Still discussing the tragedy as they undressed, the two ladies agreed that Domina evidently felt it all so much that she could not speak of it, and so they had better not speak of it either. But it was strange how Laura had always had a feeling of horror at the idea of being on the sea. She had been nearly ill with anxiety when Joscelyn crossed to England and again when he brought home Domina, and that was a fairly short crossing. Laura supposed that it was some sort of a presentiment—at second-hand—

"With Domina so dear to us it is perhaps understandable that I should feel a trouble coming to her. She bears it very well. But to lose an only brother so shockingly is a thing that she will not easily get over. Think, Lucy, what should we do if Joscelyn—— But Domina is very brave. She did not move a muscle as she read her grandmother's letter. She has amazing control."

This was Lettice's letter—

'DEAR DONNA,

Thank you for your last letter. I'm glad you are well and happy. I am sending you the books from your schoolroom, as you ask for them. I can't conceive what use they can be. With them I send a couple of black dresses that I have ordered for you from my own woman—two muslins and a silk. I think you can trust my taste: though you will no doubt be startled at the change of cut. The panniers will need adjustment, I daresay, but I assure you it is the moment's wear, and you will need mourning when you come over. It may not be your choice: you can order more; but you cannot arrive in your trousseau clothes, coloured and out of date. I ramble on like this because I am cowardly and dread writing down in cold words what I have to tell you. My mother was the same: when she was distressed she talked clothes.

My child, I have the most shocking news in the world to tell you. We have lost Gilly. He was drowned. Your father is nearly out of his mind with grief. All this will bewilder you, for I know what your Irish papers are, and you have not yet heard that Gilly was on his way to America. But it all happened in such a rush and the whole subject was so painful that I delayed writing: and now comes this news like a blow. Our only comfort is that Gilly died like a hero. Your father clings to that. But I must not be so incoherent. I will begin at the beginning. I promised your father I would tell you as much as is necessary. He says there is no need for both of us to write.

I have not told you in the last months of our growing anxiety as regards poor Gilly. I felt that you could do nothing to help us and that it was not right to sadden your first year of marriage, and of course we did not ourselves know till the last month the true state of affairs. Indeed, we should not know now but for Stephen, who has been like a son to your father over it all. I am not going to sadden you with details of the wretched story; but Gilly disappointed all our hopes from the start. You know how pleased your father was with him and how well he worked in the first three months of his engagement, until your wedding in fact. And I will say this for poor Gilly that to the last his stage work always satisfied me. But he got himself into an extremely undesirable set, ran up huge bills which your father paid. I know you will believe that he was extremely patient with Gilly, more patient than

I should have been, especially as Gilly never told him the whole story of his debts and your father was constantly having the shock of discovering fresh commitments. I try not to blame poor Gilly. He was always so easily led. You know how affectionate and impulsive he was, and he could not be persuaded to break off what your father considered a totally undesirable friendship. In fact he defied your father and very cruelly, as I thought at the time, insisted on leaving home and setting up for himself in rooms with this friend of his. And yet I suppose it was natural. So it went on through last winter.

I have never known anything like your father's patience. He even allowed Gilly to persuade him to employ this friend at the Glory Hole. I think that your father thought that he would be able to keep a better eye on Gilly. Your father was perhaps unwise in his criticisms, but he belongs to the new fastidious school and he doesn't understand the temptations of stage life. He never toured. He was always in authority and responsible even as a boy. But touring with your grandfather as I used to do, I can make allowances and as I told your father, how can you say that anybody drinks too much when it is purely a question of a strong or a weak head? A glass of champagne is quite enough to upset some people, and I do not believe that Gilly drank in the accepted sense. But he did come down to the theatre two or three times in a very excitable state and did not give a very good performance, and it upset your father terribly. There was a scene, I hear, and your father seems to have laid all the blame on Gilly's friend (I will not tell you his name for I know his mother) and another young man in the theatre, and dismissed them both. And then, it appears, they were very insolent and actually demanded money of your father—I suppose to hold their tongues about Gilly's weakness, though your father did not tell me details. And I am afraid your father had to pay them a good deal of money before he got rid of them.

I do not approve of your father doing that. I cannot understand such weakness. One had only to say the word 'Police' and we should have heard no more of them. But men, I have always found, are curiously weak when it comes to taking any sort of moral risk and I cannot altogether blame your father; for poor Gilly, as a result I am afraid of more dissipation than we realise, was in a state of collapse, really ill. Your father brought him home to me and I had the nursing of him, and of course I soon got him well. I understand nerves. But it was a great shock to me when your father told me that he had decided that there must be a complete break with Gilly's old associates and that he had been cabling out to Russel. Russel was most kind and offered to take Gilly into his own company—he was just starting, as you know, on a world tour. It seemed the very thing and your father most grate-fully accepted. I confess I was very much against the idea at first, but Stephen persuaded me. I had a long talk with Stephen and I am afraid, from things Stephen let fall, that our poor Gilly had difficulties of which even your father did not know. I shall never forget Stephen's goodness and sympathy. It was Robin over again. It was he who finally per-suaded Gilly that it would be best for him to leave England; for at first Gilly would not hear of it and did not seem to realise that from every point of view it was absolutely necessary that he should leave the country, if only for a time.' (And the word 'absolutely' was underlined, the heavy stroke standing out like a bar sinister on the thin paper, deli-cately networked with handwriting.) 'However, it was finally settled and in the end poor Gilly seemed relieved, and in the last day or two was his old self, Donna! I shall always be glad of that. Nothing could have been sweeter than his way with me—dear, affectionate boy! He would not leave me, and I am afraid it hurt your father that Gilly showed he was frightened of him. Your father is shut up in himself and I dare not speak to him, but later I shall be able to make him understand that he has nothing to reproach himself with. It was necessary to be stern with Gilly and I do fully approve of his bearing to the boy in the last weeks. But of course Gilly never could bear an uncomfortable at-mosphere and being in disgrace. Your father and Stephen took him down to Southampton and Stephen says that when your father said good-bye to him in the cabin Gilly was good and grateful. And when I saw your father the next night he seemed much relieved in his mind.

And so you see, my dear, everything having settled itself satisfac-torily I did not think of writing to you, though I have a letter here half written, of course, telling you that Gilly was joining his uncle.

Well, you can guess the rest when I tell you that Gilly was on the *Sylvania;* or have you not seen the news? If you have, this letter is superfluous: if not, I grieve to tell you that the *Sylvania* foundered three days out. Some were saved, but not Gilly. Having said that you can imagine there is no more to say. The business has made an old woman of me and I do not know what to do with your father. It is worse than when your mother died.'

The letter broke off abruptly and resumed after a lapse of some days.

'We are just back from Gravesend. Stephen and your father have been down to see if they can get into touch with any of the survivors.

They did not want me to go but I would go with them. The survivors were in the town's care and it was easy for Stephen to question them. He had a long talk with one of the common sailors who was saved, and then brought the man to us at the hotel. He is a very good sort of man and knew Gilly quite well. He said everyone loved Gilly and that he could have saved himself if he had chosen. He, the sailor, ran into Gilly as they were getting away the boats and he had urged Gilly to take the free place, but Gilly gave it up to him because he was married. The man was in tears as he told us. He said that Gilly had given him a message but that it was knocked out of him with the wind and the cold and he could not remember the exact words, but it was love to his father or some such phrase. He said that Gilly was leaning over the rails as the boat went down and that he waved to them.

Your father listened to it all without a word. Stephen and I have interested ourselves in the man. He has six children and they are a very poor family. I say to Stephen—if Gilly gave them his life we may as well see that they live. But your father looked at the man as if he would have struck him, and walked out of the room. And when Stephen had got rid of him and went to look for your father he was not there. He had left word that he had gone back to town, so I followed with Stephen and am but just got home.

I am very anxious about your father. I think you should come home at once, as no doubt you will. It is arranged that Stephen shall stay with your father for the present, as Harry will not come to me. So I am alone in the house and should be glad to have you and Joscelyn. I am not so young as I was. This business makes me know it. I hardly know how to deal with your father. He does not speak at all. I do not know what we should do without Stephen. He offers to forego his plans for a year abroad and join your father at the Glory Hole at once. I think your father feels this a comfort.

Remember me to dear Joscelyn and your sisters-in-law. You will, of course, bring Joscelyn with you.

Believe me, my dear granddaughter,

Yours very sincerely,

LETTICE BROOME.'

CHAPTER 29

HARRY BROOME WRITES TO HIS DAUGHTER

She was not overwhelmed though she tried to be, for she knew that her darlings expected it. She told them the dreadful story of the drowning and she told her husband something of what had gone before, though instinctively she still protected Gilly, dead and beyond protection, even from her husband. That was too old a habit to break, even though she did not miss Gilly very much, and felt more the sort of chill that she might have felt if a light gauze shawl had slipped from her shoulders at a dinner-party where she was enjoying herself too much to bother to replace it. She felt a chill, not a grief, and she did not show her letter. What regret, what pity she did feel was for gay, useless Gilly, not for her grandmother, not for her father. Indeed, her first reaction to Lettice's letter was angry panic. They were trying to get her back to England, were they?

She knew what would happen if they succeeded. She would be reabsorbed, dreadfully translated back into the girl who could never please anyone, who was the focus of general irritation, who must fight for the right to breathe and be disliked for fighting, and who would conquer and then be pilloried for conquering. What—take Joscelyn with her and see him in a month her father's right hand, snared by Lettice, ranging himself against her, criticising her, no longer thinking her a wonder? No, that she would not do! They didn't want her. It was mere sentimentality to pretend that they could possibly want her. She would not budge.

Yet she was more moved than she knew. Lying wakeful that night at her husband's side she did certainly experience a sobbing, blinding crisis of regret for the passing of Gilly that shook her from head to foot. But it was hardly grief, it was hardly affection, hardly a civilised sentiment at all. It was at best a clan grief, a sudden consciousness perhaps of her flesh that its twin flesh was dead. However that may be, it was violent while it lasted and enervating as the pang that is the preliminary to physical love. If Gilly's ghost had come dripping to her bedside at that moment she would have risen and followed him, weeping and obedient, to his bed beneath the waters. But the sensation spent itself and in the morning, when she had put on a new black dress, she took the precaution of burning Lettice's letter. Her sisters-in-law were sorry for her in her black dress, and Joscelyn told her how sad and sweet she looked, and everyone was kinder to her than ever and she continued to be heartless and happy.

She wrote to Lettice at once, explaining how impossible it was to leave Ireland and her married duties, and wrote also to her father, formally and gently. Then to Stephen with whom she had always been on fair terms, she flung in secrecy a hasty, passionate note.

'I couldn't come back to England, Steenie. I should be quite useless. I won't. I can't. You know me. What use should I be? What good could I do? Persuade them not to want me. I won't come however much they write. But, Steenie, I do beg you to send me your own news of Gilly. You needn't be afraid of hurting me. We have never had illusions about Gilly, either of us. And I don't care what he has done, but I must know. I've always known all about Gilly. That was his one virtue as a brother, that he did let one know everything about him. So it won't shock me; but I must know what has been happening in these last two months. What did he do? What was the worst of it? I can't bury him in my mind until I know the whole of it. You needn't write to me piously and say, Don't judge him! I never judged Gilly. A creature so beautiful was justified whatever he did, I've always felt that. I'm sorry for my father. Yes, this is genuine, Stephen. I pity him profoundly. But I'm not coming home. Don't be shocked at this but write to me. Please, please, write to me!'

But Stephen was a very simple creature and observed all the conventions of feeling, and was besides very busily getting engaged to a charming young actress who wept for Gilly softly and innocently. So he was shocked and did not write.

Three months later, however, Harry wrote: and this letter Donna did show to her kindly, easy-going husband. For, knowing his attitude to her family and her English life, she could rely on him to be interested, sympathetic and not at all offended by what he read. She could also rely on his courtesy and good sense when it came to dealing with the mad proposals which it contained. For Harry Broome wrote frigidly accepting his daughter's expressions of sympathy and using those expressions as preliminaries to a deal. He began by outlining with an icy frankness the state of his own heart.

Gilly, said Harry nakedly, had, of course, been the centre of his life. He, Harry, had accumulated an extremely large fortune for Gilly and Gilly's children: also a position; for, as a manager, he stood at the head of his profession. As regards his position as an actor he had nothing to say: no-one was responsible for another's creative ability: that was a thing that he could not will to his children. But the control of the largest theatrical combination in London, in England, was another matter: he might say a family matter. And then, with piteous pomposity, he traced for his daughter's benefit the Broome dynasty, from Richard's day to his own, and mentioned that he had refused a knighthood six months ago as unsuitable.

'My mother is the daughter of the late Duke of Bedenham and my father was William Broome, the son of Robert Broome, the son of Richard Broome. I do not care for a city title.'

He continued to explain still fluently and without feeling, that he had intended in due time to abdicate in favour of Gilly.

'For Stephen has his own fortune. If Gilly had cared to take him into partnership of course I should have been very well content. But Gilly was my heir.'

But Gilly was dead, and though Stephen might still be taken into partnership, indeed, he might say that that matter was settled, still Stephen was not his heir.

'I have worked all my life to see my children in my place. Now my son is dead; but my daughter remains. I formed a high opinion, my dear Donna, of your capabilities as an actress, and I have not forgotten your prudent advice to me when still a young girl as to the proper handling of my boy. I am now proposing to put you, as far as may be, in my boy's place. I should like you to arrange to come over to England with your husband. I will treble your allowance and shall be satisfied if you will take over the control of my house. I should like you to resume work on the stage and also to make yourself acquainted with the business workings of the theatres under my control. I should be gratified if your husband could be persuaded to identify himself with the Broome interest also, and will do all in my power to smooth the way for him should he care to avail himself of the opportunity. That, however, is entirely a matter for his personal decision. He is a man of vested interests and no doubt has been only prevented by money problems from exerting himself in his particular world. If he should have any idea of entering politics, as I have heard from your grandmother was once the case, I will finance him.'

And so the mad, inhuman letter ran on, but making the writer's meaning ludicrously and pathetically clear. Harry Broome was prepared to pay the half of his fortune to have his daughter in London.

And she might have come if he had left it at that. But he went on to make it clear to her that as an individual he did not want her at all. He wanted an heir.

'You will probably have children. If you have a son your interests will naturally be transferred to him. But it is quite clear that your children cannot be brought up in your present home. All the Broomes have been brought up in London within sight and sound of the theatre. I am sure your husband will see the force of my suggestion.'

Thus Harry, writing in his glass world with the snows of the ninth circle settling on his bowed shoulders, and its cold thickening the thought in his mind and the ink in his pen. Thus Harry, creating miserably some phantom third generation Gilly, born of the dark stick his daughter. Thus Harry, exhausted with grief and despair, dehumanised, writing foolishly, his pen guided by that fraction of his tired brain which must be organising, creating and foreseeing.

He signed his letter and left it to chance and his secretary to post, and went to give orders for the preparation of his house for the newcomers.

It did not occur to him that they might not come. He told Lettice when next he saw her that he expected them in a few weeks. He discussed with Stephen how much and how little Donna need be told of the workings of the business side, and went on to plan, drearily, the autumn season, with an eye to special parts for Donna. When he got his daughter's letter utterly refusing to discuss the scheme he could not understand it, but it was so great a shock that it brought him back to reality. All his grief, his despair, his weariness, contributed to his violent anger at this monstrous thwarting of his will. But also he was struck desolate by it. Donna was wrong. He was seeking more than an heir to the Broome kingdom. He did not want Domina for her own sake, but he did want kindness from Gilly's sister, from Maud's child. He hated her for her ready refusal, and yet unappeasably desired her presence as a sick woman desires abnormal food.

He wrote again, curtly repeating his orders, and this time Joscelyn answered, civilly, with friendly explanations. Donna said that it was a good letter. So did the sisters. So did Stephen. Lettice, dropping out of things more and more, was not shown the letter.

But the letter did not lessen Harry's bitterness. Who was this stranger to come between two Broomes? Lettice, ranging herself flamingly on her son's side though he did not ask her sympathy, said to him—"My dear Harry, you must cut off the allowance."

But that he would not do. Maud had not taught him many lessons, but what she had taught him she had taught him for life. He had learnt from her for one thing, how to look at money. Money is common property among people of the same blood, of the same sympathies, of the same stratum of emotion. You cannot love, hate, torment, beguile, rejoice your lovers or confound your enemies unless you inhabit the same world, and are ruled by the same laws: nor can you play your games with each other unless you have a common supply of counters. "Cut off Donna's allowance? You must be mad, Mother!" said Harry repressively: and went back to his work and was more successful than ever.

He did not answer his son-in-law's letter or hold any further communication with his daughter; but he found himself thinking of her, with anger, sometimes with absolute hate, but thinking of her intensely. He was still planning to play Lear and he could not find a Goneril. He could not forgive her for failing him. Little Madeleine Reilly would be a possible Cordelia—gentle, sweet, stubborn and very pretty. He liked her mildly and he was perfectly ready for Stephen to marry her. The matter did not greatly interest him; but Stephen's happiness, Stephen's glow, pleased him. He told Madeleine, who was terrified of him as her manager and still more terrified of him as a future all-but-father, one or two curt tales of Robin. Madeleine, listening and shooting puzzled looks at Stephen on the other side of the table, wondered if the terrible creature's mind were failing him. For everything that he said about Stephen's father Robin seemed to her like a description of Gilly Broome. But she did not say so to Stephen, for she did not want to betray how closely she had studied Gilly.

Madeleine had liked Gilly a little too much, and knew it. But everybody had liked Gilly a little too much. They liked him too much and then he let them down. Why not? The sun shines on you and then it goes in. Is it the sun's fault if afterwards you shiver? Gilly had been radiant to Madeleine Reilly. There was a time, though she could not believe it now, when she was only civil to Stephen because he had a look of Gilly, as a peony has a look of a rose. But now Gilly was gone, as the scent of the rose is gone when the wind blows too harshly: and his spectre took on little by little the less delicate hues, the earthier strength and humours of his cousin Stephen.

Stephen had grown into a very handsome man. If there was a memory of Gilly's desperate charm lingering still at the corners of the mouth, the nostrils and light blue, bright blue eyes, did it matter? At any rate he was a much more satisfactory person to love than Gilly. Imagine having children by Gilly! She shuddered at the spectral notion. But she and Stephen meant to have children. Both of them hankered after affectionate domesticity rather than passion. She would look after Stephen: Stephen would allow himself to be looked after. But romance lay outside marriage, and both knew it, and knew too that he would always have romances in his life, and that her one little romance was tenderly over. Dear Stephen! She wouldn't have married anyone but Stephen in any case. He was hers. But oh, poor Gilly!

And with that last tribute of a sigh Madeleine Reilly went happily to her wedding. Harry gave her a startling allowance, and Lettice gave her a Paris wedding-dress: and there were lords and ladies who terrified her at the reception afterwards, and a half-dozen pluperfect theatrical celebrities, and hundreds of impeccables without titles. And her own grandmother, the famous Mrs. Reilly, told her that it had been her own heart's desire to marry Stephen's grandfather, but it was better as it was: and did she, Madeleine, realise that in marrying Stephen Broome she was marrying the English theatre?

"For there is no-one to succeed but your husband," said Mrs. Reilly. "If you notice, Domina Broome did not come over from Ireland to the wedding. They say she has cut herself off entirely. That's a heartless young woman! What—she sent you the pearls? I am surprised. Her own string, are they? How very odd! How very unlike Domina Broome!"

But there the shrewd old lady was wrong. To pull off her neck her own string of pearls, the string she had inherited from her mother, to send them in a carelessly packed parcel to Stephen's bride just because Stephen was her cousin, and had been a brother to her half-loved brother—this was extremely like Domina Broome. At any rate, if you had asked her husband, her sisters-in-law and her enthusiastic and ever growing circle of dependents and neighbours, they would have agreed that it was just like Domina Pallas. But Donna in England and Donna in Ireland were two different people and in all their lives they never met each other.

Perhaps, too, that impulsive gift of the pearls was Donna's gesture of placation to Melpomene. For she had, whenever she was happy, a sense of being happy at the end of a string, like a sparrow. One day, there would be a tug on the string and she would be drawn backwards, fluttering helplessly, terrified, to be crushed in an engulfing hand.

Harry was responsible for this rooted anticipation of disaster in her. She had heard him decide, eyeing her up and down, while Lettice pointed out as if she were a filly they were thinking of buying, her peculiarities of figure, profile, gait and speech—"The truth is, Mama, she is built for tragedy!"

Her adolescence had taken the professional remark very seriously indeed. She was already aware that her mother's death had pulled down premature night on the house of Broome, and she was aware of her father as a tragic figure. She had even, under her jealousy, comprehended the necessity of his reliance on Lettice, of his passion for Gilly, of his aversion from her black-and-white self. She was his tragic mood made flesh. But though she accepted she did not the less violently resent the fact that to her would always be apportioned in life the tragic and the tragi-comic rôles—the Player Queens, the Cressidas, the ridiculous Mrs. Creegans.

Her marriage had for a time lightened her morbidity. She had escaped the tragic rôles in the theatre, so why not in life? There is no tragedy in the Fortunate Isles. Nevertheless the goddesses do not so easily let go of their servants. *Vénus toute entière à sa proie attachée*— she had once learnt that passage by heart, and shuddered over it. Artemis, Cytherea, Melpomene: Chastity, Love, Performance—it was all the same which goddess you served. A woman was the conscript of all three: and if she tried to escape, their prey. Each would mangle her and none could protect her against the other two. But her worst dread was of the third of that trinity—was of the tragic muse, Performance.

And the hideous haphazard of Gilly's death had taught her that the difference between stage and real life was this—in a stage play the performance must be intentional: accidental tragedy was bad art; but real life, thought Donna shuddering, was full of the accidental performance, full of the accidents of sudden death and unexpected sickness and never-dreamed severance of lovers and their loves. She was frightened: and when her husband caught a cold or complained of rheumatism she would be fantastic about him.

Joscelyn took her pretty young fussings good-humouredly, but he went his way for all that. And because he never crossed to the island to see a tenant without her imagining that the boat would be caught in one of the currents, never went shooting without her envisaging him stumbling into a bog and discharging the gun into his own body, never went riding without her foreseeing a riderless horse bolting up the drive with trailing reins, she got into the habit of accompanying him whenever she could. Her stage training, involving as it did dancing, fencing, riding and more strenuous gymnastics than was at all customary for young ladies of her age, stood her in good stead. She walked, rode, shot, sailed, and did these things well. Her husband, proud of her, taught her to do them better, till, from being his wife and hostess she became his companion and friend and her happiness mounted to the skies and her fear diminished.

Nothing could happen to Joscelyn while she was with him. Hers, indeed, was a curious devotion. His love for his young and beautiful wife was a natural and understandable thing, but hers, to their circle of neighbours, was less understandable. It was, in fact, much more like the passion of a child rescued from governesses by an adoring father than the normal attitude of a young woman to her lover. But Donna, at any rate, was entirely unaware that in life and in her own life there was the possibility of a devotion more intense, a passion more unquiet. She was completely contented, save always for that fear of a disturbance of her content by her father, fear of some appeal irresistible to her easy-going husband. She could trust herself to be flint, but she could not trust her husband.

But no further appeal came from Harry. He, too, could be flint. But he was not a man to be turned from his purpose any more than his daughter could be turned. Her hatred of all that he himself stood for had been concentrated and confined in one secret chamber of her personality; but her hatred had not therefore lost its strength and its power to erupt disastrously and repoison her whole nature. And his capacity for immoderate affection, though it also had been driven by misfortune into a darkened chamber of his consciousness, was not dead though it was sick and emasculate. He had now, and more intensely than ever, the desire to set up an idol, build a shrine, and flog in a congregation of worshippers. But he had no longer a warmth of spirit wherewith to fructify his desire: and without warmth his desire appeared even to himself threatening and unnatural, a stroke of lightning, not a stroke of the sun. Nevertheless, he would have what he wanted, and he set about getting it, tormented at every step by the memory of his boy's unhappy face as he had last seen it dwindling away from him, while the lurid water between the boat and the quay-side grew wider in the dripping dawn.

Then the memory would re-shape itself and he would see again his boy's happy face, rose-crowned, torch-lighted, the beautiful mouth curling as Gilly said—'There lies your love!'

"O God, where lies my love? What is Gilly's face like now? And Maud, ten years and more in churchyard mould with filth feeding on her, what is she like now? In corruption, corruption—there lie my loves!"

CHAPTER 30

NEVERTHELESS Harry set about getting what will and pride, and the arid habit of achievement told him he ought to have, and for the last time he turned to his mother to help him to get what he thought he wanted.

There had been, for a year or more now, no breach but a subtle estrangement between them. His visits to her had been as formal and punctilious as ever, but his spirit had not visited her nor once cheered her since the miserable business of Gilly had begun. She had not agreed with his methods of coping with Gilly, and age, though it did not make her less shrewd, did make her less adroit. She did not always remember to slip on the velvet glove when dealing with him, did not always remember that you cannot talk to an embittered potentate in the late forties as you can to a tentative schoolboy or an inexperienced young husband. And age and grief had not made him either more tolerant or better able to endure criticism and direction. The shock of Gilly's death had, for a time, separated them completely. He could not endure her sympathy. He was like a badly frost-bitten man to whom comfortable warmth is a worse torment than freezing alive. But time and Donna's disobedience bridged their difference and when he did return to her he came at a run. Perhaps he had a vague and pitiful idea that after this spiritual estrangement he might return, not to the vigorous old woman with her too much crystallised efficiency, her too familiar idiosyncrasies of affection, but to the vigorous, all-sufficing mother of his youth, the mother who could melt difficulties for him by merely listening to him, and could run on his errands with the unerring vigour of a hunting bitch unleashed.

And so he came to her in her pink and silver boudoir, kissed her—it was the first human touch he had had since Gilly's death—patiently let her look at him again, and smiled at her with a sort of grim understanding as he read her incurably volatile thought—'How striking he is still!'

And coming on the errand that he did, her thought pleased him. He glanced, not knowing how like to Gilly was that instinctive glance, at his own reflection in the mirror. It struck him that the golden convolutions of the frame backed against the pink wall were like the setting of a gigantic ring, and the glass its jewel on which his own black figure was engraved. But Lettice's thoughts were much more definite. She concentrated on the actual appearance of her son.

"He does dress well," she said to herself, approving his middle-aged but still admirable figure. The breadth of his shoulders was slightly accentuated: the fashionable frock-coat was dragged at the waist so tightly that it had an effect of swathing the narrow hips: and was as it should be—the latest cut. For the rest the cuff-links and tie-pin were severe. Trust Harry not to overdo an effect! She was delighted with him for so subtly failing to suggest the actor. She knew how that air of the distinguished amateur carried him professionally. "The most natural actor in London: the only gentleman on the stage: he ought to stick to comedy!" was the verdict of those who flocked to see him in Shakespeare and melodrama.

But again she approved that Harry stuck to his Shakespeare and his melodrama in spite of these compliments. He would have been less natural, less completely the social figure in a part which required of him precisely that air. Besides, his public loved him the better for being able to prophesy eternally what he would be like in parts he had no intention of playing. Meanwhile—he was too old for Hamlet, too young for Lear, too slight for Leontes, too much of a gentleman for the Jew, too mannered for Antony, too romantic for Macbeth, too solemn for Malvolio, too whimsical for Prospero. So long as they could see him in all these parts in order to say these things about his conceptions, he would never lack for an audience.

But to him she said, looking up at him and for once letting her pride in him, her love of him, have free play—

"Dear boy, I'll tell you something. As I watched you coming into the room I thought it, and now I say it to you. If you were on the stage together you could act your father off it, just as he acted his father off it. I was there. I saw it happen. So now I've said it—you are a finer creature than he was." She sighed. "I wish you would put on *Hamlet*. I'd like to see you play it once again before I die." And she continued to look at him with questions in her eyes.

For her extravagance was only her way of conveying to him that she detected in him a new bearing and liked it. The gloom was there: the oppression was there: the weariness was there as she had seen it with a sinking heart these six months. But there was a fresh determination about him that thrilled her and would, she knew, thrill any audience. She was not the daughter and wife and mother of players for nothing.

"What are you going to do?" she finished sharply.

"Marry again," said he, sitting down beside her.

She clutched her stick in her tiny, still pretty paws, and struck it on the ground.

"My son!"

His dark eyes were hard.

"Yes, Mother, you can say 'My son!'; but I cannot say 'My son!' "

"Is that why?"

In answer he pulled out Donna's letter and threw it in her lap. She read it frowning: then pulled off her glasses again impatiently.

"Cold and hard," said she, "and a fool."

"She must judge for herself," said he. "And so will I judge for myself. I loved Robin; but I cannot let it all go to Stephen, all I've made. I propose to marry again and have children."

His mother said nothing.

"Why should I not?" said he, answering her silence.

She fought with herself. Old as she was she had still to fight with herself. At last she said—

"I think you are very wise. A sweet, pleasant, intelligent woman of thirty-five——"

"I want children," said he.

"A young girl, Harry?" said she uneasily.

"My daughter was married to a man nine years older than her father."

"But younger in spirit, Harry, less cruelly used by life," she said, thinking to herself—'You look fifty, my poor boy!'

"Oh, as to that, Mother, I daresay I shall have my deserts. And I shall be kind to my wife. I shall give her a big position, money, everything she wants. I think you know me well enough, Mother, to be sure that I should be a considerate husband."

"Plenty of girls will be delighted to marry you, Harry, if you have made up your mind," said she quietly.

"I have made up my mind, Mother."

"Very well, my dear!"

For what could she say to him, with her mind shooting back across the years to her own first marriage with her elderly widower. The old man had been considerate to her and it had turned out very well, and he had left her all his money. It had not hurt her. It would not hurt Harry's future wife. 'But how Harry could!' her heart wailed. 'How Harry could!'

"Have you anyone in your mind?" she asked.

"Adelaide Wybird," said Harry.

"Domina's friend?" said she.

His manner hardened.

"She is a year or two older than Donna," he returned. "Twenty-two, to be exact."

"And she has no money. It's a great match for her. She's a very sweet girl, amiable, healthy. I don't think you could have chosen better, Harry."

"That is what I think," said he.

"When do you marry?"

"As soon as possible. I look to you, Mama, to take things off my hands. It will be easy enough. After all, there is the Wybird connection. I thought the connection would please you. And she is a dear affectionate girl and will be very ready to let you make much of her. You will help me with all this, Mama, won't you?" And for an instant an expression flickered on his face that startled and touched her, and reassured her too. Harry was afraid.

The appeal was enough for her, and she did for him all the innumerable smoothings of the path that a woman of her age, experience and social weight could do. She liked the bride, a pleasant, simple creature, flattered at her destiny, respectfully terrified of her future husband, but girlishly in love with his looks and his reputation, and not at all reluctant to adventure into matrimony.

Lettice saw her son married fashionably, saw the pair into their carriage and drove back to her lonely house—for Stephen too was married and gone—and sat that evening in her gay room over her solitary dinner, the tiredest, loneliest old woman in London. She had lost her son and knew it. He did not ask her advice any more, only her help to achieve his ends. She could not warn him, she could not soothe him, she could not make him smile. She thought to herself with horror that she had not once seen him smile since Gilly's death, not even on his own wedding day. "God help that child Adelaide!" said Lettice with a shiver.

Then she called her maid and had herself elaborately dressed, summoned her carriage and went out all by herself to see the new play and Harry's understudy at the Gloriana, and tried not to remember that this was Harry's wedding night, and came home so tired that she actually cried a little after her maid had put her to bed. Then, her own tears stinging her to familiar indignation with the world for treating a Broome so monstrously, she cast around for someone to punish. Somebody must be punished. Whom would it hurt most to know that Harry was married? Would it hurt Donna, that cold, hard, cruel, selfish, unnatural daughter, cause of all the trouble and without charm, utterly without charm? It might. If Harry had children Donna might whistle for her fortune. However romantically she felt about it now, sooner or later Donna would achingly regret that lost fortune. For money is the final desire: money is the final love: and when you are old, dis-charmed and helpless, money is the only power. One day unloving Donna would regret this week's work and the loss of power.

Lettice rang. It was three o'clock in the morning, but Lettice rang cheerfully, none the less, for her maid to bring her the rosewood writing-desk from the other side of the room. What was a servant for if not to serve? She let the maid adjust the pillows and light all the candles in the room, and settled down to write the letter that should carry a little of her own uneasiness across the land and sea to her escaped granddaughter.

But to Donna at the breakfast-table, bright-cheeked, bright-eyed from an early tramp with her husband through the startled morning woods, the letter brought supreme rapturous relief. Surprised she was and possibly faintly shocked, but oh, how relieved! Now there would be an end of these attempts to break up her idyll, an end to this talk of duty to your talents, your inheritance, your father, and your Broome blood.

"What d'you think, Joscelyn? Listen, Lucy, Laura! I can't believe it. What do you think has happened, and so soon after Stephen's wedding too! I don't know what to think about it. I don't know whether to be glad or sorry for him. I can't conceive it at all. My father, of all people! My father has married again."

And she stood looking down at her letter with an air of such bewilderment, distaste, curiosity, that her husband was reminded of one of his young heifers nosing lightly a leaf of green stuff that it would not eat.

"You dislike the idea?" said he.

"No," said she, lifting her dark eyes as if she relied on them to convey her meaning to him rather than her tongue. "I'm only thinking of the girl he's marrying. I know her a little. She's a very distant cousin. She's silly but beautiful. They're poor. I like her. Adelaide her name is—Adelaide Wybird. And she's quite young still, Joscelyn.

How could she marry my father? My father's an old man."

"He's younger than I am, Donna," said her husband.

She looked up at him again, startled, amused.

"He isn't! It's not possible. Oh, but that's absurd, my father's old."

"Not much past forty, I should say. I'm fifty, Donna."

"Are you? Oh, how funny! But I love you. Now I can't imagine any woman falling in love with my father. It would be like falling into a well of icy water—black. One would never be able to get out. One would drown. He's old. He's icy. I'm sorry for Adelaide. I suppose her people made her. But what possessed my father?"

Her husband smiled at her and gave her no answer. But he thought, good, simple man, that he understood his father-in-law. But he couldn't say to his Donna—"He wants an heir—" just because he, too, so intensely wanted his heir. Well, there was plenty of time. Donna was well and happy. Plenty of time. But he could understand his father-in-law.

And he wrote to him and made Donna write, and the courtesy and warmth of the letters did, I think, please Harry. Yet he was bitter against his daughter; for he knew well enough that if his daughter had come home he would not now be sitting at rare meals—the theatre did not absorb him the less because of his marriage—with an amiable but painfully shy young woman who pleased his taste and did not irritate his nerves, but who had nothing to say to him and to whom he had nothing to say.

CHAPTER 31

SNOW IN PARADISE

THE year of 1870 went round—a cold year with more bad news in it. Stephen and his Madeleine had a son before it was out. To please Lettice it was called Eustace after that baby brother whom she had preferred before Lionel himself but who had never struggled up into manhood. Lettice was fairly content: to be a great-grandmother was a distinction. Yet she would rather have had Harry's son on her knee. Unfortunately good pink-and-white Adelaide Broome failed in her duty. All her other duties she performed with care and, Lettice could see, with intense satisfaction. She had been the middle one of a large family of hungry girls, all pink and white and golden, all poor, all impeccable. The five of them, painted together, had been the sensation of the Academy and the two eldest had married on the strength of the sensation. Now she in turn had done her duty and went about, wrote Lettice sharply to Rosina (not caring that letters had now to be read aloud to blind, failing Rosina) she went about like an extremely well-bred housemaid promoted to be parlourmaid. It was unkind of Lettice: for Adelaide was attentive to her new mother-in-law, called on her three times a week, asked her instructions, took her advice, was grateful to have her dinner-party lists vetted for her and never said a word against Harry.

"Not that she has a word to say," said Lettice. "He is most generous with her."

Yes, but he wanted a son.

Adelaide would have been glad to give him one, and presently announced her condition with modest triumph. It was not her fault that she was one of the patrons of the famous pro-French bazaar. Was she not cousin by marriage to the beautiful Duchess of Bedenham? Had not Harry said that she had better go? Was it her fault that all the pink flannelette of the useful-stall caught fire and that, though the dreadful catastrophe of a general conflagration was averted, there was great pressure and outcry and fear? Could she prevent a miscarriage? These pink and white young women have no stamina! And down went Harry's hopes into yet another grave.

Yes, in England it was a quiet year: and not too gay a one in Ireland.

For Joscelyn Pallas was a pitiful man and the intermittent famine of his countrymen was a nightmare to him. How to get money —that was the problem! His sisters were born sisters of charity: and Donna, impulsive and Napoleonic, flung her allowance into the mouth of hunger, and conceived large schemes of relief and put them into train at once: and went to her husband for the money, never dreaming that there could be such a thing as a genteel shortage of cash as well as a proletarian shortage of potatoes. And she infected that anxious, generous humanist, her husband, with her own notion that there must be money somewhere: and as it was not to be got from his rag-and-tatter estate he began to fumble in a lackadaisical, penny-wise, pound-foolish way with his invested money, exchanging his gilt-edged securities for morning-glory mine shares. The first results were glorious. After all there was a difference between four per cent and nine per cent—all the difference between hardship and famine for his tenantry. The year ended more happily than it began, and Joscelyn told his sisters that perhaps this year Christmas might be Christmas again.

And Christmas it was! For while the rest of the British Isles shivered in damp fog the west of Ireland, which in no circumstances cared to resemble any other part of any land in the world, decided to have a spell of old-fashioned cold: and the ponds froze, and the two rivers flowed sluggishly under delaying films of ice. Also there was snow, so much snow that on Christmas Eve Joscelyn and the grooms hauled out of a shed that Donna had never yet explored such a carriage as Donna had never seen. It was a large sleigh with bells. One of the horses was harnessed to it: Christmas charities, the two aunts and Donna were piled into it: Joscelyn climbed on to the box in front and took the reins, and off they drove like people in a Russian fairy tale carrying Christmas with them.

In later life when she had come to such close grips with humanity that nature and its fields were no more to her than a green floor-cloth regularly repainted, and nature's skies no more than the blue ceiling-cloth of a dingy theatre, her years in Ireland seemed to her, as she looked back upon them, a rare dream, a fantastic illusion. It was a night spent among the good people, an enchanted night of fairy tale that lasted nearly three years.

And the memories of those simple years of magic were finally crystallised into a picture of herself, driving over the dream country with her darlings in that incredible vehicle, land-ship, Viking's galley drawn by horses, with bells ringing and bell echoes singing past her ears.

"What is Ireland like?" She often had to answer that question.

"Mountains: very green grass: the sea: the rain rains every day; but you go out in it. The clouds are alive. Flowers everywhere in summer. And in winter we go sleighing."

"I never heard of snow in Ireland. I thought Ireland was so warm and moist. Are you sure you mean a sleigh?"

But she rarely bothered to answer. She spoke of what she had known. Let them think she was dreaming if they liked.

But she was ludicrously wrong if she thought in her middle life that people imagined her to be dreaming. Hard, handsome, competent Domina Broome could not be linked with any dream.

And indeed she was out of her dream soon enough. For the unexpected and prolonged cold brought all the cousins of two counties together, united in one common idea of skating. Old skates were dug from the bowels of shiny, round-topped trunks, and new skates imported. Pond after pond was visited, cut about and left. But one day a party ventured on a backwater of the river and was too venturesome. A second cousin, a silly sixteen in her first long dress, might have been drowned if it had not been for Joscelyn, who hauled her out of the icy hole into which she had blundered and got himself soaked to the bone and half frozen in doing it. That the silly cousin should catch a violent cold and be in bed for a week and then rise again perfectly recovered, was natural enough; for sixteen can stand a shock and a chill. It was also natural that Joscelyn should catch cold and take to his bed: and perhaps it was natural that the cold and the chill should turn to pneumonia. These things happen. You cannot defy nature: fifty-odd cannot stand a shock and chill as sixteen can. Anyhow Donna was proved right in thinking to herself that in a stage play accidental tragedy is bad art, but that real life expresses her art in accidents, unexpected sicknesses and never dreamed of breaches between lovers and their loves.

For Joscelyn Pallas died: not at once, but after a half recovery and a month's convalescence, a check and a series of relapses that broke and mended his young wife's heart, and broke it again. When at last the see-saw of hope and fear ended she was stunned, resigned, but unable to believe in her evil destiny.

Women did not go to funerals in the 'seventies; but Donna went: quite intractable, trying to believe that Joscelyn was dead, and incapable of realising it. But when she had seen him buried, and drove

home again to the huge shabby house—for now she saw how rambling
and shabby and decayed it was, how weedy the drive, how damp and
overgrown the shrubberies—when she went into the huge forlorn
sitting-room with the pink wall-paper he had had hung for her, and
the new looking-glass and chandeliers, when she saw her sisters-in-law
all tremulous, and realised how old they were—then she believed it.
Then she kissed them and hugged them and wept with them, and
swore to them and to herself that she would be another Joscelyn
to them. All should go on as before. They would never forget him
and they would never be parted.

Thus strong Domina defied life and misery. But of course life was
much stronger than Domina: and in three months they were parted
for ever.

CHAPTER 32

HARRY BROOME IS GENEROUS

Can there be a worse calamity than death? Ask the bereaved, as they come home from the burial of loves and hopes, when they sit down to face the cash cost of death. Then their worst calamity stares them in the face—dispersal. Even to Laura and Lucy, those gentle souls who had built their dull happy lives about the dead man, the black cloud that had rushed up over the horizon and now blanketed their Irish sky was a bearable gloom compared with the thunder and lightnings that must presently discharge upon them. Their brother's death was an ordinary sorrow; but to leave Brian's Fort was an apocalyptic woe. Yet sell it they must. What else was there to do?

For weeks they had cast about for ways and means and none had been found. Sell it they must. Joscelyn, dear good impulsive Joscelyn (already their tone was weakening from reliance to pity) Joscelyn had been rash, misguided, more generous than just in money matters. His pension, of course, had ceased, and it seemed that the second fair flow of income derived from an annuity must now cease also: and he had re-invested their grandfather's money in glorious shares that had suddenly ceased to pay. As for rents, everybody knew how scandalously lenient he had been with his tenants. It would take decades to recover all arrears.

Yet even if they consented to sell, who would buy, with money—the lawyer's phrase—so tight? And though they were willing to do anything, they were too old to be governesses and they would die if they were parted: and they could give up the servants and fend for themselves at a pinch, and gather sticks in the wood for firing; but there was twenty pounds to be paid for Joscelyn's fishing-rod, and Lucy had an account of over seven pounds with a Dublin mantua-maker: and their cousin Martin had always said that Joscelyn was too easy-going—God forgive us for blaming him! So what were they to do, Donna? What were they to do?

The lawyer lifted his eyebrows, marvelling that the widow could bear that atmosphere of feathery sorrow, as if a pillow had been broken instead of a heart. He was teased to death by the gentle, lamentable outcry; but it affected young Lady Pallas otherwise. Here was a channel for her grief. Now she could suffer creatively. Oh, the relief of acting, deciding, directing! She was instantly, passionately up and doing for these beloved, helpless shadows of Joscelyn. She gathered the frightened creatures to her : she radiated assurance : she was stability, she was comfort, she was strength. They should not be parted either from each other or from her. As for Brian's Fort, not a field should be sold, not a stone dislodged nor a servant discharged. Only let them leave it to her! But they must not agitate themselves, for what was she to do if one of them fell ill? They must trust her and try to be happy again, because that was what Joscelyn would want. And had they forgotten that there were flowers to be picked? The hospital mustn't suffer, must it, because poor Joscelyn had died like a hero saving life? But if they would answer the letters of condolence—write in her name as well as their own to all the circles and semi-circles and orbits and spheres of relations and connections, that would help her. Then she would have time for a quiet talk with the lawyer and get things straightened out. But first and last they were not to worry! Indeed and indeed all should go on as before.

Thus valiant Donna. And the two gentle ladies believed her, and said to her and to each other that she was a prop and a comfort and a tower of strength : that they felt different women now that they had talked it out with her, and that she was their darling and their blessing. Lucy would see to the flowers at once while Laura, because she was the elder, settled to the mournful task of acknowledging the sympathetic letters.

"Ah, but it makes me cry, my dear, the way they write about him. I never realised how much he was loved. But it is only right that a young creature like you should be spared such a task. I will answer them in our joint names, but of course I will leave my answers open that you may read them all."

Domina nodded and hugged them and went off to her long talk with the lawyer. But she came away from the interview so grave that she had to put on her smile like a fine rubber mask when she was with her sisters-in-law again.

There was more than two thousand pounds owed : as much more owing without hope of repayment : not a penny of income outside the property, and the property needing money spent on it.

"How much do we need to keep it up?"

"If you could spend five thousand on it, it might pay its way in a year or two under a competent agent. Sir Joscelyn, rest his soul, was no manager. He was too easy-going, forgive me, your ladyship! Though, for that matter you can't get blood out of a stone, and the land's stony, so what's the good of squeezing the poor devils who live on it? But with money laid out it could be made to pay. I was chatting with a young cousin of my own the other day who has been to one of those new farming colleges, and he had tears in his eyes as he spoke of the opportunities the place showed to a man like him. 'But,' says he, 'capital, capital! I could make it bloom like a garden, Uncle, but not without capital.' But this is all beside the point, Lady Pallas. As I can see it you have no capital. Ah, well, I told Sir Joscelyn to stick to the gilt-edged. But he would not. He would not."

"And what would it cost us to go on as we are?"

"Well, I daresay you could scrape along on two thousand."

"And if we sold the land and kept the house and the demesne?"

"You'd scarcely sell so, for only a jumper-up would buy the place, to make a show in, you understand, and for that he'd need the house. These Dublin tradesmen, they buy to make a show and start a family tree. As I told your ladyship, one such offer I've had in already. It's a song, but I doubt if you'll get more."

She sat a long while thinking, careless or unconscious of the lawyer's presence, and he watched her face curiously. For she was a fine young woman, he thought, and had taken the blow well, and although she was in as tight a corner as could be conceived he had a notion that she would not stay quiet in the corner. But how would she get out? He knew all about her. His view of her was but little more sophisticated than that of the family town. An actor was certainly a cut above a tinker, a little more respectable than a Punch-and-Judy man; but the town had never heard of the famous Broomes. Donna's taint of vagabondage, however, was annulled in the town's eyes and his by her equally well-known relationship to the Viceroy of that day and time, and by her own carriage, speech and air. So the neighbourhood had accepted her as a satisfactory consort for a Pallas, though a surprising one. She had not surprised it, however, in the brief months of her reign. Now perhaps, he thought, the surprises might be beginning!

"How long can you give me before I need come to any sort of decision?" she asked him finally.

"Plenty of time, plenty of time, your ladyship! A month—six weeks —two months—there or thereabouts."

She nodded and rose.

"I shall let you know before the month is out," said she, and bade him good-day. Then she acted. For she would brood over a business for weeks, procrastinate, evade, and whenever possible wriggle out of the need for making a decision at all; but when she did decide upon a course she always took the next step at once. So she sat down again in the chair that her man of affairs had just quitted, drew towards her a sheet of paper that she had provided for him, picked up his still wet pen and wrote to her father.

She wrote to ask a favour of him—the first, and a big one. Perhaps Harry would have loved his daughter at least half as well as he had loved his son if she had sometimes asked a favour of him. He so liked to give, so long as he might give of his own will, so long as his generosity was not claimed as a right. "It is your duty—" Harry buttoned his pocket. "Father, do—" and he opened it. But most of all he had loved being plundered by Gilly who would put his hand in his father's pocket and help himself shamelessly and confidently, while Harry lay back letting him, eyes half shut like a cat permitting freedoms. Harry revelled in the fact that Gilly never forgot a birthday, never failed to celebrate a first night. If he had to pay the bill for his own birthday present afterwards, that was an added pleasure. It was so absurd and charming and childish of Gilly to borrow money from him to give back to him. Gilly was pretty sure of his father, wasn't he? Not many sons and fathers were as intimate and sure of each other as he and Gilly.

Thus Harry to himself before the discovery of that other sordid Gilly, and the dreadful little secrets which he could not tell his father, and the dreadful little pleasures for which he could not ask his father to pay. So Gilly wasn't sure of his father after all!

"If you had come to me, my son! My son, my son, if you had only told me—— "

"Well, Father, I didn't like to worry you."

"Oh, Gilly, Gilly!"

But Donna had a wicked pride. She had never asked her father for a farthing nor willingly given him a kiss.

But now she was to learn that pride is the weakest of the passions and that love is the most shameless. She wanted everything she could get for her two darlings. Her will and intention that they should have what they wanted, all they wanted, was a force that enlarged her common will of daily life as mountain rains swell the bulk and triple the driving force of an already swift-flowing river. The huge, dry-topped, lichened boulders where commonly flowers grow and swimming beasts find foothold and a mid-river rest, such hoary boulders in the bed of her pride were washed round, flooded, dislodged and sent rolling like little stones under which the smolts hide. So intent was she on stating her needs to her father, so eager to imbue the very paper on which she wrote with the urgency of her need, willing the message on its journey across the channel, insisting on the answer she required with every stroke of her pen digging into the paper that she had not time to wonder at herself. As she folded her letter and sealed it and sent it off thirty miles across the country to catch the mail, she did once perhaps wince at the picture of herself, Domina Pallas, urgently asking favours of anyone. Then the Broome in her mocked at the phrase disdainfully—asking favours! Father wouldn't call it that: and she had a sudden exultant sense of battle joined between her and a creature of her own size. He would deal out favours like blows, and her thanks should be return blows. For he was quick enough to understand and be jealous of the force that was driving her to ask her favours.

And what a force it was! Even in this the reek of sorrow what an ecstatic pleasure she found in loosing on the world this tigerish power born of sheer loving. She loved. Then she must make, take, break, in order to give her takings, makings, breakings to her lovers whom she chose to benefit. Pride? People who talk of being too proud, what do they know about the true pride? Well, she had written what was necessary: she had not any doubt that her father would help her. How his answer would humiliate her and how contented she was to be humiliated!

And then, suddenly, the exultation dropped from her like a cloak and left her exhausted and shivering.

"What's the good of it all, Joscelyn, when you're not here? Why am I doing it and how shall I live without you? O Joscelyn, I'm so tired and heavy-hearted. And now, I suppose, we go down into the garden and pick flowers! The ones that I threw into your grave must be brown already. How I hate these brilliant sunny days! I wonder how long it will be before Father answers my letter."

It was long, or it seemed to her long. She reckoned over every possible delay in transmission until she found the prolonged silence frightening. She had been so sure of getting what she required. Had she been too sure? No, no! She had been beaten in her first round with life and had had to ask help from a Broome. Being a Broome surely she would get her help. But almost more intolerable than having to ask for help was having to wait till her father chose to send it.

She went about with a strictly cheerful countenance, and sewed at her mourning, waiting with fair patience for the all-desired, unbearably worded message. But as the days drew into the second week she could hardly bear the strain. On the morning of the completed fortnight her self-control had so far weakened that she found herself behaving as aimlessly as a strayed cat. She wandered out of the house into the garden, weeded a bed energetically for ten minutes, went into the tool-house for a fork, forgot what she had come for, went back into the house to wash her hands, picked up her sewing, put it down again, went to Laura's room for company and then remembered that Laura and Lucy had driven across to the other side of the lough to visit some second cousins. At last she thought she would walk; but her Leghorn hat had a blue ribbon round it. She had to rip it off and twist a black one round the crown instead. She pricked her finger with the hasty pins she crammed into the bow and when she put the hat on her head she found that the pins projected inwards and tore her hair. She could have wept with agitation and unreasonable fatigue as she put the matter right; but there it was, she was Lady Pallas and must not wander about the countryside without a black ribbon in her hat. So she worked herself up into a state of graceless, barren energy, as she swept through the cool corridors of the house, out into the blazing sunshine, on what errand she did not know. But she found herself, when she came out of her thought at the far end of the long weedy drive. The drive was flanked by solid sheets of rhododendrons in flower: and the crimson, magenta and pale pink mounds of colour rose high above her head. The last twist of the drive and its brilliant ramparts flung her out between the ever open gates into the white road itself.

It was an endless Irish road, blazing white, with an unnaturally high stone wall on one side, banking up a field. A goat's head champing ivy looked over and down at her from its ridiculous elevation like a mild devil. On her right the boggy fields stretched away to the hills, and, though it was June, in the emerald hollows the unabsorbed water lingered and shone. Ten yards away the whitewashed cot of one of the grooms stood level with the roadside. As she strolled past a housewife darted out in front of her and picked up a turkey-hen that was brooding in the middle of the road, and there were greetings and curtseys. Donna acquitted herself suitably and went on for a few steps: then chid herself sharply. Joscelyn would dislike her wandering down the road by herself. It would so disturb his notions of how she should carry herself in the village.

Obedient to any wish of his she was about to turn back, and indeed had taken a few steps past the cottage on the return journey, when the sound of a horse's hoofs and the jingle of a car in motion stopped her. Again she turned and saw a jaunting car heading towards her. It drew along briskly, dust rising behind it, and she waited where the road was broad for it to pass with its dust. And this it would have done had not the hoofs and wheels become involved with the turkey-hen which had meanwhile returned to its roosting-place. Donna and the owner of the hen dashed at the same moment to the rescue and there was a general cloud of soft dust, squawking feathers, trampling hoofs and conversation. As the cloud settled the deeply interested Donna glanced up to the car itself. The bench facing her was empty, but on the further side of the knife-like spine of the vehicle sat one passenger. He had twisted in his seat and with both arms half lounging, half clutching the knife-edge, was surveying the scene with a bored amusement that at once labelled him a stranger and an Englishman. His deerstalker was pulled over his eyes against the bland wind, and the fashionable ulster in which he was buttoned to the throat concealed his person. But her eye rested on him a moment longer than it might otherwise have done because a face without a moustache and whiskers was an odd sight, and yet, to her, a familiar one. Only an actor—She took a step into the road and cried out, half in pleasure, half in dismay—"Stephen!" and as she did so the bland wind lifted the brim of her Leghorn hat.

Counting over her memories, which she saw always in bright circles such as a traveller's lantern flashes on a path as he blunders his way through dim shapes of darkness, she found that she had preserved only that bright moment when their eyes encountered each other. She did not remember how he greeted her, how he climbed down from his extraordinary perch, whether he or she dismissed the vehicle or how they talked as they walked, as they must have walked together, back along the white, uneven high-road in the blue shadow of the wall. The next lantern picture, with its accompanying recalling of lost sounds, its re-creation of movement, smell and touch, showed her herself inside the iron gates, and Stephen, courteous and strange, fastening them for her. They were never fastened as a rule and so the staple came out rustily on to the ground; but she let him attempt the business, watching him as he did it, hating him. She did not want him; for he was a Broome and he had found her out: and now she would not be able to keep anything to herself any more, not even her memories. He would walk up the drive with her and turn down her private glades with her, and note her flowers and stoop to her strawberry beds and pick her lilies, and go into her house and be liked by all her servants. And Laura and Lucy, too, would be enchanted by this Broome. This Broome would stamp his family personality upon every possession she had and show her as she truly was to the people and the place that loved her, and then they would cease to love her. She hated him for coming, and she hated her father for sending him. She would have disowned him if she could.

At the moment his eyes met hers. He had conquered the obstinate, rusted locks, but his hat had dropped off in the struggle: and now, though he stooped and picked it up, he did not at once put it on again, but turned to her bare-headed and smiled.

And at once and for ever he ceased to be the cousin of her childhood. Instead there stood before her in the centre of a circle of sunshine, against the back-cloth of huge, unnatural blooms, a juvenile lead entering to his garden love-scene, the spot-light following him. She regarded him with absolute fear. It was as if her profession in the flesh had come in search of her. She wanted to say—"I don't know you. You have come into the wrong world—" and run for her life. But of course it was too late. He had known her at once and had kissed her and held her hand. She put up her hand to her cheek where he had kissed it and then, hardly knowing what she did, moved to the middle of the road and stretched up her arms as if barring his way to the grey, dreaming house whose chimney-tops were visible behind the final curve of the crimson rhododendrons. But he only laughed as she did so, and said—

"Dear Donna, you haven't changed at all."

"I have," she said fiercely. "I have utterly changed. I'm a different person, Stephen. You needn't think you know anything about me."

"You're taller," he said. And thought to himself—'But outwardly, of course, she is much changed. She has learned to carry herself. Her skin is much whiter, surely. She has magnificent eyes. She is a little too large for real life, certainly. She is stage to her finger-tips, but really, you know, she is quite a splendid Shakespearean creature. Uncle Harry will be pleased. I wonder what Madeleine will think of her—' and spoke his thought conventionally turned—"You never knew Madeleine, did you, Donna? I think you will like each other."

She looked at him, not a whit less suspicious, but her arms dropped slowly to her sides and he noticed with keen appreciation the decisive grace of the gesture with which she took her long flowing skirt and half lifted, half directed its heavy flow, banishing it behind her. Her gesture said—'I must have room before I can cope with you. You press in on me too much with your talk and your personality. Well, and now you are here, what do you want? Your wife? What do I know or care about your wife?'

But he was still admiring the flow of her gown, and thinking to himself that he had never seen a woman carry the new bustled mode better. The flowing skirts spread wide over the sea-beach gravel, flowing as easily as waves had once flowed over that same transported beach. But beneath them was no wickerwork figure. Here was a lovely woman: and the lovely woman was Donna, whom he had last seen clumsily blooming, a little too full in the cheeks, neck, arms and bosom, like all young girls, and like them all painfully dumb when she wasn't painfully direct, anyway impossible to talk to save behind the scenes, in the schoolroom or in the back-walks of the garden. Even on her wedding-day she had seemed to him a nursery creature dressed up, as immature in her wedding finery as she had been upon the stage. And anyway, what's a cousin? A sister at second-hand!

But this mourning mistress of lands and houses and iron gates dealing graciously with her people, but less graciously with him—this was a provocative stranger. And he remembered that she was his cousin only because it gave him a certain advantage in a situation in which he had all the difficulties to conquer. He felt like a guest actor who has ousted the local lead in a provincial theatre and knows that he will get no help from the rest of the loyal company.

Thus far Stephen, before she interrupted his thoughts.

"Why have you come, Stephen?"

"Well—" he began—"Uncle Harry sent me."

"Why did he send you? He could write. Why hasn't he answered my letter?"

"I have a letter for you from him in my luggage. By the way, I suppose they have taken my luggage up to the house? I daresay you will let me stay with you, Donna, for a day or two?"

But she did not concede a smile to that jest.

"I'm not sure. I must know first why you've come. It is extraordinary of my father to have sent you. What am I to do with you now you're here? What is in his mind? I suppose you know what I asked him to do for me?"

"Yes, yes, of course, Donna! You must know that I am acquainted with his business affairs. Since poor Gilly is gone I have—"

"You have taken Gilly's place. Yes, that I can understand. But that does not give you Gilly's place with me. I write to my father. I do not write to you."

He was astonished at her panic. For panic showed in the pinch and flare of her nostrils, in her quick, agitated speech and her hand on her heart, held there in unconsciousness of the gesture as if she were guarding a locked treasure.

"There is so much to talk about, Donna," he placated her, consciously using every trick of personality with which he was accustomed to win over an audience or a woman. "Hadn't we better go up to the house? I can't stand in the middle of the road and talk to you. And there is a great deal to say."

She swept up to him.

"I will not have you in the house or seeing my sisters until I know what you are here for. But you are right. We cannot talk here. I know where we will go. Come with me." And as she put her hand lightly in his arm in the conventional gesture of the day, the conventions seemed suddenly to put their arm in hers also. At any rate she gratified him by adding graciously and much more coolly—"I'm sorry, Stephen. You startled me out of my wits. For a moment I thought you were Gilly sitting in the car. No, that was foolish: that was only for a moment. But you trail England with you and I don't know why you are here. You do see, don't you, Stephen? I can't take you to my sisters before I know why you are here. But of course I am glad to see you. Of course you are very welcome. Come this way. I'll go first. Mind the bramble, it will whip your face if you are not careful. We will go to the laburnums: there is a seat there. I sit there a great deal. My husband's mother planted them when she came here as a bride. You will not see anything like this in England. Come and sit down."

And she seated herself on the marble bench to which she had led him, a high-backed, broad-seated bench supported by sphinxes who couched breasts on paws. But he did not sit at once, though her hand moved in invitation, but stood astonished at what he saw.

For the bench stood on a natural terrace or recess on the breast of a steepish hillside, planted in the manner of an apple orchard. But instead of apple trees, laburnums flamed, so that he gazed from the natural terrace on which the bench was placed, upon billows of intolerably brilliant yellow bloom. The colour was purer than fire, purer than gold. So intense was its purity that by contrast the emerald Irish grass dimmed on the retina to sage green, and the jade and purple streamers in the dark ocean beyond were debased to mere verdigris and iron.

For this yellow shone brighter than anything in the world except the sunshine overhead. But when he stared up through the tatters in that brilliant canopy to the sun itself, for the trees met overhead, then the sky re-assumed the mantle of virginity, and blue was again the purest of all colours, the Madonna colour, and the laburnum ceiling turned dark as gold still hidden in the earth.

Dazzled he lowered his glance to the splashed whiteness of the bird droppings on the less white marble of the weather-worn bench, to the black flow of his cousin's dress, to the bold outline of her arm and bosom against the sphinx's head. Then his glance came to rest on her face. She was not looking at him. She was staring at the sky. He wondered how her wide open eyes could endure the blaze of noon. His could not, and the thunderous heat of the day oppressed him.

"How hot and quiet it is," said he. "Spell-bound. Not a bird singing. You are right. We have nothing like this at home."

She moved her head impatiently. She did not care what he thought, her gesture implied, of any beauty she could show him. Nor had she brought him here to feast his eyes.

"It's pretty," she said grudgingly. "Come and sit down—or stand if you'd rather. I don't care. But tell me why you've come. What is there to say that my father could not write?"

He began to resent the hostility of her tone.

"Well, Donna, I'm not here of my own particular wish. You should realise that."

"Oh, of course," she conceded, and for the first time flashed him a personal look, gracious, disclaiming any will to wound. "You have to do what Father tells you, I know that. But what does he want? Is he prepared to do what I've asked him? After all, it is not so much, Stephen. A share of his fortune would have come to me at his death. And now, I suppose, Gilly's share will come as well. He couldn't alienate it finally."

"Has he ever said he would?" returned Stephen.

She shrugged her shoulders.

"You know pretty well, Stephen, what my father feels for me."

"Yes, I do," he returned bluntly. "But I wonder if you do."

"I did," said she.

"But now?"

"Oh, now I don't even remember."

He thought to himself—How ungracious she is! How grasping, how heartless! He looked at her beautiful profile and was the angrier because it was so beautiful.

"The daughters of the horse-leech cry 'Give!'" said Stephen softly, for he was devoted to Harry. It pleased him to see the colour flame up into her face. She flushed scarlet, her whole cheek glowed, her neck, her very breast was tinged with pink.

"Oh, how unfair—" began Donna. Then she broke off. "I'm not going to be led into a discussion with you, Stephen, of anything I do——"

"Or ask?" said he with meaning.

"Or ask. You could no more understand me in this matter than you could understand these hill-sides when you've lived here just one week. But my father and I do understand each other, Stephen, believe me! And I'm quite sure he will give me what I ask."

"Oh, yes," said Stephen, eyeing her with angry amusement. He resented her attitude to his uncle: he resented her attitude to himself. He was filled with a very profound desire to teach his cousin a lesson, and thought with frank pleasure that his message would soon teach her that lesson, though he would have preferred to teach it her himself. "Oh yes," said Stephen softly, "he is prepared to give you what you ask. I am here to see that your wishes are carried out."

"All my wishes?" said she.

"I think so. You've asked, haven't you? for a competent man to run the place. Well, I've brought one over with me. He comes with every possible recommendation. But I will show you his papers later. He was, for a time, on one of the royal farms. He had a reputation for making two blades grow instead of one, and he comes from this part of the world. It was the luckiest chance that I secured him; for your father insisted that the proper man should be found and it might have taken three months. But we had luck. If you like him he shall be installed at once and any capital within reason that he needs he shall have. He is to be encouraged to enterprise: my uncle wishes that. For if he invests capital in the place he will look for a return, though the return shall be invested in your name. As for the question of income, he has been through your figures and approves them. He thinks you have been very moderate and he proposes to allow you five hundred more than your maximum. And he is ready to agree that the capital shall be placed in trust so that you need have no fear of its failing your sisters-in-law. You may be sure of their comfort for life."

There was a silence. A restless hot breeze ruffled the laburnums. He shifted his eyes gratefully from their intolerable blaze to his cousin's dark dress. Her face was turned away from him. She was staring down the grey aisles of the laburnum grove. She did not say a word.

"I think you will admit that he is generous, Donna," said he.

"Wonderfully generous," said she in a low voice.

"I told you that you did not understand him," said her cousin.

"I thought I did, but I see that I am wrong," said she. Then she said, using for the first time the familiar, nursery name—"I see that I must remove from my heart some misconceptions, Steenie."

They sat again in silence and his heart softened to her as he saw her face softening with relief. He thought—'Now, at last, she is womanly.' And watching her, he began to think—'What was the marriage like? What sort of a wife did she make? What sort of a lover?' .

Looking up she caught his eye fixed on her, full of these speculations, and for the first time, it seemed to him, regarded him in return not as a mere postman of wrath whose message you take because you must, but as a creature who had a right to be in her life. Her next words acknowledged as much.

"You must not misjudge me, Steenie," said she. "I am in great trouble. Think if your own wife—so soon—not three years, Steenie! And there is no-one but me to look after his people. Somebody had to fight for Laura and Lucy. They are quite old, Stephen, and helpless and unworldly. You should not think of me as unwomanly because I fight for them. They are all that is left me in life."

"Donna, you are only eighteen," said Stephen across the gulf of four whole years, and pitying her as he thought to himself—'How little she knows yet how one forgets things.'

She answered his spoken comment.

"I know, Stephen; but they are all that is left me all the same. This is my abiding place. This is my life."

"But don't you understand," said he, "that you've to come back to England? I've come over to fetch you home."

Her dark figure stiffened away from the marble background. Her right hand, tightening on the sphinx's muzzle, pulled her up.

"Home?" said Donna. "You have come to take me home? This is my home." And she leant forward a little, still swinging by that grip upon the sphinx's head, while her left hand caught and gripped the fluted edge of the seat itself. She was like a toy doll that swings eternally on a cross-bar by the locked grip of its hands. "Or do you mean a visit?" said Donna—"that Father wants to see me. Is that what you mean, Stephen? That's all you mean, isn't it, Stephen?"

"Well, Donna," said Stephen uncomfortably, "if we went up to the house I could give you your father's letter. He's told you exactly what he expects you to do."

"But you've read his letter?" said she.

"I know the contents of it."

"Well?"

"Why, Donna, didn't he write to you months ago, directly after Gilly died? You know what he wanted then."

"And I refused," said she hoarsely. "I told him that I never would, never could come back."

"No, and then he couldn't force you to come."

"No," said she thrusting up her chin. "He was mad to think that he could force me."

"Yes, Donna," said her cousin. "But he still wants you to come. And now he thinks that he can force you."

She still gazed at him intently, her teeth gleaming, her lips parted. She did not look dazed. She looked intelligent. But he was shocked to see how white she had grown.

"He won't give me this money unless I come home?" she said.

"You know him," said Stephen with a shrug. "He's set on your coming home."

"I'm to live at home again in my old room, and sit at meals between my father and a stepmother of my own age? I'm to go down to the theatre every night with Father and to throw myself into my acting, and be one of the Broomes? For how long? How long will he hold me to it, Stephen?"

He began walking up and down, not looking at her, as he talked persuasively.

"Donna, be reasonable. There's no time limit. Can't you see that he wants you at home, in his life—our life—for good? He thinks you have a future as an actress. Gilly has gone and I'm only a nephew. If Adelaide should have a child it would be different. But they're all telling my uncle that it is unlikely after the fright she's had—but you'd better talk to my grandmother about that," said Stephen uncomfortably. "Well, don't you see, Donna, there's only you left. Isn't it natural that Uncle Harry should want you? You know how he feels about the succession. While there was Gilly you could do as you pleased, but now Gilly is gone—and your husband is gone—can't you see where your place is? Come now, Donna, be human! Be pitiful!"

"I won't," she said. "I can't. I couldn't do it."

"Do you know that my uncle's hair has gone quite white? He'll go out of his mind if we can't give him something to settle his thoughts upon."

"I won't come," said she.

"You'll have to come, Donna!"

"I won't come," said she. "I won't. I won't. Never."

Then she, too, got up and began pacing up and down, agitated, oblivious of him. But he fell into step beside her.

"You've got to look at this thing reasonably," said Stephen. "And after all Uncle Harry's doing what he thinks right for you as well as himself. You can't bury yourself out here for life."

"My husband brought me here," she said. "It's his home. My place is here, Stephen, with his people."

"Two elderly ladies and a derelict estate. How are you going to live, Donna?"

"I have my allowance," said she.

He made no answer. But his silence was a menace.

She caught his eye and turned to look him in the face, for she was as tall as he.

"He wouldn't take my allowance away?" said she catching her breath.

"He'll use every weapon he has, of course."

"And you said he was generous!"

"He is generous in his own way. But you've been fighting a battle with him, Donna, and you won't own you're beaten. When you own it, then he'll be generous. Dear girl, give in!"

She looked about her over the laburnum blaze to the bleak enchanted hills, the restless seas, the sky alive with clouds. She looked round her into the dim aisles of the grove, on to the ground: she searched with her hopeless eyes the grasses and the shamrock slope. She looked round her from heaven to earth and back again to his face, seeking for help, and found none.

"Joscelyn!" said Donna vaguely. Her lips began to tremble. Then came the end that he had foreseen some five minutes, and he put out a hand to support her. But she broke away from him and sinking down once more in the corner of the great stone bench, dropped her arms across the sphinx's head, dropped her face to her arms, and broke into an immeasurable storm of tears.

Oh, tears! Stephen shuffled his feet impatiently; but he was troubled none the less. He was accustomed to the easy tempests of the stage, to his grandmother's occasional hysterics, to his pretty wife's touching little emotions. Women's tears he thought of as he thought of women's curls, rouge, furbelows, feathers, and artificial flowers. Women's tears had never yet made any mark on his memory. But his cousin Donna did not cry like a pretty woman, charmingly, into a lace handkerchief. She cried as Gilly used to cry.

Stephen's mind moved backward as he watched her, in grief and heavy regret for opportunities lost and mishandled. He felt again the weight of Gilly's head and shoulders flung across his knees, as Gilly clutched at him, sobbing and abandoned. Everybody knew Gilly's laughter and his narrow bright glances, and a good many knew a Gilly turned obstinate, leaden, the fountains of laughter quenched. But only Stephen knew the true Gilly in his despairs, in his frenzied repentant snatches at sanity and sobriety, and good, peaceful, daylight life. No other had seen Gilly tossing on his bed, beating at the wall, tearing his own heart open for Stephen to see. Tears sprung of weakness, and quenched again by utter weakness, these were the sort of tears that Stephen understood. And he had seen another sort of weeping and understood that also—

"I have bad news for you, Uncle. About Gilly."

"Can there be worse news, Steenie?"

"Uncle, his ship has gone down."

He remembered the one staccato question that followed. Then the silence. Then the horrifying tears.

But this was another sort of crying. Absorbed in her own private grief, abandoned to it without pretence or artifice, completely indifferent to his presence, Donna seemed to him less a woman than a human instinct. He felt in the presence of this natural, displayed grief of hers something of the curiosity, the exaltation and profound respect that he had felt when he had first come upon his own wife suckling her child.

Presently he sat down beside her, making no attempt to console her, but waiting until of her own will she grew quiet. Then he said—

"Donna, do you know what broke Gilly?"

She lifted her head sharply.

"I don't want to hear tales of Gilly," she said, her voice still weak and choking.

"And I'm not going to tell you any," he returned. "But what killed Gilly finally, Donna, what made it impossible for him to do anything but slip down and down to perdition, was this—he wouldn't work. He wouldn't take the trouble to work, to act. He was too weak to get rid of his poisons as the rest of us do. I'm not speaking for the world. I'm speaking for us, the Broomes. There's a devil in us, a changeling—I don't know what to call it—that has to be given work. It's like fire—a good servant but a bad master, as they say. I've proved that, I can tell you. You don't suppose I don't have my devil on my back? But I haven't got time for deviltry, Donna, when I'm rehearsing. Everything goes into the part then—everything, I tell you! I've got a new part now, as soon as I get back, which is absorbing me so much that even when I'm talking to you I can't really think about you. My mind's barely here. Uncle's the same. I think Uncle Harry would have gone mad when Gilly died if he hadn't had the theatre to turn to. And I think, Donna, when you come home, when you start work again with the rest of us, though I don't pretend you'll be happy, I think you'll find the excitement will carry you along."

How much she heard he couldn't tell, though she had stopped crying and was wiping her eyes and putting back her hair. But he felt that his words deserved some sort of answer, and as she stretched out her hand for her hat he caught it and held it.

"Did you understand, Donna, what I was trying to say?"

"Yes," said she submissively.

"There's comfort in it," he insisted.

He had for an instant the thought that he could find other ways to comfort if he chose: he pressed her hand again. She nodded, accepting the gesture with a weary tolerance that irritated him: and rose.

"Shall we go up to the house now, Stephen? It must be near lunchtime. I expect you're tired and hungry and thirsty. It's a long tedious journey, isn't it? Did you have a good crossing?" They began to walk together towards the wood. "How long are you to stay?"

"I must be back within the fortnight," said he. "We ought to be able to get things settled in a fortnight, don't you think?"

"Oh yes," she agreed, and stumbled over a stone.

He put out his hand quickly to help her.

"Take my arm," said Stephen.

But first she made her own gesture.

"Stephen, it was good of you to come. I do know that it was good of you to come."

Then she took his arm.

CHAPTER 33

SNOW EVERYWHERE

A FORTNIGHT later she had left Ireland behind her and was home, attending rehearsals daily, learning her parts again in front of the looking-glass in her schoolgirl's bedroom. She had slept well, and had sweet dreams, and now she was awake again.

She had been received in state. Stephen had brought her to the house and taken her through the hall to her father's study : had stood by while she and Harry greeted each other. She had been glad to have him by her, for she had felt a momentary, panicking need of his cheerful presence, his personal support. This was when she saw, with a curious shock of self-reproach, how right Stephen had been. Her father was shockingly aged. His hair, as Stephen had warned her, was white, and he stooped from his great height till he was no taller than Donna. But it struck her as she looked at him, shocked into attention by the change, that the real change in him was the fact that in growing prematurely old he had also grown handsome. He was so thin that his countenance appeared as a mere flaking of flesh modelled over the bones of the skull. But the bone-work which could so ill represent youth and bloom was at last revealed as beautiful. The hollows from which the eye-balls glared fiercely yet with such fatigue, the bleak mouldings of the nose, the thin lips lying flexible and expressive over the strong teeth, the fierce chin with its cleft and the rigid lines of the jaw cutting back into the neck below the cliff of the cheek-bone, all these contours had the dignity of a hill-side of rock. She could just remember her father's face ten years ago, fuller, softer, warmer, a crag in a mist. Here was the bare crag.

It was a relief to her that she had to deal, not with his remembered countenance, but with this new aspect. Then, as she stood talking to him, she caught sight of his face and her own, reflected in the over-mantel and with a sort of wonder saw—and she had never seen it before—that there was a strong likeness between them. High, narrow forehead, strong nose, cleft chin—yes, they were alike : and she felt, in her moment of complete abasement, a most curious thrill as she perceived that truth. She and her father were alike. Gilly did not resemble him. It was she who resembled him.

Why then, if she so resembled him and he her, then they might well have some pity for each other. Then perhaps she could never forgive, but perhaps understand his preference for Gilly. One could not love oneself. When he was so harsh with her, was he, in his strange mind, being harsh merely with himself? Was that what Stephen had been trying to tell her?

She looked round for Stephen and spoke his name aloud— "Stephen!" But Stephen had left the room.

Harry, however, caught up the word on a half smile.

"Yes, we all depend on Stephen," said he. "That was why I sent him to you."

"He was very kind," said Donna.

"He is a kind lad. He has not all the brains in the world," said Harry tepidly, "but I could not do without Stephen."

She was puzzled by his tone. Why does he praise at all, she thought, if he cannot speak more heartily? Why does he want me home if he does not kiss me when I come in or say—'I am glad to see you.' Accustomed to the gentle warmth of the two last years she found herself utterly unprepared for her father's manner. 'He hasn't given me one smile,' she thought. 'But it is not merely that he dislikes me: he did not even smile at Stephen.' And she said, with an impulsiveness that amazed herself—

"Stephen was more than kind, Father. He was the greatest comfort."

Harry nodded politely.

"And he has settled all your affairs according to your wishes? I gave him a free hand. You approve of our choice of agent?"

"Yes, Father, thank you."

"And your sisters-in-law? But I heard from them myself." And he put out his hand to his desk as his daughter started. "A very charming letter. You may read it."

She took the letter in silence, bewildered. Why had they written to her father? Why did they do anything independently of her? Her eyes stung as she read the letter. It was one of Laura's best—gracious, dignified. It expressed with extreme dignity all the necessary gratitudes and it was affectionate and tender on the subject of Donna.

'We realise, of course, that you are doing the best for our dear girl. She could not stay with us for ever. It touches us to see her sorrow at leaving us; but of course we realise, my sister and I, that in a year or two fresh impressions will insensibly lessen the very natural grief that she feels at our mutual loss. We can assure you, dear Mr. Broome, how glad we are that she should have this opportunity to return to her own people and her own life. The society of your wife and the affection of her cousins will restore her spirits. She is very young.

'And now you must let us express our appreciation of the delicacy and kindness of your nephew to us. He has in all things . . .'

She put the letter down wearily. 'How glad they were that she should have the opportunity . . .'

Was that how they felt? Even they? Though they had clung to her and she had directed their lives for them: though they did love her, though she knew they did love her, still they could write to her father over her head, so wisely and tepidly. They wrote to her father as two equals. She realised at that moment for the first time the power of the tie, strong as the blood tie, strong as the clan tie, the tie of period. Laura, Lucy and her father belonged to the same generation and so they had a private language. And her husband? Had Joscelyn, too, had an instinctive understanding of her father that she had not? Not at the hour of her husband's death, not on the day when she said farewell to her Irish home had she felt so lost, so lonely, as at that moment in her father's room, studying the evidence of that gracious little letter.

It was as if its reading were a signal for a hand to come ripping out of the past and grope in her brain for the figured memory of her husband, to close shadowy fingers upon it and withdraw it out of her consciousness into some dim hinterland of her soul. And in the void which its withdrawal created, there was left but one thought reverberating like an echo imprisoned in a chasm of the rocks—'But I have no-one to talk to! There is no-one who speaks my language!'

But as she thought this she heard outside the door Stephen's laugh and the murmur of his light voice as he crossed the hall with Adelaide. 'Stephen!' her heart exclaimed: and suddenly she realised how much worse life would be if there were no Stephen.

She handed back the letter.

"I am glad they wrote, Father. You have been more than kind. It was good of you to send Stephen."

"You know that Stephen is now in control of the Syracuse?" said he, nodding away her thanks.

"The New Broom? Yes, he told me."

"He is making a success of it. He does his own casting, to a certain extent controls the policy. It is principally Shakespeare, of course; but Stephen likes to experiment with modern stuff—and I indulge him. Occasionally I go over and play there myself. We do not make money,

but it is an excellent training-ground. But you know all this. After all
you have not been gone three years."

Three years! Three years of human time is but a day in the green
country. Her mind swept over time and space and was back again with
Joscelyn, driving home through the wide, marshy valley, full of
summer flags: she saw again the dim hills and the widening estuary
running level with the white road on its way to the sea, till the sight of
it was cut off by the rising stone wall. The wall topped with ivy rose
higher and higher and a goat looked over munching. Then on her left
there flashed into sight the rhododendron drive and the blue smoke of
the hidden house, and above it the cairn-crowned hill. But how brief is
a day in Fairyland!

"Yes, Father, it's not three years," said she.

"I'm transferring Stephen's present leading lady—but you won't
know her, she's since your time. She comes to me for the present.
Later she goes to your uncle Russel. Your uncle Russel and I exchange
members of our companies now and then." Suddenly he winced and
broke off.

There was a dead silence—a sick silence. She thought, mourning for
him—'My poor father!' and said aloud, fumblingly—

"Father, I've never said to you—I've never told you—Gilly—"

"Be quiet," said Harry under his breath. "Be quiet!"

Again they sat in silence.

Presently he went on.

"Her transference will leave a vacancy. You ought to be able to fill
it. I never have doubted your capacity. You need training and
experience—" his glance slipped over her expertly—"But you are much
improved in looks. You hold yourself better. You have more poise. I
feel sure you will do your best."

"Yes, Father," said she.

He hesitated.

"Have you any objection to beginning at once? Socially, of course,
you will not care to appear for some months yet."

"No," she said inaudibly.

"But this is another matter: this is your work. And for it, of course,
you will take your maiden name. Your widowhood has nothing to do
with your work."

She said nothing. Again he hesitated, as she had hesitated. Then he
said, as awkwardly as she—

"I am speaking to you so far professionally as your manager. But

you must not think, Donna, that as your father I have no sympathy—
that I do not sympathise—that I——"

"Oh, Father, don't!"

He desisted.

Presently she spoke again.

"I will try to please you, Father. I will do my best. You would like
me to begin work tomorrow?"

"Yes," said he with satisfaction, and rose. "Yes, that will be best.
And now you had better come to your—to Adelaide. She will look
after you."

And he put his arm through hers so that his hand rested on it, and he
pressed it gently as he led her to the door. She felt his approval. But
even so he had no smile to give her.

CHAPTER 34

THREE BROOME WOMEN

BUT when she returned to the sitting-room Adelaide was all smiles and her grandmother chatty. Her grandmother was also much aged, she thought, but her manner was as vivacious as ever. Adelaide was her latest crony. That was made plain at once.

"First of all—" said Lettice turning to Adelaide, after one familiar appraising look at her granddaughter—"we must get her some clothes."

Donna looked round for Stephen. She had the hunted air of an animal handed over to new masters, who seeks its former master's eye and asks—"Do I wear this collar? Am I to submit to these hands?" But Stephen had gone home to his wife. It was, surprisingly, her father who helped her. He had brought her to the drawing-room and had formally commended her to Adelaide, with the elaborate courtesy and careful attention he always paid his wife: and had then sat down as if in pursuance not of a pleasure, but of a fixed ideal of conduct. It was his duty to converse with the three women for a little while before leaving them together, and he would do it. But at Lettice's first words he frowned.

"Donna is not a child now, Mama. Choose her dresses for her when you choose my coats for me, not before."

"Harry, dear boy!" began Lettice.

"She is in mourning as I am," said he harshly. "Leave her alone." His mouth worked an instant: then he went out abruptly.

Lettice endured the savagery with a blandness that told of habit. "Your father is always overworked nowadays," said she. "It makes him irritable. But of course you must have new clothes—lots of new clothes. Adelaide will help you. She has taste. I leave you in safe hands with Adelaide. But you must show me what you buy. It—" her gay, cracked voice faltered for an instant—"it amuses me." And on she rattled while Donna listened and wondered if it was true that she had ever been away. She felt herself growing momentarily more sad, heavy, frozen, though she said yes and no to her grandmother's chatter and did her best to talk to Adelaide. She had always liked Adelaide, and Adelaide was being kind and welcoming. But already even Adelaide had taken on the tinge of the room. She wore a gay fashionable dress, but her kind, unintelligent face was pale. She looked as if she slept badly. She was only four years older than Donna but already she was a matron and her bloom was gone.

But she, too, was eloquent about clothes. She drove her step-daughter down to the theatre next day and waited placidly while Donna was re-introduced to the stage-manager and the principals of the company, and was given her script. They sat together in a box for an hour watching Stephen conducting a rehearsal, and then drove home again. In the afternoon Adelaide took her to the Park Lane house and she listened while Adelaide and Lettice and the dressmaker designed her new clothes for her, and stood for the holland pattern to be fitted. All her clothes were shockingly old-fashioned, they assured her, except the two that Lettice had sent over to Ireland. Then she was driven home once more.

Harry was playing that night, so the two women ate their dinner together with no other company: and then Donna learned a part until she went to bed. On the next day she went down again to the Syracuse in the morning, but she was not to begin actual rehearsals till the following week: so Adelaide fetched her once more in the handsome carriage and drove her this time straight to Oxford Street and they bought silks at Peter Robinson's and fallals at Jay's. Adelaide insisted that the heavy mourning should be lightened.

"If it had all happened in England you would have had to keep to black for a full year," said Adelaide kindly. "But after all poor Sir Joscelyn died in Ireland, and black depresses Harry, I find. You know that he would not let Lady Lettice wear mourning for Gilly. He is very strange, Donna. You don't know how strange he is."

And a curious look fluttered for an instant in Adelaide's pleasant brown eyes.

"He sleeps so badly," she went on. "I found it so difficult to get accustomed to sleeping in a blaze of light. But he will have lights. The gas and candles burn all night in our rooms. It makes me wake up with a headache, going to sleep with the bright light on my eyes, but of course I don't like to tell him. You know, Donna, I don't think he sleeps more than a couple of hours in the whole night. He ought to see a doctor, but I don't dare suggest it. If it were me I should go mad: I can't do without sleep, can you? Look, Donna, do you think it's too soon for you to wear this grey with a pin-head dot? You could have an embroidered muslin collar and cuffs. It would be Quakerish but it would suit you. And tell the man that you want to see that other pattern again—the black and grey stripe. If you had it made up with a berthe you would look just like Mrs. Siddons. Do you know the picture in the National Gallery? Her dress is blue and white stripes but the effect is much the same. Do have it, Donna!"

Then they drove home again in a hurry, because Adelaide had a few friends coming to dinner. But Donna was graciously excused because she was still in the first months of her widowhood. She dined in her own room and continued to study her parts.

So her days passed. Rehearsals filled the mornings and early afternoons. Sometimes she did a little shopping: always she worked in her own room at night, till her parts were learned and she found herself acting at night. Her father, she found, was only to be seen on Sundays for the theatre engrossed him. She used to hear his tired tread on the stairs round about midnight, and Adelaide's voice greeting him from the bedroom; for Adelaide did not sit up for him.

"It's the sleep you get before midnight that keeps your complexion fresh," explained Adelaide. "If I sat up for Harry, my love, I might sit up till two. Besides, it irritates him to be waited for. So I get my beauty sleep before he comes. Harry is very considerate. He wouldn't like me to sit up. I would if he wanted me to," added Adelaide, and meant it; for she was a nice kind woman.

Donna indeed grew in time pleasantly at home with her. She thought that her father could hardly have picked a better housekeeper. Adelaide had been brought up to be a good wife and a good hostess and justified her upbringing. She was fond of her husband, was grieved that she had no child, enjoyed her position as a married woman, shut her eyes as much as possible to the theatre connection: and if she were ever a little peevish or out of sorts she could always be made happy by a shopping expedition.

"I'm glad you get on with Adelaide, Donna," said Lettice one day wistfully.

"She's so harmless, Grandmama," said Donna without interest or scorn.

"That's it!" said Lettice with relief. "And that, I think, is how your father thinks of her. Don't you, Donna?"

"He's very kind to her. I don't think he thinks of her at all," said Donna.

"Why should he?" said Lettice sharply. "She was given a good marriage settlement, a handsome establishment and most extravagant pin-money. She was only asked to behave herself and see to the household. Light enough duties, I should think. But she was expected to have a child. And then, out of sheer hysteria, sheer lack of control, sheer cowardice, she disappoints my poor Harry."

"She couldn't help the fire, Grandmama. It must have been a fearful shock," said Donna.

"My girl—" said Lettice—"neither you nor I, nor your mother, nor my mother would allow any shock to happen to us. We might watch or suffer the tortures of the damned," said Lettice, "but we should not allow our feelings to affect the child. We should not allow it. Remember that, Donna, when your time comes."

"Mine?" said Donna, her face hardening.

"Yours, my girl! You have not exhausted the troubles of life, my dear! But when your troubles come on you, you are not to behave like that frightened cow Adelaide. You are to keep your head and come to me. You understand? Do you understand, my girl?" said Lettice.

"No!" said Donna, thrusting out her chin at her grandmother.

"What's that?" Lettice was jerked out of her benevolence.

"You forget," said Donna.

"What do I forget?" demanded Lettice, her eyes snapping.

"I'm a married woman," said Donna, "as much as you are. You all forget that, I think. I'm not a schoolgirl: I'm Lady Pallas. I've asked help of Father. But next time I shall not come to anyone."

"Pooh! Tragedy airs!" said Lettice.

CHAPTER 35

STEPHEN HAS IT OUT WITH DONNA

'I am Lady Pallas!' Thus she saved herself from reabsorption into her family. But because in her bearing she was always Lady Pallas, never Domina Broome, her first weeks at the Syracuse were a spectacular failure. She made no friends but many enemies. She would sail along the mean stone corridors to her dressing-room, oblivious of a half-opened dressing-room door and faces looking out, or at most mutter an unsmiling greeting to some barely recognised player as she passed. This was because she did not see them, her whole mind being else-where. But, as she was the daughter of Harry Broome and could with a snap of a finger lose any underling his place, she got no credit for short sight or absent mind. She was too good for her company, that was clear. What was she doing at the theatre, then, if she was too good for her fellow-players? And she was not only proud, they said. She had a flailing tongue. When the set, or the stage direction, or a fellow-actor's gag did not suit her, she said so, sharply, with decision. She did not argue, she over-bore, hatefully trading on her position. So they said, and said too that she was vain and greedy, that she would not let an actor have the full stage for his speech. If he forced her down to the foot-lights as the custom was, she did not submit, she turned her back on him. Then down he had to come to catch her attention and her glance. That might be modern technique, but they called it another thing, they called it pure selfishness. Selfish, imperious, entêté, trading on the fact that she was a Broome and Harry's daughter—that was the verdict on her of the company.

She did not guess it, however, for much as they disliked her, they could not afford to be uncivil to a manager's daughter. Then how should she guess? She was so innocent of dislike for them. But she did feel unfriended and out of touch, but supposed that it could not be helped. This was inhuman England, not home. You could not expect much kindness from anyone. On the whole she did not care.

And this indifference of hers showed in her work. She was con-scientious certainly: she studied her parts, and had her tenacious opinion of how they should be played. Her inherited technique and her personal talent served her loyally: she was patently a better actress already than her predecessor. But her audience, nevertheless, preferred her predecessor.

It was a noisy, direct, orange-sucking, spitting, rowdy audience, loyal, critical, familiar : always ready to prompt a beloved player when he failed in a familiar line, but equally ready to shout out its disapproval of an affectation or an innovation. It was an audience, too, that had its favourites and knew all about their private lives, and shrieked con-gratulations to the soubrette when she returned after the birth of a baby, and chaffed the comedian when he had been unfortunate at Epsom. It was, however, an audience that prided itself on knowing a tip-top actor : and Harry, broadening his style a little on his occasional guest-nights at the Syracuse, could drive that audience just as crazy as he pleased.

Stephen with his light tenor voice, his jolly reliance on personality rather than on acting, and his good looks, was immensely popular, particularly with the women. In his brief reign, too, the place had been redecorated, the temperance bars made much more comfortable : and he would persuade Harry now and then to let him put on a new play within a month or two of its appearance on the other side of the river, instead of making his clientèle wait the usual couple of years. And he had a passion for improvising scenelets, charades, impromptus, which he would wedge in between the triple solidities of the old-fashioned programme. Anything to entertain! This point of view his audiences understood : they loved sport. A tragedy was a cock-fight or a pigeon-shoot to them : 'They have tied me to a stake : I cannot fly : but bearlike I must fight the course,' was a line to be taken literally. They halloo'd, they hunted their Macbeths and their Malvolios : and they loved Harry and Stephen for showing them good sport.

But they could make nothing of Domina Broome, that correct, impeccable young actress : so modern, so frigidly refusing to tear a passion to tatters. And though they did not show any open dislike (Stephen and Harry were too popular for that), she had no following, gained little applause and was listened to in a big part with an attention that was more inquisitorial than flattering. This did not worry her, but it worried Stephen and it worried Harry Broome.

"She falls foul of them, eh?" said Harry to his nephew.

"It's not that, sir, quite——"

"She doesn't interest them?"

"No, sir, I wouldn't say that either. She interests them sufficiently, and every now and then she fires them. But they—they're almost afraid of her, sir. She makes them feel small and common. They don't like it. It's very odd how they take it. I gave her Adriana last week, you know, sir. I wish you'd seen the show, Uncle. That pair of twins is a find. And Donna played very well. She has a vein of comedy, you know. I liked her reading. But what they liked was her defeat at the end. They howled with delight and I have an uncomfortable feeling, sir, that it was Donna's defeat that they enjoyed, not Adriana's."

"What did she say to it?" said the father.

"She? I don't think she noticed. And if she did, she didn't care."

"No. She doesn't care."

"I don't think she does, sir. I wish you'd talk to her."

"I?" said Harry. "You're mad, Stephen. What induces you to think that she would listen to me?"

"Well, I don't know, Uncle——"

"Did Gilly? Had I my son's confidence, Stephen? Did he deviate by one hair's-breadth from his own road for my sake? Then why should Domina?" He moved restlessly in his seat and shuffled with his papers. "You'd better see what you can do, Stephen. You managed her very well in Ireland. I daren't risk *Lear* as we stand, and it's important to us all that it should go on this autumn."

Stephen nodded; for the scheme was one that he cherished almost as much as his uncle. The Gloriana had been redecorated: there was to be a gala re-opening in any case; for it would celebrate the twenty-fifth year of Henry's management. To put on *King Lear* would double the excitement; for Lear is the final test of an artist, let alone a management. And Russel had promised to come over. Russel, who had played Lear himself in New York, had no desire to play in easily bored London a part unsuited to him; but as a gesture of fraternal affection he would be delighted to play Kent. Besides, there was enough of Kent in Russel and enough of Russel in Kent for Russel to be sure that he would have his own special success in it. Stephen's wife was Cordelia, and Stephen, of course, was predestined to Edgar. Donna should play Goneril. Would not such a cast be a triumph for the Broomes? And if the Prince and Princess of Wales came in state to the first performance, that would be a social event indeed and each side would feel that it was honouring the other.

Mama, thought Harry, planning it all out—Mama, especially, would be pleased. Poor Mama! One must get her to the first night somehow, though the whole family would pay for it afterwards. People as old as Mama had no right to such vitality. Such vitality was irritating, grotesque. What was more revolting than live eyes in a tottering body? And Mama insisted on going about, insisted on tottering in public. But of course she must come to *Lear*—her last appearance probably, if the doctors were right. Still your heart-beats and take your last calls, Mama! But she with her terrible loving-kindness would be absorbed in his triumph, not hers. And when she had sated her pride in him she would be watching Stephen. Well, there she would have a shock. For Stephen and he had a novel notion. It was Harry's really, of course.

"Stephen, my boy, I don't want you to play Edgar. I want you to play Edmund."

"Edmund, Uncle? But why?"

"Edmund was beloved," said Harry.

"But——"

"Yes, I know. Think it over."

"But, Uncle, think of the importance of Edgar's part."

"But Edmund was beloved!" his uncle retorted. "Who do you play to, nowadays? You, boy, above all? The women!"

"Come now, Guv'nor!"

"The women! And what do the women care about an Edgar? Beware of the part of a prig, Stephen. Can you think of Edgar married? Can you think of Edgar with a mistress? Of course you can't. But Edmund was beloved. Beloved!" repeated Harry fiercely. "Look at his father, his brother, his women! Edmund was beloved! False, cruel, vicious—he was still beloved." Harry's face was grey. He continued: "It's the cruellest stroke that Shakespeare ever drew." Then, more harshly still—"Gilly should have played it. I'd saved it for Gilly. But there's a likeness between you two: there always was. If you play it as I tell you I shall see my boy again."

"Uncle—Uncle——"

"Be quiet! I am master in my own theatre." His tone changed: he was once more the persuasive, irresistible Harry, disarming all argument. "Take my advice and I'll give you your big chance, my boy. You'll have to trust me a little behind the scenes: I shall want control; but officially you shall have the putting on and management of this revival. You shall have the credit. Why not? You're to be my successor. But not if you play Edgar. You're on the stage too much as Edgar, you must see that for yourself. But if you like to give up Edgar to Russel's juvenile—you know he has written to me about it—what's his name? Angers—and be content with Edmund, well, you

shall have your chance and you shall have one, two, three Broomes—
four, counting yourself, to do your best with."

"Four?" said Stephen.

"Donna plays Goneril, of course," said the father sharply.

"I don't think she can touch it, sir!"

"It's the one part she can touch," said Harry.

"But I told you, sir, we're rehearsing it now. It's next week's piece.
And she isn't good."

"I'll come down and see it," said Harry. "She works for me. But
do what you can with her, Stephen, for I won't put on *Lear* at the
Gloriana without her. I'll have my people round me," said Harry
fiercely, "alive or dead!"

"All right, Guv'nor!" Stephen said no more. He could manage his
uncle six days out of seven, but on the seventh—whew!

He was so hot and flustered as he left the theatre that, though he was
cutting it fine, he thought he would stroll across the bridge instead of
beckoning a hansom. He wanted to think. So it was his job, was it, to
make a silk purse out of a sow's ear? It was all very well for the
Guv'nor to be glib about it. Of course Donna could act if she chose:
anyone could see that. But she wouldn't—the stubborn devil! Or
rather she was acting with a brilliance that bade fair to defeat the pack of
them—acting the incompetent. She had her own deep-seated plans, no
doubt. She wanted to be given up as hopeless, and then—home she'd
trot to her laburnums. It was clever, and a very cool piece of insolence,
too, if you came to consider it. She actually preferred that god-for-
saken hole in the west of Ireland to all they had to give her. There she
was shrugging her white shoulders at them all, at the metropolis, the
theatre, the Broomes, especially at the Broomes! She was saying—
'None of you are worth my while. You can keep me by force, but only
by force, believe me! You've no charms to hold me—no charm about
you, no charm at all.' She, she of all human beings said 'No charm' to
the Broomes.

The Guv'nor was perfectly right. Something must be done about it:
and Stephen, as Donna's immediate superior, was the one to do it. No
charm! He would not waste tact and kindness—well, charm if you like
—on a selfish, unapproachable, ill-tempered fine lady whose only value
was her profile and really remarkable figure. "But, my dear Donna, an
audience doesn't give tuppence for face and figure alone, believe me!
Cleopatra's nose wouldn't have changed history without Cleopatra's
charm to back it. But at present I would no more trust you to play
Cleopatra, in spite of your looks——"

Yes, something of that kind he would say to her. If she could be high-handed, so could he: and with better right. It was his duty to be master in his own theatre. If she wanted fireworks she could have them—a set piece—a full Brock's benefit. No charm!

And in this mood of up and doing Stephen arrived at rehearsal, rather late, and vexed to be late, for he was courteous and conscientious. Late as it was the company was incomplete. His cousin Donna did not arrive for another twenty minutes. They did not wait for her, and it was true that he had not needed her and that she had known that he would not need her. Still the call was for eleven: and if he did not arrive till a quarter past, that was no reason why Domina Broome should be later still.

"Why are you late, Miss Broome? The call was for eleven."

"I understood that you were doing the Edgar scene first."

"But the call was for eleven."

"I know, but——"

"When you have to be late I should be obliged if you would ask me for leave."

"But I'm not late. My scene has not begun yet."

"The call was for eleven."

"Yes, but——"

"Remember for another time, please."

So there, Donna! First round to me, I think!

But though she flushed she did not appear anxious to attack in turn. If the wind had lifted the brim of her hat she would have endured the tug with much the same vexed indifference.

Suddenly his memory supplied him with a picture of her—a black figure on a white road, with green fields and immense skies behind her. He saw again the look in her startled dark eyes as the wind lifted the brim of her Leghorn—'Who are you? What harm are you bringing to me?' Then the recognition—'Stephen!' And now she stood on the airless stage, submissive to the harm he had brought her. Poor Donna! His mood changed. Not much, but a little. But he went on with his thought-out plan.

He let the company play for half an hour, was patient, critical, dissatisfied. He had something not too pleasant to say to each member of the company, chivvied the supers, agitated the prompter and lost his temper with the stage-carpenter. The company stared and fussed. Suddenly everyone became aware of personal failure, ill-learned parts, fatigued utterance and a most extraordinary lack of the usual power to self-excite on which the actor depends, particularly at rehearsal. The company felt its own lack, yet resentfully, not altogether blaming itself. The building, the company felt, was to blame also: there was no more feel to it than the hall of a church mission. Also there was something the matter with Steenie Broome. What had happened to Stephen, usually so well aware of his company's moods, so ready always to throw his own vitality into the pot for the general good? He did not bluster bracingly as his habit was, only to end with a laugh and a coax: he nagged. Down went spirits into the dust, and down dropped the pitch of the voices: the pace grew duller, the verse less intelligible, and the very movements of the actors slowed down to cab-horse trot.

Only Domina Broome, entirely impervious to the mood of the theatre, the manager and her fellow-players, continued serenely to play her part as she always played it, very competently indeed. And Stephen left his cousin alone. There was neither praise nor blame for Donna. Finally, at the end of a dusty and disintegrated hour, he made his effect.

"That will do for today, ladies and gentlemen!"

He said no more, sprawling on his little cane chair, elbows on the prompter's table, his head once more buried in the prompt copy.

Such restraint was terrifying. What had happened? What was going to happen? The company trailed out, inquisitive, injured, each member of it vaguely afraid of a loss of security, of a change of policy indicated by this extraordinary breaking-off of rehearsal at a quarter past twelve in the morning. But curiously enough there was no resentment shown, even furtively, against the obvious cause of the upset, Stephen himself. He had nodded them abstractedly off the boards that were, after all, their precious living: and might prevent their return. But these things he had a right to do. Courtesy was his grace to them, not their right. No, the obscure resentment expressed itself in careful avoidance of the company of Domina Broome. There was not one of the company who did not feel the most vivid pang of rancour, suspicion, and dislike as she rose from the dusty property throne, leisurely shook out the long folds of her black dress and adjusted its fashionable shorter draperies, descended the dais and began to cross the stage, letting her skirts trail and puff up little clouds of dust as she fitted on, finger by finger, her long black kid gloves. She had reached the door held open for her by an assiduous understudy and was passing through without a thank you, when a call from Stephen stopped her.

"Miss Broome, don't go just yet, please. I want to speak to you."

At once she turned and came back to the circle of light.

"I shan't be a moment," said Stephen to her. "You will excuse me. Here, Archer!" and he beckoned his assistant.

Donna looked round her for a stool and sat down to wait placidly enough. All personal relations between the Broomes ended when the footlights were lighted. Stephen was her manager: he had a right to keep her waiting.

But she got very tired of being kept waiting. She told herself that it did not matter, that she had nothing else to do, that if rehearsal had not broken off she would be at this moment waiting in the wings. But still, as time went by, Domina Broome began to resent very much the fact that her cousin Stephen kept her waiting. Living as she did in a half sleep of boredom, home-sickness, exhausted feeling and general discontent, it was astonishing to her that so immaterial a fact as the fact that Stephen kept her waiting should have any effect on her at all. As well sit here as sit at home: as well sit at home as sit here. What difference did it make? Nevertheless Stephen was keeping her waiting.

Bubble after bubble of irritation welled up through the cloudy waters of her consciousness and burst upon its surface, till she felt livelier in her mind than she had felt for a month of Sundays, and the angrier and the better for it. By the time Stephen had finished with his scene-shifters and his stage-carpenter, by the time he had gone through the script with his prompter, shouted up instructions to the flies and inter-viewed with lightning speed three stage aspirants, the hands of the clock had moved on nearly an hour and Donna had a red spot on her cheek and very lively eyes indeed.

At last, however, he rose. White daylight, trickling down the hanging ropes from the flies like water dripping through a colander held under the tap, clung about her head and outlined him as he crossed the stage, so that for a moment he did not look like himself or human. To Donna, glancing up angrily, the likeness to Gilly was astonishing, and her quick morbid mind perfected for itself the vague impression as a sick eye sees faces of malignity in the harmless pattern of a wall-paper. In his dark figure outlined in silver, with a shadowed face, she saw for an instant a drowned boy walking on the land. The thought destroyed her anger as swiftly as Stephen's next step destroyed the illusion, and restored to himself and her his own warm breathing personality.

He came up to her and spoke pleasantly but not cheerfully.

"I'm sorry, Donna, to make you wait. Will you come to my office? I want to speak to you."

"You have made me wait an hour," said she, not exactly resentful but unable to resist making the statement.

He looked at her with surprise.

"Yes, I was busy."

She shrugged her shoulders and followed him off the stage and down the long cement corridor lined with tarnished looking-glasses, and on up the flights of stone steps that led from floor to floor: for Stephen's office was at the top of the building.

There were, as usual, three or four tired people standing and sitting in the little outer office: and, as usual, all rose with eager respect and one or two pressed forward with—"Oh, Mr. Broome!" Stephen stopped, smiling, friendly but deprecating—"Hullo, Travers? Were you waiting for me? I'm afraid there's nothing today. But come in next week." He went from one to another while Donna frowned and tapped her foot and finally went in by herself to the inner office. Once again he was keeping her waiting!

Stephen did not come in for nearly ten minutes, but when he did he forestalled her irritation by an attack which immensely surprised her. She was sitting on the low couch that ran along by the window, enjoying the pleasant airs which blew in upon her hot cheeks. There was room for him beside her, but he did not come and sit down, nor did he go to his desk. Instead he slammed the door behind him, then, leaning back against it, attacked her.

"Why couldn't you be civil to these people, Donna, as you came through?"

Donna stared in genuine surprise.

"What people?"

"Those people after parts. Old Travers—Mary Gain."

"My dear Stephen, I didn't see them."

"Well, why didn't you look?"

She was puzzled.

"I didn't know them," she said wonderingly. She couldn't understand what he was driving at.

"You know that they are actors and actresses. You know that they belong to the stage, just as you and I do. You may be playing with them any day."

"Certainly," said Donna, flushing as she caught his drift. "And when I do I shall know them and say how d'you do. Meanwhile they are strangers."

"That is exactly what they are not. They are people of our profession. At the moment they are out of a job and probably hard up, cr they wouldn't be hanging round the office when they know perfectly well that the company is full. And you walk through them as if they were the ghosts of scarecrows."

"I did not."

"I say you did. It's damned insolence."

"Stephen, I won't have you speak to me in this tone."

"It is exactly the tone which you used as you came through the office. Your manner used that tone, Donna."

"Well, and if I did?"

"Don't again, that's all! You've no right to use it. You wouldn't dare if you were one of those poor devils hoping for a job at a pound a week. But because you're a Broome and the Guv'nor's daughter, and because you know that this place will belong to you when my uncle dies——"

"I think you are out of your mind, Stephen. I never thought of such a thing."

"Well, they think it, poor brutes, when they see you sailing past. I hate snobbishness."

"I am not a snob," said Donna angrily. "Whatever I am, I'm not a snob."

He came down to the table-desk and sat down on the end of it, facing her.

"No, I don't believe you are at heart. But you do behave like one, Donna." Then, with his disarming smile—"I don't mean to be rude to you but you made me angry just now. I'm sorry."

She looked back at him with her lips pressed together. She would not smile back at him. Secretly she was amazed, not only at his attack for which she was genuinely unprepared, for her bad manners were never conscious; but for the fact that his reproaches hurt her exceedingly. She could have cried. What did it matter if Stephen thought ill of her? But it hurt her very much that he thought ill of her.

"What did you want to speak to me about?" said she, finding astonishing difficulty in controlling herself. "Be as quick as you can, Stephen. I shall be late for lunch."

He hesitated.

"Well, it's rather a difficult matter to begin——"

There was a knock at the door and a clerk came in.

"The stage carpenter wants to speak to you for a moment, sir."

"Oh! Oh, yes, of course. Come in, Staines!"

"It's about the frame of those doors, sir. I can't get it done by Monday night, not without I have help."

"What's Tolman doing?"

"Busy on the sky, sir. I daren't take him off or it won't be dry in time."

"Well, Whitman then?" said Stephen impatiently.

"Whitman's gone to the store with the van, sir. He's the only man I could trust."

"Hm! Can't you fake up anything?"

"Well, you know what it is, sir. If the Guv'nor sees it I'll get into trouble. He won't pass shoddy."

"No, you'd better cut across the Bridge to the Glory Hole, Staines, and take this note to Mr. Carfax. He'll lend you a couple of men." He scribbled a hasty note. Then, as the door closed—

"Well, the fact of the matter, Donna, is this———"

The door re-opened.

"Can you see Miss Portman a moment, sir?"

But before he could answer the lady's face appeared smiling over the clerk's shoulder.

"I'm not interrupting you, Mr. Broome? Just popped up to ask you if there is or is not a call this afternoon?"

The actress was old and privileged, so Stephen restrained himself with an effort.

"Now my dear, look at the stage door! There'd be a notice, wouldn't there? What do you come toiling up all these stairs for? Ten-thirty tomorrow. Good morning!"

He shut the door again and turned to his cousin with a look that asked for sympathy. But she was staring out of the window, lost once more in her own thoughts, and had none to give him.

Now Stephen liked sympathy, liked giving it, liked getting it. He was tired and worried and had an unpleasant job ahead of him. A pleasant word from his selfish cousin would have soothed Stephen and greatly weakened the force of his attack. As it was, righteousness possessed him, and there was, too, a vicious little desire to hurt.

"Donna, will you give me your attention for a moment?"

"They look like flies down in the street, don't they?" said Donna—"or ants."

"If you'll make room I'll shut the window." And he did so, sharply, and sitting himself down on the cushion of the window-seat, substituted his own pleasant countenance for the flies. At which Donna lost interest.

"Well, Stephen?" said she, rising and wandering idly from picture to picture on the walls. It was as unconscious a movement as ever a woman made, an idle impulse of restlessness and disjunction from the scene; but it angered Stephen precisely as her indifferent passage through the ante-chamber had angered him. He, too, got up.

"It would be civil of you to listen, Donna."

"But I am listening, Stephen."

"I cannot talk to your back."

"What? Oh! I'm sorry."

But as she turned round there was another knock at the door. Once again Stephen dealt with the interruption, once again turned to his cousin.

"This becomes a farce. I can't talk to you here."

"Come home to lunch," suggested his cousin amiably.

"No, I should have to be agreeable to Adelaide, and I don't want to be agreeable to anyone."

She glanced at him with a gleam of amusement.

"I find you bad-tempered this morning myself, Stephen. It's so exceptional that I can't help noticing it."

"I can't say that of you, Donna."

"Oh, my dear Stephen, how cross you are!"

"Well, the thing I have to say to you is this—I never find you anything but bad-tempered—bad-tempered, self-centred, indifferent and impossible to work with."

"Stephen!" began Donna and left her mouth open.

"And what's more——"

There was a knock at the door. Stephen, using the objurgation of the hour, flung it open, crying—

"Send everyone away! I am seeing nobody else this morning. I am seeing nobody at all. I don't care if it's the Prince of Wales himself. I'm going out to lunch. Come, Donna!"

And he took his cousin firmly by the elbow, hustled her dignity down the long corridor to the spiral staircase which ran up from the stage level to the flies and the roof itself, put a foot upon the perforated iron steps and began to climb.

"Come along now!" he called down to her.

"Where?"

"The roof, of course." He was struggling with the trap-door as he spoke. "Only place they don't harry you."

"But I've never been on the roof."

"Well, you're coming now!" And he heaved back the heavy lid with a clatter. "Come on!"

Shrugging elaborately she condescended to follow and as she emerged and was dazzled by the sudden sunlight Stephen's hand caught hers and helped to steady her over the ledge and on to a flat roof half the size of a tennis court. At some time or other it had been smoothed and cemented, and an incised line crossed it dividing the space as a chalk line marks a rehearsal room. There were a couple of stone benches and a table, and a high parapet enclosed the whole.

"But——" began Donna: and then as the high sweet wind laden with the lilacs of Camberwell blew across her face—"Oh, Stephen!"

"Yes." Stephen drew a deep breath, and he too felt that his fatigue and heat and irritation were being lifted away from him by the wind and the quiet. He had meant to have such a third act curtain with his cousin, for that matter still meant to; but he no longer desired to beat her about the head. He wasn't going to lose his temper. Oh, no! Leave that to her! But she, too, was momently feeling more strongly the influence of the place and showed it.

"Peaceful," said she. And then—"Why don't we rehearse here in the summer?"

"We used to—in your mother's time. She loved it. But nowadays the Guv'nor never comes near it."

Her face softened.

"If thy heart torment thee, cut it out! Poor old man!"

"I come up sometimes to get a part in a hurry. Come and sit down!"

But instead she crossed to one of the look-out places, climbed the three steps and stared down upon the sea of roofs. A moment she stared. Then—

"Oh, how I hate a town!" said Donna, and turning her back on the river and the towers of the city, she descended and crossed to the opposite corner, where, in the half distance, lay bowery Camberwell. Beyond, green ridges rolled to the sky-line where from its country home the Crystal Palace signalled to its London one.

"If I'd known of this," said she wistfully, as he climbed up beside her, "I'd have managed better. I could have got away in my mind up here. Look, the clouds are driving west." And she went on softly—

> "'Eilende Wolken, Segler der Lüfte,
> Wer mit euch wanderte, mit euch schiffte,
> Grüsset mir freundlich mein Jugendland——'

I wish you'd put that play on, Stephen. There's quite a good trans-
lation. I should like to play her."

"Which 'her'?"

"Maria Stuart, of course. Who else?"

"But don't be ridiculous, Donna. You play Mary? Never!"

"Couldn't I? That's all you know. 'Eilende Wolken, Segler der
Lüfte!' Oh, well!'"

She sighed and stepped down once again without another look at the
distant hills: and once back on the floor of the roof the stone parapet
hid view and neighbouring houses alike. It was like being in a room
with a blue ceiling. The sky above them was cloudless with noon
heat.

She touched the bench with her finger, found it clean enough and
sat. Then, as her hand rested with the sort of stage gesture so natural
to her on the arm of the bench and her hands closed over the curve, she
glanced down, lifted her hand quickly, then looked up at her cousin,
her eyes suddenly alive and glowing. There was childish delight in
her voice as she said—

"It's a sphinx's head!"

"Is it?" said Stephen not attending. For he was not yet friends with
her, and her talk of Mary had given him his chance and he was wanting
to take it.

"Why, yes——" She was impatient at his stupidity. "It's the bench
in the laburnum wood. Oh, I like it here. I shall come up often."

Ah—there was his chance.

"If I let you," said he briskly, sitting down beside her and playing
with the key.

"Let me? Is there any reason why I shouldn't?"

"None at all. I could have a second key made for you easily. None
at all if you stay on at the New Broom."

"Oh, why talk like that, Stephen?" said she impatiently. "You know
well enough that I've got to stay here—or at the Glory Hole—or at
the Genista—day in, day out, night in, night out, for the rest of my
natural life. Father has made that plain enough."

"That's while he thought of you as an asset, Domina. But now
he's beginning to wonder whether you are such an asset to him.
He's a business man. He may reckon you as one of his losses and
decide to cut his loss. Then, I daresay, he will send you back to
Ireland where you so much want to be. He never speaks till he has
made up his mind; but I foresee, if you go on as you are doing now,

that this will be the end of it. I expect you will be pleased. That is why I tell you. I'm always willing to give you pleasure."

Her hand still clutched the sphinx-head as she leant back, bewildered, prepared to be angry, completely at a loss.

"I don't know what you're talking about."

"Oh, don't sham stupid, Donna," said he, "when you've been so exceedingly clever."

"Clever? I assure you, Stephen, I don't know what you mean."

"Well, I think it is clever of you to agree to my uncle's terms. You get all the money and support you want out of him and in return you come over here and do all he tells you. Only you do it so badly that he is forced to say—'You are no use to me at all,' and send you away again. But you have kept the letter of the bargain and Uncle will admit it, and so you will keep all he gave you. But I think, Domina, that you are just a common cheat."

He expected an explosion of anger. He knew his cousin's temper and her tongue. But no explosion came. Instead she sat staring at him with so horrified an air that he found his anger, which he knew to have been half an affair of histrionics, difficult to maintain. If she had flamed up into furious self-defence, then he could have fought her well, for he thoroughly enjoyed a scene. But she did not budge: and her quiet softened his mood again and made him say to himself as he had often said before—'She is so maddening because one never quite gets hold of her! One ought to be able to get hold of her and hurt her.' And his sincere desire to be in touch with her made him eloquent as he continued—

"And then you have the audacity to talk of playing Mary Stuart. *You* play Mary? Why our audiences would only just put up with you as Elizabeth. They resent you, I tell you! One day they'll show it. Have you ever been hissed? Of course you haven't. No more have I. But they say it's deuced unpleasant."

"Oh, bother!" said she, bored.

"It ain't so easy to say bother to a mob, Donna. Do you know what a mob can do to an actor if it dislikes him? Do you know what it did to John Evans once? It made him come on to the stage and beg its pardon for being in the right. And it tried to make him kneel down."

"Did he?" said she.

"No. He said he'd kneel to God and to his Sovereign and to no-one else."

"There was a man!" said she, glowing.

"And there was a mob! You be careful!"

"Pooh! It's a hundred years ago."

"But a mob's always a mob."

"Hateful beast!" said she.

"Your master," said he. "You're the servant of the public. It'll show you one day. I thought we were near it in *Richard II*. I was ashamed of you as the Queen. How should a wife weep? You ought to know. But you did not tell us."

She put her hand to her head.

"Are you suggesting, Stephen, that I should tell those fools in the audience what I felt about losing Joscelyn?"

"You're no use to us here if you don't," said Stephen.

There was a long silence. The noonday sun pouring down, beat upon the floor of the roof and the floor threw up the heat again, so that the middle air danced blue and misty as steam above fire.

"Never!" said Donna at last. And then—"Well, go on! I may as well hear the worst of myself."

He shrugged his shoulders.

"You shut yourself up. You play for your own hand. It reacts on the company. They feel you despise them."

"I don't, I don't!" said she with a wail in her voice. "I never think of them."

"Well, what right have you to say that?" he demanded. "Isn't it an insult to people who help you to live, never to think of them? How would you feel if no-one thought of you?"

"Who thinks of me?" demanded young Domina. And at that moment, in the midst of the righteous indignation which he was thoroughly enjoying, it struck him suddenly that she was only a girl and that he was sorry for her.

"Why," said Stephen with that thought breaking the impetus for him, "all of us do, Donna. My uncle——"

"Stephen, don't cant!" said she.

"Well, I do then," he said. "I'm your cousin. I'm extremely fond of you."

"Oh—fond!"

"Yes, fond," he said. "Only you make me so angry. After all you're endangering my position as well as your own. Your father has set his heart on making a star of you, and you are in my theatre. If you won't work with me, if you will antagonise everyone——"

"But what am I to do, Stephen?" she said, piteously.

"Feel more," said he. "Don't lock it up."

"There isn't any more to feel," said Donna.

"What?" He looked at her laughing.

"There, you see——" she broke in—"you laugh when I say my true thoughts, or else you disbelieve. I tell you, you are wrong about me, all of you. I've never thought these things. I don't mean to cheat."

"Yes, but Donna, look what you're doing to us all."

"What do I do to you all?"

"Well, my dear cousin, you broke off rehearsal this morning for one thing. And that's a thing I've not seen done in my whole experience."

"Your whole experience!"

"Well, I've been in it since I was a baby. Anyhow my mother was an actress. Aunt Maud wasn't. I tell you that if my uncle had been in the theatre and you had not been his daughter you'd have been given your money and told to go."

She abandoned the sphinx's head and leaning forward on the bench beat her fists on it, crying—

"But what did I do? You don't tell me what I did."

He said slowly—

"You make it impossible for people to play with you."

"Who says I do? How?"

"D'you find the company friendly?"

She wrinkled her brow and stared at him, quite comically searching her mind. But she brought out at last an honest—"I don't know. I've never thought."

"D'you like your audiences? Is it a pleasure to you to see them, to get at them, to coax them, persuade—Oh, you must know what I mean —treat 'em womanly?"

She said again ruefully, but seeing his drift—

"I don't know, Stephen. I've never thought of them like that." And then, hastily, as if in answer to an accusation he had not spoken—"What has that to do with it? I'm not a person on the stage. I'm a part. And I do work at my parts. I don't cheat. I think of nothing else, except—" her voice shook suddenly—"except home—except Ireland—and I try not to think of that. I remember what you said to me, Stephen, about drowning oneself in work. I do try to, though I see you don't believe it. What more can I do? And after all—" her chin lifted—"I don't know why I should defend myself to you. I get good notices. No-one has attacked me in the papers."

"My dear girl, why should they? You have by inheritance, just as I have, what most people take years to learn—technique. You've had several years' training with my uncle, and you're very handsome. With all these advantages, if you can't be adequate what can you be? All the same, Donna, as you are you're no use to us. What did you say just now? That you don't know what your audiences think of you? Good God, and you pretend to be an actress! And you don't know what your company thinks of you! Good God, and you pretend to be a woman!"

"You are writing yourself in a good set speech, aren't you?" she hit back at him, sulkily.

"Oh, very well! I say no more."

"Oh, you can go on," said she, sulkily. "You will, anyway—we both know that." And then, as he did not at once speak—"Well, after all this, what do they think?"

"Your audiences? That you are a piece of handsome machinery, in good order."

"It's not true."

"Perfectly true. What else are you? You're not a woman. You're bloodless and inhuman. You can neither give nor get love."

"Haven't I been married?" she demanded.

"To a man of fifty, yes—a good fellow."

"And I loved him dearly." Her voice broke suddenly, and at that his expression changed.

"Dearest Donna, I know you were very fond of him. But—" he got up and stood looking down at her—"but you aren't quite alive yet, Donna, all the same." Then as she, too, stood up—"Shall I tell you—" he went on—"what a critic said to me about you the other day?"

Suddenly her cheek flamed.

"No, I don't want to hear it. You can say things about me, Stephen, and I let you. But I won't let anyone else. I don't know why I let you."

"Don't you?" said he under his breath—"Why do you? Donna, why do you?"

"Why?" She checked a moment: her mind stumbled, recovered, sped on. "Does it matter? I choose to. But I won't endure it from other people. Even from you it's hard enough to bear. You make me out hard and cold: and if you think that, then I'd rather you said it, of course. But I'm not hard and I'm not cold. But how can I show you that I'm not? It's cruel of you to think of me as you do. Oh, of course I know that you are being kind to me—patient—that few men would take such trouble. What—" and over her shoulder she shot him a glance—"d'you think that I don't feel that? But of course you think I don't feel. Well, I don't care. Why in the world should I care what you think? Oh—" she flung up her hand violently as if she would push away the glare of the sun—"the sun is intolerable on this lead roof. I'm dizzy with it. It beats down on me. Haven't we finished, Stephen? There is really no more to say. I can't be lectured for ever. I'd better go home. Please, Stephen, let us go down!"

And she flung away from him across the hot leads in some agitation. He followed more slowly, for she had startled him, and he had startled himself. He was moved too, by the slight, subtle agitations of her shoulders and long, slender back, under the tightly fashionable gown. He was absorbed in following. At the trap-door she paused.

"Stephen, go first. My eyes are so dazzled by staring at the sun."

He nodded, clambered in and down. The descent was a difficult business for Donna with her trailing skirts, but she managed it, leaning downwards into the darkness to seek his hand while her feet felt for the ladder foothold. Then down she came, still steadied by his hand, and they stood together, peering down over the rail of the stairhead to the darkness of the far-off stage.

"All right?" said his strained voice.

"Yes," said hers.

"We'll go straight down to the stage, shall we? Shall we?"

"Why not?"

"Let's then! Do you mind?"

"No."

"Good."

He released her hand and began to go down the twisting iron contraption with its slender balustrade and perforated steps, and its sharp, giddy twists.

But she was half blinded by the sun-blanks left on her eyes, so that illusions of inter-circling suns, red, green and brown, interposed between her and solidity. Through the steps she could feel, though she could not see, the deep drop from the flies to the stage, and she had never any head for heights. Her natural tendency to vertigo was heightened by that dizziness which always follows session in the sunshine. She felt for the handrail, missed it, stumbled, knew herself falling and cried out. Then she felt herself caught and held, held in the arms of a hunger suddenly and savagely discovering itself. Give us this day our bread!

Without surprise, as if it had been the fulfilment of a lifetime's waiting, she yielded to the demand of this hunger, not submitting merely, but returning the embrace with exaltation and delight. Here was the missing life. If this were feeling, it was easy enough to feel. If this were loving, it was easy enough to love.

CHAPTER 36

WHEN, years later, Stephen looked back to the beginning of his disasters, his love-affair with his cousin, he would groan to himself over the singular folly of it, would ask himself in a sort of despair—"What possessed me? What possessed me?"

And then he would look across the table to the worn, cheerful face of his wife on her sofa and say to himself—"It wouldn't have happened if she had been with me. But without Madeleine——"

And indeed he was right. Only Madeleine Broome, Stephen's loved but little considered wife, could have checked at that moment the gorse-fire blaze of passion which swept across the lives of Stephen and Domina Broome, and then died out as swiftly as it had blazed leaving their future blackened.

If Eustace, Stephen's first-born, had not been a frail child, had not needed a three months' sojourn in country air and his mother's incessant care, there is little doubt that the affair would not have happened. Stephen had few secrets from his wife. She had made a worker of him, and shared his work: and suited him besides so well that when he was with her the philanderer in him gladly fell asleep. But with Madeleine away he was a bachelor again, and ready for anything: even for the amusement of handling that unusual she-problem, his cousin Domina Broome.

For he was attracted by Donna and he was rather fond of solving human problems that nobody else could solve. But he had no intention of letting himself fall in love with her, though he thought her very lovely and liked fighting her, until excitement, anger and a stumble in the dark did the business for both of them.

It was their mutual revelation of strangeness that betrayed them to each other. Domina had known Stephen too familiarly ever to think of him or be aware of him as breadth, height, thickness, warmth and strength. To feel herself physically controlled by him created in her sensations that she did not understand and did not want to deny. He, for his part, was amazed at the fierceness with which she responded. Such response turned her into a stranger, a contradiction of all he had ever thought her. His own words to her of a few minutes before—'Try

398

to feel!' floated through his mind and he laughed at them irritably as one does at the memory of a foolish phrase spoken in ignorance. Feel? She blazed with feeling: she set a light to herself and him.

But no, he could not forget that it was he who had lit the blaze, he would not let her for one instant overwhelm him with the fierce flames of her vitality. He was as dangerous as she, and knew it, and for once utterly reckless, matched himself against her as he had never before matched himself against any woman, flinging into the bon-fire of their mutual passion all sense of caution, of responsibility, of tenderness or pity for the woman, the weaker creature. She could look after herself and so could he, and the fire was a fine fire. So let it blaze! For he was truly convinced that she could look after herself. It was incredible to him that her passion, her violence of attack and surrender, her delighted adventuring with him along any path, the subtlety and urgency of her desires and the completeness with which she unveiled them to him, could go hand in hand with igno-rance or innocence. She had deceived him, he thought, about herself. He had made himself ridiculous in her eyes by telling her that she was ignorant and unawakened. How she must have mocked him. That thought quickened his passion for her but it did not make him compassionate.

Yet all the while, had he but known it, his first judgment was right. But the swift maturing of her physical nature deceived them both, and demoralised them both.

They were drunkenly in love, miserable out of each other's sight. Separated they schemed, planned and wildly plotted to be together. Together they watched each other jealously for any sign of slackening. They tormented each other with super-subtleties, protesting the while their own simplicities of soul. The plainest yes or no was suspected of its double, triple meaning, was arraigned, explained, good enough for a scene and a reconciliation. The first move towards departure, the private word given to another, the eyebrow lifted a shade too high, the smile too subtle, the turned back, the look of intelligence missed—these were treacheries inexplicable until they were explained into acts of special grace.

They met of course daily at their rehearsals: and he was rude, but with secret looks at her, and she was a miracle of patience and her answering eyes were full of laughter, so that they did not dare to look at each other much before the company. And she was a new Domina Broome to the company. Courtesies flowed out of her, and kindnesses. If anyone had a grievance Domina listened to the grievance and took it across to Stephen to be put right. At night her cold audiences began to give her a hand. And as she curtsied to them, delighted, gracious, thankful, oh so intensely thankful for the invisible bouquets, and winning her audiences the more by her astonishing thankfulness, she slanted her eyes towards the wings to see if Stephen heard.

He heard. He was so proud of her that he wanted to talk of her to everyone, and would have done so had he not had some remnants of prudence left. But instead he would go over on any and every pretext to his uncle to tell him how marvellously Donna was getting on all of a sudden, and to drag the Guv'nor back with him to see her crack scene. But rehearsing all day and playing together thrice a week did not satisfy them: their mutual cry was always—"Can't we get away from people? Can't we be alone?"

It was not easy in Victorian times for a woman to evade observation; but Adelaide was not inquisitive and she was accustomed to her family's late returns. And Donna found that the madness which was upon her gave her an extraordinary facility in invention, gave her a capacity to plot and lie and forswear herself as she had never dreamed that any mere slack-mouthed liar could do, let alone her austere and fastidious self. She found an exquisite delight, first in lying and then in mocking to her lover the fools who were taken in by her lies. She would be garrulous with accounts of her tricks and deceits, making Stephen laugh; for in their high-wrought state, in their light perpetual drunkenness they laughed easily and found everything exquisitely absurd, and most absurd of all they found their acknowledged distrust of each other.

For they could not wholly trust. Each must try to appear the less eager, for that gave advantage, the hold, the upper hand. So when they appointed to meet (the roof was their usual unwatched and unsuspected meeting-place) one lover would say privately—"I will not be eager: I'll come late today," and dawdle on the way, then hurry the last ten minutes in sudden fear of being too late: and arrive panting, far too soon, to find the other there already, panting, having arrived far too soon. And so the love-dance went on dizzily till rehearsals began for *Lear*.

Then indeed there could be no meetings on the roof, no comings and goings across Waterloo Bridge, and Harry kept them working with an intensity that quenched the gaiety of their delight in each other. But the tireder they grew the more they stood to their tryst. It was simple enough for Donna to declare herself too fatigued for the drive home after the prolonged late rehearsals, and take impeccable lodgings near the Gloriana. When she did not go home Adelaide said—"She has stayed in Bedford Street." When she did not come to Bedford Street the decayed gentlewoman who chaperoned Miss Domina Broome (she is Lady Pallas, of course, really!) knew that she had gone back with her father to Regent's Park. But actually Domina had gone to those secret rooms that Stephen knew. You went down a passage roofed in and dark. Half way along there was a neatly painted door let in to the wall with a little brass knocker and a window beside it, and an innocent geranium in the window behind the blind. In the little house on the wall lived Morgan's daughter who would do anything for Master Robin's son. There Donna and Stephen could and did meet, with the more obstinate and feverish regularity because the early excitement of their adventure was over: and its charm was now its fierce habit. The pair insisted jealously on their rights: they grew more and more like children, weeping with exhaustion and the desire to rest, yet jealously insisting on their right to sit up and see the New Year in. And their fatigue, too, was like the fatigue of children, as exaggerated and fantastic as their previous vitality, for their mutual exhaustion was more infectious even than their previous mutual gaiety had been. The fierce blaze soon exhausted the supply of fuel and the flame dropped, at any rate with Stephen, as suddenly as it had flared. Stephen gave up first. He had not his cousin's tenacity: quicker to thrill than she, he was always the first to be bored: and with boredom all was over.

The breach was made one crisp September evening when Donna, huddled and half asleep in the box from which she watched scenes and awaited her call, turned at a touch on her shoulder. She knew it for Stephen and she sprang up at once and followed him into the darkness of the withdrawing-room, half closing the box door behind her. It was the room in which Robert had killed himself, but that day was long ago, a mere legend to them both.

"Donna, I can't come tonight."

She knew him well enough never to show disappointment, but, as she nodded unsurprised acquiescence, she made up her mind that he should come, he should come.

He went on fretfully—

"Uncle's worn me out. He's had no mercy."

"Of course, of course! Has he finished with you now?"

"Not for another hour. He wants to run through the second scene again. You know what that means."

"Well, when I've finished my scene I'll go."

"Yes, I think you'd better go home."

"Well, I shall go to Morgan's whether you come or not. I shan't go home. I've arranged with Adelaide to be out. Don't look worried, Stephen. It's perfectly safe. Adelaide thinks I'm at Bedford Street, of course. Why shouldn't she? Adelaide thinks I am so sensible to spare myself the drive and confesses that it does save the household work. She is so pleased at saving the maids trouble that my conscience is truly clear, Stephen. You may smile, but I have a conscience. I don't like deceiving people, not even poor Adelaide."

"Nor do I like deceiving people," said he not looking at her: and instantly, warily, she swung round upon her own words like a tethered boat in a tide.

"Oh, my darling, what harm do we do? How tired you look. Look, dear, come to me afterwards however late it is and I will make you rest so well. I'm not a bit tired, and I will have supper ready for you, and it shall be very peaceful. We won't even talk."

"It will be too late," said he.

"Will it? Perhaps you are right. You shall do just as you think. I shall understand. But look, Stephen, if it is not too late, come! I shall be awake. I shall not expect you, of course I shan't expect you, but of course I shall be awake. Do come! Is that my call? No, I have another five minutes, but I must be going down. Good-night, Stephen—unless you come. Come, Stephen——"

"I ought to go home, Donna."

"Yes, but come!"

"I don't know. Good-night!" He stooped to her for a conscientious kiss but it turned, at her touch, to a wild and hurtful embracing, to a frantic clinging together, to a struggle for release as if the locking of their bodies created in each soul a cruel, unreasoning desire to break and destroy the symbolic prison of arms, lips, love. It was as if at the same moment they experienced a passion to be one and a passion to be separate, and the two passions fought each other within the cage of their embrace. Swift come, swift go! The mood swept over them like lightning, leaving them burned and bewildered.

But bewildered as she was, and breathless, flung back against the wall, one arm outstretched against it steadying herself, one hand on her breast steadying herself, still she was tenacious. "You will come,

Stephen?" And her eyes sought his scarce seen face as if her glance had turned into hands and the hands were caressing him. For the glimmer that had travelled dwindling thither across the dark auditorium from the lighted distant stage thinned but did not expel the darkness of the tiny room: and the sense of touch was the only sense awake in it. Sight and hearing were reduced to ghosts of senses. Their very thoughts were expressed by touch.

"Come!" she murmured, and felt him, only a yard away, catch his breath, check on his words, shiver and begin again.

"I can't, Donna. I've got to go home."

"Why?" They were both whispering.

"Madeleine comes home tomorrow."

"This is tonight."

"I know. But there's much to do at home and I have to be here again so early."

"She's coming home tomorrow?"

"You knew she was."

"I didn't know. You never told me. What are we to do?"

"Do?"

She fancied that there was a chill in his voice: and then fancied that it was her fancy. But the fancy did not quiet her and her voice tightened and heightened.

"So it has come at last, Stephen! Well, it must be faced. But oh, I'm so sorry for her!"

She felt him stiffen.

"What d'you mean, Donna? Are you talking of Madeleine?"

"Of course, poor woman! She will never forgive us. I feel so wicked. Stephen, how shall you tell her? Or should I? Or had I better face Father? I want to take my share. But oh, Stephen, if we didn't love each other this wouldn't be bearable. Stephen, what are you doing?"

His voice came choked and breathless in the darkness. He said— "We must have a light!" as a choking man would say—"Give me air!" And in another instant the gas was flaring.

Stephen stood in illumination under the jet. He was white and his hands shook. He looked exhausted and angry. She would have gone to him, but his strange look held her back.

"What is it, Stephen? What is the matter?"

"Yes, what is the matter, Donna? What have you got into your head? What lunacy? I'm not going to tell my wife anything."

"You are not——!"

Then she felt rising in her cheeks that leaden blush of anger and dismay, that blush of the whole body which sets the very eye-balls burning.

"Am I to tell her then?" She tried to go on but her voice was weak.

"Good God, no! Nobody's to tell her anything. Donna, are you mad?"

"But aren't we in love?" she said. "Won't she divorce you? Shan't we get married?"

"My poor darling——"

"Why am I poor if I am yours, if I am your darling? I don't understand you. Your look has changed. You don't look at me! You don't answer me! Why don't you answer me? What is frightening you, Stephen? Shan't we get married?" Then she caught his arm imploringly. "Shan't we? Why are you so angry? What does it mean?"

She was right. He was angry, furiously angry with her for being so stupid and yet still beautiful. He wanted to hurt her for insisting to him that their position was intolerable. Why couldn't she take life as it came?

But he tried to speak to her intimately and passionately.

"Donna, don't break things! Don't spoil things! We have had a jolly time, haven't we, together? Well, it's over. It must be. Can't you see? Don't be such a child, Donna! I'm married. You've been married. We're people of the world, not children. Why do you make me seem so—— Why do you pretend—— I don't have to explain things to you, do I, at this time of day?"

Her hand dropped from his wrist.

"You're explaining very well," said she in a high voice. "But I——" she faltered. Then, recovering control—"But one thing I want to know—in all these weeks—through all that's happened to us—haven't you loved me at all? Stephen, even a moment ago—weren't you loving me at all?"

He met her gaze boldly.

"I've loved you precisely as you've loved me, Donna. We've always understood each other: at least, I thought so. Donna, my call is in a minute. What's the use of talking? This thing has got to stop sometime. It had better stop now, hadn't it?"

She ignored it.

"You want it all stopped then?" she said.

He gave her an uncomfortable smile.

"It's ways and means, Donna. It's not my doing. Madeleine is home tomorrow. It couldn't go on."

"If Madeleine were dead would you want it to stop?" said she. He hesitated.

"Say it!" she ordered him. "Give me a 'Yes' or 'No'."

His face softened suddenly.

"Look here, Donna," said he, and put his hands on her arms. She made no attempt to resist, and as he went on talking his arms tightened round her so that she swung back, lifting her own hands to hold him away, not in anger but in order to watch his face. "Look," said he, "if I said 'no' it wouldn't be true: and if I said 'yes' it wouldn't be true. But, dear, if you go to a ball and dance all night long and enjoy yourself with—with passion—what's the end of it? Do you want it to go on for ever? Of course not, of course not! The end of it is you want to go home."

"I see," said she cloudily, after an interval that seemed to him endless.

"Donna, don't look like that."

"What?" She jerked out the word with a start as if his last sentence had waked her from a profound sleep, and put up both hands to her cheeks as if by feeling them she could divine the quality of her look. "What? What do I look like then? Do I look sad? Do I look angry? Hurt? Then my looks belie me, Stephen. Truly they do. You're right, of course. It's got to stop. It has been very jolly, hasn't it? I shall never forget it, shall you? And I shall never forget you, Stephen, and all you've taught me. Don't look so agonised. You make me laugh, Stephen. You're looking now as if it were I who break things off. Listen! Yes, they are calling for you. You must go down, Stephen. But kiss me first, quickly. We shall not be alone again."

It was a good end, a better end than he had hoped. He should have been satisfied. But he escaped from that dim room, from the fierce pressure of her mouth, dissatisfied, cheated. He stumbled down the stairs of the box like a man pursued, feeling a knife between his shoulders.

"I wish you'd stand by for your cues," said Harry fretfully as he hurried on to the stage.

"I'm sorry, Uncle. I was working out some business with Donna."

"Is Donna up there still?" Harry turned, shading his eyes to pierce the gloom beyond the foot-lights, and called—"Are you there, Donna? Don't go yet then. When I've finished this scene I should like a run-through with you. Or are you too tired?"

Donna appeared at the front of the box, her white hands holding the red curtains apart. Her white face was a mere blur in Harry's eyes; but Stephen's younger sight saw it very clearly.

"Not at all tired, Father," she called. "I'll wait for you. I like watching."

"Get on then!" Harry nodded his players into position. "Now, Stephen!"

But Stephen was tired and played badly. Harry, equally tired, snarled at him and would not let him go till he had rendered to his satisfaction lines, gesture, business that should have been easy enough to Stephen.

"You're putting nothing into it," cried Harry. "What's the matter with you, Stephen? You're moving as if you were wood. Edmund must have charm, deviltry, go. I thought we agreed that you played this scene all smiles. Smile, boy! Be gay! If you can't give me gaiety the part goes to pieces."

Stephen plodded on.

From the box Donna watched the scene with precisely the sort of smile that Harry wanted.

CHAPTER 37

RUSSEL and his company arrived two days later. He had not been in England for five years but he was by now so famous, and his last visit had been such an immense success, that the bookings at the Genista were satisfactory, and engagements in the provinces could be made on Russel's own terms. Russel had, of course, to be content with the Genista until the Gloriana re-opened. But *Lear* would not at the best have a long run—very few long runs in Shakespeare! When it was over Harry promised his brother that he should have the Gloriana for as long as he could fill it.

"I shan't want it for more than three months," returned Russel, who believed in short seasons. Meanwhile a month's repertory at the Genista would suit his book, he told Harry; but he added discontentedly that he had forgotten how small the stage was.

"I didn't know what to say to him," confided Stephen to his wife. "It's not the stage. It's him. Did you ever see anything like him? He ought to be playing Falstaff. I tell you, Madeleine, I'm downright afraid of him in Kent. I'm afraid they'll laugh at him. And that voice! I wanted to cry—'Well roared, lion!' Yet would you believe me, Madeleine, when I was a little boy my uncle was the handsomest creature you ever saw. And a voice that thrilled you. Eating and drinking can be the devil, can't it? To think that he was once my idea of how a man should look—perfect carriage! He had the air of being so balanced that any attack from any quarter would always find him prepared. I've never seen a carriage like it."

"Except yours," said his wife.

"Mine?" He looked at her, astonished and pleased. He thought that he knew all about his good looks, but this he did not know.

"Do I walk like him?"

"Of course you do. Forward tilted. And you stand like Fortune on her globe."

"There's a simile!" said he smiling down at her; for she was a little creature.

"Not mine."

"Whose then?"

"Your cousin's."

"Donna's?" In spite of himself, a wariness crept into his voice. "Well, I'm flattered. What else has Donna been saying about me?"

"I don't know. She talks a deal about you. She admires your acting. She says you are so modern in your methods. I like your cousin. She's a generous praiser."

"I shouldn't have thought," said he carefully, "that you had had much time to see her since you came back."

"Oh, well, it's only at the theatre. But you know how endless the waits are. We were the whole afternoon in my dressing-room. Little Eustace was wonderfully good. But I did not keep him for more than an hour."

"Why did you bring him—a baby in a dressing-room!"

"Donna wanted to see him."

"I'm glad you get on so well," said he very slowly. "But I'm a trifle surprised."

"I'm a trifle surprised myself. She is entirely unlike the descriptions you've all given me. Sullen? Silent? Awkward? But not a bit, Stephen! She's a very good talker, and a good listener too."

"What did you talk about?" said he.

His wife's pretty face grew pink.

"I suppose," she admitted, "that it was principally about you."

"I wish you wouldn't trot me out," he said. "You're always doing it."

"I don't. What nonsense, Stephen! Don't be so vain. I only told her about the wedding. She wanted to hear. No, you're wrong about Donna, Stephen. She has all sorts of good qualities. And I don't know what you mean by 'no charm'. She has immense charm. When I am with her I want to please her: I want to make her smile. Notice her smile, Stephen, next time you talk to her."

"Oh, my dear girl, I've something else to do," said he irritably. But she did not resent the fling—comfortable, kind creature that she was. Instead he had instant sympathy from her.

"What's worrying you, Stephen? Don't tell me that you're not worried. Ever since I came back I've felt it."

"It's the *Lear* production," said he gratefully, confidentially. "How do you feel about it yourself, Madeleine? Do you feel that rehearsals are going well?"

She hesitated.

"Parts are. Donna is magnificent."

"Oh, Donna! You have an obsession about Donna."

"It's you who have the obsession, Stephen. You seem to dislike her. You don't judge her at all fairly. You told me she was a stick. But my grandmother says—I took her with me yesterday and she watched the opening scene—she says that she is her grandfather over again. And you know how Grandmama talks of William Broome. I wonder if they were as good as everyone pretends—the Kemble generation and William Broome and the elder Kean."

"We should probably find that they ranted."

"Like your uncle Russel."

"Yes, that's it exactly, you shrewd little thing! The American tradition is still in the eighteen thirties, which is why I am so worried. Uncle Harry's style is much more modern than my uncle Russel's : and they clash amazingly. I, the unfortunate nephew, am supposed to be rehearsing them both, but it's as much as my place is worth to pull either of them to pieces. I can't tell Uncle Russel that he bellows, and I can't tell the Guv'nor to exploit Uncle Russel's mannerisms. He knows them fast enough without my telling him; but he won't take an advantage. That's Broome loyalty: dog don't eat dog. But I say the show should come first."

"My love, if you want help you know where to get it."

"I'm blowed if I do!"

"Think, Stephen!"

"Well?"

"Well, I believe in picking old people's brains. Lady Lettice can manage those two: and they'll never let you."

"It turns my stage management into a farce," said he.

"But nonsense, Stephen! A successful manager is only somebody who understands his company and pulls the right strings. You've got two people in the company who won't let you control them. Well then, call in someone who can. *Lear* must be a success."

"It'll break Uncle Harry's heart if it isn't," said he.

"It'll break your career if it isn't. One doesn't get this sort of chance twice—most people don't get it once. But Grandmother Reilly calls you Fortunatus——"

"I thought you said Donna——" He stopped abruptly.

"So she did! So you see it strikes everyone. Granny Reilly says that your luck frightens her. She says you've only made one mistake."

"What's that?" he said sharply.

"Oh, it's just a joke."

"What though?"

"I shouldn't have said it, Stephen. It was a stupid joke."

"You'd better tell me now. Come along, Madeleine, out with it!"

"Well, if you must know, she said that if you'd been really prudent you'd have married your cousin Domina. She can't think why it never occurred to you. There she was for the taking—a beauty and an heiress. She's a double heiress, I suppose, now poor Gilly's gone. All the Broome property will come to her, won't it?"

"All Uncle Harry's undoubtedly. But the theatre property was left between the three brothers, you know. I shall get my father's share when Grandmama dies."

"Then it means—" said she slowly—"that eventually the control lies between you and Donna?"

"Oh well, there's Uncle Russel."

"Who will his heir be?"

"How should I know? I feel a little uncomfortable, Madeleine, trying on dead men's shoes."

"Don't be sentimental, dearest. It doesn't mean you want them to die. But of course one thinks of Eustace. If your uncle Russel had no heir he will leave his share either to you or to Donna or to Eustace."

"Well?"

"Well, it's important. I mean, whoever gets it will be in control. If your uncle Russel left it to you, Stephen, as he very well may——"

"Uncle Harry's personal fortune will go to Donna," interrupted Stephen, "so we should be level even if Uncle Russel does leave his share to me. As you say, he probably will for my father's sake."

"You ought to have the casting vote. You're a man. I wish you knew more definitely how the land lies. Couldn't you talk to Uncle Harry?"

"My dear Madeleine, I should no more dare approach the Guv'nor on such a subject—"

"No, I suppose you can't. How strange men are! They're like children over their possessions. My little brother now, he has a rag doll. If I admire it or stroke it, at once he comes, quite politely, and takes it away, puts it severely in a corner with the oddest look. It is his property. It must not be touched or admired by anyone but himself. Even the toy itself is in disgrace because it has been touched and admired."

"Yes, that's all very amusing—" said Stephen, bored.

"Yes, but you—" said Madeleine, not at all bored—"you behave in exactly the same way over your cousin, for instance. She is *your* cousin and everybody is taught that fact."

"What utter nonsense, Madeleine!"

"But of course, my dear! You do it unconsciously. You took Donna away from the new Edgar so firmly this morning that you made me laugh. But he's nice, the young American, isn't he?"

"Pleasant enough," said Stephen.

"He admires Donna, you know."

"Pooh!"

"Well, and why not? Let the poor man admire her! She likes him too."

"You seem to have observed a great deal, Madeleine, in a week's rehearsal."

"My dear, I keep my eyes open. I'm so happily married myself that I can't help encouraging love affairs: and that unfortunate Geoffrey Angers is in love. All the theatre sees it. And if you ask me, Donna is encouraging him. She's provocative in that stately way of hers. How you could ever have said that she didn't know the rules of the game! But there—I suppose people are always blind about their own relations."

"I certainly can't see my cousin behaving like a soubrette if that's what you mean," said Stephen heatedly.

"Don't be so dog-in-the-mangerish about Donna! If it amuses her to make an extremely attractive young man fall in love with her I don't see why she shouldn't."

"Nor do I, except that she doesn't and he isn't."

"Well, you watch!"

"And anyway—" burst out Stephen with extraordinary heat, "what we gain by having an American in the company I do not see. I must say that I think my uncle is treating me unfairly. I am supposed to be staging this venture and yet I am not allowed to do my own casting. My uncle is far too ponderous for Kent—"

"No, Stephen, he makes a very fair Kent, I think."

"I daresay! But I'm telling you what I think, Madeleine! Then on the top of a cast of such importance, my uncle Russel thrusts this Angers boy upon us for Edgar."

"Well, but your uncle is a partner, after all."

"I know that! You don't have to tell me that! Really, Madeleine, I do know my own business. I only say that my uncle shows a very peevish sort of vanity. Just because he himself has acquired an accent in the States, he insists on another accent to keep him in countenance. That's what it is, you know. Angers is in the play by virtue of my uncle's vanity and his own abominable accent."

"Well, Stephen—" said his wife admiringly—"I didn't know that you could."

"Could what?"

"Lose your temper so completely and absurdly. Has somebody taken away your toy too? Really, Stephen, you are being extremely unlike yourself." And she looked up at him amused and yet with a very searching air. "Stephen, my love, what have you been doing with yourself while I have been away?"

They gave each other a long look. Then hurriedly Stephen began to talk of the number of changes that Cordelia would need: and Madeleine, who suited the part of Cordelia, did not press her question.

But that exchange of looks had been as good as a dozen speeches to both of them. Her look said—'You have something on your mind. But don't be frightened. I shan't press you to tell me, and I love you whatever it is.' And his look answered—'There is nothing whatever to tell you. I don't want to tell you. I'm not going to tell you. Some day or other I suppose I shall tell you.'

But though they thus sealed their pact, each made one reservation. Madeleine thought that she would like to know what Stephen found to dislike in a nice young American: and Stephen thought that he would like to know what Donna, of all people, saw to like in a prig of an American.

Husband and wife were perhaps right in their estimate of Geoffrey Angers' character. He was a prig, but a nice prig. He came of a Boston family which prided itself on English descent and impeccable position. He was an orphan, had been well educated, had plenty of money, plenty of enthusiasm, plenty of time on his hands. Intellectual and emotional, he had the usual young man's pleasure in amateur theatricals and contempt of the fellow-amateur in theatricals. Inevitably he hankered for the footlights. What can aunts and uncles do when a moneyed young intelligent decides to go on the stage? Nothing whatever but talk. This they did, while he went to New York, where his birth and position made it easy for him to meet the celebrated Russel Broome.

The two men had at once liked each other. Russel, affectionate, childless, eternally a fish out of water, enjoyed indulging young Angers' ambition, and Russel's own social background had made it possible for Angers' family to accept the situation. Angers, too, had a fair talent and learned to imitate Russel very gallantly. It was natural for the older man to bring the youngster over with him as a member of his small picked company, natural that he should push the boy's fortunes now that he had no longer much amusement in pushing his own. For Russel's creative impulse was long over: he thought nowadays only of retiring comfortably yet with a flourish. This visit was to be his last to England as a professional: but he had yet to break the news to Harry and did not quite know how to do it. It was pleasant to have young Angers with him, so sensible, so discreet, so English in his point of view. He could talk over his problems with him almost as if he were a son, thought Russel, and waxed a little sentimental over that word 'son', and over himself for not having one. Not for one instant did he recall his own interviews with his own father, or Harry's last despairing letter about Gilly. But he enjoyed talking of his family to Geoffrey Angers, and Geoffrey was of the type that adores the friends of its friends. He was perfectly ready to find Harry Broome a genius, and Stephen Broome the handsomest young man in England, and to chuckle respectfully at Lettice's sallies, and—what was he to think of Domina Broome? Here Russel gave him no help.

"As for my niece Domina—Lady Pallas, rather—I know very little about her. She was a secretive child, a trifle morose, I should say. But I admit I never looked at her. Gilly was the light of the house. She was married at sixteen to an elderly Irishman; but he died not long after their marriage. Yes, a very sad business."

"And she is in London, sir?"

"Oh, of course! Naturally she came back to the stage."

"And will play Cordelia?"

"Oh no, not that type at all. Goneril!"

How could Russel, if he had tried, have constructed a better version of Cinderella to tinder up the imagination of a romantic young prig?

And Donna did nothing to quench the spark. But then, as everyone said, Donna was very much changed. Everyone felt indeed, uncomfortably, that they had been unjust in confusing her true nature with the superficial effects on it of grief. The grief was now worn off with a vengeance: and Donna looked better than she had done since she first came from Ireland. The colour had come back to her cheeks, though her eyes had still the dark blue look that comes of weeping: and she was certainly stouter.

But it was the change in her manner more than her looks that amazed everyone. Donna nowadays had a vivacity and a flow of gay talk not unlike Lettice's, as Russel and Harry remembered it years ago. Donna, who had never bothered her head about clothes, was always appearing nowadays in new dresses and ran up bills that made Harry stare when, quite casually and shamelessly, she laid a bundle of them on his writing-table. Donna too had lost much of her reserve : she had an air of saying—I am ready to be friends with you all. Nothing showed the change in her though more clearly than her treatment of Geoffrey Angers. She was from the first enchanting to him, and carried herself towards him with a gentleness and a submission that was bewildering to those who knew her. She had the air of understanding that he longed to be a St. George, the air, too, of being prepared for the rôle of rescued princess. Nevertheless their engagement startled everyone.

"But they've only known each other a fortnight !" was the cry. "But how imprudent ! But how romantic ! Well, young people will be young people. Lettice, is this your doing? I suppose so. Really Lettice Broome is unparalleled—quite shameless, of course, but oh, what skill !"

Lettice appropriated all congratulations, and because Russel was her pride at the moment, showered blessings on the match and talked of Romeo and Juliet, and wanted to know if there was a Rosaline left behind in America. Geoffrey found her delightful, and was at home with her at once. But he was afraid of his future father-in-law ; for Harry did not like the hasty, romantic business, and showed it.

But Harry Broome's objection was not quite sane. He had grown to have a horror of any change in the circumstances of those attached to him. He was like a wild animal who distrusts all movement. While everything is still everything is safe ; but oh, what horror may not any movement unloose ! 'Change and decay in all around I see !' Then let us inhibit all change and so defeat decay !

But he could not object to so good a match, especially with Russel enthusiastic. And if it did mean a voyage to the States, and for Donna the final assumption of the Broome position and the Broome dignity in New York rather than in London, still he could not say that thereby any of his hopes and plans were defeated. Indeed, his ambitions were being so neatly realised that again he was suspicious. He could not believe that fate could be meaning so well by him. He despised his daughter bitterly that she could marry again so soon, but it was not his business, and against Russel's delight in match-making he could raise no defence. He had to consent. There was nothing to prevent the pair being married as soon as they pleased. If they chose to be married in a month, then married they must be.

Harry blamed his mother for this last precipitancy. It was she who decided to make the marriage a preliminary to the re-opening of the Gloriana. At eight o'clock on the morning of *King Lear,* Domina Pallas was married to Geoffrey Angers in the heavy church between Henrietta Street and King Street and the market, but had no formal breakfast afterwards. The wedding feast was to be a part of the supper which always followed the first night of a Broome show.

Thus Lettice planned it, but she did not mention her plan to her son. For Harry since his first wife's death had cut down festivities. Bread and cheese and beer on bare tables was good enough for him and his company, he said : and was angry with Lettice when she suggested that Adelaide should revive the old tradition. Harry always had his way, and Lettice said no more ; but on this occasion she had made up her mind that she for once would have her way. Did not she, too, own the theatre ? One can humour a son too far.

CHAPTER 38

'THE ELDEST HATH BORNE MOST'

THE Gloriana re-opened handsomely to a handsome audience, and the press next day was handsome also. Nevertheless, it was pretty generally admitted that it had not been Harry Broome's night. It was the younger Broomes who had carried it away. Russel Broome had certainly made a lovable Kent, but the old hands said that he was too regal and overwhelming. He took the centre of the stage as a right and in the first scene robbed Harry Broome of his proper majesty. But then Russel was playing, as he always did, at his full strength, and Harry was not playing at all. "The lion and the unicorn," muttered Mrs. Reilly to the formidable Lettice.

And Lettice was not pleased, but owned that the youngsters had done nobly, especially her grandchildren, Donna and Stephen, and that Stephen's reading of Edmund was certainly hard on Geoffrey Angers who illustrated too well his own line—'Edgar I nothing am—'. She confessed also that if Donna's scenes with her father had gone for little it was not Donna's fault. Harry, as if he could not shake off the early smothering by Russel, was sullen and would not help his daughter: she could strike no fire from him and was clearly frightened and disastrously tamed by his aloofness. She was too inexperienced to act in spite of him: her gestures had said quite meekly—"I must wait till he chooses to be alive." As he would not live she had fallen back on her power of pouring out great lines for the sake of the music, and so had done, not her best, but very well. But in her brief scene with Edmund she had taken her chance. Her swift shameless kiss flashed like a knife upon the scene and at the end of the play her cry—'Ask me not what I know—' was so wild and her exit so maddened, that the company as well as the house hung for a moment on a dead pause before the Albany could falter—'Go after her: she's desperate. Govern her!'

These were the high lights of the performance, though Harry in the final scene played with a dreadful, blinded gentleness that at last, too late, gave him his limelight. He tolled out the five 'nevers' as if on each 'never' a sense died, and at his 'Thank you, sir,' a woman in the pit began to sob grievously, yet so quietly that no-one hushed

416

her. Thus, to the sound of his own harsh-drawn breath and that remote and solitary sobbing, Lear ended.

"Not too bad," said Mrs. Reilly soberly. But Lettice was merciless.

"He has muffed it. He is in one of his moods like his father before him. And exhausted, of course, I grant you that. I allow that, for, well as Stephen has done, the responsibility is Harry's. But it is worse than that: his mind is afar—worried about my granddaughter, I fancy. He hates to part with anything, you know. Well, now it is for me to do what I can. He must be roused—must. Allowances will be made for a first performance, but he must be on the heights tomorrow and all the week. It will get about, and tonight won't matter: people will come again just to see the change. I am not seriously alarmed, but he must be roused. He will not be pleased with this wedding business tonight, and that is to the good. I have always found that you must anger Harry to get the best out of him. Now with my Robin it was another thing. A sharp word nipped him like a frost. Will you come round with me? We can slip through the pass door and get across to the green-room before the others are off the stage. Oh, listen to the cheers!"

Mrs. Reilly nodded.

"You may not be fully satisfied, my dear, nor for that matter am I. I shall have a good deal to say to my granddaughter before tomorrow night—a very tame performance. But our friends in front appear content."

"Oh, friends in front!" said Lettice contemptuously. "Friends are the most dangerous critics in the world. Friends should never be listened to in your profession, my dear!"

For though they were grandmothers with a joint interest in Eustace Broome, six months old that morning, still Lettice was a Wybird and if Mrs. Reilly had her ancient marriage lines, nobody had ever seen them.

Then the two vigorous old women by sheer force of personality opened for themselves a way through the press of audience and passed down it, chatting and serene. They bustled through the pass door, avoiding the groups that hung about the stage where Stephen and his uncles conferred, and so reached the green-rooms, which were divided from each other by folding-doors now flung open, making one very long, very narrow room. It ran, as a matter of fact, the whole length of the stage, from which it was divided by a wall and passage. In later days, of course, the rooms were cut up into dressing-dens, and with this conversion went much of the glory. The Broome portraits, the

Sheridan relics, Mrs. Pritchard's mirror, Richard Broome's chair, are out of place in the entry hall and the manager's office where they still exist, piteously lacking their proper setting.

But while Lettice lived the double room kept its long state : and there a sit-down supper was laid. Lettice's plate and her treasured sets of three-branched candlesticks had been brought down from the Park Lane house. All the silver dishes were wreathed with smilax, the wedding-cake stood upon a damask-hidden junction of the long tables set end to end, and Lettice's own staff was in attendance. Specially invited guests from the front of the house had already arrived and were making a chatter : and by the time the weary actors, some twenty in all, stumbled in for a sandwich on the way to their dressing-rooms, one of Lettice's favourite parties was in full swing. How wearisome was the froth and sparkle for those tired players till, after a glass of champagne, how glorious was the froth and sparkle! And the guests were distinguished and affable, and made the company feel that all London had been present at a huge success, and that now the players were hearing at first hand what London thought. Very pleasant! Discriminating audience! Excellent champagne!

Lettice, sitting at the head of the table, gathered in the glances, and her tongue like her laugh was untiring, as she dominated the conversation at her end and signalled directions, questions and gay hints at Donna and Geoffrey who controlled between them the centre of the table, while Russel, Adelaide and Madeleine worked loyally to right and left and across the smilax. But they were slight Broomes compared with old Lettice, who wore one of her voluminous dresses of pale grey chiffon, and looked a gallantry. She might be an old woman, but she still spent a fortune on her clothes. She had taken of late to wearing an exquisitely fine lace chin-band to her cap. It freshened the curve of her cheek, hid her age-marred throat and showed up her diamonds, which were quite as fine as those of her niece the duchess, sitting at the foot of the table on the right of Harry's chair, Richard Broome's own chair.

The chair was still empty, however. For Harry, fastidious and precise in his habits, had first gone to his dressing-room to remove all traces of make-up. He could better endure fatigue of the extremest sort than grease-paint on his face one moment longer than necessary : and he hated the smell of his robes, sweat-stained and inevitably soiled by even a week's use. Stephen also had been kept upon the stage by various overseer duties : and it so happened that the only place left when he did come was the vacant chair at the bride's side. Donna, catching his eye, gave him one look and laughed: then beckoned with her finger.

Stephen hesitated, flushed scarlet, then with a sudden tilt of the head, an imperceptible squaring of the shoulders, marched round the room and sat himself down beside her. He talked resolutely to the guest on his right till the meal was half over; but when at last he turned, there was Donna and her look.

"I wanted you beside me tonight," said Donna at once, softly. "It's an odd situation, Stephen, isn't it—the sort of situation you enjoy?"

He said tormentedly—

"Donna, don't!"

"Don't what, Stephen? Stephen dearest, darling, my true love!"

"Are you mad, Donna? Be quiet! Someone will hear you."

She took no notice but rippled smoothly on. Her low voice slipped over her lips like summer water hissing over stones in the bed of a stream—the smallest of sounds.

"You played so well tonight, Stephen. I shall remember how well you played when I am on the other side of the world. But you'll forget, won't you, unless I give you a keepsake? I ought to give you a keepsake. But I haven't my flowers with me. It's orange-blossoms for a widow, you know, not myrtle. Myrtle's for a maiden. But look, there are sugar flowers on the cake. You shall have a sugar flower from me, Stephen." And she leaned forward and detached a spray and laid it beside him. Then, as he pushed it from him embarrassed and hating her, she said—"Don't you like my keepsake, Stephen? Then I must send you one from America. Shall I, Stephen?"

"Donna, people are staring at us."

"Of course, they always stare at a bride. Dearest Stephen, how helpless you are! You can't do a thing to stop me, can you? You can't even prevent Madeleine from watching us. She is watching us now, Stephen. Very well, I'll stop, because I like Madeleine. I should hate to give her anything to watch."

And she turned from him to her bridegroom: and Stephen, after a couple of minutes' interest in his plate, the knives and forks beside him and the broken posy of sugar flowers, lifted his head and looked across at his wife. As he had known, she was still watching him. He tried to turn from her, but could not: there had first to be an exchange of looks. Hers said—

'Don't lie to me, Stephen! I know everything now.'

His said—

'Wait! For God's sake wait till I can tell you about it.'

Hers answered—

'I cannot forgive you. But I suppose I shall forgive you. Why did I go away?'

While his eyes still implored her, defied her, outfaced her, she turned away and began to talk gaily to her neighbours: then stopped like everyone else to watch Harry Broome come in, and clap him and welcome him, though not perhaps with the spontaneous fury of enthusiasm that his appearances would so often evoke.

For on this night his bearing, unwilling, unthanking, all charm withheld, soon put a period to the courteous din. Everybody, guests, company, family, was anxious to be delighted to see him and do him honour, but everybody wanted him also to reassure them that he was still their unconquerable Harry Broome. For he had not on this great and long awaited occasion produced in them the desired spiritual orgasm, and his failure left them tense, irritable, merciless, yet so ready to be eased again into sleepy surrender to his art and his personality. Let him but charm, beckon, promise, gather them in, and they would be his again so thankfully.

But he would not or could not.

He came into the green-room hostile, prepared for hostility, and at the first burst of clapping paused, leaning back against the door as if he had been shot instead of hailed, and his eyes ran over his guests as if he knew them for his executioners but did not much care, was far too tired to care. It was as if fatigue were a drug of which he had taken an over-dose.

Yet he had never looked better, nor more completely, in the strict blacks and whites of evening dress, the theatre's child. He had removed all actual traces of paint, but the make-up had left his skin matt, without the faint natural polish on cheek-bone and nose, and his eyes lay dead between the rubbed and swollen lids. His head and shoulders were framed for the instant by the square green baize notice-board on the door behind him. The green made his white face whiter, and he looked, thus framed, like a self-portrait by death. With a stiff response to the already silenced greetings, he sat down quietly among his audience-guests in their fashionable clothes and stage-guests, with their rich barbaric habits and artificially healthy faces, and began, unsmiling, to talk to his neighbours.

"He's a genius at an entrance," murmured Donna to no-one in

particular. And as if her father had heard her, though the distance made it impossible, he lifted his head and looked full at her.

She sustained his look with her usual superbness.

"Goneril!" said Stephen under his breath, unable to resist it.

She shrugged, as she answered—

> "'Tis his own blame: hath put himself from rest,
> And must needs taste his folly.'"

"My wife—" said Geoffrey, charmed, to the lady on his right—"has Shakespeare in her bones. She is always quoting. They will appreciate her at home. To my mind her performance tonight—"

"Oughtn't you to be cutting the cake?" interrupted the lady brightly.

"I think you're right. I think you're quite right. Donna, my love, isn't it time we cut the cake?"

"With a tin sword?" said Donna. "Give me yours, Stephen!" And she put out her hand and tugged at the handle, and found it too much for her. For Harry was a stickler for realism in his stage properties and the hilt was heavily decorated, the sword heavy.

"It's not tin," said Stephen, giving it to her.

"My father-in-law—" said Geoffrey admiringly—"doesn't care what he spends. Let me help you, darling!"

And very gay and handsome the young pair looked as they stooped over the wedding-cake, Donna grasping the hilt and Geoffrey directing the point of the blade into the icing and almond paste, while all the guests screamed advice and directions.

There was the proper fuss and confusion about the cutting of the cake, a circle of laughter round Russel and a crackle of wit round Lettice. Stephen was indefatigable and Geoffrey, entirely unaware of moods and tenses, was, thought his wife, 'a pleasant relief from all of us.' Nevertheless, the party went but heavily because Harry would not play host. After the first efforts at conversation with his nearest neighbours he had sunk into a gloom, scarcely answering when he was spoken to, refusing all food, a death's-head indeed. Lettice at the other end of the long table, gay, helpless, furious, tried in vain to catch his eye. Her foot began to tap: her withered cheek grew redder. Russel, three seats away, cried softly, affectionately, half teasing her, half in warning—"Now, Mama—" for he knew the signs. But she would not be stopped. Instead she rapped on the table and in the half silence that ensued called out shrilly—

"Harry! You do not give the cheer!"

"That's from *Macbeth*," Geoffrey instructed his wife.

She did not answer. Like the rest of the Broomes she was watching her father. Harry's head came up slowly. He answered his mother with the familiar defiance of the chin—

"What is it, Mama?"

"It is time for a speech, Harry! Am I to make one or shall you?" And she held his eyes implacably. Her pose, her tone, her red cheeks, her sparkling eyes, all said as plain as speech—'I am perfectly ready to make a scene if you do not support me—ten scenes for that matter. And I shall enjoy them all.'

"Now, Mama——" said peaceable Russel again.

"Oh!" Lettice pushed aside the intervention with glance, gesture of the hand and testy exclamation. Her temper was rising. She would not be checked. "Harry!" She challenged her younger son again, smiling, very sweet—"Which is it to be, Harry?"

The hubbub of the guests stilled again and everyone listened for his answer, and Stephen half rose on a look from his wife. But Russel was before him.

"Come, come, I'm the uncle of the bride!" cried Russel lumbering majestically to his feet. Harry shot him a dark look, and his glance sank again to his plate as Russel threw back a—"Leave it to me!" Then Russel began.

He was a good speaker and the company adored him. He joked them all, scattered congratulations as lavishly as confetti over the show as a whole and over all performers and performances. Then, apologising for his avuncular interest, he outlined the career of the bridegroom, commented on the beauty of the bride, and did it all so happily that the tension was relieved and the healths at the end were heartily drunk.

"Long life to the bride and bridegroom!" cried Russel, emptying his glass and at once refilling it. And the response was more cordial than Donna herself would have believed possible. Smiling she acknowledged the outstretched glasses, clinked, nodded, drank with everyone in turn and ended, on a whim, by stretching out her glass to Stephen. He was not ready.

"Come, drink to my good fortune," said she, "and to Geoffrey's!" He stared her down, smiled, would not drink.

She shrugged and turned to her husband.

"Geoffrey, you must reply now. Don't be nervous. I'll whisper to you what you must say." And then, turning her back on Stephen, she sat, her face upturned to her husband, smiling, wistful, with her attention concentrated on him, the image of the perfect bride.

Lettice, from the end of the table, eyed her granddaughter uncomfortably as she listened to Geoffrey Angers.

'The girl is acting,' she said to herself. 'Now why? It's a fishy business, this marriage. If she had come to me for advice . . .' The speeches went on and on.

Lettice was toasted: the Gloriana was toasted: Cordelia and her grandmother were toasted: and old Mrs. Reilly rose demurely to return thanks in her pretty cracked voice and made them laugh. But nobody had ventured to propose Harry's health and Harry had not spoken a word.

"He's beaten you, Mama," murmured Russel impudently: and his face must have shown his thought. For just as he continued to himself —'Bless my soul, and I was once afraid of the old lady!' Lettice flashed him a look that made him jump in his seat. 'Whew!' said Russel to himself—'She's still got fangs! What's she going to do now?' Then, over his neighbour's white shoulder he saw her crook her jewel-laden finger at her nephew. At once Stephen pushed back his chair and came across to her.

"Yes, Grandmama?"

"Stephen, my child, no-one has drunk your uncle Harry's health."

"Well, Grandmama, we thought—— You see, he hasn't speechified yet. We are all out of order."

"Well, don't wait any longer! Get up and say something! Otherwise people will talk."

"What shall I say?"

"Not very much. Career, you know!"

"Very well." Then, as he turned to go, she caught him back by the arm.

"And Stephen, speak just a moment of the family! Mention your own father's plays and Aunt Maud's work at the Syracuse!"

"Won't he hate it, Grandmama?"

"I daresay. But it's right that they should be remembered."

"Well, if you're sure."

"I'm sure."

Now Harry!

Stephen spoke very well, though he was nervous. He spent some time in outlining all that Harry had done for the English theatre and in talking of what the Gloriana owed him. Then Stephen hesitated, and said floundering that he ought to speak, too, he thought, of what the theatre, his own theatre, the New Broom, owed to its other founder. As manager of the New Broom he had had opportunity enough to know how wisely the foundations had been laid. "If you look back," said Stephen feeling his way, "to those first founders, to William Broome who is before our time, to those whom some of us remember, my own father, the playwright, my—my cousin's mother to whom we owe the New Broom—I mean—we cannot forget Maud Broome——"

"That's enough," said Harry loudly. "That's enough, boy! Enough!"

There was a scraping noise that set teeth on edge as he rose, pushing back his chair. Stephen subsided, flushing.

"My nephew here—" Harry addressed them harshly—"means well, and will do better, I daresay, as time teaches him. But he forgets that this is a wedding feast. Instead he has offered you the funeral baked meats. He has seen fit to ask my guests and my company to toast the dead as well as the living. Then, forgetting, I daresay, that I am still among the living, he couples my name with theirs. Perhaps he is justified. Something of a man's spirit must die with Lear if he is to be successful in portrayal. And on the other hand to fail, as I have failed tonight, is to cut oneself off from dead and living alike."

There was an outburst, on that, of remonstrance, and cries of courtesy, affection and excitement. He hushed all, sternly, with—

"Failed, I say! In sleep a king, but waking no such matter. No such matter," repeated Harry, shaking the table a little because he was leaning forward and clutching its edge with his hands. His guests, no longer clamorous, stared.

"Harry, Harry, sit down!" said Lettice softly.

"In sleep a king, Mother! Leave me my crown! And so, my friends, out of my dream, neither dead nor alive, I pour a libation to the ghosts of this theatre. For these our actors, as I foretold you, were all spirits and are melted into air, into thin air, and now we breathe this air: we breathe the substance of our loves. That's an odd thought, eh? That chills you all." And he looked about the table as if he laughed at the general dismay: then, in a gentler voice, went on—

"Let it not. But give these airs of death their welcome at this feast. For from my coign of vantage between two worlds I can see them more clearly than you living can. I know each face—father, brother, wife, son—and I speak for them. Listen then my daughter, and you my company! Listen, Stephen! Listen, Donna! while I rehearse your duty and your rights.

"You are the priests of a temple: and also, for it is a single, ancient office, the prostitutes of a temple, serving the god with your bodies as well as with your souls. Your duty is undivided service: and I warn you now that if you stray from that service, whether through ambition or for money or in love, then the god will punish. For since I was a boy I served him, but I divided my heart. I put myself, my own glory, my own gain, before any god. Next to myself I put my wife. And next to her, as you all know well enough, I put my only son. She died. My boy was drowned. Then I put off my hope and kept it no longer for my flatterer. He is drowned: the sea mocks——" He swayed and his speech was choked.

Stephen sprang to his feet and hurried down the room to him.

"Uncle, won't you stop? Sit down again. We all know what you want to say."

Harry caught him by the arm.

"Take warning by me, Stephen! Bend or break! I would not bend till I was broken. Then at last I returned to my god and he, in his own time, comforted me. Yes, this I tell you all—my god has comforted me. I am his mouth: he knows my heart. And so I thought, having surrendered in service, that there would be no more punishments. But tonight I know better. Tonight he warns me that I may no longer be his mouth. For tonight my voice failed and my spirit failed. I accept the sign. My service is ended.

"But to you, daughter, nephew, son-in-law—I have no son—to you I say, 'Serve my god!'"

"What god, Father?" Donna was whispering: but in the silence her words were as keen as a shout.

And Harry, thrusting Stephen aside as a wind sweeps aside a light and pendent bough, bent towards her, hanging over the table, one hand supporting himself, the other outstretched.

"What god? I loved him this side idolatry as much as any—— There the worship began. For a god——" whispered Harry, his eyes staring through the thick, dancing air above the many candles as if he pursued uncertainly a winged thought—"for a god is but a man who has known all we know—love, hate, frenzy, corruption, and the dust of time. And these things have destroyed his loves and his own body: and his soul has descended into hell. But his spirit lives. What? This is no new doctrine. Each art has its Christ. And we, the priests of the oldest temple, have we not our god and our drowned and holy book? I say holy——" cried Harry hammering on the table: and he began to jerk his body as he talked, trip on his words, pant and glare like a man straining his soul after some utter prize of thought that eludes him still.

"Listen to me!" he cried. "We of the theatre are a people set apart. The world comes to us to see itself, but we do not go out into the world to see ourselves. We have no selves: we are but the mouths of the god. I went to church today to see my daughter married; but I do not find in any church the comfort that my worship gives me. But when I play his Hamlet or his Timon, his Falstaff or his Lear, then I become one with the god, then I know companionship, then I know exaltation: then, though life starves me, I am fed. And I would have you go into the world and preach this gospel——"

"Harry, Harry!" cried Lettice in a shaking voice—"You must stop. You are out of your mind. This is blasphemy. Russel, Stephen, all of you, don't listen to him! He doesn't know what he is saying."

"Mother—" he cried in a high, exhausted voice—"I will worship my god!" and he caught at his brimming glass and lifted it, spilling the wine. "I drink to him!" cried Harry. "There shall be no other god for me!"

Then he flung away the glass and crashed down into his seat with his arms on the table among the litter of scattered food, glasses and dishes.

The crazed look, the crazed delivery, held the long room silent; but in the crazy after-quiet sane tongues began to wag. The sympathetic murmurings swelled and buzzed about the central Broomes; but the guests were tractable and the company, naturally, was accustomed to outbursts of temperament and very loyally seconded the single-handed youngsters and Russel in their heroic conversational efforts. Only Stephen was left at Harry's side; but presently Adelaide got up quietly and went down to him.

Lettice, watching with glittering eyes while she raged in conversation as brilliantly as ever she had done in her life, saw that Stephen was trying to persuade Harry to rise. But Harry would not listen, would not budge, sat like a stone Lear in evening dress. So, like a wise woman, his mother continued to patter low-voiced to the notables, not of the weather or the Germans in Paris, but of what was occupying all their minds.

"Temperament, just temperament! Nothing to worry about," said Lettice, sweet, pathetic, motherly, and so obviously and effectively worrying. "No, say nothing! Much better leave him alone. He has over-worked, you know, consistently for years. My daughter-in-law has been greatly worried. And then the part—he lives in it, you know literally lives in it. Superb at rehearsals. Tonight—snapping point. I was expecting it. Tomorrow he'll be himself. Come back today week and you'll be startled. My husband was just the—yes—— Oh no, you mustn't go yet. But why go? Well, it is late. Russel, Lady Mary has to go now. And you, too, my dear? Must you? You know it's very wicked of you, you're breaking up the party. Well, if you must——" And she rose, cresting the general movement, her diamonds twinkling, her colour high, her laugh clear and ready. There was no hurry, no fuss. She forgot no-one. She omitted no ceremony nor last word.

Not until the latest guests and the latest actor were out of the door did her manner change. Then she swept round, harsh and headlong, upon her family—stout, flushed Russel, hovering Stephen, tearful Adelaide, and the bridal pair.

"He won't speak to me," wept Adelaide.

"Pooh, have you never seen hysteria? Control yourself, my girl! See if the carriage is there, Stephen! Adelaide, go home with Stephen! Harry will want you later. Donna, you and Geoffrey can do nothing. You had better go at once! I shall take your uncle home, Stephen. Russel, go below and wait for me and Harry!"

She drove them out, shut the door on them, swept her glance about the empty room, hesitated, pulled herself together, put up her head, then advanced upon her son as much in anger as in concern.

"Harry! Harry! Wake up! Look at me! Come alive!" She put her hand on his shoulder and shook him vigorously.

That woke him. He hated to be touched. He pulled himself away from her, lifted his head and looked at her with his drugged eyes. But she was not to be intimidated.

"Harry, what possessed you? Do you know that you have been talking the most arrant, blasphemous nonsense? They will think you mad."

He lifted himself slowly and heavily in his chair.

"Why, Mother, I chose to say my 'I believe'. Why shouldn't I?"

"You talk like a fool. And what sort of scandal do you suppose will spread over London? They'll say that you are out of your mind."

"They'll say that I've failed. And I have. I've failed in Lear. I dare not play tomorrow, Mother. I shall never play again. I'm done, Mother. Dead and done. That is why I said what I said. What did I say? Nothing so dreadful. Besides, what do I care? I *will* leave some sort of testament. If I could have played tonight as my life has taught me to play the part, then there would have been no need for all this. But as it was—" he turned from her sullenly—"the spirit moved me. Confession is good for the soul."

"Poseur!" said she.

"I am not."

"And coward!" She took a step so as to be once more in front of him, vigorous and unescapable in her just anger. "I am ashamed of you. You give in before your fight begins. The run is your test, not a single night. Tonight? All I asked of you tonight was to send that unhappy girl of yours away a little happier."

"You should not have sprung it on me," he said sullenly.

"Sprung what?"

"One of Maud's feasts. How could you be so cruel? And you beckoned to that boy—I saw you. When he spoke of Maud—d'you think I didn't know who put him up to it? Such witless cruelty—to call up my dead!"

"Listen to me, Harry! Blame me if you like, but I'm your mother. I care for you, Harry. I care for your reputation. I had to rouse you. You were in your mood tonight. D'you think I don't know of your mood? I am your mother."

"No-one knows," said he, "now Maud's gone."

"Maud! Maud! Always Maud! I'm your mother, I tell you. You don't choose to confide in me, you never have; but do you think I don't know all about you? I tell you you were ringed in: one could not get at you. I had to break through to you. I had to. What weapon was I to pierce with but Maud's name?"

He stared at her as if at a stranger.

"I'm your son. And all my life you've been as close to me as breathing," said he. "But now I see that I have not known you at all. You are light-minded and worldly. You are cruel and silly and very cunning. And I see that I am what I am because of you. All that you are I have become. But Father gave me a heavy heart to hamper me. Between you two I am what I am. But I'm not grateful, Mama. I never want to see you again."

"Harry, Harry!" said she piteously, and put out her little glittering hand.

"Mother, if you touch me I shall go mad. Keep away from me, Mother!"

"Harry——"

"No, I must go. I can't be with you any more." And he turned from her to the door.

But with that loving cunning of hers she darted round the other shorter way of the table to intercept him, caught her hip against a corner as she swung round it, caught at the table itself for help, clutched the cloth, and by so doing swept with a crash a plate and two of the branched candlesticks on to the floor. Then she screamed.

Harry, in the doorway, turned to see her with a white face and a mouth like an 'o' as with her tiny hands she beat at the flames leaping up her body; for the candlestick had fallen down on her gauzes and the flimsy material was flaring like so much resin.

But, as he rushed to her help, she screamed—"Keep away! Keep away! You'll be hurt!" and fled hobbling from him down the room. A moment he paused, horrified, helpless: then wrenched at the tablecloths, shook them clear of their litter and was after her. Her strength had failed, and she collapsed as he flung the cloths about her, bore her down to the floor and began to beat out the fire. A rug was under his hand. He pulled it over her. The smothering weight had its effect and the flames leaped no longer: and she, too, struggled no longer. When all was at last quiet, with movements suddenly grown slow, he began to pull away the blackened covering. But when he had taken one look he rose up in horror and rushing to the door, flung out into the passage calling hoarsely—"Russel! Stephen! Help me! Stephen! Russel!"

The last thing she heard was his voice dying away down the corridor, like life dying away.

THE death of Lettice from shock and burns may not have been the original cause of Harry Broome's mental breakdown; but it certainly hastened it and made it complete. It was months before he could resume control of his theatres. But though her passing ended a period in the history of the Broome family and the Broome theatres, the fact was not at once evident. For a time all went on, in the theatres at least, as before. The *Lear* performances were not cancelled, for Russel had stepped into the breach, and under the stimulus of excitement, anxiety and grief, played better than ever he had played in his life: while the sympathetic house, knowing the dreadful story, smothered him and his company with respectful applause. Indeed several reputations were made that season. Stephen and Donna stepped out of the ranks of promising juveniles to their places at the tail end of the London galaxy: while the understudy who played Kent thanked his luck for the Guv'nor's breakdown.

Nor could any member of the company altogether avoid enjoying the feeling of emancipation which Harry's prolonged absence permitted. A theatre is not unlike a school: and Harry had the eye of a successful headmaster. But when, at the end of his brief season, Russel sailed with his company, his niece and his nephew-by-marriage for America once more, and Stephen Broome was left in solitary control, then Harry's absence began to be felt as an evil. Stephen could coach: Stephen could direct: and he could keep his company loyal and happy: but he was not a business man. He understood routine, but he was without enterprise. By the time the Christmas season was over the management had lost their year's profits.

But in the spring of 1872 Harry was back from his prolonged sea voyage, certainly looking better, plumper, less tired, and on grateful terms with his young wife. For kind, unsubtle, lightly regarded Adelaide had been the stay and prop of the harried family in those first weeks of complete disorganisation and collapse, when Harry's reason spun like a spider at the end of a thread and there was no Lettice to control him. Donna had been useless: her mere presence was a perpetual disastrous excitement to her father. But Harry was gentle with his wife, treating her as a kind young nurse whom he liked and was content to obey. She never left him: and when time and rest had at last recovered him, he did not lose his reliance on her.

He came back a dulled man, less savage, less sensitive, fallen into premature old age and content to enjoy the comforts of his home. Indeed he got into the habit of conducting much of his business from his own library desk. He never acted again, but devoted the rest of his life to protecting, as far as it was possible to do so, the future of his theatres. He had not lost his lifelong habit of living in the future, of violently willing his daily life forward towards a goal. But his ambition had ceased to be a personal one: his goal was now the preservation of the Broome inheritance.

For when he came back from his prolonged absence, an absence in which all news, letters and intercourse had been strictly forbidden, he learned that one desire at least of his late years had been fulfilled. Donna had borne at seven months her first child, a boy who had been called after him Henry, but to please the Angers, Edmund—Henry Edmund Broome.

Round this unknown new self Harry Broome began to build up affection and to accumulate possessions. And because of this new interest, as the years went by, little by little he drew back from his position of benevolent father-uncle to Robin's son. His dear nephew was no longer the male heir. Harry had been the careful guardian of Robin's play-earned fortune, had been scrupulous in division, and had dealt with the investments that he had made on Stephen's behalf as carefully and as successfully as he had dealt with his own share. But all transactions were in his own name and should be so while he lived. He had promised his brother to do his best for the boy: and he did his best, he told himself, by continuing to control the money which would be eventually his nephew's.

But Stephen, knowing nothing of all this, and needing money, for he was naturally extravagant and Madeleine produced babies with Victorian regularity, had been the more gratified to find himself heir, by Lettice's will, to a third share in the Broome enterprises—Robin's share. Naturally he was tenacious of his rights. But Harry and Russel, always in agreement, retained of course the casting vote on matters of policy. Because Stephen chafed and they were fond of him they occasionally gave him his head; but he was not wise in business though admirable in the theatre itself. He was timid when instant decisions had to be taken, yet occasionally in love with rash policies which he pressed upon his uncle for the mere sake, Harry thought, of reminding Harry that he was junior partner.

After being twice over-persuaded, Harry began to withdraw his confidence and with it his generosities. Stephen felt and resented the change and showed it; but his resentment had no effect. For time and anxiety for his wife's poor health, the burden of family life and the sense of being at odds with his uncle, had robbed him year by year of his light-hearted ways: and with it had gone much of his charm. And without his charm Stephen could do nothing with Harry. When Donna and Geoffrey brought their son with them on their first visit to England some nine years later, the uncle and nephew, though they worked together with fair surface amity, were in reality not on good terms, as all the world knew. For it was one of Harry's grievances that his nephew was not the best person in the world at keeping a secret.

Donna on the other hand had in eight hard years not lost the habit of keeping her troubles to herself. Her marriage had been moderately successful. Russel had had a fine welcome on his return to New York, had starred his niece and been gratified by her immediate success. But after a time he decided that she lacked rough and tumble experience and would be all the better for some work on the road. He fitted her out with a good stock of plays and clothes and told her to go off and learn how to manage a company and a husband; for Geoffrey would of course want to go with her.

Geoffrey, absorbed in literature and his wife, had ceased to be of much interest to Russel, whose Falstaffian characteristics grew upon him more rapidly after his return; for all the Broomes exhausted themselves early, like arrows shot upwards instead of forward. Russel began to say that it was time he left the stage to the youngsters, and a year later he bought a farm in the country and without much regret bade farewell to city life and the occupation of a life-time, and sank with a curious enjoyment and relief into a life of early rising, huge meals, open-air labour and long nights of sleep. He had never shown in the whole course of his life any hankering for the country, but in his old age he displayed to his neighbours an astonishing understanding of earth and the beasts. If he had lived in England he would have poached unashamedly.

"I can't understand your uncle," said Geoffrey to his wife after a flying visit. "I've seen him hold a theatre quiet just by lifting his hand. I've seen them take the horses out of the carts and draw him through the streets—that happened in Dublin, you know, at our first landing—

and there he is, milking cows and dipping rushlights, and concerned about cider and homebrew. He'll finish by going to meeting, God help us!"

"The first Broome—" said Donna—"was a country lad and used to cry 'Buy a broom!' for a living until he joined a company of strolling players." And then, impatiently interpreting her husband's preliminary cough—"Oh, don't tell me again about the Mayflower, Geoffrey! I know that you descend from a clergyman who was somebody's younger son. It's written all over you; but I tell you again I don't care a spangle for gentility. Which reminds me—you can like it or dislike it—I am going to play Mazeppa."

"If you play Mazeppa," said he, "I shall leave you."

"Then you can leave me," she retorted fiercely. "It'll make little difference to me."

"Yes, you do your best daily," he returned in a low voice, "to prove how little affection you have for me."

"Oh, I have affection enough," she interrupted irritably. "I'm fond of you, Geoffrey. I don't want you to leave me if you will go my way. But you must go my way. I can't afford to go yours. While I'm young and can earn it I must make money. I can make a great deal of money out of playing Mazeppa."

"I think you're mad about money. I have a fair fortune and you will inherit from your father."

"Who is all but out of his mind. It may be all dissipated or willed to Stephen. There is such a thing as undue influence. Do you think I trust Stephen?"

"No, but you might trust me to consider the interests of our only child."

"I trust no-one," said Donna. "But I will scrape, pinch, save, beg, borrow and steal money to give Edmund when he is ready to use it. I know what it is to be dependent, and he is not to know it. He shall not be dependent on anyone—not on his grandfather, not on you, not on me—no, not even on me!"

"And you think it will please him when he is a grown man to see pictures of his mother tied naked to the back of a horse to amuse a circus?"

She made a gesture of disgust.

"Oh, you Puritans! How I hate your minds! You know perfectly well what the equipment is."

"Yes, you may be clothed. But are you decently clothed?"

"I shall wear what Ada Menken wore."

"D'you think I'd have my wife bracketed with Ada Menken?"

"I'm going to play Mazeppa. I shall make a lot of money," said mulish Donna.

"Then I say again I shall leave you," said Geoffrey, weaker, but not less mulish.

Neither of them was to be shaken. She played Mazeppa and he did leave her and the stage. For her reality had dispelled for him the glamour of theatrical life: and he went home to his property and his people very gladly. There congenial occupations and dignified little responsibilities awaited him, and family influences all the stronger for the long absence. These so worked on him that he settled down in the family homestead: and though he made no open announcement he severed for the time all connection with his former life. But his breach with his wife was not complete. He was too fond of her for that, and she had for him a certain feeling, rather less than affection, rather more than tolerance, which held her to him. She had a good deal of respect for his culture and social taste. She knew, for instance, in her heart, that he was right about Mazeppa. It had been a wild idea which she soon regretted. She occasionally played a much modified version of the part in rich primitive towns that knew nothing of modern comedy, tolerated Cibbered Shakespeare and saved their enthusiasms for travelling shows: and did make some money by it. But she soon dropped it out of her repertoire altogether and took care to let him know that she had done so.

He responded instantly with the suggestion that she would find a London audience at Boston. And when she next played there she was classical and discreet and thus rewarded him. If she had had rough experiences she kept them to herself and appeared rather as a grand amateur with an English accent and impeccable clothes. As a matter of course she rejoined her husband, ruled and entertained in the family mansion throughout the season, and had a very great success.

This reconciliation was effected when Edmund was about five years old. She had had the wisdom to leave him for months at a time in her husband's charge: and he had grown into a fine healthy boy. He was not tall for his age, but square, robust, immensely strong and blazing with vitality. Occasionally she took him with her for a week or two and was astonished by his independence, inquisitiveness, astonished too by the amount of training he had already received from gentle, priggish Geoffrey. It was no great wonder, of course, for a child of six to read, write, cipher, be at home in Latin and leading articles, when pre-cocity was the fashion: it was all a question of training. But Geoffrey had trained the child wisely, had encouraged in him not only a fury for knowledge and a passionate love of music, but also a taste for out-door exercise that long visits to Russel and Russel's farm developed. But neither Russel nor Geoffrey had been able to knock into the boy any love of acting. Shakespeare bored him and he hated to recite.

"What shall we do?" said Donna dismayed. "What will my father say if he doesn't go on the stage?"

But the boy's first tour with her lifted that anxiety. If he had no desire to act, he had a most passionate curiosity concerning the work-ings of a theatre. She, or rather Geoffrey, had prim notions of keeping the boy to her dressing-room and her lodgings; but you could sooner keep a puppy from the kitchen door than keep young Edmund Broome from the property room or the flies. The stage carpenter was his ally: the scene-shifters and the painters his bosom friends. He adored sitting on a high stool in the box-office, watching the business manager take the money. Sometimes he pulled off the tickets for him, and as a treat was allowed to hand the paper strips through the grill and take the change. Dismissed from that sanctuary he would explore the under-stage, and once broke his crown climbing the ladder to the little platform whence the more primitive lights were worked. Before he was eight he could be trusted to check programmes and ring up the curtain: and the lazy stage-hands were glad enough on the sly to leave him the handling of cocoa-nut shells, wind-tub and water-whistle. In the day-time while his mother rehearsed he would spend hours in the property room, working at his own little model of a theatre which he and the stage carpenter had constructed between them.

Donna, of course, obliged him to learn and act such child parts as came along: and he was quick, clear-voiced and adequate. But he did not like this part of the life and avoided acting as much as he could. Nor was he interested in the performances themselves, though he made it his business rather than his pride to go nightly to the various parts of the house, and return to his mother's dressing-room with the report of the audience's temper and the effect of the lighting on her make-up.

So it would go on for a month or two, and then she would have a sudden pang of terror that the boy was getting roughened by the life and was missing his lessons and the quiet of his ordered Boston

home: and would pack him off to Geoffrey. Edmund was never
unwilling. He liked his father, his lessons, his pony and his piano,
and above all he loved travelling. He was much the most pleased
of the three when Donna, who in the last year or two had been
playing principally in New York, received an advantageous offer for a
world tour, and wrote to her father suggesting that it should end in
England. Geoffrey had no notion of acting again but, it being a period
of peace between them, was willing enough to go with her. The
pedagogue in him thought it was his duty to see the world and attend
to the education of his son, for Donna wanted to show the child to his
grandfather and it was not convenient or practicable to travel a tutor.
Besides, said Geoffrey to himself, as he grew older he would not be
able to take such an opportunity even if it occurred, and he was not
sorry to return to England, see his father-in-law and satisfy himself as
to the boy's prospects. Geoffrey was perfectly contented to look after
his son's future himself, but his intense respect for the English heritage
weighed with him. If Edmund's prospects were as brilliant in England
as they very well might be, as Donna declared them to be, he would
not stand in the way. So he settled his affairs and prepared for a year of
playing, once more, second fiddle to his wife.

The tour was successful, though the three did not make the fortune
that William Broome had made fifty years before. But they saw the
world, gained friends, reputation, and experience: and Donna and the
boy throve on the venture. Physical hardships did not dismay them
so long as there was accompanying excitement: they were neither soft-
bodied nor soft-hearted, and could endure dirt as easily as discomfort,
strange food or fatigue. The unfortunate Geoffrey, on the other hand,
was worn out with weariness by the time he reached England. He
had less stamina and he could not throw himself with the ardour and
unconsciousness of the Broomes into the lives of strange families and
strange people. Life had sand-papered away Donna's surface reserves.
If the gallery shouted at her she could answer it graciously, crack a
joke with it or, if need be, shout it down. It did not disconcert her to
give interviews and deal out information concerning her affections,
her religious beliefs and her taste in lovers to an interviewer; for her
invention was quick, almost as quick as her business instinct, and she
had developed a certain sense of humour. But her easy, friendly,
contemptuous lies horrified her husband. When they found their
hotel bedroom invaded by a mob of schoolgirls in search of souvenirs,
or when she was stopped in the street and asked to sign albums or

even kiss a couple of total strangers, it was he who shrank, sneered and was unhappy, while she called him 'the sensitive plant' and laughed at him good-naturedly. But she understood his attitude though she affected to pity it and him. She said to him one day on the boat going home when the pestering and the flattery had been greater than usual——

"Geoffrey, if you had ever been really in grief you would laugh at this sort of thing as I do. It isn't real, my dear. It's part of the game. It doesn't touch me."

"Touch you!" he said disgustedly. "Of course it touches you. It marks you: it coarsens you. The very fact that you can permit it and laugh is a coarsening——"

"Not of me," she said. "I'm not here."

"Where, then?" said he, with one of his sudden flares of jealousy.

"Hy-Brasil," said Donna.

"I don't understand you," said her husband. "Any stranger can look at you and push his way into your dressing-room, and get a handshake and a smile and all manner of information. But when I ask you a question you answer me with——"

"Hy-Brasil," said she again: and then—"Poor Geoffrey!"

Edmund looked up from his book.

"Hy-Brasil is a fabled island off the west coast of Ireland. I read about it in the Encyclopædia," said he. "St. Patrick is said to have visited it. It is sometimes called the Fortunate Isles. See Atlantis and Avalon. Father, will you come and play deck-quoits?"

"There, Geoffrey," said Donna with her queer smile.

"Ireland?" he picked it up. "You weren't there three years."

"Not three years," said his wife.

"Donna——" he began, tormented as usual by her manner.

"Come on, Father!" said Edmund impatiently.

"I'll play with you, Edmund," said his mother quickly, and left Geoffrey doubly robbed.

The three arrived in London on the noon of Edmund's tenth birthday: and the fact that presents and cake were unfairly postponed destroyed to some extent his interest in meeting his English grandfather. But Donna for once bothered her head as little about his grievances as she did about those of her husband, left at the station to deal with the baggage.

Now that she was actually in England, in London, she found herself beset by an extraordinary longing to see her father and her home.

Neither love nor hate moved her, but a sudden realisation that she had been for years starved of emotion. As she drove through the much changed streets, she marked every alteration with a pang. The hansom jingled into spring-coloured Regent's Park, and entered a drive now so overgrown with flowers and shrubs that there was no sign whatever of the house. Then the familiar sharp turn of the sweep brought it before her with the forgotten old suddenness and she felt her heart thudding in her breast as furiously as if she were making her entrance on the first night of a new part.

Adelaide was waiting for them in the drawing-room with her friendly incoherence and easy tears. Edmund was greeted. His elders kissed, then drew back and looked at each other.

"You are much changed," said Adelaide.

"You are not changed at all," said Donna.

And with one accord the two handsome women turned and, standing with linked arms, surveyed themselves in the long pier-glass. Each was right. Adelaide at thirty-four had not a grey hair in her head. Her roses were scarcely dimmed, and the tight bodice and swan skirts of the eighties accentuated the pleasant plumpness of her English figure. She wore a dress of bright Prussian blue and her fair skin triumphed over the test. But Donna was much worn and looked older than her stepmother. Made up, lighted, dressed, she was a magnificent creature, but as far as daily life was concerned, her bloom was gone. Both knew it: neither owned it; but on an odd feminine impulse kissed again and in silence. The two had always liked each other. Then—

"Where's my father?" said Donna.

"In the library. Will you go to him?"

"Yes," said Donna: and she took her son by the hand. But before she was across the hall Edmund had pulled his hand free: he could not bear to be controlled. However, having asserted himself, he followed her sensibly enough. She knocked at the door: its dark red polish reflected Edmund's face for him: he pulled an idle face at himself as he waited, then glanced up at his mother. Why didn't she go in?

"Look, Mother, one can see oneself. Shan't we go in, Mother?"

"Wait, dear! Wait!" For she was racing back through her childhood as she listened for that often feared 'Come in!'

"Come in!"

Then she entered, to see her father rising from his chair. The window lights were behind him and she could not see his face. Besides, to her own bewilderment her sight was thickened over by a sudden painful rush of tears. She was much agitated. She could hardly speak as she crossed to him and took his hand. He held it, watching her intently. He was moved by her agitation. At last—

" 'Vain dew,' " said Harry gently. And then—"So this is the boy."

CHAPTER 40

EDMUND—A BROOME

THE Angers were three months in England, and in that time each of the three gathered agreeable memories. But if they had compared notes, this husband, wife and child, they would not have agreed over the value of their memories. Donna did not discuss hers with anyone; but Geoffrey often said how much he had been gratified by the attentive courtesy of his wife's relations. Formal, emotional and fastidious, he had grown to loathe the hail-fellow-well-met of stage life. His passion for the theatre had been a passion for its illusions: its facts appalled him. He had gone on to the stage to escape the coarse realities of daily life; but how much coarser were the realities that created the stage illusions than the realities of his own well-mannered domesticities! His very wife had grown, in his eyes, into a symbol of deceitful illusion. She was a magic-lantern projection, a little larger than life: a voice filling a theatre admirably but deafening at close quarters. He had even a sort of embarrassment in coming back with her to the decent immemorial England of his literary dreams, of his brief hurried love-affair, soon over, and inexplicable to him now.

But his overwhelming wife who had once seemed a figure of high romance amazed him now by appearing to understand his discomfort. With impatient kindness she had commended him to the graces of her stepmother, had said to Adelaide Wybird, that gracious English matron—

"Addie, Geoffrey is craving for Wybirds—dozens of Wybirds. He doesn't know it, but he is. Gather the clans for him, dearest Addie, and come and choose me the right dresses to go visiting in."

And on that he had been swept into a round of visits, sometimes with his wife, sometimes without her. He had stayed in the shires with a country parson who had a farm and a title besides his vicarage: and the parson, somehow, was connected with Geoffrey's singular wife. He had been carried over by pony-cart to a cathedral close and was entertained by a bishop who turned out to be another relative. He had gone with his father-in-law, his stepmother and his wife to stay with a duke, and there was formally welcomed as a second cousin through his wife. There were female relatives innumerable, and a great-uncle who was over ninety and had been Governor of the Bank of England. He, in turn, had a bachelor son of Geoffrey's own age in attendance. His name was Lewis Wybird: they all seemed to be Wybirds. And in the nursery Edmund was expected to play with a pretty little girl who was Lewis Wybird's ward, the daughter and heiress of a partner, it appeared; for Lewis Wybird himself was a bachelor. Geoffrey envied him. Yet he enjoyed himself; for all these relatives of his wife behaved formally to him because it was their habit to be formal; but yet were friendly to him because he was the husband of his wife and the son-in-law of Harry Broome: who, it appeared, was a personage rather than a player. He wondered at feeling so much at home: he had wanted the stilted pleasing visits to be twice as long as they were, and all the while he had marvelled at his wife's complete abandonment of her stage personality, had envied her for being comfortable when he was shy and forgot to say as he had said twice a week for the last five years whenever she vexed him—"I was mad to marry her."

His son's memories were very different. Edmund had loathed the round of formal visits, though he had enjoyed the ponies and the dogs and the one wild day when he had persuaded Lewis' ward, the eight year old Elinor Dale, to levant with him. They had tagged on at the back of a farmer's jogging cart and had at last, by luck and struggling, hauled themselves into it. There they spent a heavenly hour among the frightened netted calves who rolled wild eyes but after a time sucked at their fingers. And as they drew into the market town the pair had dropped cunningly to the pavement still unseen and wandered about the market. Then they had been allured by the wheeze of a gigantic musical-box and following their ears and a tail of people had come upon an Odd-fellows fête with green banners, a band, a merry-go-round, cocoanut shies and booths. Then they had made friends with a Punch-and-Judy man and Edmund had been smuggled under the curtain and talked Yankee through the horn and convulsed the crowd. They had had tea with the Punch-and-Judy man and tried to buy the dog Toby. The man would not sell, but had promised Elinor that if she sent him a proper ruffle for the dog, sewn to a leather collar so that it would not cut his poor neck, the dog should wear it. The man could not write but Edmund scribbled down his address on a dirty piece of paper and there ensued the farewells of equals. It was a grand memory, unmarred for Edmund by its conclusion; for it did not occur to his mother to punish him for amusing himself. It was Elinor who was punished by her severer guardian. Edmund did not like Lewis Wybird the better when he overheard him advising that he, Edmund, should be sent to school. But he liked Elinor. Still, he was glad when the round of formal visits came to an end and they returned to his grandfather's house.

For he soon found out that his grandfather went down daily to one or other of his theatres and liked Edmund to come with him. Once the stage door was passed, however, he would forget him for as long as Edmund chose to be forgotten.

It was the boy's chance. His curiosity ran over the buildings like a fire, and everybody was extremely friendly and told him all he wanted to know. Even his cousin Stephen, handsome, jolly, but always in a hurry and always rather tired, found time to take him up on to the roof of the New Broom and across to the separate property rooms of the Gloriana. And in the dear little Genista they were putting in the marvellous electric lighting that his grandfather hated.

He talked a great deal to his grandfather, who had in his library a toy which Edmund would have given his ears to possess. It was a table, twistable like a dumb waiter, and on it was built up an exact model of the Glory Hole, with walls that unhooked and a roof that came off. Here his grandfather would sit in the evenings shifting sets, snipping bits of cloth, cutting out scenery, and renovating the little wooden figures which for years, he told Edmund, he had been accustomed to whittle, till there was hardly a figure in the whole range of his productions which he did not possess. Easy to his hand was his cabinet with its innumerable boxes, all labelled. Each box-drawer contained a Shakespeare play, with its script, its proper scenery, its proper figures. But the figures did not interest Edmund. It was the footlights that fascinated him, and the miniature curtain that rose and fell so smoothly, and the tiny flies with their hanging threads.

"If it were mine," said Edmund fingering, "I'd put in this new electric light."

"But there is gas at the Glory Hole," said Harry.

"Well, if it were mine I'd have the other all the same."

"Why, boy?"

"Well, the man at the Genista says that electric light has come to stay: it's only a question of time. So I shall put it into my own model when I get home. I've only got lamps as it is."

"And lamps are gone for good. But I should have to take out all this——" and Harry touched the miniature tubing with a loving finger.

"Well, why not, Grandpapa? Let me rip it out for you."

"Not yet, child! You will one day, I expect. Well—" testily—"what is it, Adelaide?"

Adelaide was reproachful.

"Edmund has a party, Harry. His cousin Eustace and Eustace's sisters have been left to themselves for over an hour. Is that good manners, Edmund? You know how Eustace wants you to play with him always."

This was true; for Stephen's son, the delicate, dreamy Eustace, had conceived a passion for his American cousin, followed him patiently, receiving snubs as favours and the most casual order as an eleventh commandment.

"Oh, blow!" muttered Edmund, and glanced at his grandfather hopefully.

But Harry avoided the appeal. He knew himself weak with his grandson. Also he was curious: so he said nothing but watched the boy intently.

Edmund, deserted by an ally, got up and was courteous to his Aunt Adelaide; but his grey eyes flashed angrily and his face was red and sulky.

'What will he do?' thought Harry: and strolled to the window to watch the rest of the play.

He saw his grandson run out of the breakfast-room window and return to the waiting croquet players. He was evidently trying to be civil. He picked a female cousin as a partner and the game continued as croquet can continue when one of the players is in a black rage and all the players are under ten. In less than ten minutes the shrieks of the little girls brought Adelaide and Donna from the arbour and Harry from the house. Eustace was on the ground, Edmund on the top of him his hands at his throat, crying—

"Say 'pax' or I'll kill you! I'd like to kill you!"

It was Donna who dragged him off the victim, while Adelaide wrung her hands. He was white with rage, quite beside himself, and struggling to get back to the appalled Eustace. Strong as she was his mother could scarcely hold him.

"What's all this?" Harry's measured voice broke into the racket, and the two women waited for the instant lull that should follow. But it did not follow. Edmund continued to wrestle with his mother till Harry caught the boy's blind flailing arm by the wrist. The touch of those cold fingers did have an effect. Edmund desisted from his energies, though he wrenched uneasily at the hard clasp.

"Go away, Donna! I'll deal with this," said the grandfather.

For an instant his daughter hesitated, and her eyes spoke to his and his to hers as if there were one thought in both their minds. Then he said—

"I shan't hurt him."

"Very well," said Donna.

Edmund continued to tug till his mother was out of sight: then desisted abruptly.

"What has Eustace done to you?" enquired Harry, releasing him.

"He said I cheated," returned Edmund furiously.

"And did you?" enquired his grandfather casually. He had watched from the window and could not help setting the trap.

"Yes," said Edmund.

"Why?"

"Well, I wanted to get the silly game over quickly."

"I see." And Harry did. He would have done the same himself. But he remembered his rôle. "You shouldn't cheat, you know," he observed.

"Depends why, doesn't it?" enquired Edmund: and added—"I didn't mind his winning, but he was so slow."

"Still," remarked his grandfather, "if you did cheat, and he saw it and said so——"

"Well, teach him not to!"

"Not to what?"

"Interfere with me. Besides, he ought to know that I wouldn't cheat—in order to cheat, you know."

"No, you wouldn't, would you?" said Harry, helpless and wistful.

"Of course I wouldn't, Grandpapa. But I do hate a fiddling game. And that Eustace drives me mad with his pop-eyes and his curls and his reciting."

"I've never heard you recite, Edmund."

Edmund produced a dazzling smile and tucked his arm in Harry's.

"And you never will, Grandpapa. I hate it."

"But, Edmund—if you are to go on the stage——"

"I'm going to be a stage carpenter. I've made up my mind."

"And not have a theatre of your own?"

"Well, I might. But I'd be my own stage carpenter."

"Better be a manager, Edmund, and tell the carpenter what you want done."

"Well, I might."

"You won't if you can't act."

"Why not?"

"You can't tell people to do things unless you can show them how."

Edmund thought it over.

"Mother's always wanting me to do little Willies and Macduffs. I hate everyone cooing over me and kissing me afterwards as if I were a baby still."

"Well, if I thought there was a thing I couldn't do——" said Harry slowly.

Edmund's bright grey eyes sparkled.

"Oh, I know *that* feeling."

Harry's heart warmed to him.

"Edmund, your mother is putting on *The Winter's Tale* at Stratford this summer."

"Yes, I know. But I won't be Mamilius."

"Not if I coach you?"

Once again Edmund thought things over. Then he spoke.

"Do you give me your word, Grandpapa, that you've got to be able to act to run a theatre?"

"No, Edmund, I won't say that. But if you want to run a theatre as it ought to be run——"

"Hm! All right. When shall we start?"

"Now if you like."

"No, now I've got to find Eustace."

"My boy——" said Harry worriedly—"what are you going to do to Eustace?"

"Oh—you know!" The brilliant eyes were alight with mischief and confidence. "Cool him down! Cheer him up! It isn't that I exactly mind Eustace when I'm not busy. I'll come after dinner, shall I?"

"Very well, boy."

Harry went back to his library, his mind thick as a snowy day with thoughts and memories, and took down *The Winter's Tale*. Was he to teach a child again at his time of life? How does one teach a little boy? Let's have a look at the part!

> 'You'll kiss me hard and speak to me as if
> I were a baby still——'

Oh, it ought not to be hard to teach Donna's Edmund to play Mamilius. And next year the small Macduff: and some time or other, Prince Arthur. But never Oberon. No, never Oberon. Not till the east and west change places will a red head turn into a cap of silver-gilt.

CHAPTER 41

THE PRICE OF WAR

DOMINA might have the temper of a devil—her husband often told her she had—but she was a quiet devil and hated to be nagged. She was the masculine half of that partnership, and as she grew older and the habit of controlling her company, her child and her life grew fixed, she found Geoffrey's more feminine qualities a nuisance and a bore. If she could have controlled him completely she would have been tender with him; but he, too, had his will, which she was not strong enough to break though she was strong enough to ignore it. He was clever at putting her in the wrong and could not resist making her little scenes when she was tired or pre-occupied: and then, when her temper was at last roused from its cat-like sleepy endurance, he would choose that precise moment to resign himself to her will and, submitting, complain piteously of her lack of affection and demand a little love. And this in the earlier years of her married life she had given him as one comforts a child with sweets. But as she grew older she had found that she had no sweetness left over for him. All that she had went to satisfy her audiences and her son. Ceasing to show affection she also ceased to accept it: and then, as poor Geoffrey told her and firmly believed, she stole his own son's affection from him also.

"Pooh! Tragedy airs!" said Donna, and wondered idly where she had heard the phrase before: and did not care tuppence for Geoffrey's wince. For it was nearly two years since her return to America with her husband and son, and for the whole of that time she had been involved in one of her customary struggles with her husband. But this time the struggle was serious because it was over the boy. She wanted him educated in England: Geoffrey, with some reason, declared that he himself was an American and that his son should have the same training that his father had had. He could go to one of the English universities later.

"Later!" said Donna disdainfully. "I can hardly keep him out of the theatre as it is. Do you think that either of us will hold him when he is over sixteen? He'll be working then, with or without our leaves. That's why I want him at least to have English schooling."

"He's an American," repeated Geoffrey obstinately.

"He's my son," argued Donna.

It was deadlock.

Geoffrey was not strong enough to prevent his wife carrying out her own intention; but he remained irreconcilable: and even made his own private efforts to enlist Edmund on his side and there failed humiliatingly; for Edmund liked change and he had a romantic passion for his grandfather.

But Geoffrey could not understand that the vigorous, self-willed, farsighted boy was already independent even of his mother's influence, and that he acquiesced and indeed enthusiastically forwarded his mother's schemes only because they were as much his own schemes as hers. He was sure that the whole business was Donna's doing, and began to remember with resentment all the other occasions that had been Donna's doing, till the ordinary comfortable domestic row worked up into something much more imposing than usual and had results which Geoffrey never intended. For Donna, harried between conflicting duties and opinions, and always at a crisis hankering for the Broome voice and the Broome attitude to life, only needed an urgent summons from Adelaide to stiffen into open revolt.

Her father's state of health had long been poor. Without any actual illness his vitality was ebbing as if he had been a man in his eighties instead of in his fifties: and Adelaide wrote alarmingly. Donna had certainly no sentimental urge towards her father. She could do without seeing him again just as she could do without seeing one of her own limbs afterwards if amputation were necessary. Nevertheless she knew that she would be maimed by his death and she did want to see him once again if she could. And besides, think of the affairs that would have to be settled after his death!

"It's no use grumbling, Geoffrey! Of course I must go, and of course I must take Edmund. He's my father's heir. Why won't you come with us? You would be a help to me." And then, belatedly, with Donna's own awkward attempt to feel more than she could feel—"It would be a pity if—"

"If what, Donna?"

"Well, we have been linked people these twelve years."

"Linked people! Is that all you call it?"

"Do come, Geoffrey!"

No, he would not come.

She could not help feeling relieved: and in the extravagance of relief said good-bye to him with unusual affection. But, as if fore-warned,

she packed away all her peculiar possessions scattered about his house,
left them trunked and corded. This he noticed, but said nothing; but he
took it as a sign that the breach between them was final. And when he
heard, a month or two after Donna's arrival in England, that his father-
in-law was dead, he shrugged his shoulders, said to himself—'Either I
go over or I do not see them again—' and—did not go over.

Donna scarcely noticed his absence, though she wrote to him
dutifully at intervals: and when, in 1886, he wrote suggesting a
divorce, she did not care. Indeed she sympathised and made things as
easy for him as she could. Why not? Why should not Geoffrey remake
his life before it was too late? She wanted him to be happy if he could,
and she knew that from now on she could do nothing for him but free
him. For, in the brief months of her second return, life had shown her a
new face. The moment for which she had been waiting for twelve years
and more had come at last.

She had never forgotten her cousin Stephen and never forgiven him.
She had never ceased to pray to the god within her that one day—one
day—she should be given her chance to teach Stephen what it meant to
lose hope. Now her day and her chance had come.

She was in no hurry. What she had to do must be done slowly if it
was to be done effectively. There were elements in her life which had
not existed when she first kissed a sword against Stephen. Edmund and
his future were now more important to her than the punishment of a
lost lover: and Stephen, she thought sometimes, would be hardly worth
fighting if it were not that he, too, fought for an heir. Who was to be
master of the Broome inheritance? Edmund or Eustace? Her son or
Madeleine's? Oh yes, there was still cause enough to fight.

She found herself opening her campaign with strong advantages.
Harry's last will, drawn up not much more than a year before, revoked
most of the benefits that his earlier will had bestowed upon Stephen.
Donna was the heir. A good part of his private fortune had been
expended in buying the second share of the Broome property from
Russel, when Russel left the stage. But the two shares and what
moneys there were left over from the purchase went to her without
brake or reservation of any kind. He had seen enough of her demeanour
to be sure that she was a pelican mother, and he had disliked the idea of
leaving big moneys direct to the boy himself. He knew what the
Broomes were like in the twenties: and he had been able to see that
Edmund had more impetuosity that all the earlier Broomes put together. Harry, who trusted cunning rather than force, preferred to

leave power in his daughter's hands to be transferred, as he wrote her in a private letter attached to the will, when Edmund was old enough to bear the burden.

'We all ripen young,' wrote Harry. 'I and your uncles were all in harness at twenty. But Edmund is much more like his uncle Robin than he is like me—fantastically ambitious—and he has the physique of your uncle Russel. I am afraid of the combination. Unless he has my sobriety to counter-balance (and he is too young for me to judge of this) he will make ducks and drakes of the inheritance. Against this eventuality, my dear Donna, I trust you to guard. You love him, I know. But in all our dealings with each other, some of which I will own I now regret, I have observed that you allow judgment to rule even your affections and your hates. I expect you to use that judgment as regards Edmund. When he is fit to control the inheritance, hand it over to him, even though he is no more than twenty; but if he has no prudence then keep the control of the fortune in your own hands as long as may be. You know the rest of my wishes: you know how anxious I am that the Broomes shall work together and that the control of our group of theatres should remain ours. But I leave you no positive instructions on this score. London is moving west: it may be to your advantage to sell the Gloriana and build elsewhere. I cannot endure the idea of it, but I would rather preserve the tradition than the building. Work with your cousin Stephen as much as you can, but do not let him over-rule you. He is an admirable second-in-command; but I have never trusted his creative judgment. He is too cautious when it pays to be bold, and when he gambles he generally loses. But his wife is an admirable woman. If you find Stephen difficult to control I advise you to become friendly with his wife, that is if her health improves. She will save you much nervous irritation, for she has a good business head and Stephen relies on her absolutely.'

Thus Harry, aware that by the re-arrangement of his will he had been unjust to Stephen and was leaving his daughter a difficult task.

Stephen had already inherited his father's share of the great concern and in his will Harry left him Robin's profits. Harry had invested the proceeds and the result was an extremely handsome fortune on paper, though much of it was in shares not so valuable as they had been at the time of purchase. Everybody told Stephen that the slump was temporary and that he had only to wait to be rich, as indeed it proved. But it was hard on Stephen to be unable to realise his fortune. He had five children to educate, and his wife, mentally active enough, had sunk physically into an invalid. Also with the withdrawal of Harry from active share in the management of the Broome undertakings, these undertakings had once more flagged. They showed no loss, but there had been no profit for Stephen. He, of course, had drawn on his account for what he wanted to tide over additional expenses. There was not only Eustace's schooling: there was the support in proper state of old Mrs. Reilly, who, marvellous old lady, had at eighty-five decided that she needed a little rest and would play no more. Madeleine too, cost him large sums in doctors, nurses, treatments and winters out of England. To draw against your probable profits is all very well when you are making them, but the theatres had lost: and Stephen, within six months of Harry's death, was some thousands in the firm's debt and had to sell out a part of his legacy at a considerable loss in the general accounting that followed.

He did not lament unduly. Never truly understanding the value of money or its manipulation, he always looked upon a loss as bad luck to be endured and a profit as sheer manna. Money had been in the bank, and would be again if he went on working and didn't worry. Besides, he was considerably overset by his uncle's death: the new responsibilities made him feel heady, and he was ripe with grand schemes whereby to celebrate the new régime, and full of genuine sympathy and friendliness for his cousin and co-heir. He advised that the boy should be sent to Westminster where Eustace had won a scholarship: and he made, with perfect sincerity, the suggestion that Edmund should spend his holidays in his own family when Donna went back to America.

But Donna did not send Edmund to Westminster. She sent him to St. Paul's and herself did not go back to America. The Regent's Park house had been left to her: and though ample provision had been made for Adelaide the two women liked each other well enough to take it as a matter of course that they should live together.

"I want you," said Donna to her affectionately. "I shall be at the theatre so much. If I know that you are there when Edmund comes home, I shan't be anxious. Not, I suppose, that you will stay with us long."

Adelaide flushed and was horrified at the premature and indelicate hint. Nevertheless the two women understood each other. Adelaide the widow was a very handsome woman and her jointure was ample. Of course she would marry again. And a year later she did: but she did not again marry into the theatre. Adelaide had had quite enough of the stage. She married a country gentleman with an estate not far from Blandon, Lewis Wybird's home. There she settled to be happy. But she remained a very good friend to her stepdaughter and her husband's grandson, and later on proved it.

But Stephen did not much like the idea of Donna permanently in England. What would she do? She would want to be acting. She who had always had a company of her own would hardly like to knuckle under to him in what were, in part, her own theatres. Yet there could not be two masters in one management.

But Donna, it seemed, thought that there could be two masters. She spent some months in going very fully into the affairs of the three London theatres and all the lesser enterprises. She was critical, acute. She put her finger on money drainages. She asked why this and that had been done and why the other had not been done. Her lawyers backed her : and Stephen's lawyers were not very adroit in defence. Nor, when she demanded an active share in the control of the great business did they find any good reason against it. But Stephen did.

"You and my father worked well. I do but step into his place," said Donna.

"Well, but Donna—as a woman——"

"Don't talk rubbish, Stephen! I have been managing my own companies in America these ten years. Besides, you talk as if a woman running her own company were an event. Look at Mary Anderson. Look at Madame Vestris! Look at Mrs. Lane down at Hoxton for that matter."

"Well, you had better get Geoffrey over," said Stephen sulkily.

"Geoffrey? He shook the dust of the theatre off his feet long ago."

"But you see, Donna, when you go back to him everything will be left on my hands. You can't be in two places at once."

"I don't intend to. You may as well know, Stephen, that Geoffrey and I are separating : probably a divorce. We have nothing in common and my work is here. Do realise that I am caretaker for Edmund. The business is Edmund's inheritance."

"And Eustace's," put in Stephen quickly.

"Oh, certainly! You shall look after Eustace's inheritance, Stephen, and I will look after Edmund's : though in another eight years Edmund at any rate will be able to look after his share for himself. I have been training him to that end. Of course I don't know what your plans are for Eustace; but I know exactly what my plans are for Edmund. He is to know every detail of the business. He is to have the run, Stephen, of all the theatres. He is to be given small parts—yes, even if it means interfering with his education. If I have any difficulty at St. Paul's he is to have a tutor: when he is sixteen he is to tour and then in any case he is to have a tutor with him. But he must learn the ropes early. I daresay you have something of the same sort in mind for Eustace."

"Eustace goes to Oxford," said Stephen. "My own time there was broken off by Gilly's death. Eustace shan't be cheated as I was."

Donna stared at him.

"My experience was very similar, Stephen, though perhaps a little harsher, and I, too, have resolved that my son shall not be robbed as I was robbed."

"Well, that's all very right, Donna. There's no reason why we should quarrel."

"I didn't know we were quarrelling. I am very anxious to work with you, Stephen."

"That's another matter."

"Oh, no. I intend to work with you. I do not intend to leave you in sole control."

"I don't see how you can help it, Donna. My uncle made me Managing Director."

"Ah, yes; but he is dead: and the property is half mine. As half owner I wish to make other arrangements."

"Well, and as half owner I object. So it's deadlock, Donna."

"Oh, of course, if you want to make a dispute of it, Stephen, you can always call in the lawyers. But what is your objection to working with me?"

"I don't think it would work."

"You don't trust my business capacity? Is that it?"

"Yes, that's it, Donna."

She smiled at him.

"I have already submitted to my lawyers and yours my accounts for the last ten years."

"What accounts?"

"The balance sheets of all my undertakings since Uncle Russel launched me in management. I have saved a fair fortune, Stephen. What have you saved?"

"You know I have a large family," said Stephen flushing.

"Yes," said she. "And I have only Edmund. I have saved for ten years to advantage Edmund; but I am prepared to spend every penny, Stephen, in fighting for my rights and his. Either you and I work together as my father wished or the whole property must be realised."

"If you like to take the Gloriana," said he, "I'll take the Genista and the New Broom."

"Nothing like that," said Donna. "I'll have no arbitrary divisions with you knowing the values and I ignorant."

"Are you suggesting, Donna," said he, "that I am capable of deliberately cheating you?"

"Yes," said she hardily.

"And yet—" said he, deeply hurt and deeply insulted—"and yet you suggest that we should work together?"

"I don't see why we shouldn't. We are arranging a partnership, not a love affair," said she.

He had nothing to say to that: he could only hate her shameless tongue.

She went on hardily, perfectly aware of his sensations.

"Don't be sentimental, Stephen. Look at the question impersonally. Each of us has something to bring to the bargain. You have your experience of English theatre conditions and your personal popularity: I have my hard head—much harder than yours, Stephen. One needs hardness to make money. And then I have my capacity as an actress which, frankly, I don't underrate. I am an asset as an actress. And you are an asset as——" an odd smile flickered for a moment about her mouth—"as a beckoner, Stephen. The English public would always rather have a charmer than an artist, and we both know it. I don't say they aren't right. But a charmer must be fed by an artist, an unselfish, businesslike artist. You know, between us we could make a lot of money for Edmund—oh, and for Eustace! But if you won't work with me or if you hamper me, Stephen, then I shall insist, not on a sharing out, but on a sale. There shall be an end of the Broome management."

"It will be an immense loss in money, Donna: a loss of goodwill apart from the fact that it is a very bad time to sell. There are too many theatres on the market already."

"I know," said she. "But I have earned a fortune and I can stand the loss. Can you?"

"It is Edmund who will lose, not you," said he desperately.

"No, my private fortune will make good to Edmund any depreciations. Well, Stephen, do you want to talk it over with Madeleine? You know perfectly well what she will say. She will be extremely puzzled that you should dislike working with me."

"No, she won't," he muttered.

On that her eyes flashed with a fierceness, a very lightning of anger that dazed and dazzled him. He was accustomed to his wife's gentle guidance: he had forgotten these female masters and their ways.

"So you did tell her!" The statement leaped out at him on a note of triumph, as if she reassured her own view of him, and he actually stepped back a pace as if her fierce look of contempt spat upon his dignity. "You added even that. You couldn't even hold your tongue."

"She guessed," said Stephen sullenly. "Don't you remember the first night of *Lear?* You behaved like a mad woman instead of a bride. You flaunted our relationship. Of course she guessed. But whose fault was it?"

"Yes, I was half mad that night," she admitted.

"Yes, you were half mad and my uncle was the other half mad. Do you wonder that Madeleine guessed?"

"Did she punish you?" said Donna.

"My wife's an angel, always was and always is, and I don't want to talk about her," said Stephen. "If I've got to work with you at least keep her out of it. And anyway it's all years ago."

"You needn't be afraid," said Donna slowly, and her hands moved in a gesture of relinquishment as she spoke to those open and upturned palms—"You won't have to work with me, after all."

"Oh—" he cried fretfully and wearily—"You know well enough that I've got to give in and work with you. I know which side my bread's buttered. If you insist I've got to acquiesce. You've got the whip hand. All right, Donna! Don't let's talk any more. I give in."

"Ah," said she, "but you've talked a little too much. I'm afraid it is I who won't work with you now, Stephen. We'll sell the concern and be done with it."

"What?" He turned on her as white as a sheet.

"We'll sell the concern and be done with it," she repeated.

He couldn't believe her.

"You won't work with me? Then what is all this talk and torment for?"

"Heaven knows! Amusement, Stephen, do you think?"

"Donna, you can't insist on selling."

"My lawyer says I am within my rights. You ought to be thankful, Stephen. There are the death duties and you are probably short of ready money. Much better sell."

"I don't want to sell." He looked at her desperately. "I'm thirty-five. It's a smashing down of my whole career, my whole habit of life.

I am the Broome tradition: I am the Genista and the New Broom and the Gloriana. I've been brought up to it: it's my position. If you like, that's why I've hated the idea of your coming back into it too. But I'd rather have you in than let the whole thing go. Can't you see what you're smashing—the traditions of two centuries?"

"Not smashing, transferring," said she. "I think myself strong enough to transfer it all, through myself, to Edmund. But you say that you and Eustace are the Broome tradition! Well—Edmund and Eustace will not be of age for another nine years. That gives you and me plenty of time, Stephen, to fight it out. Let us see, nine years from today, which branch will represent the Broome tradition. Don't look so frightened, Stephen. You used to love a fight."

"Donna, I beg you not to do this mad thing."

"Yes, you always thought me mad," said she.

"Donna, you don't realise the brutality of what you are doing. I have about as many burdens as I can bear, but I can carry them because I'm in my stride. But to put them down, and re-shoulder, and start again without anyone to help me—that's another matter. With the children, and Madeleine always ill, it's more than I can face."

"We all say that," said she indifferently, "when we're in trouble. But you know one does face things and after a time one masters them or is mastered by them. It's all a question of one's nature, Stephen. One must learn to be hard, and learn to be cold, and learn not to feel too much: and then one wins."

"Donna—are you still holding against me that craziness when we were both so young?"

"Oh," said she, "I wish you wouldn't be emotional when I want to talk business. However, I can talk to my lawyer and he can see yours. You do understand, Stephen, don't you, that I mean to sell?"

He understood well enough. He was passionate with apprehension, the awful lucid apprehension of the artist whom accident had made into a business man. He foresaw all the disastrous consequences of any action in any direction and it paralysed his own power to take action in any one direction and so save himself. Another man might have leaped at the chance of complete independence with capital for a new beginning. Not so Stephen. The very idea of quitting his stronghold, dismissing his staff, securing a new theatre, weeding out the incompetents, interviewing lawyers and bargaining with the bank terrified him. The business of the Broome theatres was an established routine. A wiser head than his had laid the rails, and the baggage of business ran along them still smoothly enough. He could trust his underlings and devote himself to the part of the work he loved—the stage work and the acting. But to start again! He could not do it. He knew he had not the brains or the initiative. He was terrified. He wanted security. He did not want war.

"I was Uncle's right hand," said he in a shaking voice. "I knew all his wishes. Can you persuade yourself that what you propose tallies with his wishes, Donna?"

She answered his last throw.

"You were his right hand, but I am his daughter. Of course he wouldn't wish it; but of course it is what he would do."

She had her way, though it was long before the contracts, undertakings and future arrangements in the three theatres came to an end. But the property was valued: a reserve price put upon it: and it was announced for sale. But as Stephen had said, times were bad. There were theatres on the market already and no-one outbid Donna's own offer for the Genista and the New Broom. She spent her last penny and mortgaged her Irish property to get the money. But she bought it, let the Genista instantly, and, herself taking over the management of the New Broom, carried on.

But the Gloriana would not sell: and as neither she nor Stephen would lease to the other it fell upon evil times and had strange lessees: and on the stage where Robert had delighted the King of England there was now carried out a series of shabby experiments—a Jubilee Ball, a pantomime with a talking horse for hero, a water pageant, disreputable gala nights, circus enterprises and the forlorn ventures of closet dramatists, rich amateurs, and theatre sharks.

Meanwhile Stephen with the money that he received from the sales, and Domina with the money left after buying out her cousin, prepared to build rival reputations. Stephen took a little theatre behind Regent Street and put on modern comedies: and did, not grandly, but well enough: till Donna, doing very well indeed at the New Broom, for they remembered her, loved her experienced staginess and the grandiose dramas which she gave them, cast her eyes on Stephen's vineyard and out of her profits prepared for a second campaign.

For she had conceived the brilliant idea of reviving the half-dead comedies of Robin Broome. The castes were small. She was clever with her lighting and had brought over with her a middle-aged Russian Jew who was a lurid failure when he was given money wherewith to carry out his designs, but given a paint-pot, rolls of linen and a time limit, could produce interiors that were original, pleasing to the eye and so simple that they did not take away from the importance of the actor. These sets are thought tame enough by the post-war Broomes when they in turn revive Robin's comedies; but for a generation whose taste was only just being educated by the æsthetic craze they were sufficiently daring. And they certainly suited the new version of *Clever Kate* in which Donna, taking out a good deal of her father and Uncle's blue pencilling, herself played the lead. A very curious and not too pleasant rendering she gave; for she went back, though she did not know it, to Robin's original notion: the lollipop became again a bitter almond.

The revival shocked the public: it just escaped the censor. But the times were favourable, and the same public which went uncertainly to Ibsen and was convulsed by Wilde filled the little theatre faithfully: especially as Donna announced that the run was limited and put on in swift succession the rest of Robin's plays, including two that had never been staged before.

Meanwhile, at the theatre across the road, Stephen Broome was livid with anger. He had not thought of putting on Robin's plays: it had never entered his head to consider them still marketable. Nevertheless they were his father's plays. At the mere announcement of *Clever Kate* he had sent in his formal protest, but believing that it could not succeed and occupied as he was at the moment with a revival of *Money*, he had done no more about it. But at its raging success Madeleine could not hold him from the lawyers. They presented his complaints. Donna defied them. Stephen tried to get an injunction: Donna's lawyers defeated him. It became a matter for the courts. And with that the famous Broome lawsuits began—suits that dragged on for years: and as each party spent themselves to procure the best advice, and as Russel, on some inexplicable principle of his own, subsidised each party in turn, the war of attrition went on till Stephen was on the edge of bankruptcy and Donna had little left of her hoarded, boasted fortune.

At this point the situation altered. For after a seven years' interval the Gloriana at last found a purchaser in Lewis Wybird, the grandson of Lettice's banker brother. He was a man of fortune and the junior partner in a huge city firm. He had never married: and his hobby, like Harry's hobby in his youth, was buying land. There is no doubt that there was a slight likeness between Lewis Wybird and his father's cousin Harry Broome, not only in features but in ways of thought. Lewis had, at any rate, enough Broome blood in him, inherited from that far-away great-grandmother the duchess Hilaret, to make him hanker for contact with the stage. He was fond of financing a likely show and seldom backed a losing one, picked his mistresses from the more exclusive theatres and forwarded their careers with interest. Also he owned a parcel of land between Oxford Street and Cambridge Circus which he would not sell because he knew that one day it would be more valuable as a theatre site than as a block of shops. He would not pay high for the Gloriana; but he had watched the struggle between the cousins, sympathising with neither. When he thought them hard enough pressed he made an offer, and it was taken.

Said Stephen to Madeleine—

"Thank God! Now we can forge ahead."

"Stephen, you're not going to let this lump sum go the way of all the rest? Let's give up management. There are managements enough who will jump at you as leading man. You take a job somewhere, touring, anything. Or do you care more for besting her than for me? Because I must have peace, Stephen," said she piteously. "I can't stand much more of this strain. Let's get out of it. There is enough to be safe on here if only you stop fighting her."

"She won't let me," said Stephen.

"She will be satisfied, I should think," said his wife, "if she drives you out of management. Let her, my dear, let her! What do you care?"

"Don't you know her yet? Don't you realise," said he, "that if she drives us out of London she won't be satisfied? If I take out a company——"

"She can't touch you then," said his wife.

"She'll contrive to," said he. "I can't give up management, Madeleine, for Eustace's sake. I can't throw away position, authority, goodwill and a public. But you're right so far. It might be wisest to go to the provinces for a bit," said Stephen cheerfully. And the sick woman had to resign herself.

Yet Madeleine was right. For when Stephen took out his touring company in Robin's plays, Donna with her superior organisation contrived to be before him. She was popular with provincial audiences, and she offered the local managers such generous concessions that she was very welcome: and trailing through the principal cities reaped a harvest for those local managements and a living for herself. She left little behind for Stephen to glean when he followed her with a second-rate company. In vain he changed his bill: she changed hers. In vain he imported a star: she imported a bigger one or two or three.

And so for some years the mad pair chased up and down the kingdom, she the hunter, he the hunted. But sometimes, for you can drive a
desperate man too far, he turned on her, and contrived to outbid her
in the eternal manœuvre for position. Sometimes, too, it happened that
both companies played in the same city, and then the transient exhilara-
tion of having stood his ground would go to Stephen's head and he
would give a performance that set the town talking and for a time
mended his fortunes. Besides, the feud between the cousins became
known and the public, which always loves a contest, of course began
to take sides. And there Donna lost ground; for Stephen would always
have more partisans than she. But as time went by she was able to set
up Edmund as a coming rival of Stephen's peculiar capacity for
attracting an audience, not so much by skill as by a display of the
Broome characteristics.

He could not at first, of course, be a very serious rival. Stephen
was skilful and experienced both as an actor and as a beckoner, but
Edmund, a mere boy, could not be much more than a decoration to a
play where Stephen was its backbone. But he had the arrogant good
looks of a young bull and, though he had no notion of beckoning, he
had Russel's trick of bullying an audience into attention. Also he
developed, to the delight of his mother, a broad comic vein that
promised to be useful. He had got over his dislike of acting, though it
was the devices of the player rather than the art of the actor that
fascinated, indeed absorbed him. For, to his passionate interest in the
mechanics of the theatre, he had now added an equally passionate
interest in its history. Macready's *Diaries* were his Bible: he pored
over Cibber, Chetwood and Dibdin: collected anecdotes of famous and
forgotten players, raked the pawn-shops and small book-sellers for old
plays and prints, and one day announced that school French and
German did not suffice him and that he also proposed to learn Italian.
The knowledge he needed he then proceeded to acquire, though he
never spoke correctly, by short but intensive visits to all three coun-
tries. His method was simple. For three holidays running he armed
himself with introductions to one or two of the principal theatres in
Paris, Dresden and later in Rome, hired in each city a shabby actor
to be his body-guard, and worked the wretch from breakfast to midnight. Four hours' sleep was enough for Edmund and so it ought to be
enough for anyone else, said Edmund, asking questions, storing away
answers, thrashing at the strange tongue till it became malleable on his
own. For he was a greedy creature. He did not care what he ate or

drank; but he was greedy for knowledge, the sort of knowledge that he wanted. He even began to learn Norwegian with the same furious ardour with which he hunted whenever one of his rich Wybird cousins gave him a chance and a mount. For Ibsen was half the fashion and though not, in Edmund's opinion, a paying game, was a marvellous purveyor of parts that might some day suit his mother. As he told her, if ever she played in Ibsen she would want him to produce: so it was better to get the hang of the man's mind direct. Besides, every foreign language gave you brand-new ideas.

"I like ideas," said Edmund greedily.

His hobby was music. He had a natural instinct for handling musical instruments and could amuse himself with almost any one to be found in a theatre orchestra, though he excelled in none. And the shabby, vain martyrs beneath the roof of palms were always his friends and made him, as it were, an honorary member of their fraternity. Later he always treated them as part of the company and shared with them the after-excitements and congratulations of his famous first nights. For he never forgot a face or a courtesy and was always charming to people who would answer his questions: and people liked answering them, for he smiled as he asked, was modest, deeply interested, paid a compliment or stood a drink and then asked more questions. There was apparently no method in Edmund's self-education but by the time he was twenty he could hold his own with his cousin Eustace, who had progressed from prep-school to his pleasant rooms at Balliol by an orderly accumulation of scholarships and was modestly sure of a double first. Moreover he appalled his cousin Eustace by embarking on a study of William Shakespeare's plays as rendered by the Schlegel brothers. When Eustace raved out his horror of deliberately helping yourself to silver when you could get gold, Edmund was calm.

"Don't be a cuckoo," said Edmund. "I've heard Shakespeare spouted all my life. How can I tell what he's like? But I tell you it's fine in German. Nice as a new suit. Gives one ideas." Then, placatingly—"Ideas for production, dear feller! Nothing in your line."

For Eustace at that time had not made up his mind, although he was a prop of the recently established O.U.D.S., whether he should adorn the stage or the pulpit or be a trumpet heralding the return of poetic drama to Albion. He thought it low of Edmund to be much more interested in revolving stages.

But the cousins got on very well. They had kept up a not exactly forbidden but unacknowledged intercourse throughout their schooldays, and Edmund occasionally ran up to Oxford to stay with his cousin. Eustace adhered romantically to Edmund, admired him as a man of the world, and in return introduced him to the particular form of æstheticism in vogue at the moment, talked religion and women, unburdened himself of his own emotional troubles, and was disconcerted to find that Edmund for his own part had solved the last of these problems simply enough by inviting a charming, plump young creature to look after his London lodgings; for the Regent's Park house was let. Edmund, for his part, liked to be liked and his cousin's affection, fragile good looks and general inexperience touched him more than a woman's would have done.

But Eustace's real attraction for Edmund lay in the fact that Eustace was the son of his father, for, as Edmund once owned to Eustace, his cousin Stephen had fascinated him as a child and could still stir and trouble his imagination.

"He makes me feel nowadays as Macbeth did about Duncan, Eustace. You know——" And Edmund began rolling out the lines with an unconsciousness that Eustace envied—

> 'Besides, this Duncan
> Hath borne his faculties so meek, hath been
> So clear in his great office that his virtues
> Will plead like angels, trumpet-tongued, against
> The deep damnation of his taking-off.'

"He oughtn't to have been taken off his job, Eustace."

"Edmund, puns stink!"

"Yes, but it is damnable. And he's so decent about it."

"You needn't tell me that," said Eustace: and his face took on that air of distraction which it instantly presented when the wind blew keen in any direction. "But what can I do? I'm no use till I've got my degree. D'you think I want to be up here? But Father insists. What am I to do?"

"Do?" said Edmund: and his square, solid young face, all hard lines under the chubbiness, assumed an expression that hovered between determination, excitement and contempt—"Do?" said he. "If Cousin Stephen were my father——"

"Well, what?" Eustace was petulant.

"I dunno. Oh Lord, what's the good of talking? Of course you're right, Eustace. You get your degree, whatever it is. You're a razor: you've got to be sharpened. And anyway, even then it's no good asking you to hack down trees. But I'm born to hack. I've no fine feelings." He hesitated on the verge of a confidence. Then—"I say, Eustace, do you know at all how Cousin Stephen feels about the lawsuit and the row and all that?"

Eustace made a vague gesture.

"My dear man, he and Mama never talk in front of us. There was a lawsuit, was there? Yes, I knew of it vaguely. But I never heard the details. Mama always said it was nothing for us children to worry about. Of course, money has been tight. But with my scholarships making things easier it would have been crazy not to have come up, wouldn't it?"

"I can't understand," said Edmund, "how you could stand being treated as a child."

"Well, I don't know, Edmund," said Eustace, hurt. "Scholarships take some getting and keeping. I never had time to go to rehearsals and gossip. My duty was to get a first."

"How's your mother?" said Edmund abruptly.

"It can't last much longer," said poor badgered Eustace in a cold voice. But his eyes filled with tears, for he was fond of his mother and Edmund's direct questions always pounded upon his sensitiveness like blows.

"And what will Cousin Stephen do then?" demanded Edmund. "Will it smash him up?"

"I hope not," said the son earnestly. "For the last six months we have known it was ending. And you can't be sorry. For five years now she has been everlastingly drugged to death and then drugged back to life. First the arsenic and then the antidote. It's a ghastly thing, arthritis. You wouldn't think she is only forty, would you?" said Eustace with a choke.

"I haven't seen her since I was twelve."

"No, of course. Well, she's—she's different. It's not her. You'd not know her."

Edmund shuddered.

"Death's a filthy thing. Shall you join your father when— if——"

"Oh, not permanently. I must finish my three years," said Eustace hastily. "Besides, I haven't yet made up my mind, as you know. You see, Edmund, more and more I feel that the Church's need——"

"I don't," said Edmund. "The stage——"

"I loathe the stage," said Eustace suddenly, flushing and violent.

"Are you going down to stay at Cirencester these holidays?" demanded Edmund.

"It depends," said Eustace uncomfortably.

Edmund glanced uncompromisingly at a photograph, signed 'Marian,' on the mantelpiece.

"Depends on whether she's back from Paris, I suppose?"

"Oh, shut up, Edmund!"

"D'you write to each other?"

"Of course we write to each other," returned the goaded Eustace.

"And the Papa's a canon. Yes, I can see why you've deserted the stage."

"I'm not deserting the stage. I haven't made up my mind. I wish to God, Edmund, you'd mind your own business."

"Oh, all right, old man! All right!"

The conversation was only the first of a series, but after it Edmund knew with some certainty that he would not have his cousin Eustace either as a rival or a support.

With this knowledge to back him and being of age or near it, Edmund thought it time to elaborate for his mother's benefit the scheme that had been occupying him since he was seventeen. He was now twenty and had been for some two years his mother's right hand. She trusted him with the knowledge of all her affairs and the conduct of most, and it had been for some months discussed between them whether a second company should be taken out under Edmund's full control, or whether Donna had better become once more her own manager at the New Broom and leave the management of the tour to him. But always they had decided that to import a star would scarcely pay them and that Edmund was still too young to star. But for Edmund's solution of the star difficulty his mother was entirely unprepared.

He opened the matter to her one Monday evening when the company was at Liverpool and she was sitting in her dingy dressing-room with its blistered paint, dirty walls and wire blinds, already dressed for Mrs. Creegan in *The Colleen Bawn*.

She often played the part though it was no lead. The melodramatic harshness of the character suited her and she had the art to carry off the pathetic collapse at the end. Nobody had ever been known to laugh at a melted Donna crying—'Hardress! My boy!' Indeed, Edmund would have liked, for the sheer interest of the thing, to see an audience disrespectful to his mother; but he had no real hope of it.

She had long since lost her youthful insolence, but restlessness in an audience would always anger her, though it was never provoked by her own performance, for she had a perfect power of terrorising her watchers into fascinated attention. She could control them when she was a mere cipher in the scene, and the younglings of her companies loved her for that power; for she would exercise it on their behalf as much as on her own. Poor, lovely, much-divorced Leda Braham played her first lead with the Broomes, and those rather incoherent memoirs of hers are full of reminiscences of Domina in early days when Leda's own ambitions were legitimate and her waist no bigger than a bedpost. She tells one particularly characteristic story—

"Of course she was very severe and frightening; but she was kind to us in a head-mistressy way, and you could always be sure of one thing— however much she slaughtered you at rehearsal she'd always help you out on the night. I remember we were playing once at—well, I won't give away the town for it's been kind to me since; but it had a reputation in those days for treating all actors as Aunt Sallies. We'd put on *Othello* and I was Desdemona. The dress suited me and I won't pretend that I didn't look the part (see the photograph facing page 11) but I had only played it two or three times and I had a bad cold and the Othello wasn't good. He bellowed. Domina Broome, of course was Emilia. Well, it came to my great scene, where I enter with Emilia and Othello calls me names and then orders Emilia to—

'shut the door;
Cough, or cry hem, if any body come——'

Then out she goes and I fall on my knees and he abuses me. But, of course, dear play-goer, you remember the scene. Well, between us we muffed the opening lines. The Othello said afterwards it was my fault. Well, I won't criticise him, poor fellow, for he has long since dropped out of success and is today a box-office keeper in a No. 2 town. I was certainly nervous and my voice did squeak a little, I daresay. It was before I went to dear Lucie Volke for voice producing lessons, and my advice to young people is, if you want to succeed on the stage, look after your voice production. The Volke method is marvellous (see Appendix). Well, to go on with my story. The audience began to laugh at us and cat-call—oh, it was terrifying. The Othello whispered to me to take no notice and went tearing on at the top of his voice—

'Shut the door;
. . . Your mystery, your mystery! nay, dispatch.'

But the more he bellowed the more they went on laughing. Then Emilia, Domina Broome, instead of going out behind us as we had rehearsed, lifted her head and looked first at us and then at the audience, thrusting forward her chin a little. She looked just like one of those swans that come hissing at you over the gunwale of a boat at Stratford. Then she glided forward, not moving fast, and yet she seemed to rush past us, her skirts billowing. It was lovely to watch her move, like the same swan lifting itself on the water to beat its wings, then sliding forward again. When she reached the bar of the footlights she stood there a moment, blazing her eyes at the audience till they quieted. Then, very slowly, she put her finger to her lips, listening, as if the footlights were the door that shut us off and she were guarding it. Oh, it was a wonderful bit of business. She used it often afterwards, and so have other people, but she invented it. Poor Othello and I were so thankful that we nearly cried with relief. I know I did cry outright, for all the notices picked out my crying as the best thing in the show. Of course I always could cry. But I've never cried so comfortably as I did that evening in the lovely attentive silence she created for us. Fortunately Othello kept his head and called to her at the end—'You, mistress,' as if her place by the footlights were the proper door. And in she came between the invisible door-posts and glided back, as much a comfort to me as Emilia must have been to Desdemona.

Afterwards I wanted to thank her, but I didn't have the courage. She was awful to stand up to in her dressing-room : everybody said so."

But everybody did not include Edmund Broome who for the life of him could not understand why the company shook.

"You have only to stand up to Mother and she's as easy——" he would explain to some young, unhappy acquaintance who had to die upon a kiss with Domina Broome gravely critical in the stalls: and would conclude—"Tell her to show you how."

For he had a great respect for his mother as an actress, found her easy to manage and knew that she liked to be chaffed. He admired her, too, because she always treated him as an inexperienced contemporary rather than a son and never bored him with reminiscences of her youth, thirty years past, but enjoyed on the other hand hearing tales of his youth, three years past. Moreover, though she attacked him with vigour when his conduct displeased her, she allowed him the same liberty.

They were not a sentimental mother and son. He was severely 'Edmund' on her lips. He, on the other hand, called her 'Miss

Petowker.' Both kept up the fiction that they two knew all about each
other; but Domina daily stared upon the Medusa fact that a son does
not tell his mother anything at all about himself, and Edmund recognised with curiosity that his mother's character was as difficult to culti-
vate as his uncle Russel's garden. Beneath the few inches of easily
turned loam was hard rock, and beneath the rock—what? Sweet
springs? Silver mines? God knew what!

Well, what did it matter so long as she remained his useful, orna-
mental and manageable mother? But would she, when he broached
his plan?

"Half an hour, please!" The call-boy's bang fell heavy on the door
and Domina roused herself mechanically from her careful contemplation of her completed make-up. She was always finished early. She
liked to prowl about the stage and drop in occasionally to the dressing-
rooms to inspect an apprentice's make-up. She pushed her chair a little
from the table and began to work some wet-white on to her long fingers
as she spoke to her son, lounging on the ancient sofa.

"You'd better go and dress, Edmund."

"Not yet, Mother. It doesn't take me five minutes."

"It should do, Edmund."

"Well, it does as a rule, I swear. How did the show go last week,
Mother?" For he had taken no part in the previous week's performance. He had travelled to Manchester on Broome business, had stayed
several nights, and only rejoined the company that afternoon.

"Fairly. Not a good house. Have you arranged anything with the
Manchester people, Edmund?"

"No, Mother. It's as I thought it would be. Cousin Stephen has
been before us."

Her lips tightened, but she said nothing.

"We do get in each other's way," her son went on, "and that's
a fact. It's astonishing how he draws still, in spite of his company.
For I do think, Mother, that his company is the very worst collection
of incompetents it's ever been my penance to see."

"You watched their show then?" said his mother with a slight
chilled air of surprise at such an unnecessary proceeding. Then continued without a flicker of interest—"How did he play? Is he ageing?
Does it show?"

"Well, he's not so much ageing as looking ill. You know Cousin
Madeleine died last month, I suppose?"

"I told you of it myself," said she, "at the time. Adelaide wrote me."

"Yes, of course you did. Well, I can tell you, it's hit him."

"I expect it has," said she: then added impatiently—"But how did he play?"

"Oh, like a lion. He is rather like a lion, you know, when he flings up his head: a worried lion! You can see the jackals at him. He played in a sort of frenzy. He said—'Damn them all! Well, I've shaken them off for five minutes, so now I'll show what I can do.'"

"What was the play?"

"Clever Kate."

"He's a fool," said Donna angrily. "He's twenty years too old for the part. You ought to be playing it opposite me."

"No, Mama, I won't play big parts: I've told you so before. I'd be an exhibition. I'm a comic. But the point is that Cousin Stephen may be sick and sorry, but he made me cry. Yes, and even made the fools in front cry though they said 'too old' just as you do. Well, of course his body is too old and so is his face; but, Mother, in spite of that he was young: he did convey the burden of being very young and overborne. It was an aching sort of a performance, but most uncommon fine. I don't know how he got his effect. I could never do it even if I had his experience. But though he's sick with experience he is really young, Mother: younger than I am, not grown-up at all. That's what I found out about him. I'm much older than Cousin Stephen already. I'd never have made a fool of myself as he has, fighting you."

"Yes," said Donna to the glass, "he was a fool to fight me."

"And yet," returned Edmund eagerly, "though he is a fool, somehow one doesn't despise him. One wants to look after him and sack half his cast for him, and protect him against the row there'd be. He wants a business manager and a capable one, what's more, too, to take the worry off his shoulders and let him get on with his own job, poor harassed devil! Seems a shame somehow. I say, Mother, I suppose this feud has got to go on?"

"Feud?" said she, rising unnecessarily. And going to her closet she began counting over her dresses, shaking them, re-hanging them, pressing out flounces between finger and thumb. The work kept her back turned to him, and the stuffs billowing about her seemed to deaden and swallow her voice. "Feud? How do you mean, Edmund? Your cousin and I are necessarily business rivals and, as you know, there have been interminable money disputes. Business is business, but feud——!"

"Oh, Mother, don't bluff! Of course it's a feud. You've both had your knives into each other for years. I'm hanged if I see what you get out of it. What do you get out of it, Mother? You must get something."

"It's eat or be eaten. I have my living to earn—and yours," said she.

"Well, Mother, but you're not earning it, are you? We're much worse off than we were five years ago."

"That's the lawsuit," said she hastily.

"I can't see why you ever started those lawsuits."

"No, Edmund, it's not necessary for you to see. But if you had been in my position at that time I think you would have done as I did. And anyway your cousin started the lawsuits, not I."

"Well, he says you forced him."

"*He* says!" At last to his relief she turned her face to him again. "What do you mean—'he says'?" Domina demanded, her eyes beginning to brighten angrily. "What is all this about, Edmund? D'you mean that you've been in touch with Stephen without telling me?"

"Well, Mother, I went round to see him after the show, of course."

"You went round——?"

"Well, but Mother, why shouldn't I? You were just saying that there's no feud and I've always kept in touch with Eustace. You know that. Don't get upset. Let me tell you about it. I liked his acting awfully and as I hadn't seen him for years and as he was always very decent to me when I was a kid, I just thought I'd go round. So I went round."

"Did he see you?"

"Well, of course he saw me. We got on very well. I tell you, Mother, I liked him more than ever. Oh, and he asked after you. He isn't at all bitter. But he's pretty hard up, I think."

"Did he speak of Madeleine?"

"Oh yes. He's a stranded man, Mama. He's got a sister-in-law to look after the girls."

"And Eustace?"

"Eustace is at Oxford still, of course."

"Yes, you see," she said, "Eustace is at Oxford but my son is earning his living."

"Well, I suppose you'd have sent me to Oxford if I'd consented to go, Mother? Anyway, Cousin Stephen's half killing himself to do it."

"He seems to have told you a good deal in one interview."

"Oh, I went round two or three times since——"

"Quarter of an hour, please! Quarter of an hour, please!" The voice of time approached once more.

"You'd better go now. You'll be late. I dislike a hurried make-up."

"Yes, Mother. We'll talk about it afterwards."

"There's nothing to talk about that I can see," said Donna uneasily to her son's departing back.

The door banged.

"Quarter of an hour, please! Quarter of an hour!"

CHAPTER 42

THE PRICE OF PEACE

BUT when the tour was over and they were back in town in the re-opened Regent's Park house, he attacked her again, and again she listened. Any of her friends or enemies, equals or dependents, would have been amazed at the calmness and interest with which she listened. To Geoffrey she had been one of these New Women, not to be broken, best avoided. To Stephen she was one of the Eumenides with a whip of snakes. To her public she was a lesser Mrs. Siddons. To her business associates she was a woman to obey for the sake of peace and quiet: wrong-headed, but not to be resisted. To Adelaide she was 'darling, eccentric Donna' who would look ten years younger if she would only take life more easily and spend two hours over her morning toilet, and wear her hair as everyone else did, fringed on the top. But to all, whether they loved her or hated her, she was an indomitable, unreasonable creature, flailing her way through life, and successful, not because of her reason, but because of her sheer destructive force of character.

But her son had always found her reasonable, and he considered himself lucky to have escaped other men's mothers, fluffy, be-ribboned, sweet. He was himself so headstrong that his mother's similar characteristics had no effect upon him, at least, no demoralising effect. He did not find her intimidating, overwhelming or maddening. He took her strength, her forcefulness, her power of quick decision and quick action for granted because he himself possessed these qualities and so found it natural that she, too, should possess them. The two, in fact, lived on the same plane and at the same pace and so they were comfortable with each other, the only two normal human beings in a world eccentrically slow and flabby. No, indeed, there was nothing violent or unreasonable or overbearing in his mother! She was a usable woman: he found her easy to talk to, easy to convince and persuade, full of understanding. Moreover she had been longer in the world than he, had lived a lot and learnt a lot. It was a comfort to have her experience to draw upon, though as an actress her methods were growing a little old-fashioned and he thought that she had too many prejudices and that she did not sufficiently appreciate Geoffrey Angers.

Edmund did not intend to let the divorce affect his own good understanding with his father. But these failings of his mother's, thought
Edmund, could be well enough borne. At a pinch he would point
them out to her. He would certainly pay for it by having to listen to a
certain amount of advice in return; but then he liked her advice. It was
generally sound; for his mother was like a man, though she had female
prejudices. She had an especially absurd prejudice against his cousin
Stephen, for instance. Now that he was himself a man, said Edmund,
it was time that something should be done about this obsession of his
mother's. It was undignified: it was unreasonable: it was expensive.

"You see, Mother, we are losing money. We've lost far too much
money: and I can't for the life of me see that it was necessary. But
you're so lavish, Mother, in your likes and dislikes."

"Edmund, I believe I give you far too much freedom. It's not
many sons of twenty who are allowed to pry into their elders' money
affairs."

"No, Mother. But you have brought me up to look on all this as my
inheritance, haven't you now? You know perfectly well that you've
only been waiting for me to grow up, and that you won't be satisfied—
no more shall I, for that matter—till we're back in London management again."

"Yes," said she, and her dark eyes flashed from their dark hollows as
if two swords were suddenly drawn. "Yes, when you put on your first
play as an independent London manager, independent even of me, then
I shall have done my work in the world, Edmund. Then I shall be
ready to go home."

"Yes, Mother, that's very noble and effective. But all this touring
round the provinces isn't helping us. We're paying expenses and we're
living, but we're piling up no capital. And I'll tell you why. We're
not capitalising our name. Cousin Stephen's for ever cutting us
out."

"My dear Edmund, we more than cut out Stephen in return. For
every penny we lose he loses a shilling."

"Yes, but Mother, why lose a penny or a shilling? Why did Grandpapa and Uncle Russel succeed as they did? Because they knew how to
combine. They played into each other's hands. I tell you there ought
not to be two Broome companies on tour in the same sort of plays,
cutting each other's throats. Or if there are two companies they ought
to be linked under one management. You know, Mother, if you and
Cousin Stephen were in partnership, and if you'd each of you sack a

business manager and let me represent you both, we'd soon be back in London. Now look here, Mother, this is my scheme. I've been at it for weeks."

And he hauled a note-book from his pocket and dragged her down to a chair beside him : and for the next twenty minutes was pouring out facts and figures, reducing salaries, scheming circuits, giving a lecture upon the whole art of touring with profit in eighteen-ninety-one. He ended with—

"You see, Mother, it's no use telling me what Uncle Russel did thirty years ago. That's why businesses smash, because the old stagers will keep on saying—'when I was in the ark we did so-and-so.' No, Mother, I don't mean to be rude. Of course your experience is invaluable. You always said when I was twenty-one you would hand over the whole concern to me. Well, that's a year off still. But I swear to you though, that when I am twenty-one this is what I shall do—I shall go straight across to Cousin Stephen. So why not let me go now instead of frittering away another year ? Lord, I know I'm young. I haven't the experience to run this thing alone. But with you, Mother, backing me instead of fighting me, it could be done—I swear it could. Mother, it's a chance of a lifetime and in another year it will be too late. Cousin Stephen will have smashed."

Her eyes shone.

"I'd like to see that ending. I'd like to see your cousin smashed, crashed, wiped off the stage, wiped out of the history of the theatre."

"Oh yes, Mother, I know all about that. He crabbed your curtain or did you out of a laugh or something when you and he were both sixteen. I know ! Yes, we're a vindictive lot, and proud of it. But oh bother, Mother, this isn't twenty years ago, this is today. God, I wish I could make you see what an opportunity it is ! You can hate my Cousin Stephen as much as you like, and he can hate you——"

"Does he ?" said she quickly.

"Well, he won't discuss you, naturally. But he ain't exactly warm and cheerful when you're mentioned. But what I'm trying to say is— you can hate each other as much as you like so long as you don't mix me up in it. It has nothing to do with me. What does concern me is my chance of going into management. If you and Cousin Stephen could only be brought to see where your real advantage lies !"

"You don't know what you're asking, Edmund."

"Yes, I do. I'm asking you not to be sentimental."

She gave him an odd, furious, girlish look.

"How dare you, Edmund?"

"Sentimental, I said, Mother."

"It's not. I'm not. If you knew what you are talking about——And, Edmund, you shouldn't talk to me as if I were your own age, as if you knew as much about life as I do."

"Well, Mother, I know as much about modern life as you do."

"Yes, that's true," she said reasonably.

He got up very deliberately, came across to her, put his arms round her neck and kissed her. It was a rare gesture for him. They were not an emotional mother and son.

"Dearest Mother, I've set my heart on this."

"I know, Edmund."

"Well, Mother, what about it? You see the sense of it, don't you?"

"Oh yes, I see the sense of it."

"Well, Mother, will you meet Cousin Stephen?"

"He won't meet me."

"That's what he said."

"Oh, so you've talked to him already?"

"Of course, Mother! I crack the soft nuts first."

"Edmund, Edmund!" Donna protested, but her tone was fond and she laughed as he meant that she should. She could not resist her son. She loved strength and respected it. It was about the only quality in man or woman that she did respect: and her own son, her own making, was the strongest human being she had ever encountered, stronger than her father because he had so little imagination, stronger than herself because she loved him so much. She looked at him, her eyes running over his physical strength and delighting in it as her ears delighted in his easy decided tones, and her face told him that he was winning.

"Well, Mother? Come, Mother!"

"If I meet him, Edmund, what do you want me to do?"

"Back me, Mother, whatever I say."

"I should always do that, Edmund, whatever I was feeling."

"And—and be kind to Cousin Stephen. I say, Mother, what did you have the row about?"

"You told me to stick to the present, Edmund."

"I say, Mother, don't be meek."

"Well, dear boy, you're taking things out of my hands, aren't you? You've presented me with a criticism of the last twenty years of my life and you have told me quite kindly and definitely that I managed it very badly."

"Don't be unfair," said Edmund impatiently.

"I'll try not to be." Then, because she could not bear to see him frown—"Oh, Edmund, do you want this so much?"

"Well, Mother," said he, brightening into confidences because he felt her resistance weakening sentence by sentence—"you see it's in some sort a—a test of me—of my power to get my own way. If I can make you and Cousin Stephen do what I want, I shall be, it seems to me, pretty sure that I'm on the right lines."

"What for, Edmund?"

"For making everyone else do what I want, of course. Mother, I do want my life to be a huge success. Mastery—that's the greatest thing in life. Mastery. I want to master everybody."

"And if you meet someone you can't master, Edward, sooner or later?"

He frowned.

"I'd beat him somehow."

"Suppose you couldn't?"

"Oh, how I'd hate him."

"I don't hate you, Edmund, though you generally get me to give in to you."

"Well, if you didn't I should hate you, Mother."

"Oh, my son!"

"I should."

"Edmund, if one day your son said the same thing to you——?"

"My own son? I should see that he kept his place."

"Pooh! You'll be proud of him as I am of you."

"I'd like to see a son of mine try it on, that's all." He laughed. "I'd break him. Then I'd build him up again. But first I'd break him."

"Yet I don't want to break you, Edmund, though you are too much for me."

"Ah yes, but that's because we agree, Mother. We agree so well. You know well enough that you think as I do about this business. So make an end of it, Mother! Do what I want. You're only making objections, you know, to amuse yourself."

She folded her hands, smiling, bitter, submissive.

"Very well, Edmund! Make an appointment. But I won't go to your cousin's house."

He laughed.

"And he said he wouldn't come to Regent's Park. Childish, I call it."

"Oh no. It's just that you don't understand your cousin."

"Yes, well, they say these little things count. I can't see why. But we can meet at the lawyer's if that pleases you both. Mother, I'm awfully grateful to you, really I am. There's no-one in the world like you. I do admire you, Mother. Mother, you're a marvel, a marvel, a marvel! Oh, I'm half mad with excitement." And he gave her the hug of a schoolboy.

A week later he dashed into her room whilst she was still dressing, the morning post in his hands.

"Mother, it's fixed. They come up from Birmingham on the ten o'clock train. He'll meet us at half past three."

"Dear boy, I have my appointment at half past three for the new dresses."

"Oh, damn, they've got to go. Half past three, Mother! Can't you fit earlier? I'll call for you in Long Acre."

And at a quarter past three he was waiting for her outside the theatrical costumier's a street or two away from the Glory Hole.

The narrow dingy street was all but impassable, for Covent Garden Market, like a woman tiring half way through her spring cleaning, goes to sleep early in her emptied house, and leaves her goods to choke all the lanes and alleys for a quarter of a mile in all directions during the rest of the day. The confusion of coster barrows, wheeled crates of fruit and flowers, huge vans with dray-horses and swinging backs, hurrying market-folk, burly flower women, was increased by the hansoms in search of short cuts to the Glory Hole, the Opera, the Lyceum or to the lodging houses and innumerable private burrows of the theatre conies. Out of such a burrow—and it had once been a lord's house—came Domina Broome. She groped her way down the vast musty darkness of the grand staircase, but caught her trailing skirt on the broken last step, half fell, clutched at the balustrade end and so saved herself from a downright tumble. But she wrenched her arm badly, and came out into the bright spring daylight rather white, rather shaken, and was glad of Edmund's help into the waiting hansom.

Once in, with the apron shut upon them, she lay back, curiously unnerved, her lip trembling. She had so wanted to be alert and in full control of herself, but she could not help her lip trembling from the silly fall. She leant back and closed her eyes, letting herself be soothed by the easy springy motion of the hansom. Edmund watched her in some anxiety.

"I say, Mother, you do look white. You didn't really hurt yourself? Mother, you'd better have a nip of my brandy."

He fished out a flask and made her lift her veil and drink, which she did, between chattering teeth. The spirit did its work. She was soon herself again, enough herself at least to say worriedly—

"I'm not being critical, Edmund, but you do only keep brandy for emergencies, don't you?"

He laughed.

"It's all right, Mother."

"Yes, my son. But you know about your Uncle Russel?"

"What about him? You don't grudge him his cakes and ale, do you?"

"I do. He sacrificed his career to his cakes and ale. I despise him for it. And yet I shouldn't, Edmund. We're all like your uncle in our different ways. We all of us, Edmund, do everything to excesss——"

She broke off. "I don't know why I'm talking like this."

"No, I've never seen you so upset. You're to drink some more, Uncle Russel or no Uncle Russel."

"You must be the exception to us, Edmund."

"All right, old lady! Put it down, dear!"

She drank again and felt better, though his solicitude did more for her than the spirit. She was her usual dignified cold self when they arrived. They entered, were greeted, transacted their preliminary business with their solicitor, and were then ushered into the room that had been placed at their disposal for the conference.

Stephen Broome rose and came across to them, and, half hesitating, held out his hand to Domina. She took it limply without looking at him. Nevertheless she was watching him closely, seeing the alteration in his face and thinking that they had not met for five years.

"Well, Domina, how are you?"

"Tired, Stephen." Her hand still lay in his. "And you?"

"Yes, I'm tired too," said he, "tired out."

"You have had much trouble," said she, "since I saw you. I am sorry for your loss."

"Thank you, Donna."

"And your children?"

"My eldest girl is married. The other three are at home. Eustace is still at Oxford as I expect you know. Where will you sit?" And he pulled up a chair for her.

She put her hand upon its back, then glanced uneasily about the room as if she were trapped. It was a noble room, long but narrow, with tall, tightly shut windows and heavy curtains of bottle-green plush that hung from brass curtain poles and swept the brilliant Turkey carpet. Framed engravings of dead and gone legalities hung upon the green walls. The long committee room table which ran down the room was made of yellow mahogany: so was the woodwork of the green leather chairs. A clock in a black marble case ticked out the minutes loudly.

"Sit down, Mother!" said Edmund, coming round to her.

So they sat down: Stephen with his back to the clock, Donna opposite with Edmund beside her. Their lawyer, who had been a crony of Harry's, was unofficial godfather to Stephen and Donna, took the chair at the top of the table and opened with a little friendly speech lauding the past glories of the Broomes, deploring the late eclipse, and expressing his own disinterested pleasure at the present truce. That done he began to outline the terms of the proposed agreement. Donna declared herself satisfied: so did Edmund.

It was from Stephen that the objections came. To the general surprise he fought the conditions clause by clause, quibbled, argued, demanded last-minute explanations, made last-minute stipulations, behaved with the unreasonableness of a man who has no good objection to make but who hopes to create an opportunity for objecting to a particular injustice by an air of general discontent. The experienced lawyer, however, chivvied Stephen patiently and victoriously from clause to clause, while Edmund watched with eager unrestrained excitement, and Domina did not watch at all till it came to signing.

Domina signed. So did Edmund. Stephen took up his pen, dipped it, hovered over the paper, looked up at them, flung down his pen again and got up, agitated.

"I can't do it," said he. "I won't do it. It's signing away Eustace's birthright."

"My dear Cousin Stephen——" began Edmund.

"Yes, it is, I tell you!" Stephen Broome spoke to Donna as if she alone in the room were answerable or accusing. "I've tried to blind my eyes to it; but here it's written down clear enough: and I won't do it, Donna! If the boy here is my partner, that's well enough. But what about Eustace? If I die first is Edmund going to take Eustace into partnership?"

Domina flushed and lifted her eyebrows.

"This isn't a philanthropic arrangement, Stephen. If I stand out of this, if I give up my control of the whole management to Edmund, you must match my sacrifice. If Edmund and you choose to take in Eustace later, that's another matter; but it's clear that Eustace is useless to us at present. You know that. You chose to send him up to Oxford. Edmund has learnt his trade while he was a child. Eustace hasn't. I don't question your judgment, Stephen. You've probably done the best thing for your son. But if Edmund becomes your partner you can't expect him to promise Eustace a berth because he's your son and a Broome."

"I've got to look after my own son," muttered Stephen.

"Certainly! Recoup your losses and devote your profits to the care of Eustace. But don't ask me to step out of management in order to make room for Eustace. I won't do it."

"No, that's all right, Mama," said Edmund hastily. "Nobody's asking you to do it."

"He is. Don't humour me, Edmund! I know your cousin Stephen. He has always been out for what he can get."

Stephen turned from his agitated contemplation of the ink-stand and the years dropped from him as if he were on the stage. His eyes flashed and he rushed into an answer.

"You of all people, Donna, have no right to make me that reproach. You were always a good bargainer yourself."

"If I was a good bargainer," said she furiously, "at least I stuck to my bargains. I paid my debts. Can you say the same, Stephen?" Then, to her anxious son—"No, Edmund! Don't stop me! Let him answer!"

But at this moment came a knock at the door, and she held up her anger and Stephen his answer while a clerk entered and whispered to the lawyer. The old gentleman rose with a comical air of relief.

"I must beg you to excuse me—a matter of ten minutes. I shall not be longer. Meanwhile a little private talk between you three will clear the air. And Donna, my dear, and you Stephen, listen to an old friend and an old fox, too. It must be give and take, you know, give and take between the poultry and the farmer's wife, or else my profession grows too fat, eh? Ha-ha! Excuse me!" And he whisked out.

"Come and sit down," said Edmund, rising and going to his cousin: and Stephen sat down again half willingly, saying with the affectionate note which always came into his voice when he spoke to Edmund—

"I'm sorry to be obstructive, my boy." Then he drew the agreement to him and began to study it anew. Edmund pulled in a chair to his side and sat, his elbows on the table, his head in his hands, whispering confidentially at the older man's elbow, pointing out to him the run of a clause. But Donna, who had also risen, continued to stand at the other side of the table, the tips of her fingers playing on the polished yellow surface, watching both men and listening to Edmund's persuasive voice.

"But look here, Cousin Stephen, you've got the whole business wrong. If we go into partnership, then the two sides of the family unite. Later, if we make money, if we win back the old position, you can do what you like about my cousin. You know I'm fond of him: I'd be only too glad if he wants to join us and is any sort of use. But there's no point in thinking about him at the moment. This business of a partnership between you and me is profitable to both of us. But to drag in Eustace, inexperienced, without capital, is fantastic. It has nothing to do with common sense."

The elder man looked at the younger with a smile that said—'How young you are! How hard you are!' Then, with a sudden shining out in manner, look, smile, intonation of his worn but unexhausted charm, he appealed to his young cousin—

"Edmund, you mustn't blame me. When you are my age you'll feel differently about things. After forty you don't work for yourself any more. You shift on your ambitions to the next generation. Ask your mother: she'll tell you the same." And he lifted his head with an odd and momentary hesitation and with a—'Can I? May I? Dare I?' and smiled his appeal at Domina Broome. Edmund, glancing casually at his mother, was amazed to see her flushing, as she answered gravely, without acidity—

"Yes, the centre of interest shifts."

"There, listen to your mother, Edmund! She feels the same. And because she does she is ready to hand over her inheritance to you. Can't you conceive that I feel the same way about Eustace? I cling to the name. I cling to the remnants of prestige for him. That's why I sent him to Oxford. I couldn't give him the stage training that your mother has given you because my company is third-rate while yours is still first-rate. But I've pinched to help him at Oxford. I've pinched to give him another sort of training. And all the while I've waited for the day when he'd come to me as you've come and say—'Now then, Father, I'm coming in with you!' Am I to say to him—'There's no room. I've done a deal with your cousin.' "

Edmund leant back patiently.

"But that isn't the point, Cousin Stephen. The point is that if we join up now we may recover. If we go on separately it's just Kilkenny cats."

Stephen repeated, with the obstinacy of a tired man—

"I want to work with my son."

It was deadlock and Edmund knew it, and throwing up his hands with a gesture of despair he turned to his mother. His look said—'It's no use. I'm beaten. I didn't expect this. Can you do anything? But no, how can you do anything?'

If she saw his look she did not answer it. She was still standing as she had stood during the discussion, staring down at Stephen while her fingers played their five-finger exercises on the table. She was frowning: her look was fixed and dark. Suddenly she gave a quick glance at Edmund's distracted face, then returned to her study of Stephen, flushed, obstinate, ashamed of his sudden rush of emotion.

"There's your son," said Donna slowly, in a loud voice.

"What?"

The two figures facing her moved with the same twist of the head, the same sudden sharp movement of the whole body.

"What, Donna? What, Donna?" cried Stephen in a voice as loud and as high as hers.

"Father—son. Son—father!" said Donna slowly: turned from them and found herself repeating, still in that high, unnatural voice—"Alice —mutton. Mutton—Alice. Waiter, remove that——" began to laugh, began to cry: then, for the first and last time in her life, collapsed into a chair in a fit of good, loud, old-fashioned hysterics.

The men stared at each other. Edmund was red as fire, but Stephen's face was grey and his lip trembled.

"Get her some water," said Stephen at last, in a voice that Edmund scarcely recognised. But he was glad to obey an older voice and hurried out of the room to blunder down a long passage and break in upon a conference or two until he found a clerk to direct him.

When he returned with the water, however, his mother had stopped her laughing and crying, though she took the glass from him and drank eagerly. Neither of the men spoke till she had put down her glass. Then Edmund said, hesitating—

"Mother——"

"Talk to him, Stephen," said Donna.

Stephen turned from the hearth where he had been standing, his arms on the mantelpiece, staring at the clock, but still he said nothing.

"Cousin Stephen——" Edmund's voice was fierce.

"Well?" said Stephen's gesture, not his voice.

"Well, is there any——?   Could——?   Is this true?"

Still Stephen said nothing.   The urgent clock and Donna's long sigh were the only sounds in the room.

Suddenly Stephen came back to the table, picked up the quill, and stooping to the deed of partnership, signed it.

CHAPTER 43

A NEW BROOME SWEEPS CLEAN

IT WAS three years before Edmund took a holiday, and later in his career he would insist that those years were the happiest in his life. They were certainly the most successful. The spectacular triumphs of his maturity could not compare, for sheer weight of achievement, with the work he did for himself and his partner between his twentieth and his twenty-third birthdays. But then, as he himself confessed, never again would he find such a partner as Stephen.

For Stephen, once convinced of his own paternity, surrendered utterly to his son, thereby bewildering Domina Broome. She had thought for twenty years of telling Stephen the truth one day, and her strange, blighting dreams had always ended in a determination to refrain from revealing the secret, not because of the blow that it would be to Stephen, but because of the blow that it would be to Edmund. This absorbed woman lived eternally twenty years ahead or twenty years behind time, but never in the present day. This imperfect judge of human nature always measured other people's signs of feelings by her own signs of feeling. But now she had to recognise that Edmund either felt nothing or controlled himself better than she could have done at his age. She could detect no sign of trouble in his face. He treated the story, when in those first embarrassing hours the subject needed discussion, as a fact, even a useful fact, certainly an odd fact: and for half an hour made his mother feel that he was uncomfortable with her and vaguely disapproving. But he would show no other sign of feeling.

In point of fact he was embarrassed. There is nothing so shocking to the young as the knowledge that their elders are feeling as they do or have felt as they do. Edmund had a very keen realisation of the indecency of the whole affair, and resolutely turned away his eyes from the spectacle of his upholstered, middle-aged mother and his tired, ineffectual, middle-aged cousin, blooming and tremulous, alive and in love with each other. There was nothing to be done about it and nothing need be said about it. It certainly made it a great deal easier for him in dealing with Cousin Stephen—his father, that is to say. But he could not be expected to be full of feeling about the business any more than he could think of Stephen as his father. All he could do was to drop the 'cousin'. They were 'Guv'nor' and 'my boy' to each other from that day on: and from that day on, too, he formally took the name 'Edmund Broome.' And with that Edmund allowed the matter to run from his consciousness. He had always liked Stephen immensely. Well, now there was a reason for it. Leave it at that!

But the dismantling of Donna's secret had another effect upon Stephen. Like all the Broomes Stephen was the passionate lover and advancer of his children, so long as they were beautiful and successful. But the little girls, nice children, had no particular talent or beauty: and his eldest boy, delicately handsome, willing, industrious, all that a son should be, was yet a dependent creature: and Stephen so wanted a prop. As he owned to Edmund in that naked hour of recognition, he had had his dreams of a magnificent Eustace breaking into the management with—"Come along, Father! It's you and me now!" He would have so loved to be support-in-reserve to his own son, to lay his experience and his careful knowledge at the service, not only of ardour and modernity, but of that inspiration which, jumping his own generation, must surely reappear in his son.

But Eustace did everything he was told to do and nothing he was not told to do: and Stephen was lonely and stranded. Stephen may have been fretted by his uncle's mastery, his unreasonable eccentricities of judgment, his gambler's throws and over-ruling decisions; but oh, how he had missed Harry's mastery. "Of course when Eustace joins me——" But Eustace was still at Oxford and daily more absorbed by religion and the Canon's daughter. What should Stephen do if Eustace decided to go into the Church?

It was that secret fear of Eustace's secession which had hardened his heart against the partnership with the interloping Broome, Edmund. But the interloper, it now appeared, was his own son—"Come along, Father, it's you and me now!" Could such good indeed come out of that unforgotten, regretted evil? Stephen could not believe it, but found it nevertheless a comfortable miracle. And as he looked at his son whom he had always liked and now was ready to love, as he listened to him and felt the vigour of the boy's personality penetrating his own fatigue, he abandoned himself to the control of a stronger nature with the simplicity and completeness that was part of his own nature and part, too, of his charm.

Yes, after twenty years, that long disused charm began to work again on his son. It was not long before Edmund would do anything for Stephen, and if he ruled him always made sure that Stephen should ask to be ruled. And be sure that Stephen asked. Stephen so thankfully surrendering his accounts and his debts, his negotiations, schemes and failures to his ridiculously young and ridiculously efficient son, comforted his own pride by saying—"Tom Robertson wrote *London Assurance* before he was twenty. And look at Sheridan! Age has nothing to do with it. It's time we gave the youngsters a look in."

And, extravagant in surrender, would have abdicated utterly, would have become indeed a cipher in sheer relief, content and pride if Edmund had allowed it. But Edmund, with his uncanny shrewdness, had seen, as he had told his mother long before, that Stephen's trouble was due to the fact that the job he couldn't do was stealing all his energy from the job he could do. So he took all the cares he could off Stephen's shoulders, in order, as he told him plainly, that Stephen should devote himself to his own work. Stephen had been a star in London and was still a star in the provinces. Well then, let him shine and not be so sentimental about the second-rates in the company.

"But she's been with me twenty years, Edmund!"

"Yes, I know! That's why you can't give her parts that suit a girl of twenty. She shall play the governess and if she doesn't like it she shall go. Don't you know that I'm right?"

"Yes, my boy, you're right enough. But after all these years I can hardly tell her——"

"I'll tell her."

Thus was the company weeded ruthlessly and new plants bedded in. And, relieved of monetary cares and given proper material it was wonderful how quickly Stephen recovered poise and tone. His acting improved: so did his looks. The company and the tour prospered, and there came a day when his firm son said to him after a long evening at the back of the gallery—"Tell you what it is, Guv'nor, you're casting yourself too old."

And with that half-laughing utterance Edmund had suddenly seen his way clear to a policy. He had not been idle in the early days of the partnership. With a shrewdness and a tenacity astonishing in so young a creature he had devoted himself, not to his own direct aggrandisement, but rather to the grooming of his lion and the re-equipment of its cage. Now at last it was ready for its London public. Well, it must be got to London. How? It must not be a hole and corner return. Money must be spent if money were to flow in. All very well, but he had not any money to spend! Then somebody else must spend for him.

He said nothing of his dreams or of this conclusion, but suddenly felt the need of a holiday, suddenly explained to his mother that he wanted to see what had been happening on the American stage in the last ten years, suddenly felt that one or other of the Broomes ought to look up dear old Uncle Russel. Everybody at once told him how right he was; for everyone, even his mother, was accustomed to thinking Edmund brilliantly right. He nodded agreement with the general verdict and took the next boat.

Stephen fretted and the company got out of hand in the two months of his absence, but his mother remained serene. She always sympathised with Edmund's sudden hankering for change. New scenes cured one of brooding, said Donna. Even the smallest change was valuable. By reopening the Regent's Park house she had put an end to one entanglement. Home was more convenient than lodgings and the prettiest housekeeper, and Edmund was a practical young man. This sudden journey to America might put an end as easily to a second, most undesirable budding affair with a girl in her own theatre. Donna was far too wise to dismiss soft, languishing Nesta Marshall as coolly as she had dismissed the pretty housekeeper, but she did not urge good parts upon her and intended to send her touring as soon as might be. Meanwhile this fancy of Edmund's for travel was an excellent thing. She hoped he would stay away six months.

Edmund stayed away less than a third of that time: but he did not return with his tail between his legs. He appeared extremely well and well satisfied, in brilliant spirits and, his mother being wise enough to refrain for a whole fortnight from asking a single question, he was soon breaking into allusions, half-confidences, and at last settled down with her to a cards-on-the-table discussion of his plans. And all Edmund's plans, it seemed, centred round Stephen.

"But don't you see, Mother, if I get the Guv'nor back to London he's got to have a professional beauty playing opposite, so that he can make love. He's only forty-three and the public's wild after the middle-aged lover type of play. You know—grey at the temples, experienced, disillusioned, and then the beauty takes him instead of the juvenile! Look how handsome the Guv'nor is still. He's only got to walk across the stage and crook his finger and all the women moan and moo! Oh, I know you never come to see him, but you should, Mother. You won't know him. I've nursed him, I can tell you, in every kind of way. I've even run him up a bill at his tailor's that frightened him. Oh, I do see my way clear. But at the moment the question is—who is the right leading lady for him? She needn't act. He'll attend to that. But she's got to look like Lily Langtry and she must have a thrilling voice. An amateur would do if I could spot one. I've been putting in spare time at every amateur show from Putney to Blackheath since I've been back. But the Gaiety nobbles all the pretty girls. But there's time still, and I've got half a dozen likely plays. And I think, Mother, that now's the time to quit the provinces and start again in town, don't you? Hang it, I've been ground-baiting for three years: now's the time to drop in the float. I'm sure of it. But I've got to find a leading lady first. I suppose there's no-one coming on at the New Broom?"

For Donna was once more managing on the Surrey side. She shook her head.

"I've got two or three with looks but none with the accent," said she. "There's Nesta Marshall, of course."

Edmund, always ruddy, took the thrust without a perceptible change of colour; but he was annoyed. He had not been sure that his mother knew anything about the latest entanglement. He did not object to her knowing, but she might have told him sooner that she knew.

"It's obvious Nesta Marshall won't do," said he coolly.

"Have you seen her since you came back?" asked his mother equally coolly. But she got no change.

"Oh, I see her sometimes," said Edmund easily.

"You haven't—" murmured Domina with a sharp look at him— "any unbusinesslike idea of marrying her, I suppose?"

He found nothing to say to that; but he furiously resented the question.

"For I think she hopes," said Donna, "and waits, and I daresay says her prayers about it." And there was feeling in her voice. She had not any intention of letting Edmund be foolish, and she did not think it likely that he would let himself be foolish, nevertheless she remembered her youth.

"Hope? Oh no, she doesn't," returned Edmund comfortably. "We understand each other, Nesta and I." Then he looked up at his mother's inscrutable face—"What are you driving at, dear? You're not suggesting that I've got to marry every girl that—O Lord, on tour!" And then irritably—"What are you thinking about, Mother? I never know what you are thinking."

"I think about women—and men—and time—and you," said Donna vaguely. "Don't be on the defensive with me, Edmund. You needn't be afraid that I should ever interfere with you. But Edmund——"

"Well, what, Mother?"

"If you can contrive to imagine how women feel and think, and how they suffer over trifles, it will help you in your business."

"Poor Nesta is easy enough to read," said he.

"Yes, but all women aren't poor Nestas. Well, go on! Tell me the rest of your business. What is all this about Lewis Wybird? You seem to have made an impression."

"How do you know?"

"Adelaide was staying with me the week before you came back. She sees a great deal of Lewis, you know, and he seems to have seen a great deal of you before your holiday. You never told me."

"Do say he's a nice friend for me, Mother!"

"What's in your mind, Edmund?"

"Can't you guess?"

"The Glory Hole?"

"There or thereabouts."

"Oh, my child, will he let you have it?"

"Well, he isn't very well satisfied with the present management. I know that much. And the sub-let falls in at the beginning of June."

"The Glory Hole in June and the Genista in September? It's too much, Edmund. Don't run before you can walk."

"Oh, I should re-let the Glory Hole at once on a short lease. There are several nibblers."

"Lewis isn't a fool. Why should he let you have it rather than the rest of them?"

"Well, I've made him the longest offer. I'm prepared to renew on a rising scale for as long as he likes. Seven—fourteen—twenty-one years, if he likes and another ten years after that, as long as the first five years are cheap. And that suits his book. He's not a gambler. I am. It'll be all my risk."

"Yes, that's what worries me. You know, my child, I'm behind you to the extent of the Irish property, but I don't see Lewis Wybird being satisfied with that—or any bank."

"Well, Mother, he'll have the deeds of the Genista."

"The Genista?" She stared at him. The truth dawned on her. "Edmund, you haven't been getting hold of Uncle Russel?"

"Yes, I have. That's my news. Uncle Russel's backing me. Well, why shouldn't he? He's got more money than he knows what to do with. And he's so pleased with——" He broke off abruptly.

"With what, Edmund?"

He met her eye uncertainly.

"Mother, you'll hate this."

"What have you been doing, Edmund?"

"Nothing, Mother, except—Well, you know Uncle Russel was always talking about his will. He's worse than ever now: always shilly-shallying about who's to have the money, and who's to have the Genista, and whether it ought to go to me as Grandpapa's heir or to Stephen as Uncle Robin's son: and then off into long stories about Robin and Harry, and Harry and Robin, and all the rest of the family. Sentimental old boy! He lives entirely in the past, you know; but he's as hard as nails when it comes to business. He wouldn't lend me a farthing at first—said I should have my share when he was gone and that the Guv'nor and I were to share and share alike. Well, then I said—wouldn't he lend me mine now? Because he doesn't use it, you know. He lives like a farmer. But no, he wouldn't, because if his investments went down where would Stephen be then, eh, eh? You know the way he jerks at you sideways."

"Well?"

"Well, I thought he'd better know that whether he lent it to me or left it to the Guv'nor didn't really amount to a row of beans: that it was the same thing, so to speak."

"You told your great-uncle, Edmund? You told him——"

"Only what you told me, Mother. I had to."

"You had to tell him about me and—and Stephen? You had to tell him that you—that you— Have you no shame, Edmund?"

"Why, Mother, it seemed to me reasonable. And when I talked it over with the Guv'nor he thought so too."

"And it didn't occur to any of you that my feelings needed considering?"

"Well, I asked the Guv'nor if it was all right, and he said that it wasn't a story to shout about the green-room, but after all it was as much his affair and mine as yours, and that Uncle Russel had always been good to him and he had no objection to his knowing."

"I'll never forgive you, Edmund."

He began to get angry.

"I don't think you've any right to say that to me, Mother. Good God—forgive! I've got something to forgive, I think, if it comes to that. It's not a pleasant word—illegitimate. And for that matter, Mother, if you will have plain speaking, I'm fond of the Guv'nor, and I do think you've been a devil to him. And to Father, too—to Geoffrey Angers, I mean. I can't stop thinking of him as my father because you sprang this on me when it happened to suit you. Forgive! You're quite right, I know nothing about clever women's minds. You've been too clever for me and the Guv'nor all along. And then you fling up at me poor simple Nesta Marshall. I'm all for simple women, I can tell you: and when I marry I shall take care I marry a simple creature like poor Nesta. I'm not going to bring up other men's children."

"Oh, my God!" said Donna under her breath: and she put her hands to her temples and stared upon her son and there was a sort of horror in her face.

But Edmund was in the full flight of rage and could not stop himself. He had taken the revelation of his parentage lightly enough on the surface. He would have said that he had put the very memory of it behind him. Nevertheless there was a part of himself of which he was scarcely conscious which had not taken it lightly. The shock had been far greater than he realised. His affection for his mother and his intense respect for her, his feeling for his putative father, his queer delight in having two homes, his sense of being master and controller of his own fate in each—all these prides had been uprooted from his consciousness and the holes still ached as if teeth had been torn out. And because he had discussed these wounds with no-one, and had scarcely allowed himself to think of them, they remained unhealed, festering. Then had come the strain of the American visit. It had been no easy thing for Edmund to discuss his own illegitimacy with his great-uncle: and when he had to think of going down to Geoffrey whom he loved and telling him the truth, he found that he could not go. He could not tell Geoffrey the truth. And Geoffrey's hurt, reproachful letters did not make Edmund feel gentler towards his mother. It was not to be expected that he should have much sympathy for her, that his own sense of disgrace should give him any understanding of hers. On the contrary, he was near hating her as he stood in the library of the Regent's Park house, despising, disbelieving, and altogether rejecting as mere stage emotion the outrage and pain her face expressed.

For she had, he felt, no right to any sense of injury. All the injury was his. He would not budge from what he had said: he meant every word and now he had done. Let the next word come from her and if it did not come, well, why should he care?

But she said nothing: and presently, with a sudden, inarticulate cry of impatience, he turned abruptly and went out of the library.

What did Donna do?

Stared after him and cried "Edmund!" under her breath: and when the door closed sat a long while waiting for his return. But he did not return. She sat in the room for the rest of the Sunday peace, afraid to leave it lest he should return and not find her. For of course he would return and they would be reconciled. She pulled out books and read meaningless words, and put them back in their places. Supper-time brought a maid and she had to speak—"Oh! Is Mr. Edmund in? No? No, I don't want any supper." She sat on till midnight, then went to her room, but left the door ajar so that he might come in to her on his way to bed. Then very late she heard him come up the stairs and go to his room and shut the door: and then of course it was no good any longer expecting him to come.

For a week after that night they rarely met except with elaborate courtesy before the servants. In the theatre they did not speak to each other. Once indeed, he, softening, volunteered a piece of news that would normally have waked her to excitement.

"Mother, I thought you would like to know. Nesta Marshall is going to be married."

"I must send her a wedding present," said Donna politely.

"So must I."

"Yes."

He would do no more: and before she brought herself to the next word the silence had lengthened until it was too late again. And so the dreary quarrel dragged on, he suffering a little, she suffering greatly. For his face in anger had the harsh, inexorable look that she had seen too often on her father's face: and every day he made it clearer to her how perfectly competent he was to do without her. But she would not give in: and he would not give in. Another week went by. Then she did give in.

She came home late one night from the New Broom to find him already at home and eating his late supper in the dining-room. He looked up, rose, offered her a chair, but made no comment when she shook her head. After the one glance at him she went out of the room again, went upstairs, took off her theatre clothes, put on a tea-gown that he had liked when he first saw it, dressed her hair: then came down again looking, as he instantly knew though he would not look at her openly, magnificent in a black, white and crimson fashion of her own.

He had left the table and was sitting by the fire with a book. As they had already met there was no need for him to make any sign and he went on reading without a glance at her. She walked restlessly about the room, saying to herself that it was her room not his, her house not his: he was her property, her flesh and blood, her own made thing, her son. Yet to her distress and bewilderment she found herself, when it came to the point, afraid of her property, her flesh and blood, her son. She was more his than he was hers. Nobody, she thought, not even Stephen, had ever quite the power that Edmund had to make her feel desolate. She could not forget his anger, his recoil from her, his judgment of her. He had so many holds on her; but what hold had she on him if he now despised her for her very motherhood?

At last she summoned up her courage and came across to him. Still he did not look up. She put her hand on the back of his chair.

"Edmund!" She found that she could scarcely speak.

Then he turned up his face to hers. It was quite hard, without light, without expression.

"Yes, Mother?" said he. And then perfunctorily—"Will you have this chair?"

"No, stay where you are! Edmund, this can't go on. We cannot go on being angry with each other. You must not have a grudge against me."

She stood helplessly waiting for a change in his face. But his eyes remained black, expressionless, and he said—

"I haven't, Mother. You seem to have a grudge against me."

"You said a dreadful thing, Edmund."

"I know. I was very angry."

"You did not understand, Edmund. It—it was before I married again. I was never unfaithful to your—to my husband."

"These things have nothing to do with me, Mother."

She began to twist her hands together, utterly wretched.

"Edmund, I'm sorry, I'm sorry! I'm so sorry for everything. Forgive me, Edmund!"

Then at last he softened.

"Mother dear, forgive *me!* I lost my temper. But it all rose up in me —all my thoughts ever since I knew. It had to come to a head."

"Yes, yes."

"I didn't mean it, Mother, as it sounded."

"It was not your fault, my child."

They sat quiet a little while. Then she said, picking her words and watching him as she spoke—

"Edmund, I have been making new plans. I am transferring this house to you."

"What?" He was startled: and as always when he was moved, began to redden—"What, to me? Good God, Mother, what's in your mind? I don't want to be bribed. This is hateful. What do you think I am? How can you? I am ready to forget all our differences, and I thought you were, too. But to give me things, Mother, to give me things——" His face was cruel with distaste.

She was very humble. She was learning at last to be humble.

"No, no, Edmund! Listen, my dear boy! You misunderstand me. I wasn't trying to placate you. But dear, you have had a holiday and while you had it I have been thinking. You see, I have worked very hard all my life, Edmund, and I am beginning to want a holiday too. The house is not a gift, Edmund: it is a burden shifted. I always meant to give it up to you when you were old enough. My father would wish it. And I see so clearly, dearest boy, that you are now old enough. Listen to me, dear! Don't be impatient! Let me tell you what is in my mind! I always hated the stage, you know, and I was so very unhappy when I was young. When my first husband died and my father forced me to go back to the stage, Stephen—your father—was kind to me. No, I'm not going to burden you: I'm not going to tell you long stories. But that's how it all happened, Edmund. But now it is all over long ago and you are grown up. And so I think I might go home now, Edmund, if you'd let me—to my house in Ireland. I was so happy there. You don't need me, not very much, and I should like to go home."

But he could not believe that she was serious. He thought it was one of her clever ways of putting him in the wrong, of making him feel her magnanimity. He resented her tricky emotionalism and yet had not quite enough courage or harshness to say to her—'Don't play-act, Mother!' So he shrugged his shoulders and sighed with inner boredom, but supposed that if she wanted a scene he must play up: and did so, though he was savage with her in his heart for forcing him into insincerities which she must know, surely must know, were only uttered because she forced him to utter them.

"Mother, that's all nonsense. Go to Ireland, darling? I never heard such nonsense. You know perfectly well you don't mean it."

"I do mean it, Edmund. I've been thinking of it for a long time."

"Well, you must un-think it, Mother, that's all. What would the New Broom do without you?"

"Nobody is indispensable, Edmund."

Of course they weren't. But that didn't mean that people could run away from their jobs with no notice given. Indispensable! She was his mother—you can't sever that tie so easily : and that was what she wanted him to say, of course. Oh well—better say it!

"What should I do without you, Mother?" said Edmund radiantly.

But she only shook her head with a faint smile that put aside the caress of his.

"You think I'm not in earnest," said she, in statement not in question. He laughed, cheerful and sensible with her.

"Well, of course you're not, Mother. You know it and I know it. Why posture to each other?"

"I mean it, Edmund."

"Dearest Mother, do let's stop it!"

"But I——"

"Yes, Mother, I know all about it. We both lost our tempers, I've told you I'm sorry. Now I'm telling it you again. So all these revenges you've been brooding out in the last three weeks really haven't much meaning now we're friends again, have they? I mean we understand each other. You know perfectly well that you could no more give up acting or the control of the New Broom or the control of me than you could fly: and I know perfectly well that I couldn't do without you. Let's recognise both the facts and consider it settled."

She did not answer. But she sat looking at him still with that half smile of wistfulness mingled with amusement. Then she said—

"I'm going to live in Ireland, Edmund."

Oh, God, what more did she want? He pulled himself out of his chair, came round to her, put his arms round her neck and his cheek against hers.

"No, you're not, dearest!"

"Yes."

"No, I say."

"Yes, Edmund."

Suddenly he realised that she was serious, that he had somehow miscalculated from the beginning of the scene his own treatment of her and her mood. At that, in the oddest way, all the sophisticated understanding of life and women and his own mother deserted Edmund. It was like losing an eiderdown in the small hours : he felt suddenly chilled and uncomfortable. With a quick movement he caught her shoulders and pulled her round to him so that he could see her face.

"Mother, are you in earnest?"

"Yes, darling. I don't want to worry you or interfere with your plans, of course. It doesn't matter for a month or two. But I have decided to retire."

"But why, Mother, why?"

"I don't know, Edmund. I just want to."

"I suppose it's your way of showing me that I've been a beast to you."

"You haven't been a beast to me, my precious child. You're the light of my eyes. But you're grown up and independent, as I planned you should be. I always wanted you to be free. But that sets me free too. Edmund, you can't conceive how tired I am."

"But Mother, dear, if you want a holiday——"

"I do. And I'm going to have it."

"But then you'll come back——"

"If you were in trouble and wanted me, of course. Not otherwise."

"But look here, Mother——" For Edmund was profoundly uneasy. He had been so sure of himself: had his future so well in hand. He would back himself to handle Stephen or Lewis Wybird, and his companies and London managers and the great British Public. My word, yes! Let 'em all come! But—but—he had never conceived saying "Let 'em all come!" without having at his elbow a confidante with whom to discuss the advance. He had kept his mother in her place, but he had always recognised and thought that she recognised where her place was—just behind him.

Pushed to it, he said so.

"Mother, I can't do without you, that's flat! You just can't go. Don't you see, I must have someone to talk to. The Guv'nor's a wonder, but he's no good to discuss things with. He ain't got the brains. I don't know who else has that I can trust. It's an odd thing, Mother, when you come to think—I've got hosts of friends and acquaintances but I haven't got anybody to talk to except you. But you know how I think about things. You know how I work. I can trust you to carry on for me. So I'm awfully sorry, Mother, but I can't spare you. I really can't." (Would that keep her? Wasn't that what she wanted?)

She did not answer him though she smiled at him affectionately.

He grew impatient.

"Mother!"

"Yes, dear?"

"Well, it's understood then, isn't it, that you put out of your mind all this nonsense about retiring and going to Ireland?"

"Oh no, Edmund. I'm going."

"But, Mother, it's leaving me in the lurch. It's unlike you. Imagine me all alone in this great house, coming home tired, no-one to speak to, no-one to talk over plans with. I mean why should it be?"

"You'll soon get accustomed to being alone. You'll like it really. You know, dear boy, there are times when my authority irks you and I'm too old to learn how to lay down authority. That's one reason why it's time for me to go."

"Well, I call it pure selfishness. You're considering yourself and not me. Do you know what you're doing, Mother? You're driving me into getting married."

"You speak as if I should regard that as a misfortune, Edmund."

"Well, but most mothers do, don't they? Don't they hate their sons getting married? I thought it was the proper thing."

"I shouldn't," said she, half laughing. "I should be glad of the help."

"Mother, I can't understand you. What's the matter with you? You've always been so full of energy. Why have you suddenly gone so limp and acquiescent? Mother, you're not feeling ill, are you?"

"Only tired, Edmund."

Tired! That extraordinary use of the word! What was it to be tired? You got tired, of course, at the end of a heavy day, after a twenty mile tramp or a week of twice-nightlies; but after all it was a delightful sensation to be dog-tired and go to sleep and wake up fit as paint. But middle-aged people talked about being tired as if it were a state like being French or married. Silly!

"Well, you ought to see a doctor."

"But I'm perfectly well, dear."

"But—but always tired! After all it must be due to something. How do you feel?"

"As if I were running a race with you, Edmund: only you are running on dry land and I am running through mud or water. It slows me. You'll feel the same when you are forty and have to keep up with your children."

He laughed. It wasn't the first time he had planned out for himself his marriage and his wife and his successful ménage. It was pleasant to talk of the castle to his mother, friendly and his confidante again.

And of course marriage would solve many problems, even this problem of her departure. There was no doubt that his mother had aged in the last months, only he had been too busy to notice it. But now watching her he did miss a certain springiness alike of mind and movements. When he was once married it would not matter so much if she did go to Ireland. After all it might prove the best thing in the long run. Her advice was generally worth taking. But you couldn't just run out into the road and get married to the first passer-by: and he had never seen anybody he wanted to marry. True, he had never looked. Why should he, with the world so full of Nestas? But still, with the thought of marriage in mind one did look at the world and women differently. Only he was not going to be hurried and meanwhile he was not going to lose his mother's support until he was perfectly sure he could do without it. He turned back to her, broadly smiling.

"Look here, Mother, I'll make you a fair offer. You're perfectly right, of course. If I could find the right woman—I know exactly what I want—I'd marry tomorrow. And I will. But till I do, stay with me. Hold the fort till I'm married, Mother, will you?"

"Yes, my dear," said Donna, with the enthusiasm that he wanted, though for a moment she had hesitated. For the years-old craving for rest and dreams had grown strangely upon her in the weeks of their breach. But Edmund comes first, of course—blessed child!

"Yes, well, that's settled. Now look—I've got a mass of things I want to discuss with you. First of all, I've put it through with Lewis Wybird. It's all signed and sealed. Isn't that news? The Glory Hole is mine unless I smash—mine for thirty years to come! I'm reletting it, of course, until I'm ready. Meantime we reopen the Genista in September with *Lucifer's Love*. No, you haven't seen it yet. I'm having copies made. It's that comedy I wrote to you about from New York. There's a marvellous part in it for the Guv'nor. I wish to God it was as easy to find a woman to play with him. Oh, you know what I want, Mother, we've talked it over a hundred times. Well, she's just not to be found. I would have liked to spring an entirely new face and figure upon London. I scoured New York with a tooth-comb. But no luck. Oh well, Ada Godfries will have to play. She's the nearest in type. It's no use crying for the moon. Now another thing, Mother—you've heard about Lewis's engagement to Elinor Dale?"

For some unknown reason Donna flushed as she answered—

"Yes, Adelaide told me."

"Well, it's a pretty big event. Union of York and Lancaster! I think there ought to be a law against money marrying money. But Lewis is a fox. He's marrying her straight out of the convent, you know."

"I thought she was at school in Germany?"

"Same thing. I wish somebody'd leave me a rich ward to train up to my own taste and then marry out of hand. Ever seen her?"

"Oh yes. Lewis has opened up Blandon, you know. I went over when I was staying with Adelaide last month."

"What is she like?"

"Elinor? Beautiful brown eyes."

"I never notice people's eyes. She's dumpy, I suppose. There must be same disadvantages or Lewis wouldn't have been able to snaffle her so easily."

"She's rather Adelaide's type, but much more intelligent," said Donna carefully. "At least, as far as one could judge. She still has her schoolgirl terrors and shynesses, of course. We went for a walk together but she would hardly open her mouth."

"Oh well, you'd scare a cannon, Mother. Poor girl, I'd make her talk."

"I don't know why you should say that, Edmund. I was extremely nice to her."

"And that's more paralysing than when you're not amused. You know it is. I'm sorry for the girl."

"So'm I," said Donna suddenly, on a different note. "She's not in the least in love with Lewis. She has a sort of schoolgirl bewilderment about him, that's all. It's curious the attraction a middle-aged man can have for a quite young girl," said Donna thoughtfully. "But it's very real while it lasts."

"Then she ought to be all right," said Edmund tiring of the subject; and was surprised at the energy of his mother's—

"She won't be. You can take that from me, Edmund. Lewis Wybird hasn't any idea of handling a girl. It's a shocking business. He's marrying her purely for her money."

"Then she is dumpy," said Edmund triumphantly.

She shot a quick look at him.

"Ah, you don't remember her. Yet you were very good friends the first time we came to England, when we stayed with the duke. You and she were always together."

"Yes, now you recall it I believe there was a pinafore that I played with. Was that Elinor? I don't suppose I'd know her if I saw her. Well, I shall judge next week."

"Are you going to Blandon? You didn't tell me."

"Now, Mother, were we on speaking terms? Yes, I'm asked. Lewis is leading up to the wedding by a series of graduated festivities—the banker prince—the Medici touch. Very fine and feudal! There'll be a royalty or two with luck. And I've promised to go down with some of the company and give a show one evening. My wedding present. He offered fees, of course, but I wouldn't hear of it. I can make my gesture as well as Lewis."

"What are you putting on?" Donna was at once sparkling with interest. "Because if I were you I should——"

"No, Mother, it's all settled. It's a piebald business. The amateurs are doing some tableaux-vivants, and I suppose there'll be the inevitable recitations. We round it with some scenes from *Clever Kate.*"

Domina crossed to her writing-table and began sorting through a pile of letters.

"That must be the function Adelaide writes of," said she slowly. "It's just a week before the wedding, isn't it?"

"What? Are you going too?" He was clearly pleased.

"Well, the New Broom will be shut by then," said she, so pleased that he was pleased. "I don't see why I shouldn't. Adelaide asked me to stay over the wedding. She has asked you too, for that matter. Are you going?"

"I doubt it." He yawned.

"My dear, it's very late," said his mother worriedly. She would not suggest that he should go to bed because she knew it would only make him sit up the longer, but she did think he looked tired: she wanted him to go to bed.

"I know; but I've got some work to do. You go on, old lady!"

She hovered about the room for a minute, poured him his drink, mended the fire, hunted a book, stood looking at him, then went off.

She paused on the landing to pull apart the curtains and throw up the window; for the June night was close: and stood a little while, her arms crossed on the sill, leaning and looking out over the garden, thinking of her son. Dear Edmund—so young, so angry, so sure of himself! Was she weak with him? She found him almost as hard to resist as Gilly. How bitterly she used to resent knowing that Gilly could do anything with her. Poor Gilly! But why, after all these years, did Gilly come

into her head? Thank God, Edmund was not like poor Gilly with his
unthrifty loveliness——How did it go?

> 'Unthrifty loveliness, why dost thou spend
> Upon thyself thy beauty's legacy?'

Why did'st thou spend, Gilly?

Sighing she turned from the window and went on to her room. She
did not leave her door ajar, but she lay long awake listening for a foot-
step: and in the early hours Edmund tapped softly, and on her murmur
came in and kissed her good-night.

RROOME SEEGGE 400

but her heart—thank God, Edmund was not her poor Gilly with his ambitious schemes—how well did it go?

CHAPTER 44

ELINOR

EDMUND BROOME never spent more than twenty-four hours at Blandon in his life; but those twenty-four hours made village history. There was none to see his spectacular departure, but every detail of his arrival has been preserved in the communal consciousness. Nor are these details blurred by the fact that Albert Edward, Prince of Wales, preceded him.

There was an interval of half an hour between the two events, and it is certainly true that in this short space of time a good part of the applausive crowd had melted; for Midsummer Day had brought mid-summer weather and the Prince, God bless him, had chosen to arrive at the grilling hour of one.

The heat however did not prevent a display of loyalty. Nature herself with her sky and her poppies and her chalk-white roads, beat out the first bars of the red-white-and-blue anthem, and her village of Blandon picked up the tune with Union Jacks, pennants, archways and ribbonades. The lodge-keeper wore a cravat, his wife a waist-belt, his daughter a hair-ribbon and his dog a collar, cut from the same roll of red, white and blue petersham: and the whole population of the village ranged since noon along the road-sides, stacked like asparagus on the green or wedged and milling at the lodge gates, had followed his lead. Nor were the dog-carts, governess-cars and blue-cushioned victorias behindhand in zeal. They blocked for half a mile all turnings from the highways to the lanes, and every whip had its bow, every governess her rosette. The bored cobs and ponies switched ribbon-plaited tails and clouds of flies rose, settled, and rose again from ribboned forelocks and head-bands to which were fastened tight bunches of cornflowers, marguerites and wilting poppies. The very air vibrated with loyalty. Loud church bells in perpetual ding-dong linked the irregularities of footsteps, hoof-beats, jingling bits, laughter, conversation and occasional sudden pauses of anticipation into a charivari of tune, while high above the massed sound shrilled the larks.

But when the open carriage was at last perceived, toy-cart tiny, at the other end of the fairmile: when it grew rapidly in stature as if at once borne forward and swelled to life-size by the cheering that rose and ran alongside: when the bald head shone recognisably and that shrewd, bearded face had by its nod, beam and dignified familiarity of response convinced every English soul upon the green that here was John Bull himself driving through his own villages to dine with his own lords and ladies: when the swift proud horses had rolled him between the wreathed gate pillars and had dwindled him and his halo of personal charm and traditional glamour into a little cloud of dust at the far end of the chestnut avenue, then, with the important and final clanging of the Lodge gates upon the sight, the crowd fell apart into parched individuals still full of loyalty but longing for middle-day dinner.

So sudden and swift was the impulse to disperse, to stream homeward to Blandon village, New Blandon, and the rest of the hamlets clustered round and on and beyond the Blandon land, that Edmund Broome, striding into the dispersal, had to breast-stroke a path for himself at every third step. This he did without any deliberate brutality of movement, but impatiently, like a swimmer splashing out to deep water through surf blanketed with weeds.

Edmund Broome on this Midsummer Day of eighteen-ninety-four was twenty-two years old. But the crowd who obstructed him would not in their later description call him a boy. He had neither the grace nor the awkwardness of adolescence: his shape was solid and strong as a grown man, his movements more vigorous than elastic. He might be compared to a cudgel, a mace, a two-handed sword, but not to a rapier. Indeed, only in countenance did his actual age reveal itself. His red golden hair was still undulled, his skin unlined, while his grey eyes had still that morning lustre which, throughout the kingdoms of nature, is the royal sign of youth.

These extremely bright grey eyes, even when the spring of youth had vanished, remained till his death Edmund Broome's only claim to actual beauty. He knew it and was not perturbed. He cared in success and adversity, in riches and despair, nothing at all for the vanities. In his later days he walked for choice when others drove in his cars, dined at Appenrodt's to please himself while his sons reserved tables at the grill-room of the hour: bought his suits from the peg and had his expensive boots patched and patched again. Looks didn't matter to Edmund; but it amused him to make other people, especially women, agree with him that looks didn't matter: and he used his bright grey eyes, his grand vitality and his abominable temper to make himself loved, obeyed and feared. Only three human beings had ever outfaced Edmund Broome when, beneath his thick eyebrows that met each other, his grey eyes grew bloodshot. The modern mind finds a display of rage terrifying and indecent; but Edmund enjoyed terrifying and did not care too conventionally for the decencies.

The lodge-keeper, however, glorious within his gates, had not met Edmund Broome nor his rages. And Edmund Broome, reared in a masterless country, had not met the self-respecting English rural serf. Both were to be surprised. The lodge-keeper knew his place and his duty. His master was entertaining the Prince of Wales. He was to open the gates to invited guests; but not to journalists, sightseers, trippers, or any other strangers, and most certainly not to a dusty young man with red hair, no gloves, no luggage and no hat. He had never heard of Edmund Broome and said so not too civilly, for there was a lingering fringe of cronies on the other side of his gates to whom he must prove that the Prince of Wales had nodded to him and to him alone, though it was a fact that every member of the crowd treasured a similar conviction. So the lodge-keeper, swinging the great key on the end of his finger, turned upon Edmund Broome a negligent ear.

"Guest, sir? The guests were all met at the station, sir."

"Yes," said Edmund impatiently. "I walked. Let me by, please."

"What name, sir?"

"Broome."

The keeper hesitated.

"Very strict orders, sir."

Edmund laughed.

"I'm expected."

"Any card, sir? I mean, sir, journalists, enquiries, photographers—There's the Stone Gate entrance half a mile up the road."

Edmund who, incurably careless, had left his cards in his coat at the station, eyed him coldly, and said—

"I am Mr. Edmund Broome. I am here at the invitation of Mr. Wybird. I am in charge of the entertainment tonight. Don't keep me waiting any longer, please!"

The lodge-keeper stiffened.

"The theatre folks was met an hour ago. Nor they didn't come in at the main gate." Then, on a sharp note of anguish—"Look out, sir! Here, sir, I say!"

For the chafing Edmund had acted. He had been rattling impatiently at the locked gates as he talked to the scornful lodge-keeper. Now his right hand shot out and through one of the wider spaces of the magnificent iron-work, caught the lodge-keeper's wrist, dragged it through and bending the helpless hand sharply against the knobbed scroll-work, forced it to relinquish the key it held. Then, while the keeper yelled that his wrist was broken, he unlocked the gate, entered, relocked it, tossed the key to the bewildered keeper, flashed his grey eyes at the crowd surging against the closed paradise, and made off at full pelt down the avenue.

But he had not gone a dozen yards before he began to cool and be vexed with himself. It had been extraordinarily silly of him to lose his temper. The man was a fool but he, Edmund, was the greater fool, he thought. This habit of losing his temper was growing on him and once it started he could never stop himself. He had to go through the rise and crash of wrath, enjoying it while it lasted, but afterwards there was the wreckage to consider. He had lost a valuable recruit in America because he hadn't been able to stop himself losing his temper in an argument. Well, that might happen to a calmer man than he. But he had nearly wrecked his relations with his mother, and that didn't bear thinking. But in spite of such a steadier—look at him just now! said Edmund in candid disgust. No, the failing must be watched. There was nothing to be gained by losing one's temper with an underling, on the stage or off. Of course the man had been insolent but—what was that infernal row? He glanced over his shoulder and began to laugh and swear at himself anew.

For the justly enraged lodge-keeper was bowling after him, shouting and waving a stick. He was accompanied by a fair regiment of labourers in their best clothes, farm lads, a woman or two and a bob-tail of boys. Moreover, far behind them all, but resolute, lumbered the village constable. Edmund's American training had not at all prepared him for the solidity with which the English countryside resents the affronts of the foreigner. There was in every member of the hunt already a confused impression, momentarily deepening, not only that the village had been insulted, but that the Prince of Wales, God bless him, was in serious danger. The word anarchist was on more than one lip, and everyone in spite of the heat was passionately running.

Edmund Broome was a young man of quick decision. It was borne in upon him that though he could no doubt extricate himself from the ridiculous situation, to do so would take time, and that he had no wish to make a fool of himself in the eyes of his host or his company. Besides, why waste one's gifts? He had won the mile in record time during his last year at school and was in excellent training. "Discretion——" quoth Edmund chuckling, and began to run like a hare, encouraged by the roar of gratified execration that rose behind him at this confession of guilt.

But if Edmund could run, so could some of his pursuers: and after a few moments he began to see a very clear picture of himself toiling along endless miles of drive and arriving on the doorstep still accompanied and far too blown to explain himself. What was he to do?

On the left of the avenue the park was edged by meadows which dropped suddenly and steeply downwards to a long green ride and rose again to woods that clothed and crowned the encircling hills. Once in the woods, he thought, he could manage to evade his pursuers. So he turned off abruptly on to the soft turf, crossed it, leaped the wire fence and then added to his crimes by charging down through the tall meadow grass white with daisies and just ready to cut.

It was the wisest thing he could have done, for if he did not know that hay was sacred, his followers did and checked instinctively. But while they followed the fence till they could tramp along the border of the meadow, he forged ahead, reached the green ride itself, crossed its mossy, thymy floor, then, sheltering as much as he could behind the groups of elder bushes that did duty for a hedge, he ran diagonally upwards, stumbling over the ant-hills till he could dive into the shade of the beeches.

In that blessed shade he paused, not only to get his breath but to see how his pursuers fared. These, to his gratification, had paused: a consultation was being held on the edge of the meadow land. One or two of the boys were straying after him, but with backward looks: while the central knot of avengers was gesticulating but making no forward movement. He thought that dinner must be calling many. However, he would not risk a renewal, but struck on through the wood and presently coming out upon clean turf again, he followed the footpath till once more the valley and the park lay exposed. Then he saw that an attempt at a cordon was drawn along the bottom, parallel to his hill-top. It did not greatly disturb his peace, however, for the main body was clearly on the turn. But he did not like the look of two dark figures, one by his shape the policeman, who plodded forward like beetles along the drive.

"And I suppose," quoth Edmund, "the bobby will be hob-nobbing with the major-domo when I arrive. Awkward! Oh well, I needn't turn up till the royalties are gone: and then they will all be easing off. Besides the garden-party will be beginning. I wish I knew my way through the gardens." For though he had seen a good deal of Lewis Wybird in the last year, the great house at Blandon had been closed. From the crest of the hill, however, it was easy to see the plan of the whole place. For the house lay with its gardens, stables and lesser buildings like a tea-leaf at the centre of a saucer. Edmund thought that he would circle the cresting woods of the surrounding hills, and bear down through the beech groves that ended, he could see, where the gardens began: and in the gardens somewhere it would be odd if he did not light upon Adelaide and his mother. Adelaide, he knew, would be at the luncheon and the whole neighbourhood would gather after the Prince had gone. At the worst he could make a joke of it, though it was a singularly difficult joke to explain. Who wants to say—'I lost my temper and they chased me'? Well, he must chance it.

He stood a moment listening. The cries of his late pursuers were no longer to be heard and he flattered himself that he had thrown them off. But he went on, nevertheless at a great rate, not so much to ensure himself from their unwelcome attentions, but because it was impossible for Edmund to do anything in a leisurely fashion. He always walked as if he were running and he ran like the wrath of God.

On he went through the cool alleys, talking to himself as he always did though the streets stared and thought him mad. He cared little for stares. He wouldn't be cheated of all the news he always had to tell himself—stories of what he would do this year—next year—sometime: arguments with invisible opponents, conciliations of doubtful allies: schemes, plans, ideas. Why shouldn't he talk to himself?

He stopped now and then to stare at the vegetable shambles, now overgrown with beauty. The woods had suffered in the late winter storms, and in the clearings fallen trees had crashed down among the spindle-berries, brambles, elderberries, eglantines and dog-roses. Such trees, blooming as they died, showed a fainter green, still young and newly varnished, against the stronger greens of the surrounding woods. Some spent bluebells lingered: the ground was carpeted with the darker blue of bugloss: each isolated ruffle of spurge shone like a street lamp in a fog: and the foxgloves were everywhere. On the high ground where the true woodland gave place to hawthorn, whitethorn and gorse, he came also upon tracts of his own broom, more dazzling than the gorse, the very colour of laughter.

Presently he glanced at his watch and found that he had an hour to spare before the royal departure was likely to occur. He thought he would laze off for a little: the scent of the gorse made him sleepy and happy; but he wished he had some beer. He turned from the track into one of the broken thickets of broom where the little lanes of the animals, fox ways, rabbit runs and such, led to a sunny open patch of turf, securely walled, hot as blazes, and starred with tormentil. There he flung himself down to rest and cool, and stare up into the deep blue sky. Somewhere a nightingale sang its day-song. A spider began to lower itself from its web in the broom to a bramble flower. The spider was very busy and as he watched it he fell asleep. He could always wake at will and wake fresh, and he woke as he had planned exactly an hour later. His movement as he got to his feet swept away the spider's web and left the grass and the tormentils and the veronicas as flat as disappointment. But Edmund felt much refreshed and made a grab at a butterfly and missed it as he pushed his way out of the broom: then, stopping, stripped a twig of three or four blossoms and stuck them in his buttonhole. He said to himself that he must get into the country oftener and that it was a great pity that yellow was such a bad stage colour: then swung on at his own same furious rate but heading now down-hill for the beech grove that would lead him into the rhododendron copses and so into the grounds.

When he reached the grave beeches he found that there was no path through the wood but that the great trees were planted so far apart that it was easy to see the way. The slope, however, was extreme and he had to turn and double between the leaf pits where half a century of rains had washed away the earth between the gigantic trunks. It was quite light in the wood, for though the beech leaves made a green silk heaven overhead the sunlight shone through that ceiling, while now and then a breeze broke it, revealing the pure blues and whites of summer.

"Perfect," said Edmund aloud, as the sun came down through such a parting and splashed light in his eyes. He paused and propped himself comfortably against the flat of a beech trunk. "Perfect. Now this is exactly what I want for the second act of *Lucifer*. I wonder—"

Then he had something else to wonder at, for almost from under his feet a laugh rang out, high, ringing, delicate, as if one of the younger beech trees were amused at him.

He slipped round the huge trunk that so effectively screened anyone leaning against it from anyone on the other side. Its roots, broad with age, made a path for his feet, and one great root ran out like a bridge into the soft loam, skirting the largest pit he had yet seen. It was a hollow, twenty feet or more across, filled to within four feet of the surface by beech leaves, raw or burnt-siena-coloured as the sun dappled or forgot them. More beech trees grew on the further edge of the hollow, and the place, sheltered from all winds, was as warmly quiet as only a beech pit can be. In that grave, living quiet, for the beech is the most human of all trees, the laughter seemed to lose its quality of sound and become an expression of the sunlight: the sound of yellow sunlight bloomed in the hollow as the brooms had shouted on the hilltop.

But though Edmund liked a splash of colour, he never thought about flowers or colours or sounds when people were at hand, and here were people of the most charming and interesting kind. For two pretty girls were playing in the beech leaves directly under his feet, and as he stirred one of them looked up.

She was a handsome creature with an olive skin, new-moon eyebrows and rippling black hair: and as she rose hastily he saw that she had the figure and experienced carriage of the Latin: or was she a Jewess? He was not sure. She wore a dress of blue muslin with a blue silk jacket carrying revers and a high collar. It was a modish costume, according to the fashion books of 1894, but not at all the dress, thought Edmund, to wear in a wood. He wondered how she had climbed down; but her feet were ankle-deep in leaves and he could not see whether her shoes were as unsuitable as the rest of her gallantry. Nor had he time, for touching the leaves, she exclaimed in a pretty husky voice and a roll of the r—

"My dear, here's a man!" and began to laugh again.

At that her companion swung round and as she looked up at him he saw, and knew that he saw, the star for whom he had searched these six months.

There she sat, his nymph, the shy, lovely, laughing creature of his imagination, the find to be so well advertised, the young amateur to be let down so lightly by critics and dressed so astonishingly by eager king-dressmakers, the Maypole about whom the play was to revolve, the Andromeda who had only to stand still and be rescued by Perseus Stephen Broome. What more could he or the public want? She had masses of thick wavy hair of a colour between hazel and gilt, twisted into metal cables and wound about her small head. She had a fair skin, straight brows and a full mouth. Her profile, as she turned in a momentary glance at her companion, was delicate and regular, but the nose had a humorous tilt and her chin was obstinate. A moment she sat back on her heels, her hands full of leaves, wrinkling her eyes against the scarf of sunshine that floated across her face. Then, as her eyes became accustomed to the light, he was amazed to see her break into smiles and scramble to her feet waving a hand, and in the next moment he heard her say—

"Fina, I believe it's Edmund Broome."

"Yes," he called down to her quickly—"I'm Edmund Broome."

At that the girl ploughed across the leaves to him and stood looking up—

"I thought you were. My guardian is expecting you. You've forgotten me, haven't you? I'm Elinor Dale." And with her free hand she shook her skirts clear of the leaves that she had trailed along with her.

So that was Elinor Dale. Not dumpy—no, not dumpy!

"Can't I come down?" said he.

"You'll have to jump," she called. "It's a lovely feeling. The bother's getting out again."

She was quite right. It was a lovely feeling dropping softly into the feather-bed of leaves. He landed on his knees, close to the object over which the two girls had been bent on his arrival, which now resolved itself into a packing case sunk in the damp strata of underleaves. It was much mildewed and contained some sort of mouldering garment, a plate or two, a damp ruined box of chocolates and a pile of *Strand Magazines* whose blue covers were mere flakes of green damp. Remembering his not so far-off childhood he could guess the occasion, and said—

"How long have you left it? My cache was a hollow oak."

Both laughed; but it was the elder girl who took charge of the situation and answered in her foreign voice—

"Yes, it is her private storing-place, before I knew her, before she came to school: and you must not tell. But I am to be introduced, Elinor, before we talk. Is this the cousin?"

"This is your cousin," said her companion. And then, to the blenching Edmund—"This is my friend Josephina Adamovitz who was at school with me in Dresden."

"And I am his cousin," said the dark girl.

"And she is your cousin. She is descended from my guardian's great-uncle. But we didn't know when we met at school that she and I would ever be related."

"As we shall be," said the dark girl, "in a fortnight. My grandmother was Georgina Wybird—'alf Persian, 'alf the daughter—"

"Oh, I know," said Edmund hastily. "Great-uncle Lionel! What about the packing case?"

Elinor defended herself.

"Pure silliness; but we were so stiff at lunch. And the garden-party isn't till four. So I said to Fina that we'd get into the woods for half an hour: and then we thought we'd see if the packing case was still there. I used to keep books and cakes in it, and a rug, and it's ruined. You see I never thought of the damp, and Blandon has been shut these two years. Everything's spoiled—"

Her voice trailed off because she had suddenly no more to say. She was plainly unsure of herself in conversation. Josephina, however, allowed no pause.

"How did you get here?" said she, as if she had known him for years. "We knew you were coming, but—" Her glance ran over his clothes and his air of dishevelment.

So then, of course, he had to tell them the story of his adventures.

"And the worst of it is," he concluded, "if I go round by the main entrance I shall have to answer a charge of assault and battery as like as not: and Wybird won't be pleased."

"No, he won't be pleased," said Elinor. Her tone had changed; for the moment at least she was sure of herself or her fact: her fact, he thought.

"And if I do get in through the garden, well, look at my clothes," said he, asking sympathy. "I've got to get in and change first somehow."

The dark girl yawned.

"Does it matter? You've only got to explain to Lewis," said she.

"Oh, no," interrupted Elinor quickly. "Better not worry Lewis." And Edmund, glancing at her, found her looking at him and found himself returning her look. It was as if there were an understanding between them instantly upon the subject of Lewis Wybird to whom it was difficult to explain things. He didn't want to make a fool of himself before Lewis, and she didn't want him to either. It was, for an instant, as if they told each other all they both knew about fussy, difficult Lewis Wybird. Having faced him before they could consult together. Because of course—why, yes, of course, they had faced him before together. Memory returned in a flash. There had been an escapade in which he had had a companion, and his companion had been terrified when they both came home late because she would have to face the wrath of Lewis Wybird. And that unremembered companion was, he supposed, this tall creature in a fashionable silk muslin dress with childish ways that dropped from her as the leaves dropped from her skirts at the mention of Lewis Wybird, who was still her guardian and in a fortnight would be her husband. And because they understood each other on the subject of Lewis Wybird, though what there was to understand he could certainly not have explained, he waited with perfect good faith for her to produce a scheme that would save him from appearing ridiculous or giving any sort of information to his host. His faith was well-founded.

"I know——" said Elinor to the other girl who was watching them both with a little air of amusement—"the laurel hedge! If you, Fina, will stroll back with us to the edge of the wilderness and then go on by the gardens and, if I am wanted, say I am in my room changing my dress, then I will take your cousin through the hedge and turn him over to old Paley. Paley's safe. It's a double hedge of laurels——" she explained to Edmund—"that circles the gardens. Once you are in it nobody sees you till you are at the house itself. It's a high clipped hedge. Nobody goes there except the gardeners."

"And the courting couples," said Fina. "I saw the housemaid and the gardener's boy from my window two nights ago. You are only hidden from the lawn."

"Oh, well, Lewis won't be looking out of a window at this time of day," said Elinor ignoring the other girl's laugh. "Once your cousin is in and tidy he can manage. But of course he doesn't want it to be known that he got himself chased round Blandon, any more than we'd like it, Fina, if Lewis found out about all this." And she kicked the spoiled rubbish back into the case and let the piled leaves fall on it before she pulled down the lid and let the lid in turn be smothered by yet more leaves. "For I shan't come here again," said she. "I thought it would be so amusing when I left it, to find it again years and years afterwards. But I've greened my hands and my knees, and it hasn't been very amusing. That comes of being grown-up," said Elinor. And then——"This way."

She was as nimble as a squirrel in spite of her height and swung herself from root to root easily. But Fina, his new-found cousin, had no notion of climbing, and Edmund did think there was nothing in the world more undignified than a stout, full-figured young woman trying to be a child of nature. And then she left her hat behind. He did not like her. He disliked young women who talked to him at sight with their eyes. She would give little glances at Elinor and laugh, and then turn to him confidentially as if she said—'Isn't she a dear little slice of bread-and-butter?' And he disliked her remark about the laurel hedge and the housemaid, and the look that had accompanied it. He thought her very common. It was a relief to him when she parted from them behind the lupin clumps that ended the wild garden and trailed off to join the groups of summer dresses already assembling on the lawns.

"Isn't she a darling?" said Elinor. "We needn't worry now. She will talk to Lewis. She gets on so well with Lewis. But then she has had so much experience. She came out at home, you know, before she went to school in Europe. She lives in Brazil. But you know all about the Adamovitzes, of course. It is a romantic story, isn't it? Fina said her great-grandmother was a princess, but Enid Wybird says she was a slave girl, which is even more romantic. All the girls thought so. Fina says she is supposed to be like her. She does look Eastern, doesn't she? I do admire her. She is my greatest friend. Is anyone looking? That's only a gardener: he doesn't matter. This way." And catching his wrist, she darted across the one open space of lawn and dived into a narrow opening which, as he now saw, appeared in the wall of laurel that circled the gardens. Once inside he found himself walking beside her down a long pleasant alley, carpeted with bugloss, ground-ivy, herb-robert and spent primrose clumps. The laurel walls to right and left of them rose high above their heads and were some four feet thick. The blue path on which they walked was matched by a blue path of sky above.

"This is very pleasant," said Edmund.

"If we go slowly," said Elinor, "we may see a squirrel."

His guide handed him over to the fatherly Paley when they reached the house, and Edmund, when he had located the little private theatre, realised that he could not expect to see her again till dinner-time. For the little theatre had not been used for years, and although it was swept and clean, and his assistants amiable, he found, as many a professional had found before him, that he would much prefer to put on a Drury Lane pantomime than arrange for the smooth running of one amateur performance.

But somewhere about six o'clock Elinor Dale reappeared: diffident, and wearing over her delicate dress a pinafore that made her look fourteen, but competent. He was astonished to find her no hindrance, but a sensible underling, an underling with dodges and ideas. Nevertheless it was hard work and he did not get much support from his company. He was annoyed with himself for having delayed his own arrival, which was, of course, the company grievance also. He thought that Elinor Dale, always ready with the right sort of nails, prepared to split a curtain or sew a rent or paint a white lamp-shade green, showed up well against his leading lady, weeping with rage because she was dining with the rest of the company in an upper room: while he was expected, as a member of the Wybird clan, to attend the state dinner. Elinor, the bride-elect, should have been dressing at leisure instead of thumbing drawing-pins and sewing curtain rings; but he didn't like her the less because she grasped the situation and took his termagant off his hands, imploring her to use her own dressing-room and innocently congratulating her on escaping, by the good excuse of make-up, the stupid dinner-party downstairs.

Off the two women went at last. Edmund, hot and dirty, was left to finish off, chivvy his own factotum, and cheer up the rest of the company, also inclined to stand on dignity. Then achieved a hurried change: and all the while dwelt upon the astonishing good sense that did sometimes inhabit a girl's head and fingers, and wondered that with such good sense to guide her a girl could be pleased with a dry stick like Lewis Wybird. She wasn't in love with him, that he'd swear. Why had that really intelligent girl, with her face and her fortune, her figure, and her future let herself be heckled into marrying a man old enough to be her father? Well, it was no business of Edmund's.

In spite of the need for hurry he found himself dressing with much greater care than he usually bestowed upon his person: and ran for it at last, only to find that he was, after all, the first down. He spent ten minutes in pacing the empty park of a chamber, inspecting clock after clock, and staring at his own face reflected ghostly in the glass of the dark paintings, before his hostess, Lewis Wybird's elderly sister Enid, came in. She was gracious but he did not find her talkative: the Wybird women never had much to say for themselves. He was very glad indeed to see his mother enter, composed and beautiful and delighted to see him. Her delight in him restored his self-respect, a little shaken by all his adventures, and also by his sense of the beauty and the importance of the old stately house, now opening its gates to so many important people who had never heard of Edmund Broome: or who if they knew him, knew him only as a Wybird of sorts.

The room was beginning to fill with dowagers and diamonds, and tall young girls whose hair, piled high, made them seem taller: and important looking men in evening dress who dropped their g's and talked loudly and made him feel extraordinarily young. But his mother appeared perfectly at home among all these people and he saw with pride that the women liked her and that the men paid court to her middle-aged beauty. He was completely satisfied with his mother for once, and coming up to her as to an ark of refuge, said so.

"Mother, there's no-one in the room to touch you. If ever I marry she's got to be exactly like you."

Now why should marrying come into his head?

Domina, much pleased, looked at her dress complacently.

"It's some of your grandmother's lace," said she.

He put up his hand to finger it and she coloured faintly. Not often did Edmund show such deep interest in what she wore.

"It's like a cobweb," said he hastily; for he saw strange men bearing down on them and he did not want to be left alone until some ally arrived. It was maddening to know no-one at all. Adelaide had been swallowed up instantly. But the dark girl, his cousin, should come in soon, and sooner or later Elinor Dale would appear. Simple, pretty name, Elinor Dale. Then he realised that his compliment had pleased his mother and that she was still talking.

"I'm so glad you like it, Edmund. Yes, I think it suits me. The lace is very old, you know. It belonged first to the duchess, your great-great-grandmother Hilaret."

"Oh yes, that reminds me, Mother, who is this young woman I'm supposed to call cousin—this friend of Elinor's?"

"Oh, you've met Elinor?" lifting her eyebrows.

"Yes, in the wood, an adventure. I'll tell you sometime."

"What do you think of her, Edmund?"

For an instant they looked at each other.

"I'll tell you sometime," he repeated awkwardly. "But this other girl, Mother, I don't think she's much of a friend for—— Who is she? Is she really one of us?"

"Oh yes. She's the granddaughter of Georgina Adamovitz, your great-uncle Lionel's daughter."

"But a touch of the dago, eh?"

"Well, the mother's a Brazilian, of course. I've never seen her, but quite good family, Enid says. Why? Don't you like her?"

"Makes eyes at you."

"She's certainly a mature young person. But she is handsome, Edmund, all the same. Look!"

And then Edmund, in common with a good many other people, glanced at the door and at Josephina Adamovitz who was entering with Elinor Dale behind her. Both were in 'full evening dress': and the young girl of the nineties in full evening dress was one of the more sumptuous sights of that formal day.

Fina was a step ahead. She wore a dress of ochre-coloured silk: her full skirt was tight on the hips, and the tight pointed bodice showed how small her waist was and how full her bust. A swirl of yellow tulle framed her bare shoulders on one of which there was fastened a cluster of William Allen Richardsons. Her blue-black hair was piled high. Through the knot of curls was thrust a golden dagger and encircling it was a wreath of more William Allens. Josephina, with her rosy cheeks and golden skin, looked like a ripe nectarine: as Donna said, she was certainly handsome. But it was a foreign handsomeness, and from behind Edmund there came an indignant whisper as English milk-and-roses told her mother—"Mama, I'm sure she's wearing rouge!"

"Dear child, be quiet!" said the lady charitably, aware of Donna and her Wybird blood. Nevertheless the little feeling that though Miss Adamovitz could not possibly be wearing rouge her colour was tactlessly high, made itself felt. None felt it sooner than Josephina who, to do her justice, had not risked rouge, but had crushed a geranium petal in her finger and very carefully applied the damp stain.

Not quite able to do without help she glanced back at Elinor, ingenuous in white, put out her hand and waited, even at the risk of becoming a foil to the younger girl's beauty. And so the two débutantes came in together.

"Well, what do you think of her?" said Edmund off-handedly. But his tone said—'I invented her. Isn't she a success?'

"She's not so striking as Josephina Adamovitz," said Donna critically.

"But she'll wear better. You know, Mother, she's exactly what we want."

And at that Donna's eyes began to dance. She was in a more light-hearted mood than her son ever remembered her.

"*We* want?" said she, underlining her pronoun.

"Of course! Just think what she'd be like playing opposite the Guv'nor."

"And think, Edmund, what Lewis Wybird would say if he could ever hear you: and think, Edmund, that she will be a married woman next Monday: and think, Edmund, whether you had better not go to town tomorrow instead of coming to stay with Adelaide as I hear you are doing!" A moment their eyes sustained each other's glance: then that astonishing confidence which was always between them, that complete reliance on each other of two natures in so many things alike, prompted Edmund's next speech.

"Mother, you do delight in smoking cigarettes in a gunpowder shop, don't you?"

"I have never in my life—" said Donna indignantly—"dreamed of smoking a cigarette."

"You'll have to, Mother, if ever you play Hedda Gabler."

"I detest your Ibsens."

"Yet you could play Mrs. Alving, Mother."

"I'd rather not discuss such a play."

"Have you read it, dearest?"

"Of course I haven't read it. Why should I? Lady Macbeth is good enough for me. Why don't you go and talk to Miss Dale, Edmund? She looks pale tonight, don't you think? Adelaide is very fond of her. Ah, there's dinner. Sir George takes me in. I suppose you will find your partner." And she sailed away from him, rather like the 'Fighting Téméraire' allowing itself to be escorted by the little black tug.

But Edmund's fate was Fina Adamovitz.

She greeted him like an old friend, called him Cousin Edmund at the end of each sentence, demanded compliments on her English, asked him if he liked yellow roses, rallied him on his gloom, asked him what he thought of Elinor Dale's dress and finally, well on towards the duck and green peas, allowed him to speak a word in answer. It was all very strange to Edmund who was accustomed to be a good talker. She did, however, allow him to say what he thought about Elinor Dale's dress and into the opening she thus afforded he cast without emphasis the remark that it looked very nice.

"She is so pretty, don't you think?" said his cousin Josephina: and before he could answer explained that Elinor was the English type and that in Brazil—"where everyone is like me—black and yellow—a hornet——" Elinor would be considered a beauty.

"You wouldn't have to go to Brazil," muttered Edmund.

"Ah, I thought you admired her," said Josephina trapping him with ostentation.

"Yes, I do," said Edmund goaded.

"I tell her, shall I?"

"I'd rather tell her myself," said Edmund, turning on his dear cousin the bold and heavy look of challenge which meant that he was about to lose his temper. But the hornet was attending to her next door neighbour, so what was there for him to do but eat his dinner and look at Elinor Dale? His mother was perfectly right. She was looking pale and tired and her beautifully cut nose was a little shiny as if she had been crying. He was still looking at her when Fina's voice sounded in his ear, cheerful and unabashed.

"I wish I could take her back to Brazil with me instead of leaving her in this 'ole of a Blandon. I am very fond of Nell and when I think it is all my fault——"

"Your fault?" said Edmund. "What's your fault?" Yes, he was sure she had been crying.

"Oh well, you know, we tease her too much, all of us at school and so she goes and gets *verlobt*. You know a German Daughters' Academy? There are thirty of us, all so dowdy. You should see us, Cousin Edmund—our hair rolled up on the backs of our necks and blue aprons and bibs."

"What?" he began to laugh.

"Can you see me in an apron and bib, Cousin Edmund? But I wore one two months ago—dark blue to wipe your pen on. Oh yes, and

Elinor too! And every night before supper—*Bier-suppe,* very cold and unfriendly, and one slice of *Kalbs-fleisch* with lovely toadstools in richest sauce—yes, I mean toadstools, yellow like a wet wash-leather glove, but so good: and rye bread, of course, but only one ball of butter. Well, before supper we say a verse from the Bible and then *Vater unser,* and then we report our sins. Hole in the stocking one mark gone: untidy drawer, one mark a drawer: ink spilled, English spoken, answering back, talking in bed—oh, such a banquet of vices: you could lose seventy marks in a week. I never lost a mark the whole time I was there. I would not. Why should I? We were on honour. Most of the girls lost for probability sake—three, six, ten in a week! But Elinor was—what you call it—below par—all the time. She lost all her seventy and bad marks as well. Because she could not tell lies. She did not think of it, poor Elinor! But that is English. So of course when the other girls go out to tea with their relations Elinor and I stay at the *Pensionnat*—she because of no marks and I because of no friends. And always the girls come back with presents and things because most of them were engaged and met their fiancés for kaffee and sometimes at the Opera. And so for days because flowers are very cheap in Dresden, every *Schlafzimmer* would be full of roses and violets, even ours, for of course I sent myself some: once a week I sent myself a bouquet. I called him Auguste, and said he had followed me from Brazil and that he had tried to commit suicide on a bridge because I cut him—like Beatrice, you know."

The bewildered Edmund put down his knife and fork.

"I don't know what you're talking about, Cousin Fina."

"I tell you—my lover, Auguste. I invented him. He had a great success with the girls. But Elinor had no imagination. So she was out of it, with no flowers, nothing: and that I say, I shall always say, was why she accepted her dear Lewis. Elinor is very slow but she will not be beaten and it was a great moment for her when she said to us all, to all the girls—'I have lost seventy-five marks this week but Fräulein Krantz can do nothing. My fiancé is here.' And of course you can't deny he is distinguished. Look now!"

And Edmund's glance obediently followed hers to the foot of the table and together they contemplated their host. Fina was right: he was distinguished. Evening dress suited Lewis Wybird: its dead white and dead black gave his long sallow face warmth, and its stiffness of cut and texture, mobility. His eyes, black in the candlelight, were quick moving and his thin grudging smile was attractive.

"There, you see! When he smiles you say—This is for me! Because he does not often smile. Well, he was like that all the days at Dresden: and he did everything she wanted and we had a river party down to the Bastei in a private steamer, all thirty of us and Fräulein Krantz and Enid. Do you like Enid Wybird? She is like *Zwieback*, nicht? We call her the *Zwieback*, I and Elinor. Yes, and then Elinor wanted to make an expedition to see the cherry orchards, and he just said, 'Yes, please?' to Fräulein Krantz and we went. He twisted Fräulein Krantz round his finger. He was so very distinguished and so much money and English. You wouldn't think how nice he could be as he was then. Quite charming. He wore a face all day that said—'I have got what I want without any trouble or expense, so now I will spend.' Were you ever in Dresden in cherry blossom time, Cousin Edmund? Well, make Elinor tell you. She can be poetical better than I. Well, coming home in the funicular he was still in a good temper and I was agreeable and talked about Elinor (as I am doing now, Cousin Edmund!) and told I was his relation and showed great-grand-father Lionel's ring. So of course he asked me to stay. Here I am. I would like a salted almond. Not that kind, the devil kind. Do you know Lewis well? Do you like him?"

Edmund met once more the shrewd eyes fixed on him and suddenly decided that his frank, fair and foreign cousin was not to be despised.

"What do you expect me to say to that?" said Edmund without enmity. "I'm his guest: I'm a relation: so are you: and we're eating his blanc-mange."

"And it is *not* made with only-cream," said Fina. "That is because he wants a wife. So you mean one should not discuss one's host."

"Or else I mean that I don't know how to answer you, Cousin Fina. Yes, I think I do like him. He's very shrewd."

"You like him to be shrewd?"

"I like a man who knows what he wants and gets it."

"That is like you are also, you think?"

"Well, I like my own way," said Edmund.

"We had at school—" said Fina—"an essay to write, from the English mistress who taught us Browning. Have you read Sordello? No, I have not either. I would not try. Elinor tried. I bet—bit—betted her she would not—and she went right through. She was very tired afterwards. Well, this was the problem. If the irresistible force meets the immovable object, who gets out of the way? That was the problem. But I wrote that the interesting thing in this problem was the person who 'appened to be sitting on the immovable object when the irresistible force blew in—blew up—how do you say it? Well, I must go because Miss Wybird is catching all our eyes. I have enjoyed my conversation, Cousin Edmund, and I will tell Elinor all you said. Oh, there is one thing I have not said. Come to me afterwards and I will tell you all about the trouble with her and Lewis. You saw, of course, that she 'ad been crying?" And out she went while he, excusing himself to his host, departed also to his proper task of controlling the pandemonium behind the scenes of the cramped stage.

The evening went very well; but the tableaux-vivants were not his affair, so during that turn he slipped into the body of the room and found a chair beside Adelaide Wybird and his mother. They were well-managed pictures consisting, it is to be confessed, principally of Josephina Adamovitz in all eastern rôles, from Cleopatra to Morgiana: and a sprinkling of English maidenhood and handsome, self-conscious, not too young English married manhood in the rest of the scenes from Marcus Stone, English history and Grimm's Fairy Tales.

"Who arranged them?" said he to Adelaide.

"Elinor," said Adelaide in the hushed, respectful voice appropriate to a realistic reproduction of *The Doctor*.

"Elinor?" He was sincerely amazed.

"Oh yes, she's very good at that sort of thing. Very artistic. She wanted to go to Paris and study painting. Only Lewis, of course, would not hear of it."

"Why isn't she in one of the scenes?"

"Well, you know, Lewis is rather old-fashioned."

"But, my dear Aunt Adelaide, you don't mean that in 1894 he's putting his foot down about private theatricals?"

"Oh no, no! You quite misunderstand me, Edmund. But he did say something, I believe, about its not being quite the moment. They wanted her for Rapunzel, you know. She has such glorious hair. And he said she must do as she pleased. So of course she didn't. I think it's quite right. After all she is to be married in a fortnight."

"Well, I cannot see——" burst out Edmund.

"No, dear, a young man can't be expected to. It's just a question of taste and suitability. Your mother knows what I mean. And it isn't as if Lewis were a schoolboy, you know, and could be in the scene with her. I think Elinor showed very nice feeling."

"My God!" said Edmund to himself as he returned to his own post, cheated of a very strong desire to look at Elinor Dale lit up by the

footlights with her hair showering down to her knees. And busy as
he was for the rest of the evening and well as he played his own part—
"I don't think I have ever seen you play so well, Edmund," said
Donna who was as a rule chary of praise—still, at the back of his
mind rankled a sense of the narrowness, prudery and general offensive-
ness of middle-aged men with money and estates. Edmund had never
thought very much about the rights of youth. He had never had any
difficulty in securing his own rights. But it did seem to him, now he
thought of it, that a man of forty ought to marry a woman of his own
age and leave a girl like Elinor Dale alone. He hated these arranged
marriages. It was no affair of his, but he did think that to marry a girl
of eighteen to a man twenty-five years older than herself was frankly
indecent.

And after the theatricals were over and congratulations received and
he, once more in evening dress, slipped back to join in the informal
dance that was rounding the evening, he not only thought but said so.
For Elinor Dale was engaged and Josephina Adamovitz was engaged,
and all the rest of the pretty girls were provided with partners and nobody was taking much notice of the rising young actor-manager,
Edmund Broome. So he, joining his mother and hearing what she
thought of it all, said his say rather bitterly.

"Don't you agree with me, Mother? Isn't it downright indecent for
a girl of eighteen to marry a man twenty years older than herself?
Look at them!"

But his mother did not look at Elinor Dale in the arms of Lewis
Wybird. She looked down instead at her fan, the magnificent ostrich
feather fan that had been one of her wedding presents.

"It depends on the girl and it depends on the man, Edmund," said
Donna gently.

"Women are so conventional," said Edmund sullenly. "Just because
it's a good match——! Look here, Mother, I'm going away tomorrow.
I can't stand watching it. I'm sure she's unhappy."

"I thought Adelaide had asked you to come on to her?"

"I don't know what I'm going to do," said Edmund angrily, incon-
clusively. Then, as Lewis Wybird relinquished Elinor and went off to
do his duty at the other end of the ball-room, Edmund elbowed in and
out of the dancers till he reached Elinor, left for the moment with an
unoccupied chair beside her.

"I do want to dance with you," he said.

"I've got a partner," said she vaguely.

"Won't you dance with me till he finds you? I do wish you would. I want to talk to you. I want to say how perfectly I thought you arranged those tableaux. Do dance with me. . . . Let me hold your fan. . . . D'you valse German or English? . . . How well you dance. . . . Sorry, did I hurt you? How horribly clumsy of me. No, it was entirely my fault. . . . No, but I assure you it was a wonderful bit of staging—absolutely professional. You have an absolute gift for the theatre. . . . Do you reverse? . . . No, I'm not being polite. I do mean it. But then you love the theatre, don't you? . . . Do you remember the Punch and Judy show? Did you ever send the collar? I thought you would. I don't know, I just thought you would. . . . You look awfully tired. Would you like to sit down somewhere? Can't we find somewhere to sit out?"

CHAPTER 46

RECKON, BECKON . . .

IT WAS about three o'clock in the morning when Elinor Dale took her candle from the hands of Lewis Wybird, offered her cheek to be kissed, received the salute and dragged upstairs in the wake of Fina Adamovitz.

"Shall we talk?" said Fina on the threshold of her own room. "Come in and sleep with me."

Elinor shook her head.

"I'm too tired, Fina."

"I'm not. I would like to take a carriage and drive away to London and do something exciting straightaway—drive to Earl's Court. Let's go up in the Great Wheel. Three o'clock! We 'ave not begun," said Fina.

Nevertheless, when Elinor came back repentantly in her dressing-gown to see if her guest really needed entertainment, she found Fina already in bed, asleep and snoring lightly, her clothes scattered about the floor and her hair still entangled with dead yellow roses.

Elinor went back thankfully to her own room and began the elaborate ritual with which she always fought fatigue. She was untidy enough as a rule, but when she was tired and worried she dreaded a sleepless bed, and so made a business of folding her clothes, hanging away her dresses and brushing her hair for the regulation twenty minutes. The fore-dawn was grey against the windows before she got between the cool sheets and lay back, her head on her crossed arms, to think over the day and the evening. She remembered that she had forgotten her prayers; but she was too lazy to get out again, so she bent up her knees into the proper position and said them to the ceiling. Then she remembered that she had not brushed her teeth, and for that unbreakable law she did get up.

How hot it was! How close it was! Her feet burned from dancing and standing. She went over to the windows, flung them open and sat down on the window-seat, listening to the occasional cluck and flutter of a bird in the jasmine and watching the trees breathe in their sleep. But the peace of the night could not pass over the sill to her: she was in a fever of fatigue. Her eyes strayed over the landscape alertly, re-living the day's movements.

Yes, Fina had been right. Anyone looking out of a window could see you walking down the centre of the laurel hedge, could see whether you were alone or not. It was a strange thing that whatever you did or said or thought, yes, even thought, you were always observed. You wouldn't think that so many people had time to waste in watching you! But they had. And how they talked! Lewis had been furious with her for straying off to the beech-wood instead of being ready to receive his guests. Someone had seen her go and promptly told him: and he had caught her on the way up to dress and scolded her about it. Yes, and then he had been annoyed because she had helped Edmund Broome with the curtains. He had said she would be late and that it was unsuitable and that there were plenty of servants to knock in nails and spoil their hands. She hadn't liked to say that it had been fun. Lewis was much more difficult to please in his own home than he had been in Germany.

She yawned and with a shiver left the window and slipped into bed once more, fancying herself cold; but in five minutes the cool sheets were hot and crumpled again. She tossed restlessly, flinching as her thoughts whirred round in her mind and bumped against memories and forebodings, just as the cockchafers used to whirr and bump into her face in the garden of the *Pensionnat* on summer nights.

Lewis. Mrs. Lewis Wybird of Blandon. Only another five days. Marrying Lewis was rather like marrying God—or a governess. Not much fun. No, it's not much fun!

"I don't care what you say," said Elinor aloud and excitedly to the large night—"Of course he's distinguished, and I'm very fond of him, and I wouldn't marry a German officer for anything you offered me in the world. It's my own free choice and of course I shall get accustomed to it. But all the same you needn't think it's fun marrying Lewis Wybird."

At that there popped up in the darkness a row of shocked faces, the face of Fräulein Krantz, the face of Gertrud Herrnhaus whom they used to call *Frau Komerzienrat* because at sixteen she was already engaged to a Town Councillor, and proud of it until all the girls who were 'von' laughed at her: and the face of the good-natured, stupid, fat Pomeranian, Frida Reitz, who was an heiress and engaged to a *Freiherr:* and the face of the hotel proprietor who had bowed so deeply to Lewis and had put violets on her plate at every meal of her stay: and the face of her soon-to-be sister, Enid Wybird, who was as plain as Lewis but without his distinction and without that glint of something unexplained in his smile which had always fascinated and frightened her, and made her quite sure, when he asked her to marry him, that she was thrillingly in love. All these reproving faces she now addressed with profound irritation—"You needn't think it's fun to marry Lewis Wybird."

No, and that cousin of Lewis's didn't think it was fun! That dark woman Lady Pallas always looked at her as if she was sorry for her. If she hadn't been so terrifying it would be nice to talk to her. It was curious that she should be terrifying when the son, Edmund, was not at all alarming. She wondered what he would think, did think of her for marrying Lewis Wybird. He danced very well. He was a delightful dancer. From the moment he found her out and took her away from the man with wet hands who carried his gloves instead of putting them on, the evening had been fun, right to the very end. The Niphetos roses in the conservatory had a delicious smell. She had picked one or two just to have in her hand and smell: and he had wanted one and she had given it to him. Why not?

Edmund Broome was a very good talker. It had been most awfully interesting to hear about America and touring, and life behind the scenes. Of all lives an actor's was the most exciting. It was the nearest to romance. After all, nothing romantic happened today to anyone, no murders, no love stories, no martyrdoms, no crusades, nothing— except sordidly, with police. But on the stage you had it all—all the thrilling feelings. Of course she was very fond of Lewis; but it wasn't love as Juliet, or even Helena and Hermia knew it. Very dull. One didn't even have the fun of unhappiness and parting nowadays. 'The course of true love never did run smooth.' Not true! The trouble was, nowadays, that it ran far too smooth. If she were on the stage she would make Edmund Broome let her play Hermia. He would make a good Lysander. How did it go?—

> 'The course of true love never did run smooth:
> But, either it was different in blood—
>
> O cross! too high to be enthrall'd to low.
>
> Or else misgraffed in respect of years,—
>
> O spite! too old to be engaged to young.'

Some people said Helena and Hermia weren't real people. Idiots! Hermia was as real as the *Pensionnat*. And Hermia had run away.

But there again, you see, the stage had the advantage. You ran away and instantly everything came right—

'Egeus, I will overbear your will,
For in the temple, by and by, with us,
These couples shall eternally be knit.'

So that there really was no reason for the play, because the Duke could just as well have overborne Egeus at the beginning of Act I instead of pretending that he had no power to alter the law. But what a phrase—'eternally knit!' In a fortnight Elinor Dale will eternally be knit to Lewis Wybird!

She turned on her crumpled pillow once more. There was nothing to be frightened about. She had done it of her own free will. Nobody had forced her. He was a very distinguished man and he had been so nice to her that day at Dresden when they had left Enid Wybird sitting in front of the Sistine Madonna and had gone on together wandering round the big rooms. Whenever she stopped to look at a picture though, he said "I don't think you want to look at that," which was funny because the school had seen them all on the Friday visits. Of course some pictures were rather horrid; but Lewis wouldn't look even at a Venus. And then he had said—was she so fond of pictures? And she had told him about wanting to paint: and he had said that there was plenty for her to sketch when she came to Blandon and she could copy what she liked in the picture gallery. And she said—was he going to re-open Blandon then? And he said that it depended on her and that he didn't want to startle her and he hadn't meant to speak of it; but her father had hoped he would look after her and he had promised to: and there was no better way than being married, and that he had grown so fond of her: and that once they were married she could fill Blandon with pictures if she wanted to: it should be their hobby: and what did she think?

Well, she thought that he was rather like the thin, handsome actor who had played Mephistopheles in *Faust* last month, and that it would be wildly exciting to be engaged: and that she would hurt his feelings if she said no: and it would be thrilling telling all the girls and having an engagement ring: besides, she didn't dare to say no.

At that she sat up in bed with a gasp. Was that idiot schoolgirl herself of only three months ago? How could she have been so mad— mad—mad! A creature of no sense! A child of two would have had the sense not to say yes. As if it mattered what the girls thought! Was it possible that she could ever have bothered her head over what a silly, idiotic pack of German schoolgirls thought of her? Could she ever have believed that marks mattered, and what you had for tea, and what the school would think of her picture in her wedding dress? Was it possible that only a month ago she had written thirty letters—one to every girl in the school—to tell them all about Blandon and her trousseau and the pearls that Lewis had given her, and had sent them all invitations to come over, and had remembered birthdays and painted careful water-colours of Blandon for all the mistresses? The truth was, let her face it, she had judged the whole business of getting married in terms of what the school thought!

Idiot! A born idiot—a complete fool! Senseless, senseless girl, to be excited and pleased at the idea of being eternally knit to—to what? 'Too old to be engaged to young!' Because after all there must be more in getting married than trousseaux and pin-money and a honeymoon. And what did you do on your honeymoon? And if you felt ill and miserable whom did you tell? Your husband, Lewis Wybird? But you couldn't. It was impossible to talk about yourself to old people and Lewis must be forty-five at least. Last night, dancing with Edmund Broome and afterwards in the conservatory, she had talked more about herself in one half hour than she had ever talked to her guardian in her whole life. What was marriage? O God, she was going to be married in a week to an old man to whom she couldn't talk and she didn't even know what marriage was.

And suddenly she was sitting bolt upright, icy cold, and shaking with abject terror at the mere thought of getting married and having Lewis come into her room at night. Because then—what happened? She didn't know and there wasn't a soul she could ask. But there was something and the fear of it made her teeth chatter. She couldn't go on with it. She would rather die. And all the while, worse than all the other horrors was the horror of ever letting anybody young like herself know the fool she had been. She thought she would die with shame if Edmund Broome, for instance, ever knew that she had said yes to Lewis Wybird just because being engaged was fun and she didn't know how to say no. Better go through with it and get married than let someone like Edmund Broome know that she was such a silly miserable schoolgirl fool.

And at that, half crazed with fear, excitement and fatigue, she got up once more and going across to the window pulled aside the curtains she had drawn an hour earlier: and instantly the morning sunshine flooded the room with sanity. It was full five o'clock and heavenly weather, with the pale dawn-mists of high summer still lying like gossamer on the surface of the world. And she was not married yet. She could dress and go out without anyone asking her—where are you going?

Her hip-bath was at the foot of the bed and she poured in cold water, splashed away her fever and her night terrors, dressed hastily and then slipped out as she had often done before. Down the broad flight of stairs she went to the saloon on the first landing: without much difficulty undid the shutters and unlatched the window and so passed out on to the stone balcony with its double staircase that led to the lawn. She had taken a basket with her half full of corn, and at once the peacocks came hurrying to meet her; for they knew her early appearances and would sit on the balustrade and scream if she were late. She stopped to feed them.

The morning was marvellously quiet. The early burst of bird music was over: there was no wind, and the sounds of human day had not begun. The almost inaudible clucks of the peacocks amused her. They were such meek sounds for the splendid birds to make. She was coaxing the shyest of the peahens—"Now, Jinny! Come along, Jinny! Sweet Jinny then!" when she heard behind her the sound of a window being thrown up. A face looked out at her and was gone again before she could see it clearly and for an instant she was appalled. Lewis? Was it Lewis? If it were Lewis there would be an end to morning glories.

For she had learnt that he was extraordinarily set in his ideas of what one might do and might not do. If he heard, for instance, of that nice Edmund Broome losing his temper with the gate-keeper he would be angry and would never forget it, though he would be quite polite about it. It was a horrid thing to face, this cold disapproval. She had been tempted before now to fib to him about trifles. It had been an effort not to. Of course if you eternally were knit to a man who always disapproved of what you did, it would be a perpetual temptation to lie yourself out of trouble: she could see that. She began to see that she had been rather righteous about the way the German girls lied. Not that she ever would lie, but she began to understand the temptation.

But then, of course, she was so much older and so much more experienced than that idiot girl of three months ago. And, thank heaven, Lewis's room faced north, so whoever had seen her it was not he. And if they spoke of it at breakfast she could say that their watches were wrong and that it was nearly seven instead of five. No, she would not! She would not do it! She would not pick up Fina's ways. But if she had not committed herself to being married there would be no need to be standing on the lawn shivering for fear of Lewis Wybird's disapproval. He had never disapproved of her in Germany, he had been so nice, so different from the guardian of her governess days. But now he was slipping back to the governess days. But it would be different when she was married. He was in love with her : he had said so : and of course she was very fond of him.

The peacocks having exhausted her supplies wandered away. She thought she would go down through the gardens to the mushroom field and see what she could find to fill her empty basket. The button mushrooms of late June were the best of all, and if she brought back mushrooms for breakfast, well, there was a reason for eccentrically early rising to give a *Bräutigam*. Nice language ! She would not go back to school for anything, but how she wished she were back at school !

And so thinking and so sighing she reached the further bank of the lawn and climbed up its green steps into the flower gardens. There she loitered yet another five minutes, uncrinkling the new poppies with careful fingers and shutting up one bumble-bee inside a Canterbury bell to hear it buzz and see it crawl out again like Falstaff out of the buck-basket, dusty, tumbled and so fat. She was too much interested in her bumble-bee to hear any other sound at all through its hysterical buzz, and was startled when, releasing it at last, she found Edmund Broome standing a yard away watching her, smiling at her, looking so young and jolly. For the first time in her life she saw and realised that men have good looks as well as women.

She was taken by surprise and showed it, and hadn't a word to say ; but she showed, too, that she was extremely pleased to see him.

"I saw you from the window," he said. "I had been awake hours. I heard you talking to the peacocks."

"Did you ?" She looked alarmed. "My voice does carry. Do you think other people heard ?"

"No, I happened to be awake." He seemed to understand her worried fear of being watched. "As a matter of fact I couldn't sleep last night," said he.

"No, nor could I," said she, and flushed a little.

"Do you want to pick flowers ? Shall I pick them for you ?" He felt for a knife.

"I was going to look for mushrooms. They have just begun. There is one field—"

"Oh, come on !" said Edmund joyfully, delighting at the prospect of escape from the garden into the open: he hated being walled in: and she led him in and out between the borders and across the Dutch garden and so over a stile into fields. They went single file until they reached a lane when, as he fell into step beside her, he noticed once more that she was carrying a basket and took it from her.

"I can take it," said she.

"I'll take it," said Edmund, and as if that were a re-introduction, began to talk again. "Why couldn't you go to sleep?" said he.

"I don't know. I couldn't. Why couldn't you?"

He caught at a panicle of elder-flower hanging over his head and jerked it roughly off its stalk.

"Well—" said he. And then—"Miss Dale—"

She began to laugh.

"Why 'Miss Dale' all of a sudden?"

"When I called you Elinor last night Lewis looked as if he didn't like it."

"I don't care," she muttered. And then, as he looked at her enquiringly, grew red and said—"I mean, I am my own mistress. I'm not married yet, and we do know each other. Do you remember how we went mushrooming and found a big one, as big as a hat, full of maggots?"

"So you remember that too? I'd completely forgotten that visit till last night. But lying in bed, thinking, it all came back to me as if it were yesterday. It was June, wasn't it? Do you know I believe it is the exact date."

"It isn't."

"It's there or thereabouts. I'll look it up when I get home. I've kept a diary since I was nine."

"Have you? I've tried. I can never make myself do it. When do you do it?"

"In the morning before I get up. I was writing it this morning when I heard you."

"There's a mushroom," said she. And presently—"What sort of things do you write? This morning, for instance?"

"Would you like to see it?" said Edmund.

She looked at him. He looked at her. They both stopped walking.

"I'd show it you if you wanted to see it," said Edmund.

"It's not a private diary then?" said she, peeling the solitary mushroom.

"Absolutely private," said he.

"I don't think there are any more mushrooms in this field," said Elinor, and they walked on again for some ten minutes in complete silence.

"Do you believe—" asked Edmund suddenly—"in love at first sight?"

She did not answer him. But as they wandered along the lane she began to gather a little bunch of wild flowers—a trail of vetch, a wild strawberry, a late dog-violet, harebells, and a young sprout of foxglove that had sprung from the base of a main tower of bloom.

"Will you tell me something?" said Edmund.

"If I can," said she, and added a backing of fern.

"Wait a minute," he interrupted. "Tell me something else first. Is this a public lane? Are we off Wybird's land?"

"I think so," said she. "Why?"

"Punctilio," said he.

"Oh—" She was puzzled.

"I'm going away this morning with the company," said Edmund. "I wanted to tell you myself."

"I thought you said last night that you were going on to stay with Adelaide Powers?"

"So I was," said he. "But I have changed my mind."

"Since last night?"

"Yes."

She stooped and added a blind nettle to her bunch.

"I'm sorry I shan't see you again," said she slowly. And then— "What did you want to know?"

"I suppose it's impertinent—I don't know how to put it. I thought you might know what I wanted to know."

"Do you mean about me and Lewis?" said she, amazed at her own coolness.

"Yes, Elinor. Yes. I want to know why? I mean—he's as old as Mother. It seems so strange. I can't understand it."

"And I can't discuss it," she said.

"I'm sorry. I suppose it was awful of me to ask."

"It wasn't awful," said Elinor faintly. And then, as they came to a gate which opened on a common—"If we cut across here," she said, "we get back to the wood above the beech trees where the Blandon land begins. Can you lift the gate?"

He let her through and followed her: and presently they were out of sight of the road and wandering in and out of gorse bushes with a great hedge studded with spent primrose clumps on their right. The perfume of the gorse swept over them with every puff of the soft breeze.

"You see, I do like him," she said suddenly. "At least I did. And he says it was a sort of understood thing between my father and him. And I'd never seen anyone and—at school—it seemed somehow rather exciting and—I know it sounds impossibly silly. You must despise me so." Her lip began to work. "But I said I would: and now I don't know why I said I would: and I'm terrified, Edmund."

He put his arm round her, for she was shaking and in need of support: and drew her in silence to the bank where it was overhung with spindleberry trees.

"Sit down," said Edmund.

She obeyed, and he sat down beside her, his arm still round her. Neither of them heeded the heavy dew.

"You've got to break it off," he said.

"I can't. How can I? Everything's fixed. Edmund, Edmund, I'm going to be married in five days. There are wedding presents and invitations. I could never face Lewis. You don't know what he's like in a rage. I had one most terrible fight with him over settlements. They wanted me to sign all sorts of things."

"And you wouldn't?"

"No, I was afraid of being tied up. They are talking to me again next week. I hoped if I stood out that he'd say we couldn't get married."

He looked at her with new respect. Childish she was, but not so weak as he had thought, and not so simple. He had for an instant a dim comprehension of the extraordinary jumble of a young girl's mind. He did see for a moment very clearly that childishness and strength are much more unevenly mixed in a big creature who would grow still, than in a small creature who had come to its full growth. Nesta Marshall— not that he wanted to have Nesta Marshall and Elinor in his mind at the same moment—but Nesta could never be as childish as this girl. Nesta was a woman at eighteen; nevertheless this girl in five years would outstrip a hundred Nestas.

Meantime it was strange how the mixture of schoolgirl and woman attracted him. She was something to mould, something to be proud of when moulded. So, while Elinor still cried on his shoulder, he kissed her, forgetting all prudence and planning for the main fact that he had fallen in love with her: and, being always one to take the straight way, told her his mind.

"Elinor, you can't marry him, you know. I knew last night how I felt and that if I had time I could make you feel the same. Well, we haven't got time, but does it matter? Wouldn't you rather marry me than that old man?"

"Yes," said she weeping.

"Well then, that settles it. He can't forbid it, can he?"

"Till I'm twenty-one. He can hold my fortune till I'm twenty-one. The lawyer told me so. I mean he showed me my father's will."

"Well, I don't care. I wouldn't care—" said Edmund sincerely, and he cared for money—"if he could hold it for good."

"He can't do that," said she. "But oh, Edmund, do you mean that you would—that if it weren't for Lewis we could be married? Oh, I am so happy when you say that. Not that we can. I said I'd marry him and I'm not going to cheat. One can't do that sort of thing: you know that as well as I do. But to pretend for half an hour—even to pretend for half an hour—"

"That's flum diddle," said Edmund, devoting himself, however, to the pretence with extreme earnestness. He was quite sure of his power over her.

But though they sat together talking softly, so happy, till the sun grew hot, while the birds began their second concert and the blue butterflies fluttered overhead and the dew dried off the spider-webs: and in that hour got to know each other as well as two people can who have just found out that they are intimates—still he was not able to persuade her that marrying Lewis Wybird was all flum diddle. It was as if that hour of love had dried the silliness out of her as the dew dried off the cobwebs, and had left behind the woman whom he had discerned in the schoolgirl, a delicate, fragile spirit with, nevertheless, a certain strength. He could sway her reason by his arguments and bend her will by his appeals, but he could not break her sense of integrity. She remained at the end of the hour still convinced that it was too late to do anything, that she was promised to Lewis Wybird and that she must marry him. The very assurance that she had young love to command and a way out of her troubles if she chose to take it, seemed to destroy her previous fears and give her a curious worldly strength. She wept, but repeated that nothing could be done: and Edmund, though he knew so much about women, believed that she meant it and was furious and raved at her for a fool and a flirt, and then swung round to beseechings and passionate protestations. But in spite of his businesslike dealings with life he was yet young enough to enjoy being self-sacrificing and romantic as much as she did. So at last he found himself following her lead and saying good-bye for ever under the spindleberry trees. And very unhappy they were as they kissed under the tallow-coloured spikes of the spindleberry flowers, and kissed again on the edge of the beech wood, and parting for the last time in the shadow of the house, hidden by the laurel hedge and unseen by the blinded windows, kissed again.

And at breakfast Elinor was white and quiet, but very charming to Lewis Wybird, who was proud of her way with his guests and with him. So he in turn was affable that morning to a very silent Edmund Broome. And then Edmund, flushing, suddenly said—"Look here, sir!" in a voice that made Elinor turn white and twist her napkin in her lap, not knowing what was coming. But what came was the story of the lodge-keeper. And Lewis laughed and took it very well: so well that Elinor shot a look at Edmund which said—'You see how unfair to him we have been.'

But if Edmund saw the look he did not answer it, but bolted his breakfast, collected his company and packed them off, and then was hasty and confused in farewells to his host and his host's sister: and so came to his—

"Well, good-bye, Elinor!"

"Good-bye, Edmund! Shall I see you—?"

"At the wedding? I shall try to come, of course. I so much want to come. But rehearsals—you know—I shall try to come, of course. Good-bye, Elinor!"

And so in a high dog-cart drove out of her life.

CHAPTER 47

A WEDDING DRESS

HE DROVE out of her life for exactly twenty-four hours. She spent a miserable, restless day, entertaining the house-party, playing tennis in long trailing skirts with the younger guests, and at odd moments baffling the curiosity of Fina, who would talk to her about Edmund Broome, his prospects, his career, his antecedents and his interesting silences. Then came another heavy, stately dinner-party; but this time with no dancing afterwards, but instead a scene with Lewis who, excited and unlike himself, took her out to look at the moon, and primly kissed her. Then, at last, she was permitted to go to bed and spend another miserable, restless night.

And though she slept a little, for at eighteen even Melpomene can only keep awake every other night, she woke early once more and of course got up at once, and went out to have the pleasing misery or miserable pleasure of going over the ground—but she forgot to feed the peacocks—which she had trodden the previous morning. On she wandered, thinking of what Edmund had said and of what she had answered and of how happy they had been before he rode out of her life for ever.

But as she reached the common and the climax of her misery, there sat Edmund on the gate.

He was a little sheepish, a little truculent, perfectly ready with unanswerable explanations of why he had had to go down to see his mother after all at Adelaide's, and why, when all was over between them, he was out at five o'clock in the morning waiting for her, and why he knew so unshakeably that she would be there. But she didn't want his explanations, and after one look at her joyous face he didn't want to give them. After all, what need was there to explain? There were the facts. He had said good-bye to her for ever and there he was.

"Because I've been thinking it over, Elinor, and you know I'll do whatever you want, but I don't see why we shouldn't see each other for this last week. What harm does it do? Can you see?"

She could see well enough.

"Well, what harm?"

"Lewis," said she.

"How does it hurt Lewis? It gives us something to remember. Are you glad to see me, Elinor? Were you surprised?"

"I was in heaven," she said. "But no, not surprised. I suppose I knew, really, that you would be there, although I knew you couldn't be. Edmund, yesterday was the longest day of my life."

"Well, it was the shortest of mine! One rush! God knows what they thought of me at the theatre. I've left them to it. I don't care if rehearsals go to smash. I've told the Guv'nor so. He isn't a child. Let him run his own show for once."

"When did you make up your mind?" said she.

"Five minutes after I left you, about half way down the drive. I wired Adelaide from Blandon Station. I am staying till Monday."

She said under her breath—

"Monday is my wedding-day."

"I don't know that, do I? That's not in my mind at all, is it? That doesn't torment me at all, does it? You've got to rub it into me, haven't you, every single minute we're together? I suppose you think this is great fun?"

"Ah, don't, Edmund!" But she loved his ferocity.

"Look here, Elinor, we can't go on like this. We've got to run away. I got a licence. I got it yesterday—at least—I shall have it in time. You've got to come away and marry me."

"Oh, don't begin it again!"

"I shall begin it again. I shall talk of nothing else. I shall be here every morning waiting for you. We've got four days. And if you don't meet me I shall come on to the lawn and throw stones on to your window, and of course I shall hit the wrong window. I shall go on till you're in your wedding dress. I shall follow you to the church door. Yes, I shall. And when you're in the porch itself I shall say—'Stop, Elinor, it's not too late!' I shall go on till I hear you say 'I will' to Lewis Wybird. And that will be the end. No, I shan't—I shan't come near the church. I shall come up here." For they were sitting together on the top of the ridge and the whole saucer of Blandon lay spread before them—park, river, alder thickets, woods, house, village and the village church. "Yes, here I'll sit and I shall watch you driving down to church. Look! I can see every stick and stone of the way. And I shall listen to the wedding bells. And when they stop I shall know it's the end of you. Ding, dong, bell! Elinor's dead! And so you will be, to me."

"Don't, don't, Edmund!" Yet she liked it. How could she help but

like it? It was the most comforting thing in the world to hear him rave.
Nevertheless the conventions of her girlhood still sat on the hill-tops of
Blandon like a row of stone gods, saying—'You cannot, Elinor! You
shall not, Elinor! Elinor, you must not!'

And so on the next morning and the next, though it cost her more
than she ever cared to remember, she let him wait for her, and did not
go out at five o'clock in the morning.

But on the morning before her wedding-day she met him again: and
he was quite a different Edmund that morning, very unhappy and very
gentle, neither raving nor arguing, not persuading her any more. They
sat together in the broom on the hill-top and listened to the birds and
hardly spoke. But this time he did not come down the hill with her to
the gardens. She said—

"Good-bye, Edmund, and forgive me, and don't think about me
tomorrow. I think you'd better go back to London."

He did not say a word. She put her arms round his neck and kissed
him because she chose to, fiercely and miserably; but he did not kiss her
back. And when she looked back from the end of the ride he had
already turned away.

All through the bustling day that followed she was cool and sensible
and the pain in her mind felt eased as if she had taken phenacetin.
Lewis had never been so kind: the display of presents was dazzling: and
she thought it wouldn't be so bad. She wore the family pearls at
dinner and everybody was enchanting to her.

When bedtime came Fina came to help her brush her hair and the
two girls talked late, and Elinor found that she had ceased to resent
Fina's questions and demands for confidence. And indeed, knowing
that tomorrow she would be a married woman, she found it easy to
have already a married, cool, sophisticated attitude to life and to the
silly tenderness she had had for Edmund Broome—"because you have
been meeting him, haven't you?" said Fina.

"Certainly," said Elinor.

"Every morning since the dance, eh?" said Fina.

"Three mornings," said Elinor. "How did you know?"

"I looked up Mushrooms in the Encyclopædia," said Fina. "July,
August and September are the months, though specimens occasionally
occur at the end of June. Did he want you to run away with him?"

"Yes," said Elinor crisply.

"Poor boy!"

"He'll get over it," said Elinor.

"I had better attend to him, eh? Did he kiss you?"

"Oh Fina, don't!"

"It must have been romantic. And now it hurts, eh? I know. The first time hurts very much. Elinor, you are unhappy?"

"A little."

"That is stupid of you. He is not dead, my cousin Edmund. When you are married you can do as you like, you know. And it is a brilliant match. I wish I 'ad the chance. Let me plait your hair. Shall I sleep with you tonight?"

"I wish you would," said Elinor, forlornly. Fina was gratified, and the two girls curled up in the big double bed and talked far into the night, or rather Fina talked and Elinor listened: and whenever Fina's voice thickened into drowsiness Elinor roused her again with questions. She had heard all Fina's past history, but now she wanted to hear it again. And not only Fina's. She wanted to know all about Fina's friends and their love affairs and their dreadful troubles with their husbands. Fina was fluent.

"Troubles? Oh, because when you are a Catholic, you know, you must have babies whether you like it or not. There is my sister Aida. She conceives very easily. Each year she has a baby. Are you cold, Elinor?"

"A little."

"Pull up the eiderdown. Well, at the end of the fourth baby it is awful for her and her figure is quite spoilt. So she will not have any more. And for four years she has not had one. And so the priest he will not give her absolution. And it makes her miserable—because she is very religious."

"But, Fina, I don't understand."

"Well, you see, her husband he is very fond of her: he will not leave her alone—hardly at all—so if they do not have children, well, it is deadly sin. And this year she gives in and has gone to confession again. And now she is to have another baby. Poor Aida! Because of course, she does not love him, you understand. But she had to get away from home: and what else was she to do? And he will not leave her alone. Why should he? He is a very good husband. She cannot complain. Better marry than stay with Mama and be watched and no money. If I must go home I shall marry the first man I get. I could not stay at home. So when you are married, Elinor, you will be able to help me. If I could marry over here it would mean a great deal. Brazilian men—"

"What's the time?" said Elinor.

Fina stretched out her hand to Elinor's watch which hung on the watch-stand by its short chain with a gold knob at the end.

"Four o'clock. Elinor, if you don't go to sleep you will be a sheet of washing tomorrow."

"Let's go out, Fina!"

"At this hour? Thank you! You go! Perhaps you will see your Edmund."

Elinor sat up in bed and pushed back her bright hair.

"If you weren't a foreigner, how I should dislike you. You run about over everything nice like a dog over flower-beds."

"I am obliged. Get yourself a glass of water."

Elinor obeyed. Then—

"Fina, do you mind the light?" And without waiting she pulled back the heavy curtains. "Fina?"

"Yes?"

"You only know foreign men, don't you?"

"All men are alike."

"Fina, why are things the way they are? Why have we got to think that men are cleverer always? Is it true that women's brains are really smaller and that the wisest man in the world would always be wiser than the wisest woman? Fina, until I met Edmund—you do like him, don't you?—I never saw a man who didn't seem to despise me. They say— 'the ladies!' and look at you like that Shakespeare play, as if you were all items. You know—'Item, two lips, indifferent red—' Even Lewis does and Lewis is very very kind to me. And I do trust him and I do like him and I know I shall be happy with him. But Edmund talks to me as if I were a man."

Fina giggled.

"Then my opinion of Edmund Broome changes, Elinor. How it changes!"

"Well, I mean he talks to me as if I had sense. Think what the world would be like, Fina, if you could do what you liked and earn your living, and go about by yourself: and talk to all the men you met as much as you liked without people saying 'Aha! Oho!' Or go out to dinner with a man quite alone, and each pay for yourself—or he be your guest."

"Such a world could not be," said Fina.

"There was a woman Senior Wrangler three years ago."

"Oh, yes, if you would like to be a frump and wear bloomers and have short hair. Come back to bed, Elinor!"

"I can't. I'm going to get up."

"Silly! Come back to bed! Sleep while you can!" And she laughed. Elinor came back to the bedside.

"Fina, my head is splitting."

"I tell you what. Get into bed and we will smoke cigarettes. It will soothe you."

"But the smell in the morning when Enid comes in! She will come in: you know she will."

"Leave it to me. They are ordered to me for my 'ay fever! Besides, what does it matter what they say? Tomorrow you are a married woman. Wait, I get them."

And Fina was delighted to slip out of bed, speed along the corridor to her own room and return with the forbidden things, rather crumpled because they had been tucked at the back of a handkerchief sachet. She lit one for herself and then lit Elinor's, and laughed at her when she choked and dropped the horrid thing and only found it again when it had burned a hole in the lace edge of her pillow-slip. But the laughter did the bride good and the smoke made her drowsy, and then fatigue rolled up over her mind like a sea-mist rolling up over a countryside, and blotted out the hours for her. The sun was high in the heavens when she was awakened by Fina, fully dressed, bouncing on to the bed beside her: the maid on the other side proffered a laden tray: and her five bridesmaids in all the various stages between dressing-gown and full toilet were swirling into her room to kiss her and wish her happiness.

And then she was aware that it was eleven o'clock and that the whole house was alive and humming with excitement. There was a perpetual sound of feet in the corridors: high-pitched voices argued with obstinate basses: there were occasional rumbles as of furniture being moved and regular hammer strokes told that a marquee was being set up for the villagers beyond the ha-ha. Then her own dog which had somehow wriggled loose from chain, collar and kennel, came bolting into the room, hurled itself on to her bed, knocked her tray to the floor, licked her face and hands frantically, barked at the maid, and was hauled out again in disgrace by one of the under-housemaids. All the while Fina, as chief bridesmaid, and the five other bridesmaids came and went, thanking her again and again for the bracelets that Lewis had given them, showing her their bouquets and clustering round her to admire the bridal bouquet itself, newly arrived from the greenhouses.

"*Ach, ist es aber ein Besen!*" drawled Fina. And indeed the bouquet was solidly constructed. Arum lilies were reinforced by lilies of the valley and wired Niphetos roses, delicate but not allowed to droop. Their scent filled the room and suddenly Elinor turned so white that Enid Wybird rounded on the flock quite angrily and drove it out of the room. Then she told Elinor that she mustn't let herself get over-tired and agitated: so, though there was plenty of time, she had better have her bath and get dressed slowly, and presently Enid would come back to help her into her wedding-gown: and with that left her to the ministrations of the family nurse and her own maid. And very soon Elinor was bathed and dressed and sitting in front of the mirror in her white satin petticoat and white dressing-jacket with the *broderie anglaise* collar, having her hair dressed in a way she did not like, brushed on the top of her head and coiled there. The maid had lighted the round spirit lamp and set the tongs to heat, and the smell of methylated spirit made her feel sicker than ever.

"Must you wave my hair, Masters? It waves enough by itself, surely."

"Just a touch, Miss, for the occasion!"

So Elinor submitted until Masters in her agitation curled the kiss-curls at the nape of the neck so tightly that the hot iron burnt her and away came the hair on the tongs. The small burn throbbed painfully and seemed the worst thing that had happened to her yet: and her eyes filled with tears that she was ashamed to wipe away as Masters pinned in the wreath of orange-blossom and hurt her again with the hairpins.

"I'd really rather do it myself, Masters."

"Oh, no! Let Masters, dear!" said Enid Wybird coming in at the moment. "She's making you look so nice. And now for the wedding dress!"

As they put her into it the memory of the hours she had stood to be fitted and the stuffy air of the fitting-room and the peculiar smell of pins swept over her and added to the growing sensation of dizziness. The maid's roughened fore-finger touched the little burn at the back of her neck as she hooked the high boned collar, and made her wince. The bodice was dreadfully tight: she could not breathe. "I told them to make it looser," she said desperately. But Enid Wybird, putting out her hands and smoothing the tight bodice round the waist, would hear no criticism.

"It's a perfect fit," said she. "Masters, pull in Miss Dale's laces a little," and the maid fumbled with the corset strings. Last came the veil, and then she was to look at herself in the glass.

"May the bridesmaids come in and see you?" said Enid.

Of course they might come in. And by this time they had all got their hats on, Leghorn hats trimmed with sweet peas and the brim quilted with pink chiffon and more sweet peas tucked underneath against the ear. They wore pink satin dresses veiled in pale mauve tulle and trimmed with coffee-coloured lace, black shoes and stockings and bouquets of more sweet peas. The room was full of noise and scents and laughter and they all kissed her again: and then Fina cried out that she looked as white as a sheet and ought to be quiet for ten minutes, and bustled the bridesmaids away.

"Could I——?" she said to Enid Wybird with a gasp.

"What, my dear?"

"Be quiet for ten minutes? How long have I got?"

"Half an hour," said Enid Wybird cheerfully. "Plenty of time. Of course you're tired and confused. Would you like some sal volatile?"

"Yes, I should," said she with unexpected decision.

The nasty stuff took away the dizzy feeling; but she still felt very sick. They stood round her, a circle of concern, till she could endure it no longer.

"I think it's my frock," she said feebly. "It's terribly tight."

"Undo the back for her, Masters! Why don't you lie on the bed, my dear? It won't hurt your dress if you lie carefully. I'll sit by you, shall I? I won't talk to you."

"Could I be quite alone, Enid? I want to read through the service again. I want to be quite alone. Will you call me in half an hour, Masters?"

"Better say five-and-twenty minutes. Well, good-bye, dear child! God bless you! I shall see you at church."

She submitted to the kiss with its lingering smell of witch hazel and eau de Cologne, and watched Enid's tall thin figure, so like Lewis's but so much less elegant, disappear.

"You're sure I can't help you, Miss?"

"Quite sure. Oh, Masters, don't let anyone disturb me. Don't even come in yourself, will you? I want to be really quiet."

"You shall, Miss, you shall!"

The door closed. At once she locked it. She did not know why she did it: she only knew that it gave her a sense of relief. The dizziness had quite gone off.

Five-and-twenty minutes, Enid had said. She picked the watch off its little stand and held it in her palm. One minute was gone already. Four-and-twenty minutes. And then—'The voice that breathed o'er Eden the earliest marriage chime . . .'

She looked up from the watch and saw the bride staring at her from the wardrobe mirror. There was something repellent about dead white satin. Twenty-three minutes. She went across to the dressing-table and picked up the bridal bouquet and bore it back to the long mirror and looked at herself again. She was a bride. She was the bride. Her hands were so cold that she could hardly close her fingers round the metal holder. With the unconscious gesture that any woman makes when she is holding flowers and her thoughts are elsewhere she lifted the mound of blooms to her face: and the scent of the pale green-white roses spoke to her as only scents can speak. There was re-created for her the conservatory and the fairy lights hung in the camellia bushes and the strains of the 'Blue Danube' and the feel of a black cloth coat-sleeve on her bare arm where her glove had wrinkled down. Then she heard again a voice in her ear—"Can't we find somewhere to sit out?"

She looked down at the watch. Twenty minutes.

"I can't do it," said Elinor very composedly.

Whereupon, laying her flowers down upon the floor, she put her hand to her head, ripped off her veil and cast it from her. Then she began to fumble with the hook of her collar, and again with the fastenings at her waist. But one of the hooks was caught in the eye and as she pulled and tugged in vain, a panic took her and abandoning the fastenings she began to wrestle with the material itself till she ripped it free of its gathers: then, stooping, she kicked and trampled at the slowly dropping folds of thick silk till at last her feet were clear. Then she wrenched open the wardrobe door, pulled down from its peg a linen frock, slipped into it, weeping with rage and fear because the cuffs were hooked and had to be unhooked before she could get her hands through them, got the dress on at last, tore down a dust-cloak by ripping its satin loop, and hustled it over her dress: turned to her glove drawer, took from it the first scarf that came to hand, swathed it round her head: then, making a football of her bridal bouquet, she stumbled to her dressing-table, tore off her pearls and laid them down. All this she did regardless of the racket she made; but now with sudden caution she tip-toed to the door, and turned the key so slowly and quietly that it did not creak at all. Then she opened the door and looked out.

A maid was passing down the corridor and as Elinor watched her out of sight a clock in the room under her chimed the quarter. Fifteen minutes! She slipped out, closing the door and went very softly along the passage, down the staircase, and then raced across the landing into the saloon.

It was as she had known it would be, empty of human beings; but her wedding presents lined the walls and near the door mounds of flowers marked the spot where she and Lewis must stand to receive their guests. She gave her fate one glance, then whipped across the empty space to the open windows, ran out on to the balcony and down the stone steps, had a vision of an empty lawn, chairs, marquee and strings of bunting: then was safe hidden in the laurel hedge and running, running, running for her life.

For it was twenty minutes to the hill-top where Edmund had said he would be, and he always kept his word: and in another moment her absence would be noticed. She could never do it. She had forgotten to change her white satin shoes and already the frail fabric was splitting. She could feel the shoe give under her and came heavily to her knees: and as, gasping with the pain of the fall and the pain of utter breathlessness, she scrambled to her feet again, she heard her wedding-bells begin to ring.

She could never do it, never do it! On through the deserted gardens, twisting, turning, doubling, she ran, still gasping that she could never do it. Her run was reduced to a walk, then was no more than a helpless weak-kneed crawl as she reached the belt of shrubbery that ended the gardens.

Rounding them, she saw Edmund, Edmund himself, white with anxiety, running to meet her, crying—

"Don't be frightened! It's all right. I knew you'd come. I've got everything fixed. I've got a horse and trap. That's right, hold on to me a minute! You're all right, you know, sweetheart! You're all right!"

She clung to him. She could not get her breath. She was sick with the pain in her lungs from that mad running. She gasped at last—

"How did you know?"

"I knew you'd have to come this way," he said.

"How did you know I'd come?"

He did not give her any answer; but he held her safe, kissing her and soothing her till her shaking knees could support her. Then walking slowly, he caring but for her comfort, she with fearful glances backward, they went along the little path that cut through the plantation to the public lane. There she saw a decent trap with a mare in it, tethered to the gate. He helped her in, put a rug about her, climbed up to the driver's seat and took up the reins.

"Hark!" said she.

For a moment they sat motionless while the horse pawed impatiently.

"There's no-one," said Edmund.

She said in an indescribable voice—

"The bells have stopped!"

On that he turned to her with the wickedest boy's grin.

"We're in for it now, Mrs. Broome!" cried Edmund: then, to the mare—"Come up, old lady!" and set off at a round pace for matrimony.

CHAPTER 48

DOMINA BROOME'S LAST MANAGEMENT

It was six o'clock of the same evening when Domina Broome, still in her wedding garments, rang the bell of her own front door. The old and experienced maid who opened it received her with a look of intelligence.

"They're in the library, ma'am. Mr. Edmund—"

"Yes, I know," said Donna sharply. "There must be some sort of a meal, of course. Tell cook to send out for what she wants! Here, take my bonnet, Mary!" And she pulled at the bow and threw back the strings with a 'pouf!' of exhaustion. It had been hot in the train. The maid lifted the bonnet carefully from her mistress's hair and took her cloak. "When did they come?" said Donna frowning.

"Not an hour ago, ma'am. And Mr. Edmund in such spirits! I was that taken aback—"

"Yes, yes. I suppose the servants know?"

"Well, ma'am—"

"Yes, of course, you're all buzzing. But tell them to hold their tongues, Mary, at least till tomorrow. Where did you say they were? The library?"

She swam across the black and white tiles and was about to fling open the library door when some sad wistful thought blew across her mind like a scent, and she remembered how often she had stood outside that polished uncompromising door, afraid to go in, thinking—'The other side of this door is my hell.' And now the other side of the door was her son's heaven, and in spite of the shock of the business and her delighted worried indignation, still she felt an intruder. What right had she to enter their heaven unasked? So she hesitated and knocked: then, on a movement from within, opened the door, entered, closed it behind her, and stood leaning against it, surveying the two children. For what were they after all but two children? They had clearly been sitting in one arm-chair, but had sprung to their feet at her knock, and Elinor held fast to Edmund's hand.

"Well!" said Donna and surveyed them. There was nothing to be said, and they did not attempt to say anything. But to her daughter-in-law she was a grim figure.

545

"Are you married?" Donna addressed her son.

"Two hours ago," said he grinning. "Special licence."

"How did you get it?"

"Certain amount of lying."

"This is nothing to laugh at, Edmund. You may find yourself in prison. Well, thank God you've done it!"

Elinor regarded her husband's mother with large eyes and summoned up courage to speak.

"D'you mean you don't mind?" she said incredulously.

"Mind? Oh, my poor child, don't look so frightened. Did you think I should be angry? Why should I? I have the greatest confidence in Edmund. I'm very pleased, my dear, so long as you look after him. I hope you will like this house. I told Edmund he should have it for a wedding present. At the same time, you know, it's a very disturbing business. Mind? I mind the way it has been done. You've both behaved extremely badly. No, I mean it, Edmund. You've done a ticklish thing in the worst possible way. Why didn't you speak to me? I suppose she wouldn't let you. But it would have been much wiser, my dear Elinor. As it is Lewis will never forgive either of you. I must say I think it was cruel to make a laughing-stock of him—the whole church waiting. It was most painful."

"Did they wait long?" said Elinor in a whisper.

"More than half an hour."

"Do people know?" said Edmund.

"Well, it has been given out that Elinor is ill, that she had a fainting fit. But of course the whole village is buzzing. No, I must say, as far as the manner of it is concerned, there isn't an excuse for either of you."

"I know there isn't," said Elinor, staring at the floor.

Edmund squeezed her hand, bowing to the storm with a full sense of his mother's own sense that she must administer the necessary rebuke before she took the matter in hand and sent them into safety.

"How did you guess?" said he.

"Guess? My dear boy, I'm not a fool. I knew something like this was bound to happen sooner or later. And I don't say that I should have stopped it if you had told me. At the same time it is very serious. Lewis can do infinite harm."

"To Edmund? What can he do?" said Elinor lifting a white face.

"It's all right, darling," said Edmund reassuringly. And then—"Yes, Mother, I've thought of it all. I've made an enemy for life. But it's done and well done: and I'm the happiest man in England. Now help us!"

"But of course I shall help you. What else do you think I should do?" said Donna indignantly. "You had better get away tonight—Italy, I think—and leave me to cope with Lewis Wybird. We have always got on well. He was very fond of my father. I will go down tomorrow and tell him the truth. Elinor, you had better give me a letter to him. Sit down at that table and get it done at once while Edmund and I talk over ways and means."

And with that Donna, for the last time, went into management.

She took her son out into the garden and had a long talk with him, and gave him much good advice, while Elinor wrestled, not without tears, over her letter. Also Donna undertook to get into touch with Stephen and interview the lawyers and, if she could, stave off the storm clouds from Blandon. She stood over son and daughter to see that they ate a good supper, packed a bag with necessaries for the embarrassed Elinor, and saw them off by the midnight train. But at the last she clung to her son like any foolish mother, as she kissed him and told him not to worry. She would let him know everything that happened and meanwhile he was to be happy—dear, dearest boy!

"And remember what I told you about women, Edmund!"

"What did you tell me, darling Mother?"

"Yes, you see, you've forgotten. Never mind! Give me a kiss, Elinor. Be good to each other, my children! Oh, be good to each other! Good-bye! Good-bye!" The train streamered out.

But late as it was her day's work was not over, for when she got back to her own doorstep she found the parlour-maid in tears of excitement.

"He's in the library, ma'am, and he won't go."

"Who, you foolish woman?"

"Mr. Wybird, ma'am."

She compressed her lips and once more went straight to the library. And again, as was always happening in that haunted room, the hands of time spun backwards, and it seemed to her that Harry Broome himself rose to meet her. She had noticed often enough in the last years that Lewis was growing like her father: the Broome and Wybird blood had mixed in both with much the same effect. But tonight it was more than a mocking come-and-go resemblance. Lewis at that moment, standing with one hand on the back of the green leather chair, the light of the tilted reading-lamp blaring on to his hands and watch-chain but leaving his face dark, was so like her father as she remembered him waiting to rehearse her twenty years ago, that for an instant she could not speak.

Familiar, long forgotten sensations swept over her: the feeling of being in disgrace, the need for wariness and humility, the cunning perception that even this all-powerful and implacable creature could be mastered by a study of its weaknesses: and the revulsion from all these feelings expressing itself again in that movement of the head which all the world found so irritating. 'Chin up! I'm not going to flatter him!' And thus far it was the mind of the young Donna.

But in the mind of the mature Domina these sensations were banished in turn by a strange new feeling of affection, of wayward, baffled, immortal affection for the powerless wisp of memory that had been Harry Broome: so that she all but cried out to that black thin figure with the heavy Wybird countenance, the pinched proud nose and narrow eyes—"Father, dearest Father, I will do anything you want."

And then she pulled herself together: because, of course, it was not Harry Broome, but the thinner, more modern figure, the meaner mouth, the higher forehead, the arider glance of Lewis Wybird. 'A dry stick, Lewis Wybird, compared with my father,' she thought. Then— 'A look of the Broomes, no more. I can manage him,' and went forward with concern, with great dignity, feeling herself in comparison with him a creature of almost florid ease, warmth and graciousness.

"My dear Lewis, what can I say to you?"

He waved aside her offered hand with a fierce irritation that suited her. The more human he was the easier it would be.

"They're here? Then that woman lied. Where are they?"

"They've been here. They've gone."

"Where?"

"Italy."

"When?"

"The night boat."

He picked up his hat and stick at that as if he were prepared instantly to go after them, over land, through seas to Italy, to pluck them out of honeymooner's Italy. So menacing was his movement that instinctively she got between him and the door as she cried out—

"No, Lewis! Listen! It's quite useless. They're married." And at that he put down again his hat and stick.

"When?"

"This afternoon."

"It's not legal."

"He had a special licence."

"She's a minor."

"He lied about her age. He doesn't deny it. They were quite beside themselves. He can be punished for it, of course. I know that. But it won't help, Lewis. They were married. Nothing can unmarry them."

He took a step towards her. Anger glowed from his still, composed face like heat out of a smoothing-iron.

"And you? How much had you to do with this business?"

"I knew nothing, Lewis."

"You would say that, of course."

She did not answer. But if he could glow with anger, so could she. Their looks battled for a moment; but she was a noble looking woman. He gave in.

"I beg your pardon, Domina. If you say so, I believe you, of course. But why did you come up to town? Adelaide says that you came straight from the church."

"I guessed, of course."

He was shaken by his pale rage, till then so carefully controlled.

"Guess? What had you to guess? You know your son, no doubt. I understand he has his reputation. But he was in my house and so were you. You say you guessed. Then what did you guess? What has taken place in my house?"

"Lewis, they fell in love. It happened under all our eyes. I saw it happening myself. But he left next day. What could one say or do? Was I to come to you and say—what could I have said?"

"All at one meeting?" said he—"one meeting only?"

"Well, Edmund went on to Adelaide's, you know," said she.

"I see. Yes, I see everything." Then—"I'll break him. I will. If it costs me my last penny. And he's your son, Domina. Well, I know where I stand now, so—I'll say good evening."

"No. Sit down, Lewis!"

"Sit down? Sit down? Do you expect me to hob-nob with you?"

"Yes! Why not? We are cousins still. Lewis, you must see sense in this matter. They have done an outrageous thing and they will be punished for it, believe me. They will not have an easy time. You have too many friends for that. Everyone must disapprove and show it. But you mustn't. I am speaking to you now as your cousin and your old friend, not as Edmund's mother. I tell you you can't afford to be active in punishing them."

"Can I not?"

"Not unless you are prepared to make yourself ridiculous. The situation for you is on the edge of the ridiculous already. You have been left whistling at the altar, a middle-aged Don Juan." And she drove her words at him with intent to make him wince. "Can't you see that is how people will phrase it, if you let them? But, Lewis, you can't afford to let them. And after all, though those two wicked children have put you in this false position, they have not done it wantonly. There is no malice in them. They fell in love—that is their excuse and your defence. It is mere policy for you to be generous, madly generous. Turn the tables! Be fantastic now in your generosity! That is the only way to save your face."

He watched her face, his cold eyes shifting ceaselessly to and fro as if he were reading a book.

"That is perfectly sound," he said at last.

"And Lewis—"

"Well?"

"There are other sides to this business."

"I do not wish to hear them."

"Ah, but you must. Look, here is her letter."

He took it, read it, looked at her.

"Have you read this masterpiece?"

"Of course not."

"Then you'd better read it."

She skimmed through it hastily. It was a girl's letter, but it had its dignity: and it ended—'You mustn't blame Edmund. It was all my fault.' Then, with ill-advised, childish pride, Elinor had signed her married name.

Said Donna, smoothing the paper—

"Lewis, can't you see now that the girl who wrote this letter could never be a fit mistress for Blandon? It's pitiful."

"It's the letter of a fool. You're right, Donna. I'm well rid of her. 'Frightened to get married!' And in the afternoon she marries."

She began to grow impatient.

"Just so. That is why you should be so thankful. Good God, Lewis, you're well out of it. You are indeed. Suppose she had married you? Do you suppose you could have stopped—"

"What?"

"Precisely such an affair as this? Does she make you less of a laughing-stock if she runs away from you after you are married?"

He was sneering openly.

"So your opinion of her character does, then, coincide with my own? A loose wench!"

She disdained him.

"Oh, please, that sort of thing is not necessary. I cannot talk to you if you take that tone."

"I'm not aware, Domina, that I've any craving to be talked to. You point out to me that I am well rid of a slut and I agree. And I agree that the course you suggest is the most likely one to protect me from ridicule. But I do not think you can expect me to be choice when I speak of my ward or of your son. If you detain me you must expect to hear the truth." Suddenly his mouth began to work. "For that matter, Donna, I am not a creature of stone. I was deeply attached——She gave me no reason to dream that she was not happy." He put his hand to his mouth, worrying at his finger-tips, and his hand shook. "Thankful! For what I have received I am to be truly thankful, am I? This is my wedding night."

She put her hand on his arm.

"Lewis, you took a risk. Eighteen—forty-five—is a gamble!"

He turned on her.

"You say that to me? You who married an older man than I? Were you unfaithful to him then in the first twenty-four hours?"

"Hush, Lewis! God forgive us all. Yes, you are right. I married an elderly man: and you know, you must know that I was a happy woman while he lived."

"And no older than Elinor."

"Younger than Elinor. Yes. He made life heaven for me. There was no other face in the world. But now, Lewis, now that I am a middle-aged woman and look back upon my life, now I can say—perhaps it was as well that he died. I did love him. But if in ten years or so, when I was twenty-six perhaps and he was an old man, if then someone had come into my life, someone my own age, young, handsome—then Lewis—"

"Then, Donna?"

"I don't say—I cannot say—I dare not say that I should have been faithful." Then as he looked at her, devouring her face with his cold clever eyes—"Youth needs youth, Lewis." And with that her hands dropped to her sides. She had done all she could. She was exhausted.

He nodded, opened his mouth to speak, hesitated, did not speak:

took up his hat, stick and gloves and without another look at her went out of the room and out of the house.

She sat on long after he had gone, too tired to move. She felt as if she had just come from her own funeral. Everything was over. Edmund was married and, in spite of the scandal of the business, well married. A flurry was very good for him: nor could a little social disgrace hurt him, though even there his luck might hold. For it was a romantic business whipping a girl away from the altar steps, and Lewis Wybird was neither young nor popular. No wonder that Elinor had run to Edmund's beckoning. But had she character or was it merely Edmund's will that had controlled her?

Donna thought that she must have a talk with Elinor, and then again, that no, she must not! They must fight it out between themselves or love it out between themselves. She could do no more for them. Your son's your son till he gets him a wife. . . .

Donna was a free woman at last and a very tired one. But she had her home waiting for her like any other married woman. Yes, though she had denied Joscelyn and her youth, he had left her his home.

'I am so tired, Joscelyn. You have been asleep this quarter century. You're rested. You're dead. But how tiring it is to be alive and alone. I've done all I can. I've acted to please you, Father. And if I hated you as much as I loved you, Stephen, still I gave you your son. And you, Geoffrey, did I do you so much harm? I never meant to. Edmund is married and happy and doesn't need me any more. I will see Stephen tomorrow, and the people at the New Broom, and I will put everything in order: and I think I have spiked Lewis's guns. It will all take about a week, I suppose: and then I shall go home for good. I'm too old to shift about. Joscelyn, I'm nearly as old as you were when you died. Only seven years between us now. Isn't that strange? I am already twenty years older than my own mother. And my boy is on the sea at this moment with a girl I hardly know. And Stephen has forgotten me and I have forgiven him. And in a week I shall be at home.'

CHAPTER 49

KINGDOM COME

IT SEEMED to her as she stepped on to the platform at her journey's end, that in more than twenty years nothing had changed: not the voices, nor the cheery, toothless porter, nor the conglomeration of carts and pony-carts and tumble-down conveyances gathered in the yard. The town had not changed, though here and there a house-front had been whitewashed, and on one side of the interminable road a hut had fallen down and two or three had been built beyond it. But everything was damper than she remembered, and the hills were lower and greyer, and she had forgotten that the long road was so bumpy.

She caught her breath as they turned into the drive; but there was nothing to distress her: the place was well kept, better kept than when she had left it, and the elderly caretaker whom she remembered as a young maid was on the doorstep to welcome her. There was no other welcome; but it was home. Fires had been lighted in the sitting-rooms and in her bedroom, delicious peat fires that burnt noiselessly and filled the grates with white ash. The maid brought her tea and repaired to the kitchen again: and Donna was left alone at last with her desire.

She was tired, and she could rest. She was at home, and she need never leave it.

Presently she wandered from room to room. They held the furniture she remembered but stiffly arranged by a servant's hand. The walls needed paint and paper, and the whole place cried out for daily care. Well, the house should have love again: she would care for it: and presently she would entertain a little and see Joscelyn's old friends. She would have the tennis courts kept up for the boys and girls to use, and presently Edmund and Elinor would be over. Later on there would be Edmund's children.

She did not know if she was going to be happy. Only time could tell her that. Well, she could always return. Edmund had said so. For a moment her thoughts dwelt on Edmund with a longing that made her sick: and yet—my son's my son till he gets him a wife! Had he not already ceased to be Edmund? Would she long for him less if she lived in the same house with him? Hardly.

No, she did not think it was in her to be happy anywhere; but at least this was home and she would never leave it. She flung open her bedroom windows and watched the sunset. It glowed upon the hillside and turned to crimson the white chalk-mark on the hill. On the branch below her there was a rustle and a chirp where the robins used to nest.

Presently she went to a remembered shelf and took down a much worn volume with illustrations—Mark Twain's *Tramp Abroad*. She propped it in front of her over the evening meal, and lay on Laura's sofa all the evening, reading it.

But she did not sleep well and the first week was a hard one, for she had been mistaken in her first impression of an unchanged home, and it was not easy, as she went about the place disentangling fact from memory and memory from illusion, to accustom herself to the changes nature and man had made. The rhododendrons had grown enormously: she was wrong about the length of the drive: a sapling wood beyond the laburnums spoilt her view of the sea. Laura's parrot was alive and remembered her; but Gambetta, the poodle, was gone. The recent graves of the two sisters were white and neat, but on Joscelyn's grave the headstone had slipped and the lettering was green with lichen. The fort was a desolation, and the roses had deteriorated into mere briars. On the other hand the bailiff had faithfully tended the red walls, though to do it he had stripped away the ferns and wild roses and snapdragons that used to grow along the coping: and the well-kept garden scarcely needed her care. It was a pleasant garden, but she remembered it brighter, gayer, more luxuriant. And how small the poppies were!

She soon saw that she would be lonely, though she was not forgotten. She renewed some old friendships, went out to dinner occasionally and gave dinners in return; but her neighbours were not near ones and she did not join in the life of the town. Well, it was her own choice. She wanted to put off the world. But something in her nature still longed for the world, so that she hovered between two moods. She was either saying to herself—"This is what I wanted. This is peace. How happy I am!" or she was saying to herself—"I shall go mad alone in this place. I can't bear it."

Yet week by week and month by month she bore it and the days grew up like briars between her and the rest of the world and fenced her in. Only in the evenings when, in the other world, she would have been sitting in her dressing-room and making up, did her sense of desolation grow acute. Then she longed for the smell of the theatre and the roar of the house at the end of a good scene. Yet it was a purely momentary longing: she had no desire to resume her stage life. But something was missing, and as the months went by she knew it. She felt as if she had walked out of the world in the hope of walking into another, as you walk out of a room into another; but she had walked out of a room into a mere blind passage, and she could not find any door.

Edmund and Elinor, coming over to see her three months after the birth of their first child, agreed to be worried about her. But then they generally agreed with each other. The fifteen months that they had spent together as well as the birth of Richard Broome had solidified their relationship and they had not justified their ill-wishers. The light brilliant love that had sprung up between them so swiftly, that might have proved a mere gaudy annual sown in April to bloom in June and die out utterly by the end of summer, had grown instead into a sturdy plant. The boy and girl soon disappeared: Edmund and Elinor were a young single entity, a young married couple, already much more partners than lovers. For though Edmund took the lead he was not an independent creature, and his successes were dependent on her constant co-operation. He loved to know that he could not do wrong in her eyes. She was passionately in love with his strength, his energy, his capacity for doing what he wanted to do: he was aware of it and the knowledge steadied him. He could not resist telling her every detail of his plans for the sake of the encouragement her intense interest, her utter confidence in his rightness gave him. But it also made him the more cautious in perfecting his schemes before he brought them to her. He could not afford to prove himself wrong in her eyes nor to let results falsify him.

For he was aware after a year's close intercourse in which they had not had too much time for illusions of lovers, but had to settle down quickly to the business of knowing each other, that his wife, though she gave herself and her judgment so utterly into his hands, was not a weakling either in body or mind. He knew that he valued her approval because she had brains and, when she judged other people, used them, and so he took good care that she should not use them against him. She was ignorant, but passionately eager to learn: conventional, but from training rather than from instinct: and he knew that he could make what he liked of her while she was still in the first flush of her passion for him. Nevertheless he perceived that if he neglected to make her to his pattern she would make herself to her own. She was as easy to break as quicksilver; but she broke into the shapes of her own nature. This he had discovered about her, not too willingly, for he preferred to take human beings as they were, to judge them and use them without thinking of how they came to be what they were. But the need to think about her was good for him and heightened his respect for her.

"Best day's work I ever did in my life," he told his mother. "We think alike in everything and I can trust her with my business as if I were there myself. And she's very sweet."

Donna smiled, as she often did, at Edmund. And he, though he could not criticise himself, was quick to note criticism. He demanded an explanation.

"Well what, Mother?"

"What, my son?"

"What have I said now? Isn't she very sweet?"

Donna looked across the lawn. Elinor sat under the cedar in a comfortable basket chair, her child on her knee. It was awake and crowing with delight as it thrust its fist against her mouth. She, too, was laughing as she kissed it. The slanting September sunlight was directly behind her and her pale brown-gold hair shone like a halo. She looked up as they spoke of her and rising, came across to them. The child, slung easily across her shoulder, was still laughing and signalling with blind fingers to the sun.

"Sweet? You always use the wrong word," said Donna.

"Oh, pooh! You know what I mean. The Guv'nor says the same. He says she's the sweetest thing. He thinks she's got a future, you know. He takes the greatest interest. He's been training her solidly all these months. She goes to him every day. He thinks she'll be a sensation."

Donna shook her head.

"It's not the actress temperament, Edmund."

"No, but she's so sweet: and with her looks! And I tell you what, Mother, if sheer hard work can make an actress she'll make one. Nothing's too much trouble for Elinor. Ah well, you can say I'm in love with her; but the Guv'nor says just the same. It's plod, plod, plod, and she doesn't know what conceit means."

"That's what I say: she hasn't the actor's temperament. She's very beautiful, Edmund, and if she works in the way you describe it's quite clear that she'll be an asset. You can get a long way with hard work. But she'll never be of the theatre as you—I—as the Broomes are. But she's very sweet."

"There, you see, it is the word for her."

"I wonder," said Donna, rising and holding out her arms for the child as Elinor reached them. "We've been talking of you," she said, with the stiff friendliness that was customary with her when she talked to her son's wife. She had not the art of talking to young girls. "Edmund tells me that you are going to become a true Broome. You are going on the stage like the rest of us."

Elinor looked at her husband.

"He wants it," said she, "and of course I'd always had a hankering for the stage."

"What schoolgirl hasn't?" said Donna rather sharply: and Edmund frowned while Elinor answered uncertainly—

"I know, of course, that it means years of hard work."

"You will be here another fortnight, I hope," said her mother-in-law softening again. "Would you care—would it be of use to her, Edmund, do you think, if she read with me in the evenings?"

Elinor flushed scarlet and Edmund answered with an eagerness unusual to him—

"She would give her ears, wouldn't you, Nell? But she wouldn't let me suggest it."

And thereafter Donna's days were full; for the readings soon overflowed the evenings and the two women worked together all day long, while Edmund rode and walked or went shooting with the bailiff.

"Well, how do you get on?" said Edmund to his wife at the end of a week.

"I'm worn out," said Elinor simply. "It's like running races with an express train. It's like being arm in arm with the Gunpowder Plot. I'm so tired I want to cry. But I shall be thankful for the discipline when I get home, I know. I'm going to electrify Cousin Stephen when I've had time to recover. But oh, I'm tired! Did you read a book that came out last year by that man who writes about India? The Jungle Book? Well, I feel like the little boy who saw the elephants dance—'I have seen it and I die.' She's a shattering woman. But, Edmund, how she can endure living here alone with all that force shut up inside her, I can't understand. What she'll do when we're gone—"

"I know, I know," said Edmund worriedly.

"Why does she stay on here? Does she think you don't want her?"

"She can't think that. Of course, I don't mind owning, Elinor, that she used to be rather overwhelming. One likes to run one's own show. But I'd put up with that to have her back at the New Broom."

"Can't you persuade her? She ought to be acting. It made me

ashamed to have her toiling over me. I felt such a squeaking Cleopatra. Talk to her, Edmund! You always get what you want. Make her come back with us!"

"I think you're right. I think I will," said Edmund, but doubtfully. For though he had gained strength and the power to control and order and be obeyed in the last fifteen months, he could not feel that the experience had given him any fresh power to deal with his mother. Rather the contrary. There was a tie between them they could not break, but he no longer felt her taut at the end of the rope which bound them to each other. The line had slackened and as fast as he ran after her she paid out more rope.

"Mother, Elinor and I have been talking. We think Ireland doesn't suit you. You don't look a bit rested, though you said you wanted a long rest. I think, and Elinor agrees with me—she's very much attached to you, Mother—that you're missing it all."

"All what, Edmund?"

"Being in the thick of things."

"Don't be so local, Edmund. I'm in the thick of things here just as much as you are at the Glory Hole. I'm planting four thousand bulbs this autumn."

"Yes, and I want to put the Guv'nor into *Macbeth* this autumn and who's to play Lady Macbeth?"

"Dear Edmund, you've invented that on the spur of the moment. Stephen could no more play Macbeth after the diet you've been giving him for the last three years than that pretty creature of yours could play Lady Macbeth."

His face fell.

"Then you don't think much of her, eh? Tell me the truth. I purposely left her to you. Oh! I *am* disappointed."

"You needn't be. I've been very favourably impressed. I think you are more likely to be right about her than I am. Tragedy, no, she couldn't touch it. Never. But her comedy was a surprise to me, I own. She has real humour, and I'll tell you what, Edmund—she's got one real gift. She can clown, and clown like a lady. I shouldn't go on coaching her too long: the freshness is half the charm. If you can put your hand on some suitable plays I should throw her in, neck and heels. She'll draw on her looks and humour for a time, and the rest is a question of work and the position you can give her."

"Oh, she'll work," said Edmund.

"Yes, but you mustn't overwork her," said Donna innocently.

"You know, my dear, you're as strong as a horse yourself, and with all that energy and vitality of yours I daresay you don't quite realise what it costs a young girl like that to keep up with you."   Then, as Edmund smiled—"I'm not interfering, dear child: it is only a private hint, but I thought her looking very fagged this last day or two.   I don't like it. I hope you have a proper staff.   Do you do much entertaining?"

They entertained, it appeared, a good deal, generally after the theatre. Elinor's fortune had made a considerable difference to Edmund's way of life.   Some building had been done at the Regent's Park house.   The staff was large and experienced, and Richard Broome had two nurses all to himself.

"So I don't think, Mother, that Elinor has too much on her hands. She's very strong, you know. You mustn't think I slave-drive her.   Her heart is in the profession, I do assure you."

"Her heart's in whatever you want her to do, Edmund.   That's the truth of it."

He laughed.

"Yes, I'm pretty lucky. I *am* lucky.   Where's wood? I'm frightened, sometimes, of my own luck.   Lewis Wybird was wonderfully decent, you know.   I wouldn't have believed it. He turned over Elinor's affairs without a murmur.   I tell you, Mother, I'm ashamed of myself when I meet him and he nods."

"He doesn't?   My dear boy, he doesn't?"

"Yes, he does.   And there's a general impression got about, and I can't help thinking he's behind it, that the whole affair was a relief to him: that he'd thought himself bound and was going through with it— nothing definite, you know, but that sort of impression.   But a pal of the Guv'nor's was dining with him the other day and he says Wybird spoke of it quite openly.   Damned genial he was about it, I hear.   And Enid Wybird answered Elinor's letter: and the Genista's playing to packed houses and I take over the Glory Hole in the spring, Mama. Fixed policy—children's plays at Christmas and for the rest spectacular drama.   Always has been my line.   Come back with us, Mama! You'll love it.   Come now, I'll give you a job—leading lady or wardrobe mistress. I don't care.   But you'd better come back with us I say!"

"No, dear boy."

"Oh come, Mother, why not? You must be bored to tears."

"No."

And he got no more out of her.

But she wanted to come.   How she wanted to come!   Custom tore at her as if it were true feeling, and almost she succumbed to the yearning voice of custom, crying—"Own you are beaten and return!" Hardest of all it was to stand up to the reasonable self in her which argued so justly, so sanely—"But why not return? What keeps you but sentiment? Why are you behaving as if you were an anchoress bound by a vow?" And her only answer was her instinct, stronger than reason, that here was life for her and a future, and anywhere else exhaustion and an inner death. It was a mere instinct and sometimes it failed her. It all but failed her when she saw the real disappointment in her son's face and the dawning of affection and understanding of her in her daughter-in-law's eyes. Women had never liked Donna very much, but here was a girl who liked her. Elinor even came to her timidly hinting that the Regent's Park house was still hers, and that Elinor would not feel deposed but would be so glad to have her and give her back the big bedroom if she wanted it. The dear child! But no, she would not go.

She saw them off at the station, son, daughter-in-law, grandson, nurse, maid and baggage, cheerfully. But it was a hectic cheerfulness. As the train wound out of the station and she saw it dwindle down the line she said to herself—"That match-box carries my flesh and blood, my house, my goods, my chattels. That tiny dot between two parallel lines is the most important thing in the world to me. And yet it cannot be terribly important, for I have let it all go, dead woman that I am!"

Then depression rolled up over her and engulfed her, and she felt herself move down the platform and through the toy station and out into the road, not as a human being but as a homunculus, living inside a glass globe, for ever separated from her kind.

She waved away her coachman—"No, no, I'll walk," and tramped on through the main street of the town, heavily, seeing no-one. A dog-cart swept by and as it did so one of the yellow curs that infest an Irish town ran out into the road. The wheel caught it: there was a yelp: and then she had a blurred impression of a crowd surrounding the poor cur that writhed in the road a moment and then lay still. She went on, feeling sick, still seeing its white eye-balls and its look of death, but thinking to herself—"It is not much more cut off from life than I am. It sees nothing: nobody cares: it is gone, the dead dog. And what else am I? Who remembers me? Can I call up my own son's face?"

She tried and could not.

Yet her common sense, so much stronger in her than in the forebears from whom she had inherited her hours of isolation, fought insistently for a hearing, told her—"You are not here again after twenty years for nothing. You have been brought back—why? You are cut off by your own will—why? Do you not know that out of the strong cometh forth sweetness and out of death resurrection?"

And as she listened, the perception grew in her mind that she was on the eve of new life: that her pangs were the pangs of a creature still in the womb, and that the hour of delivery was very near. Aud then, as these moods do, her depression lifted and was gone, swiftly, inexplicably as it had come, and she was herself again as she had always been, a rather tired, rather lonely, sufficiently contented woman, saying—"It has been pleasant to see the dear children again, and Richard is a fine little fellow; but I shall be glad to have the house to myself."

On she tramped. Her heavy skirts made her wrist ache, and she thought she would have in the dressmaker to chop out a breadth. Edmund's love of walking was in her too, and had grown upon her lately: and what did it matter how she looked? She planned long walks and a talk with the bailiff. Then her eye was caught by a circular rosette of lichen on one of the stones of the wall. Her mind lifted it and carried it on with her as a thing to be examined.

As she came at last to the short cut across the field, she realised that she had thought of nothing but the orange of the lichen and its delicate, frilled edge for the last ten minutes: and then there surged up in her mind a curious exultant realisation that worded itself thus—"I can think. Everything in the world is my book now. I needn't read books to keep my hunger down any more. I shall never need books again, because I can think. This is the pleasure of pleasures, to use one's own mind violently and skilfully, as a tennis player uses his body. I have got years and years of thinking ahead of me. How I am going to think!"

On she went across the fields. With every step her mind worked more rapidly. She was in a state of tension, and knew it and enjoyed the sensation. Her thoughts would move neither forwards nor backwards, but were furiously active none the less, consuming the spectacle of an eternal present. She found herself rejoicing over the quantities of grass-blades in the field, over the fact that a hill faced her and that a sky was above it. Sky, hill and the grasses pressed in upon her mind, embracing her, and she thought that voices must be urgently speaking to her also; but she heard nothing. She was all sight and touch, but her ears were stopped and her quivering soul said to her—"You are not yet born."

She went along by the hedge on the further side of the field. It was more of a bank than a hedge. There were brambles and fruiting wild roses: and presently she came upon a small beech-tree that had clawed away the green covering of the bank and left a scar of bare earth beneath itself. Beyond it the hips and haws began again and there was a scatter of late flowers. It was a common bit of hedge, not striking or beautiful; but as she passed by, it looked at her and smiled, and she saw quite clearly that it was Joscelyn. There was his unaltered personality imbuing the hedge with life, passing through it, part of it and then part of her. She felt him become part of her and stood still, shuddering with delight.

The strange, inexplicable moment passed, and she put her hands to her eyes and rubbed them like a child that has come out of a dark room into a garden. For now she could hear as well as see: now it seemed to her that she was born. She was part of the grass on which she stood, part of the sky, part of the hill before her, part of the eternal air. She was an appearance, at one with all other appearances, and enjoying that reality indescribable of which appearance is but a symbol. The dead dog, the iron of the hoof that had killed it, the book lying open at home waiting for her to finish it, the baby Richard, Edmund in the train, her parts that she had played a thousand times, the minds that wrote those parts, the tears that she had wept, Joscelyn, the clouds, the earth—all these were hers: all these were in her: all these were herself and she them.

"What is it?" said Donna. "What has happened to me?"

Out of her dreary childhood and her dreary youth came the recollection of the inevitable ending to a dreary hour—"The peace of God which passeth all understanding keep your hearts and minds——"

The sun dropped behind the hills as she pulled herself together, picking up her dusty skirts.

"I must hurry," said Donna to the listening universe, "or I shall be late for tea."

CHAPTER 50

EDMUND BROOME AND HIS FAMILY

It was part of the conditions of her new life that she could not speak of it to anyone. That did not greatly irk her, for her old life had taught her to do without intimacy. But her grandchildren discovered that she could tell a fairy-tale or any other sort of tale with most uncommon ease, and kept her to it.

For the children of Edmund and Elinor were constantly with her. Henry had been born eighteen months after his brother Richard, and in Jubilee year Geoffrey arrived—but they called him Gerry. After that there were no more children for a long time. For the death of Stephen, some months after Gerry's birth, had a revolutionary effect on the households of his sons. Eustace married on the extra income: and Elinor became too important a figure in the economics of the Broome theatres for her to be permitted to continue in domesticity. Though her first years of stage life had been much interrupted by child-bearing, she had nevertheless been popular. Motherhood had developed her beauty, and, during a period in which a full figure was an asset, she was admired; while her capacities as an actress had been much increased by good training. Her husband had left her entirely to his father: and Stephen, who adored her, had coaxed, laughed, talked, drilled and comforted her into the conceit of herself which she needed. She soon picked up his lightness of touch: she had evolved a feminine version of his beckoning look and his laugh: and as she had taken, of course, the name of Broome, a great part of her public thought of her, not as a wife of a Broome, but as an actual member of the clan, and the gayest of them all.

And indeed Domina's judgment of her was not far off the mark— Elinor was a brilliant clown. It was as if the mere coming on to the stage, certain of the exquisite response which the experienced older man gave her, freed her true nature. She was bound down and repressed outside the theatre by early marriage, early motherhood, the responsibility of a household and the overbearing and exigent personality of her husband. In the theatre she was like a dog released from a chain: and her wild high spirits carried many a poor part and many a poor play.

563

But outside the theatre she was meek : and Stephen watching his two favourites, and wishing that Eustace and his pink and white young woman were half as amusing, had shaken his head sometimes over Edmund's treatment of his wife. Edmund expected a lot. He expected a female self that should display all the qualities that made him a masterful man, yet never display them to him, only to the rest of the world. He wanted a mistress and a business manager, a hostess and a pupil all in one. He wanted a mother who put her children first, but never let the children or her motherhood get in the way when he wanted her. He wanted a kind shadow, who would yet be a woman of importance when he took her about. Stephen, remembering his own young days, was amazed that Edmund got so much of what he wanted. Never had there been such a teachable creature : and when Edmund occasionally complained that his wife's one fault was her knitted brow, Stephen would retort indignantly that the public did not make that complaint. In the theatre at any rate, she could laugh and make her audience laugh with her. And this he told his son, who was too much occupied with the launching of his new policy at the Glory Hole to watch his wife's work very closely. Stephen always ended his comments with the advice—"When I am dead and gone, mind you let her star at the Genista ! She has learnt a lot and she'll learn more if you let her have her head." For Stephen was whimsically sorry for Elinor and for himself, servants of the strong-willed Broomes. Domina and her son were hard on the graces of life.

And now Stephen was dead : and Edmund had to ask himself if he should follow his father's advice?

He would half follow it, he decided, not quite sure of his wife's strength, and perhaps a little jealous of her. So he inaugurated a joint reign for himself and her in those worthless, amusing domesticities which were the policy of the Genista for the next ten years. Edmund, who had never forgotten his grandfather's advice—"You must be on the stage yourself if you want to keep the company together——" had always played a part as a matter of course in any piece in which it was possible to make his burly figure and downright methods acceptable, and he had become a sound and fairly well-known actor. He had the Petruchio manner, and the public of the late 'nineties, disturbed by the New Woman, adored above all things the taming of a shrew.

So for the next ten years, disguised as a financier, a miner, a copper king, a ranchman, or any other strong man of the people with a million in the bank, an iron will and a heart of gold, he mastered an aristocratic

Elinor garbed in a becoming tea-gown. The policy was vastly success-ful, though Elinor missed Stephen and high comedy. The public liked knowing that it watched the business side of a successful domesticity: and Edmund did not know, and Elinor did not let anyone guess, that the domesticity was perhaps not quite as successful as it appeared. But Elinor thought to herself sometimes that the modern playwright knew very little about married life as she knew it. The heroines whom she depicted with her well-known grace, comicality and charm, always had their bedrooms on the ground floor, or at any rate at the head of the staircase in full view of the lounge: and if there was a nursery it never interfered with the opportunities for suspicion, physical violence or grand reconciliation scenes. She thought that if she had any temptation to ill-treat her husband, and she certainly had none, the difficulties of coping with three lively, healthy, high-spirited and intensely affec-tionate small boys would have gone far to keep her in the straight path.

Her private problems, at any rate, were curiously undramatic. Edmund was never jealous of her, but he could be extraordinarily irritable if she was not at hand when he wanted her: and their quarrels were generally occasioned by nothing more romantic that the fact that he adored the children as much as she did, but treated them much more injudiciously than she would dare to treat even a puppy. He gave them sweets and money for the asking, encouraged them to beclamber the conversation when he was in the mood for them, let them stay up for supper when they wheedled, and was amused if they wanted to sip his sherry or experiment with his cigars. On the other hand, when he was not in the mood she thought him brutal. He made nothing of a box on the ear, and the curt, last-minute withdrawal of a treat if he was bothered or not in the mood to honour his promise. He would encourage them to be impudent to him and delight in their cleverness one day, yet on another a small boy would be thrashed for a harmless mutiny or a fit of the sulks that came, often enough, from sheer mis-understanding of a command.

Yet she did not know how to fight him. He worked magnificently and incessantly, was always over-tired, and his passion for his children, ill regulated as she thought it, seemed to her nevertheless a touching and beautiful thing. Besides, the children were bold little things, and where she, at their age, would have sunk into bewilderment and misery, took their chance of tips or thrashings with uncommon fortitude, and developed early an uncanny skill in recognising and dealing with their father's moods. She had not, never would have, such skill.

The character which he had exhibited to her at the time of their marriage, his furious decision, his adroit execution of a scheme of which at the time she had been barely aware, his deft adaptation of her irresponsible impulses to fit his scheme, his tenderness and his passion for her in that troubled hour, had given her a sort of worship for him which made it difficult for her to judge him justly in their later life. He had been too much god in the first year of marriage for her to accept him later as the moody, faulty, headstrong, well-meaning human being that in truth he was. She saw his faults but would not, in her own mind, admit them as faults. They were attributes of a superior creature which she must first accept and then learn, slowly, humbly, wisely, to understand. If he lost his temper with her she must have no peace until she plucked out of her own personality the quality which irritated him. If he appeared to contradict himself grossly, she must realise that it was her lack of subtlety that could not see the real link between the two apparently opposed points of view. If he were unjust to an underling then, though she went behind his back to repair that injustice, she and the underling much each understand that he himself was not aware of his own injustice. If, to her bewilderment, he behaved in a way that did not square with her idea of perfect courage or perfect rectitude, then it was for her to learn that there were many sorts of courage and many sorts of rectitude, and to beware of sitting in judgment on his faults when she had so many faults of her own.

Only when some trifle, too long brooded over, called into being one of his sudden fits of rage, had she no mental defence of him against himself. Then she sat under the storm with bowed head, loathing the noise and the violence, trying to think of nothing at all till it was over, hating to see him as a ridiculous object.

For she loved him the more steadfastly because she was physically a cold woman. Sex in her was much more a thing of the emotions and of the intellect than of the flesh. Like so many women of her day, the actual facts of marriage had been a shock to her : and later in her life she would recall with pity that young girl Elinor lying in bed beside her husband, watching him satisfied and asleep, turning over the leaves of her Bible in search of reassurance. Was it right, this strange, repellent business between a man and a woman? Was there anywhere in the Bible a justification of this adventure of the flesh? She accustomed herself in time, and with the coming of her children her sense of revolt died : but it was never a violent need of her life.

But Edmund, she knew, looked at things differently. Emotion he saved for his children : for his wife he had only passion and trust. She wondered, sometimes, that he could be so patient with her during her pregnancies. He was always most kind and most gentle when she was ill, easy with her fancies, pliant to her whims, and ready enough to let the children at such times go to their grandmother in Ireland. Nothing could be kinder than Edmund at such times. This she said to her old friend, and cousin now, Fina, and Fina, a little grudgingly, said that she was lucky.

For Fina could not quite forgive Elinor Broome her fortune and the fact that she had slipped out of a marriage with the wrong man into a marriage with the right one. Fina could not quite forgive Elinor her success on the stage, her assured position in the world of the theatre, her pleasant Sunday night salon, her friendships not only in Bohemia but in the world in which she had lived till her marriage : nor could Fina forgive her the fact that three attractive boys had not diminished her friend's English beauty nor weakened her English constitution. Least of all could Fina forgive her Fina's own marriage.

Elinor, much against Edmund's will, had been good to Fina in those early days when Elinor was a young matron and Fina slim-hipped and the more striking of the two. Elinor thought it dreadful that Fina should have to go back to Brazil and did her utmost to match-make for her in comfortable London. But Fina was too flamboyant for the Broomes' friends. In a couple of years she had grown, besides, so fat that Elinor, who was a practical soul, suggested a diet rather than the perpetual spending of three guineas and five guineas on ever-unsuccessful corsets boned to the knees. Indeed they had a little quarrel about it : and the next thing that Elinor heard was that Fina was engaged to an actor in one of Edmund's own companies. And the next thing, of course, was to get work for Fina's husband, and the next that Fina hated touring and that Fina's husband drank a little and could not save enough to provide for Fina's confinement or the baby's outfit. Elinor came to the rescue, for she was very fond of poor Fina ; nevertheless she was relieved when the husband secured an engagement in America and took off himself and his wife. There he did well enough : well enough at any rate to let his wife come over for a holiday some seven years later. And where should she stay, but with her dear friend Elinor and her dear cousin Edmund Broome ?

Elinor, who could never learn that the past is not the present, that yesterday is a frightening ghost, was delighted to see Fina and thought her improved. Fina was thinner and the dark blue coat and skirt, veil and pince-nez of the American matron suited her. She said that her husband had left the stage and was dealing in land : and that their one child Alys, the same age almost to a day as Elinor's Henry, was bright and a beauty. No, Fina for the first twenty-four hours had no troubles at all. At the end of a week she was hinting that she had of course her troubles like other women, and on the last night of her stay, before she went off to her husband's people in the north, the truth came out. She was not in England for pleasure : she was in England because her husband was infatuated with another woman, and because there was no-one to help her but her husband's people who were strait-laced and would be shocked and would say so—"For of course he wants a divorce, and I'll die rather than let him have it. It isn't as if it were the first time."

And then, Elinor, in the innocence of her heart, was just a little too much horrified and just a little too ready to say so, and up flew Fina in defence of her own husband, who was not after all any worse than other men. At that Elinor, so secure, smiled too pityingly, and all the long-stored envy, all the illogical resentment, streamed out.

"Oh, my dear, don't be a hypocrite and look at me like that! As if everyone didn't know that you have as much to bear as other women, and more. Ah, you put a good face on it, as you should ; but Elinor, at least do not pretend to me! Why put a look on your face—my cat would not touch cream! Ah, pah! You are wise to shut your eyes, of course! But to me, to such an old friend as me, it is a farce when you do it. Though, of course, if you choose you may put me at a distance——"

Elinor sat down with an air of bewilderment, half amused, half annoyed, much puzzled.

"Dearest Fina, I seem to have upset you, but I don't know what you're talking about."

"My dear, I talked of me and my troubles, and you gave me much sympathy, and I say thank you very much! But now when I talk of you and your troubles——"

"But I haven't got any troubles," said Elinor with her little gurgle of amusement, and thinking to herself that Edmund's faults of temper and Henry's trick of fibbing, and Richard's curious moods of depression were at any rate troubles that she scarcely admitted to herself.

"Ah well, you are discreet. I admire you. And after all I daresay it gives you a hold."

"But what gives me a hold, Fina ?"

"On my word, Elinor, I lose patience. You know nothing of that woman—oh, no!—who was married so soon before you, and the little boy has such red hair! Oh, no! How should you know? And you do not know why the little Letty what's-her-name who got on so well at the Glory 'Ole and is now a star on tour in that part of yours from five years ago—you do not know why she gets on, oh, no! And when your babies come, such a kind husband, so considerate for such a long time! Oh, Elinor, you bore me! We are no longer at the *Pensionnat* and Fräulein Krantz will not come in in three minutes to turn out the light."

Fina ceased, panting, and Elinor, putting down the ornate heavy teapot, rested her hands on the railing of the silver tray and regarded her friend with a countenance in which indignation, disgust, perplexity and concern were ludicrously mingled.

"My dear Fina, you mustn't talk like this. You shock me, really you do. I don't think you're well. I know you've had a terrible time and that you hardly realise what you're saying, but why attack poor Edmund? Edmund, of all people!" Then, as if the iniquity of the thing had only slowly grown clear to her, her voice grew stern. "It's degrading to talk like that. People who don't know you will think you have a base mind."

Fina opened her mouth with an indescribable expression; but Elinor, once started, had to say her say.

"Yes, I know you're upset, Fina, and I know you don't realise—but truly people who don't know you would think you abominable. No, don't let's talk about it. It's horrid. Poor Edmund!"

Then she began to laugh a little uncertainly, for the attack had shaken her. She hated malice and she hated dirt, and encountering these things was as frightened as a child offered spirits. Also her real affection for the older woman was stirred. She thought the poor creature had had her mind turned by her troubles and she burned with indignation against the wicked husband who had brought darling Fina to such a pass. How hateful, hateful, men could be! So she was distressed for Fina and wanted to show it, but could only say—"Forget about it, my dear! Have another cup of tea."

But Fina, though she took the tea, continued to look at her strangely, the fire and fury all gone from her face, a curious, almost a professional interest shining in her black eyes. Elinor, still nervous, but with her sense of humour always on the wriggle when she was with Fina, thought her friend looked at her exactly as her monthly nurse had done.

"Nell—" said Fina at last, respectfully, using the long forgotten name of their schooldays—"Nell, have you always had a dressing-room to yourself on tour?"

"I haven't toured much, you know."

"But always the lead, eh?"

"Why?"

"Never heard the girls talk to each other, I suppose, in the big dressing-rooms?"

"Well, I suppose I have," said Elinor regarding her, puzzled.

"Do they tell good stories, eh?"

"What d'you mean? Oh, *that* sort of story! I won't listen."

"And you have no women friends?"

"Of course I have—dozens of women friends," said Elinor indignantly. "You know perfectly well there are people here every night. I'm rushed to death, what with the acting and the entertaining, and Edmund, and the children. I never have a minute to myself."

"That explains it, I daresay," said Fina slowly. "But you were the same at school. I'm sorry, Nell. I thought you were patronising me."

"Fina, that's not fair."

"I know it isn't. I tell you I'm sorry that I—chattered. Don't think any more about it. I say things, and they mean nothing."

"No, dear, I know they don't."

"Then forget 'em, eh? We are friends again. I love you though I kick at you, eh? So you think no more of my nonsense. And I say, Nell, don't speak of it to Edmund."

Elinor stiffened.

"My dear Fina, you don't suppose that I should insult Edmund——" but at that moment Edmund himself came in.

"Elinor, where's Richard?"

She turned to him a little anxiously. She knew the tone. The fatigues of a heavy business day, some trouble or other with one of the company, a bolted lunch—such a day's history was in his tone: and he was always querulous about the children when he was tired. He liked to have them with him for that free hour before he and Elinor went down to the theatre, yet nine times out of ten he could not bear their noise and they had to be turned out of the room again in a hurry lest he should lose his temper altogether and ruin the evening's performance.

So, in spite of herself, the deprecating note that irritated him crept into Elinor's voice as she answered—

"Why, my dear, I don't know. In the garden, I think, with Henry."

"Well, that's just where he isn't. And anyway, Elinor, how can you allow the children to be out so late? And it has been raining."

She glanced at the lilac spring twilight, and rose hastily.

"You're quite right. Of course they should be in. But Nurse went out for me you know, and I was talking to Fina."

"Yes, exactly. And meanwhile Henry is all by himself at the edge of the canal."

"My dear Elinor—" Fina broke in excitedly—"do you allow it? If he fell in——"

"Exactly. If he fell in!" said Edmund. "I sent him straight into the house."

Elinor laughed at them both good-humouredly.

"My dears, there is a good six feet of wire fence between him and the water. What do you take me for? And if he likes fishing through the holes why shouldn't he, bless his heart?"

"Well, all I can tell you—" said Edmund, warming himself at the fire and surveying the room sharply and irritably as if he thought every chair in it were in the wrong place and Fina the ugliest woman he had ever seen—"all I can tell you is that I found Henry loitering by himself in that damp corner of the garden with not a soul to speak to and no idea of where his brother was. And I've told you before, Elinor, I won't have Richard going off by himself, never asking whether his brother wants him or not. They're brothers: and they should play together. Henry has a sweet temper and I won't have it spoiled by enforced loneliness."

"Oh, my dear Edmund—" Elinor brought her husband his tea cheerfully—"can't you leave the children to fight it out between them? They're very good friends. If Richard occasionally chooses to go off by himself——"

"Yes. And where has he gone? Ring for Nurse!" And Edmund drank his tea in a gulp and went off, while Elinor, red-cheeked and frowning, and wishing to goodness that Fina wouldn't sit there all ears and eyes, obediently rang the bell. But before the nurse could answer an outcry arose from the other side of the hall and Elinor, hastily excusing herself and hurrying to the rescue, found her husband in the doorway of the library, confronting a howling eldest son. The little boy held a hand to his ear and in the other clutched one of Harry Broome's wooden manikins in its rumpled black velvet cloak. Round about him were spread the contents of Harry Broome's famous

cabinet, arranged with such care and neatness that his mother wanted
to catch him up and hug him. He had laid out the theatre on the floor,
and there were rows of pin-legged, pin-backed chestnuts for seats. All
the figures not needed in the present production were seated on the
chestnuts as audience: and what is more they were a carefully graded
audience; for the lords and ladies sat in the stalls, and Bottom, Gobbo,
Autolycus and the rest made up the pit. The tiny curtains were drawn,
and on the stage itself the trap-door, no bigger than a match-box, was
open, and Laertes was up to his knees in the draperies of a prostrate
Ophelia. Richard, it seemed, had been interrupted in a performance of
Hamlet, Prince of Denmark.

"So there you are," said Elinor cheerfully to the child. "What's the
matter, darling?" And then, on a dreadful, quick change of note—
"Edmund! Edmund, dear, please!" and instinctively she put herself
between him and his son, her heart sinking to see that he was in one
of his rages again. She knew so well the signs, and, as ever, with her
unquenchable optimism, prayed that a smile and the right conciliatory
word would hold up the storm and that it would pass over this time.
But it never did pass over. It did not now.

"D'you see what he has done? He sneaks out of the garden although
he has my strict orders that he is to be out of doors between two and
four, and he comes into my own room! Did he ask your permission?
No, of course he didn't. He comes into my room and he has the
audacity to go to my drawers, to pull open everything—look at the
disorder! Really, to have my private papers and affairs——"

"But, Edmund, he hasn't done any harm. He thought he was
allowed. Didn't you, Richard?"

"We played last Sunday," Richard gulped out.

"There, you see, Edmund——"

"Elinor, I won't have you prompt the boy. Because I have the
children into the library and play with them on a Sunday afternoon and
allow them to handle a delicate and valuable collection like this, under
my eye, does it mean that the child is to come into my room in my
absence and pull the whole set to pieces?"

"No, of course he shouldn't, Edmund. Of course he shouldn't. But
he didn't understand, did you, Richard? You know, dear, it's naughty
to touch things without asking Father." And then, in a low voice—
"Edmund, dearest, control yourself, for pity's sake! It's all right,
Richard. Father only means that you must ask someone first. Look,
dear, help me pick it up and put it away in the right drawers."

"You will leave these things alone, please! The child goes to bed and stays there. And another time, Richard——"

She got him away at last and bundled him up to the nursery still frightened and sobbing, into the arms of the nurse: then turned back again to the library, came silently in and knelt down to pick up the small properties and put them away, praying in her heart as she did so— "Oh, let him be kind about it! If he could be kind about it!" But her husband watched her out of the black gloom that would not, she knew now, lift for the rest of the evening. The silly tears fell on her hand as she gathered up the chestnuts and ordered and straightened, and all the while she said to herself that one must not judge, *must* not judge. Edmund had confessed to her once in their earliest best days of marriage that he knew well enough what his temper was. That confession came after their first quarrel, when she had been so frightened that her terror had quenched the outburst: and Edmund, so humble then, so remorseful, had told her that, because it was impossible for her to understand the sensation, she would never understand either how impossible it was for him to control or even regulate its comings and goings. Bad as it was for her it was worse for him, because at such times he did not know what he said or did, yet had afterwards to bear the burden of the things he had said and done: and so she must be patient with him.

And she was patient. She treasured up those confidences of their love days as if they were precious and holy sayings, and repeated them to herself at such times as this, when she was so near judging Edmund, resenting him and hating him. She said then—"His temper is not Edmund. It is a separate thing, a physical curse. I haven't got a temper, so how can I understand?" But the more Edmund's temper oppressed the children, the harder she found it to bear. And she had other things to bear. In the old days he had come to her after such a bout to say— "All right again now, dear," or—"Forgive me, Nell!" Or he would merely kiss her tempestuously and go off leaving her heart light. But now his bad days were as much a habit as his good ones.

She rose stiffly and stood a moment looking at him, wondering should she speak? Then knowing it to be too soon, went away, went brightly back to Fina in the drawing-room saying—"Mischievous things children are! Richard had been playing in the library and Edmund does so hate it. Won't you have some more tea? Are you coming with us to the theatre, Fina, as it's your last night?"

But Fina was going to friends and must hurry off to dress. So Elinor saw her thankfully to her room and then went across to the nursery where Henry and Gerry sat at tea. Gerry merely gave her a quick look from his brilliant dark eyes and then returned with a slight pathetic snuffle to his cold, his cake and his kitten, which he had just started on a journey down the sleeve of his Norfolk jacket. Gerry called it travelling by tube and enjoyed the ticklish business more than the kitten, which presently emerged, wild-eyed, at Geoffrey's wrist.

But Henry, in the best of health and spirits, looked up at her entrance, his whole face lighting with delight. But then he was always such a friendly little creature with a dimple of humour on his chin, blue impudent eyes and a free tongue. He never cried and didn't know what fear meant : he was not even afraid of Edmund. And this fact enchanted Edmund, who was in consequence downright enchanting himself when he played with his second son. With Henry on his knee Elinor saw sometimes that he was still the very Edmund who had jumped down into the leaf pit and run away with her from Blandon so long ago. Dear Henry!

Before she could say a word Henry had jumped to his feet and was dragging out a chair for her and then not letting her sit down in it because he had so much to say.

"Mother, why is Richard sent to bed? Mother, do let Richard get up! I say, Mother, we've got such a lot to do after tea. It isn't fair. Because we did play theatre last Sunday and Father played too. He talked an awful lot about teaching us to act, and to do it every rainy day like his Grandpapa. So Richard did. Mother, do let Richard get up! Do, Mother! Mother, do!" And he seized her wrists and shook at them, and then as she stooped to him caught her round the neck and swung himself up, his small boots linked together behind her back and his arms clasped round her neck. "Let's go and get Richard down! Do, Mother!"

"Has Master Richard had any tea, Nurse?"

"No, Ma'am, he won't touch his tea. He's in one of his moods, Ma'am."

"Put something on a tray, Nurse! I'll take it up."

"Let me carry it, Mother! Do!"

"No, Henry, you must finish your tea." Then, as she lowered him on to his chair and unclasped his arms, he scuffling, laughing, clinging for all he was worth—"Henry, be good! I want to talk to you while you finish your cake. Listen, your father thinks you weren't happy playing by yourself in the garden. Did you miss Richard so much?"

Henry stared at her.

"No, Mother. I nearly got two sticklebacks."

"Then why did you tell your father, Henry, that you wanted Richard?"

"I didn't. He said where was Richard, and I said I didn't know: and he went gobble-red, you know, the way he does. And then he went away."

"Didn't you know where Richard was then, Henry?"

"Richard was playing theatre," remarked Gerry. "I knew."

"So did I," retorted Henry.

"I knew first."

"No, you didn't."

"Yes, I did."

"But if you did know, Henry—I think that's enough cake, Gerry—why did you tell your father you didn't?"

At this the dimple deepened and Henry anointed and then bit into a large piece of bread-and-butter without remarking until it was too late that the golden syrup was running off it into his hand.

Said Elinor, dealing efficiently with the matter—

"You mustn't fib, my son."

"Well, I don't, Mother, to you."

"Not to anyone, darling. I've told you so, often."

"Well, I only do when he gets red."

"You mustn't ever, Henry. It's wrong."

He smiled at her sweetly and ate more bread-and-butter.

What was she to do? What could she do? She took up the tray and went across the passage to the night-nursery.

Richard was lying in his bed, curled up like a puppy, and, at an angle which made her despair for his eyesight, reading a book. He looked up at her from it, scowling: a black-haired, black-eyed child, strong and sturdy, inches taller than the radiant, golden-haired Henry. He looked much older: was a bigger piece of work altogether and much less easy to manage. After that one look at her he went on reading; but so formed his nine-year-old personality that she frankly did not dare say to him at that moment—"Richard, don't strain your eyes," or "Richard, put down your book." Instead she came over to him, put down the tray on the night-table, pulled up a chair and sat down.

He took no notice of her whatever.

"Richard!"

He turned a page.

"Richard, listen! I want to talk to you."

He turned another page.

What was she to do? As always her own incompetence in dealing with those she loved was dreadful to her. Oh, for surety of touch in human relationships! Should she sit still and wait, or should she put out a hand and take away his book? He was Edmund's child—what would she do if he were Edmund? Sit still, of course, and wait till he was ready. She sat still and waited. The pages were turned with great rapidity. At the end of five minutes she spoke again.

"Darling, do eat your tea!"

"Don't want it."

But she took the cup from the tray and put a sweet biscuit in the saucer and said—"Come on, Richard! Come on, now!"

And at that Richard closed his book and sat up and allowed himself to be fed, and indeed drank thirstily. His face was stained and puffy with crying. He ate and drank in silence, but when he had finished and she moved to put the tray out of their way he said hastily—

"Don't go!"

She smiled at him.

"I won't. Not until it's time for the theatre. What are you reading?"

"Swiss Fam."

"Shall I read to you?"

"No." And then—"Mother, when can I get up?"

"Darling, it'll be bed-time in an hour."

But the evasion was noted: and Richard's face set more sullenly than ever and his grievance began to merge.

"It isn't fair. He let me on Sunday."

She would not answer the challenge. But, answering it indirectly by trying to turn his exile into a treat, she began cheerfully—

"Shall I get Henry to come in here and we'll have a game, the three of us?"

He eyed her, half attracted, half suspicious of her good faith.

"May he?"

"Of course he may."

Suspicion won.

"No, I don't want him."

What was she to say? What was she to do?

"Richard, we're trying to decide what to put on next at the Genista.

There are two plays with lovely parts for me. I can't make up my mind. Shall I tell you the stories so that you can help me to decide?"

"Go on," said he more graciously, but not committing himself.

Never had she tried so hard to tell a story well as she tried in the next hour: acting the parts to him, telling him why she was afraid of one, why she was tempted by the other, trying to restore his pride by an appeal to his intelligence.

He listened solemnly: and his comments were shrewd. When she had quite finished he felt under his pillow and, producing a bag of chocolate drops, offered her one which she took. He ate one himself, then restored the residue to its place. Out in the passage arose a hullabaloo of voices and laughter and bath-taps turned on.

"Oh, they're coming," said Richard savagely. "Just when———"

"Yes, and I must go now, darling," said she regretfully; for she knew she had not succeeded in winning him: and yet had not failed—not utterly failed. For he replied half grudging, half commanding—

"Come and see us when you're dressed!"

"I will."

He let her get as far as the door; but then called to her urgently:

"Mother, come back! Mother, I want to say something."

She came back at once. He knelt upright in bed and caught her hands.

"Darling, you'll catch cold."

"Mother, tell me something! You must tell me something."

"What, my precious?"

"Mother, do you—do you think Father was fair?"

She stared down into his unwinking black eyes. What could she say to him? How could she go behind Edmund's back? Life would be impossible if she undermined Edmund's authority, if she shook the boy's faith in him as a creature who must be in the right. What was she to say? Phrase after phrase rose in her mind and was rejected. We mustn't discuss your father . . . what Father says is right . . . you mustn't question what your father says . . . when you're older you'll see that your father was right . . .

"Mother, *was* it fair?"

She said, distressedly—

"No, Richard, I don't think it was." And was instantly horrified at what she had done. Her words would be quoted against her, would be told to Henry: one day in a passion would be flung at Edmund himself. What unwise thing had she done?

Then as she looked at her son she saw more deeply into the matter. For Richard was regarding her, not with naughty satisfaction, not even with the absurd delight of a child exonerated, but with an uncanny and unchildlike air of relief. And suddenly she saw that she had stood, quite blind and unawares, on the very edge of an abyss. So he had understood her dilemma: it had been a test question. God help her if she had answered him dishonestly. As it was, said his look, he was sure of her, now and always. If she had answered him in any other way he would not have been deceived, would not have swayed in his attitude towards his father. Nothing in him would have been altered; but for her everything would have been altered. She would have lost her son.

"Good-night, my darling boy."

"Good-night, Mother." He reached up lazily and kissed her, then with a sudden chuckle kissed her again as hard as he could.

"Mother, give us back my book!"

She gave him back his book and before she was out of the room he was absorbed in it once more.

As she drove down to the theatre with Edmund in the new car that was his toy, Elinor was making up her mind, as she had done for fifty times in the last three years, to tackle him about his dealings with the children. For he was always so reasonable, so brilliantly sane, when he was not in a passion. If she could only catch him when he was in a good mood she ought to be able to make him see that you cannot treat a child as you treat a promising novice in a company, excite it, favouritise it, cast it down brutally, lift it up again. You must not discipline a child thus: it is criminal cruelty to eight years old, whatever it be to eighteen.

She said these things over and over again within herself, and had just screwed herself up to saying them aloud when he cut the ground from under her feet, as he too had done fifty times in the last three or four years. For he had the most infallible and uncanny fore-knowledge, it seemed to her, of any sort of attack due: and always he would forestall her by something so reasonable, by something often so generous, that again and again she had to put away her grievance and admit herself wrong once more.

"Elinor, I don't know what you think about it, but I think it's time those two boys were at school. You know what it is—I come home so tired that I quench them unduly, I know that well enough: and you spoil them, of course. That's inevitable too. But it's not a normal atmosphere. School's the place for them. Will you see about it or shall I?" And then he went on with that note in his voice of complete kindness and understanding which rarely as it came and because it came so rarely, always disarmed her and made her his worshipper again, content to trust him—"It's hard for you, Nell, I know. But it's got to come, old lady. And you've got Gerry for another year."

"They'd better all go together," said she bitterly.

"That's rubbish. But of course Richard ought to have gone a year ago. See to it, won't you?"

"There's a very good day school—" she began—"out at Kensington. Eustace told me of it. Gore House I fancy it's called——"

"What?" He withdrew his hand and looked at her sharply. "Kensington? Rubbish! Out of the way place! What on earth put Kensington into your head? Really, Elinor, some of your ideas are too fantastic."

He was angry again. What on earth had she said now to make him so angry?

"Besides, anyway—" he swept on—"I don't approve of day schools. I won't have it. Pick out a good preparatory school for them and I'll come down with you and look it over. They'd better go at Christmas. It's no good arguing, Elinor! I've made up my mind. Richard wants handling and God knows I haven't time to do it. But the boy's got too much brains and spirit to be left to women. Oh, damn that fool, he's in a block again!" And he tapped at the glass in front of him and gesticulated angrily at his unmoved chauffeur. There were few people who did not fear Edmund Broome, but Hammond, his chauffeur, was one of them: and when Edmund talked angrily of modern independence and the Kruger spirit, he really meant Hammond. When the car began to move again he sank back. "Yes, well! Now another thing, Elinor. Have you thought any more about those two plays—*Candlesticks*, I mean and *Wild Clematis?*"

"I could play either part," said she, switching her thoughts obediently. "But, of course, *Candlesticks* is wiped out, isn't it? There's no part for you. It's a pity. It's a fine part. I'd have liked to play it."

"You can play it if you want to," said he with a sideways look at her. "Don't bother about me."

"My dear Edmund, can you see the Genista continuing without you? What would your matinée girls do?"

"I could easily put on *Candlesticks* at another theatre if you want to play it," he persisted, ignoring her smile. "I could get any of the Shaftesbury Avenue theatres tomorrow."

"What? And let the Genista?"

"Of course not, Elinor! Don't be silly! No, I did half wonder whether I'd put on t'other thing—what's its name—*Wild Clematis*—at the Genista and give the woman's part to Polly Traill. It's a little heavy for you."

"Polly Traill?" said she, slowly. "Do you mean the girl who is understudying Lucie at the Glory Hole?"

"Well, there aren't two Polly Traills, are there?" said he irritably. "She's had admirable notices."

"When?"

"Well, as a matter of fact I asked in one or two critics when Lucie was ill. But you know all that as well as I do, Nell, or you could if you took the faintest intelligent interest. Why are you always so obstructive? Why do you always set yourself against me? It's only an idea. I'm asking you what you think of it. Wouldn't you like to star on your own?"

She gave him an odd little smile.

"Edmund, I should adore it."

"Oh, would you?" He was taken aback. "Well—that's all right then. Mind you, it's only an idea. We'll talk it over later." For the car had drawn up at the stage door. Then, as he helped her out—"By the way, Elinor, did you say Eustace told you about that school in Kensington? When did you see Eustace?"

"He and Marian came in last week. They're thinking of sending the boy to a co-educational school later. They're hesitating between Bedales and this place at Kensington."

"Co-education? Stuff and nonsense! Eustace always has some bee in his bonnet. Well, what are you waiting for? Get on, my dear, get on! I can't make up in five minutes, if you can. And I've got to go through to the front of the house."

Elinor played badly that night and knew it, and for once did not care. She felt as if she had had a tumble and did not yet know how much hurt she was. The minor injuries occupied her, the cuts and bruises, and gravel on her hands; but she had a suspicion that there was a graver injury of which she would only later be aware. The cuts and bruises hurt enough in all conscience. The two boys taken from her at one stroke, though, of course, Edmund was right—Edmund was always so right—and now this strange idea of launching her at another theatre and putting another woman in her place at the Genista! She couldn't like the idea. And yet, what was there to dislike? She had expressed a wish and he had instantly, very charmingly, made her wish a possible thing. It was perfectly true—the part in *Wild Clematis* was not obviously a part for her, though she thought she could play it. Edmund must feel pretty certain of the Traill woman to risk the change . . . Oh, well, if Edmund could make a new star and have her on a long contract, cheap, it was all to the good.

But her mind went over the conversation again and again, restlessly, unhappily: and afterwards when she dressed for the after-theatre party to which she and Edmund were going, though she made herself look beautiful she could not make herself look happy. As she looked at herself in the glass she wondered that her worry showed so little. She thought without pleasure that she looked more like twenty-five than close on thirty, but as for feelings, she felt forty! It was the result, she supposed, of the graver injury that was—what?

But at the sight of Josephina whom they were to meet and take home with them, she thought she knew all about that other injury. If you touch mud, said Elinor to herself, what can you expect? Fina had flung mud all over her and she had not been adroit enough to stop the discharge. And now the mud stuck everywhere; for when she looked at Fina she remembered every word of their conversation and when she looked at Edmund——

She stopped herself. She would not injure Edmund in her own mind by letting herself even wonder why Fina chose to say such things about him. Gossip swirled round everyone. No doubt they said filthy things about her as well as Edmund, and no doubt Edmund heard them. But had he told her? No. Could she not do as much for him? Yes.

Then she saw him talking to a pretty, willowy young woman with a common voice, vivacious eyes and noticeable movements and turning to Fina asked before she could stop herself—"Who is that with Edmund?" And suddenly, inexplicably, knew who it was before Fina had time to answer her, and herself said quickly—"Oh, of course, it's Polly Traill, isn't it?"

Yes, it was Polly Traill.

CHAPTER 51

A REHEARSAL

EDMUND's plans were carried out. Having launched the glorified Christmas entertainment, the poeticised pantomime for which, under his reign, the Glory Hole had grown famous, he took the Shaftesbury Avenue theatre and produced his wife successfully in *Candlesticks*. It was her first play without him or Stephen to hold her hands: and she was half terrified, half exultant. But she was lucky in her play and in her author, who fell in love with her as rehearsals went on and re-wrote the part for her, gilding it. She was lucky, too, in her clothes and lucky in the moment. For the Boers were beaten; peace had just been signed: all the world was preparing for the coronation of King Edward, and everybody was in the mood to be merry.

And she, too, just because things were going ill with her outside the theatre, was in the mood to be merry within it. As a girl she had envied Edmund because within the theatre he could experience all the emotions that she, busily preparing for her marriage of convenience, could never know. Ten years later, not quite so happy in her love match as she had expected to be, she realised how right she had been to envy him. Edmund had broken the bars of her cage certainly, but it was only, she thought sometimes, to put a collar on her and take her out for walks on a lead. Even at the Genista, though she adored the theatre and her own position in it as its mistress, hostess and star, still she was under her husband's eye. He was the centre: he was the actor-manager: her gaiety must be the decoration of his solidity.

But here she was now, in management on her own. For Edmund made it part of his policy to announce that she was in management on her own: he was shrewd enough to see how much her value would be enhanced by such an announcement and he could afford the experiment. He really wanted to discover how much she had learned, how much he could trust her. Besides, half his mind was busy on his own part in *Wild Clematis*. So soon as Elinor was launched he could go on with his plans. He did not think that she would be able to run very long without him, but he thought she would run long enough for him to establish *Wild Clematis* and Polly Traill.

But Elinor emerged nightly from her dressing-room freed and drunk with freedom. Her company loved her and was infected by her own excitement, her child-out-of-school attitude to her part and to the play. Her unknown author's very fears gave her, too, a curious courage. The gods could not be brutal to two people on a first venture, however much they might disregard the prayers of one.

She was right. *Candlesticks* and June came in together, and *Candlesticks,* as everybody knows, is still making money, and its author still blesses Elinor. For Elinor, after years of 'manager's wife' stardom, that unsubstantial demi-fame, knew at last real success, personal success, the sort of success which concentrates on the individual and is rude to his friends, relations and all his past life, and says flatteringly—"You are god: there is no other god before you: stand still and let your head be turned!"

And turned Elinor's head might have been if all had not gone on just the same at home, with as many duties and worries as ever, and Edmund rushed to death, grimly aware of but not particularly excited by his wife's personal success. And Richard and Henry had been at school five weeks and Gerry, though she loved him, could not fill their empty places in the house.

But it was strange to come home daily from the fuss they made of her in the theatre to her own unimportance at home. She got a certain comfort out of visiting Marian Broome who knew nothing and cared less about stage stars, and in talking over preparatory schools with her when she ought to have been helping at the Theatrical Garden Party. She liked Marian because the canon's daughter was so completely absorbed in her husband and children. Eustace had done well for himself. With a little influence, pushing and the Broome advantages of good looks, attractive personality, voice and eloquence, he had become a popular preacher and filled his west-end church as easily as his cousin Edmund filled his west-end theatre. He and his cousin remained close friends and the two nurseries played together; for Eustace had a son, Hubert, and two daughters. But though Eustace was doing well, he had not married a wife with a handsome fortune and so his sons went, not to the wildly expensive preparatory school in the Cotswolds, but to the good school at Kensington.

"And I wish," said Elinor sighing to Marian, "that Edmund would have let the boys go to Kensington too. It's so lonely for Gerry. You know how old he is for his age, from always being with the other two. He doesn't know what to make of it, left alone."

"Why don't you let Gerry go for a year with Hubert?" said Marian practically. "It wouldn't hurt him. They have an excellent Kindergarten."

"Oh, Marian, he's far too old for Kindergarten. But it might be possible to let him attend for a time. I should be glad to be rid of Mademoiselle."

"Come down and see it."

"I can't. I've got to go to rehearsal."

"My dear, you're not rehearsing *Candlesticks* are you, at this time of day?"

"No, but Edmund is in full swing with *Wild Clematis*. They open in a fortnight. I thought I should like to see how they're getting on and I know it's one of Edmund's scenes today."

"Come tomorrow then."

"Matinée. But I tell you what, Marian, come down with me now— it's barely two."

"And see a rehearsal? Well—I might. Papa would be horrified, of course. You wouldn't believe it, Elinor, but I'd never been inside a theatre before I married Eustace. When Eustace talked of 'the lay pulpit' the other day and it came out that he meant the Glory Hole and His Majesty's, I thought Papa would have a fit. Some more coffee? Well then, let's go!"

And down they drove to the Genista in the brilliant June sunshine, through streets in which decorations for the approaching coronation were already beginning to appear. And then Marian had to watch, with interest, amusement and a certain envy, the welcome Elinor had from the doorkeeper and the stage carpenter and the wardrobe mistress in her black alpaca apron, as she paused at the door of the little office behind the stage doorkeeper's rabbit-hutch and found the three of them drinking tea and munching sandwiches.

"Half an hour off for lunch, ma'am!" said the stage carpenter with a glance at the clock which stood at two-fourteen. "We start again in a minute. Shall I tell the Guv'nor you're 'ere?"

"No, don't disturb him. Mrs. Broome and I are going into one of the boxes," said Elinor: and then to Marian—"I never tell Edmund when I'm watching. It puts him off." And she rustled down the corridor and slipped along the side of the set stage unseen, though she could hear Edmund's voice within the set haranguing someone or other. The two women squeezed through the pass door and on to one of the upper boxes, and in the half darkness pushed aside the dust-sheets and made themselves comfortable. The curtain was up and the stage itself brilliantly lighted, but rehearsal had not begun. Edmund himself was in argument with the stage-manager, the assistant stage-manager and the scene-painter. And presently the stage carpenter himself came running. Something was wrong with the colour of the walls, and the men were holding up samples of colour—crushed strawberry, salmon and terra-cotta. Edmund came down to the foot-lights, shading his eyes against the glare.

"Any good?" he shouted.

The elegant figure of Polly Traill sauntered down the aisle. She was a slight creature and with her bell skirt and bell sleeves, her long fussy jabot and her floating boa, she looked as if she could float right over the orchestra and on to the stage itself. But the brass rail of the orchestra arrested her and leaning over it she issued her directions. Pink would not do. No shade of pink at all. "If I've said once I've said fifty times that we must have three sets, Edmund!"

"And if I've said once I've said fifty times that three sets are going to cost too much."

"I can't talk to you up there," said she fretfully: and Elinor saw with bewilderment that Edmund, without any air of annoyance, at once made his way round the footlights and down the wooden ladder to join her. She couldn't understand it. It was so unlike the Edmund who couldn't bear to be thwarted.

"What is the trouble?" hissed Marian Broome at her side.

"They're making special features of the dresses—some sort of an advertisement in conjunction with one of the big dressmaking firms," whispered Elinor. "I don't quite like it, I must confess. It isn't the Broome tradition. But Edmund says one must try new ideas. The dress in this act is called 'Risen Love', I believe, and she's quite right, it won't do against prawn pink."

"All right! Scrap it!" came from Edmund at this point. "We'll have a new set. Tell Dukesbury I'll see him afterwards." He bent to Miss Traill again, and though her matinée hat made it impossible to see his face or hers, Elinor, watching the crown of the hat, was visited again by that uneasy sensation of disquiet. She felt very angry with no-one in particular, and she felt as if she wanted to cry. She wished rehearsal would begin.

It began soon enough, but it did not make her happier. For as time went by she saw that Polly Traill was allowed to control the whole rehearsal as she herself had never been allowed to do. The willowy, bright creature was at Edmund's elbow save when she was on the stage, and when she was on the stage it became momentarily more clear that she was not easy to direct. "I needn't say that line, need I?"—"Can't I have that line re-written?"—"Must So-and-so stand with his back to me?—it makes it very hard for me"—Thus the stream of complaints flowed on, but always with such a helpless air, such appeal, such a charming smile, such confidence in her director's power to remove all difficulties, that Elinor thought to herself—'I don't like her, but I don't wonder Edmund does. She asks for everything more prettily than anyone I know.' And then realised with a shock that she was taking for granted that Edmund liked Polly Traill very much indeed, and that Polly Traill had found a new way of managing him. But it was true, they were intimate, they understood each other, they were a pair: and Edmund was unjust when Polly Traill ordered him to be unjust, and extravagant when she required extravagance, and played very badly a part that didn't suit him in order, as it seemed to his wife, to remain upon the stage with his leading lady.

'I'm jealous of that woman,' said Elinor to herself. 'That's what it is, I'm feeling jealous. I ought to be ashamed of myself. But why does he let her take his arm whenever she speaks to him?'

Then, as she watched, she began to hear Fina's voice as clearly as if Fina were sitting beside her—'You do not know why she gets on—oh no! Oh, Elinor, you bore me. We are not in the *Pensionnat*.'

"Oh, my God!" said Elinor suddenly aloud in a high, frightened voice.

Edmund, down in the stalls, turned in his seat and Polly Traill turned with him.

"Who's making that noise up there? Who is it up there? I will have quiet at rehearsal. Who is it?" Then, to the stage manager—"Go up and see who it is, Queans. I will not have people coming in without my permission."

"It's Mrs. Broome, sir," said the stage manager in a low voice.

"What? Oh—Oh, that's all right then! No, wait a minute, Queans! Ask Mrs. Broome to come down to the stalls. Tell her she'll see much better. Carry on there!"

But when Queans reached the box he found it empty. Elinor, touching Marian on the shoulder, had said—

"I'm feeling so shaky. It's the heat, I think. Do you mind?"

Marian, who had been heartily bored, nodded, and in another moment they were standing in the box-office entrance, blinking in the sudden sunlight while Elinor continued to apologise—"But we've seen enough, haven't we? Rehearsals are very dull, you know, till the last day or two."

"It's only three now," said Marian absently. "I've got to fetch Hubert. Come down with me to Kensington."

Why not? Elinor, feeling stupid, without any will of her own, nodded. She lay back in the car and closed her eyes.

"It's tiring watching rehearsals," she said again.

Marian, yawning, agreed, and they drove in silence along Piccadilly. The Park was alive with flowers, riders and pretty frocks, and they chit-chatted about acquaintances in carriages, the theatre, the children, and the new bell-sleeves, Eustace's most unsatisfactory second curate, and the coronation, as they drove on into Kensington: and all the while Elinor was saying within herself—

"It isn't true. If it's true about that woman, then it's true about little Letty James who went out in *Clever Kate*. Then it's true about— Oh, it isn't possible! When I've been ill? When I've been on tour? It can't be true that Edmund's been unfaithful to me over and over again! I've seen him in this mood with women before now. There was that girl whom Stephen discovered, and Edmund was so nice to her and gave her that part of mine in the No. 2. You don't mean that it was only because—No, it's not true! It's because I've always thought the Traill girl common: it's because I'm not playing myself: it's because I'm jealous: it's because I've let my mind be poisoned: it's because Edmund's too gentle to put that woman in her place!" And then she began to laugh at the idea of Edmund accused of being too gentle.

"You look so peculiar," said Marian glancing at her in uncomfortable reproof, "letting your lips move. You might be praying."

"I was," said Elinor harshly. And Marian lifted her eyebrows and wondered at Elinor.

The last classes were still being given when they reached the Kensington school: and when Marian Broome, pleased to be received with a good deal of fuss, was asked to watch she barely looked at Elinor for consent.

They began with the babies in the garden, who were all, as it seemed to Elinor, rather grumpily happy, completely occupied by toys of which she could make neither head nor tail. She was relieved to get indoors again to a proper schoolroom, with desks and blackboard, and breathe the more familiar atmosphere of ink, childhood and chalk. She sat down on a hard round chair a little in Marian's rear, listened to the lesson and observed the rest of the children while Marian admired Hubert for both of them. Elinor amused herself by imagining her own pleasure if Henry or Richard had been sitting among the big boys at the back. Then her heart jumped; for at that moment one of the big boys at the back lifted his head and looked at her: and she thought for a good quarter second that it actually was Henry. For catching her eye, he smiled at her, half in embarrassment and half with the friendliness of a good child, and smiling showed a dimple.

"Marian," said she under her breath—"look there! What a curious likeness!"

"Hush!" said Marian sharply. "Hubert is going to recite."

But it was an astonishing likeness. His hair was redder than Henry's and he was a sturdier child, but they might have been twins for all that. The more she looked at him, the more fascinated she was by the adorable resemblance. She could hardly wait for the lesson to be over to put her question to the young mistress.

"Who is that child with the red hair at the end of the room? He does so remind me of my own little boy."

"Would you like to speak to him?"

Yes, she would. Meanwhile—

"Elinor, here's Hubert," said Marian. "Say how-do-you-do to Auntie, Hubert!"

"Yes, dear, you did recite well." And then—"Marian, look at that child! Do you see the likeness?"

"Who to?" said Marian, twitching her son's jacket and producing a handkerchief.

"Don't you see it? Henry—"

"So there is! Quite a likeness! Funny! Wet it, darling, so that I can rub the smut off your nose." Then, as the strange little boy came up shyly under escort—"Elinor, we must be going."

But Elinor stooped to the introduction.

"What is your name?"

"Willie."

"Willie who?"

"Willie Marshall."

"And where do you live?"

The pretty young mistress interposed.

"He is one of the boarders." Then, under her breath—"An orphan. His people are in India."

"Oh, I see. Will you come and have tea with me and my little boys one day, Willie?" And then, as the dimple reappeared—"May he? I suppose there's no objection?"

"We should just have to ask his guardians, Mrs. Broome. But I'm sure they'd be delighted."

"Yes, do ask, will you? You see, my own little boy——"

Marian dragged her away.

"Couldn't you see, Elinor, that the poor woman was dying to get rid of us?"

"And can't you see, Marian——" And Elinor looking over her shoulder laughed as she waited for the exceedingly shy and pink Miss Martindale, running after them down the long corridor, an autograph album in her hand. "Sign your book? But of course I will, Miss—Miss Martindale, isn't it? Where shall I put it? On a page to itself? But isn't that rather——? Oh, very well! Then the pink page, I think. Pink's my colour. I'm so glad you enjoyed *Candlesticks*. It is a pretty play, isn't it? Ah, but think what a lovely part for me it was! What, you've been three times in a fortnight? Well, I do call that being a support! I hope I haven't blotted it. Good-bye! I was so much interested by every-thing. Good-bye!"

"How silly and gushing people are," said Marian irritably, as they drove off.

"Silly? Oh, I don't know. It's rather pleasant of them. I don't think they mean to gush. Wasn't that a curious likeness, Marian? Are you friends with Willie Marshall, Hubert? Is he nice?"

"Oh yes." But Hubert didn't know much about him: expect that he was one of the big fellows, older than Richard, and that he lived at school even in the holidays and never saw his mother, but liked his guardian who gave him lots of pocket-money.

"Have you ever seen his guardian?"

"Oh no. Willie doesn't either, not often. But he writes to him sometimes, and in the holidays he takes him for a day in the country now and then. He has a car."

She was sorry when Marian and the child left her. Their busy talk had prevented her from thinking, but no sooner had she dropped them than, of course, in poured the thoughts of Polly Traill again, black and bitter.

'Trifles light as air, are to the jealous—' The words went round and round in her head while she fought with her jealousy, still refusing utterly to believe what seemed now, as she ran over the history of her married life, so damnably easy to believe.

There was no proof, there was not a word of proof, but the sup-
position explained so much. 'Confirmations strong as proofs of Holy
Writ—' She clung to the phrase. She was so simple a creature that she
must always turn in trouble to a teacher of one sort or another, and
good phrases helped her to clear her judgment. 'Confirmations strong—'
But such confirmation had executed innocence, so often. Then let her
beware! Jealousy was driving her into wild surmises against Edmund.
But suppose Edmund were guiltless of offence against her? How
could she face him if he ever learned of the suspicions Fina had put into
her mind? She had a wild idea of speaking to him, of clearing up the
wretched business and of getting the comfort that he must surely,
surely be able to give her. But in giving her the comfort, how Edmund
would despise her for her mean and abominable suspicions. No, of
course she could never speak to him. She must put the whole thing
out of her mind and pray for charity and to be kept from a slanderer's
imagination.

Edmund was in the library when she came in, patiently exhausted.
He had a dinner tray beside him and looked up as she entered with a
curious expression, half apprehensive, half aggressive.

"Ah, there you are, Elinor! Forgive me for going on with this. I
have to get back. We shall be at it till midnight, so don't wait for me to
fetch you, for God's sake! I may not be in till three. No, I'm all right.
Don't worry about me. Go and have your own dinner." And then, as
she turned—"Oh, by the way, Elinor, I wish you wouldn't come down
to rehearsals just at present."

She stopped and stared at him in pure amazement.

"Not come to the Genista? But—but, Edmund—?"

"Well you see, today, you shouldn't have laughed up there. Upsetting! You thoroughly upset Polly Traill."

"I'm sorry if I upset Miss Traill, Edmund. I turned a little faint and
I'm afraid I—"

"Yes, yes, it's all right. I understand, of course. I understand
perfectly. But the fact is Polly's a sensitive creature and she's got it
into her head that you don't like her—"

"I don't like her? But Edmund, I've scarcely met Miss Traill."

"Yes, well, she thinks you might have taken a little more trouble
about it, I fancy, considering she's been working in one or other of
the theatres for two years. Oh, it's hot weather, you know, and—
well, the fact is, Elinor, she doesn't seem to be able to rehearse when

you're there. After all, you're a star, you see. It's a bit of an ordeal for a young girl. Better keep away for the present, I think."

"If you turn me out of my own theatre at another woman's orders, Edmund, I warn you I shan't come back."

"Now, Elinor, don't be a fool!"

She turned on him, white with anger. He saw a face that he had never seen.

"Yes, I am a fool. I've been a fool too long. Of course I won't come back to the Genista. I will never play with you at the Genista again—"

"Now look here, Elinor—"

She went quickly out of the room.

CHAPTER 52

ELINOR WALKS HOME

IF SHE had been free she would have gone straight over to Ireland to her mother-in-law. She liked that strong remote woman : she could have talked to her : she might have taken advice from her. But she was tied by the immense success of *Candlesticks :* and though she could have run away from London and the house and Edmund to Domina Broome in that other world, she could not ask Domina Broome to come to her. For Domina could not bring her world with her, and without her world of low, magic hills, wild clouds and immeasurable Atlantic air, Domina Broome would be just a stern relative by marriage to whom she could not talk. She must wait till she could go to Ireland, and *Candlesticks* might run for months. She had told Fina so confidently that she had hundreds of friends, but now when she came to review them, was there one friend to whom she could go for comfort? There was not. She began to realise how she had centred her life on Edmund and the boys, and thought : 'How unwise I have been! Love is very narrowing.'

The days went by. She contrived to be out a great deal and she did not see her husband more than twice in a week. She had taken over the high light attic of the ridiculous Victorian tower which pepper-potted the house, and there she now slept. Edmund made no sign. And sitting up in bed in her tower room, one morning, looking out over the roofs to the sky-line, an idea came to her which was to solve, for the time at least, her problem. She would take a house out in the country.

The more she thought about the notion the better she liked it. Cars were beginning to be generally used and it was much easier to get about than it had been five years ago. Ireland was a long way to send the children when they wanted a change, and they would make nice friends in the country. When the elder boys brought their friends home the Regent's Park garden was a cramped playground. London schools and London nurseries were closed cities. Except for Eustace's brood there was no to-and-fro between Gerry and other children : and when she wrote to ask the Marshall child to stay she heard that he had left the school quite suddenly. The children needed country life and country friends. She was making a great deal of money. She could buy her house in the country outright and have her own car too.

The more she considered the notion the better she liked it. She had always been content to let her handsome income flow into the general use, for what did it matter who paid the bills or how the moneys of husband and wife were spent? Half her fortune was invested in theatre concerns, but a half had been retained, at Edmund's own insistence, in her name. He could not touch it without her leave, though the income had always been devoted to keeping up the Regent's Park house. But Edmund was making plenty of money nowadays: she herself did not know half his enterprises or undertakings. In future her money should pay for her own house, her own car and her own concerns. She would have a place for the children if anything went wrong.

And because she was a woman who always met calamity by instant action the scheme comforted her out of all proportion to its importance. She knew herself that she was stunned, and that it would take her a long time to realise the full evil which had befallen her. As for the future she did not dare to look far into it. She could not believe that she had lost Edmund for good and all. On the other hand she did not think that she could ever forgive him for being other than she had believed him to be. What would be the end of it only God knew. Meanwhile one did the next thing. It was only sensible to prepare a refuge.

She wrote to the older boys—if you could live in the country what would you bargain for—hills, woods or water? But she knew what the answer would be long before the letters came. Of course they wanted the river!

Well, they should have what they wanted while they were young. She didn't believe in delaying the little happinesses. So she spent the next fortnight in the country, driving from house to empty house, lunching at small inns and getting back to the theatre in bare time to slip into her clothes. But the sun and the fresh air did her good and calmed her. Troubled as she was she could not help enjoying house-hunting as much as any other woman. Besides, there was a sullen devil in her that thrust up its head now and then to say—

"If Edmund were with you, you wouldn't be allowed to choose what you liked."

Near Marlow she found the house, a roomy William-and-Mary Manor, well lifted above the river level, with gardens all about it, sheltering woods behind and straight ahead level kingcup meadows. A tributary wide enough for bathing and boating cut through the garden and wound away down the meadows to join the Thames, its path marked by kneeling alders. The house was just what she wanted. It had three big panelled sitting-rooms, a wide entrance hall and a stairway which led up to the landing of a long corridor running the length of the house. The bedrooms and bathrooms gave on to the corridor: the attics were above.

So far she was soberly pleased with her find, for the house was old and well built; but she was childishly delighted when, at the end of the garden, she discovered a two-storied cottage, much older than the house. Its entire ground floor had been turned into a studio by a former tenant: there was a minstrels' gallery, and above were a couple of bedrooms. What a place, when they were just a little older, for the boys!

She came back to town bubbling with excitement and went next day to her lawyer's and settled the matter out of hand. But not until all was signed and sealed did she say to her husband coldly, at one of their formal meals—

"Edmund, I have decided to take a house in the country. I have seen the place I want."

"I haven't got time to come and see it now," he protested hastily, "with the first night a week away."

"There's no need," said she vaguely, and he said no more. But he had answered in a way that disturbed her, angry as she was with him. She thought he looked very tired: she thought he looked harried: she thought that he looked as if he missed her. And she could not help wanting to make him comfortable with enquiries and listenings, and a good long talk. But he said no more, and she went on playing to packed houses in the evenings, and spending her days at Shoolbred's and Maple's and would not ask any questions or concern herself at all with the fortunes of *Wild Clematis:* nor did she go to the dress rehearsal. She could not, of course, attend on the night: and though she heard him come in very late she would not go down to him to hear how the play had gone, and he did not come up to her.

The papers were divided next morning. There was plenty of praise for Polly Traill: there were a good many references to her own unavoidable absence. Edmund's part, it seemed, had not suited him. On the whole, the notices were good, but they were not enthusiastic, and it soon became clear that the critics had felt the pulse of the public and been doubtful. It seemed that their doubts were justified, for at the end of the week Edmund found himself faced by the fact that he had a charming play and kind notices but no audience. Little as he liked acknowledging it, he had a fair notion of the reason. He had played too long with Elinor: he had built up too securely the legend of a devoted couple: and the public, always a little uncertain as to whether the theatre is not, after all, the devil's church, a mere brothel in disguise, loved the assurance that their linked appearance gave. They were a guarantee that art was respectable and that the seven sins were make-believe. Here were two good actors, married, with three children, in love with each other! How delightful it was to watch them pretending to have lovers and domestic troubles, when one knew they had none! But when the devoted husband played with another woman, and his name was coupled with hers rather too openly, then the public coughed: and the play alone not being good enough to draw it, the public stayed away. It was a temporary thing: it would blow over; but meanwhile Edmund was losing a great deal of money every week, and Polly Traill had lost her head and was playing shockingly. Still, he would weather it, even though it meant jettisoning Polly Traill. He had no use for women who could not stand rough weather, and the last rehearsals had taught him a great deal about Polly Traill that he had not known before. But he would weather it.

And so he would have done, if a piece of bad luck had not befallen poor Edmund which neither he nor anyone in England could have foreseen. *Wild Clematis* opened on the seventeenth of June: on the morning of the twenty-fourth the shaken country learned that King Edward was dying after an operation, and they rang up in the theatre that night to a house that not even paper could render inhabited.

Edmund was no fool. He knew when to fight and when to run away. The notice went up at once and by the end of the week the Genista was closed.

But Edmund was not beaten: and when, with the King's almost equally rapid recovery, the slump ended as quickly as it had begun, he rushed on a safe revival, starring Polly Traill and himself. Thus he saved his pride though he could not save his public. For the safe revival failed, and failed, he knew, because Polly Traill in Elinor's part was younger and prettier, but not Elinor. Still, he ran it till the Coronation was over: then, after heavy losses, closed down again.

The double failure was almost his first defeat. He was frightened, and, studying the returns of *Candlesticks,* there were moments when he hated his wife. He flung himself at once into preparations for the autumn campaign, himself produced the tours he sent out, went down personally to pay surprise visits to the launched companies, scheming, planning, fighting to retrieve the lost moneys. He would recover. He knew it. Meanwhile he stifled in the August heat, refused to take a holiday, and wanted his wife.

But Elinor was out all day and playing every night, and the children were in Ireland on their regular annual visit to their grandmother. He began to wonder what Elinor did with herself all day. Now that he had a little leisure it was hard that he should never see his wife. At last he told himself that it was time he went to see what had gone wrong with *Candlesticks:* he hadn't been near it since the first night: everybody was sure to be over-playing by now.

Down he went that very evening. Taking care that nobody should report that he was in front, he pushed his way up into the gallery and stood at the back of it, leaning over the wooden parapet. Elinor and the second act were well under way, and he watched her with growing admiration, thinking that it had done him good to be away from her in the theatre. He could judge her more dispassionately after the separation. His mother might be right: Nell might not have been born an actress, but, by God, she had made herself into one. He wished that his mother were there so that he could say—"See what she's done! See what I've done with her!"

For Elinor at that moment was being very delicately and delightfully drunk and the whole house was rocking: yet she offended nobody, not even him! Brilliant clowning! After the Traill fool, with her languishing twang, and her obstinacy and her mechanical tricks, what a comfort it was to watch an artist and a gentlewoman. He did not know a woman in London who could put over a broad line more gracefully. She had such a complete air of not knowing what she was saying. Sometimes he was near believing that she did not know.

At the end of the act he hurried down the stone flights, out along the asphalt alley and so round the back of the theatre to the stage door. There was his wife, standing in the doorway, wrapped in a cloak, gasping for breath, taking the cool night air in the little sheltered yard that gave on to the pit exit.

He went straight up to her.

"I was up in the gallery. You were magnificent, Nell."

"Was I?" Up went her hand to her cheek in the familiar childish gesture of embarrassment. Then, careful for her make-up, she took it away quickly with the experienced gesture of her trade, and turned as if to go in.

"Don't go in yet," he said. "You're not on for a quarter of an hour, are you?"

"No," she said.

"Nell—" He, too, was grandly embarrassed.

"Yes, Edmund?"

"Nell, I've sacked Polly Traill."

He looked at her expectantly, but there was a long silence before his wife said—

"Was that quite fair, Edmund?"

"Well, I've sent her out on tour. Same thing."

"I see."

"Nell—" His eyes held hers. The entreaty in his voice was very real. It was clear enough what he wanted. For an instant as she looked at him her mind stiffened and hardened with resentment. Her essence drew away from him crying, 'I can't and won't forgive. I won't. I won't.' But then, as she looked, she began to remember how good he had been to her when she was in a trap. He had got her out of the trap. He had loved her and been good to her. If she had thought him divine when he was but a faulty creature, well, whose blame was it, hers or his? Did he ever ask her to put him on a pedestal? But he had rescued her and loved her, and she had borne him three children, and he had been unfaithful to her, brutal and selfish. But now he wanted, as she had once wanted, rescue, comfort and to be loved. Better to give and give in—always better to give. She put up her hands, pulled his head down to her and kissed him.

"Come in and wait for me," said she. "It's the shortest act."

But he caught her hands and kissed them with fervour. He was relieved and embarrassed, and very happy again, and he wanted to tell her about his losses and his plans quickly.

"You get on," said Edmund, almost pushing her from him into the narrow entry. "And be quick afterwards, old lady! I'll wait for you here."

Then he walked up and down, up and down in the cool blue evening, waiting for her: and when she came out, hurried to her and sheltered her arm and elbow into his hand as she loved him to do, and walked her off into the darkness, waving away the car.

"You're not tired, are you?" said Edmund. "I'd so much rather walk as I talk. I've got a good deal to tell you."

She was very tired; but she walked home with him.

CHAPTER 53

RICHARD, HENRY, GEOFFREY AND JOHN

SHE was simple enough to imagine that her troubles were over. She and Edmund had been estranged: now the estrangement was ended. Well then, one had only to be happy. And happy she was for a few months, and happier still when their last child, John, was born, though he came prematurely into the world, nearly cost his mother her life, was from the first a delicate child and kept them all in a state of lively terror for the first few years of his existence.

In spite of this, or because of this, he was the best loved of Elinor's children. She would never own it, but everyone knew it: and, strangely enough, no-one resented the fact, not even Gerry, who always thought himself ill-used. Nor did Edmund resent it. Edmund who adored his elder sons and spoiled and bullied them almost as jealously as a woman, had been profoundly irritated by any sign in his wife of a like adoration. He would empty his pockets to any of the boys if they wheedled him; but Elinor always had the utmost difficulty in persuading him to let her spend for them. He must be first with them and also first with her, and he hated his sons when he saw her absorbed in them.

But he did not resent her absorption in John, though he treated her occasionally as if she were a highly incompetent nurse who needed a good deal of direction if his son were to have his due, and watched his elder sons jealously to see if they showed any sign of jealousy of the late-come youngest, the darling, the son of prosperity. But the school-boys disconcerted him by being as much attracted to the baby as he was.

At five John was the centre of the house. His brothers' quarters were his chosen nursery in their absence, and when they were at home, there he was still to be found, very quiet, very watchful, and, infant though he was, a useful and obliging shadow, never in the way, obedient as a well-trained pet, only flaring out into a rage of tears when he was dragged off to take walks or play with other children or lead the life proper to a child of his age. His elders handled him as if he were a puppy and disciplined him when they thought of it, but they had also a rather charming admiration for their toy. They always had stories to tell of John's latest. Richard, Henry and Geoffrey quarrelled among themselves with acridity and gusto, constantly found each other's presence a nuisance and said so, but they never apparently found John a nuisance. Even when they filled their cottage with school friends, John was never actually kicked out, though he might be kicked into a corner. He was handsomely bullied by his elders as was only right; but all three would, singly or combined, have half killed any other human being who attempt to do the like. John took it all very quietly. As Richard said, you never knew what John thought.

But it was Donna, over for one of her rare, brief visits, who classified John. Henry, who was her especial favourite, had given her no peace till she came over to see the country house. Because he reminded her of Stephen and was as persistent as she herself had been in her youth, she surrendered and came. Edmund was greatly gratified by the visit and took a day off to meet her and bring her down, and himself took her over every room in the house and every stick and stone of the garden. For he had quite forgotten that Elinor had bought it and expected a good deal of praise from her at the cheapness of the place, and the wisdom of the step, and the admirable taste with which the River House, as they called it, was furnished.

"And that's the boys' house?" said Donna, as they came round the syringa bushes and saw it suddenly fifty yards away across the little lawn.

"Well, yes—" said Edmund grudgingly—"for the time being they're allowed to use it as a playroom. It keeps the noise from the house. I haven't decided yet what I shall eventually do with it. It's too damp for a library."

"How well Henry serves!" returned Donna, firmly leading her son's ideas and steps towards the distant tennis lawn. For till the boys asked her to their room she wasn't going near it. Edmund should know better than to suggest such a thing.

"He and Gerry think of nothing but games," said Edmund taking the bait. "You know Henry has got his cricket colours this summer?" And he shepherded her leisurely across the tennis lawn while Richard waited to continue the game.

Elinor greeted them gaily and made room for her mother-in-law beside her; but Edmund wondered that Elinor could see the game at all with the glint of the river in her eyes, and was sure that his mother couldn't: and insisted on moving the iron seat and the deck chairs to the other side of the court—

"Now then, Richard—Henry—give a hand! Can't you see that we want to move the seat?"

He settled them all where they did not want to be, and then stood beside them watching the resumed game for some five minutes. He remarked to Richard—and with justice—that it was not like him to serve double faults twice running and that he must pull himself together, suggested—and rightly—that the net needed tightening and insisted on its being done there and then. If you were playing at all you might as well play properly. He told Richard sorrowfully that he had asked for that one when an easy return was smashed at the net, called off John to fetch him his own racket, decided that after all he had not time for a game, and at last strolled back to the house, while small John, unruffled as ever, trotted back to his place behind Richard and began once more picking up the litter of balls.

"I say, John, you might fag our side a bit!" shouted Gerry.

But John, smiling, did not budge. Richard was his owner.

"Odd thing, family likeness," said Donna to her daughter-in-law. "John's as obstinate as Edmund, you know, although he looks so frail. And then again he's so like my poor brother sometimes that he makes my heart ache. His colouring—his figure—it might be Gilly come alive. Only looks of course. In character he's more like my father."

"John always seems to me singularly individual," said Elinor, not very pleased.

"Ah, but when I look at your three boys I don't see them as you do. For me each is a palimpsest."

"I don't think I know," said Elinor cautiously, "exactly what a palimpsest is."

"A new writing on an old manuscript. When I look at Henry I see Stephen and I hear Gilly laugh: when I watch Richard I hear my grandmother and my father quarrelling and I see myself sulking with them both."

"I have never known three children more entirely individual," said Elinor crisply.

"No, Elinor, not individual: only variations on an old theme."

"I believe—" said Elinor reddening—"that each soul comes from God and goes to God and is responsible to God alone."

"The sins of the fathers—" said Donna.

"That's Old Testament and I don't believe it, and what's more if it were New Testament, still I shouldn't."

Donna was grimly amused, and not for the first time, by the incongruous simplicity of that well-known actress her daughter-in-law, and showed it so plainly that Elinor had to laugh.

"Well, I mean—as if the children weren't themselves," protested Elinor.

"I've seen that dimple of John's on Gilly," said her mother-in-law, "in exactly the same place. And Gerry's little patch of red hair on the side of his head——"

"The left side," said Elinor. As if she didn't know her own son's hair!

"Well, I have heard my grandmother say that Uncle Lionel had it when he was a boy, just such a patch the size of a halfpenny. It merged with the rest of the hair later. You'll see, it will with Gerry. And I tell you, in character as well as looks, some sentence or so of the old writing will show in each of them."

"Not in John," said John's mother firmly, watching the group on the lawn. The game had ended in a discussion at the net and John, overlooked, but firmly wedged between Henry and Richard, was sitting balanced on the handle of his racket, watching each speaker in turn. "Everybody says he's like me if he's like anyone."

"He's got your patience, Elinor, and your half-buried sense of humour. That's all. He's not in the least like you really. Don't you see what he is? He's all the Broomes."

"I don't see it," said Elinor obstinately. "He's such a quiet little boy."

"He can afford to be quiet. He's at the centre. Have you never heard the family rhyme?"

Elinor laughed.

"Reckon—beckon—? The children brought it home the last time they were staying with you. What does it mean?"

"Charm. That is if you know the last two lines. It gives you the power to get your own way and be loved for getting it. My father should have taught me the spell by rights, but he taught my brother instead. That's why, my dear, I am a woman without attraction. My brother threw it up at me once that he knew the rhyme and I didn't, and I took it very seriously. Oh, I was bitter about it. But that small boy of yours looks as if he were born knowing the last lines, the lost lines. He *is* them. He has only to crook his finger——"

"Don't tell him so," said his mother.

"He knows, my dear. I wish he weren't so delicate, Nell!"

Elinor looked harried.

"I know. He's always giving us frights. My heart's in my mouth each time Edmund looks at him for fear he should say it's time for him to go to school. He isn't fit for school. He wants keeping back, not urging."

"Yes, I should keep him with you."

"But that's what I ask myself—what am I to do? Edmund is urging this American tour. I hate leaving the children. Of course I can send the elder boys to you: you are always so good to them. But leaving John is another matter."

"And leaving Edmund?"

Elinor looked up quickly and the two women's eyes met.

"There's all the difference," said her mother-in-law, "between your leaving Edmund and Edmund leaving you, you know. I shouldn't go to America if I were you."

"No, I don't think I shall."

The two sat in a thoughtful silence as they watched Henry begin a pat-ball game of instruction with John: Geoffrey came over to be agreeable: Richard, of course, went off as usual to his books.

For Richard had persuaded his mother to line with shelves the room that his father thought too damp for a library, and it was already half full of the oddest rag, tag and bobtail of print. Thither Richard retired by the hour to be happy; for he was a greedy reader. This irritated Edmund, who had gradually enlarged his own collection of theatre books until it was valuable and interesting. He was constantly adding to it still and was always delighted to display his finds. But though he genuinely loved his reading he yet could not be contented to let other people read what they wanted to read: and he would drift into the boys' common-room and run his finger irritably along the shelves, and wonder where Richard got the money to spend on the rubbish he bought. Then, like as not, he would carry off Richard to his own room to talk of the books of his own boyhood and read aloud to him from one of them.

And Richard would listen for a time with interest and an air of real respect; but always, to Edmund's intense annoyance, the look would change at last, with no apparent reason, between the beginning and the end of a random sentence, to a look of polite boredom: and Richard would say—"Yes, Father! Thank you, Father! I'll take it away and read it, sir!" Richard admired his father and thought him a great man, but he also thought him an intolerable bore.

He never thought about his mother at all. She was there: she was his: why should he analyse her? But he was always analysing his father to his brothers, and being a brilliant mimic, did not stop at analysis. One day he wrote a series of scenes which he called 'The Acts of Edmund Broome', and Henry and Gerry were convulsed by it.

Edmund coming down to breakfast in a good temper: Edmund criticising the grilled kidneys: Edmund prodding the imperturbable Hammond in the back and pulling down the window to curse foot-passengers: Edmund arriving at the office: Edmund devastating a rehearsal: Edmund taking a call—all these phases of the well-known actor-manager, Henry Edmund Broome, his irreverent eldest was accustomed to enact, working it up into a little revue, with Henry at the piano, Gerry taking all the other parts, and John sitting under the piano glancing up from his drawing and chuckling now and then.

But their mother wandered in to them one winter's evening and stood listening in the doorway for a good five minutes before they saw her: and that was the end of this particular entertainment. She was furiously angry with them, the more because her sense of humour had been tickled; for Richard had caught every trick, every intonation, every fierce, pompous or sentimental note.

"How dare you, Richard, make fun of your father?"

Henry, with his delightful and disarming smile, interposed.

"Darling, there is no harm. You must admit he is funny sometimes."

"Richard, do you hear me? I am speaking to you."

"I say, Mother, it was all of us." Henry still fought the losing battle.

"Richard!"

"Yes, Mother?"

"Richard—I've never punished you yet——"

He looked down at her with a half smile. He was taller than she.

"Well, Mother?"

"I'm going to punish you now. You are not to use this room for the rest of the holidays."

"Very well, Mother."

"You know why, Richard?"

He gave her a quizzical, yet intimate look.

"Oh, yes."

"Then move out your things tonight. John!"

"Yes, Mother?"

"It's time you went to bed! Come at once!"

At which very meekly and soberly John emerged from under the grand piano and went off with his mother.

"Whew!" said Gerry as the door closed, and fell back dramatically into the best arm-chair. But Henry went off into fits of laughter.

"Would you believe it?" said he. "And I've known her fifteen years!"

"Oh, shut up!" said Richard roughly.

"Shut up yourself! Why? That's what I want to know! Why? She knows Father just as well as we do! What possessed her? D'you know, Richard?"

"Oh yes, I know," said Richard irritably, stuffing a stack of his books into a satchel preparatory to the move.

"Well, why?" said Geoffrey.

"Oh, don't go on squeaking why, why, why! You know Mother. It was because John was there."

"Little beast's getting a nuisance," said Geoffrey.

"Oh, John's all right," said Henry hastily. "But I say, this is rot. Shall I go and talk to her, Richard?"

"Oh, shut up!"

"Yes, but——"

"Will you kindly leave me to manage my own affairs?" and Richard humped his parcel on to his back and departed.

Gerry stretched out his legs and yawned.

"Well, she hasn't turned us out, that's one comfort," said Gerry.

Henry laughed again.

"Mother ought to be more sympathetic. She doesn't much like budging herself. Have you heard them both over the American business? She's refusing to go now. The old man's livid."

"He needn't be. He'll make her go," said Gerry yawning: and, as usual, was right. Edmund was always too strong for Elinor: and when John was eight years old she went to America just as Edmund had planned. But she would not go till she had extracted his unwilling consent for John to be with his grandmother during her absence. Edmund was quite sure that school would knock the delicacy out of him! But he had to agree because he very much wanted his wife's co-operation.

For his enterprises had enormously grown in the last two years. But Elinor, formerly so docile, had grown stubborn and difficult. It was as if, in spite of their reconciliation, some spring had broken: he never induced her to play with him again at the Genista, for instance. But, of course, he had become with the years far too much occupied by the business side of his enterprises to appear before the public: and, as he said, his wife in management was as good as himself in management.

For years Elinor had had her season in town with a tour to follow, a fair average of success, and a steady increase of popularity, while Edmund, having invested by mere shrewd chance in a modern children's play that instantly became a huge success, was able to put it on every Christmas for twenty years, risk the inevitable profits on a big spring show, and yet be sure of a margin at the end of the year. Naturally success merely bred in him a more furious ambition and by the time Richard was ready to go to Oxford, Edmund Broome, though he had dropped out of the public eye as an actor, was one of the biggest figures of the English theatre world: and, still dissatisfied, was talking about getting a footing in America.

He had, indeed, already a legitimate interest there. Russel, who had died a year after John's birth, had been complimented by being asked to stand godfather to John and had left him the Genista, with the proviso that John should not assume control till he had been to and left one or other of the Universities. Russel had missed his last years at Oxford, and knew just what he wanted a Broome to do: and had no idea of losing part control of the family fortune by the mere accident of mortality. The rest of his property was equally divided between Eustace and Edmund. Eustace had the cash and Edmund the property: and part of the property was a valuable New York site on which Edmund erected a theatre called The Russel-Broome. He enjoyed the gamble, but knowing nothing of the American public and its tastes, had dropped more than he could afford before he had the brilliant idea of bringing over his wife and exploiting in a series of English plays.

But he found her hard to move: indeed he perceived with dismay that she would no longer throw her cap over the moon because he asked her. That day was dead. They had never had a quarrel since John's birth, but within a year he was going his own way again and she hers, and there had been many successors to Polly Traill. If she knew of them she never showed that she knew, and he would have said if he had been asked that they got on as well together as any married couple in the kingdom, though she was damned obstinate about the boys and spoilt them. But that was natural. Still it was hard nowadays to make her fling her cap over the moon. He had to tell her a good deal about the state of his finances, and about that very awkward deal with the Hatzfeld Brothers, before she would do what he wanted. And then, only a week before departure, she once more nearly threw up the whole thing and put him in a deuce of a hole, just because he had dealt as he thought fit with his own eldest son.

God knew, thought Edmund, that he was fond enough of the boys. Nobody could call him a harsh or unfeeling father. Didn't they have everything they wanted? Didn't they cost him a good five hundred a year apiece? Hadn't he given in to Elinor's fancy for letting them have the garden house to themselves? Was ever a set of youngsters more pampered? Why, at their age he was touring the country, earning his keep and a little over. He gave them every mortal thing they wanted and what did he get back? Evasions, insolences, disobediences, at the slightest crossing of them for their own good. That was because he tried to do his duty as a father instead of being a mere slave to them like Nell. And it was not only to him that they were insolent. She might choose to ignore it but he greatly resented their manner to their mother. They mimicked her to her face and she seemed to think it a joke. Yes, she allowed these fifteen-year-olds to criticise her, and what's more it seemed to him that there were times when she accepted their criticisms. And all this nonsense about diet, and Geoffrey lecturing her about not taking exercise! Really, what these children permitted themselves nowadays! And she actually listened to them and agreed that she was too fat and what's more had actually fined herself down with too much tennis and food fads, and what not.

Well, perhaps it was as well in view of the American tour; but he hated a scraggy woman himself, and anyway to see Elinor permitting them to treat her as they did, to watch her solemnly respecting their opinions, their whipper-snapper, ginger-pop opinions, well, it made him sick. He was thankful that John was in Ireland that holiday, though he missed him. Yes, he did miss the child. But he was not going to have John led astray by his brothers' influence, thought Edmund, though Henry was harmless enough, bless the boy! Good boy, Henry! And Geoffrey was well enough. No, Richard was the problem. Richard could thank his father's leniency that he was not at this moment hunting a job at a pound a week. He hoped he had done right in letting him go to Oxford. Discipline was what the boy wanted and never had. They had always spoiled him, he realised that now. And so, as Elinor said, you must make allowances, and of course the boy had left school, but hang it all, if he was allowing Richard four hundred a year he had at least the right to criticise the spending of it. First editions of the moderns! Conrad! Who'd ever heard of Conrad? Oh well, if the boy liked to waste his money it was, he supposed, no affair of his. But the boy must understand that he wasn't going to pay his debts. He had said so to him. "You understand, my boy? And you're not to come running to your mother every time you're overdrawn either!"

Well, that was a harmless warning enough, wasn't it? Nothing to make the boy sulk and glare at him, in a friendly, fatherly warning like that! Couldn't Richard understand how anxious his father was? He had spent a full hour telling Richard how much harder he had had to fare when he was young, when sixpence had to do the work of a shilling, and he at sixteen had been business manager of a company and had had to keep his head among sharks and sharpers and fools. But the boy simply wasn't interested. "So you understand, Richard, no more throwing away money on this sort of thing!"

"For that matter, Father, it has gone up in value since I picked it up, by nearly a pound."

"That's not the point, my boy! That's not the point."

"Well, Father, I thought as long as I don't run into debt, I could do as I liked with my own allowance."

(His own allowance, you see! His own allowance!)

"Well, my boy, when you have to work as hard for money as I do—"

"If you'd rather, I'll try to manage on less, Father. Of if you don't think I ought to go to Oxford——"

Good God, did the boy think he grudged him the money?

But when it came to making an hotel of the place then he had put his foot down. Certainly he had said that Richard could use the London house while he was getting his kit together. Yes, and he supposed it was reasonable that the boy's friends should come in to see him, and if Elinor had given permission for a supper party, well that certainly put part of the blame on Elinor. But to come home unexpectedly at one o'clock in the morning and find a dozen youngsters at their ease in the music-room, with the piano going and the whole pack of them shouting at the tops of their voices (did they call that singing?), well, it annoyed him! It might be unreasonable, but it annoyed him. He didn't grudge them their fun, of course. But the whole affair was unsuitable, noisy and unsuitable—mere schoolboys and a bottle of whiskey on the side table! Yes, there was! He must say, he thought he had been very gentle with Richard. Many a father would have handled the situation very differently. But he had merely beckoned Richard out of the room and told him quite quietly that the thing must stop, at once, and that he was to come to him afterwards in the library.

Elinor could say what she liked, and no doubt the boy had told her a long story, but he had been anxious to control himself and had controlled himself till the boy's insolence made it impossible. Richard confessed that he had actually bought the bottle of whiskey and brought it in! If he had helped himself from the sideboard it would have been bad enough—youngsters of seventeen drinking whiskey! but to go out and buy it and sneak in furtively, that Edmund could not forgive. Elinor was simply childish with her talk of the boy having bought it for the look of the thing! Trying to give his first grown-up party correctly indeed! Good God! The boy had only left school five weeks. As he told the boy—"If you hadn't left school and weren't supposed to be a responsible human being, I should know how to deal with you!" And then the boy had been insolent. And, well, of course he had lost his temper. And then——Edmund hurried over the rest of the scene. But he would never forget the boy's tone—

"I don't see that smashing up the place does any good!"

And then the boy had actually walked out, had left him and walked out. And he himself had rung up Elinor and she had come up by car, the foolish woman, and arrived at five o'clock in the morning and God knows what Hammond thought.

And that was not the end of it either. A fine dance Richard had led them after that—not a word from the boy for nearly a week and he with all the last minute preparations of the journey to make, and a thousand-and-one final arrangements in the theatre, having to put it all aside to concern himself with a schoolboy's vagaries: and Elinor in such a mood and swearing she wouldn't come to America, as if one could smash a contract like a beer bottle! Of course the boy had gone off in a huff to one of his friends! Was he to run round to the parents of every boy of Richard's acquaintance saying—"Is my son staying with you?" The boy had plenty of money: if he chose to behave like a fool let him sink or swim. And then, after three days, Richard rings up his mother as calm as you please—

"Don't worry. I've got a job."

And what sort of a job? Bottle-washer to a cinema operator! A Broome in one of these bastard photographer's Punch-and-Judies! A Broome! Fifteen shillings a week, and Elinor actually proud of him! As if she and Richard didn't know well enough his feeling about the cinemas—the ruin of the theatre—the great threat and peril—only nobody but himself had the sense to see it, except Tree. Tree said precisely the same thing. But nobody listened. But the impudence of it, you know—authors putting in their contracts 'Cinema rights reserved!' Let them take their rights! Well, he'd have Richard out of that hole quickly enough. After all, he knew how to handle Richard. The boy might be an insolent young devil, but the boy was fond of him and he was fond of the boy. And Elinor might be right: young people were so literal. Richard might have thought that he was really angry with him. "Yes, my dear, don't worry. I'm the boy's father, aren't I?" He'd show her how to handle a youngster.

"Come now, Richard, what's all this about? You've thoroughly upset your mother. She's been chasing half over London after you. Drop all this nonsense and come home at once, and we'll say no more about it."

"I'd rather not, Father. I'd rather stay where I am. I like the work."

How angry Richard made him! What a stubborn face he had! And there was Elinor watching them both. Well, he could set an example in self-control, if that was what she expected or didn't expect. But he'd have to be damn quick about it. He'd got the appointment with the Guild syndicate at eight. One could always do so much better over a dinner. Well—to settle the matter—

"The truth is, Richard, we've both been hasty——"

"I'm awfully sorry about the whiskey, Father. I never thought you'd mind. Only there were one or two older fellows——"

"Yes, yes. Your mother explained all that. Very well then, that's settled."

"I'd rather stay on where I am, Father, if you don't mind. It's a frightfully interesting job and——"

"Elinor!"

For he found himself turning to her, although he hadn't meant to call her in. However, let her try if she wanted to.

"Richard—" said his wife—"you're not going to throw up Oxford for the sake of a gesture?"

Queer phrases she used, and look how the boy's face changed. She could always tickle him up somehow. He wished he had her knack.

"It isn't a gesture, Mother. It's the most interesting stuff. I've been to every show I could get near for the last year. There's a future in it."

How maddening the boy was with his tone of authority! How Elinor could defer to him as she did! Women were amazing. Well, he wouldn't. He'd show who wielded authority.

"You don't know what you're talking about, my boy. Take it from me this cinema craze will run its course like other crazes."

"I don't think so, Father."

"Well, I'm sorry, my boy, I do! And at the moment it's my views that matter, not yours. When you've had my experience——"

"That's why I want to stay where I am, Father, for the experience. You told me only a month ago that you'd begun getting experience at sixteen."

"Yes, well, I don't choose you to have the same sort of experience."

"But I do choose, Father."

"Elinor, am I going to be defied by my own son?"

"I'm not defying you, Father. I only——"

"Well, I wash my hands of it. I'm sending you to Oxford: I'm giving you a princely allowance. You have a career waiting for you afterwards. If you choose to fling it away and if your mother chooses to let you, it's your own look-out. I'm sick of the business, and I'm sick of you, my boy, I can tell you that. Unlicked cub! You can make what arrangements you like, Elinor, and Richard can give me his decision tonight. I'm not going to waste any more time over him."

And so he had got out of the room, angry and sore and bewildered, with that damned word cinema rankling in his mind. And when he next saw the pair of them it was plain that there was to be no more trouble. But there never was trouble if you showed that you meant what you said. But if you gave an inch they took an ell. Oh yes, he had certainly taught the boy a lesson. He could afford to let him down lightly.

"Well, Richard?"

"I've thought over what you said, Father, and what Mother said, and if you and Mother think I ought to go to Oxford, I'll go. And of course I want to go, Father, only——"

"Yes, my boy, that's all right. Glad you've come to your senses." But he wondered once or twice what Elinor had said to Richard, and presently in his own way asked her.

"Did you have much trouble with him, my dear?"

"Oh no, Edmund. You know how he's always set his heart on Oxford. It was only his pride that was upset. I think he wanted to show you that he could support himself if need be. He got into his head, you know, that you thought him——"

"Well, what?"

"Edmund, can't you understand how a sensitive boy feels about money? Has Richard ever asked you for money? Can you ever remember him doing it?"

"Well, I don't know. Henry is a sensitive creature enough, I should have said, and when he wants anything he comes to me for it without hesitation. He has no false pride at any rate."

"He's younger, Edmund. He has a different nature."

"Well, I wish Richard were more like him, that's all I can say. Henry's never given me a day's trouble."

Poor Edmund! He was not three months in America before Henry gave him more than a day's trouble. It was precious hard, when everything was going so well, and Elinor having a real success, and the contract with the Hatzfelds' going through after all, and Richard safe at Oxford, and good reports of John's health coming in from Ireland, that Henry—Henry of all people in the world—should break out. Henry at sixteen had got himself involved in a shady dancing-hall disturbance. The boy must have been mad. In term time, in the sixth, throwing away his record and his position! What did he want to philander with women for, at sixteen? Disgraceful! He could thank his stars he hadn't been expelled.

"No, he should thank Richard," said Elinor, putting down the house-master's letter with a grave face.

"Yes," said Edmund with satisfaction. "Richard's got his head screwed on his shoulders. I'm very pleased with Richard. Oxford's doing him good."

For Richard, it seemed, had taken on himself the responsibility of elder brother with great discretion, had dashed down to the school and his old house, and had fought his brother's battles with some success.

"There's been the hell of a rumpus," wrote Richard to his mother. "But he's not expelled. The Head's been comparatively decent, and Pocock of course, as usual, was a brick: and I've talked to Henry like a Dutch uncle. Silly ass! You needn't worry. I didn't really worry, though it was a bit serious. What it is to be popular! He's wriggled through again."

Edmund put down the letter, breathing heavy relief; but Elinor drew it to her with a frown. It was the word 'again' that worried her. Edmund needn't be so shocked. Some boys were men at sixteen. Why, Edmund himself—She couldn't forgive Edmund for being angry with Henry and sneering when Edmund himself—— She did think it was Edmund's job to be understanding, not hers. But he was like a maiden-aunt sometimes. She wished her mother-in-law lived with them. She did understand boys, although of course she went too far always. What was that she had said—"You may as well face it, Elinor! Some boys want girls to play with and some want women to go to bed with—and if Edmund can't grasp the difference between Richard and Henry and Gerry, refer him to me. I still know more about him than you do, my dear! I'll talk to him."

But how could Elinor do anything stuck in New York? You couldn't write: you had to be on the spot. The truth was she had been away from the boys too long. The tour round the world had been a mistake, and now Edmund was booking her for another season in the autumn of 1914. It was difficult to be a mother and an artist at the same time. And yet, it always seemed to her that the more worried she was in her mind the better she worked. Wasn't that strange? The more unhappy you were the better you worked. She couldn't understand how her mother-in-law could exist without a career and an audience. Suddenly at the height of your career to throw away your career—no, that Elinor couldn't do. More and more the theatre, the actual theatre itself, with its gruelling work, its artificiality, its squalors, its swift excitement, its opportunity for incessant emotion, became her actual home, and her home the mere comfortable hotel which she kept for husband and her sons.

She came home to that hotel early in March. Edmund had gone on ahead of her and she was to re-open the Genista so soon as Easter was over with the light comedy that had done so well in New York. And when she arrived at Southampton Richard and Henry were there to welcome her, enormously grown, both of them. She hardly knew Richard. She had left a sulky, uncertain schoolboy, all self-assertion and shyness, suspicion and enthusiasm, a male variant of that stupid schoolgirl of twenty years ago, raw from the *Pensionnat*. Strange that she had never seen the likeness before! It was not a true likeness, of course. Richard was a Broome, not a Dale. Only because they both passed through the same state of transition was there a passing likeness. But the comparative emancipation of university life had already defined and settled him, at any rate physically, as the honeymoon had defined and settled her. He would never be handsome: his face was too heavy, too square and mask-like for handsomeness; but she thought that she had nevertheless an astonishingly attractive ugly son. His pose was the sulky and sardonic, till he was pleased. But, touched by an idea, an emotion or a humour, he would crackle, sparkle, send up a rocket or two, and then, all in an instant, would become a Fifth of November bonfire. And she approved the ridiculous care with which he was dressed, and his black hair carefully arranged to look like lacquer. She liked, too, his authority with her and with his brother.

Henry was completely unchanged: taller, of course, but that was all: and better-looking than ever, with not one of his familiar, summer-day tricks of laughter and good-temper and self-mockery missing. Yes, he was still her own Henry, whom no woman could resist, and adorably unfilial in his care for her. But then, as she said to herself, Henry would be possessive and protective with Christabel Pankhurst. There he was, giving everybody precedence and being charming with rugs and wraps : yet pointing out with some pride that he was contriving to sit exactly where he wanted to sit, and insisting that, though he was pleased to see his mother, his real reason for being on the quay was the need for visiting a particular Southampton shop. His mother didn't imagine that she was the excitement!

Dear Henry—how blessed it was to hear his nonsense again, and be soothed by Richard's silences. But where was Gerry? Wasn't he home from Ireland yet? Surely.

"Oh yes! Turned up a day or two sooner than we expected. So he came instead of John. There's only room for three. And John didn't seem very keen."

Thus far Henry. But Richard said nothing.

"Where's my Gerry then?"

"Well, he thought that if he were dropped at Winchester he could have lunch with a pal of his. We're to pick him up. Gerry always kills two birds with one stone," said Richard solemnly; but whether in sarcasm or excuse his mother did not know and did not ask. She was sensitive on the subject of Gerry, who was always so pleased to see her when she was at home, and so entirely capable of getting on without her when she was away. Gerry always had some tucked-away reason for anything he said or did, even for being pleased to see her. The reason was generally quite harmless, but there it was, and every member of his family save Edmund was aware of the trait. But Gerry was proud of handling his father so much better than Richard could. "Leave him to me! I can do anything with the old man," was a favourite saying of Gerry's. And indeed Edmund was fond of him and responded readily enough to his attentions.

But it was curious how little Gerry entered into Edmund's calculations when he discussed the boys' futures. Richard and Henry were both to go on to the stage; but Richard, he thought, would probably be best on the business side. As for John, John, of course, could do anything. "We won't hurry John, my dear! He must find his own way among his own talents." Edmund was always understanding about John. But when it came to Gerry—"We'll find him something," he would say comfortably : and as often as not pull out a letter from Gerry himself and tell his wife to get the boy what he asked for. It would be—"By the way, my dear, Gerry seems to have been having some trouble with his teeth, and he wants you to write to his house-

master. He says the local dentist ruins all their teeth. So Halley had
better see him. He says he could get leave next Wednesday."

"Wednesday is dress rehearsal."

"So it is. Well, perhaps the boy will have time to see a little of it."

And then Edmund would wonder why John listened intently and
intelligently to the trifling debate.

Such long forgotten incidents were in Elinor's mind as they drove up
through the English spring. But, when they got to Winchester and
picked up Gerry, he was as usual so charmed to see her, so loving, so
possessive, so anxious to be two against the world, that she hated
herself for the unmotherly thoughts she had harboured. She should
remember that life with Edmund, for ever fighting suspicions of
Edmund, had made her abnormally thin-skinned. It was foolish to
expect a schoolboy like Gerry to think of anything but his own concerns. As long as he loved her what did it matter if he also made use of
her?

So she drove home very happily with her three boys, and when they
reached Marlow there was the household joyously and sedately welcoming her, but no Edmund and no John. A wire explained Edmund's
absence, but why was not John at the gate? She found him in her room,
a quiet little boy.

"Well, John, here's Mother! Here's Mother, John! Aren't you
pleased to see me?"

Yes, he was very pleased to see her, but in a small aloof voice: and
though he received her kiss, did not give her one. She had to make
friends with him as if he were a strange child, very shy, very polite.
Was it possible that less than a year could have made her a stranger to
him? What was the matter with John? He sat in her room and watched
her unpack, but he said very little, and he went off to bed unbidden.
She worried over him all through dinner.

"Has John been very quiet lately?" she asked Richard as the meal
drew to a close.

"Not more than usual. Why?"

"Well, he's hardly spoken to me. It's as if I'd offended him."

"He was excited enough about your coming," put in Henry. "He's
been talking of nothing else for days. I wonder he didn't ask to sit up."

Elinor, too, had wondered.

"He won't find it easy at school," remarked Gerry, "after always
hanging round grown-up people."

"I suppose you call yourself a grown-up person," said Henry, who had left school at Easter, would be at a crammer's throughout the summer and go up to Oxford in the autumn.

"Yes, I do." Gerry was snappish. "And John's got to learn that he can't do everything that we do."

"You gave him a lesson on the subject yourself, didn't you?" said Richard smoothly.

"What do you mean?" Elinor looked from one to the other enquiringly.

"Well, Mother," said Richard, who was uncommonly flushed—"I promised he should come in the car, but Gerry took upon himself to alter things."

Gerry also flushed.

"If I've got to forego meeting Mother to please a spoilt kid——"

"Yes, you met her at Winchester," said Richard quickly.

"But Father himself said it was far too long a drive for John. It's not my fault. I don't want to coddle him, God knows! It's not going to do him any good at school."

"Oh, school!" Elinor sighed. For John was to go in a fortnight, and would have gone a year ago if it hadn't been for his health. It was inevitable, and she knew it. But she dreaded his going. Well, there it was!

"He couldn't have been upset about not coming, could he?" she said to Gerry.

Gerry bent his candid brows over the problem.

"Who? John? I don't think so. He quite understood. I must say that for the kid—he's sensible. I say, Mother, are you driving up to town tomorrow? I'd so love to drive up with you."

"My dear, it'll be rather dull for you, won't it? I shall be at the theatre all day."

"Oh, I can put in time. As a matter of fact I've got a——"

Richard laughed softly.

"What's the joke?" demanded Gerry with instant truculence.

"You amuse me."

"Flattered!"

"Children, children!" Elinor rose. "Coffee's in the library. I'll be down in a moment." And off she went to say good-night to John. She met the nurse on the stairs.

"I was coming to look for you, Ma'am! I can't do anything with Master John. He won't lie down and go to sleep. He won't even try. He's been watching for you."

"Excitement."

Elinor passed on to her son's room. There he was, bolt upright in his bed, looking such a baby in his correct little pyjamas.

"Mother, shut the door!"

She obeyed and sat down beside him. So now the trouble was coming out, was it? She half guessed what it would be. But only half guessed.

"Mother—" he caught her by the shoulders and clung to her, shaking her in his agitation—"say it isn't true!"

"John, darling! Gently! Say what isn't true?"

"That I'm being sent to school because I'm in the way?"

"Did Gerry say that?" Her voice grew stern.

"Yes. I told Gerry you'd think I didn't want to come to meet you, and he said that they couldn't talk in front of me, so I might as well give him my place. Mother, it wasn't the drive I wanted. I did want to see you. I did! I did!"

So that was Gerry left alone for a year! It was not Gerry's fault, of course. It was her fault, wicked mother, for being out of England for nearly a year. But how could Gerry be so cruel to such a little boy? Thoughtlessness, of course, and not cruelty, but—how Gerry could! Well, it was easy enough to comfort the child. John was not Richard revolting against injustice, at war with the world since his seventh year. John only wanted affection. Baby as he was he could rule his own life better than Richard had ever been able to do. He could cope with Gerry better than she could once he was reassured. Tell him he was loved and his wits would do the rest, must do the rest. For Gerry, of course, was right. It was because he was nearly always right that he could be so deadly to the young and tender. And yet Gerry was right— one must not coddle John.

But one might love him. Sitting beside him, allowed to treat him as the baby he would always be to her, it was easy to teach him that he was loved and wanted.

"John, do you know it's half past nine? Richard will be up to fetch me. You'll go to sleep now, won't you?"

"Yes, Mother." John, reassured, was getting sleepy. But, like all the Broomes, he could not sleep until he had arranged his immediate future. "Mother, will you come in a punt with me tomorrow?"

"I've got to go up to town. But you can come if you like."

"Oh, but Gerry is going if you do."

"Is he?"

"Yes, he said he was this morning."

"Come too, John, all the same."

"Can I come to the theatre?"

"Won't you be dull?"

"I like watching. Oh, Mother, it's so lovely to have you home. Mother, shall I like school? Gerry says I'll hate it. Mother, we've only got a fortnight before I go to school."

CHAPTER 54

ELINOR AND HER SONS

RICHARD asserted that his mother manipulated dates so that he might attend her first night before he went back to Oxford. Henry, who was being coached, came as a matter of course, and Gerry was also present; but Elinor was too anxious and rushed even to enquire how Gerry contrived to be in town two days after school reopened. But there was no John. John was in exile: not even at the familiar Cotswold exile of the other three, but because of his delicacy in an establishment on the east coast within an hour's run of town. It was very well sponsored: and he could be sent up easily to the family doctor if necessary. She had left him with a heavy heart, but saying to herself that she was a fool to worry. One mustn't coddle John. Gerry was quite right.

It was a weak-kneed play, but it went well. She foresaw three months, not more. Indeed, the main pleasure she got out of it was the fact that Richard had struck up a friendship with the author. This pleased her: Richard saw far too much of the theatre world and not enough of all the other worlds, she thought anxiously.

And her other pleasure was the sight of Lewis Wybird in the stalls, clapping away as heartily as if she had never run away from him and made a fool of him for all the world to see. And afterwards he actually came round with his wife, a handsome man of sixty and a handsome woman of forty. He looked contented and his wife wore the family pearls much better than Elinor would have done. Talking to them she thought she had done Lewis a good turn after all. "Heart's blood is only dust when it's been dried twenty years," said Elinor to herself.

Then she introduced Richard, and Lewis was gracious to the young man and told him that his own boy, Philip, would be going up in the autumn and perhaps they might see something of each other. What a change was this from averted eyes and old hate! Time is a blessed god, a prince of peace.

So Elinor enjoyed her success, and was pleased that the play ran better than she had expected, so that even in the hot July weather it was necessary to put on an extra matinée.

She was living at the time entirely in the Regent's Park house, for her engagement book, after her long absence, was unusually full: so full that she had no time to go down and see Henry and Gerry, and would not go down to see John. It was mere cruelty to re-stir the dreadful home-sickness every three weeks. Richard and Henry had told her that she must not do it. Edmund, who had returned to America directly after the new production, wrote in vain for first-hand news. "Aren't you going down to see the boy?" demanded Edmund in surprise. But Richard had told her she must not, and so she did not go down.

Term was over for Richard and he was at Marlow with a friend when Donna's letter arrived, full of the Irish situation. Her house had twice been searched for arms, and she thought that the children had better not come over that summer. But she was amused at Edmund's suggestion that she herself should shut up the house and come over to England. Why, they might burn down the house if she were not there! Elinor smiled as she read the vigorous pages. Her mother-in-law's happy assumption that her mere presence could hold the country-side in check was so characteristic in its unconscious arrogance.

She worked through the letters in the waits with her secretary and at the end of the show she had half a dozen strangers to welcome like old friends, and one or two friends to say "Don't go!" to, and keep a little longer after the mob had dispersed, and say good-bye to at last so thankfully. Then she could take the smile off her face and clean off her make-up and get into her street clothes without having to bother for a quarter of an hour at least about anybody's feelings except her dresser's; for even her dresser needed humouring. It was amazing to her that everybody, almost without exception, needed humouring. Oh well, she supposed, she was humoured too, if only she knew it. The boys humoured her, though not so much, surely, as they humoured Edmund? She tried so hard to cure herself of asking them questions and worrying if they did not come in for meals till all was cold. She had triumphantly cured herself of saying "You won't be late?" to Richard, and she took nowadays more pains with her clothes than she had done since she was twenty. No, she did not think that they often blushed for her. And she definitely knew that, once in the theatre, the positions were reversed: then they took a pride in her: then they respected her authority, not as a mother but as a star.

For she was a fixed star nowadays. She had worked like a beaver in the last year or two, going from theatre to theatre in New York to watch the old tricksters and the new importations, polishing, modernising herself. She knew that she had greatly improved. She realised perfectly well that the play would not have run a week if it had been trusted to her five years ago, and now it was booming. Well, she owed it all to the boys for keeping her up to the mark, even though Edmund had not liked her performance. She did not expect it. She thought that nowadays he was curiously old-fashioned in his judgment of acting, though not of actors. He still had a marvellous flair for winners.

Elinor picked up his letter again. So there was yet another find—and the offspring of dear Fina of all unlikely creatures. That was really very funny. Edmund wrote unusually fully of the girl—'just Henry's age, much more delicate-featured than Fina, impudent but promising.' Fina had sent her along saying that she couldn't keep the girl off the stage, that after all she was a Broome, and would Edmund please give her a big part in his new show. Instead Edmund had packed her straight off to a theatrical training college, little as he approved of those dens of elocution. But as he rightly said, it would keep her out of mischief till he was ready to take her in hand. The girl was a find, no question, and he didn't want her to be snapped up by other people. So, though he was not using her at the moment, he was giving her a long contract. Edmund believed in giving young people long, long contracts, and so controlled, as the years went by, a good many fretting stars.

Elinor wondered what the girl was like. She must be kind to her when Edmund brought her over, for Fina's sake.

She left the theatre at last and made her way through the little yard to the waiting car. Hammond grinned at her as he touched his cap and opened the door.

"Surprise packet inside for you, ma'am!" said Hammond, who never, never could learn that an employer was not a human being, and went to turn on the lights. She stumbled in, deadly tired, feeling with her foot for the flowers, box of chocolates, or whatever it might be. Then, as she groped in the dim light of the street lamp, she saw John, John himself, sitting up in the corner of the seat, exactly as he used to sit up in bed, his eyes fixed and watchful.

"John!" She could hardly believe her eyes. "John, where have you come from? What's the matter? O my precious child!" Then, as she bent to kiss him and found his face cold—"Why, John, what is wrong? Has school broken up?"

He shook his head.

"But what are you doing up here, dear? Yes, home, Hammond. As quickly as you can."

"Yes, I've come home," said John on that. "I'm not going back, Mother."

"What's that, my darling?"

"I'm not going back." They began to move through the streets.

"Where are we going?" said John with a clutch at her.

"Home, darling."

"You're not driving me back to school?" said he suspiciously.

"No, dear. We're going to Regent's Park. Now tell me all about it."

"Well——"

"John, have you run away?"

He began to cry, and presently became hysterical, and after that fell asleep in her arms, and she and Hammond between them had much to do in getting him into the house and putting him to bed. But she could get nothing out of him, except that he didn't like school and had come home and no-one, not even his father, should make him go back. She did not think that he was ill, but it seemed to her that he had had some sort of a shock, and she would have rung up their doctor had she not known that he was away on holiday. It was no use calling in a stranger to John. She hardly knew what to do, for though he seemed to sleep, if she moved to the door he woke at once and screamed for her. But about two o'clock she got to the telephone and rang up Marlow.

Almost at once Richard's deep voice answered the telephone.

"Hullo—is that you, Mother?"

"Oh, thank God you're not in bed, Richard."

"We've been out on the river." And she heard him give a low laugh of enjoyment. "It's a marvellous night. Show go well?"

"Richard, can you come up to town?"

The quality of his voice changed.

"What—now?"

"Yes, now. John's here. He's run away."

"My god! The little devil! What's he been doing?"

"I don't know. I'm very much frightened."

"Mother!" His tone was at once intimate. "D'you mean it? I say, Mother, is he——? Oh, damn, they've cut us off."

And for twenty minutes Richard wrestled with the telephone and could get no answer but the most courteous—"If you'll hang up again, sir, I expect the other party will come through." And when Elinor did at last get through she was answered by a voice she did not know.

"Is that Mrs. Broome? I'm Kenneth Bruce, Mrs. Broome. Yes, one of Richard's friends. He said you'd know. Yes, since Monday, having a great time. Richard went on his motor cycle, Mrs. Broome, ten minutes ago. I was to tell you he was coming straight along. I'm awfully sorry John's ill. Yes, of course, absolutely understand. Richard said he'd ring me up in the morning."

She put down the receiver, breathing relief. The blessed boy, what a comfort he was! And how like Edmund when Edmund was young—so good at making decisions. She had better have something ready for him when he got in.

He was there as the sun rose; but before she had time to give him bite or sup the maid came running—

"The motor cycle's wakened Master John, ma'am. He's screaming his head off."

"Oh!" Elinor was on her feet in an instant, but her son stopped her.

"Let me go up, Mother! I can generally manage him." And up he went.

The maids were downstairs and had set an early breakfast before he came down again. She knew better than to go up and disturb them, but she was waiting at the foot of the stairs, pacing to and fro across the chess-board marble, in an ecstasy of worry, when at last she heard the door go and Richard reappear. But he smiled as he hurried down to her.

"It's all right, darling. Don't look so tragic. He's all right now. I say, have you got some milk or anything?"

"Breakfast's ready."

"I'll take him something up."

Again he was gone a long time.

When he came back at last to his own breakfast she let him nearly finish it before she cross-questioned him. But at last she could bear it no longer.

"Richard, what is it?"

"Oh, there's been a rumpus." Then, seeing how tense she was, he smiled at her easily—"It's all right, darling! But hadn't you better have some coffee too? You look worn out."

"I've had what I want," she returned impatiently. "Go on, Richard! What is it? Is he ill? Ought we to get a doctor?"

"Don't think so. I gave him his breakfast and now he's asleep. He'll be all right when he wakes up: at least, I expect so. I think I managed him. Don't worry, Mother! He's had a shock and he was frightened, but he'll be all right when he wakes up."

"But has he got into trouble? He hasn't done anything, Richard?"

"Good Lord, no!"

"Well, but tell me what's been happening. Don't let me have to cross-question you. What have they been doing to him? A child like John doesn't run away and turn up in the state he was——"

"No, you're quite right, Mother. No, of course not."

"Well?"

"Oh, well, it's the usual business, you know."

"What usual business? What do you mean? Have they been bullying him?"

"Well, I suppose you could call it that. He's a decent little chap and he doesn't know his way about yet. And he saw things he didn't like, and——"

She stopped him.

"What things?"

"Oh, Mother dear, you must know the sort of—troubles—that crop up sometimes among small boys."

"You mean he was unpopular?"

"Oh no, just the other way." Richard cut himself some more bread but did not seem in a hurry either to eat or speak. "The fact is, Mother, he seems to have come up against a couple of rotters, and as he didn't know how to cope with them he just walked out. He's a plucky little devil. He waited till they were all asleep and walked out of the dormitory. Caught the ten o'clock train. I daresay they haven't found out yet. We shall have to telephone. I think I'd better go down. I'm not at all sure, in the circumstances, that he ought to go back."

"But what *are* the circumstances, Richard?"

"I told you, Mother," said Richard uncomfortably.

She got up and came across to him.

"Richard, what is it that has upset John so dreadfully?"

"Well, Mother, you know the sort of little beasts small kids can be sometimes, don't you?"

"I thought you said it wasn't bullying. I'm sorry to be so stupid, Richard, but I don't know what you're talking about. What has happened? Why won't John talk to me? I seem to be knocking at a closed door. I thought John told me everything."

"Oh, no, Mother, not by a long chalk." Thus Richard, mocking her gently.

She could have wept with anxiety, irritation and fear. Why wouldn't Richard talk to her comfortably? What had gone wrong? John had done—what? What were the silly, poor little crimes?

"Richard?"

"Yes?"

"Richard, he hasn't been stealing or anything, has he?"

He made no answer; but as he sat drawing patterns on the table with the point of a fork his abstraction answered for him. It wasn't that.

"Then what, Richard?"

He said, with a sort of uncomfortable airiness—

"Oh—sex, Mother."

"Oh!" She was dumbfounded. It was some time before she said— "I'm dreadfully sorry, Richard. I'm afraid I've been very stupid at seeing things. I am—stupid. I was stupid for so long about your father when—when everybody else saw."

And then at last he looked up at her, meeting her eyes, and she saw by his expression that he was aware of all that she meant, and she was ashamed. And yet she was thankful that at last he was her grown-up son and not her dependent child, and that she could talk to him and ask help.

"Richard—if I take John away from this school and send him to the Cotswolds, will he be all right then?"

"Well, Mother, nobody can guarantee that he won't come up against beastliness."

"What, in every school?"

"Well, dear, it's just chance. If the house is a decent house he'll be perfectly all right. Besides, now he does know what he's up against, you can be pretty sure he'll look after himself. Tell you the truth, I blame myself a good deal. I ought to have talked to him before he went. I might have known that Father wouldn't warn him."

"But those babies, Richard—those babies!"

"Well, he'll have to know about things some time or other."

"What, does it go on later?"

"Oh, Mother dear!"

"Richard, how do you know all this?"

He hesitated.

"I, Mother?"

"Yes."

"Do you mean—how do I *know?* or—how do *I* know?"

"Is there much difference?"

"All the difference."

She said desperately—

"I don't understand you. I'm all at sea. Can't you explain to me? I want to know how to look after John."

He hesitated again. Then—

"When you were at school, Mother, didn't anybody have hero-worships?"

"Oh, *schwärmerei?*" She was relieved. "Oh yes! Oh, is that what you mean? Is that all? But then, Richard—no, I haven't got it right yet, because—— Why has it been such a shock to John?"

"Well, dear, I suppose it's different with men. You get romantic friendships, and protective friendships—every sort of shade and grade. But behind lots of it, Mother—you can't get away from it—lies the physical."

"Do you mean they fall in love with each other?"

"Sometimes, yes."

Some guardian prudence held her rigid at that moment so that she did not give utterance to her first instinctive thought—'But that's unnatural—that's horrible!' It was her reward, perhaps, for long years of saying to herself—'Never judge!' For, looking at her son, she saw that he was watching her as intently (the memory swept over her) as he had watched her years ago in the nursery. So it was as she suspected—a test had been repeated. At nineteen as at nine he had comprehended her dilemma and once again she had stood, blind and unawares, on the very edge of an abyss. If she had let him see, even for one moment, her sense of sick repulsion, she would not have altered him, but she would have lost her son, both her sons; for only Richard could help her with John. So, though she knew he was at the end of his patience, that he was sick with her for pestering him, she went on:

"How did you find out, Richard?"

"Everybody knows, Mother."

"Does Henry?"

"Surely."

"I can't believe it."

"Of course, dear, there are people who can go right through school without noticing anything——"

"But you, Richard? What about you?"

"Oh, I'm perfectly all right, Mother."

Now he was lying to her. She knew it instantly. She had asked too much of him and so he had to lie. What did it matter? They understood each other. She loved him. It made no difference. Besides——

"Richard, people grow out of it, don't they?"

"Most of them, Mother. They grow right out of it and forget all about it as a rule."

"How d'you know?"

"Well, dear, I just know. They forget it so utterly that half the time they swear it doesn't exist. D'you suppose that if you told Father what had upset John he'd believe you?"

"But, Richard, if John himself told him?"

"Yes, but John never would tell him. What's the matter, Mother?" for there was wrath as well as pain and fear in Elinor's face.

"D'you mean to tell me, Richard, that all over England fathers can know that there's a risk of their own sons, boys of ten and eleven, being frightened as John has been frightened, and that they let it go on? It's not credible. D'you suppose, if women knew—d'you suppose if I'd known, I'd have let it happen?"

"Can't alter human nature."

"What, Richard? Haven't wise people——? What's the remedy?"

"God knows. I don't think there is one. But I say, Mother—Mother dear——" for he saw that she was crying.

"No, I'm all right." She turned from him abruptly. "I was only thinking——"

"What?"

"I wonder you can ever forgive me and your father. You were only nine when you went to school. I never dreamed—how could I dream——?" She turned suddenly—"Richard, it's you——"

"You mustn't bother about me, Mother."

"Richard——"

"Look, Mother, you must leave me to shake down. I shall probably end up like everybody else, fall in love with somebody you've picked out for me yourself and settle down, and send my children to school, perfectly sure that I'm doing the best for them." Then, with keen distress—"Dearest Mother, you made me talk to you. I didn't want to talk to you——"

"It's all right." She pulled herself together resolutely. "Tell me what I'm to do with John."

CHAPTER 55

JOHN'S WAR

RICHARD was very helpful about John. He dealt with the school for her: had a long talk with the head-master and another long talk with the doctor who overhauled John. The doctor, too, was helpful—helpful and terrifying. Elinor began to realise that it was all very well to be proud of a child's brains and sensitiveness and self-flowering ways, all very well to say sometimes to oneself— There is a difference between him and the other boys: everyone says so. Suppose it should be the difference between talent and genius? But you couldn't expect to say such things to yourself without paying for it.

Her doctor frightened her. Extraordinary excitability—a total unfitness for school—thinks too much—feels too much. Knock him off all books for a time—let him run wild—open air—plenty of milk. Not the faintest cause for alarm if he's handled carefully, but he mustn't go back to school just yet: not for a year at least, perhaps longer.

But what would Edmund say? Edmund with his fixed idea that she hopelessly spoiled John, with his conviction that school was the panacea for all in a growing boy that irritated a father? She foresaw a scene, a series of scenes, with John involved in all of them.

"I should like you to talk to my husband."

"I'll talk to him, Mrs. Broome."

Meanwhile John went to the sea with Richard and came home rosy, and so happy and easy to manage that she could not believe he had even frightened them. Was it possible, thought Elinor, shocked into extravagant maternal bitterness, that some children are actually better for being unhappy? Was it possible that to inflict an agony of homesickness thrice a year on a nervous child of nine or ten was not always the best way to form its character and prepare it for the practice of the Christian virtues? Elinor thought that sending some children away from home was rather like waking an insomnia patient at five in the morning to wash him.

But Edmund wouldn't see that, of course: and although Richard's talk had set her mind travelling, thinking, reading, making discoveries, still, she couldn't discuss such things with Edmund.

But she need not have been anxious. By the time she saw Edmund again so many things had happened that she could have sent John to a Barnado Home for all Edmund would have cared. First came a wire— "Autumn arrangements cancelled: returning next boat"—and then came Edmund, worn and anxious, but more the vigorous captain of events than he had been these ten years. And there was a long talk that first night between him and Elinor and Richard, and for the first time Richard was allowed to know some details of his father's innumerable commitments, enterprises and schemes, all now endangered. For Edmund was in touch with Germany and in touch with Austria, and knew all that America was saying. So he had sold his American ventures while the going was good, had cancelled his wife's contracts at heavy costs and still thought himself the gainer, because, in that all-powerful world behind the scenes where the money was made and lost, it was an open secret that war was a question of weeks.

And Edmund spent the rest of that white night trying to make a shuddering wife and a kindled son understand what war would mean to the world, to England, to the profession and to the Broomes: and having, with complete justification, scared the life out of them, went to bed much relieved. Next day there were more talks: Henry was summoned home: and there was, for a time, a strengthening of all ties between the father and his sons. Edmund showed up well in an emergency. His pettinesses fell from him: the blacker the situation the more cheerful he grew, and his sons marvelled at his energy, his good temper, and at the amazing flow of schemes and alternatives which that big brain of his, working at full speed, was able to conceive, survey, discard and put into practice. They marvelled, too, at his sudden abandonment of his habitual secretiveness, his readiness to discuss ideas with them and to listen to their ideas.

Only Elinor did not share the curious wave of mutual admiration which ran through the house in those days. She knew the significance of that sudden, overwhelming irradiation of charm. Things must be pretty bad, and Edmund must know it. Yet inevitably she felt a certain re-awakening of the old sleeping tenderness for him. He was a fine fighter and lovable in adversity. She had to laugh and cry over wary, hostile Richard's sudden enthusiasm for his father, and Henry's bewildered response to a gaiety not unlike his own. It couldn't last, of course. When the bad times were over and prosperity came again, back would come the other Edmund. But she was glad that the boys should see, for once in their lives, that side of their father. She addressed them in her heart—"Now you see what he was! Now you see why I loved him!" She was justified in her sons' eyes for the father she had given them, if only for a week or two.

It was only for a week or two indeed: for the storm burst even as Edmund had foretold, but sooner than he had foretold: and by the end of August Henry and Richard were in uniform and every member of every Broome company working on half salary. No, there was little time to worry about John, who had in three months so completely recovered his health and spirits, and was tutored by an elderly protégé of his uncle Eustace, and for the rest left to a curious, solitary happiness: till, with all the rest of the stay-at-home world, he was swept into the agonising, hysterical activities of the 1915 homes-front.

For Elinor, working desperately in a wild, salacious farce to keep the theatre open and keep people's spirits up, was involved in an endless series of charity matinées, war performances, flying visits, here, there and everywhere. It was the peculiar war duty of her profession to distract, amuse and entertain those about to die. War work was not asked of her, but laughter, incessant, irrepressible laughter: gaiety, flare, fuss, flurry, bright looks, lively spirits, warm impulsive maternal speeches at little gatherings and big gatherings, and smart clothes, and a good make-up on a haggard face, and an air of knowing that God was in His heaven as well as the Zeppelins, and that all was right with the world.

And in this light easy work of hers, John was gradually involved. A clever child, accustomed to the stage, with a clear voice and no self-consciousness, was a gift on the improvised charity platform, in dialogues, little sketches, charades. He and his mother between them made a great deal of money in that moneyless time for the endless, rattling boxes of the war charities.

For Elinor, for a loving woman and a tender mother, so terrified a year ago when a little son's finger ached, had become singularly ruthless. Richard and Henry were 'out there', and now Gerry had enlisted and was to be swallowed up in turn. Was this a time to spare herself or John? And so for two years John led the life of a grown-up man, caught back among the women. And what he saw, felt, thought, what sort of dents and grooves the home-front spectacle made in his mind, what sort of shafts were sunk in it, only John knew, and he never told. But he kept his diary, and followed his mother about, and was efficiently there when he was wanted and effaced himself when he was not wanted, a miniature man: not in the least afraid of an audience and invaluable at those gay entertainments in hospital wards and hired halls and country drawing-rooms where the audiences were sometimes people who could see but not hear, and sometimes people who could hear but not see, and sometimes people who could not move, or sometimes people who were merely frightened. Well, it was all the luck of the war, and why should John, at fourteen, escape?

Then, at the end of 1916, came the news of the death of Henry. Henry had been home just before—such a gay leave. John remembered it as he remembered the bright, blurred excitement of his first Christmas tree. There was Father coming home at unexpected hours and buttonholing Henry and taking him off to the library, and Mother and Henry talking very little, and Henry coming to a charity matinée and taking John off afterwards to a dinner and a revue, just the two of them. But they picked up two or three of Henry's friends in the foyer, and the whole pack of them came home afterwards to the Regent's Park house and they all sat round in the music room till three o'clock in the morning, and Henry poured out rag-time. But sometimes one of Henry's girls came and pushed him half off the piano stool and they played together, and everybody shouted at the tops of their voices: and Elinor was in and out of the room in a restless sort of way, and when John got to bed at last he was sick with tiredness and a curious longing to cry. He could not sleep, not for ages. Henry's face would come back into his mind, looking, not a bit like itself, but as it had looked on that queer night after the great matinée at—where was it? He had forgotten—seaside somewhere—he went to so many places.

Gerry and Henry had both been on leave and came down with them, but Mother had to dash back to London for the evening show. She left directly after her turn, but John had another by himself. So the boys said they'd wait and drive John back to Marlow after dinner: which of course was grand fun for John, having dinner with them at the hotel. Gerry and Henry had been ripping to him, too, and he'd been introduced to some of Henry's friends who were all very grand, with lovely clothes, and they were very polite to him as if he were grown-up.

Then came a confused recollection of laughter and light, and cocktails, and dancing, and everyone in uniform: and Henry had disappeared—now was that before dinner or afterwards? Then Gerry was in the lounge looking bored, saying, where was Henry, because it was his suggestion to drive John home, not Gerry's! So they went and looked for him down a corridor, and they opened a door and there was Henry with all his friends, sitting round a large table playing cards, and some of the women were standing up and leaning over the men's shoulders and shouting, and they all looked different from what they did downstairs: and so did Henry, and John was horribly upset: he didn't know why, but he was. Henry was his, not those people's, and they oughtn't to look different all of a sudden, and why was Henry so angry with Gerry? He had got up and came to the door and shoved them both out into the passage, and said to Gerry—"You must be mad bringing the kid in there!" and Gerry flared and they had a row under their breaths. John had forgotten how he got home, but it still made him furious and miserable to remember the evening. Why couldn't he go and sit by Henry? If he oughtn't to be there why was it right for Henry? And none of the women even looked at him, though they'd been so lovely to him downstairs.

John turned and twisted, and thought he'd never go to sleep. Yet he must have been fast asleep when his mother came in to him for he screamed out as she put her hand on his shoulder and said—"Is it air-raids?" And she said—"No, darling, Henry's just off. The car's round. He has to be at Victoria at nine. I'm going to see him off. D'you want to come?" And he did and then he didn't, for the silly, sleepy side of him hated being wakened, and yet, of course, to go in the car was something, for they weren't allowed to use the car except for business at a time like this, because of petrol.

And then he shook himself quite awake and out of his silliness: and of course he wanted to come. But he didn't join in the excited talk that went on in the car all the way, with Henry so frightfully funny about a dump being blown up, and Mother laughing all the time as if she couldn't stop, even when Henry stopped. But half way there John pulled out his scribble book that he always carried and began to draw, as well as he could for the jolting. And Henry said— "What are you up to, John?" and made him show. And then Henry said—"He's a marvel at a likeness. And yet—Do I look like that, Mother? I don't think I look so down in the mouth as all that!" And then he began to sing—"Pack up your troubles—" and put on a wonderful simper for John, and kept very still for John to draw another of him laughing. And they were at Victoria, and the train went out sooner than they thought and so they never said good-bye to Henry properly.

When the news came, only a fortnight later, that Henry was killed, he felt he couldn't bear it, that if the war went on much longer his head would burst. And it was more difficult to talk to anyone, but it seemed easier and easier to listen.

Father talked a lot to him. Father told him an interesting story about a boy he knew, a ripping kid, rather like Henry to look at, who was awfully good at books and got scholarship after scholarship. He had a father who was an awfully busy man, but sometimes they had a day in the country: and this boy, his name was William, was going to be in the office with his father when he grew up, because he liked everything his father did much more than his father's other boys: and he had gone to college. Oxford? God forbid! No. Cambridge! And when the war came he had enlisted: and as they were doing gun drill he tripped and got run over by a gun and crushed, and he had to have morphia for four days, and then he died. And it was all useless, useless, useless! And what was the good of it all? And then they used to talk about Henry: and then they used to talk about this boy.

The boy William became so real to John that one day he settled down to write a play about him. He didn't get very far, only an act and a half, because he always stopped to illustrate; but he found himself enormously enjoying the work before he got bored with it. His tutor was working him pretty hard and he was always breaking off for concerts and matinées and things. And then when he came back to the stuff three weeks later it always looked so silly, as if someone else had written it. But he copied it out as far as it went, as he copied everything he wrote, into a common-place book, and illustrated it. He wrote quite a lot of poetry too, though when he looked at it a year later it seemed to him the most extraordinarily sentimental rubbish, and made him feel hot when he re-read it and he thought he had better burn it, but he could not quite bring himself to do that. Suppose it should be good, after all? But of course it was pretty bad. Still, why burn it?

And he went on filling his book in his minute handwriting. He thought sometimes that when Richard came home he'd ask him to have a look at it. Richard hadn't had leave for two years and he ought to be home any day. He longed for Richard to come home: for he saw less of his mother and more of his tutor in 1917. There had been trouble between his parents early that spring, a row behind locked doors. His father had been in one of his rages: you could hear him from the hall. Then his mother had come out, white and worried, and sent him flying for brandy while she telephoned old Cummins, the doctor. Cummins came: and his father, it seemed, had been working too hard for years and had got blood-pressure and had got to knock off whiskey and tobacco and was in bed a week and really must take more care of himself. At the same time John knew perfectly well that the row had not been about his father's health. And the end of it was, for his mother and father always seemed to mix up their rows with business and engaging casts, that his mother went down to the New Broom and ran a Shakespeare season there. She was jolly good, though she had never played Shakespeare before: and there was a lot about it in the papers. And he played Mamilius and Prince Arthur, and the fried egg in *Macbeth:* only then his voice cracked rather early and he was out of the fun again. But having played himself he had a different feeling for the theatre, and spent half his holidays there, prowling about the wings and the property rooms. But when, one night, he went down to the Genista and prowled about behind the scenes, there was a hell of a row and all the talk came up again about his going to school. But it came to nothing, because his tutor said that he was a bit too old and war conditions were difficult, and he'd much better be coached direct for one of the universities. And Richard said the same when he came home. For Richard was wounded early in 1917.

When his mother got the telegram she turned white and said— "Thank God! Thank God!" And as John watched her, something happened to him. It seemed as if there streamed out from her to him a most horrible sensation of fear, pain, longing, and then relief: as if the telegram's arrival had broken down a dam and loosed the flood. Suddenly he saw his plays lying open before him, all the plays at once, and thought to himself that they were kid's work, and that he understood absolutely now why she said 'Thank God!' instead of 'Oh, my God!': and that he realised for the first time the awfulness of the war, and the inner meaning of the innumerable interesting scenes that he had witnessed with such curiosity: and why people looked as they did, and why Henry had been so cheerful, and why London was such a feverish gay place. And he thought that for two years he had been afraid his head was going to burst, but now that it had burst, he was better for it. He felt horribly tired, and he felt that he adored his mother and knew exactly what she felt about Richard, because in an extraordinary way he was feeling the same. He wanted to get Richard back and Gerry back more than anything in the world.

Then his mother began to talk, talk, talk, as she hadn't talked for months: and he listened and realised how strung-up and overwrought she was, and found that he knew quite well how to manage her and how to make her rest. But he felt singularly lonely. He had never felt so lonely in his life as he did that night after she had gone off to the theatre. He dined with his father, and his father went on to the

Genista: and he curled up on the sofa and thought about Richard and Gerry and how marvellous it would be to have people of his own age to talk to again: for they were his brothers and his own group, even if they were older. But his father, of course, was an old man. And his mother, the darling, well, she was his mother and of course she wanted managing.

But Elinor said to Richard, when at last they let her see him, that he wouldn't know John, John was so grown and that he was the comfort of her life.

"Which means that he's getting a bit of a prig," said Richard. "Oh well, I'll deal with him."

When he got home at last on sick leave, Richard prepared to take a good deal of trouble over his young brother: and was very much amused to find that John was in the same mood as regards him. John evidently proposed to treat him as one of the lesser gods. He fagged for him devotedly, wanted to talk and did not plague him with interest in life at the front, but, watching Richard dress at nights for his parties, fidgeted with the photographs in his room, asked questions and sometimes got answers.

"Richard? Are you going back to Oxford when the War is over? Lots of people are."

"Depends on when it's over."

"It would be ripping if I were up with you. The War's bound to end this year."

"I'd be too old, John."

"Twenty-three."

"I wouldn't like it any more. There'd be nobody up I knew."

"Yes, but Richard—if all your crowd came back too?"

"How many are there left, John, do you suppose?"

John fidgeted anew with the trifles on the mantelpiece. He had reached the particular stage in the conversation which he had intended to reach: for he wanted to find out just how to be nice to Richard over friends lost and missing; but to do that he must find out if Richard had lost them, and if he missed them. But of course he mustn't ask questions. He must unobtrusively know. So he continued to fidget, till Richard, watching him in the looking-glass as he tied his tie, came to the rescue with a half laugh.

"It's all right, John. You're not embarrassing me. But of course most of my crowd are gone. What else did you expect?"

There was a silence. Then—

"Richard," said John, rebuttoning the snap of the photograph—"Who's that?"

Richard turned his head, then returned to his tie as he said carefully—"That's Kenneth. He's still alive all right."

"Then when is he coming down?" said John quickly.

"I haven't the faintest idea. Never, I should think."

"Oh!" John did not see that there was any need to continue the conversation, so he did not; but when Richard had gone out John wandered back to fetch his book, which he had left in Richard's room, and also to have a good quiet stare at the photograph whose original wasn't coming down for any week-end.

But when Alys Broome began to come down for week-ends John's pride in possession was disturbed.

Alys Broome, poor dear Fina's girl, was Edmund's new star. She had refused to stay at the Dramatic School of his choice, but instead had knocked about playing small parts, and writing at intervals to Edmund defying him to enforce his contract and enclosing cuttings and photographs and recommendations by the pound. And Fina Adamovitz wrote half a dozen times to Elinor. Nothing had come of it, however, till last autumn when Alys got a part in New York without any reference to Edmund, and made a hit in it.

Edmund, who had the English rights of the play, had already decided on his cast; but the author wanted the little American and was a nuisance until Edmund cabled for the girl to come over. When she came over he thanked his stars that he had cabled: the author was right. She was just what they wanted—a husky-throated, silken witch with the new boy's figure and the new Dutch-doll head and the new sexual appeal that infuriated all the older women and puzzled all the older men. He decided at once not to waste her on the little play for more than two months. Then he shifted her from it into *The War Bride,* that curious piece of modernity which seems so old-fashioned today, but which scandalised London in 1917 : while Elinor, very unwillingly, went on to the New Broom. The success Alys Broome made is still the talk of the dramatic academies.

Richard was furious when he heard that the Genista had been given up to the newcomer : and it was not till Gerry came home on leave that the two of them together went to see Alys Broome. Elinor, who was scrupulous in her attentions to Fina's daughter, had arranged a little party for her afterwards, and watched Gerry amusing himself mightily with Alys Broome, and Richard, of all people, obsessed by her. She did not wait for Richard to ask the girl down: it was bound to come: she had no sooner seen them together than she realised that it was bound to come, and she was glad. If Richard once fell in love, how much anxiety she could put behind her. She would not set herself against anyone who could charm Richard out of his isolation fort. Besides, as Alys came down oftener, she too began to feel the spell of the girl's personality.

"She's a new broom," said Edmund, nodding amiably. He was excessively proud of his find: and the needed sudden success—for times had been critical with Edmund—had done him more good than the rigid diet on which his doctor had put him. "She's got a tang—a war tang. Didn't you see what the *Times* said?—'All the essential graces and none of the superfluous ones!' She's the easiest person to coach I've ever met in my life," said Edmund proudly.

"You used to say that of me." Elinor smiled at him.

"Ah well, but she's so modern, so alert."

"I don't like the way she does her hair," Elinor could not help saying.

"Well, the public does," said Edmund jealously.

Yes, and Richard did. Elinor was amazed at Richard's capitulation, and, for that matter, at Alys's capitulation. All the qualities in him which frightened his mother and too easily hurt her, his abruptness, his sarcasm, his sardonic matter-of-factness, his nervous revolt against any ornament of speech or thought, his restlessness, his self-mockery, Alys Broome appeared to find attractive. At any rate she plainly enjoyed provoking their display. Still more curious, she herself began to display similar qualities as if for Richard's special benefit. The two had an air of sharing an enjoyment.

"They understand each other. They are both the war world," said Elinor sighing, and wished that Richard had chosen out a lovely kind girl, fair and slow, instead of this sophisticated eighteen-year-old woman of the world, with her clinging dresses and her clinging ways and sudden boyish austerities of manner when you tried to talk to her and find out just how well she and Richard understood each other. Were they engaged? There was no word of it. Elinor thought she could not bear it if they walked in on her one day, as the fashion was, and said that they had been married that morning. They so easily might. Yet she thought that Richard would not do that to her unless Alys made him. He would say a word to her surely: so far he had not said a word, though it was plain enough that he thought of nothing but the girl. Though, for that matter, he was not the only one. Alys was always a centre-piece. She could light up a room in two minutes merely by entering. Everybody always wanted to laugh with her and at her and over her: and their laughter was champagne to her. She would stand in the centre of a group sparking off little arrows of comments and questions in all directions: or tell a little story about herself, and there would be a peal of laughter and half a dozen voices urging her to go on: and she would go on, too, hurriedly, as if she knew that in another moment everybody around her would begin to clap if she did not. But then, on a stray word or thought, she would be grave again, and her brown liquid eyes would overlook insolently the human interests of the moment, only to glide away from them like a breeze passing over the corn-fields or a ray of sunlight sliding through a wood. And then she would look round for Richard.

Gerry was sulky, because, though she was charming to him and talked to him a great deal, she always stopped talking if Richard spoke, and often quoted Richard: and he grumbled to Elinor, and then got his own back on the universe by chivvying John, till he had a better idea.

He gave a party for Alys to which it was no use asking Richard, for how could Richard dance with his leg not yet right? She came willingly: and while they danced he told her all about himself and what he thought and liked and did: and was enormously flattered that she wanted to know what he proposed to do when the war was over, and what his profession was to be, and what his prospects were? And he told her that he hadn't a notion, and that he'd like to stay on in the army, but that that, of course, would depend on the old man. And she said how hard it was, as she herself knew, to have no private income: and he agreed heartily and wished to God he had Richard's luck.

"My grandfather left five hundred a year to the eldest grandson, to encourage Father, I suppose. And old Russel Broome has left John the Genista. It's damned hard luck on me. Richard's like Father: money sticks to him: he's got his whole career mapped out already. Has he talked to you about films yet? No? I'm surprised he hasn't. I suppose he's afraid of the old man hearing him."

"Your father?" said she softly.

"Oh, Father loathes the films. They're a worse menace than Hindenburg."

And then Gerry went on telling her stories of adventures that had happened to him, or might have happened to him: she listened and gave him a happy evening. Poor boy, he was going back in four days. Why not?

Nevertheless, on Geoffrey's last week-end she left him to his parents, and was more than ever Richard's partner. Elinor said to Edmund—

"Edmund, have you noticed those two?"

But Edmund, after a moment's amused surprise, was extraordinarily irritated, and said—

"What utter rubbish! Most unsuitable!" and added that he saw no sign of it at all. But John saw signs of it. John was deeply interested, but withdrew himself a little as he always did when emotions were in the air, and suffered a strange pang of jealousy to see Richard, his own brother, absorbed in a stranger: and knew his mother felt the same, and wondered if his father felt the same. And Gerry noticed it, and was frankly furious and showed it, as he always did, by violent high spirits and a teasing restlessness that made him blow cigarette smoke in the dog's face, and ring three times in ten minutes for small unnecessary services, and ask his father inconvenient questions about the way things were going at the Glory Hole. And then he told Alys a long story about Richard running away to become a film operator, and told it very funnily so that everybody had to laugh: though Edmund, in spite of his laughter, scowled a little. Then Richard said uncomfortably that Alys didn't want to be bored with his mis-spent past: and took her off down the garden to the punt: and Gerry muttered that it wasn't everybody who was lucky enough to have a wound that kept them at home this weather! And John said surprisingly—

"You are a cad, Gerry!" And then Gerry said to Elinor—

"Why don't you send him to school, Mother? He ought to have been at school two years ago. That would knock the nonsense out of him," and went over to the window-seat where John was sitting doing his preparation: and before John saw what he was doing, picked up the fattest of a pile of exercise books and began to look at it.

"Give me that!" said John loudly.

"Half a second! I only want to see how your studies are progressing." And Gerry began ostentatiously examining the pages, only to give a hoot of laughter—"My God, John, you've a nerve!" and would no doubt have said more had he not been at that moment borne down and flattened upon the window-seat by the sudden, utterly unlooked-for onslaught of John, the harmless John, the shadow John. It was a ludicrous spectacle; for Gerry was broad and burly, and John a slight creature who did not come much above his shoulder. But John, hurling himself on his brother, kicking, biting, tearing at those strong wrists, was quite beside himself. He wanted his book and he would have it: and so startled was Gerry and so much amused, that John for a moment did have the upper hand. He was able, at any rate, to get hold of the book and wrenched himself and it away together with a force that sent him spinning against the table: and he knocked over a bowl of roses and there was a mighty crash.

Elinor, who had seen this sort of scene before between her elder children, hastily insisted that it was all very funny and began to pick up the roses. But Edmund was furious.

"How dare you, John? At your age—behaving like a spoilt baby!"

"He had my book," said John.

"Well, and what if he had? There's nothing you're ashamed of, is there, in your books? Why shouldn't he have a look at them?"

"You ought to go to school, that's what it is," said Gerry angrily, "kicking and scratching like a girl."

"Yes, and I'll do it again if you touch my things," said John, amazing them. "It's always the same when you come home. Everything's spoilt."

"John, your brother's home on a week's leave, and he's been fighting for his country and for you. Do you realise that you may never see him again?"

"Oh, come, Father!" protested Gerry enjoying himself.

"Hold your tongue, Gerry! John, beg your brother's pardon at once and give him that book."

"Edmund, I don't think——" began Elinor.

"That'll do, Elinor! I've left the boy to you too long. I won't have this sort of exhibition. D'you hear me, John? Tell your brother you're sorry for being so babyish, and give him that book. D'you hear me?"

"Yes, Father."

"Then do as I tell you."

John backed to the wall, his hands behind him and the book in his hands.

"Oh, it's all right, Father!" Gerry, comfortable now that he had created a commotion and ridded himself of his own ill-humour, swung round to his brother's side. "I oughtn't to have chaffed him. It was my fault."

"Will you kindly be quiet, Gerry?" Edmund's face was dark with rage, and Elinor said in a low voice—

"Edmund, don't excite yourself! Remember what the doctor said! Let me deal with John."

And at that Gerry chimed in—

"Yes, honestly, Father, do drop it! Here, I'm going. Oh Lord, there's always a strafe on in this house." And he ran down the steps into the garden. His going did not help his brother.

"John! You have never disobeyed me before, John, and I'm trying to excuse you; but if you don't give me that book I shall punish you severely. Do you want me to punish you, John?"

"No, Father." The tears were pouring down John's cheeks.

"Then give me that book."

No answer. No movement.

"John, give me that book!"

And then, for Edmund was terrifying in his rages, and John was but fifteen and, though he had often watched, had never faced that wrath, John gave in: and brought out his hand with the book in it.

Edmund took it, and began, as Gerry had done, to look it through. It was an odd sort of book. There were pages of dialogue, scrawled illustrations, poems, notes, and exceedingly lively caricatures. Gerry had had justice done him more than once. There was a sketch of Hammond and several versions of John himself. He turned a page.

"Father, please give it to me," said John suddenly.

But his father only looked at him, looked back at the drawing, shut the book, put it in his pocket and without another word walked out of the room.

In his own room, however, Edmund opened the exercise book again and sat for some time staring at a certain picture—a drawing of himself, half portrait, half caricature, that he recognised at once. And yet—was it himself? Was this how he looked? So brutal, so overbearing, so ridiculous? The boy had the mind of a devil—a heartless young devil! And what was this he had written underneath?—

'Or some fierce thing replete with too much rage,
    Whose strength's abundance weakens his own heart.'

Looking at the crude drawing and the subtle words, and thinking of the scene that had just passed, thinking of the past, and thinking of the future, Edmund Broome, who so seldom strayed out of the present, had a mortal fright. Where was he heading? What was he to do? Was this how his son thought of him? But he was so fond of the boy, and surely the boy was fond of him? Elinor, wasn't he?

"Elinor?" he appealed to her as she came in to him—"What's got hold of the boy?"

"He's dreadfully upset, Edmund. He's downright ill with worry. Won't you talk to him? You know he draws everybody. He's always doing caricatures. What is it? He told me he'd done a caricature of you. Can I see it?"

His fist came down on the book. He tore out the page, ripped it into tiny pieces, flung them into the basket: then said—

"Tell the boy to come to me."

John came.

"Here's your book, my boy. You mustn't make fun of your father. You can caricature whom you like, but don't play tricks on your father and mother."

"Father, I——" John got no further.

"Yes, I know. And I can take a joke. It was all a joke, wasn't it? You don't think your father can't take a joke, do you? Give me a kiss, boy, and run along!"

The relief of it—the blessed, unutterable relief of it!

CHAPTER 56

The War Bride showed signs of running a year, but they were not far into the autumn before Alys, restless, ambitious little thing, grew very tired of her part. What did it matter if it suited her to perfection? Three acts of doing nothing tensely, but suggesting a whole world of passion by her special art of standing still intently and letting the rest of the cast work for her—that was her gift. And she galvanised her men. They had their own lives, their own love affairs, but while they were on the stage they were in love with her. She radiated sex as a rose its perfume. The women in the company did not love her and maintained that she played for her own hand. But Alys went her own way.

"And are you pleased with me?" she would say to her author when he came into her little windowless dressing-room. Pleased with her! Hadn't she made his play for him?

"Are you pleased with me?" she would say to Edmund in her amber voice. He would answer with emotion, and she would give him her sad, haunted little smile, and out would come the story of her latest trouble with the rest of the women. Oh no, he wasn't to do anything. There was nothing to be done. But oh, how tired she was of standing still, night after night: no change, no opportunity to improve herself or enlarge her art.

"And tell me about the new play at the Glory Hole. Costume, is it? Shakespeare? No, I suppose I couldn't possibly play in Shakespeare. Of course, I've always wanted to play Juliet. Who hasn't? But what's the point of talking about Juliet when you're putting on *A Midsummer Night's Dream?* It's horribly expensive, isn't it? D'you think it's the right time for *A Midsummer Night's Dream?* Don't you think people want something more rousing? Something with war in it? Oh yes, of course, Elinor would be marvellous as Lady Macbeth."

She had the modern trick of calling them all by their Christian names.

"And you would be a wonderful Macbeth, Edmund. You could play it. Oh, I know you haven't played for years, but what does that matter? You ought to come back to the stage. Money, money, money-making all day long. But there it is. One can't do without money. You know, Edmund, I'll have to have a rise if I'm to go on playing this beastly part. Oh, I know the part's not big enough to carry the salary I want. But if I were playing a lead? Oh, Edmund, I wish there was a part for me at the Glory Hole. Everything's not absolutely fixed yet, is it? I'm sorry you're doing *A Midsummer Night's Dream*. You ought to do a martial play. *Julius Caesar?* My God, no, Edmund! Leave that to the public schools. Edmund, darling, I suppose it never occurs to you that I'd make rather a good Cleopatra? Oh, do put on *Antony and Cleopatra*. Why shouldn't you play Antony? I don't see why you shouldn't play Antony!"

A month later she wrote to Richard, once more in France, that she had a great piece of news for him. His father had got it into his head that she was wasted on *The War Bride* and possibly, probably, he was putting on a Shakespeare show in the spring, and possibly, probably, she was to play the lead.

Elinor wrote to him by the same post that she wished he would write to Alys and dissuade her from this preposterous notion of playing Cleopatra—'You know what your father is when he gets an idea into his head, and of course we all know how brilliant Alys can be in a part that suits her; but honestly, my dear boy, she hasn't got the experience for Cleopatra. I doubt if she will ever have. She has the temperament, I daresay, but she hasn't the physical strength. Oh, this weary war—if only you were home to point things out to her. She listens to you, doesn't she? I am certain your father would not have put on *Antony and Cleopatra* unprompted. I wish you were home. Oh, what a cruel and foolish thing to write to you! But, my dear, it can't go on much longer now. London is alive with rumours. They say we may have a truce at any moment. (I wonder if they will censor this?) We're doing very well at the New Broom. I am Lady Teazle this week—the greatest fun in the world. I'm worried about John and have had Dr. Cummins to him. He says he is over-growing his strength, and we have to go very carefully with him for a year or two. John has just shown me a really remarkable little curtain-raiser. I've had some copies made and am sending one on to you. Oh, Richard, if you could be home for Christmas! Somebody must get leave at Christmas: why not you?"

A fortnight later the Armistice was signed, and though poor Gerry did not get home for months, Richard had good or bad luck for once and was home for Christmas.

It was a strange Christmas. They kept it at Marlow and Donna came over. They had urged her to come, but it was curious how her coming shadowed the house. She seemed taller and darker than ever and she had very little to say to anyone except John. She talked a good deal to John. Alys Broome told Richard that his family was too much of an ordeal for her—

"Christmas dinner with your grandmother watching everything I do and saying nothing, and you and John playing into each other's hand all through the meal—"

"We do not!"

"Of course you do. You keep things as smooth as snow and you sparkle like icicles, but ooh, it's chilly! Oh Richard, take me out somewhere to dine by ourselves and we'll dance afterwards. Oh, bother, you can't dance! I wish Gerry were home. No, darling, of course I didn't mean that, except to dance with. All right, I'll come to your family party, but I'll behave so badly."

But she didn't. She behaved beautifully in a delicate make-up and a soft little clinging frock of crimson velvet: and after they had eaten, dragged Richard to the piano and sang enchantingly. And then she made John dance with her.

"What d'you think of her?" said Elinor to her mother-in-law.

"Cressida," said the older woman.

"Why d'you say that?" said Elinor. "Yes, I suppose she could play it. Doesn't John dance well?"

John overheard and stopped.

"I don't. Alys makes me dance well. She's a heaven to dance with." Alys laughed and slid him into the dance again.

" 'She will sing any man at first sight,' " said Domina. "I don't like her, Elinor."

"Oh, but we're all so fond of her."

"Yes, she's an attractive little piece, but I don't think she's going to do your Richard any good. She's too soft and hectic."

"They all are, nowadays," said Elinor. "It's the excitement of the peace."

"Ah, their peace," said Domina with a sigh. "Your Richard looks ravaged. He has his memories, I daresay."

"That's why I'm so thankful—" said Elinor. "She'll make him forget things."

"Or give him things to remember. I see no hope for those two," said Donna with her strained look.

"Don't! You talk as if you saw the future."

"I do," said Donna calmly. "It comes of living alone. I knew about Henry two days before you did."

Elinor turned white, and said in a strained way—

"It's easy enough to say—"

"I keep a diary," said Donna indifferently. "I note these things down. I lead a strange life, Elinor. I know which grain shall grow—sometimes. Don't be frightened. I'm not going to talk about it. There's only one of you all who'd know what I meant if I did."

"Edmund?"

"Good God, no! John. That grain will grow. I could teach John, if he were ready to learn. He has the capacity to see, but then he hasn't the will, no more than any of these modern children. They have learned to accept death so wholly, that if you talk to them of life they think you are doing them an injury."

"I suppose you're a spiritualist," said Elinor reflectively.

Donna laughed.

"Oh, Elinor, how young you are! Because I say I believe in the Holy Ghost, the Lord and giver of life, who proceedeth from the Father and the Son, you ask me to tell you a ghost story! But you teach me what a fool I am to talk like this. I've always sworn I wouldn't. Only, when you see a thing clear ahead, it's hard to hold your tongue."

"What do you see?" said Elinor fearfully.

"Trouble."

"What sort of trouble, Mother?" And not twice in her life had Elinor called Domina Broome mother.

"Trouble for you all from that young woman."

"You mean you don't think she'll make Richard happy?"

"Do you see any happiness in Richard's face?"

"That's the war."

"I suppose so, Nell, I suppose so. How unhappy this modern music is! What are you playing, Richard?"

"It's that song of Violet Lorraine's—"

" 'Some day I'll make you love me!' " Alys crooned to the tune as she slid by, still in John's careful arms. Donna rose.

"D'you know it's late?"

"Late? It's only eleven," said Richard.

"My good youth, I go to bed at nine in Ireland, and I sleep till eight in the morning unless they rouse me at three to see if I have pistols concealed. Good-night, my children. This is the first Christmas of the peace. Pray God we keep it. Edmund, will you see me up the path?" for they were down in the garden house.

Alys sprang up.

"We'll all see you!"

"You're not going yet, are you?" Richard reproached them.

Edmund, his mother on his arm, hesitated in the doorway. The wine he had drunk had flushed him and, commanding as his mother was, she did not overshadow him. His wife, looking across the room, thought what a fine pair they were, and wondered that she could think it without any tremor of pride in him, without any anxious look that he should include her. It was dreadful to her to realise that instead of hoping he would say—"Come, Elinor!" she was hoping that he would go on with his mother and leave her with her sons. She was hoping, as desperately as she had once hoped for his look and his smile, that one or other of her sons would say to her—"Don't go, Mother!" But that was foolish. Richard was saying "Don't go!" to Alys, and how natural it was. They wanted their quiet hour, the three children.

She rose hastily, very careful not to say to John—"Come with me!" because it was good for him to be with the elder pair. But then she paused again, as Alys said, yawning prettily:

"I'm not going to stay up tonight, Richard. You're on holiday; but I'm a worker. I haven't had a weekday off since the first night."

"Pooh, that's only a year!" Richard smiled at her.

Alys was indignant.

"A year and three months. September the twenty-eighth, nineteen seventeen, if you please, was the dress rehearsal."

An indescribable look passed over Richard's face: and John thought —'Doesn't she remember that that was the night of Paschendaele?'

"Stay half an hour!" Richard was very humble; but her smile was almost petulant as she shook her head. Nevertheless, as he put her cloak round her and drew her out into the darkness, she was exquisite to him. So much Elinor saw before the shadows of the path swallowed them, as a moment earlier they had swallowed Edmund, Donna on his arm.

John gave his mother an odd look as he stood at the book-case, idly fingering the loose volumes that lay along the tops of the shelves.

"D'you like her, Mother?" said he significantly.

It was his pride to put into words, a fraction sooner than his companion, what his companion was thinking.

"Very much," returned Elinor loyally.

"You know, it's awfully curious, I never thought of Richard in love. Doesn't seem like him somehow. I don't believe he is either."

"Why not, John?"

"I don't know. He wants to be, I know. He kids himself that he is. But—I don't know." A look of caution veiled his eyes for a moment. Then the desire to talk swept caution almost aside. "I don't know, Mother. I see him with that lovely creature—I do think she's the loveliest thing I've ever seen, don't you?—and I wonder why he looks at her at all. I think I know why, too," he said half under his breath.

"Yes, I think I do too," said Elinor.

"Do you? Then you're clever, Mother; because I'm not sure. But I think it's because she's—"

"Like Richard himself, do you mean?" said Elinor.

At that he stopped wandering about the room and came over to the hearth and sat down.

"Then you have noticed it too? This is exciting. I didn't know, Mother, that you—that a woman—could ever quite understand Richard. But you do, don't you?"

"I think I do," said she painfully, not fully understanding, but so desperately anxious not to check him.

She succeeded. John was absorbed in his subject. Never had he been so much at home with her. It was as if their mutual affection for Richard endowed them both with unusual power to develop their thoughts.

"You see, Mother, as I see things, Alys is all that Richard would like to be—brilliant, heady, making everyone mad about her and not feeling a thing. I don't think she feels anything at all, you know. And that's what Richard envies. That's the difference between them. He feels. She doesn't. He feels how dreadful it is not even to know what he wants and yet to be sure he'll never get it."

"What does he want, John?"

"Don't you know, Mother?"

There was a silence. Then John picked up his argument.

"But she, she knows what she wants: and what's more she knows she'll get it."

"What does she want, John?"

"Don't you know that either?"

"I'm not sure."

"Money."

"What?" Elinor was startled. "I thought you'd say power, power over men."

"Oh no. Money. That sort of power. She hasn't got any imagination at all, I think.   Mother, d'you know that flower. Love-in-a-mist?"

"It's my favourite flower," said Elinor.

"Yes, and when the petals fall off they call it Devil-in-a-bush."

"John, go to bed!"   And then, as Richard came in: "Make John go to bed, Richard!"

"John, it's time you were asleep. Is that what you want, Mother?" and Richard flung himself down on the couch, smiling at John: and as John went off in supreme contentment, Elinor too, gave a little pleased sigh.   Richard heard, and answered it instantly with: "Dearest, this is like old times—peace times!" and then forgot her.

She sat in silence, watching the smile die out of his face.   Yes, her mother-in-law was right.   He had had bad times: it was written all over him.   As he sat, staring at the fire, thoughts played over his face exactly as the flames played over it: and she thought: 'Where has he gone?   In this one second my son has gone such a long way from me, and will go further.'   Her face showed her pain, and he had not strayed so far after all, for he put a hand on hers.

"What's the matter, Mother?"

She started.

"Oh, how quick you are!   I was thinking about you.   I was thinking you were four years of time away from me, and at once, here you are back beside me."

"Yes, I'm home," he said, unsmiling.

"And happy?"

"I ought to be," said he.

"You do love her, Richard, don't you?"

He moved his head restlessly.

"I suppose it's that.   She fills my mind, anyway.   Whether she cares for me or not I don't know.   I daren't test it, and yet I think of nothing else and am thankful to think of nothing else.   It's a strange thing.   All through the war, the real things have been Kenneth—and you and John—at least, until Kenneth went—"

"Oh, Richard, I didn't know."

"How should you?"

"When was he—"

"Killed?   Oh no!   He's far too good at taking care of himself."

"Richard!"

"No, I suppose I shouldn't talk like that but—oh, Mother, it's hard to see someone you love making himself cheap—"

"Yes," said his mother.

"And then, because you like them enough to say—'Stop it!'—to have it all broken up—"

"Yes," said his mother.

"You see, he's nice really—"

"Oh, Richard—" said Elinor, and her despairing hand lifted and dropped again to her lap.

"But he is! You'd have liked him, Mother. That's why I hated the whole silly business so at the time. But afterwards, when I'd been out long enough, I wondered if I blamed him so much—or them. I wondered if it wasn't just envy. Oh, well, I'd got you and John. But as soon as I got home, Mother, neither you nor John seemed real any more. You came to see me in hospital, you remember—my God, how I waited for you!—and you came in at the door and you did look such a darling with your flowers, and I did so rejoice to see your dear face, bless you!" He touched her hand again affectionately. "But as you came up the ward you got shadowier and shadowier, till when you bent over me, Mother, you weren't there at all. Just a scent of flowers. I did feel lonely. And the same with John, and the same with Father. And I said to myself—'But my people aren't real! They haven't been out with me and they don't know what I know. They're just shadows out of my past.'—Ugh, it was filthy!" He shivered.

"Dearest, it was shell-shock. You know they said—"

"Yes, I know what they said. Useful word, shell-shock. I think I kept it up jolly well. You never spotted, did you?"

"Oh yes, my son. And so did John."

"How d'you know?"

"How does one know things? I understand John. At least, I think I do. I used to think I did. But you all grow up so: I am afraid to say I understand you any more. But I know he noticed what I noticed. And then you met Alys—"

"Yes. You see, Mother, she didn't care tuppence about the war. That was so real of her. I can't explain myself. But there she was, thinking about her career and just how much she could twist Father round her finger and how her frock suited her and how much money she'd make—oh, it was heavenly! She was flesh and blood, not spirit. I love her selfishness. I suppose I always have loved selfishness."

"Richard!"

"Joke, Mother, that's all! But I'm nearly sure I love her. I get myself back when I'm with her. Our minds work the same way."

"That's what John said."

He looked at her oddly.

"John must be fond of me. Yes, and that's another thing I love her for. She's given me back you and John and everyone. She's made you all real again." He looked at her with his strange smile. "I suppose you hate her for being the one to do it? I should."

"D'you think I could hate her, Richard, if she's done that for you?"

"No, but you don't like her, Mother, that's plain enough. And yet you should," said Richard.

"Well, I see her faults."

"Yes, so do I. I always see people's faults so damnably clearly. And my own! That's what's the matter with me." He stared at the fire, his lips pursed, remote as the unshed snow above them in the deeps of the winter sky. Presently he turned to her again, kindness in his eyes—"Mother, you must go to bed."

But she did not stir. She, too, was absorbed in the leapings of the last flame.

"When I was young," said Elinor at last, "we fell in love so differently. For years I never saw a fault in your father."

"I think Father hates me," said Richard abruptly.

"Richard, don't talk like that."

"Ah, but you don't know how strongly I feel it. If it weren't for you I shouldn't have stayed at home a week. I feel he's always saying 'Get out of here! Find a den of your own!' And yet he's talking to me about producing with him at the Glory Hole. He's mad. He must know it wouldn't work."

"My son, the war's been over six weeks. You don't suppose you're going to get over all that it's done to your mind and body in a fortnight? You don't suppose your father's normal either."

"Oh, don't compare me with Father!"

"Your mind's been blown about for four years, Richard, and so has his. I'll never judge any man who's been through the last four years—"

"If I once started judging Father—" began Richard slowly.

"Richard, you mustn't be so bitter. I know what's in your mind. If I can bear with it, can't you?"

"I've often wondered how you can," said he.

"My dear, this is Christmas night. Why do we get on to these subjects? See me to the house, my son, and try not to think of anything but home and Alys, and that the Peace has come. Where's my coat?"

He put it round her and they stepped out into the dark night, and on along the path to the main building. One light streamed out from the corner room.

"Isn't it strange not to have to pull one's blinds," said Elinor. "I shall never get out of the habit."

He laughed.

"Alys won't worry herself, the darling," said he. And then—"She's reading very late."

They moved on noiselessly across the crisp grass.

CHAPTER 57

EDMUND AND HIS SON RICHARD

GERRY came home some two months later—dear Gerry, grown so tall and broad and important : and being the last comer and the novelty, was instantly Edmund's darling. And because Gerry asked for it he was not only given a very handsome allowance, but encouraged to take a flat in Half Moon Street : and somehow or other the bills for the furniture and the cigarettes came in to Edmund, and Edmund at first did not even storm before he paid. Good God, the boy had been through four years of the War! Something must be done for him!

So Gerry had his flat and his allowance instead of being packed off to the New Broom to play in Shakespeare as had first been planned. That plan had not suited Gerry at all, for the New Broom had become a rough and ready training ground in theatrical virtue, where good clothes had no background, and the women had brains and voices but were hardly smart and the discipline was the discipline of an up-to-date girls' school. No place for Gerry, taking his father out to dinner, and lunching with his mother when he wanted sympathy, but not getting much sympathy because her mind was on other, heavier matters. He soon got the truth out of her. There was trouble brewing again between Edmund and Richard.

Richard had defiantly flung himself into the world that fascinated him, and as he had asked no allowance from his father, but lived in two rooms on his own income, Edmund had not a word to say, although he said it, sullenly or furiously or with venom every time they met.

Gerry, listening to his mother's confidences, and his father's confidences, and going off for long drives on Sunday with Richard, was very sympathetic with each in turn and gave very reasonable advice which would inevitably precipitate the storm that he knew to be brewing. As he said to himself, the disinterested observer could always see straightest, and whatever else he might be or might not be, at least he was disinterested.

So he told Edmund that—"Of course, sir, I know Richard's heart has always been in the films. It doesn't seem to me much good forcing him on to the stage."

"Forcing? Force a Broome on to the stage? If Richard doesn't realise his privileges as my son and a Broome, he needn't be afraid, Gerry, that I shall force him. But I tell you this, my boy—if Richard throws away his birthright, he needn't think he can come to me whining to be taken back when his movies, as you call 'em, move him on."

"No, sir, I'm sure he won't."

"Oh, he won't, won't he?"

"Well, of course, if you listen to Richard——He has got big ideas. He was talking of chains of picture houses all over the country. One studio, you know, controlling a whole circuit."

"Gerry, I will not listen to such nonsense."

"I don't mean that I agree, of course—"

"I should think not! Why, d'you realise, my boy, what the position of the theatres—of our theatres—would be, if your picture houses once got a strangle-hold?"

"No—yes—yes, of course, sir! I didn't think."

"No, and your brother doesn't think."

Later Gerry would outline the conversation to Richard, with perfect justice emphasising the fact that, as Edmund grew older, he was less and less capable of perceiving new ideas, and that really after the war, with all conditions so changed, if one had to sit down and listen to a long rigmarole of—'The way I started, my boy, in 1885—' one would get nowhere. There the movies were, a fact, an existing fact—"and if Father can't or won't see it, Richard, I don't see that you can be blamed for taking your own line. God knows I'd take mine tomorrow if I'd got a chance. I suppose there's no opening? I wish you'd introduce me sometime to those fellows you're working with."

But to Elinor Gerry deplored gently and with absolute justice the tactlessness of Richard with his father.

"It would be so easy for Richard just to humour Father. He's only got to play a part now and then, when Father pushes one at him. He's only got to show himself occasionally in the theatre and shut his mouth till Father settles down to the idea that he's going to have a son in the movies, and everything would be smooth. And then when he did make a success Father would be bursting with pride. But no, he will go bull-headed for what he wants, just as Father does. I think Richard's a fool. No tact."

Elinor would sigh and feel that things were worse than she had realised, and tell Gerry that if he did get a chance of influencing his brother, for pity's sake he was to take it.

But Gerry held that the only person who could influence Richard at the moment was Alys, and that he would do well to see a good deal of Alys and prime her as to the line she ought to take. And Elinor would beg him to do what he could.

Gerry continued to do what he could. The harder he worked, the bitterer became the situation between the father and son, until Edmund's attention was deflected from the activities of Richard by uncovering the fact that Gerry in six months had contrived to run himself hopelessly into debt. Edmund paid the debts after terrific interviews: only to discover a week or two later that Elinor had also paid the debts. And there, for the time being, was the end of Gerry's flat and the little supper parties at the Savoy, and so on to the night clubs. But Gerry, who hated rows, feeling them, as he told his father and mother, to be undignified and unnecessary, remembered in time how handsome he was and how extremely attractive to his elders: so he told all his troubles candidly, humorously, caressingly, to one of his many women friends, an exquisitely dressed American divorcée ten years older than himself, who had wonderful hair and wonderful pearls and a wonderful capacity for enjoyment. She enjoyed, among other things, Gerry's good looks, blatant charm and blatant selfishness, and she could afford herself any whim. Her whim was to marry him.

As she told Elinor, with complete simplicity, she was going to enjoy mothering him, and was perfectly prepared for him to be unfaithful to her so long as he told her the details afterwards. Later, indeed, she was to falsify a good many of Gerry's anticipations and her own ideas of give-and-take. But at the time it was a grand, devotional business, and on the whole the Broomes were not ill pleased.

Alys, with that curious tolerance of the modern woman for another woman's admirable points, adored the widow's clothes and figure. Edmund, after a long talk with her, pronounced his son well settled: while Elinor talked anxiously of dear Constance's beauty and sweetness, and wrote to her mother-in-law that though it was not generally wise for a man to marry a woman older than himself, here, Elinor felt, was a genuine exception. As for young John, he fell gloriously in love with Gerry's Constance for a fortnight, and as he had already the full use of his uncanny capacity for analysing what he admired, and his own sensations while he admired, he has since pilloried his unconscious sister-in-law in at least three plays. But Richard did not like her, and Gerry knew it, and was piqued that his brother did not envy him. And although Richard was to be best man, the strain grew between them, with Richard definitely the aggressor, nervy and restless, and not too pleasant about some of the bride's presents to the bridegroom. And Gerry told malicious, funny little stories about Richard to his Constance, and sometimes to Alys who had a keen sense of humour : and went about arm in arm with Richard whenever he could, for one should always stick close to an enemy's side. And so it came to the farewell supper of Gerry's bachelordom, which on the night before his wedding he insisted on giving to his five oldest friends.

For Gerry, who had an extremely affectionate nature and never forgot a birthday or an anniversary, took very seriously indeed the idea of having all his oldest friends with him at this great moment of his life. Two he had not seen since their schooldays, and one was a war alliance, and one was his best friend in real fact, and the fifth was Richard. And they all met in a private room at an extremely expensive restaurant, to eat and drink and be merry.

The food was good and each course had its wines; but the feast was scarcely a merry one; for Gerry was in a high state of sentimentality and could not crack a joke to save his life, and Richard sparred with the best friend, and the three others sat making conversation and wondering why they had been invited; because, as a matter of fact, the school friends had never seen Gerry since all three left to enlist, and the war friend had put Gerry with the war into the extreme background of his mind. However, they could always drink. And they continued to drink, steadily and with a fervour, which would have been more comprehensible if it had enabled them to enjoy themselves. But the drinks were even more mixed than the party, and so the evening ended with a certain grimness.

Gerry, who had drunk carefully, but not quite carefully enough, was sure that it had been a grand evening. Richard, however, fully occupied by the problem of getting Gerry home and producing him in fair condition next morning, forgot to say how grand the evening had been, and Gerry resented this loudly. Richard listened tolerantly to the flood of Gerry's resentment, which soon engulfed not only Richard but John and their father, most of their friends and all their acquaintances, for Gerry was at home in all the dressing-rooms and had a good memory. Richard, though he winced once or twice, contrived to remain unshockable and unsurprised, and so gained his object, which was to get Gerry to bed. Thereupon Gerry, touched by Richard's attentions, forgot his resentment utterly. Indeed, he began to reproach himself, always at the top of his voice, for that he was going to be married tomorrow, leaving poor, poor Richard without a brother to turn to in trouble.

"So listen to me, Richard! You listen to me. Let me give you some good advice now before it's all too late. You came a cropper before, all through not listening to me. I could have told you a lot of things about a lot of people if you'd asked me. You go about with your head in the air and your eyes shut. Kenneth! I could have told you all about Kenneth."

"Yes, Gerry. That's all right."

"'Tisn't all right. And look at Alys! There you are with your eyes shut again. Tight! Shouldn't ever be tight."

Richard said—

"You'd better shut up, Gerry, and go to sleep."

But Gerry was furiously indignant at being told to shut up and go to sleep, and repeated very loudly the advice about Alys and eyes, and coupled it with a piece of information that struck the weary Richard dumb and shaking, and so changed his voice that Gerry's mood turned to truculence once more: and he repeated his information at some length. Then, getting no answer, he began to weep monotonously, was sick, was better, drowsed a little while, then rolled over onto his pillow and fell fast asleep.

But Richard, dead Richard, murdered Richard, patrolled the streets till the town roused itself: then limped across the Park, down Piccadilly, and so presented himself at the door of Alys's flat, and, brushing past the maid-servant and her brass rags, walked into his love's room.

There she lay under her yellow silk eiderdown, with the French pierrot dangling by his neck from the bed-post and grazing her pillow with his toes. Her black hair was in a boyish disarray, and she blinked sleepily as she pushed back the tangle from her flushed young face with an arm bare except for Richard's jade bangle. She stared up at Richard for a minute as he stood over her, with an enchanting look of extreme amazement and extreme amusement, before she said—

"My dear Richard, what on earth are you doing here? Haven't you been to bed? And how did you get past Mariette?" And then, in real concern—"Richard, what has happened?"

He stood looking down at her, his lips working, totally incapable of speech, and she was frightened by his look. Her mind ran swiftly over the possible reasons for his state, even as she stretched out her lovely little hands to coax him to sit down on the bed beside her and—"talk to me quietly, Richard, and tell me what is the matter. My poor, darling boy, what is it? What's wrong?"

Then he found his voice.

"Gerry said that you were my father's mistress. Is it true? And that everybody in London knows it. Is it true? Ever since you came over. Is it true?"

Only for an instant did she lose control of her expressive features: then she broke out into peals of sweet, derisive laughter.

"Richard, my lamb—how heavenly! Your poor father! No—aren't people wonderful? Who said it? Tell me all about it!"

But he had seen her face in that first moment, and as he watched, it was as if a thousand never heeded trifles rose out of his memory like fireflies to circle her, lest he should miss any detail of expression. So he looked, and was presently satisfied. And while she still laughed, and then, springing out of bed, would have detained him, he pushed by her as if she had no existence for him, and left the room and her.

And so home to his flat and bathed and dressed, transforming himself at great length and with great care into best man: made sure of the ring and went off to the assistance of his brother, who by that time badly needed assistance. Richard was admirable with Gerry, took him out for a walk, walked him back in time, was sympathetic, brought him down to church (for Constance would not be cheated of the full splendours of an English wedding), performed his duties admirably, was charming to the bridesmaids, saw that the bridal couple were released in fair time, came back intently into the house, passing his father without a look, and entertained the dwindling guests till the place was cleared.

But when at last he was free, he went to look for his mother, and found her at the foot of the garden steps, radiant, but very tired, and crying a little, carefully, so as not to hurt her make-up.

He caught her arm by the elbow in a grip that made her cry out.

"Mother, I want you."

At that moment Edmund appeared at the top of the iron staircase.

"Ah, there you are, Nell! Richard, don't keep your mother waiting."

"Mother," said Richard urgently. "I've got to talk to you at once."

"But your father—"

"Mother!" His grip became unbearable. "You've got to come, Mother!" And again in that pale voice, "Mother!"

She was yielding after one quick look, only to stop dead and step a little in front of him as Edmund came down the steps saying bluffly—

"Now Richard, my boy, don't keep your mother standing about when she's tired! Nell, I want you in the library."

"You want everything, don't you, Father?" said Richard, and his tone was intolerable. Edmund reddened with surprise.

"What's this? Control yourself, Richard! Are you ill?"

"Sickened!"

"Richard, darling, what's the matter?"

"Mother, I think I shall go into the Church. I should like to preach a sermon on the fifth commandment—Honour your father and mother! But there ought to be another commandment—a post-war commandment. Honour your sons, for their days have been short in the land! How sick you must have been, Father, that I came back at all!"

"He's mad," said Edmund staring.

"Yes, I am. I should think I am mad, and have been these four years. Why, for four years I've been doing the work for you. I've been keeping you alive, Father, and while I did it you couldn't even leave me my one chance——" His voice failed suddenly.

"Be quiet!" said Edmund violently at the top of his voice. And then to Elinor—"I think he's out of his mind." His face was crimson: he was breathless.

"Careful, Edmund, careful," said the wife mechanically. Then the mother turned to her son. She knew her son.

"What is it, Richard?"

"It's Alys, Mother! It's Alys. That's all. That's all it is. Nothing to get excited about. Only there isn't a club in London that doesn't know all about it, Mother—all about it!"

"I would never have let you marry her," said Edmund thickly.

"D'you hear that, Mother? O my God, let me get out of this!"

"Elinor, Elinor, stop that young devil!"

Elinor caught her son's arm.

"Richard, you can't go off like that!"

Richard flung round.

"Young devil!" repeated Edmund. He was fumbling at his collar. He had the air of a man choking.

Richard regarded him and began to laugh.

"You needn't work it up for me, Father. I'm going." And he went.

"Richard!" Elinor made a half step after him and he turned on the iron stair. On the wall behind him the blood-red sheet of Virginia creeper glowed in the sunset: and to his mother his immaculate wedding garments were suddenly ridiculous and horrible, and his face, lit by the same sunset, was twisted in unnatural torment. He had the look of a roasting heretic, yet, and it was dreadful to her, even at that moment the Broome charm was not roasted out of him. He used his trick to the last as he cried out to her, to her, only to her—

"You know where to find me, Mother, if you want me," turned again and the black doorway swallowed him.

"Mad," said Edmund on a huge sigh of relief, and he pulled out his handkerchief and began to mop his face. He was panting and exhausted. He might have been at the end of a second act, shaking with effort and relief as he faced his audience.

But his wife was his audience, and she looked at him unmoved. His eyes met hers and outstared her defiantly, but he could not make her look away.

"What are you staring at me for?" said Edmund at last truculently.

"Saying good-bye, Edmund."

"What's this?"

"Good-bye, Edmund."

"Nell, you don't mean to tell me that you believe—that you're influenced—that you take any tale—"

"No, no, no—" said she wearily.

"Yes, but look here, Nell—listen! What d'you mean?"

"I'm going to leave you. There's no reason to stay."

His eyes blazed.

"Well, leave me then! What? You think I can't get on without you? But if you leave me, you don't come back."

"No, I shan't come back," said his wife.

"Nell—I—if I—"

"It's finished, Edmund."

"All right then, it's finished." Again they stood staring at each other.

"I shall go down to Marlow," said she. "You can make what arrangements you like. I'll divorce you or separate from you, whichever you prefer, so long as I never see you again."

"You can't do it."

"I can and I will."

He said incredulously, childishly—

"Elinor, you can't. We've been married twenty years. You know me: you know what I am. You've always taken me for what I was.

There never was a wife like you—I know that well enough. Can I help it if that boy fancied himself in love? Nell, you know me. You've always understood—you've always condoned. Now, all of a sudden, to smash up everything——? Don't you see, it's damnable?"

It was so hard for him to abdicate, to wrestle, to plead: it was a skin-changing beyond his power to accomplish. He was like a struggling creature that could not be born. But to her own secret horror she watched his struggles with no more emotion than a faint distaste. She suffered, certainly, but she did not suffer for him but for herself, and then she only suffered from a sense of waste. She thought to herself— 'It is ten years since he could move me in any way. I see that now. When John was born and it all started again: then I found out what he was. Then I saw that he couldn't change. Then I should have left him. But I couldn't give up the legend of being in love with him, of being his faithful wife and martyr. That revolts me now. I have been, in my own way, as self-indulgent as he. I bear him malice because he has made me ashamed of myself.'

But aloud she said—

"There's no need for any malice, Edmund. Don't let's be emotional. But of course we must part."

His face was ludicrous with concern. She perceived that the idea of losing her was a hideous distress to him, and could not understand it. Losing him was no distress to her.

"You know the sort of scandal there'll be?" he muttered.

"There needn't be. So long as we are separated, I don't care what story you give out."

"What about John?" said he. And she saw the fear in his face, the intense and abject fear of losing a beloved possession. She saw very clearly at that moment how she could avenge Richard on Richard's father, and was tempted. Yes, then for the first time in her strong gentle life she knew temptation and the reason of that prayer which she had uttered so glibly morning and night since her babyhood—'Lead us not into temptation; but deliver us from evil.' She longed to use the weapon his look had put into her hands, as drought longs for water, as a woman longs for her delivery. She could take John from him. She could pay Richard's debt. 'Lead us not into temptation: deliver us from evil—'

"Nell!" cried Edmund.

At that moment John himself came out on to the top of the steps and called to them cheerfully—

"I say, aren't you two coming in? It's a bit chilly for your rheumatism, Father. I've had a bath."

He had indeed. He was pink from hot water, honey smooth as to hair, and his dressing-gown was remarkable. The virginia-creeper, dulling in the after-sunset, had not a chance against John's virgin taste. As for John himself, he also was cheerful, and he carried a far too early cocktail in his hand.

Elinor saw her husband's eyes turn to his son, and seeing, had some dim glimmering of the truth of the matter. She had loved Edmund's youth, not Edmund: and now Edmund had given his youth to his sons. Richard, Gerry, John—these, to the man himself, were Edmund: and he loved himself in them.

Her mind hardened. She loved the boys for themselves, not because they were Edmund renewed. But he—what did he do for them but attempt eternally to confine them within the bounds of his own outlived youth? She would not pander to his horrible self-love. He had slain Richard and spoiled Gerry: he should not have John.

She left him unanswered, unregarded, and went up the steps to her son.

But she had reckoned without John and John's character, and her own careful training of him. Edmund disregarded, Edmund without attention paid him, Edmund left alone in the garden, rather bowed, rather forlorn—that was not in the Broome tradition at all. John, with his unerring sense of situation, had of course perceived instantly that something was going on between his father and mother, and his brother. One of the rows, probably, to which he was entirely accustomed, and to which he adapted himself with the tact of a corn-field in the wind. He had not asked—"What's up?" when Richard stumbled past him, and he had given his father and mother plenty of time to have out their difference before he emerged innocently on the steps. Now, his mother's rigid face was enough to let him know that the matter was more serious than usual, so when she said to him in passing—"I'm going up to lie down, John, before I go to the theatre. Come up with me!" he squeezed her arm affectionately and said—"I'll be up presently," and then went out to his father. His mother was his ally; but his father looked wretched, and he was fond of his father, was John.

CHAPTER 58

RICHARD'S STAR

AND in the long run it was John, tenacious, tactful, subtle and affectionate, who determined the future relations of the hopelessly estranged pair. It was inevitable that he should know something of the magnitude of the breach, for neither his father nor his mother could help talking to him: they knew nevertheless that John knew all about it, all about Alys, all about Richard. And though in sheer embarrassment they both evaded discussion of the actual reason of their estrangement, they could not conceal from him their bitterness, their anger and their weariness of each other.

Elinor was the wilder. She, for so many years a patient woman, had now a drunkard's craving for utter freedom. Emancipated by shock, her attitude to her husband had become the fiercer, the more intolerant, because of her previous submissions. She insisted on complete separation, and she would have liked a divorce. Yet for Richard's sake she would not involve Alys Broome. Edmund was careful to give her no other cause and his previous lapses she had condoned. For Edmund also had swung away from his mood of half-despairing acquiescence in his wife's decision, and was preparing to fight: and a good deal of Broome linen would have been washed in public had it not been for John's determination not to lose any possession of his own. His father was his possession, so was his mother: and he wanted to keep them both. Too astute to fight the battle of either with the other, he did yet contrive to soothe, mitigate and delay action till time accustomed them both to their situation. Edmund, finding that he still saw as much as he chose of John, ceased to talk of asserting his rights as a father. Elinor, her nerves soothed by a long holiday and always wax in her children's hands, acquiesced in John's plannings, until there came a time when, for the boy's sake, she even agreed to be seen occasionally with Edmund.

So Elinor attended first nights at the Genista, and Edmund took his wife and son to dine occasionally in the restaurant of the moment. Officially there was no breach, and never had been a breach. But their only common interest was their interest in John, and the only private interview they ever had again was on the occasion of John's breakdown.

662

For John, who had worked with the Broome fury at the business of managing his father and mother, was, after all, not the entirely experienced person he thought himself, not altogether the prop and stand-by that he appeared to his mother, nor the complete companion that Edmund found him. He was also a frightened boy of seventeen, over-emotionalised, over-sensitive, precocious, with an imagination shaken to pieces by the home-front panics of the previous five years, and already, like his great-uncle Robin before him, the mere wick for his own devouring talent. This child had been, for some months, concentrating energy, capacity, will, magnetism, spirit, on securing for himself the safety of his home. His father, his mother, his brothers, these were the furniture of his soul. He had lost Henry, he had lost Gerry, then he had lost Richard. He clutched, desperate as vertigo itself, at the two affections remaining. When at last he was able to relax his efforts, when at last he was able to feel secure again, he collapsed and was exceedingly ill, and frightened them all to death: and had to have a year of lying fallow and so did not get to Oxford till he was twenty.

Edmund worried himself to death over John's delicacy, and Elinor agonised, but neither guessed what had caused John's illness, but wondered to themselves that two such robust people could have so delicate a child, and yet were thankful for his delicacy because it kept him tethered to them. At least they had one child left. It was in vain that Edmund brooded over Richard and longed for Gerry, and Elinor tightened her lips over Gerry and ached for Richard. Longing did not bring either son home.

Gerry's honeymoon was an indefinitely prolonged affair, for his wife owned a yacht as well as an estate in Florida, and the sub-tropical life suited Gerry very well indeed. When he was tired of lazing they went to New York. Why not? There was nothing to come home for.

As for Richard, he had departed for Hollywood a week after Gerry's marriage. He wrote regularly to his mother, and sometimes to John, brief letters, chronicling the details of his professional work and generally throwing in a comical adventure, encounter, dialogue or mishap, but saying nothing of coming home. Why should he when it was so clear that he was in his right place, and that by an astonishing chance he was among friends. For Lewis Wybird's only son Philip was also at Los Angeles, learning the job—'Not my side, but the business end. We rather fell on each other's necks. Apparently old Lewis Wybird has dropped all his theatre interests since the war, and is backing Philip to an unlimited extent. There aren't any British films to speak of, you know, but Philip doesn't see why there shouldn't be.'

Six months later came news of Richard's luck in being chosen out of heaven knew how many rivals for a big part in one of the new pictures. And a year later Richard was a full-blown star, making thousands and investing all he made in Philip Wybird's companies.

Other bits of news he gave from time to time.

'Saw Gerry the other day. He and Constance have taken a house out here for the summer. Gerry's grown horribly stout. Very pleased to see me.' And later—'It's astonishing how many Englishmen are drifting out here. I've met two or three old college friends. I'm sharing a place with a man I used to know at Oxford. He can't get a job; but I'm so overwhelmed with work that it's become absolutely necessary to have a secretary, so the arrangement suits us both very well.' And again—'I've just finished my first independent picture and it looks like being a success. Now I'm hesitating whether I'm to build a house out here and be naturalised, or whether I shall come home and lose my money gloriously making films at Elstree. I think I shall come. I'm homesick sometimes, and so is Kenneth.'

Elinor wrote out eagerly—'Is the Kenneth you speak of that friend of yours who once stayed at Marlow? So you've made it up! I never met him, did I? What a difference it must make to you to be in touch with English people and friends. What is Philip Wybird like? I see his father occasionally at first nights and he is always very gracious. It is curious to feel that his son and mine are good friends.'

But he did not answer her questions or make any comment on her letter, and she was working too hard to let herself worry.

The four years had not greatly affected Elinor in the theatre. At forty-nine she was still a handsome woman, just able to play young parts still, but as steadily refusing them and striking out her own line in elderly comedy. She carried on her work independently of Edmund, seldom lacked an engagement, went about a great deal and dressed better and better.

John had already written her two plays which she had firmly refused to put on, but she saw well enough where he was heading, and lived for the day when she should open, in her own son's theatre (for the control of the Genista was to pass to John when he left Oxford) in her own son's play. The early talent for drawing had fed the main channel of creation, and so soon as she was able to cure him of disliking God violently in free verse she thought he would be safe.

Well, what more could she want? Here was Gerry safely married and looked after, Richard was on the screen, more discussed than Balkan kings, and John himself bade fair to be one of the after-war crop of prodigies, whom John so prodigiously admired, whom she also secretly admired. How could they do it at their ages? And the girls, too, were as astonishing, contesting elections, controlling businesses, flying. . . . Producing a couple of babies had been enough for her at that age—she had known a full ten years of marriage before her brains began to work properly. Marvellous, terrifying post-war boys and girls, how she envied them! How she admired this generation that had bought itself bloodily a freedom of which her youth had but dreamed. Oh to have been born twenty years later in the world! Well—if she could not keep as young as she wanted to keep, and could not think as youngly as she wanted to think, at least she could watch with excitement and appreciation the younger generation. And what did it matter if they thought her grand and comic? She was grand and comic: she owned it, chuckling, for she was happy. With John content at Oxford, filling the house with his friends, in close touch with her, outgrowing her, but never ignoring her, with Richard in America, writing so cheerfully, and cured, surely cured at last of Alys?—she was happier than she had ever been in her life. She worked hard: she enjoyed her work: she was not torn any longer by any personal passion: she had put off Edmund and her past life: and she had her children. If ever a woman had received with bitterness and despair the strokes of fortune that woman was herself; yet, now, looking back, how all these miseries had worked together to bless her. For twenty years the horror of losing Edmund's love had hung over her. She had lost it, and now she rejoiced daily in the loss, because of the freedom it had given her. Strange! She wished him well: she was thankful to be quit of him. She supposed he was happy in his own way: she hoped so, but thanked her stars that it had no longer to be her way. Poor Edmund!

She looked at him closely and critically on their occasional formal meetings. His face was much coarsened, she thought, in the last few years, and he was far too stout. There was nothing, nothing at all left of the young Edmund. He was not tragic; but it was tragic that the boy should have died out of him so utterly. There had been no youth in Lewis Wybird: that had been his sin: and now there was not a pin to choose between him and Edmund save that Lewis was withered and Edmund was gross. Yet Edmund's father, the adored Stephen, had been young to the hour of his death. And because of that, after all these years, she still missed him and wished that John could have known him. Little as she now cared for Edmund she felt a rage against fate because the lasting power to charm had been given to the failure of a father : and only the passing power to the successful son. Yet there was still something about the eyes when Edmund smiled. Oh, well, life was strange! Poor Edmund!

Edmund was poorer than his wife knew. The War had caught him a year or so too late: he was a pre-war Napoleon: he could not adapt himself to the entirely changed conditions of the post-war theatre world. He could not accept the fact that new audiences had grown up which knew not the Broomes and had no use for the problem plays, the honour dramas, and the elaborate but old-fashioned spectacles on which he had built his fortune. He began to have a rage against his public, flinging it play after play in the spirit of 'if you don't like it you can lump it' and of course, lost money. Then he began to panic, and, swinging round from his position of infallible isolation, began to take every one's advice at once, and lost yet more. The day came when he was faced with the fact that he could no longer run his three theatres. Well, the New Broom could go. He had never made much money out of it, and he was offered good terms.

So he accepted, and instantly found himself held up to public obloquy and the Press seething with indignation at the idea of the historic theatre, traditional church of St. Shakespeare-in-the-Slums sacrificed to common need of cash. Then some whipper-snapper or other from the provinces stepped in and paid the purchasers a far larger sum than they had offered or paid Edmund, public subscriptions poured in, and the New Broom was saved.

But that did not help Edmund, impoverished, affronted, sore, and no longer a symbol of the great traditions of the English theatre, but a commercial manager who had miscalculated his public's mood, and lost much money when he might have made it. Meanwhile, his touring returns dwindled as the cinemas sprang up like mushrooms in the old circuit towns, great cities, and watering places. Everywhere on the gaudy posters, the family name blared at him, cheapened, overdone. His hatred for the cinemas grew into an obsession, and his hatred for his son into a mania.

And he had no one to talk to; for Alys had long since left the Genista for a more modern management and had had no successor. He generally dined and lunched with a pretty face or an old client, but he had no friends; he had only a thousand acquaintances : and they were running up a cinema next door to the Genista, and the bank was beginning to be troublesome. And God knew what Wybird would want when it came to renewing the lease of the Glory Hole next year, with rents going up so monstrously. Once, not so long ago, before the accursed war and Elinor's desertion, he had dreamed, nay, more than dreamed, had planned and determined to buy back the Glory Hole. Now he must be thankful if he could still find the money to rent it!

Suppose now that he let the Genista for the last year before John took over his property? It would not make any difference, for of course he would manage it for John; but suppose he let the Genista, drew in his horns as much as possible as regards the tours, cut out the American project altogether, and concentrated on the next Christmas season at the Glory Hole? His children's perennial had life in it yet, though it had worn very thin in the last year or two. Suppose he could persuade the author to treat it as Hammersmith treated the classics or import one of those clever fellows from Russia, and give him a free hand—new production, new direction, everything modern and mad? It wasn't his taste, but there was no doubt that Lewis Wybird would require a pot of money spent on the Glory Hole when he renewed the lease.

All right then, they would spend! They would out-modernise the moderns! There should be lighting systems from Berlin, direction from Russia, an American chorus brought over, and, if that was what the English public craved—a nigger band! Ideas ran about madly in his brain like cats with their fur afire. He'd show 'em! Little men do the work themselves, but big men pick lesser men to do the work for them. He'd show 'em. But he wished he had someone with whom to talk over his plans.

He would look sometimes at the photograph on the table by his bed, studying it intently. But there was no use thinking of that. That way madness lay. And it was only because he was tired and overworked, and worried as everybody else was worried, that he so longed to talk to somebody, anybody. Besides, there was John. John's time at Oxford would be up at the end of the summer. And then they'd show the world, the two of them! Father and son, shoulder to shoulder—that was the way to do it! A man needed his son. And John was a good boy, a dear boy, always thoughtful, always affectionate, never giving him a day's trouble.

By the way, he must write to John about the Genista and outline his plans for the autumn. He chuckled: he would have to explain to John that, comical as it sounded, he was asking John for his formal consent.

"You will have to realise your responsibilities, my boy, once you've left Oxford!"

Well, there was no hurry about that; but there was surely something else in his mind, wasn't there, connected with John? Oh yes!

"Isn't there a formal invitation of sorts, Miss Needham, invitation to the O.U.D.S. show? Haven't I accepted?"

His secretary laid the papers on his desk.

Ah, there it was! He thought so—a guest of honour! And John wanted him to go. Dear boy!

He fumbled for his son's letter.

A great night for John. Mercutio, eh? He'd rather like to see John play Mercutio. It didn't clash, did it? When was that appointment with Wybird's people to discuss the terms for the new contract? He'd written them a fortnight ago. Very dilatory they'd been about answering and he'd had to write again. He supposed that they took it as a matter of course. But still, business was business, and he'd tell them so when they foregathered. But that wasn't till next Monday, was it, Miss Needham? And the O.U.D.S. show would be Saturday. No, he needn't put them off.

"Ready, Miss Needham? Take this, please:

'DEAR JOHN,

'I am looking forward to coming up on the—fill in the date, Miss Needham—and have written formally to that effect to the Club. I shall be glad if you will dine with me before the performance, as I have one or two points to discuss with you in connection with the Genista, and no doubt you will have little time afterwards. So it would be better if you did not invite friends to join us——' "

"I beg your pardon, Mr. Broome; but he'll be rather busy beforehand won't he?" said his confidential secretary, who was Somerville and privileged.

"Eh? What's that? Nonsense, nonsense! If I want to see the boy—"

"Very well, Mr. Broome." She waited, fountain-pen poised, while he fidgeted.

"Eh, what's that? You don't think he'll be able to come, eh? Make it difficult for him? All right then. Cut it out, cut it out! Where were we? Oh yes. 'No doubt you will be too busy to dine with me before the performance,—' No, cut the whole thing out." Then—"Hm—Oh, by the way, Miss Needham, d'you know if Mrs. Broome is going up? No? Then you'd better get on to her."

He waited impatiently till the connection had been made.

"Hullo! Is that you, Elinor? Yes, it's Edmund. Are you proposing to go up to this affair of John's? . . . Oh, earlier in the week, are you? . . . One moment, Elinor! Er—(I shan't want you for a few moments, Miss Needham, if, er—) Yes! Well, Elinor, it occurred to me that it would be suitable if we went up together. I have an invitation to speak at the dinner afterwards, and no doubt John would want to include you. . . . What? What's that? . . . Richard? When does he arrive? . . . Oh—yes, I see. . . . No, naturally. . . . Have you told John? . . . I see. You've only just heard. . . . I'm sorry, Elinor, but I thought it as well to make the suggestion. . . . Quite. . . . Good-bye."

He shoved his fist on to the bell.

"Ah, Miss Needham—that letter! Give it to me. I'll finish it by hand."

And he took it from her and added, in his slanting, rather large, curiously feminine hand—

'I have just heard from your mother that Richard is returning to England. He has not seen fit to let me know and it is unlikely that we shall meet. I hardly think it necessary to point out to you, my dear John, that though he will, no doubt, come to Oxford to see you, he had better not be invited during my visit. I have never discussed with you the details of my difficulties with your brother, and I hope it will not be necessary that I should ever do so. But if your brother should in any way poison your mind—' (No, no! That would not do!) He slashed and double-slashed out the words and began again—'Of course I know you will be very glad to see your brother, but you must not forget that you have promised your old father—' (No! Not that either!) 'But you must not forget that you are coming home to me at Easter. I shall have a good deal to discuss with you then, or even earlier. Meanwhile I greatly look forward to seeing you, and trust that your Mercutio will do the Broomes credit. If you have time to run up to town before the night and are in any difficulty about your part, you know, John, I could make time to coach you.'

Then he signed himself John's affectionate father, shoved in the envelope a ten-pound note, and turned, with a queer sense of pleasure ended, of the last page closed on a book of escape, to the weary piles of his correspondence.

But all through the rest of the day's work, interviewing applicants, the important business lunch, the telephone wrangle with Wybird's manager, he found himself thinking, not of John whom he was to see so soon, but of Richard, who was arriving at Southampton during O.U.D.S. week, and would have his mother to meet him, no doubt. Richard would look for his mother to meet him; but would never again in this world look for his father to meet him. Well, Edmund had John. John cared much more for his father than he did for his mother, that he'd swear.

But Elinor was not on the quay to meet Richard, and was, for that matter, not able to go up and see John act. For she was with a strict management, and was a star, and it was quite impossible for her to get off. But she had posted letters to the boat: and Richard, reading his mail in a private room at the Southampton hotel, opened her letter and was first pleased and then worried, and then looked up uncertainly as Kenneth Bruce came in.

"Look here, Ken—" Then Richard hesitated again as his secretary flung himself down in a beautiful exhaustion on the unpromising hotel sofa, and remarked fretfully that Richard was getting too much of a celebrity to be endurable as an employer and that he was worn out.

And indeed his grievance was justified, for the boat had been tempest-tossed and had not got in till the late afternoon. Kenneth Bruce, who prided himself on doing his job as quietly and unobtrusively as he wore his clothes, was vexed to the soul that his time-table should be upset. Moreover he had been harried by the reporters, and he found that his carefully acquired American methods of coping with them did not go down so well in soberer England. His fair skin showed that the March winds had nipped him: his brown eyes showed that he was very ready for sympathy: his petulant lower lip showed that he would make trouble if he didn't get it.

But Richard, still deep in his letter, did not see the signs as he went on—

"Got rid of them all?"

"God knows! I cleared out about ninety. Swore you'd a conference on and I didn't dare disturb you. I promised you'd see 'em in London."

"I say, Ken, you were tactful?"

"Of course! I oiled and I buttered. What else am I for?" Then, with his attractive half smile slipping out as if in spite of himself and his bad temper—"Don't worry, Dickon! I've fixed them."

"Saint!" But Richard, deep in his letter, did not see the smile as he went on—"Now look here, Ken——"

"Why? Anything up?"

"No, no! I only wanted to talk plans with you." Then turning again to his letter—"I suppose you didn't think of that call to the Genista?"

"I did. I put it through at once."

"You're a marvel. Thanks awfully." Then as a waiter came in with the beginnings of a meal—"I ordered you a sherry."

"Oh! Oh, thanks! Did I want some?" Kenneth's ill-humour returned as he sipped.

Richard smiled at him indulgently; but there was a note of deprecation in his voice as he continued—

"I say, Ken, you've booked us somewhere, haven't you?"

"Of course. I wirelessed for a suite. The Ritz. Why?"

"Well, I've just got a letter from Mother. She's mad for me to come straight to Marlow. Of course, as she says, it's practically on the way, and tomorrow's Sunday. I suppose you'd mind awfully if you went up to London alone?"

There was a moment's pause before Kenneth said—

"You mean you drive to Marlow and I go up by train?"

"Well, that's as you like about trains. You could drop me and take the car on if you'd rather," said Richard persuasively.

Said Kenneth even more persuasively—

"Oh, Dickon, surely you can go down tomorrow?"

"You know I meant to. But she wants me to be there when she gets in, and—well, I'm rather keen to see her."

"Oh well, that settles it, doesn't it?" said Kenneth.

"It would only be for a few days."

"A few days? Oh, I see."

"See what?"

"Oh—nothing!"

"Rot! What? Why do you say 'Oh, I see', like that?"

"Well, I didn't know I was going to caretake for a week in London by myself. That's all. I just didn't know." Kenneth put down his sherry with a clatter on the brass tray. Richard watched him in a fuss of distress.

"Ken, don't be an owl. 'Caretake!'"

"Well, I was under the impression that we'd planned one or two things together, Dickon."

"Yes, Ken, I know. But it's only putting it off for a day or two."

"I see. You've made up your mind. Lovely!"

"Look here, Ken, are you trying to make a scene?"

"I? Good God, no! I'm far too humdrum. Scenes are your specialty."

"That's damned rude."

"Well, it's damned rude of you, I think, to ship me off to London—"

"Oh, for God's sake, control yourself!" and Richard, quick-eared, cast a look at the door. A moment later the waiter re-appeared, hovered, clattered, stepped back.

"Dinner's served, sir!" said the waiter.

Neither moved. Then Richard said obliviously—

"Put the stuff down. We'll wait on ourselves."

The order was bowed upon. The door was shut.

Said Richard gently, persuasively, and his asking hand lay outstretched on the table between them—

"Ken, what's the matter?"

At that the other turned on him.

"Oh well, I think it's rather curious of you. You might have made up your mind on the boat, I think. I've got relations too. D'you suppose I haven't got anyone? I should have made my own arrangements. But it never occurred to me that you wouldn't—that we shouldn't—that on our very first evening in England——"

"But Ken——"

"After all, I've been at your affairs since seven a.m. I'm all in. I don't find it amusing. Oh yes, I know—I'm paid to do jobs, and you're a genius who mustn't be worried with details—but all the same—our first evening——"

"All right," said Richard with passionate decision, "I won't go."

Kenneth swung round as if the capitulation acted as a fresh irritant instead of a salve.

"Of course you must go."

"Well, I shan't. Don't worry, Ken! I'll make Mother understand."

"But that's silly, Dickon! That's just silly. You know you want to go."

"Silly or not, I'm not going to have you call me a slave-driver."

"Oh well, you might allow for one's being disappointed."

"Well, now you won't be disappointed. So that settles it." Richard took off a cover and helped himself to food.

Kenneth, staring out at the dreary sea, did not move.

Said Richard at last—

"Hadn't you better have some dinner?"

"I don't want any."

"You ordered it. Is it absolutely necessary to make a scene before the hotel people, Ken?"

"I didn't know that refusing a cutlet constituted a scene."

"Christ!"

"Who's making a scene now?"

"Kenneth, I do think you might behave. I've told you I'm not going. You'll be ill if you don't have something to eat."

But Kenneth, though he sat down sullenly, would not meet Richard's eyes. And they continued in silence the pretence of eating till the waiter intruded upon them anew with cheese and brandy. As he did so the telephone bell rang.

"Shall I answer?" said Kenneth, the perfect employé.

"If you don't mind," said Richard, the perfect employer, and helped himself to watercress as he watched the younger man cross the room.

"Hullo? Is that the Genista? Mr. Richard Broome would like to speak to Mrs. Broome." And then, to Richard—"They're fetching her. Half a second." But the call was half over before Kenneth's face radiated sudden charm into the telephone—"Hullo? Is that Mrs. Broome? Hold on a minute, please." And as he held out the receiver to Richard he appeared to forget that he was not as friendly with Richard as with the voice seventy-five miles away, and Richard smiled.

"Don't go," said Richard, as Kenneth made for the door. "Hullo! Is that you, Mother? Yes. Me. Richard. Well, darling, isn't this grand? What? I can't hear you. You sound as if you'd been running."

The dear foolish boy! Of course she had been running. She had run so fast that she could barely speak when she reached the telephone in the door-keeper's office, the stinking, old-fashioned telephone with the press handle. She was quite oblivious of the door-keeper and of the loungers as she spoke to him across the counties.

"Richard—is that you, Richard? Oh, my dear boy, where are you?"

Then Richard's voice—

"Just starting for London, darling! I shall see you tomorrow."

And she—

"Tomorrow? Why not tonight? Aren't you coming straight across to Marlow?"

"Well, dearest, I've got a whole mass of baggage and business and stuff. I thought I'd settle in at the Ritz and drive down tomorrow afternoon."

"But Richard, dear—" Elinor's voice came outraged over the line—

"of course you're making your head-quarters with me. Where else should you go?"

"You're an angel, Mother. But I should turn the house upside down."

"But, dear boy, I like it turned upside down."

"I don't think I will, Mother."

"But Richard, why not?" He could hear that she was nearly in tears.

"I don't think I'd better, really. It would be too much for you. The stuff's all gone off already with my man. And then, you see, I've got Kenneth with me. (Shut up, Kenneth!)" For Kenneth, his fair skin showing his sudden discomfort, was interrupting in signs and under-tones.

"Well, but bring him! There's plenty of room. Is he there? Let me speak to him."

A pause.

"I'd better come down later, Mother. I really think it would be better. (Kenneth, be quiet!)"

But the telephone conversation seemed to have dispersed Kenneth's strange, petulant, master-mistress mood. He was once more the Kenneth whom Richard was so lucky to have found and who, of course, must find Richard rather a trial, but managed him wonderfully.

This normal, hearty, public Kenneth Bruce here snatched the receiver from Richard with one hand while he fended off attack with the other, as he spoke irresistibly into the telephone.

"No, no, that's all wrong, Mrs. Broome. Good evening, Mrs. Broome. This is Kenneth Bruce speaking. Yes. No, but we talked over the telephone once ages ago. Imagine your remembering! But look here, Mrs. Broome, really it's all nonsense about Richard not coming. He's got a crazy notion—(Be quiet, Dickon!) he's trying to get hold of the receiver, Mrs. Broome—(Shut up!) No, honestly, it's sweet of you, but I really ought to go straight up and see to things. It's frightfully kind of you, but——"

Here Richard wrenched the receiver out of his hand.

"Hullo! Is that you, darling? Now listen!"

"No, my dearest child, you listen!" Elinor would no longer be over-ruled. "Of course you'll both come. Why shouldn't you? I've always so much wanted to meet your Kenneth. I shall drive down directly the show's over. I may even be there before you."

"But listen, Mother——"

"My dear, I must fly. It's my call. I shall see you both tonight then!"

The telephone went dead.

Richard jammed down the receiver and turned blackly.

"I'd rather you didn't interfere another time with my private calls."

Kenneth, perfectly restored in temper, grinned disarmingly.

"Well, I know I shouldn't have. But I put you in a hole, so I had to get you out of it. Of course I'm not coming, Dickon. And of course you're going. And of course I was—impossible. There! That's handsome!"

With touching eagerness to be gone, the anger died out of Richard's face.

"You see, she'll be so horribly disappointed," began Richard instantly, intimately: and his companion nodded understanding.

"That's why. You've just got to go, I tell you."

"I suppose I ought to." Richard wavered. "I know I ought to. Besides, I want to. But after all, why shouldn't you come too? I know she meant it. I know Mother. I know she'd like it. Yes, Kenneth, you shall come."

"Well, that's your affair entirely, of course," said Kenneth.

"Will you come, Ken?"

"I'd like to if I shan't be in the way. If you want me——"

"Want you! You were jealous, weren't you? Wasn't that it? Wasn't that all there was to it?"

"Yes, I was jealous." But Kenneth smiled comfortably, almost in amusement, at Richard's searching look. "I'd better order out the car," said Kenneth severely.

But as he passed the sofa Richard's long arm shot out and caught him by the shoulder, and he turned willingly.

"So now that you know what it feels like—" Richard challenged on a dark flash—"how do you like it?"

"What?" said Kenneth's look.

"Being jealous."

Said Kenneth with his disarming smile—

"Don't be silly! There was never anything. It's finished! Over!"

"It's never over," said Richard.

CHAPTER 59

EDMUND BROOME WATCHES TWO SHOWS

When Edmund stepped into his limousine he had a packet of papers clutched in his hand and his face was so black with rage that Hammond actually refrained from pointing out to him that they were already twenty minutes late and that the roads were greasy, but sped upon his business with a cautious recklessness, while he wondered what the bloody hell had gone wrong now? He was the more ready to soothe his master's mood because the car was a grand car. Yet it worried him, even as he enjoyed handling her, for he knew the symptoms. And Hammond was right—Edmund never committed an extravagance unless he was singularly worried in his mind. The more he lost, the more reckless he was apt to be in his buyings. There was no need at all for the new town car; but he had fancied her and bought her only a fortnight ago, and Hammond, for all his pride in her, wondered whether he had not better be looking about him. Things must be pretty bad with old Broome in a new suit and a new car! Nevertheless, she was a grand car, and he got her up to Oxford, not indeed in time for his master to dine, but in plenty of time for the performance.

Edmund roused himself from his papers and the incomprehensible, insolent letter from Wybird's people as they slowed down into Oxford: glanced at his watch, then directed Hammond to the Randolph. He had just time for a sherry and a biscuit. Hammond was not pleased when he got instructions to call for his master at the Town Hall as late as one o'clock. "I may be later, but you'd better be there."

Edmund went in, gulped his sherry, booked his room provisionally, went out. He knew his way to the theatre. He lumbered along Magdalen Street in such haste that he scarcely noticed the grand new cinema, though if he had been leisurely he would have stopped to stare and sneer, and hate it. But he was thinking that if he hurried he might have time to go round to wish the boy luck. What was the time? Seven minutes to . . . H'm—better not. He'd see John afterwards. Much best to slip in quietly.

But that, he found, was impossible. He had no sooner asked for his ticket, than he found himself received as one to whom honour is due, and his hat, his coat and himself taken in charge by an unknown but beautiful young man with a programme seller's sash who came up to him and said firmly—

"I think you must be John's father. Can I—— my name's Ronald Curtis——I think you wanted a seat at the side?"

It was true. He had bargained for a seat at the side, not knowing how much amateur acting he could stand at a stretch; but so much attention made him feel as if John had put him into a crêche for safety and that he would not be allowed out until John was ready to take him home. It was impressed upon him that John was a person of importance; but whether he himself was a person of importance as the father of John or as Edmund Broome, he could not tell. But he liked the young fellow, who got him a programme and told him where he might not smoke, and answered all his questions. For Edmund, deeming that here was one of John's friends, made himself delightful, and asked many more questions than he really wanted to ask for fear of appearing unfriendly. He was just a little relieved, in fact, when the boy left him with a warm promise to come back to him between each act, and he could settle back in his seat and look about him.

Instinctively, he began to count the small house. Not a vacant seat! That was natural, he supposed; but it was pretty damnable that you could always pack a house to see somebody who couldn't act, though the Glory Hole was paying half salaries, and even Hal Anderson on a hundred a week couldn't fill the Genista. The theatre was the preserve of the films and the amateurs nowadays. Richard, no doubt, was making thousands. But who cared for the real thing any more? How many of this eyrie of children that was now to cry out on the top of question, and would shortly be most tyrannically clapped for it, would take the trouble to go to the New Broom when they came to London? No, they'd go off to their revue or their musical comedy or go to see Richard eroticise on a screen for them! Do the boys carry it away? Ay, that they do! Hercules and his load too! But he wondered bitterly what this houseful of young men, all financed by their fathers, would do if they had to carry his load?

He shrank into himself, for the moment unnerved by the sense, smell, movement, voice of youth all about him. He had a sensation of being buried alive in youth. But as he began to heave himself up in his seat to get clear while he could, the saw of music ceased and Chorus came out.

> "Two households both alike in dignity,
> In fair Verona where we lay our scene
> From ancient grudge break to new mutiny."

The familiar words soothed Edmund like a glimpse of lamplight in a window of his own house. He settled back and composed himself to listen, and, if they all spoke as clearly and stood up as shy and straight as young Chorus, to be lulled.

And lulled he was, though the acting was much as he expected it to be, careful, earnest, dull. But he did enjoy the quality of the voices. Natural vigour could hold its own against training—for one week! And though he did not bother to follow the playing, the general effect was pleasant. But it was very hot in the theatre, and he had had a long drive and no supper. He did not exactly drop off to sleep, but he did not attend very sincerely, till he was roused by a line and a voice—

"Nay, gentle Romeo, we must have you dance——"

and came to attention with a jerk. What? John on already? Come now, let's have a look at the youngster!

And Edmund fumbled for his glasses and put them on and examined John with the utmost care and beamed as he realised that the boy was not only looking very well but playing excellently. Oh, he had the knack of it! He was playing as Stephen had played in the very same part; but he was lighter, airier, slenderer. Admittedly he was not near so handsome as the Spanish-eyed Romeo, who was traditionally romantic and very good indeed, though not quite experienced enough to carry his own swagger. But he had his own looks, had John! The black and silver clothes suited him: so did the colourless make-up. Edmund could not take his eyes off John, flitting as coolly through his Mab speech as a fish through water. Why, the boy had wit! He knew what he was doing, and what his author was doing. How delicately he contrived to be unromantical, modern, gay and voluble, and yet keep his hand on his heart as if he held the two sides of a wound together with his long Veronese fingers. Fanciful—but no doubt it was the modern view of Mercutio. These moderns identified Mercutio with Shakespeare himself—he had heard Richard hold forth on that notion once. That was where John had got the idea, no doubt. A good thing that Richard had cleared out when he did with his unsettling notions. Not a good influence for John. But the reading was clever—and what bright eyes the boy had.

There, the speech is over, and though Romeo is a promising young actor and must be noted, the pleasure of the scene, of course, is over too.

And when John's excited laughter, his stream of mocking maddening verbalities had ended chokingly on the remote and bitter cry, "A plague o' both your houses. Your houses!" when John's twisted face, all Wybird now, a long, white boy's face with agonising eyes, and the Broome laughter fled from it for ever, swayed out, propped between two other palpable boys, then the play was over for Edmund. Regardless of the fact that he was a guest of honour and John's father and that his exit would be noted, he got up and went out upstairs and across the foyer to the street.

He was pleased, he was agitated, he was shaken. He had not known that his son had it in him. He had never thought of John as doing anything in particular, except be about when his father wanted him, and, of course, go on the stage in due time; because all the Broomes went on the stage. But now he had found himself moved by an utterly unexpected display. The boy seemed actually to feel and suffer. Why, you could have heard a pin drop! If John could do that at twenty, what was John? Something out of the common, surely!

He turned the corner of George Street, and walked on blindly, his thoughts completely occupied by his last sight of John, his hand at his breast and his face twisted in rebellion against the sensation of pain. He was to have a son to be proud of at last then? Little John was to make his mark in the world, and Edmund would live to see a new Broome name on the hoardings. He looked up, blinking in the light of the cinema, and saw another Broome name on other hoardings.

He was staring into the naked shallow forehall of the picture house that he had passed on his way from the Randolph. The programme was posted up on easels, and on other easels there were coloured photographs of his own son, life-sized varnished photographs of Richard's popularised face. Oh, there was no mistake, the name was everywhere —Broome, Broome, Richard Broome—in every type of lettering. And when, on a strange, dry-throated impulse he first peered and then pushed through one of the swing doors into the inner hall with the booking-office on the right, opposite hung yet another oleograph of his son.

"Shan't say I'm not fair," muttered Edmund savagely to the oleograph. Then, turning to the grille, he fumbled in his pocket a moment, then slammed down a note.

"Best seat you've got!"

A machine clanged and a strip of ticket was obtruded. He took the alien voucher with distaste and marched on, through the mirror-lined café and up the stairs, along the covered passage that burrowed through the circle and emerged half way down. A girl with a torch caught him, and he followed her mechanically to his seat, his eyes already glued to the screen.

Edmund knew nothing of film technique. Though he talked a great deal about the films, and on every occasion thrust his hatred for them into the limelight, the truth was he had seen but half a dozen pictures in his life. He knew so little of the business that the mere attempt to read the captions regularly delayed him in following the plot, and in ten minutes he was in a fever of irritation, because he could not make out what it was all about. Also the silence of the presentation curiously oppressed him, though he found a certain pleasure in the open-air scenes. He said to himself with a sigh—"Of course the theatre can't attempt this sort of thing," as a girl in a sunbonnet came swaying and fluttering down a swaying fluttering noiseless garden. But it was all very un-English: the bamboos, the gleaming white porch of an unreal-looking house and the intense sweetness, the arch looks, the bloom and the arts of the actress in the sunbonnet bored him. He fidgeted throughout the love-scenes, and turned in his seat to stare and rejoice when two or three groups began to catcall and whistle. His own gallery gods slept not then!

But, except for the undergraduates how intent the audience was, and how tense. It was doing more than half the work. Or was it? Two seats away a boy and girl sat huddled together and, as he glanced at them, the girl pulled off her hat and dropped her head on the boy's shoulder. There was an intimacy, an innocence about the gesture that immensely affronted him. They might have been with sanction in bed together. And yet they were both watching the screen.

Aha! Richard at last!

But that can't be Richard? Richard was a boy, for all his four years' fighting. This black and white shadow, showing his teeth in a laugh, represents a man who knows his worth and his strength and is quite aware that it is his shadow, not himself, which holds his cheap audience. The old ring-master conceded, not without some pride, that the boy did know how to use his whip. Now, in one of the old plays that *was* a play, a Bernstein or a Sardou, how Edmund could have used him! D'Artagnan, now there's an idea! Revive the *Three Musketeers* at the Glory Hole with Richard as D'Artagnan. But before anything could be done about it, comes this cursed fuss over Alys, and off goes Richard to sell himself and the Broome name. Yes, that's what the young devil was doing. He wasn't just prostituting himself: he was auctioning the name. Watch him at it now, and using all the family tricks too, the Governor's tricks, old Uncle Russel's tricks, tricks of laugh and look and beckon. Yes, here was an Americanised version of the Broome charm, blatant, mechanised, reconstructed. Worst of all, thought Edmund, with a discomforting flash of insight, the young Judas didn't even enjoy what he was doing. He was bitter about it and sold his bitterness, too, as an added charm.

> 'Dickon, Dickon, cats and mice,
> Crook your finger——'

Lord, he hadn't heard that since he was a baby.

Edmund wished uncomfortably that the boy didn't look so mature and unhappy. He had never dreamed of course that Richard looked twice at Alys. Surely anyone could see what the girl was, clear enough? But if the little devil had really turned the boy's head he could understand it if Richard had a grievance. He wished he could explain to Richard—what was he doing now? Oh, good boy!

And Edmund suddenly found himself clutching his seat in quite uncontrollable excitement as Richard Broome, riding a fine horse, appeared on the crest of a hillside nearly as steep as Cleopatra's Needle and proceeded to precipitate himself down it, reaching the bottom in safety to escape down another of the quivering, leafy, noiseless drives, while a dozen riders came to grief fifty yards behind him. What Richard was doing on horseback with a woman across his saddle at this stage of the story was beyond Edmund's comprehension, but it clearly didn't matter what the story was about. It was plain that the story was a mere vehicle for Richard. And no wonder they exploited him. You couldn't get away from it, the boy had that priceless gift of personality for which Edmund himself would always pay a hundred a week and think cheap at the price. Why, on the stage, properly handled, properly directed, he'd have every woman in the pit half mad. What possessed Richard to throw himself away on this muck when he was a Broome and could act, and had a father in the profession only too ready and willing to make all easy? Why, if he and Richard chose to pull together, with young John coming on and Elinor——

'You needn't work it up for me, Father!' . . . 'Good-bye, Edmund . . .'

Ah, he was a sentimental fool to let himself dream when they were all, all against him. Henry had got himself killed: Geoffrey had cheated him and lied to him: Richard hated him: Elinor had left him. He'd spent his life planning for his children, toiling, saving for them, and always putting them first. And when they had got all they could out of him, they just said—'Thank you! We can't put up with you!'—left him—and took Elinor with 'em. Everybody left him, public, money, wife, sons, and he couldn't do a thing to stop it. He didn't want it to happen, but it happened, and he couldn't do a thing, not a thing.

Edmund, choking with self-pity, beat his fist on the velvet elbow of his seat at the thought, and, as he did so, his son's face swelled out at him in a close-up. Shadow and substance stared into each other's eyes, and the shadow narrowed its eyes at the substance, laughed, and disappeared again.

This was nightmare! Edmund rose, blundering heavily over knees and feet, and stumbled out of that devil's peep-show into the five-hundred-year-old street and stood blinking miserably at the calm church opposite him, a dignity of stone with dark blue night behind it.

Well, he must go back to the boy's show. He looked at his watch under a lamp. Indeed, it must be very near the end. He hurried on and broke into a lumbering run as he neared the theatre. John would be slighted if he weren't there for the end. Mustn't upset John. John was the only son he'd got left.

He slipped into his seat as Juliet died, and sat very quietly, regaining breath and contentment through the familiar, unfamiliar scenes which followed the final dropping of the curtain. The audience letting air out of its lungs, the groups of friends energetic when the applause slackened but resting from their labours when they had worked it up again, the company call, the delivery of bouquets to the actresses—all this was familiar. But the President's speech was a new thing in stage effects: so was the series of figures in evening dress which he summoned forth to walk or shamble or bolt across the stage. And when the audience, not content with the President's speech and the producer's speech, appeared bent on getting a speech out of every member of the company also, Edmund quailed.

" 'What, will the line stretch out to the crack of doom?' " he chuckled to the faithful Mr. Curtis who materialised at his elbow soon after Romeo's speech of thanks: but was soothed by—

"It'll be 'God save the King' in a minute."

And the audience being by this time extremely languid, 'God save the King' it was. After which Edmund found himself skilfully run out before the press became impassable.

"Where do we go now?"

"To the Club, sir, just across the road."

And then he was piloted into a doorway between a picture shop and an ironmonger's. It was a dark entry with an air of having had packing cases opened in it, and smelt mildly of dust, damp, straw and cookery. Edmund blundered up the uncarpeted stair, reached the landing and at once headed with his usual decision for the half-open door on his left.

"No, that's the dining-room. No, not there either, sir! That's kept for the ladies in the cast. Here you are!" And the hard-working Mr. Curtis was at last allowed to shepherd Edmund between coat pegs and umbrella stand into the Clubroom itself.

Edmund refused an arm-chair, but, established on the hearth-rug with his back to the over-mantel and his coat-tails as near the fire itself as the fender-seat allowed, looked about him benevolently.

"I see—and you all gather here. But—we don't dine in the other room, eh?—because I told my chauffeur——"

"Oh no, in the Town Hall. That's right. John will be over in a minute to fetch you. He said I was to tell you. But of course he'll be kept till the last. I say, sir, can't I order you a drink?"

Edmund left alone continued to look about him. The white-walled room was already beginning to fill and grow stuffy, as heat, cigarette smoke and the occasional cigar overpowered the brisk day-time odour of furniture polish. The steady influx of men in dinner-jackets drove the first comers round the walls of the cloak-room on which the notice-board hung, towards the closed folding-doors which cut the main room in half. Corner seat, raised window-seats, and all settees were occupied: so were the arm-chairs and the sofa against the wall. But though the room was filling fast John did not appear, and Edmund began, after the manner of stranded visitors, to perambulate the walls, examining with real pleasure, because he himself possessed a copy, the Reynolds engraving of Kean, and feigning, after he had tired of the prints on the right of the fireplace, a deep interest in the frames on its left. Each held an assortment of small photographs, former casts with officials in the bottom row, players above, and each photograph neatly labelled.

He had exhausted the fascinations of the *Bourgeois Gentilhomme* company, had glanced at *The Pretenders,* and was considering a diagonal cut across the room towards the *Rhesus* frame, when Ronald Curtis returned with renewed devotion, followed by a waiter and a whiskey and soda.

"Come up into the window, sir! You can see the room better.

Mind the step up. Yes, it's getting full, isn't it? Nearly everyone's here. John ought to be over any minute now."

Edmund, thankful for his drink, nodded affably.

"That's all right. I like watching. That's the Romeo, isn't it, just come in? Very sound performance. What's his name?"

"Allenbury. Guy Allenbury. Yes, he was pretty good, wasn't he? Would you like——? I mean, I expect he'd like—I say, Guy, can I introduce——"

Edmund soon had a group round him and began to enjoy himself. Then John slipped in, as usual so quietly, and made his way to Edmund silhouetted against the bright blue window curtains. He was welcomed graciously.

"Very excellent performance, John! Excellent production. Your women, I thought, were particularly good. Very well chosen. I was surprised how well they blended. Because as a rule, you know, my boy, I don't consider that it's wise to mix two types of performance. As I was saying, the professional actress has her technique and her experience and it's not easy to disguise. But I realised tonight that you young men, you've got something of your own, too, there's no doubt of that. There's something about your voices——"

"I'm frightfully glad you liked it, Father. I did think it went quite well myself."

"That's what I'm saying. Astonishingly well. Not that I quite agree, my boy, with your reading of the quarrel scene. I remember, when I played it—poor Tom Heriot was the Romeo—I handled it more soldierly on the whole. 'I will not budge for no man's pleasure, I——' "

The noise made by some two hundred voices was nearly as dense as the atmosphere itself. It had breadth, height, and thickness. Nevertheless Edmund's voice, trained to fill the Glory Hole, trumpeted through it, and several people turned round as he continued, instinctively gathering in glances—

"And then, there's that later line——"

"Yes, I know, Father, I know," said John hurriedly. "I say, Father, where did they put your coat? Because we ought to be going in a minute."

But it was a long and much interrupted minute, and Edmund's eye followed his son with surprise and amusement. The full room got much fuller and Edmund began to feel extremely hungry before John and John's party surrounded him and carried him on with them to the Town Hall.

There Edmund found himself placed at the top table between the Nurse, old Lena Marlborough, who was on the President's right, and a young man rather older than John who said he belonged to the same college. He had been the Friar, he told Edmund; but did not seem much interested to learn that Edmund failed to recognise him. Indeed he appeared to take very little interest at all in *Romeo and Juliet* but was exact and passionate about *Cyrano,* which, he told Edmund, was the sort of play that the O.U.D.S. ought to be reviving if they had a scrap of enterprise, and was Dean ever in this world going to put on *Hassan,* did Mr. Broome suppose?

Just then John, at the other end of the table, leaned forward to catch his father's eye, and nodded and smiled, which comforted Edmund immensely. And then John caught the eye of Edmund's neighbour, whereupon the neighbour smiled for the first time and afterwards said something really shrewd to Edmund about John's performance, and Edmund's prejudice began to melt. Nevertheless he was thankful for the company of old Lena Marlborough, a woman of his own school who had played under his mother in her young days and knew all about Edmund. She agreed with all he said to her about the decay of public taste, but owned that she herself was thankful to eke out her salary with film work. But still, that didn't alter the principle. He was going to speak tonight, wasn't he? Why didn't he say something about it? Weren't the toys amusing?

"What toys?"

She directed his attention to the pile in front of her, and he then perceived that nearly everybody in the cast had a similar pile of absurdities, threepenny trifles, toy animals, toy furniture, mascots, babies in baths, bottles, and even less delicate objects, each attached to a label at least a yard long and 'wide as a church door', as Edmund said with a chuckle to the young man next to him, who retorted that it was all very silly and childish of course, and rather reluctantly allowed some of his own labels to be inspected, inscribed as they were with improbable and surprising quotations from the play.

Edmund observed also that the size of the piles of toys varied. His acquaintance had a dozen: the Nurse fifteen or so: lovely Juliet more than she could do with: and Romeo, John and one or two personalities at the other tables were snowed under by the immense labels which must really, observed Edmund laughing to his neighbour, have cost more than the toys.

"Oh quite!" responded the neighbour.

But at any rate, thought Edmund, counting rapidly, John's pile was bigger than anyone else's. That pleased him immensely: and when it was time for his own speech he got up happily. He told them how well they had played and gave them an anecdote or two about Irving, and, encouraged by a look at John, warmed up into a violent denunciation of the cinema habit and an appeal to all of them, feeling as they did about Shakespeare (for they had proved that night how they felt about Shakespeare!), to do their best to make the English theatre what it had once been and might so easily be again.

"I think that got home," he confided to Lena Marlborough under cover of the clapping, and turned to receive with much pleasure the murmurings of the young man on his right. But when he looked about him again Lena was talking to the President. He yawned shame-facedly. Now that his own speech was over the glow was dying out of the evening. Juliet was on her pretty legs; but he hated listening to women speakers.

He found himself wondering what the letter from Wybird's people really meant and whether he'd be able to get back to town that night, but roused himself again to listen to John's speech, which revealed to him a new and entirely unintelligible John. All he appeared to do, as far as his father could make out, was to stand up, looking extremely shy, and begin rather trite sentences which nobody let him finish. The quarter sentences and the gales of laughter seemed to go on for hours. John sat down at last, pinkly, and hid himself behind his toys while the young man on Edmund's left murmured resignedly—

"Of course, it's not fair!"

Edmund had not understood a word, either of the speech or the comment, but he gathered that a compliment was intended and laughed in flattered agreement: and as he listened to the storm of applause he suddenly realised that for the first time in his life he was perfectly happy, blessedly happy, blissfully happy.

Listen to 'em! Look at John! Look at the pile of toys in front of him! That showed, eh? But he wished that he himself were in it all a little more. He sat fiddling with one of the labels that had come loose and passionately wished that he could show John publicly how proud he was of him. He ought to have mentioned John in his speech, of course, but he had a feeling that John might not like it. But suppose he—Wait a bit! Yes, that was a notion! That would do! He turned to his steadily mellowing neighbour.

"How much longer do we go on?" asked Edmund.

"Hours," said the neighbour with an air of exhaustion which seemed to Edmund not perfectly genuine.

Edmund looked at his watch.

"Well, er—look here—would it matter if I slipped away for a minute? Got to give my chauffeur instructions. Don't want to keep him hanging about."

The neighbour half rose.

"No, of course not, sir! I'll come with you, shall I?" and cast a look about him. But Edmund's hand, which still abstractedly fingered a torn label, pressed him back into his seat.

"That's all right. Don't you move. There's that friend of John's by the door. He'll look after me." And with a word to the President as he passed his chair, Edmund, less conscious than his son of the notice he was attracting, worked along, encountering and circumventing chair-backs, till he reached the end of the long table. At a touch on the shoulder his programme seller—John's friend—what was the lad's name?—jumped up eloquently and went out with him, while Edmund's late neighbour gazed with faint perplexity upon their conjunction.

Yet another speech was just ending as Edmund came back. He settled into his seat again with an extremely satisfied air and continued to enjoy himself so thoroughly that he won a friend or two at the top of the next table. There was a talk across the glasses about London and Edmund's latest play, and he had another glass of port and would have had another after that had not everybody just then begun to make a move.

John came for him at once, but so many other people came for John that the room was nearly empty before their group began to move down the room and so out to the landing railings and the stairway.

"You coming on with us, Father?" said John.

"I don't think so, my boy."

"Do come, sir," said Romeo. "It's a squash, but it'll amuse you."

"Yes, come along, Father," said John affectionately.

But Edmund, far too much of an artist to spoil a planned curtain, was firm in refusal as they went down the broad staircase and turned down the passage to the cloak-rooms.

"I like that friend of yours," said Edmund approvingly to John as he helped him into his coat. "Nice intelligent boy. You'd better ask him down, hadn't you, next vac?"

"Do you mean Charles, Father? The man next to you at dinner?"

"No, no, that nice fellow—what's his name?—Curtis. He looked after me all the evening."

"What? Ronnie?" John was amused. "No, Father, I don't think so."

"Why not? Nice young fellow."

"Yes, Father, I know. He's very decorative. But if I asked him I'd have to ask so many. I want to ask Charles, though, sometime." Then, as they emerged on the Town Hall steps—"Have you got your car there, sir?"

"Oh yes," said Edmund, heavily demure as he descended. Then he stood aside, beaming, to watch his son's face.

And indeed John's face was worth watching as he took in the glories of the new Rolls with the grinning Hammond at the wheel, and, tied to the door, a label—'wide as a church door.'

John stepped up to the label, examined it, glanced up at his father. Then John began to blush—face, neck, ears, forehead, hands, and continued to blush as the crowd on the steps charged down upon them.

Edmund could hold his tongue no longer.

"Like it, John?"

Because, for an absurd instant, it had seemed as if John were almost too surprised to be pleased. But at his father's question he burst into exquisitely reassuring activity.

"Oh, but look here," cried John in a high excited voice and with a great deal of gesticulation—"I say, you people, look at my toy! Isn't it too marvellous? I mean, look at it! Father, you really are—— I say, do look at it!"

"Read what's written," commanded Edmund proudly.

The neighbour thrust his arm through John's and read aloud over John's shoulder, so pleasantly—

" 'You ratcatcher, will you walk?' "   And everybody, after an instant's hesitation, saw the joke and laughed eagerly.

"No, but Father——" John continued to protest.

"That's all right, my boy! It's yours. Bundle in! Come round and see me in the morning!" And Edmund lumbered off.

Well, it was worth working hard all your life to be able to give your own son such a pleasure! He paused at the corner, pretending to light a cigarette, and watched the group disputing as to who should ride in his present to John. Most of them got in and the car slid off up St. Aldates. But that nice young fellow who had looked after him strolled off with another friend. They were just behind him when he reached the Randolph. He nodded to them paternally as they passed him: then, well satisfied, turned in.

Said the nice young fellow to his companion as they walked on—

"God, what a present!" He sighed in a luxury of good-natured envy. "Did you see John's face? Wasn't he charmed? Did you see how red he got?"

But the friend grunted—

"You went out with the old boy. Why didn't you stop him?"

"Stop him? Why?"

"I should have thought you'd know that John would simply hate it."

"He wouldn't! He didn't! Did he?"

"Well, of course he did, you goop! In front of everyone—a great town car that he can't ever use, with the De la Mare label stuck on it. Having to call it a toy! Can't you see how he felt? I felt hot all over."

"I say—does—will John think I ought to have stopped it?"

"I don't know what John thinks. But I should say you've put your foot in it all right," said the friend. "Up to the neck!" he added with conviction.

CHAPTER 60

TAKEN IN EXECUTION

EDMUND spent the Sunday with John, who would not hear of letting him go off by the early train. John drove the car and Edmund sat beside him. Edmund enjoyed himself thoroughly, and had a half impulse to tell John about his business troubles; but it was such a relief to put them utterly out of his mind. Let the dogs lie. Besides, it did strike Edmund that John would enjoy the car less heartily if he knew.

But when Edmund got back to town that evening he slept badly, and on Monday his troubles began. For the ambiguous letter from the Wybird people meant that he could get no definite word from them about the renewal of the lease. They shilly-shallied and they put him off, and when at last with some difficulty he got their principal man to meet him, then the truth came out. They had had a better offer. They did not propose to renew.

"A better offer?" How dared they have a better offer and give him no opportunity to cap it. Was that decent, courteous business dealing? What were they thinking about? Let him know what offer had been made, and they would soon see whether or no he was prepared to cap it! Good God, he had been a lessee for thirty years! Edmund, in the right, and with his temper in full blast, could intimidate most men, and the end of it was that an appointment was made with Wybird's people.

"I believe Mr. Wybird himself will be up on Friday, sir, or at any rate Mr. Philip. I'll telephone through for instructions, and confirm."

Edmund was left raging. Had he not paid his rent on the nail, these thirty years? Had he not improved the Gloriana out of all knowledge? If it was fifteen times as valuable today, whose doing was it? Of course it was some mismanagement of the underlings. Old Wybird was all but a sleeping partner, and Philip, only just back from America, was a nincompoop, as he had heard. He had never met him. Well, he would meet him and teach him what courtesy and decent business give and take meant.

Nevertheless Edmund was no fool, and he began to be afraid, bitterly afraid that he was going to lose the Glory Hole. He wasn't a millionaire: he was prepared for an immense rise in rent, but—but there was a limit.

Suppose they wouldn't let him have the Glory Hole at his final price? Where would he be then, with his principals engaged already, and all his other huge commitments? You couldn't get the sort of show that he was planning ready in three weeks. Where else in London could he find a home? No management was going to step out of its quarters because he'd been a fool and bitten off more than he could chew. He'd be stranded. Oh, well, he could wriggle out of his commitments. It would cost him a fortune, and he'd make a fool of himself, but at any rate, if the worst came to the worst——

Deliberately he wiped the Glory Hole and his schemes temporarily out of his mind and asked himself what other irons he could put into the fire to warm. He was not popular; he had been realising that lately. He had long since lost his reputation as a luck-bringer. But someone must be found to go in with him. What about the Genista? The Genista would be free next September. He and John at the Genista, launching a new policy—now there was a notion! Young blood, young blood! Impulsively he sat down and wrote to John, and sent the letter off, expressed. The action soothed him for an hour; but then he began to brood again. Where could he get money? Elinor of course would come up to the scratch, at a word, he knew that. But no! Confess to Elinor that he had overshot his mark? Not he! Besides, he was letting himself be stampeded. He flattered himself that once he got in touch with young Wybird, it would be easy to adjust the situation. Good God, he'd been at the Glory Hole thirty years! A boy like Wybird hadn't much to teach him.

But when he came to his appointment on the Friday afternoon, early, because young Wybird was going down to Blandon with his partner for the weekend, and was shown into the large, formal office, there sat, not only young Philip Wybird, but old Lewis himself. Lewis must be seventy-five if he were a day, but he did not look more than an upright, biscuity sixty-eight, with his high collar propping up his long chin, his shoulders square, and his figure stayed into rigidity. They had not spoken for eight years, though Lewis had never cut him, always nodded at first nights. Yes, it was just eight years ago that Lewis had come up to him at the Garrick to condole with him on the loss of Henry.

Lewis greeted him now just as he greeted everybody, primly and formally, making Edmund, though he was a man of fifty, feel young and unlicked. Odd, the effect Lewis always had on him! He shook off the feeling angrily, and Lewis's quick eyes noted the gesture, ere they travelled on in an imperceptible glance at his son.

Edmund got down to business at once, and spread out the whole situation for them. He felt that he was unusually eloquent and that they listened with interest. But when he had quite finished, young Wybird, with a look at his father, said that he was terribly sorry but he didn't know at all what could be done. It wasn't exactly the question of another offer. Mr. Broome had misunderstood his representative. Of course there had been other offers——

"Which I'll cap," interposed Edmund.

Yes, but they weren't at all sure, he himself wasn't at all sure that he wanted to re-let the Gloriana. He and his partner had some notion of running the place themselves.

"Perhaps you would like to meet my son's partner?" whispered old Lewis Wybird, and touched a bell. "Wouldn't it be more satisfactory, Philip?"

"No doubt, no doubt. But do I understand——" the big heave of Edmund's shoulder shut out doddering Lewis Wybird—"that you yourself are taking over the Glory Hole? I understood you were in the film business?"

"Exactly," said young Wybird. "I'm considering—we have been considering plans for turning it into a picture house——"

"The Gloriana? Are you mad? You couldn't do such a thing. Your father wouldn't allow it. It couldn't be done. The family theatre! It's been the Broome theatre this hundred years! Wybird, you couldn't allow it?"

Lewis Wybird shrugged his shoulders.

"It's no good appealing to me, my dear Broome. I've turned it over to my son there. It's for him and his partner to decide."

"Who is your partner?" thundered Edmund, the louder because of the sudden meaningless check and pound of his heart. "Let me see him. I'll talk to him!"

"In a minute," smiled Lewis Wybird, and as he spoke Richard came in.

And then they'd been charming to him. That was what he remembered clearest, as he sat alone in his library on the Friday night. He might have been a pet rabbit. They'd set a filthy trap for him and caught his paw, and then when he had agonised long enough to please them they had very kindly and gently released his broken paw.

The insolence of their concern! They'd have got a doctor to him if he had let them. First they baited him till he lost all self-control—yes, he knew he had, though he'd promised Elinor—oh, but that was ages ago! Then they worked him up till he began to choke, and then they talked about a doctor. Let them leave him alone! He didn't want their offers and concern, and the rest of the hypocritical tomfoolery. He wanted to go home, and he knew his own way out, thank you! Couldn't he stumble on the step when he got outside if he chose, without Richard, that beast, his own son, coming running, and getting him a taxi and looking at him like that, and wanting to see him home? Christ—Richard! Richard, the ally of that crew!

"I say, Father, are you all right?"

"Drive on!" he had said to the taxi-man. "I'm paying for this taxi. I'm your fare. Drive on!" That's what he had said, and left Richard on the pavement staring after him with that damned nursemaid look on his face. And then Richard had rung up. He had dared! Edmund had answered him. "You're too soon, Richard. I'm alive still. And I shall stay alive long enough to make you regret this little game of yours, my boy. Ring off!"

And after that he had not answered the telephone however much it rang. But he had had a good dinner and it had done him good. And now he felt heavy and sleepy, but so hot still were the cinders of his rage that he knew he should never sleep. But he did feel tired.

He had gone up to his room and changed into his dressing-gown, and then somehow it didn't seem worth while to come down again.

Thus Edmund, lying on his bed listening to the tick of the clock and his own red-hot thoughts going round and round in his heavy head. Of course he couldn't sleep. He knew he should never sleep sound till he punished his son. He had always been weak with Richard. Well now, there must be no more weakness. He must teach Richard his lesson. But how? And when? What was the time? Past eleven. He must have dozed without knowing. And that damned woman hadn't put the soda water in his room. How often had he told Elinor—no, no, of course!

He got up wearily, re-tied the cord of his dressing-gown and shuffled downstairs. As he crossed the hall he saw the evening letters lying on the table. Bills, bills, bills, catalogues, bills, bills—— A letter from John, a fat letter. Good boy!

He slipped the letter into his pocket, beaming, fetched himself his drink and wandered slowly upstairs again, for if he didn't go straight up he would fall asleep in his chair, and that meant a cold awakening. Dear boy! He patted his crackling pocket, reached his room, went in, shut his door, put down his glass by his bedside, then slipped off his dressing-gown.

There was no hurry. He did enjoy John's letters: one of his treats, a letter from John. The boy wrote as he talked: one could hear his voice.

He got heavily into bed, arranged his lamp to suit himself, picked up the letter from where it lay on the flat photograph-case, opened the envelope methodically with a paper-knife, put on his spectacles, pulled out the sheets, lay back luxuriously and began to read. Then he stiffened and shifted anxiously nearer to the light. What was it? What was the boy driving at?

'MY DEAREST FATHER,

'I've got so much to tell you important and exciting, that I hardly know where to begin. I can't believe that I only saw you a week ago. But first I must thank you most awfully for your letter. Of course it would be a perfectly heavenly scheme for us to be together—I mean, for me to run a show under you—and I'd adore it. Only I do wish I'd known about it before——'

What was this? What was this?

'——because, of course, as the Genista's been let two years now I thought you'd really lost interest, and it never occurred to me that there'd ever be a chance of anything at all like what you suggest.

'Well, Father, what has happened is this. Richard's been staying with me this last day or two, and he put up a scheme to me for using the Genista, that did seem most frightfully tempting and I've decided——'

So John had gone too. He might have known. John too.

He folded the paper with a shaking hand, and with the orderly instinct which all his life had served him so well, fumbled for the envelope. It slid from him over the silk eiderdown and glissaded to the floor. Mechanically he leaned over the edge of the mattress, dangling his arm after it, and at last he touched the paper with his fingers, but could not grasp it. It only slid forward from him under the valance. He leaned further out. A rage of anger at the thwarting filled his soul and beat in waves about his body. Still he could not get hold of it. He continued to stretch and claw and strain. . . .

CHAPTER 61

RICHARD AND JOHN

ELINOR'S two-seater, with Richard at the wheel, came slicking down the Marylebone Road, in and out of the ten o'clock traffic, and almost collided with John's great car already drawn up at the door of the Regent's Park house. John dashed out on to the steps as Richard got out and the two brothers caught at each other's hands as they exchanged first words.

"I came as quick as I could," said Richard. "I started within five minutes of your call, but the lanes are tricky coming from Blandon. When did you get here?"

"Half an hour ago. They got on to me before eight. I got through to you and came straight on."

"And——" Richard hesitated—"it's true?"

"Yes," said John. "He must have died round about midnight." His face began to work.

They moved into the dark hall and stood irresolute.

"Have you been up to him?" muttered Richard at last.

"No. I—not without you."

"Have you seen Cummins? How did it happen? Heart?"

"I suppose so. Cummins said it might have happened any time. They only found him when they went up with the tea. Cummins couldn't stay till I got here, but he's coming round to see us at twelve. I 'phoned through saying we'd be here."

"What about Mother?" said Richard.

"Well, I waited to ask you. It's the last show at Manchester. She can hardly get away tonight. Besides—what could she do? Shall I wire her, or shall we wait till I meet her tomorrow?"

"No, you'd better wire. No, I tell you what. Wire her to put through a trunk call at midday. One might sit hours at the telephone."

"And then miss her. Yes." John went to the telephone and took off the receiver, but his hand was shaking so much that he had to put it back again. He steadied himself against the radiator as he turned to his brother—"Can you realise it, Richard? Father's dead."

"Yes."

"Dead." John's eyes asked for contact of some sort—glance, gesture, touch; but Richard kept his eyes lowered as he said—

695

"I'm going up to him. Coming?"

John shrank.

"Ought I to? Richard, I can't. Not now."

"All right. You get the wire sent."

And Richard went upstairs alone, into the stately bedroom, straight up to the bed, and stood there looking down at his father.

He was well enough accustomed to the look of violent death, but the look of civil death was new to him, and some of the forgotten church-yard awe of childhood settled upon his spirit as he stared. It was not the dead body that made him quail, but its surroundings—the yielding textiles, the brilliant dyes, slick woods, bright metals, glass, cane, ivory, oils, essences and waters, and the warm, breathed air of the room. The transmutation of living-room into death-chamber was unnatural and flippant. He was curiously distressed by it, though he felt no actual grief for the actual dead. His antipathy against his father was too explicit and his wrongs too recent for any such sentimental pretence. And yet, emotional as he was implacable, he did grieve, not for Edmund, not for himself, but for the waste of a relationship.

'If he had been fond of me we might have had good times together,' thought Richard, looking down upon his father, and deliberately choosing timid words to clothe his dismay and passionate regret. And the cold flesh prostrate on the bed could not, nor no longer desired to explain itself to the warm, kindred flesh which it had injured and adored.

He turned away at last and as he turned his eye was caught by the little heap of trifles on the night-table. The heavy gold watch and chain brought back childhood and his father's loving face and voice— "Blow! Blow hard!" Open springs the lid and his father chuckles.

'O God, don't!' cried Richard to his soul in the silence, and fumbled unsteadily with the litter on the night-table: slit envelopes, a little pile of money, and a leather photograph case—

John had finished his telephoning and was standing on the steps, shivering in the light March wind but too miserable to get an overcoat, too miserable to do anything but wish his father weren't dead, when he felt his brother's hand on his arm.

"Let's get out of this," said Richard. "I want some air."

"I'll get my hat."

"Damn your hat! Come on!"

And they went off together down the drive, out of the garden, along the sweep of the Park, and cut into the Marylebone Road, walking aimlessly along it without a word exchanged, till they found themselves at last jostling the passers-by in the traffic at the Euston end of the Tottenham Court Road. Said John suddenly—

"Richard, I've got to have a drink."

"Well, you can't get one," said Richard out of his dark cloud.

"Well then, I've got to have some coffee. I didn't have any breakfast."

"Nor I. Yes, we'd better get something. Where do you want to go?"

"Anywhere. I don't care."

"Do you think I do?"

"Well, we won't go anywhere then. I can manage."

"Oh, shut up! Where?" said Richard irritably, but concerned for John.

"I really don't mind." John's gentle smile was eloquent of his determination to transfer to his brother the burden of decision: and they walked on for a few minutes in deep depression.

"What about my club?" said Richard at last, heavily.

"All right!"

"Very well, we'll go there. That is, if you're yearning to talk to people?"

"Of course I'm not!" The usually sweet-tempered John answered so angrily that his brother shot a look at him, and then said affectionately—

"John, do you really want something?"

"Yes, I do. I feel rotten."

"Well, where do you want to go?"

"I don't care in the least where we go."

"Then let's go in here!" And Richard paused doubtfully in front of a steaming eating-house.

John, after one look, changed his mind.

"Oh, not there! Let's walk on a bit."

And because the two brothers understood each other's round-about way of expressing disturbance, distress, grief, Richard made no irritable protest, but instead took his brother by the arm a little above the elbow and walked him forward. John's strained face relaxed at the touch.

"I mean—may as well put in time," he elaborated gratefully.

"Yes." Richard, too, was resolutely businesslike. "Can't do anything till I see Cummins. By the way, you'd better talk to Mother on the 'phone, I think."

"Had I?"

"I think so. She'll hear it better from you."

"All right."

But John's face whitened and his eyes and lips began silently to rehearse that conversation, till his brother paused again, this time before a Lyons tea-shop. Then the natural John came back with a rush.

"We can't go in there!" ejaculated John reproachfully.

"Why not?"

"Well——"

"Well?"

"Oh well, if you want to!" said John resignedly.

"Want to?" Richard in turn jetted up a flare of irritation. "What does it matter? I don't care what we do. Go in there or take a taxi to the Ritz—I don't care as long as we don't stand shilly-shallying."

"All right, all right!" And, recovered, deeply affectionate and entirely in touch with his brother's mood, John took charge in turn and, a slim Cortes, pulled open the door and entered that practically unknown world. Richard followed sullenly and they sat down at one of the coffee-stained, marble-topped tables. The floors were still wet and a kneeling charwoman flapped a flannel to and fro under the stacked chairs. They ordered some sort of a meal, drank coffee, ate drearily, but felt the better for it. A cat came along and John fed it with bits of toast and Richard wished he wouldn't: and at last, wild with irritation, said so.

"Do leave the beast alone, John!"

John looked into his brother's face, dark against the background of glass window and spring daylight.

"Sorry," said John, and shoved the eager creature gently away with his foot. "Shall we go? Have you done?"

"Yes." But Richard leaned his head on his hand and made no movement to go. Said John, for the sake of something to say—

"What's going to happen now, Richard?"

"God knows! Everything'll have to be wound up. And I suspect it'll be a messy business. His affairs must be pretty involved."

"Oh no, they aren't," said John. "He only bought the Rolls a week ago."

"That proves nothing. I think we shall find that he was hard hit, John."

"How do you know?"

"I don't. But I guess. I can't go into it now." His voice flagged. John looked at him anxiously but with a resolute eye. For the food had done John good, and though he was pretty unhappy, of course, about Father, he was feeling much more himself. And John's first object when he was himself was to be as comfortable and acceptable to Richard as Richard would allow him to be. John knew perfectly well that his elder brother was suffering violently in a tortuous, underground way of his own, and he was awed, troubled and intrigued by the spectacle and longed to be in close, possessive touch with Richard and his emotion. Also he knew that if Richard was to begin that extremely important piece of filming tomorrow, he would need nursing, gentling, and keeping in heart today. So—

"Richard, d'you know you're looking ghastly? You ought to have had a drink instead of this mess. Look here, let's go down to your club now and I'll get you some brandy. You sit here while I get a taxi. I won't be a second."

"Oh, for God's sake, shut up!"

John shut up.

"I can't get his face out of my mind," said Richard at last.

"I've never seen anybody dead," said young John.

"I have." Richard laughed harshly. "That doesn't worry me. But I say, John——"

"Yes?"

"Have a look at this." He felt in his coat pocket and pulled out a leather photograph case and pushed it across the table to his brother.

"Why, it's Henry," said John. Then, looking again—"No, it isn't. But it's awfully like him. Where did you get it?"

"In Father's room. By the bed."

"Who is it?"

"Yes, that's it. Who is it?"

John turned over the case and a cutting fell out, together with a snapshot of the same boy in uniform.

"It *is* Henry," John asserted once more.

"No, it isn't. It's signed 'Willie.' And look at this cutting—'Killed in action—William Marshall.'"

"Willie? Willie? . . . It must be that boy Father used to talk about. What on earth——I never thought he existed. I thought Father was telling me a tale. Then—then—? Why, Richard, he must be——"

"Yes."

"I wouldn't show that to Mother if I were you," said John, watching Richard put away the leather case.

"I shan't," said Richard, with that curious tenderness which always

came into his voice when he spoke of Elinor. He went on, still gently—
"But I wish I'd known."

"Why? What could you have done?"

"I don't know, John, exactly. But if I'd known Father was suffering from that sort of cancer I don't believe I'd have hated him so."

"Hate?"

"I loathed him."

"Well, I didn't," said John slowly.

"I can't help it." Richard was sullen. "He was different with you. You saw the other side of him. You see straight and I'm warped, I know that. But he—Alys—and he judged all of us—and he was so deadly old."

John's eyes, which had averted themselves in a sort of horror from his brother's distorted mind, were fixed on the movements of the street. A wind tore along it, blowing forward the skirts and scarves of the women, lifting paper and straw. A few doors away a gramophone shop was loosing two tunes at once on the public ear. At the other end of the cross street there was a glimpse of spring green, blue sky and scudding clouds.

"We shall have to wire to Ireland," he said absently, staring at the clouds. And then—"Can't you remember him young, Richard?"

"I can remember him in white flannels, once, when I was a tiny kid: I suppose he wasn't much older than Kenneth. And once in the garden in a hammock. He made me a buttercup chain. I can see his neat fingers—square tips. Good hands he had. O God, what's the use of talking?"

"Did you know—" pursued John, his eye on the clouds—"about his running away with Mother? Grandmama told me. He whipped her off half an hour before the wedding, she said."

"Wedding? Who to?"

"Lewis Wybird," said John, informative.

His brother stared at him, his mouth a little open.

"Are you inventing, John?" said Richard at last.

"Of course not. I could hardly believe it either. Oh, but I've heard heaps about the family. I could tell you stories about all the Broomes right back to Queen Anne."

Richard put his elbow on the table and leaned his head on his hand.

"I don't want to hear them. I've heard enough now to guess——"

"What?"

'Oh, leave it! Are we going on for ever, talk, talk, talk, about what we can't help? He's dead, but I'm filming tomorrow. John, have you made up your mind about the Genista?"

John shifted thankfully off his quick-sands.

"Yes. I wrote to Father definitely two days ago."

"What? What did you write?"

"Only that I was going in with you. Why? What's the matter now?"

"O my God, John!"

"What, Richard?"

"Don't you see what we've done?"

"What have we done?"

"I met Father yesterday on business: and old Lewis turned up. Philip and I couldn't think why. And then we turned down the offer for the Glory Hole. You know, we're going to run it as a cinema and we told the old man so—kicked him out, in fact. That's all. And then he gets your letter. Pretty, isn't it?"

Not a word from John. Richard at last looked up from the marble whose veins he was retracing with a stump of pencil, and questioned his brother with his eyes and the twist of his mouth. Still no answering look. Richard could not bear it.

"Isn't it?"

Then John's lip began to quiver and his eyes filled.

"My letter? But I didn't know, Richard!"

"You didn't think he'd be charmed, did you, at your going with me?"

"No, I didn't think he'd be charmed," said John with miserable honesty. "But, Richard, I'd got to do what I——"

"Wanted to do. Of course! You were perfectly justified. I was only—trying to get company. Don't worry. I killed him. You didn't."

"That's just hysteria," said John sharply, instantly roused, as he would always be throughout his life, to passionate defence of Richard, especially against Richard himself. "It wasn't either of us. It just happened. And what's more I'll tell you why it happened. It happened because Father was almost a great man. Oh, can't you see—" and John's face, fully exposed to the daylight, showed a bleak concentration of intelligence, bright and cold and inhuman as the brilliant March morning. "Don't you see—" said John, tussling with his thought and his brother—"that we oughtn't to be sorry for him at all? If he'd ended as we all thought he would—just another rich man dead—then yes! Job with everyone giving him a penny—I despise that end. But

Job on the dung-heap—that's greatness, Richard? That's worth writing about. You can't have greatness without a crash."

"Oh, talk, talk, talk!" said Richard wearily.

"Well, I write plays. 'The fall is the measure of the climb!' That's the theme which always attracts me. And Father has fallen so far that it makes one dizzy. D'you realise, Richard, that he'd just about lost everything—wife—children—honour—estate? O God, I wish I hadn't written that letter! You think that because I talk like this I wasn't fond of him. But I was. I didn't loathe him: I loved him: I liked him awfully: he was nice. Remember how he used to boast about the Broome tradition, and how he was stage-manager at sixteen, and made a star of Mother, and how marvellous Henry was, and you, and Gerry, and the way he ran the Glory Hole, and refusing a knighthood like old Harry Broome? Mine is the kingdom, the power and the glory!"

"He was monstrous," said Richard with his dark flush. "It was the boasting that humiliated one so. And when he boasted about us——"

"Ah, but we were part of his triumph. 'I live again in my children.' He was always saying that. Don't you remember?"

"Remember! He told me once I was his immortality. Can you beat it? He never dreamed I'd a life of my own. I'd have gone mad if the war hadn't come. That taught me at last how unimportant he was."

"But it didn't teach him," said the younger brother.

"No—that's why I despised him. He was incapable of learning."

"Well, that's just why I don't despise him. Think! Even a world war didn't shake him. Everything changed, but he wouldn't accept the change. He was a Broome, and he was going to carry on as the Broomes have always carried on, in the direction he wanted to go, although the whole of theatrical England, Richard, had decided to turn round and go the other way. There he stuck and they couldn't topple him over. Only he himself could do that."

"How do you mean?"

"You say we kicked him out between us. Well—but aren't we his children, his extensions of himself? If that's true, then only Edmund Broome has conquered Edmund Broome. Now that's tragic, and it thrills me."

Richard looked at his brother with tired eyes.

"Death doesn't thrill me and I don't believe in tragedy. Life's farcical, not tragic. I've got over the romantic stage."

"Yes, but that's the point. He hadn't. He wouldn't. He was the last of the romantic Broomes, and he behaved according to pattern. But it's not our pattern, of course. Can you see yourself raping your Sabine and founding your family?" cried John on a swing of words, and then stopped himself suddenly.

Richard flickered one keen look at his brother, then went off into a fit of good-tempered laughter.

"No, John, I can't. Art for me! But I'll be godfather to all your children."

"Children? I'm not going to have any children," said John in alarm.

"Aren't you going to marry?"

"Oh, probably." John's tone, the gleam in his eye, the deliberately schooled muscles of his mouth, made it clear that this province of his future was already fully dreamed out, but that he didn't propose to talk about it.

For a long minute Richard watched the thoughts come and go on his brother's still ingenuous face, like the shadows of little flames playing on a wall: then completely and extravagantly lost interest.

"O God, how sick of it all I am!" muttered Richard from his pit. And then, one eye on John—"But that public of mine——!"

John would not laugh with him.

"I am going——" said John, setting his teeth—"to write three brilliant failures before I'm thirty."

"I'll film them for you," said Richard comfortingly. "And then what are you going to do?"

"Make money. Make a very great deal of money."

"Like Father."

"No, not like Father." John's face clouded. "He didn't know what to do with his money. But I know." His eyes began to lighten. "I'm going——" proceeded John, "to taste—touch—smell—see—hear—feel—think. I'm going to fall in love. I'm going to have a huge success. I'm going—I'm going—— Oh——" cried John on a climax of anticipation, as he crooked a beckoning finger at the waitress and the world—"Oh, Richard, I'm going to enjoy myself!"

New Year's Day—New Year's Eve, 1930.